WAR IN THE DESERT

"Ugashe!" Dandy Bill called out. The braves sidled but did not really retreat, hard faces turned toward the major. The Dreamer slowly chewed his meat. Cutler saw the violence congeal in that slow helplessness of catastrophe observed in a dream. The major drew his revolver, cursing as his horse still pitched and jerked against the bit. Several troopers near him cocked their carbines. Symonds fired into the air.

Immediately there was fire from the canyon wall and the two troopers who had cocked their pieces were slammed out of their saddles. Others fired back, horses wheeling. Another trooper fell, yelling for help. Bunch spurred, dismounted, and helped the wounded man up behind his saddle. Cutler saw Benny Dee, rifle raised, aiming. Malcreado was caught among the other milling horses as he drew his Colt. He saw Pizer spur up to where the Dreamer had risen and empty his revolver point-blank. There was a steady yelling, hoarser from the troopers, shriller from the Apaches.

The firing ceased when the troops had passed out of effective range. Cutler saw four, five, six empty saddles. Higher on the ridge, brown bodies could be seen filtering among the trees, cutting off further retreat.

APACHES
OAKLEY HALL

"A novel rich in history... Classic Western action from Oakley Hall, who may be the living master of the genre."
—*Kirkus Reviews*

"All kinds of fascinating lore about the Old West... Solid characters in a gritty, believable world."
—*The Washington Post Book World*

Also by Oakley Hall:

WARLOCK
BADLANDS

APACHES

Oakley Hall

BANTAM BOOKS
TORONTO • NEW YORK • LONDON • SYDNEY • AUCKLAND

*This edition contains the complete text
of the original hardcover edition.*
NOT ONE WORD HAS BEEN OMITTED.

APACHES

*A Bantam Book / published by arrangement with
Simon & Schuster Inc.*

PRINTING HISTORY
Simon & Schuster edition published August 1986
Bantam edition / November 1988

ISBN 0-553-27541-0

Published simultaneously in the United States and Canada

*Bantam Books are published by Bantam Books, a division of
Bantam Doubleday Dell Publishing Group, Inc. Its trademark,
consisting of the words "Bantam Books" and the portrayal of a
rooster, is Registered in U.S. Patent and Trademark Office and
in other countries. Marca Registrada. Bantam Books, 666 Fifth
Avenue, New York, New York 10103.*

PRINTED IN THE UNITED STATES OF AMERICA

O   0 9 8 7 6 5 4 3 2 1

The historian must not try to know what is truth, if he values his honesty; for, if he cares for his truths, he is certain to falsify his facts.
—*The Education of Henry Adams*

BOOK ONE

Following his Apache trackers up the swale through the jumbles of paddle cactus and ocotillo whips, Cutler saw them gathered on the ridge, pointing, laughing: six of them, dirty brown legs under their filthy shirts astride brown ponies, long black hair in turbans. Nochte pumped his carbine up and down twice in a signal.

Cutler spurred on up the slope, so tired from two weeks of chasing hostiles he could hardly dig his heels in, and Blackie too tired to respond. Tazzi shouted down to him in the Indian way, as though white men were deaf, "Ho, look, white-eye loco!"

Down the far swale were two prospectors and their mules, ragged and dusty, with sweat-dark hats pulled low on their faces. One sat on the ground with his pick across his legs and rifle cradled in his arms, staring down at it as though afraid to look up at the catcalling Apaches on the ridge. The other scrambled up a red-earth cutbank, not quite gaining the top down, keeping to his feet with difficulty. He took another run and failed again. He also carried a rifle, and he too never looked up at the ridge.

"*Mucho miedo!*" Nochte said. Much fear! Skinny and Lucky cackled to one another in Apache. Jim-jim stood in his stirrups to flourish his carbine threateningly.

"Ho, white-eye, do not frighten!" Tazzi shouted. "This friend!"

Cutler could hear the one prospector panting to split his lungs as he tried again to run up the ten-foot bank. He waved his cap and called, "Cavalry! Scouts!"

Neither responded. The seated prospector seemed paralyzed. The other made one more despairing run at the bank. Cutler realized that he himself must not look much different

3

from the Hoyas. Although he was issue-trousered and -capped, he was as filthy as they were, and the silver bars on his shoulders would be invisible. Chockaway and Benny Dee came up with the pack animals.

"What see? What see?" Benny Dee cried.

The prospector who had been trying to run up the bank now leaned panting over his rifle, bent like a question mark. The other carefully laid his weapon on the ground beside him and used his pick handle to brace himself to his feet.

Skinny and Lucky continued their catcalls and leg-slappings. The Apache sense of humor! With laughter they would lash a captured teamster to one of his wagon wheels, head down over a slow fire until his brains boiled out his ears. With laughter the Hoya scouts would prepare an ambush for warriors of their own race, escaped from a reservation and so branded "hostile" by white-eye law. And the same hostiles would laughingly return the favor. Many soldiers in the territories of Arizona and New Mexico had died listening to Apache laughter. It rang through the horrors of war, defeat, depredation, and retaliation, of pacification, concentration, and extermination.

When Cutler had received this command as an aide of General Yeager's, he'd had the usual soldier's mixture of contempt and respect for the Apaches, who were gut-eaters, torturers, ruthless savages, Stone Age men. At first he'd made no attempt to learn their guttural, harsh tongue, since he could make his demands understood through Nochte, his interpreter, who had been captured by Mexicans as a child and brought up on a ranch in Chihuahua. Many of the other Apaches also knew some Spanish, with which he was familiar out of his own peculiar boyhood. Little by little they had captured first his interest, then his reluctant affection. Where once they had seemed to him indistinguishable, one from another, now they were as individual as white troopers. Confidences had passed between him, Nochte, and Kills-a-Bear, although Cutler maintained a reserve with them as a proper officer. Those two were both serious, intelligent men. Tazzi was a jeerer, whose scoffings covered some vulnerability. The others were more shy with him than he was with them. He had begun a dictionary for his own use, with Nochte's help, puzzling what seemed an excess of consonants

into phonetic spellings, and aware that slight mispronuncia-
tions could carry dangerously different meanings.

He found himself more and more interested also in their
beliefs and customs, founded in great good sense. Living in
family groups as they did, at least they knew their own
ancestors. There they had the advantage on their officer.

Cutler considered himself a good soldier, despite black
marks in army books—the chief one, he knew, being that he
was a "mustang" lieutenant and not a product of the Good
Gray Battalion on the Hudson. So were the Hoyas good
soldiers, for all their dirty faces and tangled long hair. Kills-a-
Bear, with Nochte translating, had told him that he was
almost grown before he found out that men died any other
way than killed.

If the cavalry, without the help of Apache scouts, caught
up with a band of hostiles, it was most likely an ambush, and
all the soldiers would ever see of their quarry was puffs of
smoke from behind rocks. Still, stiff-necked officers like Col.
Abraham Dougal, commanding at Fort McLain, distrusted
the scouts and resisted their employment. Although Cutler
and the Hoyas were stationed at McLain with the 13th
Cavalry, he was on detached duty as an aide-de-camp to
General Yeager, commanding the Department.

He told Nochte to hold the scouts on the ridge and
headed Blackie down toward the prospectors' camp. He held
a palm up in a peace sign and hoped the idiots wouldn't take
a potshot at him. "Scouts from Fort McLain!" he called.

Neither of them moved, staring at him from under their
hat brims. They had done some hacking at the cutbank.
Beyond their tent two mules cropped at tough weeds with
jerks of their heads.

As he came up to the man with the pick, the fellow's jaw
began to work. He spat tobacco juice. His eyes were pale
blue and blank, and Cutler had the sensation of looking
through them into the hollow of his skull. The man sighed,
coughed, shook his head once. "Jesus God Almighty, thought
those devils had us certain-sure. Holy Jesus!"

"Caballito's busted off the reservation. We think he
passed by not far from here."

"Holy Jesus!"

"What's he say, Georgie?" the other called.

"Says Caballito's on the loose again."

"He's heading for Mexico," Cutler said. "A couple of
hundred Sierra Verdes with him. It's a big breakout."

"Those fellows up there's with you, huh?" the panting
one said, straightening. "Thought we was goners, we did."

"There's been some killing, sheepherders and soldiers.
You'd be safer in town just now."

"Can't you soljers keep them murdering Pache devils on
the reservation?"

"We keep trying. So you won't have to worry so hard
when you're out here digging holes. I'm telling you to head
into Madison until this is over." He swung Blackie around and
started at a slow walk up to where the Hoyas waited. They
looked like part of the earth, queer earth-colored excrescences in a country of excrescences, man shapes on horse
shapes blending with the earth except for a white foreleg on
Kills-a-Bear's pony, a white blaze on Lucky's. They had
stopped laughing at the prospectors' antics and now looked
merely watchful.

Cutler waved an arm: forward. Nochte and Tazzi copied
his gesture. They started on, hoping to cut trail on the Sierra
Verde band before it found refuge across the border. Somewhere beyond these hills was Major Symonds with A and D
Troops. All the cavalry within range had headed immediately
for the principal passes and water holes, in the hopes of
intercepting Caballito in his flight, while the scouts moved
more slowly at first, tracing the renegades' progress.

Nochte and Kills-a-Bear rode ahead in their distinctive
hunch of cutting for sign. So called for their ancestral home in
the Sierra de Hoyas, the Hoyas were Western Apaches, the
rest of their band settled on reservations in Arizona, although
they knew this country well from their own days of raiding.
They were scouts by nature and training, as were all Apaches.
By fingering a horse turd they could tell hostile mounts from
cavalry. They could distinguish by a partial moccasin print
Chiricahua from Mimbre, Mescalero from Sierra Verde, determine from a hoofprint whether the horse had been shod
by Mexicans or Americans.

Kills-a-Bear beckoned to Nochte and the two of them
slipped from their saddles to squat in the brush. They
nodded together, Nochte's face intent and young, aquiline for
an Apache, Kills-a-Bear's older and terribly marred, with his
destroyed eye and scar-plowed cheek. Nochte rose, dusting

fingers together in his precise, almost finicking manner. "Verdes!" he called. Sierra Verdes. Green Mountains. Red Stripe People. Caballito's band.

They followed sign. Whenever they lost the track the Hoyas would arc out to either side, hunching in the saddle as they peered at the ground. They were no friends of the Sierra Verdes, and, when a band broke out of a reservation and began raiding, it made life difficult for those left behind, for all Apaches, for all Indians. The Territorial newspapers would renew their clamor for the extermination of the Apaches, bucks to be shot or hanged, squaws and children to be parceled out among the pacified tribes of Indian Territory.

Cutler could read some of the sign himself, a broken twig showing a light-colored center, scuffed earth, once a chain of bruises on soft ground. The scouts hurried ahead and he could sense their certainty in the cock of their heads. A band even as big as this one, encumbered with old people and children, could travel faster than cavalry, encumbered by pack trains and rolling stock. The scouts were faster. However, traveling faster than Caballito involved the chance of catching up with him at a place of his choosing.

Late in the afternoon they heard the faint percussion of firing. Hills rose ahead, among them a saddle where, Cutler knew, Rock Creek snaked through a narrow defile. There Major Symonds had caught up with Caballito, or more likely, Caballito had ambushed the "Iron Major." The tired mounts responded briefly, he, Tazzi, and Nochte now in the lead, the others stringing out, the pack animals falling behind. The sun was at their backs.

After a silence the firing picked up again, nearer. They came in single file along the creek, almost dry this time of year, a rivulet connecting pool to rocky pool. Here the tracks of many horses were clearly evident, cavalry shod, A and D Troops catching up with Caballito at a place of his choosing.

Cutler picked up the pace again heading into the canyon, steep fall of cactus cliff to the right, shelving volcanic balconies on the left. Firing resumed, very close now; he spotted a puff of smoke from the steep side. The scouts had stripped to their breechclouts for a fight, grinning dirty faces under red turbans, carbines in hand.

A bullet splatted against a rock beside Cutler. As though it had been a signal, the red sun sank behind the curve of

canyon wall. He dismounted and took cover behind a boulder, Kills-a-Bear and Tazzi with him, the others sheltering
where they could. The pack animals had been held up further
back.

"Go see," he said to Tazzi. The squat, big-shouldered
Hoya threaded his way, crouching, among the boulders ahead.
There was another lull in the firing. Kills-a-Bear made a sign
indicating riflemen and jabbed a finger at points on the cliff
ahead. Of course he had spotted more than one hostile.
Cutler beckoned to Jim-jim, the best shot among them, and
pointed to a puff of smoke. Jim-jim rested his carbine barrel
on the boulder, squinting. The carbine cracked. He levered
and fired again. A bullet whacked stone and squealed off.

Tazzi and a trooper appeared, crouching; a sergeant of A
Troop, his face grimed and powder-blackened.

"Plenty trouble, blue soldier," Tazzi commented.

"Lieutenant Cutler, sir!"

"Didn't the major have the sense not to follow Caballito
into a trap like this?"

"Din't know we was anywhere near hostiles, sir! They've
got us split up. Major and Lieutenant Helms and teri-twelve
others trapped up ahead. Some deads! I don't know if they
can hold out till nightfall, sir! Captain Smithers'll be mighty
glad you've come up."

He doubted that either Captain Smithers or the Iron
Major would take any pleasure from being relieved by Apache
scouts, nor Lt. Lonny Helms from being relieved by Pat
Cutler.

"Tell him I'll try to set up a diversion to take the
pressure off." He said to Nochte in Spanish, "See if anybody
knows a shortcut around to the other end of the canyon. The
major and some blue soldiers are boxed in over there."

Skinny knew the way. He looked no more than a boy,
with legs thin as licorice whips, bushy hair, and a carbine
almost as tall as he was. Leaving Tazzi with the sergeant and
summoning Chockaway from the pack animals, Cutler set out
with the six scouts. Cartridge belts X-ed over their bare
backs, they hurried ahead of him along the riverbed to
another canyon, where Skinny led them scrambling up a
shale slope. Here the sun reappeared, and Cutler sweated in
his canvas uniform, panting with the exertion of keeping pace
with his command. Presently he could hear firing below. He

pointed Jim-jim to cover on the cliff edge and instructed him to shoot at targets of opportunity when he, Cutler, bounced a shot off the granite face as a signal. From the edge he could glimpse the black heads of several of Caballito's bucks, and, further over, movement where the women, children, and old people were hiding. He couldn't determine the whereabouts of the horse herd—stolen cavalry remounts with it. There was another lull in the firing.

Below, to the left and close by a round pond, were two dead troopers and a dead horse. He couldn't make out where the Iron Major and his detachment were concealed until he saw a cap ducking behind a boulder. The Apaches were poor shots, but, with repeating rifles, made up in firepower what they lacked in accuracy. The troopers were not much better. Thanks to the government's stinginess, many recruits fired their first shots in battle.

He saw swift movement on the opposite canyon wall, two brown bodies in concerted action. A boulder began to roll downward, slowly at first, almost halting, then gaining momentum. Bounding off a steeper transition, it slammed down toward the harried advance guard of A Troop, to crash among the rocks on the canyon floor.

Skinny led them on, downward now through brush they had to cling to in their descent. Cutler cursed Major Symonds's stupidity and ill luck. Around a shoulder of granite the creek reappeared, a hundred feet below. He sent Lucky back up to the ridge to pick off any Verdes who were flushed, and stationed others at vantage points, depending in this situation on Nochte as interpreter rather than his own crude Apache. Another boulder began a crashing descent into the canyon. This time one of the warriors exposed himself too long, flipping his breechclout in defiance, and Cutler had time to draw a bead and fire. The man spun, fell, and crawled to cover. Shots whined past.

Ducking from rock to rock, he and Nochte hurried on down the last slope to the riverbed. Among the boulders there they came upon a dead corporal spread-eagled prone, with a bloody mush of a back. Beyond him the other lay on his side as though asleep, one leg drawn up. Crouched further along was a trooper with eyes wide as fried eggs.

"Jesus Christ, Lieutenant, we're in some bad position here!"

"Where's the major?"

Another boulder bounded down the cliff and shot up in a high arc with a shattering cannon crack. "Jesus Christ, they'll mash us all." the trooper moaned. "Major's over there somewheres, if he ain't dead!"

"Major Symonds!"

"Here!"

Cutler ducked from cover to cover, Nochte close on his heels. The major crouched beside a dead gray horse. His expression reminded Cutler of the prospector named George; his mustached face was pasty white, and a bandana with a bloody stain over the ear was bound around his forehead. He stared at Cutler with an expression of idiot terror.

"Get us out of here, Cutler!"

A corporal crawled in beside them. "Major—Lieutenant Cutler—Lieutenant Helms is bad hurt. See, you can see his leg there. And there's hostiles getting close. Somebody had better do something!"

"Never mind that, Cutler!" the Iron Major said in a galvanic whisper. Sweat gleamed on his cheeks, and he kept levering his carbine back and forth, sliding his bottom toward Cutler. "How're you going to get us out of here, Cutler? You have got to get us out of this, man!" He grimaced painfully as another boulder crashed down the canyon side.

Cutler pointed to Lieutenant Helms's one blue leg, extending beyond a boulder, and said to Nochte in Spanish, "Lieutenant Helms is hurt. Can you brink him back here?"

Nochte glanced at the leg with a flash of eye white. He set off at a crouching, weaving run. The crack and whack and ricochet squeal immediately picked up. Nochte tripped and rolled out of sight. Hit!

"Cutler—" the major started, and covered his head with his hands as another boulder crashed down the cliff.

Cutler said to the corporal, "Can you get the word around? My scouts are up behind Caballito's bucks. When they start firing we'll have to move fast to clear out of here."

"Give me five minutes, sir!" As he slid away, the corporal studiously avoided looking at the Iron Major.

Symonds meticulously brushed grains of sand from the barrel of his carbine. "Grateful you've shown up here, Cutler," he said. "This has been a terrible afternoon! We've lost some men. Good men! The rascals caught us very clever. Never a sign of them!"

The rule was that when you saw Apache sign you must be careful and when you saw no sign you must be very careful. "I've got my scouts well up behind," Cutler said. "On my signal they'll start firing. We'll want to move back to join Captain Smithers then."

"Very good, Cutler. Depending on you, now."

The corporal slid toward them again, panting. "Ready, sir. Looks like they hit the scout you sent after Lieutenant Helms. You are not going to leave the Lieutenant behind, are you, sir?"

"I'll try to get him out."

"You are not to try such a damn fool thing, Cutler!" the major bellowed. "Told you we're depending on you now! Get us out of this hellhole, Cutler!"

The corporal's eyes flickered once. Cutler swung his carbine up toward the granite crag and stroked the trigger; the butt jarred his shoulder. Smoke plumed from Jim-jim's carbine, and the other scouts joined him firing down on the Sierra Verdes below them. Cutler hooked a hand under the Iron Major's armpit and hauled him to his feet. "Go!" Then he sprinted across the dry riverbed to where Nochte had disappeared and the blue leg and black boot protruded from behind a rock.

"Come back here, Cutler!" Major Symonds screamed. "Cutler, God damn you, that is a goddamn *order! Cutler!*"

Cutler ducked behind the rock where Helms lay face-down in the sand. Nochte was huddled beside him, black hair springing wildly around his face. He had used his headband to bind his leg. "*Muerte!*" he said, jerking his head at Lieutenant Helms's body.

Cutler knelt to listen for breath. Helms's blood stained the sand. Dead. "Broken?" he asked, pointing to Nochte's leg.

"*Sí!*"

He grasped the scout's arm as he had the major's and pulled him erect. Nochte balanced on his good leg, and Cutler ducked and took him on his shoulders. He staggered back across the sandy creek bed and in among the boulders, where he stumbled, fell to his knees, and rested there, panting. Then he thrust himself and his load upright and started on again.

Suddenly he was among soldiers, and there was no more firing. Caballito and his warriors, his women, children, and old people—called the Red Stripe People from the slashes of red painted on their cheeks, and Sierra Verdes from their home mountains—would be slipping away to some prearranged rendezvous, and from there to their haven in the Sierra Madre, south of the border.

When Cutler had eased Nochte to a seat on a rock, the Iron Major lunged at him, his face black with rage beneath his bloodied bandana. "That was direct disobedience of an order, Lieutenant! I intend to have your balls! Corporal, you're a witness!"

The corporal stiffened to attention but did not otherwise respond. Cutler saw disgust on the faces of the grimy, blood-stained, exhausted troopers watching this display of Major Symonds's. The Iron Major goggled at him, his mouth working like a fish's out of water. He knew, and Symonds knew, that there were no charges the major could bring against him without showing himself a fool and a coward. The colonel detested his second in command, but the major was a conniver and Cutler had made a deadly enemy.

He saluted smartly and managed to say nothing, the major turning from him to attend to other matters.

Before dark they had recovered the bodies of the dead. Those of Lieutenant Helms and one of the troopers had been mutilated by the retreating Red Stripe People.

Caballito crossed into Mexico not many hours ahead of Cutler and the Hoyas, who were constrained at the border as though the international boundary were a stone wall. Cutler settled in at the hamlet of Ojo Azul, where there were a cantina and *tienda,* a few adobe hovels, and long-abandoned ranch buildings with melting adobe walls narrow-ported for rifle fire. The place had been fortified against Apache raiders, for this was one of their main routes into their sanctuaries in the Sierra Madre.

During the afternoon the cavalry troops came in, pennons flying, the Iron Major with A Troop, and Captain Smithers, a tall, aristocratic Southerner, with D. Pack trains and water wagons lumbered in, with all the impedimenta that made chasing Apaches possible and catching them impossible. Tents were set up in neat, brown, pyramidal rows beside the muddy pond. Lieutenants Farrier and Olin brought in F and H Troops, trailing a pale tan cloud of dust against the western sun.

Tequila, mescal, and whiskey were available at the cantina, and a hog ranch of Mexican and Indian women materialized beyond the pond. The four troops of the 13th Cavalry from Fort McLain waited at the border for General Yeager, the departmental commanding officer, to arrive from Fort Blodgett near Santa Fe.

First came two officers with a detachment of troopers, one of them the 13th's fat adjutant, Jumbo Pizer, the other a stranger, a captain, a suddenly familiar captain, a hulking man with a fierce blond mustache and a chin like a ram. It was Sam Bunch, whom Cutler hadn't seen since he had left Dakota Territory.

13

He found himself running toward his friend, who was dismounting. "Sam!"

"Pat!" Bunch's big hand grabbed his. "Long time!"

"What're you doing here?"

"Just got transferred. I guess the general figured you birds'd never catch Caballito without me." He winked ponderously. Cutler could feel himself beaming as though his face would crack. His only friend at Fort McLain had been the contract surgeon, Bernie Reilly. Now here was Sam Bunch, transferred from Dakota Territory. It more than balanced the major's enmity.

Pizer stood by watching the reunion with an unfriendly squint. "You two know each other?"

"Served at Fort Meade together!" Bunch said. "Pat and I went on a scout together one March, like to got us froze to death. Sioux country! You run a pack of Pache scouts, I hear, Pat. I had a company of Crow constabulary."

There seemed a connection Cutler couldn't quite figure. A bright squalling of a bugle announced the arrival of the general, aboard his famous gray mule, Aggie. He wore a pith helmet and his many-pocketed canvas campaign jacket. His shotgun was slung across his back, and a brace of wild turkeys swung from saddle thongs. With him were a squad of Negro troopers and Captain Robinson, his chief aide and secretary. The troopers proceeded to erect his tent, a vast affair that looked as though it had been designed to house some desert sheikh. From its central pole the Stars and Stripes and Yeager's two-star pennon were unfurled.

Yeager had an ugly, coarse-grained face framed by reddish mutton-chop whiskers. He scowled at the soldiery drawn up for his inspection and casually returned Major Symonds's flourish of a salute.

"At ease, at ease!" he called, and began to shake the hands of officer in order of rank. Cutler heard him say to Captain Bunch, "Your arrival has been very speedy, Captain!"

"Hello, my boy!" he said to Cutler, his grip swift and hard. He strolled on to greet noncoms who had served with him in Wyoming Territory, leaving Cutler with the familiar mix of emotions that possessed him whenever the general reintruded in his life—distrust and gratitude, an expectation like a fox gnawing his liver, along with a sour resignation, but affection and respect despite himself.

The general presided at supper in the big tent as soon as retreat had sounded, and offered the required first toast to the cavalry. Sour red Pass wine was drunk, and glasses were refilled by the Negro trooper waiter. Yeager conferred with the Iron Major on his right and Captain Smithers on his left. Jud Farrier and Petey Olin, with his red-haired face tough as a Bowery Boy's, were installed below the salt, and Jumbo Pizer across from Cutler, who sat between Farrier and Sam Bunch. Bunch whispered to him, "Hear you've been at it again, eh, Pat? Disobeying orders! In the most flagrant manner, I have no doubt." Bunch was a Marylander, and his *outs* and *doubts* rhymed with *boots*.

"I don't know what the fuss is about," Cutler said. "I was ordered not to bring out a wounded officer, and I didn't." He had not spoken in a whisper and the major's eye rolled at him, hot as a coal. There must be gossip about the Rock Creek fight if Bunch knew of the dispute already. It seemed to him that the other officers were ignoring him more particularly than usual.

"Yes, passed him up for one of your precious scouts, I'm told," Bunch said.

"My scout weighed less than a dead white-eye. More useful, too."

"Ah, you'll be a lieutenant all your life, Pat! Pummeling captains in Dakota and bedeviling your superiors down here."

It was probably true. He had ranked Bunch a few numbers in Dakota, but now Bunch was a captain, where he had been seven years a first lieutenant. No doubt this was due in good part to a drunken brawl with Captain Howie in a Deadwood saloon two years ago. He would not have even Bunch think he cared.

"A officer can always resign his commission," he said, and wished he did not sound a prig saying it.

"Ah, there's only this one trade we know! What else would you do?"

"Play cards. Billiards. Pimp."

On the other side of Cutler, Jud Farrier avoided his glance, sawing on a tough turkey leg. He had a narrow, clean-shaven face and long upper lip and resembled a Methodist preacher. Now his lips were pursed with disapproval. Major Symonds must have been active broadcasting his version of the events at Rock Creek.

At the head of the table the general rose, one hand slipped into the side pocket of his jacket, while Percy Robinson tapped a wineglass with a fork.

"You will be interested to know, gentlemen," Yeager announced in his rather high voice, "that the army has not been under such an attack from the Territorial press since the Victorio war. The news that Caballito and two hundred Sierra Verdes have *again* escaped has raised a hue and cry for my scalp. 'Evil news rides post while good news baits,' eh?"

He chuckled, smiling around the table at the attentive faces of the officers of the 13th. Cutler was interested in his effort to be charming to his subordinates, and also in Captain Robinson's expression as he regarded his master, at the same time smug and obsequious, but a hint of irony also in his fat, middle-aged face, with the rash of broken capillaries in his cheeks and his nose like a plum. Percy Robinson was a man of accomplishment in his own right, an authority on historical cavalry warfare and an Indian scholar, who had published a number of booklets in an army information series, slim volumes bound in green canvas: *Shamans Among the Navajo, Native Flora in New Mexico Territory,* and others.

"Ah, the Rings!" Yeager continued. "Our newcomer, Captain Bunch, will be familiar with the Indian Rings of Dakota Territory. These are but frail circlets of grass compared to our local products! The Tucson Ring, the Santa Fe Ring—you from Fort McLain are of course familiar with the Madison Ring, an offshoot of the Santa Fe. What hamlet in the Territory within range of an Indian reservation and its government contracts is so poor-spirited as not to possess its own Indian Ring?"

There was laughter, and Yeager smiled and leaned his free hand on the table. "Who are these gentlemen, gentlemen? Perhaps Captain Bunch does not know. They are Republicans, unfortunately, capitalists, carpetbaggers, many of them, who arrived here with the California Column during the war and remained to make their fortunes. They are easily recognized, for there is no lean and hungry look about them. They are well dressed, well shod, well spoken. One cannot find better friends than these men, if all goes to please them. They are merchants, bankers, traders, editors, politicians, and their lackeys, the Indian agents; even, I am sorry to say, some corrupted officers..."

Or some like Colonel Dougal, Cutler thought, who were not even corrupt, only dim-witted and loyal to old friends. He had heard before this Yeager's sentiments on the subject of the Indian Rings and the Territorial press, which had often made the general's life miserable. Tonight it was as though the general had been speaking specifically to him, which was a knack of Yeager's, for those men he had listed in Madison were all of them Californians, and had been Cutler's friends in Ran Boland's card room above the Boland & Perkins store. It was understood that they ran town and county, and made good livings supplying the fort and the Bosque Alto reservation. He had half shared and half resented their jokes about the cavalry, and more than half resented their jokes about the Apaches, especially sexual rumors, which were a special interest to the poker club. He had become increasingly uncomfortable with his fellow Californians, his friends when he had no friends at Fort McLain, until two months ago he had encountered Lily Maginnis and had deserted the card room for the Maginnises' soirees.

"They are filled with righteous indignation that Caballito has escaped our grasp and will soon again be raiding north of the border," General Yeager continued. "Not to speak of the depredations he has committed on his flight south."

He leaned on the table with both hands, gazing from face to face. "But they are hypocrites, gentlemen! Secretly they rejoice. They rub their hands together like Shylock. They prepare their ledgers for the figures that will soon be written there. Because in periods of Indian warfare their profits are enhanced. New army units are moved within their reach, for which they furnish the provender and the liquor, all those necessities of an army that must travel on its stomach. They become wealthy in times of war, gentlemen. In times of peace they are comfortable, but impatient—cheating the Indians on the reservations and having their way with the poorer classes of settlers, lending, collecting, foreclosing, buying cheap and selling dear.

"In these quiet times they furnish the reservations with tainted beef weighed on doctored scales, weevily flour and sanded sugar. Are you all aware of the Sierra Verdes' history, gentlemen? I will let Perce here inform you of the intricacies of their hierarchies."

Cutler watched Robinson flush and straighten and care-

fully place his wineglass beside his plate. The captain said in
a schoolteacherish voice, "You must understand that Dawa,
not Caballito, is the true chief of the Red Stripe People.
Caballito is what is called his *segundo*—his second—and is a
shaman of considerable powers connected with the thunder.
That is, the thunder speaks to him and is the source of his
power as a seer. He is a medicine man and war chief much as
Sitting Bull was in the Sioux wars. Dawa's actual heir is
Joklinney, presently languishing in prison on Alcatraz for the
bloody raid he led during Caballito's earlier breakout—"

"Thank you, Percy," Yeager broke in smoothly. "That
other breakout was three years ago, as some of you will
remember," he went on, "but a little prior history is necessary. The Sierra Verdes had made their peace and were
granted a reservation in their home mountains, the Green
Range. There was the usual pattern, however, of pressure
from settlers and miners, and it became the Bureau of Indian
Affairs' policy to abrogate the treaties and concentrate the
Apache bands on fewer and larger reservations. The Verdes
were relocated at San Marcos. That was their 'trail of tears,'
to a place they hated—hot, flat desert country, insect-ridden,
with bad water. In addition it was near Tucson and the Indian
agent was under the sway of the Tucson Ring. The first
breakout was for the reasons I just mentioned—men become
desperate when they see their families going hungry. The
reverse of the 'trail of tears' was the 'trail of blood,' back to
the Green Range. There, after an extensive campaign, we
were able to force their surrender and return them to San
Marcos.

"This time the Ring has been cleverer in precipitating a
breakout. A sheriff and his deputies came to San Marcos with
papers to serve on Caballito and Dawa, and many of the
braves as 'John Does,' for the depredations they had committed—
despite the terms of their surrender signed with me. Apaches
are terrified of the white-eye's 'papers,' gentlemen, and with
good reason. Prison metes a swift death from the 'white-
sickness'—tuberculosis. So I accuse the Ring of directly con-
spiring to force this breakout. They are vultures, gentlemen!"

He was silent for a moment, grimly glancing around the
table again.

"And now through their newspaper lackeys they are
making their pious fraud of an outcry against the army. 'Shall

we upon the footing of our land / Send fair-play orders, and make compromise, / Insinuation, parley, and base truce—'" He grinned his sudden, gap-toothed grin, and Cutler marveled again at the charm he purveyed. "Nay, nay!" Yeager went on. "Let them flay me for my attempts to befriend a defeated foe as his 'Nantan Lobo.' Let them rail at our ineptitude, stupidity, lack of resolve. But not at our cowardice, nor at our loyalty to the nation we serve! And they shall not cast their aspersions on our comrades who have already perished in this pursuit!

"And in an extended campaign how many more will die?" he continued earnestly. "Soldier and civilian—not to speak of Mexicans—some horribly murdered. How many hundred died thus in Victorio's war, how many tens and scores in Josanie's raid, in Chato's, in Joklinney's, and in Caballito's earlier breakout?

"I have pled, gentlemen, for a treaty of 'hot pursuit' whereby we may cross the border to follow renegade Indians into Mexican Territory. To no avail. And so we are held up here at an invisible line that Apache raiders may cross with impunity. When they do, we all know the depredations and the death of brave men that will result—on this two-thousand-mile border, which is impossible to patrol. Until that consummation that the civilians of this Territory claim devoutly to desire and which the vultures of the Rings proclaim in their hypocrisies—the erasing of a tragic people from the face of the earth."

He paused again before he raised his clenched fist and brought it down without force on the edge of the table. "But gentlemen, we who have fought them can afford a more magnanimous view. There remains one course, which I am determined to pursue—to find the means of persuading Caballito to return peaceably to another reservation than San Marcos. I believe we can afford this one concession to a brave enemy!"

The general seated himself amid the applause of his officers. Cutler thought he had brought everyone to his side, even Major Symonds from his expression. The major rose to propose a toast to General Yeager. With his nutcracker jaw and black cavalry mustache, he resembled an oversized and vividly painted toy soldier, and he represented everything that Cutler detested about this postwar army. He was a martinet and a bully, at the same time a coward and stupidly rash. A hypocrite as well, for Cutler had heard Symonds declaiming on the necessity to "exterminate the devils!" Cutler thought that Colonel Dougal, mad in his own way, would be gratified if Major Symonds galloped off to extinction in some Little Bighorn among the Apaches. As the major indeed had almost done at Rock Creek.

Bunch whispered to him as they reseated themselves after the toast. "Robinson says Nantan Lobo wants to see me after supper. What do you suppose?" "Chief Gray Wolf" was the Apache name for Yeager, whom they trusted over all other white-eyes.

"Something to do with the persuading he mentioned?"

"Ah!"

The black waiter poured more wine, and Cutler cautioned himself that he was imbibing more than was good for him. Overindulgence led to his insulting his fellow officers and pummeling captains.

"Enjoy your turkey?" he said to Jud Farrier.

Farrier nodded, purse-mouthed.

"It's Ring turkey, actually vulture."

Farrier didn't respond, eyes wavering nervously. Captain Robinson leaned over Cutler's shoulder to say that the general expected him to remain for a conference when supper had been concluded.

In a smaller compartment of the tent the general stretched out in a folding chair, his tunic loosened at the neck. He indicated chairs to Cutler and Bunch, and Robinson seated himself at the battered camp desk with pen and paper before him.

"I propose to go into Mexico to talk sweet reason to Caballito," Yeager said. He grinned at the two of them. "Can we get word to him, do you think, Pat?"

"I think we can, sir. A sister of one of my scouts is married to a Sierra Verde."

"I want to arrange a meeting south of the border. Caballito and, say, nine bucks. Ten on our side also. He's vowed never to return to San Marcos. Very well, if he'll return to Bosque Alto Reservation all will be forgiven. Indian Affairs will just have to go along. Do you think that will tempt him?"

"If it doesn't, there may be a dead general and nine of his people," Robinson said.

Yeager squinted at his aide, opened a cigar box, plucked one out for himself, and handed the box to Robinson. "Pass these for me, would you, Perce?" Robinson handed around the cigars and lit them, his lamplit figure throwing bulky shadows on the canvas walls.

"I'll trust the old cutthroat, and I think he'll trust me," Yeager said. "I can't blame him for being unable to get along with Dunaway at San Marcos. How those greedy buggers cut our work out for us! No rest from the wicked, eh?"

If the Boland & Perkins store was the Madison Ring, then Chet Dipple, the Bosque Alto Indian Agent, was a part of the Ring too, Cutler thought. Bosque Alto, the reservation of the Nahuaque band of Apaches, Fort McLain, which had been established to oversee it, and Madison, the town that had sprung up to service fort and reservation, formed, if not a ring, the three points of a triangle. "I'm not sure Dipple is much better than Dunaway, sir," he said.

"He can hardly match Dunaway's arrogance! Can't be helped anyway, can it? The Bureau has jurisdiction while they are on the reservation, and we have it when they're off. The only Indians we can have to do with is hostiles, it seems! Well, sufficient unto the day, sufficient unto the day. We'll take your Hoyas, Pat. And Dandy Bill to translate. Now, Captain Bunch, I requested your transfer to my command because you've got high marks for training Crow scouts up north."

"I will say I was some help to Major Nixon in that endeavor, sir," Bunch said, coming to attention in his chair.

"And the duty suited you, did it?"

"Yes, sir. A Crow isn't just a regular Indian, you know, sir; they are kind of white Indians. I will say Major Nixon and I trained a pretty regimental troop."

"Apaches are not just 'regular' Indians, either, are they, Pat? But I would not say they are 'white' ones. Now, Captain, how would you feel about a place on this expedition I'm planning?"

"It sounds like a grand adventure, sir!"

"I believe you are able to get along with Pat Cutler. Served with him up north?"

"Yes, sir," Bunch grinned. "We used to call him Old Cutlery. He was quite the pugilist, Pat Cutler."

The general cocked his head to one side to look at Bunch closely. "Ah well, Pat does require some protection from his own rash nature, doesn't he? He has vowed never to strike a superior officer again. Except under the most extreme provocation, of course."

Bunch chuckled. Cutler could feel his face burning. Percy Robinson was smiling at him blandly. It was maddening to think Robinson might know things about him he did not know himself, from General Yeager's dictated memoirs.

Yeager asked Robinson to pour a round of brandy, and again the broad shadow moved stooping against the walls of the tent, while Yeager spoke of the use of native scouts:

"The British have long embraced the principle. Gurkhas, Sikhs, Afghans. They did have the one mutiny, certainly; but overall the system has proved itself again and again. It is effective and cheap. This country has rarely used its own resources. I've run into a devil's own amount of opposition in my own efforts. But certainly the Crow scouts have proved themselves against their hereditary enemies, the Sioux. And certainly Pat's trackers have proved themselves in action against other Apaches. Now, Sam, if I may call you that, when we have brought Caballito back to Bosque Alto, I intend to establish a company of Sierra Verde scouts!"

Grinning his malicious grin, Yeager exhaled smoke and brought his brandy glass to his lips.

"Sierra Verdes against Sierra Verdes!" Bunch exclaimed.

"Exactly! We have found that Indians serve well as scouts against an enemy tribe and against an unfriendly band within the same tribe. Now we will see if we cannot subdivide a band against itself, so as to keep hotheads like Caballito in chancery. I propose to put you in charge of their training, Sam."

"Thank you, sir!"

"You will recruit them. They will become an elite. Rich men! How quickly six dollars a month becomes a necessity! Caballito on the loose is an embarrassment to me, Sam, Pat. We will subvert a proportion of his braves. I intend that this will be his last breakout. I am sick and tired of being flayed in the newspapers!"

"You plan well ahead, General," Robinson said.

Yeager laughed. "I will also have another restraint on Caballito. Tell Captain Bunch about the Joklinney gambit, Perce. You already know of this perhaps, Pat."

"Something of it," he said. He knew that Yeager was as clever as Caballito in setting ambushes, and, as Percy Robinson had said, planned far ahead.

Yeager sat grinning as Robinson spoke. "You heard me say earlier that Joklinney, who is old Dawa's legitimate heir, was imprisoned at Alcatraz. Actually, the general has seen to it that he has been released to Fort Point, in San Francisco Bay also. There he has been given some freedom in order to observe the white man's ways, his numbers, his machines and ships and wealth—his power, in other words. Eventually Joklinney will return to the Red Stripe People."

"Oh, very good, sir!" Bunch said.

"I believe that Joklinney along with a company of Sierra Verde scouts will immobilize Caballito in the future," the general said. "And I will adopt similar procedures for other restive bands. A 'hot pursuit' treaty, whereby we could pursue hostiles on into Mexico would finish the whole matter, of course."

"It is the atrocities that accompany their breakouts which are impossible to contemplate," Robinson said soberly.

"That is, of course, the point of it all," Yeager said.

Cutler had seen some of those horrors in his years in New Mexico, but he had come to understand also that those who had seen more horrors than he had, who had lived in the Territory longer, respected an enemy fighting for his life. Through Nochte he had heard some of the other side also: of the murder of Juan José, of the treacherous capture of Cochise, and the torture and murder of Mangas Coloradas by the California Column. Nor had the Apaches been the only depredators.

Yeager said, "Pat, you will endeavor to arrange a meeting with Caballito not far south of here, and as soon as possible. We will be no more than ten, and will expect to meet with that same number. Nantan Lobo will speak to Nantan Caballito about returning to Bosque Alto rather than San Marcos."

"I'll start Lucky off first thing in the morning, sir."

"Very good!" Yeager made a bustle of bringing a gold watch from one of his pockets, consulting it, and winding it. Cutler and Bunch rose promptly to say their goodnights.

In the darkness outside the big tent, Bunch halted to piss, sighing as the spray splattered on the hard-packed earth. "Crazy old bird, ain't he? I'd better tell you what I've heard them saying about you, Pat. Sleeping with some shave-tail's wife, the one you didn't bring out of that ambush."

"I didn't bring him out because he was dead." He could feel a cool lace of sweat on his forehead.

"Ah, well, forewarned and so forth," Bunch said. "And speaking of which, I'll sleep better before this mad expedition of Nantan Lobo's if I have a bit of coont before bed. Come along?"

"Not for me, thanks," he said. So they thought he had not brought out Lonny Helms because he had slept with Emily Helms. The affair had been over for some time, burnt out to Emily's damp recriminations that he had forsaken her for another.

"Spoiled by white meat," Bunch said. "Like fucking a bowl of clabber, in my opinion. I like a bit of color. Nigger wenches, Injun maidens—wash the bear grease out of their hair and sweeten them up with a whiff of perfume between their titties, and they can be damned fine. They're anxious for money to buy pretties with, and I'm anxious for some coont that's not all slathered with white-meat grief. Simple economic exchange."

"It's the same economic exchange that the general would use for his Sierra Verde scouts."

"Ha!" Bunch said. "Ah, there's a light to guide me." He lumbered off toward the red lantern, while Cutler turned toward the cantina.

His fellow officers would be there, and, almost certainly, unpleasantness. Might as well face it.

There were five officers of the 13th in the cantina, faces turned toward him, then away, play of shadows from their movements against the lamplight. At the bar beside Captain Smithers stood Jumbo Pizer, the fat-faced State-of-Mainer's patent leather hair parted in the exact center of his head. Two Mexicans sat in a far corner with a checkerboard on the table between them. Cutler bellied up beside Smithers and asked in Spanish for a glass of whiskey. His jaw muscles ached as he watched the sad-mustached Mexican proprietor pour a potion from an unlabeled bottle. Smithers turned to regard him down his nose.

"Mighty poor show at Rock Creek, Cutler," he said, Alabama thick in his mouth. He was the descendant of a proud military line, whose father had forsworn his West Point oath to take up arms for the Confederacy. On the third finger of Smithers's left hand was his own fat, gold Military Academy ring.

"Very poor," Cutler said. He didn't think Smithers meant the Iron Major's falling into an ambush.

"Like to hear your side of it."

"My side of what?"

"Lonny'd been dealt with pretty hard by those Red Stripers."

"I'm sorry, I don't understand. You'll have to spell it out, Captain."

The silence was intense, Jud Farrier staring at him past Smithers, Petey Olin and the adjutant further along the bar. The major was drinking alone, hunched grimly to the bar, trying to pretend he heard none of this.

Smithers said, "Why, bringing out one of your niggers instead of Lonny Helms!"

The whiskey tasted like coal oil seasoned with red pepper, and a swallow of it turned into a coughing fit. Smithers stared at him like a sharpshooter along the rifle barrel of his nose. "It is only fair that we hear your side of it, Cutler," he said, as though he had been protecting Cutler from the judgment of the others.

"Ah well, I was ordered *not* to bring out Lonny," he said. He raised his voice. "You'll attest to that, won't you, Major?"

The Iron Major chose not to hear.

"Nevertheless—" Smithers started.

"Lonny was dead," Cutler said. "So I brought out my scout, who wasn't."

"An order is an order, Cutler," Pizer said severely.

"Orders are not the point I'm raising, goddamnit!" Smithers said.

Bunch had told him that the motivation had already been supplied. Lonny Helms had been a skinny young man with a Presbyterian haircut, a sorry officer, whose unfaithful wife had been wont in social situations to discourse on his inadequacies. She had had at least one affair before the one with Cutler, but he seemed to have been chosen to bear the blame for her fallen reputation.

"You say he was dead, Pat," Jud Farrier said, without looking at him directly.

So that was it. "Dead," he said, nodding. "My scout will also tell you that, though I suppose Captain Smithers wouldn't take the word of a nigger."

Major Symonds was gazing over at the Mexican checkers game as though that was where the interest lay. Cutler kept an eye on Smithers's glass, in case Smithers was considering disposing of the bad whiskey elsewhere than down his gullet.

Smithers said, more in sorrow than in anger, "I'm not sure I'm prepared to accept your word in the matter, Cutler."

"What?" he said. "A fellow officer? I know I'm not West Point–trained, Captain, but I thought an officer's bond and oath were all-important to you Southerners!"

He supposed it was just as well that Smithers didn't understand to what he was referring, although Pizer did, gaping at him open-mouthed. Just then Sam Bunch stamped in to halt beside him.

Cutler grinned at him, feeling drunk, from the Pass wine, the general's brandy, the coal oil whiskey, or pure hatred. In the shard of hazy mirror behind the bar he regarded his tough, short-bearded, blue-eyed face. No doubt he looked like a man who would leave his mistress's husband to be tortured by vengeful Apaches. The silence, with only a clink of glasses, was of a satisfying duration.

"How did you find the local poontang?" he asked Bunch.

"A bit smelly," his friend said grouchily.

They left the jolly company of the bar to seat themselves at one of the tables in the dim rear of the cantina, and the little barkeep brought a bottle of whiskey and a glass for Bunch.

"Why don't you tell me what happened, Pat?" he said, hunching heavy-bodied forward over the table. He stank of sweat, semen, and female juices. "Rumors and speculations! You were under arrest for spoiling Charley Howie's good looks in a saloon fight, bound over for a court-martial, no doubt you'd be cashiered. Poof, the whole thing blew over and you were transferred down here. Everybody knew it was Yeager's doing! Rumor was you were bastard get of his." Bunch squinted at him in the semidark.

Cutler contemplated a familiar inner turbulence. Had not the same possibility occurred to him? Still occurred. He had looked for some resemblance to himself in Yeager's ugly face, framed by rusty sideburns. There was none, whereas there was considerable in the photograph of Yeager's legitimate son, a captain of engineers, that stood on the general's desk. No resemblance in his own Irish mug to Yeager, and none either to Ruth Anna's remembered dark-eyed beauty.

"Do you think I look like him?"

"No offense," Bunch said, grinning. "Since if he had a tail instead of a nose he might be mistaken for the south end of that mule of his headed north. *Some* connection, though," he said.

Cutler remembered the first time he had encountered Yeager, on the second floor of a building in Washington. He had never seen so many high-ranking officers since, so many buttons in that era of double-breasted frock coats, so many starred shoulder boards.

"I was sent to him by a woman friend of his in sixty-four," he said. "He was to make a soldier of me." ("A decent man of you," was what Ruth Anna had said in actuality.) "He was a staff officer in Old Brains's headquarters then. He turned me over to a colonel, who turned me over to a captain—I ended up serving in a Pennsylvania regiment right at the end of the war, when things were coming apart. I captured a pack of rebs in a schoolhouse. I was given a field commission—"

"The mustang lieutenant," Bunch said. "But did Yeager have to do with that?"

"Not with that, but he arranged for me to remain in the army after the war, with the commission in force. He probably had to throw some weight around to do it."

"Why would he?"

It was another familiar question. Cutler swallowed another dose of the whiskey. If he had a friend in the army, it was Sam Bunch. "It must have been the woman who sent me to him," he said. "She was a San Francisco madam."

"Oh, yes, yes, you were raised in a whorehouse, as everyone has heard."

"I'd gotten into some trouble and the Hounds were after me—"

"*Dogs?*"

"They were a gang of pimps and gunmen. The madam was an old friend of Yeager's. He likes to brag that she was in love with him. 'The most beautiful woman in San Francisco in love with a young lieutenant at the Presidio,' is the way he puts it."

He checked his machinery: some tremor in his chest, a queer ache in his arms, hands clasping the whiskey glass like some kind of handle. But it was a relief to be saying these things to Sam Bunch.

"Anyway, he's kept track of me all these years. I'll see him every six months or so—more frequently in the two years I've been down here. We'll talk about Ruth Anna. He'll tell stories about those days in San Francisco—before I was born. Gold Rush times. Once he showed up at Fort Meade to tell me Ruth Anna was dead. He got drunk that night, so she had meant a good deal to him."

It was that night that he realized that the "young lieutenant at the Presidio" had been in love with the most beautiful woman in San Francisco. He had realized that all the women he himself had been interested in had in some way resembled Ruth Anna. She had died in Sacramento, in "reduced circumstances." Of course she died of some foul disease, Yeager had said bitterly, repeating and repeating the phrase, as though to make himself believe it. He himself had not even been able to believe she was dead. How could anyone so alive in his memory be dead? And if she lived on in his own life, what of that of the "young lieutenant at the Presidio"?

Bunch was regarding him, squinting one eye and then the other, perhaps feigning more drunkenness than was the case. At the bar some argument was in progress.

"Whenever I'd see him like that, I'd think there was going to be some revelation," he went on. "I'd thought I might be a bastard of his—by some girl in the house, say. But there's never been any revelation. Perce Robinson's always on hand, and since he's helping Yeager with his memoirs, I suppose all that's said is grist for the mill."

"So he got you out of a court-martial for striking a superior officer in a brawl over some whore," Bunch said.

"I'm exceedingly grateful that he used his influence to talk certain interested parties out of seeing me cashiered," he said, tapping fingers to his forehead in a salute of obeisance. "And having me reassigned down here as one of his aides.

There was a civilian chief of scouts then. I took over the Hoyas when he died of lockjaw. There was talk of my expanding to a company, because of Yeager's belief in Indian scouts. But there was peace then, after Caballito's other bustout, and so he lost interest. I report directly to Yeager, so Dougal doesn't have much say as to how I conduct myself. Or rather I report to Percy, and my orders come through Percy. Still, every once in a while Yeager will have an attack of nostalgia, and he'll show up, or summon me to Fort Blodgett. I guess I'm fond of the old buzzard, and I know I have to be grateful to him—he will remind me of that. But he can be a pain in the butt."

"Famous for it," Bunch said.

Cutler reminded himself that he had been drinking since retreat, wine, brandy, and now this terrible forty-rod; he was in danger of talking too much, like a dam broken. Confidences such as these had not passed between him and Sam before, even snowbound for ten days in a Dakota blizzard, huddled together with all their blankets and the buffalo hide piled on top of them. In those days Bunch had had no question to ask, and Cutler no impulse to reply if he had. When General Yeager had interceded in the court-martial proceedings, Cutler had found himself en route for New Mexico Territory so swiftly that he had not had time even to say good-bye to Sam Bunch.

He said, "I wonder if you can understand a madam being the most sought-after woman in San Francisco. That was in the fifties. San Francisco was a special place then, and so were the madams."

Probably Ruth Anna had indeed died of a "foul disease," he thought, but something in his head balked at the idea that she had had clients, or even lovers. When he had known her, she had had gentlemen admirers.

"I went to school with the nuns," he said. "I'd get into fights there, and I remember once Ruth Anna was summoned to the school. Maybe I was seven then." He had to stop himself from giggling. "It was like seeing a battle cruiser appear in that pond outside. She wore a hat that made her appear eight feet tall. She had a beautiful, olive-skinned face with enormous eyes—she was so nearsighted that she had to wear queer little round eyeglasses when she did her accounts. She had on a rust-colored gown that must have had ten yards of material draped and tucked and fitted, maybe forty pounds of velvet. She had an impressive bosom, and they wore bustles then, and in between a waist you could've put your two hands around. Well, there she was, and there was little dried-up Sister Joseph in her white cowl. She wouldn't even look up at Ruth Anna's face, she just fixed on the owl-headed gold pin Ruth Anna wore for a brooch at her throat—" Enough.

"Interesting," Bunch said, nodding judiciously. He poured more whiskey for himself. "And later, when you were pulling a field commission, I was dancing with pretty women at the Academy. I thought an officer's life was all levees and balls, with a few fights with rebels in between. I married one of those pretty women, too! But didn't she love her Daddy, that one! I believe she loved him because she thought he didn't have a cock. It surely was a shock to her to learn I had one! Never got over it."

Cutler was relieved that they were off the subjects of Yeager and Ruth Anna. "Well, here's to women, Sam!"

"Can't live with 'em or without 'em," Bunch said, ticking glasses. He lowered his voice. "So you were fucking the wife of the shavetail that was killed, and some lawyer's wife in Madison too. I don't know how you do it, you scaly bastard."

"It must be my gentle nature and good looks."

"Old Cutlery," Bunch said fondly. "But it don't look like you have a whole lot of pals in this outfit."

"Not many," he said.

That night in his bedroll, listening to Kills-a-Bear's snorting snores and gazing up at the uncountable stars with his head spinning and his stomach lurching from too much bad whiskey, Cutler saw a dead man hovering in his memory's eye. It was not Lonny Helms, but a pimp named Big Ed Raines. He had seen many dead men in his career as a soldier, but the deadest man he had ever seen was Ed Raines. He had shot the pimp in the eye for the bloody beating of a young whore he, at seventeen, had convinced himself that he was in love with. Raines lay spread-eagled on the floor with blood puddling in his eye and coursing down his cheek, while Lizzy crouched on the bed in her shift, stuffing her fingers into her mouth to keep from shrieking. And so it had been perfectly natural, when he heard a captain he detested anyway brag-

APACHES 31

ging in a Deadwood saloon of the beating he had given a whore, to say that in his, Cutler's, experience, it was only pimps who beat their whores and that he was surprised to learn that pimps were admitted to the Academy, much less commissioned as officers in the Army of the United States. His speech, and Captain Howie's response, had resulted in his punching a superior officer, who, in falling, had bumped his head on a table corner hard enough to be rendered unconscious.

For the earlier crime and other abuses in which he, as darling of the parlor house on Delight Street on San Francisco's Nob Hill, had indulged himself—the free tricks scrounged, the cigars, liquor and laudanum sampled and appropriated, the general arrogance of a seventeen-year-old male, whorehouse bred and attractive to women—he had been banished to Washington, D.C., to Ruth Anna's old friend, General Yeager.

"It is time that gentleman took you in hand," Ruth Anna had said. "Let him make a soldier of you, since you choose to disport yourself with firearms. You will inform him that it is his duty to make a decent man of you." She looked like an angel of banishment in his memory. He would never forget a simple aspect of her face or figure, especially those great eyes in which he could still drown, the cloud of dark hair that wreathed her features in their disapproval, their disappointment, even dislike; yet still, for all her severity, there remained that tenderness of aspect that had perhaps been the very basis of her beauty, so that even in his disgrace he could feel that one day he might be forgiven, summoned back, as though it had only been a temporary punishment—

But he had never seen her again, and four years ago General Yeager had told him that she was dead, in Sacramento, in reduced circumstances, of a foul disease.

3

They made camp in volcanic terrain fifteen miles south of the border—Cutler, Bunch, and the Hoyas Tazzi, Kills-a-Bear, Lucky, and Jim-jim. They were to meet with the emissaries of Caballito, with whom Lucky had made contact. When the time and place of the meeting had been settled upon, General Yeager would proceed to the chosen site, to parley with Caballito and Dawa.

Cutler and Bunch waited, sweating in oven heat in the shade of cottonwoods along a dry creek, the scouts on watch on higher ground. Tazzi hissed penetratingly, raised his rifle and pumped it above his head, four, five, six times. They waited. Cutler watched a drop of sweat thread its way down Bunch's blond-stubbled cheek.

Six bucks appeared on the ridge, long-haired, turbaned, wearing the high Apache moccasins, bare-thighed beneath their breechclouts, one in a white-eye vest, two in buckskin shirts. Red paint striped their cheeks horizontally.

"War paint?" Bunch whispered, lounging at ease against a patchy-barked trunk.

"Just Sierra Verde identification. Red Stripe People."

"Pretty tactical for savages."

Lucky led two of the bucks down toward them. They carried their rifles ported at exactly the same slant, a middle-aged warrior with a flat, dark face, and a younger man with a filthy headband.

Tazzi, puffed by his role as interpreter in Nochte's absence and before Dandy Bill's arrival with the general, stood and barked at the Verdes. He and Lucky conferred. He nodded portentously to Cutler and beckoned with the Apache paddling motion for the emissaries to approach. Cutler and Bunch stood to face them. Cutler recognized the older man

32

as Cump-ten-ae, pinned to whose filthy vest were a number of gimcrack badges. The younger man looked frightened, eyes slipping right and left. A breeze rustled in the branches above them, cooling.

With Tazzi's and Lucky's help, some sign language and Spanish, and the Apache he knew, Cutler got the message across. Nantan Lobo and Nantan Caballito would meet at the place decided upon, to the end that Caballito and the Red Stripe People could return to the United States in peace. Not to San Marcos, that was understood; to Bosque Alto. Lucky would already have broached that idea. Cump-ten-ae looked scornful at the name of the Madison County reservation, and railed at Tazzi: the Sierra Verdes could not trust the white-eye, who had many times broken his promises!

Lucky, Tazzi, and Cutler exchanged glances. Bunch stood frowning, thick arms folded on his chest.

Cump-ten-ae gestured that Caballito was far from this place.

"Nantan Lobo is also far from here. Perhaps in three days' time they will meet," Cutler communicated. At this place, or elsewhere?

The two Sierra Verdes conferred. The brass cartridge cases in their ammunition belts glittered in the sun that filtered through the light green leaves. A half day south of here there was good water and better forage.

"It is well. In three days." Cutler held up fingers.

Cump-ten-ae nodded and made a palm-up salute. Without another word the Sierra Verdes turned their ponies and started back up the hill toward where their comrades waited, rifles at the ready. When all had disappeared, Bunch dropped to his seat against the cottonwood trunk.

"How did it go, Pat? I couldn't make out much. Three days came across."

Cutler was sighing with his own relief. "It may have gone better than it will when Dandy Bill shows up. One of their complaints is that the interpreters tell lies."

That afternoon he and Tazzi went hunting. Lucky had taken a message to the general, and Jim-jim rode into the nearest town to return with two bottles of mescal. That night they feasted on wild pig and the scouts got drunk, staggering, clowning, and shouting with laughter at their own antics: Cutler knew that they could turn very ugly when drunk.

Brutal fights erupted on the reservation from orgies of the Apache beer called *tiswin*. Women were beaten, men killed. The record of the blue soldiers was not much better, however. Drunk on whiskey, he himself had battered Captain Howie unconscious in a Deadwood saloon.

"The difference," he told Bunch, "is that they don't have the sense we have, that tells us if we do x, y happens inevitably. They will go ahead and do x anyway."

"Just like you, you crazy mustang," Bunch said. "Just the same, I'm looking forward to training a company of scouts. I wonder how Caballito'll take that."

"In that same no-y kind of way, I'd think," Cutler said.

The next day they moved to the meeting ground, where there was a thicker grove of cottonwoods and water standing in pools in the stream bed. The area was alive with Apache sign, the scouts were jumpy, and Cutler was more affected by their nervousness than he liked to admit. The hours crept. Bunch seemed anything but nervous, whittling from a chunk of white wood a square box with a ball inside. In his jeans trousers, leather chaps, checked shirt, and broad-brimmed hat, he looked like a cowboy on a south-of-the-border hunting trip. Cutler was similarly attired, in case they were intercepted by Mexican troops.

On the third morning he was awakened at first light by Kills-a-Bear poking him, whispering, and pointing. A *ranchería* had magically appeared on the next hill, five wickiups of branch ribs caught together at the apex, two of them already covered with blankets, canvas pieces, and hides. Women moved among them and feathers of smoke rose.

About noon General Yeager arrived aboard Aggie, wearing his pith helmet and many-pocketed khaki jacket. Following him was an army ambulance and a pack train of mules driven by a tobacco-spitting packer. Captain Robinson and two squaws popped out of the ambulance, dusty as museum pieces. Yeager explained that the squaws had been left behind in Caballito's breakout and had been transported here by way of Bosque Alto so they could describe the reservation to the renegades. One was a wife of Dawa, Pow-ae, an ancient, flat-faced matron clad in elaborate layers of skirts, a short blouse, and graying hair in braids. The other was young, plump, and silent with fright. Dandy Bill followed them out, a dark, sour young man, swinging a black hat to beat the dust from his white-eye suit. He was a half-breed who had been captured by Apaches as a child and had grown up among them.

"'They that stand high have many blasts to shake 'em,'" the general declaimed, stalking up and down before Cutler, Bunch, and Robinson. "'And if they fall they dash themselves to pieces.' That's *Richard Third.* Ah, but it's taking chances that puts the ginger in life. If we succeed here we'll all be hailed as heroes for a little while. If we fail I may get my comb trimmed."

"*Zigosti,*" Kills-a-Bear said, approaching with a pale, fragrant loaf of mescal bread. He had been trading with the Verdes ensconced in the visible *ranchería.* "Nantan Lobo, Nantan Bigotes, Nantan Tata," Kills-a-Bear said, offering the loaf. Cutler took it and thanked him.

"What's that mean, *bigotes* and *tata?*" Bunch asked.

"*Bigotes* is mustaches. *Tata*'s a kind of kindly uncle—that's me. *Lobo*'s the gray wolf."

Yeager looked pleased; sometimes he was so devious Cutler thought he would never understand him, at other times he was childishly transparent. The scouts had begun calling Cutler Nantan Tata after he carried Nochte out of the Rock Creek fight. Kills-a-Bear stood watching Cutler hunk up the loaf and present pieces to the general and Sam Bunch. The three of them chewed the starchy, sweet Apache staple, the general nodding and pointing to his throat in appreciation, until Lucky took his leave.

"Tastes like perfume," Bunch said.

"If soldiers would eat it, we could chase Indians with fewer encumbrances," the general said, munching his handful with apparent enjoyment.

From the clearing beyond the ambulance, the scouts watched, grinning and whispering together. They were an exotically shabby bunch in their filthy clothes and red headbands, their wild hair and dirty faces: savages of a murderous and desperate race, Cutler thought. He knew in his heart that Apaches who had been raiders all their lives, whose fathers for centuries had been raiders, could not be changed to fit the white-eye model in a generation. On the white-eye reservation they found their lives hemmed in by boredom and diminished by indignities and injustices. They had to learn to steal in order to feed starving children, and to buy the whiskey that was the universal palliative for hopelessness. Some of them might join the scouts to earn the blue-soldier dollar, and others in desperation would break out of the reservation to become raiders again, hostiles who would eventually be wiped out. For if a warrior was killed, a generation was required to raise another; if a trooper died, Nantan Lobo simply requisitioned a replacement. They called themselves Indeh, the dead, even these Hoyas. Maybe the young Sierra Verde chief, Joklinney, would be changed by Yeager's San Francisco into something his fellows could never be, but that remained to be seen.

Tazzi cried, in his hectoring voice, "No plenty pretty squaw Nantan Lobo bring. Ho!" His humor convulsed him. "Ugly squaw cook for scout-fella, ho?" He spouted Apache at the two women who stood close together for protection, their eyes sliding from Tazzi to Dandy Bill, as he stalked up. Arms folded, he questioned the older woman in his harsh voice.

After a moment Dandy Bill said contemptuously, "This old one say she left behind by Dawa. Too old to live off reservation. Knees hurt too much! Cannot walk so far." He barked questions at the younger one.

"This one frighten her husbin beat her. She hides when Nantan Caballito say they leave San Marcos. They cannot find! She do not like San Marcos, but do not like live Sierra Madre, very hard." Dandy Bill strode away, as though his duty had been accomplished, to stand alone in the shade, frowning into one of the pools.

Cutler considered the fact that these two had rebelled against the departure of the Red Stripe People from San Marcos on Caballito's orders. What if a majority of a band did not wish to return to a life of raiding? Was their leader obliged to bow to their will? If this wife of Dawa's had aching knees, what of Dawa himself, who must be over seventy? He watched Lucky offering mescal bread to the squaws.

"I will wager that Caballito accepts my offer after the proper amount of argument," General Yeager said.

"And here he is, I believe," Captain Robinson observed.

On the ridge a squad of Apaches with red-striped cheeks gazed down on them. One, slightly in advance of the others, wearing a buckskin shirt, was Caballito.

Three rode down into the camp in single file, headbands over mud-dark, red-striped faces, ragtag clothing, fine stolen horses, and Springfield breechloaders: Caballito, Big Ear, and old Dawa. Seven others remained on the ridge, rifles at the ready.

Big Ear was young, shark-mouthed, squinting right and left, a white band around his forehead, black locks falling to his shoulders. He held up to ride beside the old chief, a tiny man with a face as wrinkled as a black walnut. But it was the first rider who captured Cutler's eye: the infamous chief of the Sierra Verdes, a medicine man who was supposed to speak with the thunder, a war chief reviled as a ruthless murderer, but famous for the cunning of his ambushes, the ferocity of his warriors, the swiftness of his movements on a raid, and the courage of his stand against General Yeager in the Green Range three years ago, a leader who had made his Sierra Verde band the epitome of the word *Apache*.

He was younger than Cutler would have thought, with a big-nosed face, deep, close-set eyes, a slash of a mouth, and a gold ring winking in his left ear. He looked savage, arrogant, and intelligent as he turned his head with slow dignity to examine the clusters of men who waited for him.

The three dismounted, Big Ear helping Dawa down. General Yeager advanced to meet them; he and Caballito embraced stiffly. Dawa toddled over to seat himself beside the root end of a down timber. Caballito spoke in a deep voice in Apache, Dandy Bill facing him in his rusty black suit.

Cutler did not like the half-breed, nor trust him as an interpreter. He said, "I beg your pardon, General, but I believe Nantan Caballito knows enough Spanish for me to conduct this parley."

Yeager gave him a steely glance. "I prefer to manage this through a proper *Apache* interpreter, Cutler. For the sake of *precision. Comprende?*"

Dandy Bill, who had reddened angrily, said, "He say 'Why have you come here, Nantan Lobo?'"

"I have come to persuade him to return to the United States and live in peace."

"He say he will never return to San Marcos."

"I ask him to return to Bosque Alto."

There was a pause for Caballito's reflection. He looked proud and remote. Cutler thought he would consent to return to Bosque Alto after the proper amount of argument, as the general had predicted.

"If we do not?" Caballito said in slow English.

Yeager tapped his riding crop against his boot, paced two steps to the right, returned, drew himself up dramatically. "Then I will pursue and kill you all if it takes fifty years."

Dandy Bill translated this into a harsh bark of Apache. Caballito broke into a broad grin.

"Say true?" he said.

"Say true!"

"Then I will remain in Mexico!"

"The Mexicans will kill you and take scalps, and sell the women and children!"

Caballito laughed harshly and made a slashing gesture with his right hand. "Indeh kills Mexicans with rocks, saves cartridges for white-eye!" The Apaches hated the Mexicans more than they hated Americans, out of centuries of massacres, scalp-hunting for bounties, and the enslavement of women and children. The Mexicans hated and feared the Apaches even more than the Americans did, out of those same centuries of raids and massacres.

Big Ear was also laughing, making the same gesture. "Yes! With rocks!" Dawa giggled and nodded vigorously. Caballito strode up and down before them, speaking loudly and at length, Dandy Bill translating in short bursts of speech.

"I lived at peace at San Marcos. I promised Nantan Lobo I would live at peace and I lived at peace. That man Dunaway is very bad. Always he cheats the Indeh. The weight of the meat is not enough. The flour is very bad. Still I lived at peace until men came with papers against me. They say they will take me to prison, also these two with me here, Nantan Dawa and Big Ear, also others. As Joklinney was taken to the white-eye prison. Nantan Lobo has promised that this will not be. These men have come with papers against me so I can no longer live at peace at San Marcos."

He halted, folded his arms, and gazed challengingly at Yeager, who faced him standing militarily erect.

"These papers are for crimes of the Sierra Verdes when they broke out of San Marcos three years ago. The papers cannot be served so long as Caballito remains on a reservation. Only when he is off the reservation, and a hostile, can he be taken to the white-eye prison like Joklinney."

"Caballito's promises have met the promises of Nantan Lobo," Caballito said.

"Nantan Caballito must tell me of these papers instead of running away to Mexico. At Bosque Alto the Sierra Verdes will be with the Nahuaque, who are their friends. There are blue soldiers at Fort McLain who will see that the sheriff from Tucson will not bring any papers to take Caballito to the white-eye prison. But the blue soldiers cannot help you when you are off the reservation, for then the law says you are hostile, and they must pursue and try to kill you. You must return where you will be safe, and live in peace there."

"I am safe in Mexico!" Caballito said, drawing himself up tall.

"I believe you are not safe. The Mexican army will pursue and kill you."

Big Ear shouted, "You talk of killing, Nantan Lobo! We kill you also!" At his yell the guards on the ridge jerked their weapons higher, half aiming them. Cutler felt the butt of his revolver in his hand in the lock of tension. The squaws had hunched their shoulders as though against blows. Caballito made an expansive gesture and the guards lowered their Springfields.

"There will be no killing here. Here is talk. The wind, the rocks, the trees, hear what we say here. I say to you, Nantan Lobo, that I will trust you. Other white-eye I do not trust." His eyes met Cutler's for a moment, hard, dark, and hostile as splinters of obsidian.

"Then you will return to Bosque Alto?" Yeager said.

It seemed to Cutler that Caballito vibrated where he stood. There was a silence. Yeager summoned the two squaws. They hurried forward and presented themselves to Caballito. Dandy Bill told them to describe what they had seen at Bosque Alto. At least there were woods and running streams in the hills of the Nahuaque reservation, Cutler knew—unlike the desert that was San Marcos. Dawa's wife spoke eagerly; the other, overwhelmed by the great men who surrounded her, had to be frequently prompted. Big Ear grated a question and the young squaw recoiled as though she had been struck. Dawa spoke to his wife in a blurred voice, smiling and patting his plump belly.

Caballito glanced from face to face, and again Cutler felt

the pressure of those fierce eyes like a hot breath passing over his face. "I will return to Bosque Alto," Caballito said.

He and Yeager embraced. Now the black eyes glistened with tears. Stepping away from the general, the Apache declaimed something in a deeper voice, and Dandy Bill paused before he translated:

"How the white-eye squeezes the Indeh, until we are fewer and fewer, until the Indeh will be gone from th᠎ earth. It is as you wish, then, great Ussen?"

When Caballito stalked over to seat himself with Dawa and Big Ear, he appeared to have recovered himself. Arrangements were made. Yeager would return to Bosque Alto immediately to make certain that the reservation was ready to receive the Red Stripe People. Captain Bunch and Lieutenant Cutler would remain here in order to accompany the band across the border. From there on they would be guarded by blue soldiers. All of this would take some time, as the Sierra Verdes had broken up into family groups and some of these were already on their way deeper into the Sierra Madre.

Cutler thought that old Dawa was pleased at the arrangement. Big Ear wore a scornful expression, but Caballito now seemed resigned, fires banked. He embraced Cutler and Bunch, and nodded and grinned thanks for the cunning little carving Bunch had created—the carved ball rattling in its carved cage. The three remounted and rode back up the ridge to join their guards. They disappeared.

"Well, sir," Bunch said. "It don't look like you are due for a comb trim just yet."

Yeager strutted up and down, hands clasped at the small of his back. "Ah, but they have not come to Bosque Alto yet! We will hope for no slips between this cup and that lip. Then how long will it be before he breaks out again? Here is an order, Lieutenant Cutler. You will make it your business to ensure that Caballito has no cause to break out of Bosque Alto. You may count absolutely on my support, I want this breakout to be his last, and *the* last. They are terrible setbacks to pacification, to the relationship of the two races, for Apaches settled upon the reservations, for the citizens of the Territory, of course; for the army, and"—he leveled a finger like a revolver barrel at Cutler—"for me! That is a direct order you will attend to, Lieutenant!"

"Yes, sir," Cutler said. Bunch stared at the general with eyebrows hunched like interrogation marks.

"Write that down in economical form, Captain Robinson," Yeager said.

Robinson said, "I thought Big Ear was not entirely pleased with the solution. The old fellow more so."

"You will write that down also. Keep written records, gentlemen," Yeager said to Cutler and Bunch. "The future moves more smoothly when the past has been carefully recorded." He paced again, shaking his head. "How discouraging it is to think that some men are cynical enough to wish Apaches back raiding because there are more profits in war than in peace."

"Caballito has got a force to him, all right," Bunch said. "I guess I would follow him if I was Pache."

Cutler had been very moved by the tears in the war chief's eyes when Caballito had appealed to his god. To be squeezed and squeezed, fewer and fewer, until the Indeh were gone from the earth. He thought he too would have followed Caballito into the Sierra Madre if he had been Apache. He was contentious enough to look forward to laying down some law to Agent Dipple of the reservation and Ran Boland of the store, but realistic enough to know the general's command was as hopeless of execution as forbidding the wind to blow.

General Yeager on Aggie, with Captain Robinson and Dandy Bill in the ambulance, departed the next morning with the pack train of mules following. The scouts dug a mescal oven and rode out in pairs to bring in game. Bunch began whittling another ball and box, whistling tunelessly. Cutler remembered that nerveless waiting of Bunch's, in a Dakota blizzard, for a thaw that had come none too soon. Several times, riding out, Cutler observed small groups of Apaches, sometimes all mounted, sometimes only the bucks, with burdened squaws hurrying alongside the horses, babies in backboards. More *rancherías* sprouted in a broad half-circle south of the camp.

One night, wind rustled in the cottonwood branches with increasing force, and suddenly rain came down as though flung from some celestial bucket. Within half an hour the creek was roaring. Cutler crouched with Bunch under the covering of two shelter halves hurriedly buttoned together. He had a strong sense of anxiety, a kind of frightened hollowness, an anticipation of loss, that he did not understand. Bunch grumbled and shifted, trying to get comfortable while keeping dry. The rain came in violent squalls with bouts of thunder, ceasing before dawn.

In the morning Cutler, Bunch, and the scouts stood beside the swollen, muddy creek, looking across at the far hillside where the closest of the Sierra Verde *rancherías* had been visible. The frameworks of woven branches remained, but the coverings were gone. No figures moved on the slope, no horses either. Lucky had been sent to see if he could find any of the Sierra Verdes.

He held up empty hands as he rode back into camp. All were gone, all. Lucky pushed a hand south.

"Plenty bad sign!" Tazzi said in his harsh voice. In Spanish he added, "Caballito son of thunder. Thunder speak to Caballito!"

The Apaches had many fears, many signs and portents, Cutler knew. How easy it would be to think that the storm carried a message. So Caballito would not go to Bosque Alto at this time, and all had been in vain.

"I'd say that was some order the general gave you," Bunch said philosophically, "keeping the Red Stripers at Bosque Alto, when we ain't even going to get them there in the first place."

With Bunch and the scouts, minus Tazzi, who had gone ahead with the message for General Yeager at Bosque Alto, Cutler rode out of the last pass of Live Oak Canyon, and the fort came into view. In the fading daylight he could still make out the bit of red, white, and blue, so small from here it might be only imagined, at the top of the flagpole in the center of the parade ground—that bit of symbolic color that never failed to push his heart to beating faster, whatever his dislike of his fellow officers and his contempt for military stupidity. Or maybe it only signified that tonight he would sleep in his own bed, in his own cubicle in the bachelor officers' quarters.

McLain was no more a fort than any other such frontier establishment, a post situated in a stand of cottonwoods planted by some past commander—or more likely a commander's wife; on a low hill between higher hills, six adobe-walled and corrugated iron–roofed barracks and mess halls, and a stone administration building all on one side of the parade ground, a string of bungalows for married officers on another. The scouts lived in a clump of sun-faded tents out beyond the corrals. Cutler worried that, if pacification finally was maintained, the Scouts would lose the pittance upon which they had become dependent. He realized that this was exactly the imperative that motivated the Indian Rings, with their profits from the Apache wars.

At the gate he and Sam Bunch parted with the Hoyas to ride past a saluting guard. Jumbo Pizer sat at his desk in the anteroom of the regimental commander's office, as though awaiting their arrival, rising to greet Bunch but ignoring Cutler as he ushered them into Colonel Dougal's office. The colonel greeted them heartily, a skinny, sour-faced old soldier

43

with hair and chin whiskers as pale as his desk-bound face. He was an inept and timid officer, who was, however, well connected in high military circles. Cutler respected him neither in his official capacity nor at the unbuttoned evenings at Ran Boland's, where he was apt to become maudlin about the good old days of wartime. His ambitions had been fulfilled, after a minor feat of arms at Antietam, when he had been brevetted major general. Colonel Dougal longed for the recovery of at least one of those stars as Cutler sometimes longed for the felicities of his own earlier years.

"So General Yeager failed to capture that rascal Caballito this time," Dougal said, looking pleased as Cutler had rarely seen him. "Could've warned him his luck would not always hold! Well, well!"

"A bundle of bad luck, sir," Bunch said. "A thunderstorm, and the thunder's known to speak to Caballito personally. It did seem hard!"

"We think we'll hear from him pretty soon that he wants to come in to Bosque Alto, though," Cutler said, to Dougal's glassy stare.

"Is that so?" the colonel said cheerfully, and turned to Bunch. "Well, Captain, I see you have joined us in the same capacity as Lieutenant Cutler, detached duty as an aide-de-camp to the general—some pet project of his. Cutler, I will expect your report on the major's debacle at Rock Creek as soon as a general's aide can be expected to find the time."

"That report would be appreciated tomorrow, Cutler!" Pizer said forcefully, still without looking at him directly.

"I suppose it will still be appreciated the day after, Mr. Pizer?"

"Is the general still at Bosque Alto, sir?" Bunch inquired.

"No, no, he's returned to Santa Fe," the colonel said. He leaned back in his chair and locked his hands behind his head. "Well, well, general officers can afford to be headstrong and erratic in their ways, if I may say so. Ha, ha! As of course Lieutenant Cutler is aware—no bed of roses being a general's aide, eh, Cutler? Well, well, I won't keep you gentlemen longer; you must be very tired from your exertions, fruitless though they have been. The major's in a perfect dudgeon, complaints about everything under creation." He winked at Cutler, flushed with his pleased expression again. Then he leaned forward until his chin whiskers brushed the table top, and said in a loud whisper. "Penetrated deep into Mexico, did you gentlemen?"

"Fifty miles, it might've been, sir," Bunch said.

"And what did you see there, may I ask? Were you looking for fortifications, military strength, antigovernment sentiments? Surely, man to man, you will not say you were in Mexico merely chasing renegades?"

"Why yes, sir," Bunch said, "that is exactly what we were doing." Cutler wondered what this tack of the colonel's was; he thought it was not mere asininity. He was so tired his legs seemed to be disintegrating into atomized muscle.

Dougal winked at them roguishly. "Never mind it, never mind it, gentlemen. One becomes perhaps overly suspicious at adding twos and twos after thirty-two years in his nation's service." The colonel exhibited a mouthful of yellowing teeth in a stuffed-predator smile and flipped a hand in friendly dismissal.

"I'll have that draft day after tomorrow, then, Cutler?" the adjutant asked, scowling at the window of the anteroom.

"I'll make you a copy of my report to the general," he said offensively, and preceded Bunch outside.

"Will you Christ's sake tell me what that was *aboot* in there?" Bunch said, as they descended the hollow-sounding steps to the street.

"After thirty-two years you put two and two together and get an invasion of Mexico. Then you might make brigadier before you are retired."

"Ah, they are all the same, these old fart colonels," Bunch said.

In the officers' saloon at the Trader's, Jud Farrier leaned against the bar while the enlisted barkeep poured whiskey. He glanced up at Cutler's entrance and quickly away. At a table Pete Olin and little Phil Tupper of E Company studied hands of cards, and beyond them the Iron Major and Captain Smithers were engaged at billiards at the rickety table. Cutler had not been asked to play billiards for months because of a superiority of attitude as well as skill, but this was the first time he had been totally ignored in the officers' saloon.

He asked for whiskey. The place smelled comfortingly of the flour, coffee, bacon, and dried apples stored behind the green curtain, and sourly of whiskey. The two at the table muttered over their cards, as though he was not to be allowed the pleasure of their voices, either. He asked the barkeep if Dr. Reilly had been in tonight.

The contract surgeon had not been in yet. Farrier had turned his back. Smithers's eyes rolled toward Cutler, to be jerked away.

He realized that this was the Silence, a conspiracy inflicted by cadets at the Academy upon one of them who had offended. A cadet guilty of a dishonorable act that had not caused his dismissal might be given the silent treatment by his fellows, who would never speak to him or even appear to notice him except unavoidably in the line of duty. He had heard West Pointers brag of continuing a Silence throughout an officer's career. Grown men. He was being Silenced.

His own dilemma was how long he must remain at the bar in order to establish his contempt for their contempt. Of course the Iron Major, who would doubtless have to face a board of inquiry into the Rock Creek ambush, was keeping himself covered. For his own part he would do well to write his report of that episode for General Yeager tonight, and make a copy for Colonel Dougal.

It pleased him that there must be a good head of curiosity built up over the south-of-the-border sojourn, which no one here could ask him about.

"Quiet tonight," he announced to the enlisted barkeep, signed his chit, and departed without waiting for Bunch, whom he had planned to meet here. Let Bunch tell them about the Mexico expedition. Walking to his quarters in the cool breeziness beneath the cottonwoods, he fought down a hot surge of nausea.

He wearily climbed the stairs to his room, lit a candle, and sank down on the bed, listening for the friendly rat who shared his quarters.

There was a soft knock, his name whispered through the door. He felt a new crush of fatigue, a disgust at himself: his filthy uniform, his unwashed body, the bowel rumble of all the careless errors, spites, and rancors of his life. Emily Helms slipped inside, gowned in black, a black veil concealing her face. She knelt before him in one of her precipitous movements that he had once thought he admired. "Pat!"

"I'd thought you'd be gone by now, Em."

"Tomorrow." Now he could make out by the candle's little light the swimming eyes fixed upon his from behind the veil. Her black-gloved hand caught his.

"I'm sorry about Lonny."

"You left him to be—" She broke off in a sob.

"He was dead, Em," he said patiently. "They mutilated him *after* he was dead. They do that." The Apaches mutilated their dead enemies so they would have to spend the hereafter mutilated, as Mangas Coloradas, murdered and mutilated by the soldiers of the California Column, would have to spend eternity without a head.

"They said you—"

"They don't know. I know. I'm sorry his body was mutilated, but I can assure you that he was not tortured."

"You left him there!" She whispered, "Was it because of *me*, Pat?"

Her thought processes were as complex as her widow's weeds. Did she want to think he had left her husband to be mutilated—or, still alive, horridly tortured—because of his insane love for her? He breathed deep of her scent of lavender powder and dried flowers, but he could smell his own exhausted stink as well.

Should he argue that he had not seduced her, as she seemed convinced? She had nagged him to take her hunting, to teach her to shoot—Lonny had not liked to hunt—to take her, in particular, to shoot wild turkeys. On that hunt no wild turkeys had been shot. She seemed to believe that he had instigated the affair, and, having had his way with her, deserted her for another. He knew she had been unfaithful before him, but for some reason his desertion of her for Lily Maginnis had aroused the ire of the other officers' wives. Lily posed some threat to the whole institution of marriage, so he could understand their closing ranks against her and any man who dared to frequent her. Whereas Emily was only pathetic.

"There was nothing else I could do, Em," he said. "Lonny was dead, and the scout I'd sent to try to bring him out was badly wounded."

"You brought out an *Indian* instead of Lonny! You left Lonny to be mutilated by *savages*! Do you hate me so much, Pat?"

He listened to her sobs, trying to muster the strength for a gentle rebuttal. It seemed to him that everyone else's thought processes operated on the oblique. But maybe the slant was in his own head.

"I know you love—another," she whimpered. "But don't hate poor Em, Pat!"

"I don't hate you. I'm sorry for you. I'm sorry for everything. I wish it could all be done over."

"You even hate the love we once had! You'd even change that!"

"I never promised anything, Em. We both knew it was a temporary insanity."

"I think you've never promised anyone anything, Pat." She rose, taller than he now where he still sat on the edge of the bed. Her gloved hands were clutched together at her breast. Her eyes glistened through the veil.

"Someday, somewhere, Pat, when you promise something—remember me!"

"Good-bye, Em," he said. When he made no move to embrace her, she slipped silently out the door.

Bernie Reilly was the post contract surgeon, not an officer but a civilian employed as an army doctor, a sandy-haired, lean, slightly stooped man with apologetic brown eyes, an ironic tilt to his head, and a wry mouth nestled in his sandy beard. He wore an officer's uniform without insignia except a small patch sewed to his breast pocket, displaying an embroidered caduceus. Cutler knew little about him. On the frontier you did not inquire into a man's origins and anteced-ents unless information was proffered. The postwar army had been a haven for volunteers with plain names and Southern accents, and it was still a destination for men who wished their pasts forgotten. Bernie was a New Englander—from a slight bray that resonated in his voice—a competent and compassionate medical man, married to a childless woman of fading prettiness and the slightly pinched, anxious expression of one for whom life was spinning by too fast.

The next day, after Emily Helms had departed by army ambulance for the railroad, Cutler was invited to tea at the Reillys' quarters, as he often was. Rose Reilly poured from a worn silver service, and Cutler balanced his cup and saucer on his knee.

"Has Pat heard yet, Bernard?" Rose asked.

Bernie's brown eyes peered at him sideways. "There's

been a new order, Pat. Junior officers will not attend Mrs. Maginnis's socials, nor in fact enter the Maginnis house unless so authorized."

He felt himself grinning like a skull. There was an impulse to stretch, but he concerned himself with the cup on his knee. The Reillys watched him, Rose worried, Bernie wry.

"When was this?"

"A week or ten days ago."

He laughed and said, "But I'm the only junior officer who goes there."

"It is simply unbelievable that that silly man would do such a silly thing," Rose said. "I'm sure it will only make you more determined to call on Lily Maginnis, Pat."

"And you don't like her, Rose," he said.

"You know I do not," she replied. "I may agree with Colonel Dougal in certain aspects of the matter, but I do not believe he has the right to make such a promulgation." She smiled at Cutler limply. "Nor do I believe you would obey such an order, Pat."

"No."

"I don't know how much of a name for yourself you wish to make as a disobeyer of orders, Pat," Bernie said mildly.

"Everyone has heard about Rock Creek, then."

"I've heard of it from the major, but also from some enlisted men," Bernie said. "Still, it would take a Pat Cutler to make allies of the major and Colonel Dougal. Nor am I so certain this new prohibition is an illegal order. I think it might be justified on some 'good of the service' basis."

"I take my orders from General Yeager, not Colonel Dougal," he said, and wished he did not sound smug saying it.

"I'm only concerned that it will strengthen your affections for *that woman*," Rose said.

"He does seem to have a certain knack," Bernie said. "Emily Helms, and then Lily Maginnis. It's been a relief to me in my life not to be attractive to married women."

"You are to one married woman, Bernard," Rose said, and colored as she bent to pour more tea. She added, "Bernard and I will not criticize you about Emily, Pat. Others are more than ready to, however."

Rose Reilly was interested in his affairs to about one

degree more than he felt comfortable with. He thought that if anything came up to prevent him from seeing Lily Maginnis this evening he would shatter like a crystal goblet. Nor was it even the powerful anticipation of Lily herself. Her musical evenings radiated a golden glow of good listening, good companionship, good talk—the most culture a frontier community had to offer, and some beauty too, for Lily was beautiful. There was a degree of sumptuousness, there were events that were not merely over when they were done, but could be savored afterward and continued on another occasion.

"The factionalism in Madison has become much more severe," Bernie said frowningly. "William Prim tells me that Maginnis and the Englishman intend to open a competitive store. The colonel is expressing his support for Ran Boland, who is, after all, a former military man."

Colonel Dougal might have benefited by General Yeager's lecture on the Indian Rings, although probably he would not have recognized the Boland & Perkins store as a Ring, nor himself as one of the "corrupted officers."

"You were a regular at Boland's poker game, Pat," Bernie said. "And were seduced away to Lily Maginnis's musicales. You can understand the colonel's tactic as a friend of Boland's."

"I don't think Ran Boland is a friend of his," he said. But he missed the male good-fellowship of the poker sessions above the store, and, although he had come to regard the other regulars there as bullies and toadies, he was sorry that it must seem that he had deserted them for their professed enemies. "Do you know what Frank Maginnis calls the store?" he asked. "Usury, Malefaction, and Collusion, Incorporated."

Bernie chuckled and said, "And I know what they call him." The original enmity between Frank Maginnis and Ran Boland seemed to have arisen over the will of Boland's dead partner. Boland damned the lawyer as a troublemaker and spiteful devil, although his venom seemed to Cutler excessive for the cause. For his part, Maginnis's bayed denunciations of the store's perquisites and tyrannies seemed excessive also.

Rose said, "Surely our friendship is well enough established so that I can tell you what I have learned of Lily Maginnis. My cousin lives in Albany, New York."

Their friendship was well enough established to be the only amenity Fort McLain offered him. It had taken Cutler some time to get over thinking this couple's liking for him was a kind of condescension, but he had got over it, and now their good opinion had become of consequence to him. But Lily Maginnis was another amenity he could not imagine losing.

"I know," he said. "She was a bad wife and a bad mother. She left her husband and child to run off with Frank Maginnis."

Rose shook her head so sharply a lock of brown hair fell over one eye, and she brushed at it in an irritated manner. "That's not all. She was very active in the woman's suffrage cause. I do not disapprove of that, Pat! But there was a handsome young minister in Albany who was also very active and very effective as a preacher. There was an affair. It was a great scandal, my cousin writes me. Albany was shaken to its roots, and the suffrage movement was much discredited. It became a laughingstock in the newspapers there. Lily Maginnis did not leave her husband and child. She was banished in disgrace, and there was a great deal more dirty linen washed over possession of the child. Frank Maginnis was a young member of her husband's law firm. And that was still another scandalous affair."

"People often come West leaving behind them scandals in the East, Rose," Cutler said gently.

Her blue eyes clouded, and she glanced down at her cup. He was afraid suddenly that she would burst into tears, her upper lip stretched down tautly like that of a child who has been rebuked.

"What I have told you does not matter to you," she said.

"I'm afraid it doesn't, Rose."

"My dear," Bernie said, "I believe that Pat is hopelessly enmeshed in the toils of this scandalous female."

"Yes, take his side," Rose said.

"I'm afraid that what Bernie says is true," Cutler said.

"Then you are in love and there is nothing to be done about it, I see," Rose said.

When he took his leave he patted her shoulder awkwardly and gave her the smile that he thought she wanted.

Madison was an easy hour's ride from Fort McLain, and he headed into town with his spirits tight and high after almost a month in the field. The sun on the eastern slopes brightened the spangles of late snow there, above the dark fringes of evergreens. The nearer hills were already in shadow. He passed a wagon, ox-drawn, heading toward town also, the wagoneer napping on his seat. Once in these parts teamsters had kept a sharp eye out for hostiles, rifles loaded and within reach. Now the Apaches were concentrated on the reservations, except for the Red Stripe People, deep in the Sierra Madre in Mexico.

Thinking of Lily at her grand piano, playing for this evening's guests, he found himself remembering Jimmy Blazer. If, in his youth, he had been a foundling with a houseful of "mothers," so there had been men who had acted the part of fathers. Jimmy had been one of these, the "professor" who played the piano in the three-story house on Delight Street. In his neat suit, bed-o'-flowers vest, and cravat, hat tipped back on his head and his whole tiny body back-tilted as though in ecstasy, he had tinkled away with many flourishes, entertaining the girls of the house and their clientele—businessmen from the City, miners down from the Sierra, ranchers from the valleys, swells from the great estates down the peninsula. Those evenings singing along with Jimmy Blazer emanated a powerful glow, a promise not even so much of delight as of felicity, and he knew he looked for the same thing in Lily Maginnis's musical evenings.

Like other figures out of his youth, Jimmy had had an education in a mysterious past. He read poetry, reciting and declaiming it with grand gestures. He talked of books with Ruth Anna and with one of the older girls, named Gwen, who also had a cultivated background. Jimmy had taught the boy Pat Cutler to play billiards for money. Another man, a frock-coated Southerner, with long, white, clever hands, had taught him to play poker.

He did not remember when he had first realized that his home life was different from that of the other boys he knew. He lived in servants' quarters with two Mexican maids, plump, jolly sisters, who were the first women to spoil him and who taught him Spanish. He saw the girls of the house, who also spoiled him, at early supper, after which Ruth Anna sometimes invited him to her third-floor parlor, to serve him sarsparilla and herself sherry from a cut-glass decanter. Often one of her swells would be with her, and the three of them would chat as though Pat Cutler were also an adult. The business of the house did not start until after his bedtime, and, if he did peek in a window at night, he saw the girls in their spotless shifts and the gentlemen, almost all of them in fine clothing, crowded around Jimmy Blazer's piano with their arms around each other, singing. It was much later that he had understood that the purpose of the house was not singing with Jimmy Blazer.

Ruth Anna had placed him in St. Catherine's School, where he had instinctively sought to conceal from his schoolmates the fact that he lived in a parlor house. It was at St. Catherine's that he had determined a First Principle. You did not try to conceal a shameful or shocking circumstance, you proclaimed it.

As he rode on into Madison in the fading day, his spirits rising with the distance from Fort McLain and the proximity of town, he reflected on adultery. Frank Maginnis was a very different complacent husband from Lonny Helms, as their wives were very different in the conduct of their affairs. Lily Maginnis's license seemed to come from some established independence, so that Frank's acceptance of it—if he even paid it any attention!—seemed to come from strength. Emily Helms's had come from contempt for her husband, which contempt Lonny Helms had seemed to share. Adultery was a very different matter to the Apaches. The squaws were usually chaste, but in the exceptions the wronged husbands were honor-bound to cut off the nose-tip of the offending wife. The practice had been forbidden on the reservation, along with the brewing of *tiswin*. Where the ban was enforced, offended husbands beat their wives terribly, sometimes to death, and he knew of one lost honor that had resulted in a murder and a suicide. Surely nose-bobbing was the more humane course in the punishment for adultery.

Lily would point out that guilty men, for their part, were not punished at all.

Coming into town he encountered Sheriff Smith and another man seated on their horses in conversation before the Mexican *tienda*, a big-hatted Mexican watching them from the veranda of the store. The sheriff raised a hand in greeting, a friendly man with disturbingly mismatched eyes in his pale face under a tall pale hat, the star of his office pinned to his vest. Cutler recognized the other as a town hard case named Mortenson, a rangy hatchet-faced man of bad reputation.

"Long time no see, Pat," the sheriff said. "Chasing Paches, I expect."

Pogie Smith was a regular at Ran Boland's poker evenings, along with the prosecuting attorney, Neill MacLennon, and Judge Arthur, and he had been a regular loser. Where did he find the funds, with a wife and a number of children to support on what must have been a small salary? No doubt Usury, Malefaction, and Collusion, Inc. was the answer.

"Stopping in to see Ran, I expect," Pogie said, and, when Cutler made a noncommittal sound, gave him a long, judicious look, jaw set to one side. "I would do it, Patsy. Ran is sort of counting up his friends just now."

"Maybe I will drop by," he said. "I have a purchase to make, at that."

"Good, good," Pogie said, grinning. "Miss you on poker nights, Pat, I do *not*! He's one to look out for over a hand of cards, Clay," he said to the other.

"That so?" Mortenson said, without interest.

Cutler rode on to dismount before the store, tie his reins to the rail, and cross the boardwalk under the big BOLAND & PERKINS sign to buy something for Nochte, who would have one leg shorter than the other for life because his officer had sent him to rescue an already dead white-eye. The interior of the store was dim and cool, with curls of flypaper hanging from the fans. Two armed men lounged against the counter at the far end. Cutler had a sense of them stiffening as he entered, relaxing when the clerk called out to him.

There were racks of clothing, articles of harness tacked up on the walls, shelves of chambray shirts, jeans trousers, and canned goods, stacked sacks of rice, wheat, and cornmeal, a pleasant granary smell. Except for the two guards, a new addition, the store itself had a fusty, old-fashioned innocence. It was upstairs that the feudal power of Madison County was concentrated.

"Something for you today, Lieutenant Cutler?"

He had already seen what he wanted, hanging on the wall—a flat-crowned straw hat sporting red and blue ribbons. While the clerk was dusting his purchase with a brush, Cutler saw the two gun-toters glance up at the stairs. Ran Boland had appeared on the landing, narrow-shouldered and thin-legged, with a gross middle.

"Hello, Ran."

"Come to call, Pat?" Ran Boland leaned heavily against the railing. His fat cheeks sagged as he gazed downward.

"And buy a fancy hat."

"Ah, well, it's Thursday, ain't it! I know where you are heading—new interests, new interests!" Boland grinned with his red lips like a bloated circus clown. "Why, I can remember not so long ago when you came by to talk to Ran and the boys about San Francisco. You would name those streets on Nob Hill like a mackerel snapper telling his beads!"

The two hard cases gaped up at their employer, while the clerk busied himself wrapping Nochte's hat in a sheet of newspaper. In 1863 the California Column had been mustered to march east and drive out the Texans who had invaded New Mexico and Arizona. Many of them, like Ran Boland, had remained after the war, to become the founding fathers of the new Anglo power. Cutler had been very pleased, when he had been transferred to the Department two years ago, to meet a circle of fellow Californians.

"I appreciated the company, Ran," he said.

"I'll bet you've been off chasing Caballito. Old Lobo made a mistake or two there, I hear. Sneaked south of the border to capture Caballito and the Red Stripers captured him instead. Oh, that is a funny one! I suppose you'll tell me it's wide of the mark, though, Pat."

"It's a clear miss, Ran."

Boland laughed. "Well, we'd admire to see more of you, Pat. But I expect you got tired of the kind of poker we could deliver." The fat man turned to labor up two steps and disappear through the door.

It seemed a pun he would have to ignore, his neck aching from gazing up at the clown face. He paid for the newspaper-wrapped hat. As he started out, one of the gunmen—a pudgy fellow named Duffy—glared at him belligerently. It seemed he was established as a Maginnis partisan.

Outside, squinting in sunlight like a blow, it seemed to Cutler that his tenure in the poker sessions upstairs had run the course of Ran's sickness. That first evening he had been welcomed there, the subject of conversation had been the daughter of a rancher all the others knew well, a pretty child of eight who had been thrown by her pony and suffered a broken leg. A collection had been taken, excessive it seemed to him; they had got together a buggyload of candy, dolls, toys, dresses, shoes, a parasol—all the wonders a frontier child might not even know to dream of. Ran Boland, who was then a stout, jolly, red-cheeked man in the best of health, had driven the buggy himself and delivered its contents to the dazed child. But at the other end of that spectrum was the case of a farmer named Cobb from near Riveroaks, who was in arrears to the store. Cobb had tried to hide some fine California riding stock he possessed by having his dim-witted son conceal these assets in a box canyon in the hills. The store had learned of this through an informer, and Boland had sent two riders wearing Mexican Day of the Dead skull masks that could be purchased at the González *tienda*. They had scared the idiot boy into running: "Looked like he was headed straight through for Chicago!" All the stock had been expropriated. "Served him right," the ill, swollen Ran Boland had said bitterly dealing cards. "Teach him and some others a good lesson!"

It was a time too when the disparaging remarks about Colonel Dougal had increased. The poker players referred to him as "old mush balls," from their jokes about battered cavalry testicles, and ridiculed him as "the leastest Injun-fighting colonel in the army," at first behind his back but more and more to his face. It was a fine joke also that Dougal retained his position only because his wife was "keeping company with generals in Washington"—this with knowing winks and grins. Though Cutler had disparaged his commanding officer himself, he was embarrassed that Dougal was so insensitive as to consider this cruel joshing evidence of friendship rather than of contempt.

One afternoon he saw a man and half-grown boy in a spring wagon drawn up before the store, the man descending and crossing the boardwalk while the boy sat in the wagon with a boot up on the brake, staring into his lap with a battered straw hat shading his face. His father took off his own hat before entering the store.

That night Cutler cleaned out the pot in the poker game, and the next day he took the two hundred and sixty dollars out to the tumble-down soddy on the farm near Riveroaks. He almost had to fight Farmer Cobb, hysterical with fear and suspicion, to make him take the money, while the dim-witted son stood by working his hands anxiously together as though washing them.

The next week, for his sins or his reward, he met Lily shopping in the store, a handsome woman dressed in the height of fashion, with a scent like a whiff of another world. She introduced herself and invited him to her Thursday evening soiree. And that first Thursday evening she had summoned him to look at her library, and, while he was examining the shelves of books in their rich leather bindings, called to him from the adjoining bedroom. There she lay naked on the bed, her flesh so white it seemed to illuminate the space around her.

At the door Frank Maginnis clasped Cutler's hand in his two hands. "Come in, come in, Pat!" He was a portly man in a heavy suit and vest, a high, stiff collar, and a striped cravat with a diamond-headed pin. In country where every man and not a few women considered themselves not fully dressed without a firearm, he never carried a weapon. Cutler had formed the opinion that the great love of Frank's life was justice. More particularly, he was obsessed by the injustices perpetrated by the Boland Ring. Farmers and ranchers were forced to purchase their equipment, supplies, and seed from the store because of both propinquity and ongoing debts, on which they paid interest of twenty-five percent per annum, with speedy cooperation of sheriff, county attorney, and judge on the foreclosure of property that became in arrears.

Because of this preoccupation with justice, or injustice, Cutler guessed, Lily was left free to pursue her affairs as a liberated woman in what she called a "free union." And yet it was clear that this married couple cherished each other.

Lily said that Frank had rescued her from bondage. He had been a junior partner in her first husband's law firm, and Maginnis was a name of some political importance in Albany, an uncle of Frank's having been a lieutenant governor. She and Frank had come west, Lily said, in search of a freer, cleaner atmosphere than that of Albany—first to Santa Fe, where Lily had relatives, and then south to Madison, where Frank had immediately become Ron Boland's adversary, as though it had been fated, as though they were two mastiffs locked upon each other's throats.

Lily stood beside the piano, swung half around so that

she resembled a flower on a stalk in her lavender gown. She
was in conversation with a man whose tweed-jacketed back
was turned to Cutler. Dr. William Prim was seated hunched
forward in conversation with Tom Fletcher, the surveryor,
who flipped a hand in greeting to Cutler, and Penn McFall,
the biggest stock-raiser in the county, a broad-framed, white-
haired, noisy oldster, who, like Cutler, had once been a poker
player in the upstairs room at the store.

Two young ranchmen, both armed with revolvers, stood
not far behind Maginnis, one a slim, fair young cowboy not
much over five feet in height, his hair slicked back into a
pompadour from girlishly handsome features. His companion, whose hard, narrow face looked familiar, was a head
taller, with striped trousers stuffed into battered boots, and a
crisply ironed blue shirt.

Lily's hair was folded into a dark roll at the nape of her
neck, and her high-colored face was raised to tweed-jacket.
She smiled absently in Cutler's direction. Frank introduced
him to the fair-haired cowboy, whose name was Johnny
Angell. The taller man was Joe Peake. Frank's gun-toters
were more attractive than Ran Boland's had been.

"Back from chasing Red Stripers, Pat!" Dr. Prim called,
and Penn McFall, as though echoing Boland: "Chased them
until they caught you, *I* heard!"

"Back," he said, nodding as he shook hands with Peake,
who was identified as Martin Turnbull's foreman. He had
heard of Turnbull, new to the county, an Englishman. That
would be Turnbull with Lily, then. Lily's flower pose shifted,
and the pale round of her arm gestured in some response to
the Englishman. Cutler was startled to see smoke rising
between them. Turnbull shifted slightly to reveal his pipe.
He was undistinguished in profile, of medium height, with
brown hair carefully brushed, and heavy brows. Cutler noticed
that young Johnny Angell was as attentive to the two at the
piano as he himself.

"Sure, I've seen this soldier before," Joe Peake said.
"Runs that pack of Pache trackers. So you've been chasing
Injun, Lieutenant. Any luck?"

"Yes," he said. "Bad."

"Some of us out here was fighting Paches while you
soljers was still wearing three-corner britches," McFall all but
bellowed.

Frank ushered Cutler toward Turnbull. Lily's eyes fixed on the Englishman seemed to him a repayment for his casual cruelty to Emily Helms, for it appeared that in the month he had been absent chasing Sierra Verdes he had lost her. She was in love with Martin Turnbull.

Turnbull had a shy manner and an unaggressive English accent. "So pleased to meet you, Leftenant. One has heard a great deal about you."

"You have the advantage on me, sir."

"Martin has recently come up from Texas, where he was looking into investments," Lily said. "He is an English capitalist, and the nicest man in the world, Pat." Her face had a damp sheen to it, and she held her white hands with their several rings clasped beneath her chin. The flesh of her bosom and shoulders gleamed in the lamplight.

"Martin has bought the Peters ranch from Penn," Frank said, standing in his characteristic back-tilted stance, thumbs hooked in his vest pockets. "We have formed a partnership, and we will be setting up a store in competition with Boland & Perkins."

"Yes, I've heard that."

"Met Mr. Boland early on," Turnbull said. "Wanted me to purchase a ranch of his, quite insistently. Said I would never get on in this county if I did not. I sought legal counsel from Frank, and we discovered that we were kindred spirits—not to speak of the bewitching Mrs. Maginnis. We hope to turn a decent profit while benefiting the community."

"We will join in competition with Randy in every one of his enterprises," Frank said. "Every legitimate one, that is. We will lend money, but not at twenty-five percent. We will certainly not demand the condition that all supplies be purchased from us or crops be sold to us."

"What about a 'miracle herd,' Mr. Turnbull?" Joe Peake asked, and there was more laughter. Boland's miracle herd never seemed to get any smaller, however many head were sold to Bosque Alto reservation and Fort McLain.

"No, I don't believe we intend to go into the rustling business, Joe," Turnbull said.

"Martin has already been threatened," Frank said. "A dead coyote on his doorstep. And of course I have been the recipient of many such offerings." Frank glanced meaningfully toward the young cowboy with his holstered revolver.

Johnny Angell winked at Cutler, then drew a severe face. "We are keeping a hard watch on those coyotes!"

"Martin doesn't take such threats seriously, and no doubt that is the correct attitude," Frank said. "But this young man has been employed at my insistence, and Joe will be running the ranch."

"You seem to have landed in Madison County with both feet, Mr. Turnbull," Cutler said.

"Indeed it has been pleasant to land in such a nest of like-minded citizens. It was not like this in Texas, I can assure you."

"Lieutenant Cutler plays the piano beautifully," Lily put in.

"I shall hope to hear you both this evening!" Turnbull replied, and set the bit of his pipe between his teeth.

The Mexican servant, in spotless white with a red sash, passed a tray of punch cups.

"And do you play this instrument, Mr. Turnbull?" Cutler said. Cynicism at the pretensions of this provincial social gathering seemed the only antidote for the poisons he was trying to digest. But Lily was what she was, as she had warned him. And he must remember what he had said to Emily about temporary insanity.

"Oh, I am an appreciator merely!" Turnbull said. "But I do insist that our hostess exercise her talent for us immediately!" This was seconded, and Lily swept to the piano. Seated, her skirts arranged, she leaned forward nearsightedly to shuffle through the music on the rack. Cutler bet himself that she would begin with a Chopin étude. Right. Applauded for this, she would proceed to the humoresque. Right again. "Bravo!" Martin Turnbull cried, applauding.

The doctor stood beside Cutler, red round of face between gray sideburns; he was a Philadelphian of fine old family, a friend of the President of the Republic, who had chosen to immerse himself in this western backwater: rumors of a murder, of a tragic marriage—many rumors, no facts. Dr. Prim applauded by tapping the wrist of his hand that held a punch cup with his fingertips. Lily swung around on the piano seat to summon Cutler.

Seated before the gleaming keys, he thought of Jimmy Blazer and that other piano appreciation society—not so far different in mood from this one tonight. He leaned back on the seat as Jimmy had leaned back, he imagined a straw hat tipped on his head, a cigar dripping ashes on his bed-o'-flowers vest. He played "The Last Rose of Summer," swinging from that into a Blazer medley, proceeding next to soldier favorites and acclaim. Especially enthusiastic were the young gun-toter and Penn McFall, who stood close behind him, singing.

A broken heart lent his fingers facility. He played "Mother, Kiss Me in My Dreams," "Susan Jane," "Little Annie Rooney," "La Paloma." When he stopped and rose, his repertory exhausted, grinning and shaking his head to calls for more, he felt more cheerful. Lily could bear being upstaged this one time.

"Most enjoyable, sir!" Turnbull said. He had refilled his pipe. "You have the popular touch!"

"Ah, that brings back old memories, Pat!" Dr. Prim said.

Conversations began again. Cutler saw that Johnny Angell kept a constant eye on Martin Turnbull, as though he took his job seriously even here. Dr. Prim had been reading Leo Tolstoy's latest novel in its French translation and was filled with enthusiasm and, Cutler thought sourly, self-importance. Turnbull had also read it, but made less of the accomplishment. In fact, it was difficult not to like the Englishman, who must already have been invited to Lily's library.

"When I read of the more mature Natasha Rostov, I think of our lovely hostess," Dr. Prim said. "She is a fascinating, headstrong lady."

"I believe that is an apt comparison," Turnbull said, nodding.

"Oh, I must wait for the English translation," Lily said. "My poor French is simply not equal to the task."

"I was taught to read in the Good Book," Johnny Angell said. "That is a book with some headstrong people in it!"

All laughed. Cutler thought this handsome little man a curious choice of gunman. Johnny had worked for McFall, Peake said, more recently for him, and now for Martin Turnbull.

"You watch that little feller, hear!" McFall said to Turnbull. "He would play his tricks on the devil himself!" He excused himself to Lily with lengthy thanks, citing the lateness of the hour, his age, joints, and digestion.

When the rancher had departed, Johnny said, as though

explaining his position to Cutler, "I rode with Mr. McFall's Regulators a year or so back. Me and Joe here, and Jack Grant and Jesse Clary. Called ourselves the four Jays. There was some pestiferous rustlers up from Texas we persuaded to change their ways. But there was other work I didn't take to, so I quit the PM and dodged around till Joe took me on. Now I'm working at Mr. Turnbull's place, like he said."

"Tell them the time you played a trick on Old Mac himself, Johnny!" Joe said. "Oh, it was pure marvel!"

Johnny said, modestly enough, "Well, this prospector came out to the home ranch—the Citadel, Mr. McFall calls it. Older fellow, and graybeard cranky like those fellows get, eyes like they was looking at something about three ranges over. He'd come to ask Mr. McFall some favor or other, and I told him he would have to speak up, Mr. McFall being pretty deaf. Told Mr. McFall the same thing about him." He proceeded solemnly. "Well, they got to shouting at each other. You know how Mr. McFall is about letting anybody get the better of him, and he wasn't going to have that prospector yelling louder than he did. There was some of the hands listening to the conversation stuffing their handkerchiefs in their mouths, but I guess in the end it was one of them that went and told Mr. McFall he'd been sold, and I don't believe Mr. McFall has ever quite forgive me."

Joe Peake whooped with laughter, but now Johnny looked abashed as he accepted another cup of punch.

"That's not all there was to the matter," Martin Turnbull said. "As Johnny has suggested, McFall turned his Regulators to other tasks than driving off rustlers."

"Got to thinking he owned all the land where he grazed stock," Joe Peake said. "Land he hadn't got around to filing on. So the work was running people off that tried to settle by water, and after a while anybody at all."

"A fellow does get mixed up about the right and wrong of a thing sometimes," Johnny said. "But there was Mexes there that had been there before Mr. McFall drovered up from Texas. That are friends of mine, too."

His voice was earnest, and there was a respectful silence. Frank Maginnis said ponderously, "Regulators are not the law. The law is the law. Penn McFall will have a hard time defending the use of his Regulators."

"To whom, Frank?" Tom Fletcher said, and immediately looked as though he wished he hadn't.

"To himself," Frank said. "To me. To posterity. To heaven."

Cutler was asked to tell of the Caballito campaign, and did so. He found himself not making light of it, in the face of Johnny Angell's sincerity.

"But one would think it a perfect solution," Turnbull said, waving gray smoke away from his face. "They will not remain in Mexico, is that the problem, Leftenant?"

"No, sir, they will have to take up raiding again, to keep themselves in horses, and beef, and guns and ammunition."

"Are the Mexican authorities cooperative?"

He explained that Mexicans were fearful of another invasion from the north, and when Apache renegades disappeared into Mexico, American troops were not permitted to follow them.

"More powerful nations tend to be disrespectful of the rights of lesser ones," Turnbull commented. "My own nation is the worst offender in this respect, and I would venture to guess that the United States has learned much at the knee of her mother."

"I know many fellow citizens who believe that the proper southern border of this country is the isthmus of Panama," Dr. Prim said. "And many out here who believe the Apaches should be exterminated, buck, squaw, and papoose."

"The principle that nits make lice," Tom Fletcher said softly. He was a tall, stooped, balding man in a black suit, with those pale blue chips of eyes that came from staring at vast distances. He was chief of party on the survey of the railroad's new southern route across the Territory. He usually managed to find himself near Madison on a Thursday evening, and was another who regarded Lily with devotion.

"What about you, Lieutenant?" Joe Peake said. "You that's shot at 'em."

"They have a side," he said.

"I can remember my father speaking of the Afghans as the Apaches are spoken of here, and Comanches in Texas," Turnbull said. "But he respected them for fighting for hearth and home."

"*Apache* means 'enemy' in Injun lingo, I heard somewhere," Johnny Angell said.

"Have you learned the Apache language in the course of your service with them, Leftenant?"

"Some," he replied. "We converse in Spanish for the most part."

"Please speak some Apache for us, Pat!" Lily said.

"*In-gew*," he said. "That means 'all right.'"

They waited for him to continue. Turnbull laughed first, Johnny Angell joining him.

"It's clear enough," Frank said after a moment, "that if you treat a people unjustly, they'll become your enemies. When they have become your enemies, then you're able to justify having treated them unjustly in the first place. How often this has taken place in the course of empire."

Cutler thought that if anyone else but Frank Maginnis had made such a statement, he would have agreed. With Frank it seemed you must disagree or feel yourself patronized. With his swollen eyeballs and tight trap of a mouth, the lawyer resembled an indignant frog.

He watched Johnny Angell watching Turnbull, a kind of luminosity to his expression that matched Lily's. They were both in love with the young Englishman. He felt a spiraling descent of loss.

After a light supper they adjourned to the parlor again. Lily played Liszt's "Reminiscences of the Opera *Norma*." She played Chopin. Cutler prophesied that the culmination of the evening would be Liszt's "Love/Death Theme from *Tristan and Isolde*." Right.

As goodnights were pronounced in the front hall, Frank and Martin Turnbull disappeared into Frank's office, and Lily drew Cutler around the corner into the darkened dining room. There she pressed herself into his arms, face against his chest. Then she forced her face up until her mouth caught his.

Twisting his lips away, cursing the shortness of his breath, he said, "You've in love with Martin Turnbull!"

The sharp fingers dug into his back. Her face was raised still for his kisses. He could feel rather than see her eyes searching his. "Yes!" she breathed. "Yes, I am. More than I could have thought possible. Yes! I love you too, Pat!"

"No, thanks."

"Can't you accept that?"

Maybe he could. Half a portion better than none? A

quarter? His voice sounded as though his throat has rusted. "If I have to."

"Oh, Pat, it is wild and exciting—and terrible. I can't think how it can end. Not well, not well. But please understand. Once you said you did."

"I know it."

She rose to her toes to kiss him again, with warm lips. He did not respond.

"Good night, Lily; I'd better go along."

Outside in the starlight he saw that Joe Peake and Johnny Angell were already mounted, one sombrero silhouette a head taller than the other.

"A fellow surely enjoyed your piano-playing earlier, Mister," Johnny Angell said. "That was music to stir a fellow up."

"Why, thanks," he said. He unhitched Brownie and mounted and called goodnights. He started back to the fort in the starlit night. The horse knew the way.

Two mornings later, en route to the mess hall, he saw a brown figure on horseback approaching down Officers' Row. Nochte, wearing his brave new hat. The scout came off his pony with a graceful twist to land on his good leg, drew his crutch from the rifle scabbard, and fitted it under his shoulder.

"Nochte!"

"Yes, Nantan Tata. See, I am well!"

"The leg has healed?"

"It has healed well enough. Meanwhile, the crutch!" He raised the crutch in salute, a thin smile on his handsome dark face. "Pow-ae has come here," he said, "the wife of Dawa. Also the younger squaw. Caballito is ready to come to Bosque Alto, if Nantan Lobo will return to the place where they have made talk."

"I will telegraph Nantan Lobo immediately. I am pleased that you are almost well, Nochte."

Nochte's smile indicated that none of the difficulties with Caballito would have ensued had he been on hand.

General Yeager, however, ordered Captain Bunch and Lieutenant Cutler to receive the Sierra Verdes' capitulation without him, and to arrange to deliver them to the cavalry at the border, who would then bring them to Bosque Alto.

They left the Hoyas at Ojo Azul, except for Tazzi, who accompanied Bunch and Cutler as interpreter—Nochte, still on his crutch, having remained at Fort McLain. The three of them established themselves in the cottonwood grove where Caballito had previously shown himself. Cutler was worried by the lack of Apache sign.

Tazzi made one scout of the adjoining canyons and ridges, returning with a melodramatized expression of worry. He dismounted, shaking his thick-shouldered body from side to side, pouting. "*Ese pe!*"

"What's he say?" Bunch demanded.

"SPs," Cutler said, "*seguridades públicas*. They're a kind of private army of the governor of Chihuahua. They're scalp-hunters."

"Plenty," Tazzi said.

"I don't see that we have to avoid these birds," Bunch said. "We're Americans down here on a hunting trip. Do you think they've run the Red Stripes back to the Sierra Madre?"

Cutler conferred with Tazzi about this. With Tazzi the give-and-take of interpretation was shaky, and he longed for Nochte's cool Spanish. Bunch paced, hard-breathing. "I'm not running from a pack of chilipeps!" he said.

"Nobody with long black hair is safe around here," Cutler pointed out. "So you're all right, Sam." He said to Tazzi, "Go back to Ojo Azul to the others. If we don't return you must get word to Nantan Lobo."

The hard black eyes that seemed not quite human stared into his; Tazzi's all-too-human grin flashed. "*Sí,*" Tazzi swarmed back up into the saddle, flourished his carbine over his head, and departed.

"I don't think old Lobo'd thank us if we scared out of

here just because of a bunch of irregulars barging around," Bunch said.

"Absolutely," he said, but he began constructing a flag of truce, fastening a spare pair of white drawers to a length of branch by their side ties. Once there was a distant volley of shooting, drawn out, that seemed to come from the southwest. It was difficult to determine the direction of sound in this canyon country.

"Uh-oh," Bunch said. Cutler promptly held up the underdrawers on the branch, waving it slowly. From the ridge four horsemen gazed down on them, three Indians and a white man in a tall-crowned Mexican sombrero. The Indians were Tarahumaras, deadly enemies of Apaches. The SPs used them as both troops and scouts.

"*Amigos!*" Cutler shouted. The four made no response. He waved his flag of truce. The white man, rifle in hand, headed his horse down the slope, the three Tarahumaras following.

"*Norteamericanos!*" Cutler called, flourishing his drawers. Bunch stood at attention. The Mexican rode close, and prodded Cutler in the sternum with the muzzle of his rifle.

"*Vámonos!*" he said in a harsh voice. "*Vámonos, gringos!*"

In a broad creek bottom the squalid army was encamped, twelve or fifteen sunburned tents, one twice as large as any of the others, flash of the red and green Mexican flag on a pole. Soldiers in soiled white cotton lounged there, some with rifles. A corral of branches had been woven among the trees of the bottom, and horses there threw their long heads inquisitively over the barrier. Preceding their captors, Bunch and Cutler rode down into the bare-earth area before the flagpole, where soldiers scowled at them.

"Not extremely regimental here," Bunch said in a low voice.

"*Silencio!*" the Mexican said savagely. More soldiers, half of them Tarahumaras, began to assemble. Cutler estimated a force of about two hundred. One Indian carried a battered brass bugle.

An officer stepped out of the big tent, a young man with carefully combed black hair, a ravaged, cynical face, a mustache that looked pasted on. His brown tunic was unbuttoned. He wore a revolver on his hip.

"So what is this, please?" he demanded in Spanish.

The officer with them responded, spitting his words. These gringo spies had been discovered at their evil work not far from here. They had immediately been brought to the colonel.

Cutler saw that there was another barricade, beyond the horse corral, this one guarded by soldiers sitting on the bars. He could not see what was inside.

They were ordered to dismount. The young colonel paced before them, looking them up and down in silence. Soldiers crowded around.

"So you are gringo spies," the colonel said.

"No, señor," Cutler said. "Hunters merely."

Bunch whispered, "What's he *say*?"

The colonel inserted a brown twist of cigarillo between his teeth. "Spies," he said.

"No, señor."

The other halted to stand facing him, arms folded, cigarillo slanting from his jaw. "And what do you do in Mexico if you are not spies?"

"We hunt peccaries, turkeys, deer—"

"You lie!" There was muttering from the crowd of soldiers. Bunch squinted right and left. "I believe you are North American soldiers spying in Mexico," the colonel said. "You will be shot."

"You will not shoot American citizens," Cutler said, as calmly as he could manage. Bunch whispered fiercely to inquire what was being said.

"He says he will shoot us for spies—" The colonel's fist exploded against Cutler's cheek, and he staggered.

"Speak Spanish!" the colonel bellowed. More calmly he added, "You will tell me where you come from, spies."

"From Ojo Azul, señor."

"And before Ojo Azul?"

"From Madison, from Santa Fe, from the capital of the United States, Washington. We are friends of General Yeager of the Army Department of New Mexico, who has told us of fine hunting south of Ojo Azul."

"Liar, you are spies," the colonel said. His smile was not reassuring. "You are spies for the gringo invasion of Mexico, and your evil plans are discovered! You will be shot when it has been determined that you are spies who lie in your teeth. This other speaks no Spanish?"

"No, señor."

"Chinga-voos!" Bunch said, and spat at the colonel's boots. The young man drew his revolver and smashed the barrel across Bunch's face. Bunch stood stiffly, hand covering his nose, blood leaking down his chin. The colonel returned his revolver to its holster.

"Tell the little prick I'll kill him," Bunch said in a muffled voice.

"No, I won't tell him that."

"Tell your companion I will surely kill him," the colonel said. "Julio, you will tie up these spies so they cannot escape, and make a good guard, eh?"

"Sí, *mi coronel!*" their captor said, and they were hustled off down the line of tents. From here Cutler had a better view of the further corral, black heads within it—Apache women and children. No way of knowing whether they were Sierra Verdes or some Mexico-based band. The women and children could be sold to the *hacendados* of Chihuahua and Sonora, an even more lucrative crop than the scalps of the bucks, although he saw no scalps displayed.

Inside one of the tents their hands were tied behind them around the center pole, so Cutler sat back-to-back with Bunch, in discomfort if not agony. A couple of mestizo soldiers with muzzle-loading rifles stood guard.

"In the morning you die, gringos!" one said cheerfully.

"What's he say, Pat?" Bunch demanded, in the muffled voice.

"He says we die in the morning."

"Tell him if we die the United States Army will come down here again, and this time we'll take away their whole ramshackle country, not just half of it."

"Speak Spanish!" the other soldier said, with a threatening gesture.

After a while one of the guards left the tent, to return with a small olla of liquor, mescal probably, which the two guards shared. Presently, seated, they began to play cards, slapping down battered pieces of pasteboard. They did not indulge in the mescal to the point where Cutler felt any hope.

"They won't shoot us, just because I've always wanted to be shot at dawn by filthy greasers in their filthy greaser country," Bunch said.

"Speak Spanish!" one of the guards said, and jabbed Bunch with the muzzle of his rifle.

"What is the name of your colonel?" Cutler asked.

"He is Don Pascual Molino."

"He is the son of the governor of Chihuahua?"

"The nephew."

"What's he say?" Bunch whispered.

Soon it was dark. Some dry tortillas and evil-smelling cheese were brought to them, and they were given sips of fiery mescal from the replenished olla. "Do you think we'll get out of this, Pat?" Bunch whispered.

He lied that he didn't think it was as serious as it appeared, and was cautioned again to speak only Spanish. He managed to recline in a position that did not cut off the circulation in his arms, and tried to resign himself to waiting for night to pass. Horses padded by outside. A sentinel made some unintelligible cry at long intervals. Bunch groaned from time to time.

He wakened to a thrashing, then silence.

"Nantan Tata?"

"Here!"

"*No miedo*, Nantan Tata!"

He felt the chill of a knifeblade rubbing past his wrist; then his hands were free. Gripping the centerpole, he forced his aching limbs erect. "What is it?" Bunch muttered, as a thick, dark shape knelt to cut his hands free. Tazzi and Kills-a-Bear, at least two others in the tent. The two guards were sprawled out, not in sleep. Bunch rose to his feet, murmuring, "My God! My God!"

"Come, Nantan Tata! Nantan Bigotes!"

They stumbled outside through the slashed wall of the tent. Horses were there, stamping nervously, two riders up against the paling sky. One wore a flat-brimmed, flat-crowned hat outlined against the darkness—Nochte! And led horses!

They mounted and started out of the SP camp. There was a shout and the crack of a rifle, more shouts. They swept up the long slope out of the creek bottom at a dead run. Higher, the eastern sky was pale with dawn.

"*No miedo*, Nantan!" Tazzi shouted. "Tazzi here!"

They were all there, riding hard in a pack together—Tazzi, Kills-a-Bear, Skinny, Lucky, Benny Dee, Chockaway, and Nochte, who had joined them somehow. Cutler heard himself laughing like a crazed coyote. He raised a hand in greeting to Nochte, who raised a hand in return. The gay ribbons floated out behind his hat. There were scattered shots. Then they were over the ridge and away.

"Caballito and the Red Stripe People are at Ojo Azul," Nochte said in Spanish. "They are ready to go to Bosque Alto, Nantan Tata."

They were three days at Ojo Azul, waiting for the last of the Sierra Verdes to cross the border and for the two troops of cavalry who were to accompany them to Bosque Alto. Caballito's band had had two separate encounters with Colonel Pascual Molino's SPs, and had killed "many." Twelve women and some children from Cump-ten-ae's group had been captured. However, a fine herd of cattle had been brought across the border, and it was clear that in the United States again Caballito felt entirely safe from the Chihuahua irregulars.

There were more than four hundred head in the stolen herd. It would be impossible to persuade Caballito the animals should be returned to their owners, so the only solution seemed to be to allow him to drive them to Bosque Alto. It amused Cutler to think of the rustled cattle accompanied by a cavalry escort, as he and Bunch sat over coffee in camp chairs on the ruined adobe ramparts, watching the brown backs of the herd moving in the dry grass of the meadow beyond the pond. Mounted bucks armed with Springfields cruised among them, like any other stockherders.

The next day Cutler scouted north with Tazzi and Nochte, hoping to find the overdue cavalry troops, but without success. When he returned Bunch came running toward him, troop-booted, shirt unbuttoned past the sunburnt V of his neck. Even his Viking mustache stood out in alarm.

"Pat, everything's gone to hell again!"

Bunch grabbed his arm and led him around the corner of the ancient, fortified adobe. "These two birds turned up early this morning. I didn't think anything about it. Then they started showing me badges and warrants. One's a U.S. marshal and the other's customs. There's warrants for Caballito and Dawa, and the other one, Big Ear, and for Cump-ten-ae. And a bunch of John Does too. And customs is after the stock they brought across." He stopped, panting, to scratch at the scab on his nose from Colonel Molino's pistol-whipping. "Christ, they will head straight back to the Sierra Madre!"

The white-eye papers that Caballito feared; fate did not

mean for the Sierra Verdes to accept their pacification at Bosque Alto.

"Not only that," Bunch went on. "The marshal's *deputized* me. Help him bring Caballito and the rest over to Tucson. I told him what would happen if he tried that, deputies' guts spread all over the landscape. He's sent off to Tombstone for some more deputies."

"They couldn't get here for a day or two."

"That's still not all, Pat! The customs fellow wants about fifteen hundred dollars duty on that stock. He got up on the roof with a pair of binoculars and counted them. Wrote the tallies down on a little form he has. He's going to collect or attach the stock."

Cutler laughed; Bunch laughed a snort. "I tell you, Pat, while we haven't been looking, there is goddamn civilization out here!"

"I've never heard of a U.S. marshal deputizing an officer."

"Son of a bitch swore he'd prosecute me to the fullest extent of the law if I didn't cooperate! Spouted some laws and numbers. I just don't know!"

"Act like you are cooperating, and I'll stay out of sight and try to get Caballito on the move for Bosque Alto tonight. If there's one thing they are supposed to be good at, it's moving out quick and quiet. We ought to meet cavalry on the way."

Bunch groaned dramatically. "He won't want to move fast! His herd will lose weight. God *damn*, I wish old Lobo was here to run this!"

"They'll just have to move fast or be caught by the white-eye papers. I'll take Nochte with me, and leave the rest of the scouts to look like Sierra Verdes—through binoculars, that is."

"Ha!" Bunch said, sounding more cheerful. "Little red paint should do the trick!"

"What're they doing now?"

"Drinking in José's cantina."

"Here I go."

"Wait a minute!" Bunch said, drawing himself up. "I'm in charge here! All right, go to it. That's an order!"

He and Nochte proceeded out to the Sierra Verdes' *ranchería*, Nochte mounted, crutch thrust into the rifle scabbard beneath his crippled leg, Cutler leading his horse and keeping it between himself and the adobe, in case the marshal or the customs agent were sighting in from the ramparts. A buck with red-striped cheeks and rifle at the ready rose from behind some brush. Nochte spoke in Apache and the guard signaled them on with a jerk of his chin, what Bunch would call "very regimental."

In the camp bushy-haired women watched with alert black eyes in brown faces. Babies in backboards were propped against the wickiups, and there was the sweet stench of baking mescal. Now two half-grown boys with rifles trailed them. Nochte, dismounted, stumped along swiftly enough on his crutch, an arrogant set to his head beneath the fancy hat.

Cutler was trying to think how to explain the hegemonies of civilian and military powers, when already divisions between the military and the Bureau of Indian Affairs must seem mysterious enough. The simple fact of the matter was that, between the border and the refuge of the reservation, the Red Stripe People were not only "hostiles" in military terms, but subject to civilian prosecution. If the troops from Fort McLain arrived, they might be able to ignore the marshal and the customs agent, but it would be well, for General Yeager's sake, if a great newspaper fuss could be avoided. Caballito was in a precarious position.

Caballito, Big Ear, and three others were engaged in a hoop-and-pole game, thrusting the pole at the rolling hoop and shouting like boys at play. They were surrounded by an appreciative audience—women in their complicated layers of skirts, aprons, and blouses, children naked or half-naked. Caballito wore his buckskin shirt, long loincloth, and high moccasins, his hair wrapped in a red turban. He confronted Cutler with an eagle glare, the corners of his mouth slashed down beneath the red cheek stripes.

He addressed Cutler in a hectoring voice, the gathering of Indians behind him stricken to silence. Nochte faced him, looking not quite so arrogant as he hung on his crutch, and translated:

"Because the Red Stripe People have come to this place of meeting, they have been attacked by the SPs. They have killed SPs, but women and children have been taken. Nantan Tata must promise that these women and children will be returned to their husbands and fathers before the Sierra Verdes will leave this place to go to Bosque Alto."

Cutler felt the working-against-fate debility. He said, "Tell him that if the Sierra Verdes had come across the border a moon ago, this would not have happened. Tell him I cannot make such a promise."

This was relayed. Caballito looked even more savage, arms folded high on his chest like a cigar store Indian. Not only was Caballito more wily than he, more experienced at this, but he argued from a desperate posture as responsible for the welfare of his band. Cutler himself only argued out of a rather vague command from General Yeager, and no real conviction at all.

"He says that Nantan Lobo must promise this," Nantan said.

He shook his head. He saw Dawa among the squaws, Cump-ten-ae standing holding a pole slanted to the ground. In evidence were maybe fifteen other warriors, most of them armed and well clad for Apaches. Evidently their sojourn in Mexico had been profitable. Caballito abruptly seated himself on the ground, the other players following his example. Cutler seated himself also; it was parley position. Nochte slid down his crutch, following suit.

Cutler said, "It is necessary that Nantan Caballito move very quickly to Bosque Alto. Two men have come to Ojo Azul with papers like those of San Marcos. These men have power over Nantan Bigotes."

The men had of course been observed by the Sierra Verdes. Who were they?

"One has the papers against Nantan Caballito, Nantan Dawa, Cump-ten-ae, Big Ear, and some others. The other will take the cattle back to Mexico."

Caballito laughed scornfully. His eyes were fixed hypnotically on Cutler's, as though the chief were trying to look inside him. A shaman was usually discovered as a child, Percy Robinson had told him. Something was foreseen by the child, either in time or space, which was brought to the attention of the reigning medicine man, who, if he was convinced, began the training of his successor. The training was rigorous. Failing real clairvoyance, there was simply seeing in a more insightful way, or maybe a kind of hypnotic power, which Caballito was focusing upon him now. He wondered what Caballito's child-vision had been, maybe something to do with thunder—voices out of thunder. What did Caballito see

in the future for the Sierra Verdes? A peaceful future at
Bosque Alto, a third breakout, death? Indeh.

"Others will come to help these men." Cutler continued.
"There will be bad trouble if they come before the blue
soldiers. Perhaps it is best if Caballito returns to the Sierra
Madre, where he can free the women and children himself."

It seemed to him that Caballito smiled slightly at that
transparency, as though he had foreseen each of Cutler's
moves in the kind of checker game the Indeh could not afford
to lose.

In Caballito's silence, Cutler went on to say, "Once it
was known the Red Stripe People could leave a place by night
so quietly no one would hear them, no one would know.
Perhaps at San Marcos they have forgotten how to do this."

Caballito smiled more widely, looking at him almost with
affection. They both knew that in the end Cutler would
promise at least Nantan Lobo's effort to bring the captive
women and children back from Mexico.

In desperate moves the Apaches bound the horses' hooves
in buckskin, slit the throats of the dogs and light-colored
horses, and had even been known to strangle the babies so
that a cry would not give them away. This move was not so
desperate. At nightfall the women began packing their be-
longings into bundles that could be lashed aboard the horses.
There was little whispering. No dog barked, no child
whimpered. In admirable time all was loaded, and the two
hundred and twelve men, women, and children of Caballito's
band, the Red Stripe People—and accompanying them, Lieutenant Patrick Cutler and the Hoya scout Nochte—set out
with the herd of cattle for Medicine Pass.

By the time the sun had cleared the chocolate ranges to
the east, Cutler thought they had made fifteen miles. They
mounted toward the pass up cactus flats like steps, and were
through it by noon. In a pause in which mescal bread and
jerked meat were consumed, he and Nochte conferred with
Caballito and the principal braves. They could continue directly
up the valley to the Bucksaws, and through one of the passes
to Bosque Alto, or, if there seemed to be pursuit, they could
use the Apache tactic of maintaining the heights where they
could keep their pursuers under observation. If these were
blue soldiers, they were constrained to the valley floor anyway by their cumbersome water wagons and pack trains. There

was still no sign of their cavalry escort, or of pursuit either. Straight on, then; he felt what must be the Apache emotions in flight: anxiety, exhilaration, contempt for the enemy.

They headed up the valley at a good pace, the men all mounted, the younger women jogging along afoot with their bundles or backboards—small, rotund, bushy-haired figures weaving through the cactus and the rocks as they easily kept up with the horsemen. Cutler noticed that one buck or another always rode close to Dawa, the frail old man jouncing in the saddle like a sack of grain.

Drinking water was stored in a section of horse gut about twelve feet long, sealed at one end and tied closed at the other, and draped over one of the horse's necks. Cutler's gorge rose when he wet his dry mouth with the warm and none-too-clean water, and he was aware of Nochte's straight-faced amusement. That night they camped among boulders on a hillside in a perfect defensive position. He smoked Apache cigars with Caballito, Dawa, Big Ear, Cump-ten-ae, and several of the other bucks, more than one of whom spoke some Spanish, but there was little conversation. He had, however, somehow incurred Caballito's favor, was, in fact, trusted. He knew he could not entirely trust the Sierra Verdes in return, for complicated reasons: because of the chief's responsibilities to these hundreds of people who had placed their faith in him and their welfare in his hands, and because of the long, dismal history of their treatment by the white-eye. No doubt there were fine, rational, and historical reasons for the broken promises, for the snatching away of treaty-promised lands, for official corruption, venality, care-lessness, and pure racial hatred. None of that must be his concern, for it was a quicksand into which an officer could sink without a trace.

So they came through Benjamin Pass and down onto the Nahuaque reservation at Bosque Alto, where the Sierra Verdes had been expected for some time. Before the Agency build-ings, where the Stars and Stripes billowed from a pole, the Nahuaques watched—the men seated on the corral rails, the women standing, giggling—as Young Eagle, their chief, on his pure white pony, silver concho belt and eagle feathers in his hair, waited to greet Dawa and Caballito. Agent Dipple, known as Nantan Malojo for his walleye, stood beaming from his high veranda. This was a banner day for him, salary and perks, with two hundred more rations to issue—more profits for everyone along the line in Madison County, with the Sierra Verdes come to Bosque Alto.

As the Red Stripe People hurried down the twist of road into the Agency, mounted bucks, laden squaws, the cattle herd kicking up dust, Cutler began to whistle "Garry Owen," the cavalry's own marching song. He furnished his own band accompaniment to this historical moment, whistling to burst his cheeks, the Sierra Verdes glancing at him in surprise, some grinning at him as he whistled their pacification, their salvation.

The cattle were driven into the corrals, and the Red Stripe People milled in the area between the warehouse and the corrals, where rations were issued to them and to their Nahuaque hosts. Cutler tramped up the steps of the Agency to shake hands with Dipple. A Nahuaque young man, with a white-eye haircut, sat with a tablet on which he had been keeping tally.

"Well, here they are finally," Dipple said. "I hope they're going to get along together."

"Maybe."

"I hope they're going to like the place I laid out for their *ranchería*, over a couple of valleys from here."

"Maybe," Cutler said.

"That's a fine-looking herd! How many head do you figure? I mean Injun. We get two-twenty-five."

"Two-twelve."

"We count babies in backboards."

"There must've been a dozen born on the way, then. Well, you'll be seeing a good bit of me," Cutler said.

Dipple frowned at him, the walleye wandering off and pulling back. "That so? Why is that?"

"The general says I'm responsible for seeing nothing disturbs them into busting out again."

"Yeh, three strikes being out," Dipple said.

6

Cutler, Percy Robinson, and General Yeager, all in civilian clothing, descended from the Ferrocarriles de México cars in Chihuahua City, in a bitter wind blowing down out of the north. The general was honoring Cutler's promise to Caballito with little hope of success. He was more hopeful that he could convince Mexican authorities of the necessity for cooperation in the matter of hot pursuit.

In the depot they had a sensation of being watched, loiterers with serapes drawn up to their eyes, Mexicans spying on North American spies. They installed themselves in the station hotel, General Yeager in a large room, his aides in the smaller one adjoining. In the saloon they downed brandies before sallying forth for a turn around the *plaza mayor*.

"Your command of this rapid tongue is very useful, Pat," Yeager said. His wool hat was pulled down to his ears, coat collar turned up. "Of course I can make myself understood in a pinch, but an interpreter is more suitable to my station."

"Learned it in San Francisco, did you?" Robinson asked.

"From Mexican sisters," Cutler said. "Off and on from a Chilean pimp who may have been married to one of them. He taught me swear words and a bad accent."

"What an advantage for a young man!" the general said in a jocular tone. "To grow up surrounded by feminine pulchritude. In the abstract it should produce a beautiful spirit. Tell me, Pat, were their favors available to a young man growing up in their midst?"

"Yes," he said, and, aware of a prurient interest, was pleased to say no more.

"Ah, I had thought Mme. Bellefleur might have run a very puritanical establishment," the general said. He turned to Robinson. "Pat and I have in common that we knew a woman without equal among her gender. A woman of constant surprise and conjecture, a setter of styles, the center of attention in any room she entered, the subject of the conversation in the homes of the highest levels of society. How she dazzled the affections of a young lieutenant at the Presidio. 'He never told his love, but let concealment, like a worm i' the bud—'" He sighed dramatically, ceasing.

"What restraint not to have mentioned this lady in your memoirs, General," Percy Robinson said.

"Ah, some matters are too tender to be broadcast to every ninny with a dollar to buy a book. Besides, the wench is dead. 'Death lies upon her like an untimely frost,' eh, Pat?" he said, and laughed.

Cutler cursed him under his breath. But he knew Yeager had not taken that death lightly, with his bitter insistence upon "reduced circumstances" and "foul disease." He himself had wept that night, after maintaining a wooden countenance in the general's presence, but Yeager had been celebrating his own grief in his own way.

They rounded a corner into the plaza, for a moment out of the teeth of the wind. The buildings here were cornered and corniced with cut stone, and stone figures of the Redeemer and the Apostles occupied niches in the facade of the cathedral. When they crossed the plaza the wind struck at them viciously. Cutler saw that the beam ends above the porticos were decorated with queer black growths that swayed in the wind like sea plants.

He realized what they were just as Robinson said, "Those objects—"

"Scalps," the general said in a flat voice.

"*Good God!*" Robinson said. He counted, his forefinger dipping and rising. "One hundred and seventy," he said finally. Cutler had counted one hundred and sixty-eight. Before this, scalp-hunting had been only a nasty abstraction. Now he felt ill with anger.

"The bounty is one hundred pesos," the general said.

"At a hundred dollars apiece—about seventeen thousand dollars here," Robinson calculated.

"These may have been here for some time," the general said in the flat voice. "Older ones retired as newer ones produce themselves."

"Butchery," Cutler said in a voice so thick he himself could hardly understand what he had said. He stood hunched with his fists straining in his trouser pockets, watching Robinson breasting the wind across the square to examine one of the scalps more closely.

"An attitude of cool irony is advisable," the general said. "These people have suffered Apache outrages for generations. If emotions run high at home, they run higher here."

"Indeh," he said.

"The dead. Yes."

Robinson returned to say that the several scalps he had examined were dry as boot leather. Caballito had claimed to have lost only two bucks, after all, besides Cump-ten-ae's women and children.

They walked along before the cathedral, their steps hastened by the wind at their backs.

"I see no prospects at all for this mission you have devised for me, Pat," the general said. "We must be talking about hundreds of pesos per captive, if captives are indeed more valuable than the scalps that might be harvested from them."

Uniformed, they met the governor and his secretary in the green-tiled *sala* of the gubernatorial palace, beside a patio filled with verdure. Don Victoriano Molino was a smooth-shaven man with gold molars that gleamed at the corners of his mouth when he smiled. He was proud of his English, but deferred to his secretary for translation. There were hearty handshakes, greetings, platitudes. Cutler felt his breath constrict in his chest as a young man appeared, strolling toward them through the patio, in a green uniform and high black boots, a young-old face decorated by a mustache that looked pasted on.

"My nephew, señores! Coronel Pascual Molino!"

Hands were shaken again. Cutler met the young colonel's uninterested gaze and thought he was not recognized. He gave thanks for a forgettable countenance. Sam Bunch of the golden mustachios was not so forgettable.

The secretary arranged tall, straight-backed chairs until all had been seated to the governor's satisfaction. The governor spoke. "Señor General, it is well that we gather here to speak of the Apache devil Caballito, who has once again confined himself to the—what does one say in English?"

"—to the reservation, Señor Governor!" the secretary said.

"To the reservation of the United States," the governor continued, gold teeth glinting. "From which, no doubt, he will again run away, to kill and destroy in Mexico as he has done twice times."

"We hope he will remain on the reservation for good, Governor," the general said. Robinson scribbled in his notebook.

The colonel said in Spanish, Cutler translating, "Have no fear, sirs. We will kill Caballito if he returns to Chihuahua."

"Tell them this," Yeager said. "Caballito knows he must remain upon the reservation. If he flees again, the Sierra Verde band will be obliterated, by my troops, or the colonel's." He bowed to the nephew.

The colonel said, "Sirs, I will welcome Caballito coming again to Chihuahua, for the next time I will destroy him. Have no doubt of this fact."

Yeager came to the point. "Caballito has promised to return to the reservation and remain there if the women and children of his band, who were captured, are returned to their people."

The Mexicans conferred, frowning, shaking their heads. The governor said, "But señores, these *indios* would not wish to return to their people. Good Mexican families take them in, they treat them well. There is enough to eat. They are not hunted, they become people of reason. The children are educated. Their lives become godly. It is much better for them. I promise you, señores, that none, none, would wish to return to their old life."

"You will understand, Señor Governor, that a promise has been made to Caballito."

"Ah, a promise to a savage!" the governor said, with a glint of gold.

The colonel leaned forward to speak, in Spanish. "I tell you, sirs, that we will welcome the return to Mexico of these savages. We welcome them with open arms!"

Yeager said, "Would it be possible for me to talk to some of these captives, to see how they feel about returning to the United States?"

Another conference, although Cutler was certain the

answer would be that it was impossible. "It would be impossible, my General," the secretary said. "These *indios*, you understand, they speak no English nor Spanish either. It would be impossible."

Cutler said suddenly, "Would it be possible to purchase back any of these captives, Señor Governor?" He was conscious of Robinson's shock, beside him, and the angered flicker of the general's eye. The governor scowled.

"But of course they are not for sale, Señor Teniente. These women and their children have been given to good Catholic families who can afford to take them in and will treat them better than they deserve. We say to them that they must 'take the devil' out of these unfortunates. Slavery has been contrary to the laws of Mexico for longer than it has been in your country, Señor."

"It is known that, in New Mexico, and not long ago, it was the custom to purchase Apache children from men who made a living capturing them, like wild animals. This was common practice."

"Ah, once perhaps, but so many years ago—"

The colonel leaned forward again to interrupt in rapid Spanish. "But they *are* animals, Lieutenant! One might say that a pretty, young such animal was worth six hundred pesos. An ugly one less, an older one much less. Sometimes the puppies half so much, when they have amusing ways." His eyes blazed suddenly at Cutler, and his face seemed to grow taut over his skull. Colonel Molino recognized him perfectly well. "Understand, sir, the males we kill without hesitation," the skull face said. "For they are animals all. We will kill them all, and also those who give them aid. Such would be well advised not to visit Chihuahua. Do you understand me, Lieutenant?"

"Yes, I understand that there are animals in every country, Señor Coronel," Cutler said.

The commander of the SPs leaned back, smiling faintly, the hard bones of the skull receding into flesh. His uncle and the secretary stared at him and at Cutler, shocked.

The general quickly brought up the subject of hot pursuit across the border, if the Sierra Verdes or another band should flee their reservation and head into Mexico. Such temporary incursions had at one time been permitted if certain regulations were observed.

The governor and the secretary shook their heads and spread their hands in helplessness. Such a thing was contrary to the laws of Mexico, although perhaps General Ordaz, in Guaymas, could make some provision... Cutler saw that Yeager had given it up, relaxing in his tall chair with a tolerant smile.

"There is no need for this pursuit you require, sirs," Coronel Pascual Molino said, Cutler translating. "There is no need for gringos to come to Mexico to pursue the Apache." He tapped his fingers lightly to his chest. "Mexico will dispose of her own enemies."

All rose, shaking hands, bowing, expressing flowery pleasure at the advancements in understanding that had resulted from this meeting between gentlemen of friendly nations. The North American officers would enjoy the magnificent scenery of the railroad line to Guaymas...

General Yeager said, "You brought me down here because of what you claim was an absolutely necessary promise to Caballito, and then you blow everything up in my face! Of course they cannot admit those captives were sold for hard cash!"

"The colonel admitted it," he said.

"What was that diatribe he launched upon, Pat?" Robinson asked.

"He wanted me to know he recognized me and would have me shot out of hand if he catches me down here again under the right circumstances."

"And you retaliated with a bare-faced insult," Yeager said coldly. He leaned toward Cutler with a gat-toothed snarl. "You will let me do the dealing you induced me to come down here for, do you understand? I will not have translators interfering with negotiations!"

"What will you do, have me shot?" Cutler asked. The general leaned back, stone-faced; Robinson's eyes bugged. Thoughtfulness, if not cool irony, returned. "Sorry, sir," Cutler said.

"I believe I have been the recipient of the impertinence of which your commanding officers complain," the general said. "Most recently Colonel Dougal. I will not tolerate it again, Pat."

"Yes, sir," he said.

"Stand at attention when you say, 'Yes, sir,' Lieutenant."
He rose to attention and said, "Yes, sir."

They were in the general's room, Robinson seated at the little writing table. The general stamped across the floor to lie down on the bed, boots propped up on the scrolled iron foot.

"Do not write down that little exchange, Robinson. We will let it go by. Have you got the chat with the governor and his nephew?"

"With Pat's help, yes, sir."

"Truth is beauty and beauty truth. And neither should be left to memory. I don't suppose we can ask those latin gentlemen to attest to a statement."

"Not when taking scalps and selling women into slavery is the Molino family industry," Cutler said.

"You seem to have quite lost your balance, my boy," the general said. "I urge you again to adopt an attitude of irony rather than this bumbling partisanship."

"Yes, sir," he said.

"Next we will see if General Ordaz of the National Army has any power over private industry in Chihuahua."

"I think you should see the Bishop of Chihuahua before we leave here, sir," Cutler said, looking down at his fists with their white knuckles.

"Oh, very well," Yeager said crossly. "But you will behave with a bit more circumspection, Pat. You arrange the appointment, will you?"

The bishop received them in his apartment in the cathedral, a plump, sleek, beringed little man. He was even less helpful than the governor had been.

Cutler translated. "Sirs, these children are much better living with these Christian families. They will be taught the lessons of the Holy Church. They will receive some education from the good friars. Their lives, which would have been lived in darkness, will be lived in light . . ."

Under the general's warning stare, Cutler did not ask about the women. The next morning they embarked on the weekly train for Guaymas, on the coast of the gulf of California, in Sonora.

Guaymas lay between red dragonback mountains and a filthy waterfront. Through notches in the mountains further ranges were visible, paling with distance through many shades of blue. Mexican gunboats rode at anchor in the harbor, and a red, white, and green striped flag flew over the fortress. A grand church sported two spires and a blue-tiled dome. On the waterfront they ate fresh shrimp, and small, copper-tasting oysters, and waited upon General Ordaz's siesta.

The departmental commandant was a three-hundred-pounder in a Colonial chair as big as a throne, toiling to his feet to greet the North Americans. Sweat stained his white uniform with its massive, gold embroidered epaulets and a chestful of medals. He was surrounded by young officers in sparkling whites. These were more friendly than those of Chihuahua City.

Cutler translated. "Señor General, it cannot be by the present laws of the Republic that foreign troops cross her borders, even in such a worthy cause as the pursuit of the evil Apache. Still, means should be found for these two great nations to cooperate in this common cause."

Yeager forced this opening as far as he gracefully could against increasing vagaries and obstructions, although General Ordaz promised to correspond with the Minister of the Army in this regard.

"It is very complicated, Señor General," General Ordaz said cheerfully. Sweat gleamed on his fat, dark features. "It is very slow, these matters between nations."

Cutler thought that if Yeager did not bring up the matter of the Apache captives, he would have to exceed his role as translator again, but, squinting briefly at him, Yeager said, "General Ordaz, there is another matter for which I beg your attention."

Ordaz listened to the translated request, mopping at the sweat that collected on his chin. The other officers listened silently. Ordaz said, "It is a grave matter, as you describe it, Señor General. I can only say that it will be looked into."

Yeager bowed and said no more. Everyone looked relieved, smiles returning to the faces of the staff officers. A servant was despatched for cool drinks. Over these the North American officers were invited to a grand *baile* that evening, at the house of General Ordaz's friend, the *hacendado* Don Fernando Palacios, who was by good fortune in residence in Guaymas at this time.

It was an occasion for dress uniforms, and Cutler trimmed his beard and mustache with small scissors borrowed from

Captain Robinson, regarding this ordinary face Colonel Pascual Molino had indeed recognized, more than a few gray hairs accumulating now, a little half circle of them like a brand on the left side of his chin. Lily was in love with an Englishman with a face even more ordinary. He should have known better than to let his emotions be caught by her; he had thought he could enjoy her arms while eluding her grasp. The general would have advised an attitude of cool irony toward women, as toward the world's injustices to the Apaches. Instead the ground had shifted beneath his feet. It was time to collect himself. The shoulders in the glass, with their silver bars, straightened; he admired his blue dress jacket, which, however, could have done with the touch of a sadiron. He turned his anticipations to the *baile* at the mansion of Don Fernando Palacios.

The three of them rode in an open carriage furnished by General Ordaz and drawn by a handsome pair of mules sporting red, white, and green cockades. The general and Captain Robinson lounged in the front-facing seat, Cutler less comfortably ensconced facing them. With the sun setting behind the red crags, they toured cobbled streets and rutted dirt ones, to a high, whitewashed facade on a narrow lane, music sounding faintly from within. They drew up among other carriages, from which the elite of Guaymas were descending—many white-uniformed officers, and women in mantillas and lace, young and old, slender and plump. Inside the gate, in a jungle of fragrant flowering plants and spreading trees, the music was louder and there were glimpses of dancers through the greenery.

The first time Patrick Cutler saw María Palacios was when she broke over his head an eggshell containing flecks of gold and silver confetti and ran away from him, her laughing face, framed by dark red hair, turned over her shoulder, the skirt of her white lace gown held off the floor by both hands as she ran. He thought her deliciously pretty. It was not cool irony he needed as the antidote to Lily's abandonment, but the attention of a pretty girl.

He knew this Mexican custom and laughed at the general's and Robinson's startled faces, thinking of the captain recording this bit of Guaymas folklore in his journal. He soon abandoned efforts to pick the bits of paper from his tunic.

"Is it some courtship rite?" Robinson asked, with his eyebrows arched like peak roofs.

"It's just coquetry. It's as forward as young ladies are allowed to be."

General Ordaz rolled toward them, thick, black Indian hair gleaming with grease. He introduced them to their host, Don Fernando, lean, tall, white-thatched and -mustached. One side of his Don Quixote face seemed to have been frozen by some paralysis into a bitter expression. The other was smiling with hospitality.

"Welcome, welcome!" he said in English. "General, Captain, Lieutenant, please make yourselves welcome here!"

In a high, dim room open to the gardens, with the pale flicker of candles everywhere, a uniformed band played from a dais decorated with pine boughs, ferns, and flowers. The dancers circled handsomely, the young women in white or pastels, many with flower coronets, the men in white uniforms or black suitings. Cutler kept an eye out for the coquette who had broken the eggshell on his head, finally locating her in the arms of a young officer, the two of them sweeping around the floor with dash and style. They halted, laughing into each other's faces as the music ceased.

Cups of punch were pressed upon the North American delegation. The two generals nodded in a conversation that evidently Cutler was not needed to translate. He wandered off purposefully, and found his assailant and her dancing partner taking refreshments from a long table just as the music struck up again.

"May I have this dance, señorita?"

"Of course, señor," she said with a dimpled smile, and her escort bowed and retired.

Hand poised beneath but not quite touching her elbow, he guided her to the dance floor. She walked close beside him with her face turned down to the little fan she wore on a band on her wrist, tiny pale earlobes tucked into her hair that swept up into a crown of white roses. He introduced himself. She was María Palacios.

"The daughter of Don Fernando?"

"The granddaughter, señor. And listen, they play the song that is dear to him." The band was playing "La Golondrina," and as he swung her out onto the floor she explained that Las Golondrinas was the name of her grandfather's hacienda, much further south. She was light in his arms, her face turned down, the cheek presented to him was soft and pale as a petal. Silver slippers appeared and disappeared beneath her lace hem. She smelled of unidentifiable flowers and of perspiration. There was a faint fretwork of tiny pimples at the corners of her lips. Their hands stuck together moistly. It seemed to him a long time since he had felt like a young cavalier.

He commented that it was warm in Guaymas, she that he spoke Spanish very well. He explained that he belonged to the United States Cavalry, stationed in New Mexico, and that he came originally from California, where Spanish was also spoken.

"From San Francisco, señor?" she said, glancing up at him with interest.

"Yes, from San Francisco." Had she ever visited that city?

Never. Sometimes they came to Guaymas, sometimes Hermosillo. She had never even visited the capital! How she wished she could travel, to see the grand cities like the capital, San Francisco, Paris! It was very lonely at the Hacienda de las Golondrinas. No, she had no brothers or sisters, and her mother and father died when she was very young. She was just nineteen.

A handsome young white-uniformed Mexican asked for the next dance, soft pale face, small mustache, dark, melting eyes. He bowed over María Palacios's hand for what seemed to Cutler, who was loathe to release her, a moment too long. This was her cousin, Pedrito. Teniente Cutler, Alférez Carvajal. Cutler shook a soft hand and released it, and relinquished this delicious señorita to the arms of her cousin, the naval cadet.

In the billiard room he found the general, Robinson, Don Fernando, General Ordaz, and an aide, taking sherry. General Ordaz airily waved Cutler and the other aide to the billiard table. It appeared very quickly that Teniente Vaca was an expert player, and this match had been set up by the two generals. Cutler lost the first game, resenting Yeager's manipulation instead of concentrating. In the second game Vaca in his confidence began to rely on bank shots, at which he was luckier than he deserved. Cutler barely pulled the game out. In the third game Vaca's bank shots missed by a hair, and the carmos kissed a hair too hard—too much spin in a mist of chalk dust. As Jimmy Blazer had said once, "When their luck begins to go, they compensate with spin." But he let the game go on just to see General Yeager shooting him glares out of the corner of his eyes while pretending to make conversation with the Mexicans. Finally he made his run from fifteen down, and ended it with a draw shot that had everybody's attention. He and Vaca shook hands and congratulated each other with mild hatred.

"Ah, you are a very fine player, Señor Teniente!" General Ordaz said, patting him on the shoulder with his cushion of a hand. "You are to be congratulated, General, on the skill of your subordinate!"

"He is good at most things," Yeager said, leaning easily against the rail of the table, as though he had never had any doubts. "Our young officers are well trained."

"Ah, but I believe this one to be more experienced than young," General Ordaz said. He excused himself with many flowery expressions, and he and Teniente Vaca departed. Cutler saw Don Fernando squinting at him curiously out of the mobile side of his face.

"I believe you could have won more quickly had you so wished, señor," Don Fernando observed.

"His actions are deliberate, whether he is playing billiards or chasing Apaches," Yeager said with his raffish grin. "Eh, Pat?"

"I also have fought Apaches," their host said. "Still, I must have sympathies for a people whose race is in danger from more powerful peoples."

"I understand that this sympathy is rare in Mexico, Don Fernando," Captain Robinson said.

"In my veins runs the blood of a people once also considered enemies by all."

There was a digestive silence at this. Don Fernando produced a wintery smile.

"Do you know of the history of the Jews in New Spain, señores? Isabella the Catholic decreed that they must leave Spain or become converts. They were persecuted, señores. Many were tortured by the Inquisition, many were burned. Some came to the Indies, and some of these accompanied Hernán Cortés to New Spain. These men congregated together and were given lands in the Panuco. There they raised

horses and mules that were famous for their quality. But the
Inquisition followed them to Mexico. Some were burned,
some were imprisoned, and all saw their lands taken from
them. A few fled west. My ancestor took land south of here,
and raised horses and cattle and the finest mules in all
Mexico. As I do to this day, after three hundred and fifty
years."

Cutler saw that Yeager was watching Don Fernando with
the frowning stillness of complete attention that meant he
was hearing something he might find of use.

Captain Robinson said, "I believe the Apache also con-
siders himself the chosen of Ussen, Don Fernando."

Cutler remembered Caballito reproaching his god. He
wondered if the Sierra Verdes could find peace and self-
respect raising horses, cattle, and fine mules on lands allotted
to them.

"Lieutenant Cutler commands a detachment of Apache
trackers," Yeager said. "Moreover, his mother was a Jewess,
and a very beautiful woman."

Under Don Fernando's intent gaze Cutler felt raw and
exposed. He had never heard this before, this was a revelation at last. Jews were people out of the Old Testament, they
were drummers selling dry goods, pots and pans, and notions
out of cluttered wagons. There were schoolboy jokes about
Jews with stinking feet. But the "Jewess" was not what
mattered, it was that Yeager had called Ruth Anna his mother.

"*Converso?*" Don Fernando asked him.

"Yes," he said, recalling St. Catherine's school. He told
the grandfather, as he had told the granddaughter, that he
was from California, from San Francisco. It was there that he
had learned his Spanish. On this occasion he did not announce that he had been raised in a parlor house.

He had the sense of the general playing some chess
game with Don Fernando, having to do with their mission to
Mexico, in which he, Cutler, figured. He felt shaken and
confused as he excused himself to wander back into the
dimmer light and music of the great *sala*. This time he didn't
find María Palacios, but contented himself by dancing with
another flower-scented Guaymas darling, this one neither so
slender nor so pretty.

In the open carriage, in the warm night, as he jolted
back to the hotel with his superior officers, he watched the

moon path on the gulf, sucked smoke from his cigar, and permitted himself to think of Ruth Anna with that tangle of emotions like lowering himself into a pit. Of course she had not been his mother. Motherhood was simply not a part of her character. "So she has sent you back to me!" Yeager had said. How had he ever thought that the statement implied paternity? He regarded the two officers opposite him, dim figures punctuated by the embers of their cigars. "But why did he?" Bunch had asked, inquiring about the quashed court-martial and the transfer to New Mexico Territory. He knew that the general manipulated people for the enjoyment of it. "Pat and I have in common that we knew a woman without compare among her gender," Yeager had told Percy Robinson. Was that all there was to it?

Now the general said, "Don Fernando implies that he may be helpful with General Ordaz. I believe he is influential in Sonoran politics. Moreover, he seems to be acquainted with Porfirio Díaz."

"He mentioned the President a number of times," Robinson said.

"He has invited us to his hacienda, three days journey south of here," Yeager went on. "Las Golondrinas. He will give us fine hunting, he said. Billiards also."

"He was quite insistent as to your coming, Pat," Robinson added.

Cutler found the prospect pleasing. The granddaughter of Las Golondrinas had been attractive enough to dispel some of his depression over Lily's new lover.

"I gave you an excellent report," the general said, pale dot of his cigar end glowing. "Fine officer. Dedicated. Loyal. Responsible. A truly competent man is very rare!"

Cutler's face prickled at the praise, although he knew it was flattery and again for some purpose. It was as though he could never get his balance in the general's presence; it was like facing a superior boxer.

"I wish you had shown off your command of the language a bit more. But of course his English is excellent. I had to excuse myself and Percy from visiting Las Golondrinas. But you will go there, Pat." He laughed and said, "Don't forget to come back!"

"I'd like to know why you told Don Fernando my mother was a Jewess," he said.

"Why, so she was! I do believe she was. Of course she told so many conflicting stories of her romantic background." He halted a moment before he said, "It was expedient."

"My *mother*?"

"Ah," Yeager said. "A manner of speaking only. Foster mother would have been more precise, of course."

His head felt stuffed with some warm substance heavier than air. "When she sent me east she said it was your duty to make a man of me."

"Why, so I have! And a fine officer, too."

He shook his stuffed head. "Why was it *your* duty?"

"As her friend, of course!" Yeager chuckled fatly. "She had done favors for me, Pat! Of course she was presumptuous. She was cunning, she was flighty, she had been a pursuer of the main chance all her life! She was a marvel of nature and infinite variety itself. Yes, I believe she was a Jewess. As I've said, I must've heard a dozen versions of her origins. Old Hungarian nobility! And yet her mother was a Parisian Jewess. A childhood in the sun and flowers of Provence, and yet as a child she also sold matches in the filthy alleys of London. Locked up in the cupola room of a great plantation house in the Mississippi Valley. She lied as freely as she breathed! In fact, she did not come from anywhere. She just *was*, like light and air. Let us not question her!"

"I have some interest in discovering who I am, sir!" he said.

"Of course. We have spoken of this before, Pat. She told me you were a foundling. Found on her doorstep. It was not an uncommon occurrence at parlor houses, you know."

He suspected that Yeager, also, lied as freely as he breathed.

Robinson changed the subject. "I wonder if you know the Apache theory of the origins of man, Pat." He didn't, and Robinson informed him. "The earth is the mother, facing upward. The sky is the father, facing down. The rain is the semen."

"There you *are*, Pat!" the general said, and laughed again.

The rage in his skull swelled unbearably, focused upon Robinson; then it seeped away. There was no point in any of this except his own continuing hunger.

"I believe Don Fernando said they will be departing for Las Golondrinas day after tomorrow," Robinson went on.

Yeager said in a different voice, "We hope that an agreement on hot pursuit can be obtained through his good offices."

Cutler closed his eyes, leaning back, his head lolling with the motion of the carriage. "I believe I must pursue the matter of Cump-ten-ae's women and children as well," he said.

"I wouldn't bother with that, if I were you, Pat," Yeager said.

"I know you wouldn't."

7

A faint track led through red plains, snaking east toward a purple range that hazed the horizon like smoke. The great Palacios coach, a huge vehicle out of the last century, with its uniformed but unshaven attendants, rocked on its thoroughbraces up a broad river valley. Cutler sometimes rode inside with a grimly enduring Don Fernando, a pasty-faced María, and the duenna, Doña Hortensia, a stumpy, middle-aged woman with a mole on one cheek, a thin mustache, and a monitory gaze which she often fixed upon Cutler. Other times he rode alongside on one of the saddle mules. Once a troop of horsemen galloped up with a flourish of hats and animals pulled to their haunches—soldiers in much-embroidered, dove-gray uniforms and tall-crowned hats. The officer saluted Don Fernando and rode beside the coach. These were *rurales*, one of the attendants whispered to Cutler, the Mexican rural constabulary.

When they had ridden off, Don Fernando lounged in his corner of the coach, dust hazing the late sun pouring through the window. A cigarillo slanted from the frozen corner of his mouth as he stared out the window. Cutler was fascinated by that double aspect of his face, the paralyzed expression that of severity and arrogance, the other gentle and anxious. He was enjoying this interminable trip, for all its hardships, through the kind of high desert country he knew well from two years campaigning in the Southwest. His Spanish expanded as he stretched it to make conversation within the creaking old coach, and he liked María Palacios and Don Fernando better the better he came to know them.

María was at one moment petulant at having had to leave behind the assemblies, *bailes*, and white uniforms of Guaymas, and at the next excited at seeing her beloved Las Golondrinas

94

again, and her beloved horse Güero. Cutler was fascinated watching her lexicon of moues, petty and grand grimaces, and melodramatic gestures. She had, almost, an ability to converse with her eyes alone. How had she learned all these feminine tricks, sequestered on a hacienda deep in Sonora, with infrequent visits to Hermosillo, and a month each year in Guaymas? Either she had learned them from Doña Hortensia, who spoke with awe and nostalgia of grand affairs in Mexico City, or they were genetic in young Mexican ladies of high estate.

Certainly she was shallow. She expressed no interest in the United States, in his life as an American officer, in the Apache wars, even in his mission in Mexico. She did speak often of her cousin Pedrito, the cadet to whom he had been introduced in Guaymas. Cutler noticed that mention of Pedrito caused Don Fernando and Doña Hortensia to glance at each other sourly. María seemed to him the most thoroughly spoiled young woman he had ever encountered, but even dusty and sallow, her pouting face could be fascinating, and when she lighted the flame of her charm she was beguiling.

When would she marry? Her grandfather, whom she referred to as "mi abuelo" but addressed as "Don Fernando," would take her to the capital to meet the eligible young men there. She had hoped that would be this year, but her grandfather had been ill. Certainly next year, in the fall. Throughout the discussion Don Fernando stared out the window with a frozen, gargoyle glare.

"Yes, it must be next fall, without doubt," Doña Hortensia said firmly. "Time runs very swiftly for the young."

"Much care is necessary in the selection of a mate for life," Don Fernando said.

María patted her hair expressively, made a moue, rolled her eyes until they almost crossed, and said, "So you have told me, Don Fernando."

"Look!" the *hacendado* said, pointing with his unlit cigarillo. "We have come to Las Golondrinas!"

In the broad valley of cultivated fields, rectangles, and contoured curves, harmonious patchworks of color, shade, and texture—green spikes of agave, the breeze-blown softness of corn, the brown stubble of fields held fallow—a castle, a mud fortress, had appeared. The scale, the mass of the place, with the green explosion of treetops over the fortress walls, took Cutler's breath away.

They entered into sudden shadow through an enormous gate that might once have supported a drawbridge. Tall doors looked rusted open. Suddenly the coach was surrounded by clamoring peons and administrative staff running, calling greetings, jumping to look inside the coach, crying out. Dogs barked. Cutler identified the *mayordomo*, a thick-necked fellow in a striped vest, a heavy chain of office around his neck. There was the padre, gowned and tonsured. House servants also wore the striped vests. An ancient crone, bent over a heavy cane, was identified as the sister of Don Fernando. A plump, officious little butler kicked a yelping dog out of the way and helped Doña Hortensia and María down a portable step. Dogs scampered underfoot, along with a pair of proud-headed, yellow-legged cocks.

The tumult lessened, and Don Fernando took Cutler's arm and indicated points of interest inside the vast courtyard, six broad steps leading to a doorway framed in cut stone, the two spreading oaks on either side, the flowerbeds. Lining the inside of the wall were the habitations of the house staff, chimneys spewing smoke over low, tiled roofs, kitchen gardens, chickens and red-wattled turkeys in fenced yards. Beyond these was the chapel, surmounted by a crude stone statue of the Savior, a limp lamb like a pet dog in the crook of his arm, the other hand raised in blessing.

The padre approached them, the skirt of his brown cassock caught up in one hand. He nodded solemnly when introduced to Lieutenant Cutler.

"A pleasant journey, Don Fernando? Don Patricio?"

At first Cutler did not realize that he had been addressed. Don Patricio!

"Long, Padre!" Don Fernando said. "Longer with each journey. When one does not have much time left in the world, one regrets spending so much of it shaken in a coach." He looked at Cutler with the gentle, almost apologetic expression on the left side of his old face.

Cutler was absorbed observing the functioning of this feudal domain. Indeed, Don Fernando seemed to be showing it off as though to a prospective purchaser—the working areas, stables where two grooms brushed down handsome horseflesh. The famous saddle mules of Las Golondrinas stamped and fed in luxurious stalls. The granary was shown, and the corn cribs and tortilla factory, where silver-painted

patented machinery mashed out the flat corn cakes from
yellow dough, attended by a brawny woman in an apron; the
dairy, where butter from a churn was patted into molds and
impressed with the Palacios crest. In the cellars, gray and
rusty casks extended into murk. All the peons they encountered
snatched off their hats to bow to Don Fernando, who inquired of Juan and Pablo, Caterina and Adela. Cutler thought
they revered their *patrón*, who unfailing introduced him as
Don Patricio. Tomorrow, Don Fernando said, they would ride
out to survey the herds, the mules, horses, cattle, sheep—
there were pigs also!—and the hacienda lands. And tomorrow
they would hunt! Don Patricio would shoot the beautiful
Belgian rifle that was one of the innumerable prides of the
hacienda. María had already planned a picnic on the river, but
no doubt the *patrón's* plans took precedence.

They returned along the walls of the casa grande, where
swallows fluttered and nested among the eaves, Don Fernando
with a stiff-legged stride in his short, black, silver-frogged
jacket, tight trousers, and the broad-brimmed, silver-decorated
hat that Cutler admired. Inside were gleaming, russet-tiled
floors, blue- and yellow-tiled wainscoting, high ceilings, broad
cool rooms, ferns, flowers, great dim portraits, window glass
catching fragments of sunlight, a clatter of boot heels on tiles.
In one room a servant mopped, flipping a cloth on a pole over
an already shining floor. Beyond it was a gallery, more of the
murky paintings lining the walls, stern-faced men and women
in the costumes of past generations. In the grand *sala* was a
fireplace couples might have danced in, heavy dark furniture,
tall vases containing flowers or sprays of peacock feathers.
Here they halted.

"It is very beautiful, Don Fernando," Cutler said in
Spanish, with gestures.

His host looked childishly pleased on the one side, sour
on the other. "Thank you, señor. It is very dear to its *patrón*.
Perhaps not so dear to his granddaughter."

"In time, no doubt."

Don Fernando shook his head sadly.

Cutler continued, "She has told me that her mother and
father are dead."

"Her father, who was my son, was shot by the victorious
army of Porfirio Díaz. He was a traitor to Mexico, you see; a
toady to Maximilian and the French. It is said that his wife

then died of grief. She died of shame. This hacienda has been deeply infected with treason, Don Patricio. I think it is only in recent years that a Palacios may hold his head up again, and I am fortunate that Don Porfirio still calls me friend."

"I am sorry," Cutler said.

"It is a paltry life that has no tragedy in it," Don Fernando said, sour ferocity twisting one side of his face, old pain the other. "But come, let us sample this amontillado."

Cutler knew that the stuff, poured with care from a leather-covered bottle, must be very precious. It tasted like dry nectar.

Don Fernando smiled again at his compliments. "At Las Golondrinas we make our own mescal, aguardiente, and red wine that I am told is not bad, but for sherry I send to an old friend in Jerez, in Spain. This is the very finest he has sent me."

Cutler had a growing, breathless sensation that something momentous was expected of him, which was yet to be announced. Standing together, the old Mexican almost a head taller, they sipped the sherry.

Don Fernando clapped his hands, which instantly produced one of the liveried servants. "You will take Don Patricio to the quarters of the oak, where he will wish to bathe and dress after our long journey." He said to Cutler, "Perhaps you will join us here later, my friend?"

Cutler followed the *mozo* up stairs whose tile treads were worn almost through by the generations of Palacios feet that had trod upon them.

The oak quarters looked out through the branches of one of the entrance oaks. His valise had been emptied, the clothing hung in the armoire or folded into the drawers of a squat, dark wood chest, dirty laundry borne away. Servants arrived bearing ollas of hot water, which they poured into a blue- and yellow-tiled tub. He bathed, luxuriating in what he conceived to be the proper hacienda manner, than scrubbing himself with soap and a cactus-fiber wad. He donned his dress uniform before a cloudy mirror in an ornate gold frame. The face regarding him was neither the ugly one of a son of General Yeager, nor the aristocratic one of the son of a Jewess connected with Hungarian nobility. He looked like an Irish private who had just immigrated from the Ould Sod.

What was wanted of him here? Don Fernando seemed to consider him someone of importance. Was it because of his skill at billiards, his recommendation by General Yeager, his Jewish blood? A dim possibility tugged at him for notice, and had to be ignored.

He braced to attention with his chin tucked in and marched downstairs to encounter his host again. This time a collection of people watched him enter the sala. Don Fernando wore a frock coat that looked too large for him, as though he had shrunk with his age. María, moving her shoulders as though to the beat of some music audible only to herself, also wore formal attire, an elaborate pink dress, flowers in her dark red hair, a wide-eyed, rather stunned, expression on her pale face that seemed often to be inspecting him in somewhat the same way as her grandfather. Present also were the padre, Doña Hortensia, and the aged sister, slumped like a dead brown bird in one of the thronelike chairs with the black stick slanted against her knees; also an officer in the gray uniform of the *rurales*, introduced as Colonel Kandinsky, commander of the Sonoran constabulary. He was a man as tall, narrow, and erect as Don Fernando, and of some indeterminate age between forty and sixty. He had fair, graying hair and spoke European-accented English as well as he did Spanish.

"So, the young American officer has come to Mexico with the famous General Yeager to negotiate for the future pursuit of Apache renegades!" Kandinsky pumped his hand and beamed at him.

Cutler asked the other if he was Russian.

Kandinsky waved the Mexican finger of negation at him. "Polish, my dear fellow! Consequently I understand the suspicions of the neighbors of more powerful nations. Mexico has well-founded fears of opening her borders to American soldiers."

"I am also interested in trying to secure the release of the women and children of Caballito's band, who have been sold into slavery by the SPs of Chihuahua."

"But that is quite another matter, Don Patricio. Mexican property rights must be considered, eh? And surely these Indians are better off, surely the circumstances are easier than their native ones!"

"I promised their chief that this effort would be made."

"This young man is a keeper of promises!" Kandinsky said, glancing around at the others. "It is an admirable trait, and all too rare! But tell me, is it necessary to keep promises to bloody-handed murderers, who have borne into captivity many Mexican children?"

"Perhaps if we treat such men with honor and the respect for promises, they will cease to be bloody-handed murderers," he said with more Mexican suavity than he had thought himself capable of.

Kandinsky laughed and tapped him on the arm. "Very good, señor! Very good! The other matter, at least, will be broached to Don Porfirio by myself and Don Fernando. We will see, we will see!" He swung to face María. "And, my beautiful goddaughter, have you had a sufficiency of the grand fiestas of Guaymas?"

"No, not enough, Lalla! Grandfather insisted upon leaving there after only two weeks!" She grimaced an obscure message to Cutler.

He was assigned to take her into the long table in the dining *sala*, where she was seated between him and Colonel Kandinsky. Don Fernando presided at the table, with his sister at his right, next to the padre.

"Tomorrow we will have the picnic at the bend of the river that I have promised you, Señor Teniente," María said.

"I believe your grandfather has other plans."

She made an explosive cluck. "Oh, pouf!"

"He mentioned a hunt."

"Oh, a hunt, pouf!" She complained rather shrilly, causing Kandinsky to frown at her. Don Fernando only laughed and said there was time for all things.

"Tomorrow you will ride the fine horse Malcreado," he said to Cutler. "There is a horse who can be a man's best friend!"

"There was a saying in Cracow that a swift horse has the worth of a plump wife," the colonel said, as wine was poured.

Cutler considered the import of that statement.

"The Mexican learned his relationship with the horse from the Spaniard," Don Fernando said. "And the Spaniard learned his from the Arab. And the Arab perhaps from the Jew, for once Arab and Jew called each other cousin, and the Jew rode horses while the Arab rode camels. In Spain, at the time of the Reconquest, the knights rode *a la brida*. Do you know what that style means, Don Patricio? The cavalry of the United States rides thus, feet planted well in long stirrups, guiding with the bridle. For it was in this way that the mailed knight steadied his great weight and thrust with his long lance.

The horse was his support merely. Then came the Arab on
horses he rode as a brother, *al jinete*—the rider leaning forward
in the saddle with short stirrups so he was almost kneeling. He
turned his mount with his knees. Thus it was that the Saracens
of the knees massacred the knights of the bridle with their
scimitars, cutting between and around them so nimbly.

"*Al jinete* came with the Spaniards to Mexico, and from
it the Indians have learned their own riding style. The
horsemanship of the savage is Saracen and that of the cavalry-
man that of the mailed knight." He laughed at his flight, even
the frozen side of his face less bitter than usual. "But as the
great Napoleon said, God takes the side these days of the
heavier artillery, and not of the swifter cavalry."

Kandinsky laughed also, applauding with a soft patting of
his hands.

"There is a difference, however," Cutler said. "Apaches
do not treat their horses as brothers, but cruelly, and ride
them to death."

Later, at the billiard table, Kandinsky explained that he
had left Poland "because of a concern, imbibed with my
mother's milk, for truth, justice, and national honor."

His family had been citizens of the Republic of Cracow,
he continued, suppressed by the Austrians in 1848. "How
these dates reveal my great age! Thus I learned to fight the
Austrians in the Italian wars of independence, until, as an ally
of Napoleon III, I learned it was the French who must be
fought. And so I came to Mexico to fight at the side of the
good president, the Indian Juárez. I have remained here at
the request of his general and my friend Don Porfirio Díaz.
Who had proven once again the international adage that the
military man always supplants the civilian whom he has
assisted to power."

He squinted comically at Cutler. "You are thinking, my
friend, that this adage is not true of that great virgin, the
United States. I will inquire if your presidents who have
followed that good man Abraham Lincoln have not been
military men?"

He admitted that this was true, and Kandinsky's delighted laugh rang out.

"For military men are insatiably ambitious for rank, you
see, my friend!"

It was an aspect of General Yeager that Cutler was

shaken to consider, but it was a reason for those memoirs Percy Robinson was working on, which did not include all the aspects of Yeager's life.

In bed that night he gazed out the window past the pale grid of the oak branches to the jeweled night sky. He laughed at his waking dream of himself riding toward the hacienda that hulked up like a warship out of green fields, wearing one of the short, tight-waisted, much-embroidered suits. Dismounting, he handed down from the great Las Golondrinas coach his pretty, laughing bride with her dark red hair, her translucent skin with the beauty spot at the corner of her bright lips. From all around appeared the peons, hats in hand, to group like the chorus of an opera as they chanted a paean of greeting and reverence. He saluted them with his heavy sombrero, and, with his wife on his arm, strode on into the *casa grande* in his tight, conchoed trousers. Gone like trash flung out of a closet were General Yeager, Colonel Douglas, Major Symonds, Captain Smithers, Caballito—even Sam Bunch and Bernie and Rose Reilly, even Lily—that other life, that desolation.

The stars blinked bright and cool, a meteor streaked across the sky like a match scraped there. He did not even dare to wish, laughing in delight at the marvel of himself at Las Golondrinas.

The next day he was furnished with a vaquero suit exactly like the one of which he had dreamed, richly made, with narrow leather *chaparejos*, a silver-frogged jacket, and a sombrero laden with metallic embroidery. He admired his image in the mirror, laughing at himself. With Don Fernando and the colonel, and a squad of vaqueros, he rode up out of the valley into eastern hills to inspect vast cattle herds. Sheep, goats, and pigs were mercifully left to another day, and they joined María, Doña Hortensia, and her niece, Ysabel, who seemed to be a confidante of María's, at the river bend, where they were tended by house servants. The picnic was formal, ponderous, and many-coursed, with plenty of the Las Golondrinas red wine to wash it down. After lunch they lounged in the shifting shade beneath the trees to the chording of guitars. He tried to find something to chat about with María while Don Fernando and Kandinsky nodded together in some solemn conversation he couldn't hear. Ysabel kept an eye on the space between him and María, and the two older men also frequently glanced his way.

In the late afternoon he again rode out with the men, to a thickly wooded canyon where the precious Belgian rifle was removed from its fleece-lined case and presented to him as though it were Excalibur. He properly admired its carved and beautifully oiled stock, the chased steel breech, the blue-gleaming barrel and tall front sight. He was stationed behind a rock, with the two older men slightly behind and above him, while attendants beat down the canyon toward them.

The buck appeared leaping pole-legged, a high, fine rack of antlers. He could hardly have missed. His shot took the animal directly behind the shoulder and he was instantly dead, plowing on for another ten yards like a full-rigged ship driving ashore.

"Bravo!" Kandinsky called out, applauding with quiet patting. Cutler had the impression of a crucial test passed and good omens perceived.

"One day we will hunt tiger," Don Fernando said, standing and stretching. "There is a tiger in the hills that sometimes will take a goat and has killed two dogs. One day we will hunt this jaguar, and you will bring him to his end with this beautiful rifle, Don Patricio."

In the stables Kandinsky excused himself, and Don Fernando led Cutler to one of the stalls. A big gelding turned an intelligent eye on him. As with so much at Las Golondrinas, this was the most beautiful horse Cutler had ever seen, small-headed, pale dun, muscles rippling beneath his coat, which gleamed from currying, like wind on water.

"This is the horse Malcreado I have promised you," Don Fernando said. "He is an animal of Arabian blood and Mexican training. He will serve you well."

"He is beautiful," Cutler said, and stammered thanks, which Don Fernando waved away. The horse regarded him serenely. It was as though the filaments of some powerful web were falling upon him one by one.

He and Don Fernando again took sherry in the high-ceilinged dimness of the great *sala*. This time his host directed him to a seat and sat opposite him across a low table, veneers of light and dark wood laid into a chessboard on the top. He was offered a cigar, which he accepted. His shoulders ached with strain as he watched the old man's mismatched face, the sad side turned toward him.

"The young men of Sonora, the young men of Mexico," Don Fernando began, "are not what they once were. They are still much influenced by the French who were here. Those officers were more dandies than soldiers, you understand. They postured in their handsome uniforms, they strutted, they waxed their mustaches. Many of our young men chose to emulate them then and do so still. They wear their hair in just such a manner. Their clothing as well. Perhaps you have noticed it in Guaymas. There is an expression, such a one is 'more manners than man.' They know no work, these empty fellows. They live for *bailes*. They ride in carriages and speak with a drawl and misuse French phrases. They speak of Paris as though it were their home! Her young men dishonor Mexico. My own son was like this. When the French were driven out, I thought that it was over. But it is not over."

The old man leaned stiffly forward to knock his cigar ash into the tray beside Cutler's ash and sip from his glass. "I cannot grieve for my son because I disinherited him when he became the monkey of the French. Have you understood what I am saying, Don Patricio?"

He could feel sweat cooling his forehead. "I must tell you that the mother General Yeager spoke of, who was a Jewess, was only my foster mother."

Don Fernando smiled bleakly. "Nor am I much of a Jew myself. Such a few drops remain, so many years have passed . . . But it is blood of which I am proud, as you have heard.

"What concerns me, Don Patricio, is that there seem to be few competent young men in Mexico. *None* that I know. *None* who are capable of the hard work, of the friendships one must maintain with peons and with presidents that a great hacienda may survive and, please God, prosper. Of the courage and the cunning, and—the luck! The luck, Don Patricio!"

Was he being offered some kind of managership? "Sir, I have had no experience in these matters an *hacendado* must deal with. If that is—"

Don Fernando raised a hand to halt him, frozen face glaring. "I beg your pardon, Señor Teniente, but you have. General Yeager has spoken of you in the very highest terms. Nor does the actual experience matter so much. When I am

gone, a competent man must be in charge of all this—" He
swept out a hand, comprehensively. "A man of force who is
also a man of reason. Or all will be lost. The *patrón* may have
to fight for Las Golondrinas, Patricio—if I may call you that.
For I believe a revolution is still to come to this tragic land. I
believe a soldier is the man I seek."

He still did not understand. "When I am gone," Don
Fernando had said.

The *hacendado* leaned back in his chair, waving away
the cigar smoke that rose before his face. "You have said that
you find Las Golondrinas beautiful, Patricio."

"I find it enchanting, Don Fernando."

"And what of my granddaughter. Do you find her beautiful also?"

He took a deep breath. "Very beautiful."

"Enchanting?" Don Fernando asked, with a gray eyebrow hooked up.

"Yes, certainly; enchanting." He watched his fingers
move across the squares of the chessboard to wrap around his
glass, then release it and draw back. He said carefully, "I am
certain your granddaughter does not care for me in that way,
Don Fernando."

"She cares only for her cousin, Pedro Carvajal."

"I have met him, the naval cadet."

The sour ferocity twisted the old man's whole face. "He
plays at being a naval cadet! As he plays at everything, that
perfumado! As he would play at being María's husband. As he
would play at *patrón* of Las Golondrinas! Neither of these will
he ever be, by my life! But yes, she does care for the
perfumado in that way. It does not matter."

"It matters to María."

"I say it does not matter! In this country, of this class,
one does not marry for love. To marry for love is to spend a
year, two, in the nopal blossom bed, and forty years on the
thorns. I ask if you will do this, Patricio."

It surprised Cutler that he would be suspicious still in
examining this offer, as though it were some joke of heaven
instead of a gift of staggering proportion. A soldier did not
have much occasion to meet marriageable young women,
especially one who had never had access to the marriage
market of officers' daughters at the West Point balls. He was
being offered a beautiful young woman of aristocratic stock,

and so much more besides, a dream he had not even realized he longed for until it had burst into actuality, the lottery he had not even thought he had played.

"Yes," he said.

Don Fernando rose. Cutler rose. They embraced. The old man's body was an armature of warm sticks. Silently the *hacendado* turned away, to take up the leather-covered bottle once more and replenish the glasses. Cutler saw the tears blurring his eyes. "*Salud*, my son!"

"*Salud*, Don Fernando."

"And to the heirs of Las Golondrinas!"

They drank in silence. Now Cutler felt an edge of panic. This was moving too swiftly!

"She has been much spoiled," Don Fernando said. "You will make a woman of substance of her. The wife of a soldier, living in rude circumstances, in danger sometimes. I must believe her blood will tell! Then in two, in three years, you will return. With the child. I believe I have that much time left to me."

"In two years' time the Apache wars must be finished," Cutler said. It was as though General Yeager's hand restrained him until that time.

"As the wife of an officer, María will learn to be a woman, and not this pouting, dancing child. A wife and a mother."

Cutler asked when the wedding would be.

"Immediately!"

They raised their glasses again. His voice was thick when he said, "She is very beautiful, Don Fernando."

The white head nodded jerkily. "You will take her away to the United States, for two years, three. But Patricio, if I begin to fail—if it becomes clear—you understand? Then you must come sooner. Can you promise me that?"

He promised.

And so the wedding was arranged for in three weeks' time, after which he would return to Fort McLain with his bride. When María was informed of the arrangement, she did not leave her rooms for two days. Then, with a red face and puffy eyes, she informed Cutler that she would become his wife.

Las Golondrinas outdid itself in the glamour of the wedding festivities: coaches and horsemen coming in from the north and west; handsome men and beautiful women, with style Cutler had not seen this side of San Francisco; forty-

eight hours of drinking and celebration, of dancing, hunting,
and billiards, his grandfather-in-law now displaying his prow-
ess. His bride was beautiful in her mantilla and white lace
wedding gown as spotless as her reputation, with her red,
leaking eyes and her self-pity.

On the wedding night there was a fumbling, prayerful
failure on the matrimonial bed, in which he came to suspect
that María was no virgin.

They came east from Tucson by army ambulance, Cutler,
his wife, and his wife's attendant, Ysabel, with a burly
corporal driver, four mules, and the beautiful gelding Malcreado,
the gift of Cutler's grandfather-in-law. Cutler rode alongside
the ambulance through the cactus plains and the rocky defiles
where once hostiles might have lurked in ambush. There was
no longer any danger, for General Yeager, the great pacifier
of Indians, had "concentrated" the Apaches on reservations,
most at San Marcos and Fort Apache, the Nahuaques and the
Red Stripe People at Bosque Alto.

The ambulance creaked along the hard-beaten track that
snaked through the boulders and organ cactus. The canvas
side curtains were rolled up, and through the dust his wife
and Ysabel watched him from their hard, wooden seats,
removed against their will from the comforts of Las Golondrinas
to this crude, dangerous, prickly country. Ysabel glared.
María's expression was one of suffering reproach, and often
she pressed a sodden handkerchief to her eyes. Her tears, he
knew, were for the loss of Pedrito rather than her removal
from the hacienda.

Her misery had first touched him, but now it irritated
him, although he was certain that in time he could win his
bride's affections. He had a suspicion that he had been
manipulated by another cunning old man, but the prize
remained a glittering one.

Captain Robinson had sent a telegram on the general's
behalf, congratulating him and assuring him of the leave he had
requested. Cutler had Don Fernando's promise that he would
speak to the president of Mexico on the subject of hot pursuit, if
not on that of the captive Apache women and children.

Where the roadway narrowed and he was forced to rein
Malcreado closer to the ambulance, María called out to him,

"Please tell me again of the accommodations we will be given at the fort, señor."

"Lieutenant Olin, whom I rank, and his wife will have to move out of their quarters. They will replace Lieutenant Tupper and his wife in theirs." Such were the perquisites of rank in the army. "There will be two rooms with scorpions in the walls, a kitchen and a place for Ysabel to sleep adjoining it. Outhouses across an alley. We will all be up before dawn for reveille, and breakfast will be served in a hurry. A corporal will be assigned as our servant—what is called a 'striker.' He will be a very bad cook, and Ysabel will have to instruct him."

María gazed up at him with her red, prayerful eyes, Ysabel with her hate-filled ones. The irreconcilable part of his wife had come to be personified for him by her attendant, whom he detested roundly.

"But you have promised that there are *bailes*, señor!" María said.

"Yes, yes, the band plays, and some of the men play mouth organs and banjos." He stopped himself from speaking more of these dreary affairs.

"I believe you wish to make this life sound very bad for reasons one cannot make out, Don Patricio," Ysabel said. She had a witchlike profile, nose and chin inclining toward each other.

"You will find that I do not exaggerate, señorita."

María pulled her cloak more tightly around her, despite the perspiration that gleamed on her pale face. As their marriage remained unconsummated he had found his thoughts turning back to Lily Maginnis more and more. He tried to shake them off.

"In Madison there are people you will find simpatico," he said to María. "The lawyer, his wife, the doctor—you will like them and they will like you."

"The wife of the advocate—she is beautiful?"

"Yes, beautiful," he said, with a horseback bow and a smile that felt as false as paint. "But not young and beautiful, señora."

He spurred up alongside the teamster, who slouched on his seat with a boot propped on the brake. "Yessir!" the corporal said, with a sloppy salute.

"What do you think, Corporal? Tomorrow noon?"

"Most likely by first dark, sir. Pulling a lot of weight."

This was true, for María had brought four trunks in preparation for the grand balls of Fort McLain and Madison. When he drifted back to inform her of the teamster's estimate of their arrival, she called to him, "But Ysabel cannot cook either, señor!" It was a cry of pain.

He bent toward her out of the saddle. "Your grandfather wishes you to see another side of life from the hacienda and *bailes* in Guaymas and Hermosillo. In a year or two we will return to Las Golondrinas. It is not forever!"

Cutler had become acquainted with Colonel Dougal over poker hands at Ran Boland's. The colonel did not try to fill inside straights. He bet little unless he held winning cards, and even then cautiously. Cutler could only equate his military capacity with his performance at cards. It was well known that his colonelcy of the 13th was due to a fortunate marriage by Dougal's sister. Cutler understood Dougal's anger with him for abandoning the male companionship of Boland's poker games for the proscribed, female one of Lily's soirees. It was a matter of basic loyalties, and Colonel Dougal was a man of basic loyalties. He understood also the colonel's antagonism to the Iron Major, the dislike of a timid incompetent for a rash one.

A bachelor by the fact of his wife's residence in Washington, and occupant of Officers' Quarters 1—the only accommodation with a shake roof and impervious to rain in bad weather—the colonel chose to receive Lieutenant and Mrs. Cutler in his office. He was sufficiently courtly with this addition to Fort McLain's feminine society. When María raised her hand for his kiss, however, he either failed to understand the cue, or else a greaser's hand was never to touch Scotch lips. María, no doubt with her own set of prejudices, seemed unaware of the colonel's. Probably she put the oversight down to simple barbarian ignorance of proper manners.

Dougal stood at presence-of-females attention, shoulders squared, one foot advanced, his right hand tucked between the buttons of his tunic and the left behind his back.

"Your quarters are in readiness, ma'am!" he said with the loudness of address necessary to communicate with non-English-speakers. To Cutler he said, "The Olins have removed themselves. I've assigned you a striker, Corporal Brent, a good man!"

"Thank you, sir."

"Well, well, Cutler, another expedition into Mexico, eh?" He winked. "And you have brought back this fair hostage!"

"Yes, sir."

"I would be most interested in hearing the details of this foray, of course. Unless you have been sworn to secrecy by General Yeager, ha, ha!"

When they took their leave, María offered her hand again. This time Dougal bent over it. Straightening, red-faced, he blared, "Happy to make your acquaintance, ma'am! Hope you will be happy among this company!" He said to Cutler, "I'm sure the ladies will be paying their calls. Mrs. Reilly speaks a bit of Mex, I believe."

"What did he say, Patricio?" María whispered, as they thumped down the steps outside.

"He said you are welcome here and he hopes you will be very happy."

"He is a nice man," María said.

Married Officer Quarters 5 had a parlor with a corner fireplace, in the Mexican style. The Olins had covered the ceiling with unbleached muslin. This was considerably stained with brown blotches. The rough pine floor was also brown-stained. The walls had been plastered with newspapers to keep out the winter chill, these thickly whitewashed. Adjoining through one door was the bedroom, with a crudely made wooden bed frame; through another was the dining room, with three chairs and an unpainted wood table. Beyond this was the kitchen.

María stood in the parlor, gazing around her. Her face gleamed with perspiration, her white-mittened hands were clasped to her breast. "It is simply a horror," Ysabel said with satisfaction. "It is simply an impossibility."

Cutler, pacing from room to room with arms folded on his chest, trying to look at this hovel through María's eyes, had to agree that it was an impossibility. Nor could he see how living in it would help to make his wife into a woman of substance. "Glittering misery," a general's wife had said of the lives of married junior officers. He himself had never seen any glitter at all in the army, except once in a while a dress uniform in a cloudy mirror.

None of the other officers' wives called upon María, so he was still being Silenced. Rose Reilly came in with a rush and a bouquet of her precious roses to sweep María up in her warmth and offer spare bedding, glassware, china, and flatware. Bernie Reilly brought a bottle of good Cucamonga wine. María and Rose chattered and misunderstood each other while Cutler and Bernie smacked their lips over the wine, and Ysabel sat in a chair just inside the dining room doorway, watching this little festivity disapprovingly.

"Still Silenced, Pat?" Bernie asked.

"Evidently."

"Beautiful girl, Pat," Bernie said, squinting at María. "Beautiful. And a blue blood, Rosie tells me," he said on parting. "Quite an addition to post pulchritude, Pat!"

After this visit María was more cheerful. In the kitchen Corporal Brent, who had scraped together some cooking utensils, prepared slumgullion. Cutler noticed that Ysabel's universal disapproval did not include the striker, who was tall and blue-eyed, with fair hair parted in the exact center of his head.

That night, on the lumpy bed, he tried again to make conjugal love to his beautiful, blue-blooded Mexican wife. Whispered in his ear were not endearments but Hail Marys, and he encountered her hand crossing herself. He desisted angrily. The enchanting coquette, who had broken the confetti egg over his head in Guaymas, had turned into this lachrymose creature. The heir to Las Golondrinas was yet to begin his existence.

The next day he dropped in upon the Hoyas, in their *ranchería* behind the stables. They were glad to see him, congregating around him and laughing with pleasure. He presented the two cans of pears he had brought with him to Jim-jim, who was handy with a can opener. They squatted around the cans and scooped out pearly white, sweet pear halves. "Good!" Kills-a-Bear said, juice dripping from his chin.

Nochte's leg was much healed. He could limp without the assistance of a crutch, although squatting before the pear tins was painful and he retreated to lean against the fence. Benny Dee and Chockaway rattled at each other in Apache,

Chockaway bursting with giggles. Nantan Bigotes was training Sierra Verde scouts at Bosque Alto, Nochte said.

"Many!" Tazzi said. "No good! Hoya good, no many!" He
pointed to each in turn, slapping his thighs with laughter.

"Does Caballito rest easy at Bosque Alto?" Cutler asked
Nochte.

"I believe all is well, Nantan Tata," Nochte said. He
wore his new hat with its ribbons hanging before one shoulder, and he patted the hat and smiled his thin smile to show
Cutler he valued the gift.

"Good pear!" Tazzi said, in the loud voice he also employed
when addressing those who did not speak his language.

With the assistance of Rose Reilly, Quarters 5 achieved
some order, although Cutler suspected that Rose's affection
for María was influenced by her dislike of Lily Maginnis. In
the cool of evening María would sit under the veranda shade
of ropy cactus woven through rough laths, waiting for her
husband. She had come to take pleasure in the bugle calls of
the post, and one of the first pleasant intervals he had with
her was instructing her in these. He supposed it was a
gesture of conciliation that she told him if she had not
consented to marry him, her grandfather would have made
her marry Colonel Kandinsky, who was *old*.

Corporal Brent was a handsome, erect young Ohioan,
who had served as a striker before, and was grateful to return
to this easy duty. He was a resourceful cook, especially proud
of his turkey ragout. Cutler complimented him upon his
production, seated at supper with María in the little dining
room, with Ysabel maintaining a post just outside the doorway, knitting. Cutler had been amused to discover that she
was knitting baby clothes. Ysabel had become an ally. The
misery, if not glittering yet, did seem to have taken on a little
sheen.

The first Thursday he drove with María into Madison he
was very pleased by her reception at Lily's. Lily was at her
gracious best, and Frank was hospitable in his welcome.
Martin Turnbull was on hand, and the doctor, Tom Fletcher,
and Turnbull's henchmen, Joe Peake and the little gun-toter,
Johnny Angell. Penn McFall arrived late, with his usual fuss.

Cutler did not like the old cattleman, who was pompous
and self-impressed, a rangy, restless arthritic, loosely slung as

though his joints had separated from long years on the hurricane deck of a cow pony. The evening was restrained, as though Lily had cautioned everyone to be attentive to Cutler's new wife, and McFall seemed to feel he was responsible for the entertainment, for he embarked upon the long story of his coming to New Mexico. Ranging up and down the *sala* bent at the waist in his arthritic crouch, gesturing with his gnarled, gray hands, he described the cattle drive up from Texas; the confrontation with old Torn Foot, chief of the Nahuaque Apaches and father of the present chief; the lightning storm that had spooked the cattle, and the storm of hailstones the size of brickbats that had stampeded them; the crossing of the flooded Pecos; the desertion of half his cowboys; the death of his brother from appendicitis. He described the selection of the site of the home ranch, and the building of his ranch house, the Citadel; his bearding of the El Paso banker who had tried to renege on the promised loan; his disputes with the Mexicans who thought they still owned the land from pre–Gadsden Purchase days; his battle with the Davey Stovall gang; and his continuing fights with rustlers.

As the story progressed, his heavy, resonating voice took on the rhythms of a campfire Homer. And in the lamplit room with McFall's great shadow lurching and gesturing against the walls, Cutler saw Johnny Angell miming the exaggerated movements—hands raised with McFall's to illustrate that terrible hailstorm; or bent tenderly to tend the dying brother while at the same time illustrating the pain; chest out and chin up to face the offending banker, Nahuaques, hidalgos; spread-fingered hand brushing his revolver butt in response to the rustlers. The movements were restrained and small rather than exaggerated, as though reflected in a concave mirror, and as the recital continued the mimicry became broader, although never mocking. Johnny's small, handsome face was intense with concentration, and, as McFall's deep voice deepened and the pulse of the action resounded, the mimicry became more graceful, like some Oriental dance. Cutler realized he was observing not one but two precious bits of frontier art. He glanced around to see who else was watching the counterperformance instead of the main one. Not Frank, intent upon McFall, or Tom Fletcher or William Prim; but Joe Peake was grinning broadly, Lily's upper lip

looked as though it had been glued to her teeth, and Martin
Turnbull gave him one glance of rolling eyes. María's hand
rested on his arm, and from time to time pressed it
communicatively. McFall himself, however, did not notice
the sideshow, and Johnny's earnest, forelocked face never
broke into a smile, as though he was oblivious to his audience.

When the performance was finished, fat Berta served
supper, and after supper Lily played Liszt. During an inter-
mission Cutler overheard an exchange between Frank and
Martin Turnbull over some legal action.

"They have no possible claim to that herd," Turnbull said
in an irritated voice.

"They have acquired a writ of attachment, Martin. I will
of course counter their moves as I perceive them, but it
would be well not to underestimate either their determination or their capacity for mischief."

"I have little patience with these maneuvers," Turnbull
said. He grimaced with a motion of his shoulders, as though
shaking something from them.

"You must have patience. This is not England."

"Frank has been dealing with them longer than you
have, Martin," Dr. Prim said, who had also been listening.

"Yes, yes," Turnbull said again, and raised an expectant
face as Lily resumed playing.

María was quiet in the buggy rolling back toward the fort
under a high slip of moon, as though digesting what she had
seen and heard tonight.

"The big man is an *hacendado*?" she asked.

"He runs more cattle than anyone else in this part of the
country. There is no hacienda as you would know it."

"He talks very much. The other I liked better, Don
Martín."

"Everybody likes Don Martín."

"The wife of the advocate is beautiful, but she is not
young, as you have said, Patricio."

"Yes."

"She plays the piano very well, but there are many who
prefer it when you play, when you can sing."

"Well, that is what we all do at the house of the wife of
the advocate. We play the piano, and sometimes there is
singing. There is much talk. Sometimes it is gossip, and

sometimes it is good talk. And everybody admires Lily Maginnis, and now everybody likes Don Martín."

"I liked best the pretty little man with the fair hair that comes down on his forehead." She made a gesture with her hand.

"The gunman," he said in English.

"Pardon?"

"The *pistolero* of Don Martín."

"That one. He is very droll." She settled herself on the buggy seat with a satisfied air, drawing her cloak closer about her, her hand accidentally brushing his in the process. All evening she had competed with Lily Maginnis, without any show of it, and she must know, Cutler thought, that she had come off very well. And had she not been competing for her husband's admiration?

"Tell me, Patricio, what is this war they speak of? Is it *indios* one must fear?"

"The war is civilians fighting each other. The *indios* are all on reservations."

"But who is it who fights, please?"

"These you have met tonight, against others. The others have a store by which they have long been cheating soldiers and Indians and lending money to farmers and cheating them also. Don Martín and the advocate will open another store. It is thought that their enemies will fight this."

"It is always money that causes wars, my grandfather says," she observed primly.

"I was very proud of you tonight," Cutler said. "You were very beautiful. All the men had eyes only for you."

"Oh, that is silly, Patricio," she said, adjusting her cloak. Again her hand brushed his, this time not accidentally. He took the hand in his.

"I believe your grandfather awaits the news of a child," he said.

"Yes, he has written me, Patricio," she said, her hand remaining nestled in his.

When Johnny Angell was fourteen, he, his mother, and his half-sister, Dewey, lived with a blacksmith named Matt Gleason in Broadfield, Indiana, in a shacky house just off the pike. Between the house and the cornfields was a grove of fruit trees, the pear tree there the biggest he had ever seen. In the springtime it would fill with grackles quarreling in their voices like breaking sticks. He hated those birds. He hated quarreling and contention, for his mother and Matt fussed at each other all the time, until Matt would smash her in the face to shut her up. Then he would not know what he was supposed to do.

He did not have much chance to play ball when he was a boy because of working for Mr. Garrett at the livery stable, and for others too, but a couple of times playing ball he had found he had a quick eye, for he could eye-to-hand hit the ball every time, fastball or curve, even though he hadn't the strength to hit it very far, being small for his age. Fellows noticed that of him, though, looking at him in that queer way they would do later on when he could keep a can jumping firing a Colt, or knocking bottles off a fence rail, or shooting wild turkeys from cover. He had just been born that way, a gift from the Lord.

For a while that year he had a half-grown, splay-footed pup called Bitty because of being undersize, just as he was. Bitty squatted at his feet, shivering, until Johnny knocked off one of the grackles, then the pup lumbered out to catch the dead bird just before it hit the ground, and—head up like a real hunting dog, a wing sticking out here and a leg there—trotted back to lay it at his feet.

One time Bitty came back with a robin instead of a grackle. His eye was not good enough to tell at a hundred feet and through leaves whether a bird was a grackle or a robin, so he left off slingshotting. He would just peg a stone into the tree full of birds, which more often than not would jar the flock into flying off.

Before Bitty was full grown, Matt Gleason kicked him to death for moving his bowels on the veranda. His mother said he must not blame Matt for it, it was the liquor that had done it.

The next thing was that Dewey told him Matt had been coming into her bed at night, trying to force her. He told his mother he was not going to stand for it. He never in his life could stand that kind of outrage and crying evil. His mother sat opposite him at the scrubbed white-pine table, with sunshine streaming in the window, a skinny, red-eyed woman with her looks already gone and a bruised cheek from Matt hitting her. "Oh, please don't make a fuss, Johnny," she said. "It's only when the liquor gets at him."

"He kicked Bitty to death and he beats on you and would me if he could catch me, and now he is trying to force Dewey, who is only twelve years old. There has got to be somebody in the world that will protect her, and I guess that person is me."

She clutched his hand across the table and begged him to pray for guidance. She promised to talk to Matt Gleason.

But Dewey said Matt kept coming to her bed, so he told Matt himself he must not do it anymore. It was at breakfast, Matt with a stack of hotcakes before him, pouring molasses on. Dewey sat with her hands clasped before her, her hair in pigtails and her eyes round. His mother stood behind Matt with her apron mashed to her mouth.

Matt just laughed, though his face turned red. "This is my house, boy. I do what I want in it. If you don't like the hospitality you can make tracks out of here, and take these women with you."

His mother started crying out, "Oh, Matt!" and "Oh, Johnny!"

He told Matt one more time he must leave Dewey alone, and Matt asked him what he would do about it if he didn't.

"I will have to kill you," he said. Matt sprang up and swung a big fist at him, both his mother and his sister screeching, but he ducked out of the way. When Matt had gone to the blacksmith shop, his mother begged him not to make any more fuss, for they would all starve if he threw them out. He packed his few things while she was talking, and then went down to the livery stable and got the old Colt he kept hidden there in a leather pouch tucked into the rafters, and went to the blacksmith shop and shot Matt dead. Then he rode the cars to Denver.

In Denver he found work in a stable, but it was an unfriendly place, with contention and bullying, and finally there was a scrape and he had to leave town. He worked awhile punching cattle in cattle cars bound for the stockyards, ending up in New Mexico Territory brush-popping. He threw in with a rustler bunch. They stole stock from Penn McFall's PM outfit, the biggest around, and sold to Boland & Perkins, who turned around and sold to Fort McLain and the reservation. They told themselves that rustling was not the same as stealing, for Penn McFall had himself rustled his cattle, mavericking and overbranding in the old days. But rustling just didn't sit right with Johnny, he had not been brought up that way, so he went to work for Mr. McFall as a thirty-dollars-a-month cowhand. Then on a Fourth of July he won all the target-shooting competitions in Jeff City. That was when fellows began looking at him in a queer way.

Just then Mr. McFall was setting up his outfit he called the Regulators. Jack Grant was foreman, and there was Joe Peake and himself, and for a while Jesse Clary, so they called themselves the four Jays. They went after the rustler bunch and sent them back to Texas in a hurry, only not so many of them as there had been. They cleaned out two other rustler gangs, too, and there were chancy scrapes with some of those ducks.

Jesse quit to go to work for Ran Boland, and Joe quit because he had got married and wanted to set up ranching on his own, which he did with Mr. McFall lending him some stock to get him started. So then there were only two Regulators, two Jays, and not much work for them either with rustling quieted down, until Mr. McFall set them to running off some families of Mormons squatting on bottom land Mr. McFall considered prime range, though he had no more title to it than those Mormons did. And Johnny didn't like that any more than he had liked rustling.

In those scrapes with rustlers, some of them fellows he

had ridden with not long ago, he would shoot to break a gun arm, but Jack would go for the center shot every time. It was not just Jack's not taking risks, there was something in him that when he was on a different side from another person he was all the way over, and no quarter given or asked for. Jack came of mountain people in Pennsylvania and a different kind of Christian religion from the one Johnny had been brought up into. It didn't seem to have much to do with the Redeemer, but straight through to the Almighty with no middleman, not much forgiveness to be had nor hope for a seat near the Throne either, for those were all used up. Jack was so honest, fellows made jokes about it, how he had ridden forty miles to pay back two bits borrowed for beer, and once he had tried to give Mr. McFall back some of his pay when he had mashed his hand roping range cattle and couldn't work for a week. But Jack could get himself as bucked up as the next fellow over riding into town after poontang, and he was fine company and jolly when the occasion was right. "Everything in its season," he would say, but when it was serious season Jack was serious all the way, like with everything else.

Sometimes it seemed to Johnny that Jack took his boss, who was Mr. McFall at the time, as a kind of junior Almighty. What he laid out for you to do was the Law, and what Jack set out to do would get set up like cement too. Still, the two Jays were the kind of pals you got to be when one had got the other out of a tight squeak, and the other'd got the one out of a hard place. He was Little Jay and Jack was Big Jay, from the Four Jays' days of the Regulators, though Jay-O-Joe Peake and Jesse-Jay Clary had moved on to other things. Now it was getting to be his turn.

The night he decided he must quit the Regulators, he and Jack were sitting by a campfire under a yellow moon, waiting for the coffee to come to a boil. He told Jack he was not going to help run those Mormons off Mr. McFall's range.

"How's that?" Jack said, sounding surprised.

"It's not right," he said.

"It's the work we do," Jack said. "Anyhow, they're moving on along. I talked to that fellow with the chin whiskers."

"Talked him into moving along."

"It's better than trouble, Little Jay." Jack leaned forward to pick up the coffeepot, hissing when he singed his fingers. He poured scalding coffee into their two cups. "What would you do? Tell Old Mac you're not going to do what you're paid good wages to do?"

"Well, he don't pay me good wages for doing what is not right to do, because I'm not going to do it. Because next thing is to run those Mexes out of those meadows along Willow Creek."

Jack sighed, and nodded, and said in his careful way, "Yes, I expect that is the next thing."

"Those people are friends of ours! We have eaten their chow. We've gone into the *placitas* to the dances, and they've let us dance with their daughters. They've treated us just like their own folks!"

"Well, it is a hard one," Jack said uncomfortably.

"We are working for a man that thinks he can run people off land they have been on longer than he has been in the Territory. Land their fathers settled, maybe grandfathers. They have got more right to it than he has."

"Well, they are Mex, you see," Jack said in the uncomfortable voice, though Johnny knew Jack was no greaser-hater like Jesse Clary. "One time this place was all Mex," Jack went on. "And it was just cactus and bandits and murdering Apaches, and no kind of control of anything. Now it's U.S.A. and halfway between cactus and civilized, but in between times there is only Old Mac in the south county to keep things orderly."

"I see that Arioso is pretty orderly, Mex-run. Well, it surely is orderly seeing everybody run off the range but *you!* So we have Mr. McFall and the store for order and the law out here, you are saying."

"Maybe that's the way it has to be for now," Jack said, sipping at his cup.

"Well, I say it's not right even if it is order and the law just now. I believe it is outrage, Jack."

Jack stood up then, tall and tall-hatted against the moon. Johnny sat looking up at him, trying to understand him. Maybe you could never understand someone who did not think like your own self. "You buck up against things before they've even happened yet, Johnny," Jack said quietly.

"There is right and wrong before and after."

The coffee steamed up past Jack's face. "So I guess you're quitting here, then, Little Jay. I'll miss you pretty bad," he said, like it hurt him to say it.

"Me too," Johnny said. "Well, like you say, it is too bad. But Jack, what if sometime Mr. McFall told you you had to take after me?"

Jack just shook his head. "He wouldn't do that, Johnny. I wouldn't work for a man who would do that."

But when he told Mr. McFall he was quitting, he didn't say he would buck him if he tried to run those people out of Willow Meadows as he had thought he would have to do. Instead he remembered he had seen the old man going into the little 'dobe church in Corral de Tierra, and he went to the Flores brothers and Manuel Abrigo, whose families had ranched those meadows for maybe three generations. Luz Flores had a new baby that hadn't been baptized yet, and he persuaded her and Carlos to go to Mr. McFall and ask him would he be the godfather. They did, and Mr. McFall said that he would. After the ceremony there was a barbeque out along the creek, and Mr. McFall came to that too, with Jack riding alongside, two men so tall Johnny got a crick in his neck looking up at them from the ground.

"Good job," Jack said, which was about the highest praise you could expect from him.

What Mr. McFall dearly loved to do was tell the story of his coming to the territory with his cattle herds, which story added a couple of new misadventures or triumphs of Mr. McFall over the forces or circumstances trying to stop him every time Johnny heard it, which was plenty of times. And he made sure that Mr. McFall got to tell his story this time too, even though half his audience didn't speak English well enough to know what he was telling them.

He bummed around a bit before he went to work for Joe Peake, and then onto Mr. Turnbull's payroll, the man Joe worked part-time as foreman for. Mr. Turnbull was what Johnny had been searching for without even knowing it, the finest, fairest, book-smartest man he had ever known. Mr. Maginnis, who was going to be Mr. Turnbull's partner in a new store in Madison laid out against Boland & Perkins, was the next finest, and Mrs. Maginnis the finest and most beautiful lady he knew of.

Still he would see Johnny from time to time in Arioso or wherever there was a fiesta or a *baile*, and once Jack dropped in at Mr. Turnbull's place, which had been the Peters Ranch

before old Ben Peters died. It was a comfortable house with
Mr. Turnbull's furniture and fixings, three rooms with stacks
of books from a wagonload that had just come from England.

Mr. Turnbull invited Jack to supper with Johnny, Joe
Peake, and two other Turnbull hands, Pard Graves and
Carlito Rivera. The Mex woman helped them all to *menudos*,
white hunks of cowbelly in the soup soaked in chili to set
your mouth on fire. After supper Mr. Turnbull poured whiskey, and Carlito played guitar in the Mexican way, with his
box held straight up in his lap, leaning his ear to the strings
as he strummed out fine old Mex tunes. Joe and Pard sat by
the fireplace with the checkerboard between them.

Mr. Turnbull lit his pipe and sat down at a table across
from Jack, three stacks of books between them so Mr. Turnbull
had to peer over.

"Everybody I know down in this part of the country is on
your side of the thing," Jack said to him, with one of those
long, straight looks that made some people nervous.

"Yes, I have been pleased by those people who have
come by to say so." Mr. Turnbull winked at Johnny, and
added, "However, it is a great comfort having the best shot in
the county at my side."

"He's only the second-best checkerplayer, though," Joe
Peake said, stretching. Jay-O-Joe was almost as tall as Big Jay,
always turning his head to one side as though trying to
stretch a crick out of his neck.

"Didn't amount to a hill of beans as a cowpuncher," Jack
said in his solemn way. "Might've taught him something if
he'd stuck with the PM."

"Too much range over there to watch out for," Johnny
said, and grinned at Jack.

"Have you had any education, Mr. Grant?" Mr. Turnbull
said.

"I've had some schooling, reading and writing and sums."

"I've just received a large shipment of books and I would
be very pleased to share them. Johnny here was never
allowed to read anything but the Good Book as a lad."

Chin cupped in his hands, elbows on the table and his
legs crossed so he was all long shanks and sharp angles, Jack
said, "A man takes up reading books out here, it is usually law
books. That's a step up a fellow can take in the world if he
had a mind to it."

"And you are such a one?" Mr. Turnbull asked, feathering smoke out of the corners of his mouth.

Johnny was interested to see the color climb in Jack's cheeks. He had never thought about Jack and the law before, but maybe that was exactly what Jack had been looking to serve, just as he, Johnny, had been looking for Mr. Turnbull without knowing it.

Jack said, as though he had been caught out, "Maybe I am."

"My brother is an advocate," Mr. Turnbull said. "I cannot say it has made him a jolly person." He struck a pose, gesturing with his pipe, and declaimed, "Your pettifoggers damn their souls, to share with knaves in cheating fools!"

Johnny thought he could die happy if he could just talk that fine.

"This country could use a good dose of law, all right," Jack said.

"Nest of rattlers," Joe said, without looking up from the checkerboard.

"Ranching and raising a family are Joe's ambitions," Mr. Turnbull said, rising to pour more whiskey. "And so the law is yours, Mr. Grant. Carlito's is to be a concert musician, and Pard's to be a gourmand of international stature. And yours, the beau of the ball, Johnny?"

"Beautiful girls pining for me, but rich and famous too."

They all laughed, glancing at him. Pard said, "You've made a good start with the girls, Johnny-A!"

Mr. Turnbull raised his whiskey glass and said, with his laugh that made it hard not to laugh along with him, "May all your ambitions be gratified!"

"And a fine new store in Madison, too!" Johnny called out.

The Mex woman brought in a plate of small, sweet dessert tamales, corn meal dough steamed with just a trace of meat juice at the centers, wrapped in damp cornshucks. Mr. Turnbull all but crowed to see them, wringing his hands together. He did enjoy Mex food. While they were finishing off those tamales in record time, Johnny heard Mr. Turnbull tell Jack that if he was interested in reading law he could help him, and Frank Maginnis would be glad to also.

At that Johnny saw a shadow brush over Jack's face, for he did not like Mr. Maginnis. There were more than a few who disliked Mr. Maginnis, a man with that kind of swagger of knowing he was always in the right, and flat left out of him the quality of taking a look inside himself and finding something there to laugh at. Mr. Maginnis was a self-righteous man, but, in Johnny's opinion, a good one.

Jack got to his feet and said, "Why, that sure is fine of you, Mr. Turnbull, but I know I just could not get through all those books. But you let us know, now, if there is trouble. A bunch of us will be on hand in a hurry."

He had been noticing that Jack had not said what side he was on in the fuss with the store, and now he felt easier. He worried about Jack ending up on the wrong side of things out of pure stubbornness.

"My regards to Penn McFall!" Mr. Turnbull was saying, following Jack Grant to the door.

That night Mr. Turnbull and Joe turned in inside, and he, Pard, and Carlito unrolled their soogans under the stars, gossiping and dozing and waking to quiet voices. He thought he had never been so content as he was that night, just before it all started.

Rounding up strays for Penn McFall, Johnny had found the place, southwest of Arioso and due south of Corral de Tierra. A vast slot had opened in the desert, invisible unless you were right on top of it, canyons leading out right and left in a network of erosion as though a mighty river had cut through and then sunk straight down into the earth. Now there was only a stream, that had freshened as he rode up it, past the canyon mouths that all looked alike. He didn't know why he had picked one particular canyon, but he had; it kept running deeper and deeper, walls rising to high cliffs that were stained rust and white and ochre in horizontal stripes. Some of these were mashed and crumpled to form caves, and pretty soon the caves looked different. They were doorways framing black shadow, tier on tier of these, sometimes as many as five stories, with broad terraces stitched together by ladders made from peeled branches. Where the canyon broadened out, there were worn-smooth adobe walls enclosing nothing, and, beyond, a grassy meadow with willow jungles along the creek. When he explored the cave dwellings he found every one as clean as though it had been swept out just last week. He clambered up the frail old ladders that were fastened together with pegs and crumbled rawhide, half-excited and half-scared, as though wild Indians, or ghosts, would come whooping out at him any minute. There was a silence to the whole place that was scary until, just sitting on one of the low walls, measuring the sun arching overhead between the canyon walls, he had learned to love it. It was a silence beyond silence, so you couldn't hear the creek, or the wind blowing, so that any sharp sound seemed a violation you almost ought to apologize for. He would find himself tiptoeing on the hard-packed red ground so his boots wouldn't scrape on the pebbles.

He had visited it time after time over the last two years, and there was never sign of anyone else having been there. It was a rare feeling thinking he was the only one who knew of it. He knew there were places like this scattered all through the desert country, *ruinas* the Mexes called them, built, hollowed out rather, by a long-gone-away people called the Old Ones, who hadn't been Apaches or Pimas or even Pueblos either. He had found a *ruina* all his own. He never told a soul about it until one day he took Mr. Turnbull there, for he knew his employer would feel the same way he did about the place.

They rode up along the strata-ed walls, Mr. Turnbull gazing up at them from under his English flat-brimmed hat like a surveyor's hat, his pipe in his teeth. "Those are impressive cliffs, Johnny!"

"Just you wait," he said. Pretty soon the caves started showing, first a few, then the ranks of squared-off black holes, and the ladders slanting from terrace to terrace, and from the cornices brush and trees fringing over. And Mr. Turnbull said quietly, "What is this place you have brought me to, Johnny?"

"It's ruins," he said. "Long-time-ago Indians they call the Old Ones. There must've been a heap of them!"

"And only you know of this?"

"*You* too, now."

Mr. Turnbull swung off his big bay to walk along staring up, leading the horse. He stopped to peer into some of the ground-floor doorways.

"That's the one I call the post office," Johnny said. "See how it's got a window for passing out mail?"

"What a marvelous discovery you have made here," Mr. Turnbull said.

They secured the horses and explored, climbing the ladders. He had been nervous about Mr. Turnbull hallooing to hear the echoes rumble off down canyon, but Mr. Turnbull was solemn and respectful, which he should have known. All the cubicles were just as clean and swept-out as he could have wished, but in the big, round room Mr. Turnbull scuffed through loose dirt to turn up some pieces of broken pottery, tan thin flakes with bits of crude animals traced on them.

"This would have been a meeting room," Mr. Turnbull said. "Imagine it crowded with people. The chief is explaining that they must leave here. There is no more water, or the crops have failed for several years, or terrible enemies like the Apaches have come against them. For something like that must have happened, Johnny." He had a slow way of speaking that sounded as though he was thinking a thing over before he said it.

"I know it," he answered, for he had worked that through too.

Back outside in the sunlight he built a fire, and they boiled up some coffee and ate some hard cheese and dry tortillas from Mr. Turnbull's oiled-silk lunch bag, and Mr. Turnbull told him some things about himself, why he had come to this country and what he wanted to do. It seemed that younger sons, for a reason Johnny could not quite get a handle on, had a tough row to hoe in England, so often they went abroad with funds to invest in order to make their fortunes. The West was popular just now because of a book that told how much money could be made investing in cattle. Mr. Turnbull had discovered in Texas that this was not always the case, for there were ups and down in the cattle market and many other problems; nor did he like Texans, whose attitudes had seemed to him excessively commercial. He wished to invest his funds in such a way that they brought a decent return but also built something that would be a benefit to others besides himself. Things seemed just right in Madison County, where he had acquired the Peters Ranch and two fine herds. There was also the opportunity of a store in town, where Boland & Perkins had had things their own way for too long, and to the detriment of the citizens of the county.

His father was an old Tartar, he said, who had made a fortune manufacturing shoes and leather goods in the Midlands. His brother was a successful advocate, with political aspirations. James was a stuffy bully Mr. Turnbull didn't like at all.

"It seems to me that had I remained in England, I would have become like him," he said. "And that would never do. I believe its very smallness makes England small-minded, Johnny. Men are stingy there, and do not wish their neighbors well. I cannot think of anyone I know there who would share a secret in such an openhanded way as you have shared this one today—with a comparative stranger."

He was engaged to be married to Lady Mary Rose, who was an angel, and who would join him in New Mexico as soon as he was settled.

Mr. Turnbull lounged against one of the low walls, squinting up at the dark patches of openings above them. "I will order some books to see if we can't find out something about the Old Ones. Their history. Where they disappeared to."

"Maybe we will go the same, someday," Johnny said. "Just like this, and a long time later some cowboy out looking for strays comes onto a town of buildings—" He broke off with a chuckle, since he didn't know how to finish the thought.

Mr. Turnbull said, "The homely Nurse doth all she can, / To make her Foster-child, her Inmate, Man, / Forget the glories he hath known, / And that imperial palace whence he came."

"Yes," Johnny said, nodding hard. "That is surely right."

"How this place can make a person forget the petty tribulations," Mr. Turnbull went on. "Writs and counterwrits, attachments and counterattachments." He sounded discouraged, all at once. "They are making as much trouble for me as they can in Madison, Johnny."

"That is why Joe has me and Pard sticking close by you. In case there is trouble."

"I simply cannot believe there is danger of actual violence," Mr. Turnbull said, scowling cross-eyed down at the bole of his pipe as he filled it with fragrant tobacco. "Surely this is a civilized nation."

"When the Apaches went out and on the prod, this was no civilized place."

"Oh, they have got Caballito back on the reservation; surely that is the end of that."

"There is other Apaches than Caballito, and others than Paches, if you take my meaning."

"Joe thinks they will try to attach that herd I have bought," Mr. Turnbull said, leaning back and gazing up. "I simply cannot believe that!"

"I guess it's time we started along," Johnny said. "Pard will be worrying."

Pard was waiting at the creek crossing beyond Corral de Tierra, sitting in the shade chewing tobacco and spitting into the water, his pony grazing off a way. Further along they caught up with Carlito and the pack mules, loaded with grain sacks and store goods from the Corral de Tierra *tienda*. Where the ridges started building, getting on toward Mr. Turnbull's spread, Johnny angled away from the others to ride the high trail and survey the scenery. He loved this country so much; when he had first seen it he knew it was home. Plane on plane slanted at different angles up toward the horizon, gray and brown and gold and red climbing toward the going-on-forever blue of the sky. The land was polka-dotted with clumps of brush, a few head of cattle grazing. He watched a dust devil swirl up, exploding into gold when the sun caught it. He loved the sunrises out here, the great yellow disk popping up so sudden and enormous it seemed to be addressing itself just to you, and the sunsets the color of a red-hot iron cooling.

Below him Mr. Turnbull, Pard, and Carlito rode in single file, the pack animals trailing behind. He turned Whitey downhill, gave a whoop, and started down toward them, waving his hat. Pard whooped, drew his piece and fired in the air. They all broke into a gallop, Mr. Turnbull looking back from under his flat hat brim with a big grin. They scared up a flock of wild turkey that took the air in a flapping fury, whizzing low over the brush and into the ravine tucked behind the low ridge.

"Why don't you fellows bring in a big turkey or two for supper?" Mr. Turnbull said, as they waited for the pack mules to catch up, so in their high spirits Johnny, Pard, and Carlito raced up the ravine after the turkeys. They snapped off revolver shots, hitting nothing but sagebrush, until Johnny halted and unshipped his rifle. He brought down one bird at ten yards and another at thirty.

They chased on up the ravine, Carlito finally racking up a turkey with his Colt, yelling, *"Ayyy carrramba, guajolote!"* Then they trailed back, halting to pick up the birds they had shot—nine in all, and fine fat fellows too.

"We'll show him that big turkey he wanted!" Johnny said, and, working fast, began tying turkeys by their feet so the wings hung spread out from Whitey's saddle and straps, so Whitey began to look like one great turkey wing. Whitey didn't like it one bit, tossing his forefeet and backing, Carlito and Pard shouting with laughter. When Johnny had the decorations all rigged, they headed back down the ravine.

Mr. Turnbull and the mules had gone on out of sight, and they trotted on over the next ridge. Here there were more bunches of Turnbull cattle in sight. Mr. Turnbull was raising a drift of dust about a mile ahead.

"What's that?" Pard called out, drawing up, for coming from the north a big dustcloud was rolling toward Mr. Turnbull, underneath it a pack of riders, it looked like at least thirty of them. Four were a good way out in front and coming fast. "Who the hell is that, Johnny?" Pard yelled back at him.

He was making slower time than the others, Whitey hampered by the turkeys slung all over him. He felt like one big fool with his turkey-horse. He spurred Whitey on, at the same time jerking his knife free and cutting loose the birds he could reach.

"It is posse from town!" Carlito cried. The two of them rode hard after Mr. Turnbull, Johnny trying to catch up. Leaving the mules behind, Mr. Turnbull had veered off to meet the front four. All the posse was spread out at a gallop now, hurrying shapes flowing across the grama grass.

Mr. Turnbull and the four riders slowed to come up together. There was the lazy, distant thump of a shot, and Johnny felt a sound come out of his throat like pain. It was like it was all some bad dream, with that hazy slowness to it, his pulse jumping and that queer strangled sound he didn't even mean coming out of his throat.

Pard and Carlito had pulled up, and he halted with them. It was impossible to see what was happening, the five riders circling; no, only four of them. Another shot thumped. The rest of the posse galloped toward the four. His belly came up against his chest so hard, Johnny thought he would puke his lunch.

"They have kilt him," he heard Pard say. Now he could see that Mr. Turnbull's sorrel was down—just a glimpse of it among the moving horses, no sight of Mr. Turnbull. He jerked his rifle from its boot, aimed, and snapped dry; he had run out his magazine shooting turkeys. There was the heart-stopping snatch, snatch, snatch of bullets passing over, followed by the shots. The main body of riders was coming straight on toward them.

It finally got through his head that they were store men who had killed Mr. Turnbull.

"We've got to clear out of here, Johnny!" Pard yelled, and the three of them swung around and lit for out-of-range, more lead flying past their ducked heads. He was panting, his nose running, his belly jerking like that. Hooves whacked on hard ground. Pard's hat brim was blown back against the crown, his chin out like he was trying to lean out ahead of his pony.

Their job had been to stand by Mr. Turnbull just in case of something like this, and they had been out chasing turkeys. Playing boys' games with turkeys. That had been his doing.

On the next high ground they halted. The posse had broken off chasing them and now the whole bunch was circling where Mr. Turnbull had disappeared. Pard propped his rifle up at a high angle to fire, but Johnny chopped a hand down to stop such foolishness. There had been too much foolishness. He knew it was done. Beneath the hollow in his head was a consciousness of a kind of great engine starting up, a locomotive puffing with a heavy, slow acceleration that didn't yet know which direction to turn.

"What we do, Juanito?" Carlito asked.

"Watch," said the queer deep voice that was his. "Make out which one is who."

"Goddamn murdering buggers—" Pard said, and stopped to rub his shirtsleeve hard across his eyes.

Now the whole bunch got moving in the same direction, heading back north, toward Madison. There was no rider on one of the horses, but something that must have been Mr. Turnbull's body slung over the saddle, though he couldn't make it out so far away, even with his good eyes. The three of them rode for a while in the posse's wake. They passed the laden pack animals, cropping at the grass. Twice there were rifle shots, but no lead came anywhere near. He asked Pard if he had made out who anybody was.

"Clay Mortenson," Pard said through his teeth.

He had thought so too, the one of the out-in-front four in the black hat, the kind of man Boland and them would hire for dirty work.

"Can figure some others then," Carlito said.

"That's right," Pard said.

They came up to where they had last seen Mr. Turnbull. The sorrel was dead, shot through the head, saddled and tack stripped off. Carlito dismounted to scour the ground, bent over like an Apache on the scout. He turned up a rock the size of a packet of coffee with blood, brains, and hair stuck to it. Carlito stood up, holding it out, facing them.

"What'd they want to bash his head in for?" Pard groaned. "They had already shot him."

Johnny dismounted also. Leading Whitey, he prowled the hoof-scuffed earth. He bent and plucked up the revolver from where it lay half under the dead horse's knee. He smelled the muzzle.

"That's Mr. Turnbull's," Pard said.

"Hasn't been fired." He secured the revolver under his belt.

"Goddamn murdering buggers," Pard said.

There were still two turkeys strung from his saddle, and Johnny cut them loose and let them fall, Pard and Carlito watching him with similar expressions.

"What we do now, Juanito?" Carlito asked.

"We'll head for Joe's. You bring along those pack animals, will you?"

"Joe will be wild as a rabies wolf," Pard said.

Joe Peake's little spread adjoined Mr. Turnbull's. His house was an old line camp fixed up, logs chinked with mud and whitewashed inside, very neat and clean. Sheds had been thrown out on three sides, with doors cut through: kitchen, bedroom, and a room for the little boy, Chuckie, who was the light of his mother's and father's life. Joe stood in the exact center of the main room, arms folded high on his chest, staring past them as though he had been poleaxed but hadn't dropped yet. Then he stretched his neck and glared at Johnny.

"Where was you?"

"Up a canyon hunting turkeys for supper."

"Damn you," Joe said, without fire.

"Mr. Turnbull sent us after turkey, Joe," Pard said.

Joe looked at him.

"When we come back they was already on him," Carlito said, hat in hands. Fanny Peake stood by the range in her floury apron. From his room Chuckie called out, "Da! Da!"

"The war has started," Joe said.

"It was my fault," Johnny said. "We took too long. Shot more turkey than we needed. Got to fooling."

Joe's dark disks of eyes turned back to him. Joe nodded as though that was enough said. "It wasn't the sheriff, you don't think?" he said.

"I don't believe Pogie Smith was in that first bunch," Pard said.

"Clay Mortenson was one of them," Johnny said. They went over the scene again, what they had seen, what they had figured out since. Sometimes his belly would jerk like that.

"Clay Mortenson would do a thing like that, I expect," Joe said in a tired voice. "Pound a man's head in with a rock after he was already dead." He made a sucking sound, like getting rid of a lot of spit. "We'll see about that," he said. "Who else, do you think? Ed Duffy, probably, if it was Clay."

"Probably," Johnny said.

Joe paced, rubbing his arms as though getting the circulation going. He threw off his wife's hand when she laid it on his shoulder. "So many of them," he said. "Must have been sent out to take in that herd they was squabbling about, or else arrest Mr. Turnbull. Must've been that. Except kill him instead. If it was a legal posse, Pogie Smith must've deputized them—even if he wasn't along. The judge had to make out an attachment, or a warrant. Of course everybody knows the judge and Boland, and Jake Weber in Santa Fe, was old partners from California Column days." He threw up his hands. "All we can start with is Clay Mortenson, anyhow."

Fanny Peake came over to lay an arm around his waist. "What about his people back in England?"

"There's a Lady Somebody he was engaged to—" Johnny started, and quit.

"Frank Maginnis will know how to tell them," Joe said. He moved away from his wife again, as though her touch jiggered him. "We'd better ride in and see Frank," he said.

"Now you let Mr. Maginnis deal with the whole thing," Fanny Peake said. She was a big woman, broad-hipped and low-bosomed, with a loose red face and blinking eyes that looked like she was afraid of getting hurt. "He's a lawyer, after all. You listen to Frank now, Joe!"

"He will just say that guns never settle anything," Joe said in a thick voice. "They just settled as good a man as we'll ever know."

"That's for certain," Pard said.

"I guess I can't see it any way but guns now," Johnny said carefully. "But I will be glad for Mr. Maginnis's advice."

"Let's go there," Joe said. He took down from their peg on the wall his cartridge belt and holstered Colt.

"Oh, Joe," Fanny Peake said.

The graveyard was on a shelf of hillside just north of Madison. Cutler guided the buggy in among the other buggies there and helped María down in her lacy black. They joined clusters of black-clad men and women where the red earth was mounded beside the dug grave. Defensive iron was in evidence, and grim faces, eyes slanting toward him and his wife, as, supporting María's arm, he guided her along the path. The white boards, crosses, and rock markers faced them out of the stony ground. There was a pressure from María's hand on his arm.

Lily stood with Frank Maginnis, pile of glossy hair beneath a black straw hat taller than her husband's bare head. Her face was veiled, her tight-fitting black jacket faired into a narrow skirt. Frank's bugged eyes in his bearded face searched the other faces restlessly. Once he took from a vest pocket a gold watch on a gold chain and consulted it. He raised a hand to Cutler in solemn greeting. Lily was moving toward them, shining black boots slipping out beneath the hem of her skirt.

"I'm so glad you've come, Pat. Oh, Mrs. Cutler, I am so sorry that we must meet again on such a tragic occasion." She kissed María showily.

María murmured in response, not understanding. Lily's damp eyes fixed on Cutler's through her veil.

"Pat, they murdered him!" she said. "They simply shot him down in cold blood!"

"Yes, I've heard," he said.

Frank approached in his stately, slightly backward-leaning walk. He kissed María's hand in greeting and smiled his pursy smile at Cutler, red mouth tucked into his beard, curiously inhuman eyes set too far apart. Coming up also were Joe Peake

134

and the little *pistolero,* Johnny Angell, for whom María had expressed a liking, both with neatly combed hair, Peake's black, the boy's tow-colored. They wore holstered sidearms, and Angell carried a rifle by its barrel. Dr. Prim drifted toward them from another group of armed men. No one spoke much, except for muttered greetings to María. Eyes on Cutler were reproachful, resentful; he had not yet declared his allegiance.

The doctor wiped his forehead with a white handkerchief and said, "Of course you've been out of the country for a great deal of the belligerent maneuverings, Pat. Have you been told what has happened here?"

"It was a posse, as I heard it. He fired on them. Or didn't."

"That is correct," Frank said. "The posse claims he did, of course." He also daubed at his forehead with a handkerchief. "Ran Boland placed a lien on the herd Martin had purchased. There were legal manipulations and a writ of attachment was issued, which Martin chose to ignore. A warrant was issued for his arrest and a posse organized. You can imagine the caliber of the men who were deputized."

"I suppose so."

"It would seem that Martin rode to meet them. He simply could not believe in the corruption of legal processes with which we are familiar. He had not lived out here long enough to distrust anything emanating from Madison—"

"He had not lived long enough in the world!" Lily said through her veil.

"Claimed he rode at them fogging and fanning," Joe Peake said in his harsh voice. "So they had to shoot him down in self-defense. Loaded him up like a butchered hog and brought him back to town."

"We saw some of it, from a ways off," Johnny Angell said. "Me and Pard and Carlito Rivera." His small, almost pretty face with the blond forelock falling toward one eye was tight as a fist with anger.

"Tried to ride them down was how he got shot in the back of the head," Joe Peake said.

"And his piece wasn't fired, either," Johnny added. "For I found it on the ground there."

María's hand gripped Cutler's arm questioningly, and he patted it once.

"Here comes the wagon," Tom Fletcher said. The mule-drawn wagon slowly climbed the road from Madison, on its bed the coffin, of shockingly pale pinewood, shaded by a tarpaulin.

Frank Maginnis and the others started down the path to meet the group that had ridden along with the wagon. Six men in lockstep carried the pale box up the path, the Methodist minister from Santa Fe striding ahead with his prayerbook in his hands. All the pallbearers wore sidearms. Cutler watched Lily walking beside her husband, mourning Martin Turnbull, who had replaced him in her affections and her bed. It occurred to him that María must be confused and alarmed by this militant scene, a new act in the "war" that she had inquired about on their first visit to town and that he had treated as a joke.

"You and Mrs. Cutler must come to supper, afterward," Lily whispered. "Will you, Pat?"

"Of course."

"What does she say, please?" María whispered, as Lily drifted away. He told her, watching the coffin set down across from the heap of red dirt. Men stood wiping sweat from their faces and necks. The minister read in a voice that did not carry to where Cutler stood with his wife's hand on his arm. Joe and Johnny Angell tossed in the first shovelfuls, then turned the shovels over to others. Frank Maginnis led Lily away, his arm around her waist.

Cutler followed with María. In the buggy he told her, "These men are angry because their friend was murdered. In the war you asked me about."

"The wife of the advocate is very sad."

"She loved him," he said, riding the brake as the buggy rolled down the hill in the line of buggies and wagons.

The procession passed along Main Street, where Mexicans watched from in front of the Mexican store and cantina, and rolled slowly on, past the two-story courthouse with its upstairs jail, the hotel, adobe residences set behind greenery, one that had burned with only a chimney still standing, and past the store with the BOLAND & PERKINS sign. A dim figure was visible standing well back from one of Boland's upstairs windows, and a bonneted woman hurried along the board-walk there. Cater-cornered was the new building, pole-ends of rafters casting oblique shadows on the adobe front, and a new sign brave with paint and bigger than the one it confronted: TURNBULL & MAGINNIS. The door of the new store was closed and barred. Sheriff Pogie Smith stood on the stoop of the courthouse, arms folded on his chest, face shadowed by the brim of his hat. To Cutler he appeared small and frightened.

The procession moved on past him toward the Maginnis house, a mansion by Madison standards, striped by the shadows of the trees on the curve of street. María's hand continued to rest on Cutler's arm with a trust that pleased him.

At Maginnis's the armed men who had attended Martin Turnbull's funeral removed their hats as they filed inside, Lily and María the only women except for Berta the cook, who carried in laden trays and steaming platters from the kitchen. Men loaded their plates and edged toward walls or corners, where they rested in uncomfortable attitudes. Frank took up a post on the dais where the piano gleamed. Lily removed her veil and stood watching her husband with tragic eyes. Conversations ceased.

"In Greek there are two words for justice," Frank began. "*Themis* means justice dispensed from above, the judicial power of kings and nobles. The power of *themis* was more often misused than not, and over the centuries people began to demand written, codified laws. There was conflict between the nobility with their inherited privileges and free men of low birth who began to demand equal justice. The word for this other justice is *dikē*. *Dikē* was written law, the law for everyone, the process of law, the dispensation of justice. 'Due share' is the actual meaning of the word. *Themis* is the authority of justice, *dikē* is the equality."

His bulldog eyes in his dark, heavy-jawed face glanced around the room. "What we have in this part of New Mexico Territory is a kind of old nobility, early settlers, those who came here first. These men have risen to positions of power and consider that they possess the ancient rights of *themis*. Their power runs back to the frontier days when those strong enough could assume the mantles of authority. It is natural that they would seek to hold onto their old privileges and their power.

"But these men fail to recognize, refuse to recognize, that the frontier has changed. Civilization has come. Towns have been chartered. There are local governments. Our nation is a democracy. *Dikē* has become the order of justice. But still Jake Weber in Santa Fe wields his old *themis* as United States District Attorney, as chief of the Republican caucus and bosom friend of Governor Dickey. So do his old comrades in Madison—Barron Arthur, the justice of the peace of this county, Neill MacLennon, the prosecuting attorney. And Randolph Boland."

Again Cutler felt the questioning pressure on his arm, and again he patted María's fingers. He had never met Jake Weber, but he had played poker with Neill MacLennon and Barry Arthur, both of them big-bellied, comfortable men, Neill bald and bespectacled, Barry with a thatch of graying hair like a shake roof; Neill a collector of dirty jokes, the judge a hunter and fisherman; both of them radiating good fellowship, ready to help a friend in need, no doubt kindly to widows and orphans and devoid of mean bones. And yet they were the local power, and their comfort and good fellowship depended upon things running exactly as they had always run. He had heard them joke with Ran Boland, not of illegal maneuvers or conspiracies, but of solving an awkward problem with a word of warning or a reminder of favors past or still to come, and especially he had seen them enjoying the evidence of human weakness in others. The only sign of viciousness he had ever come upon was Ran's violent dislike of Frank Maginnis, but he would never forget the farmer, Cobb, approaching the store with his hat in his hands, and he knew that violence was only the next step beyond Ran Boland's usual methods of persuasion.

"*Themis*," Frank continued, "is favored, or at least rationalized, by many because often it seems more orderly than the complicated demands of *dikē*. However, a war of revolution was fought by Americans to bring *dikē* to America. That war was won, but it seems it must continually be refought. Friends, it is apparent that it must be refought in Madison County."

Frank waited in an effective silence, looking rather pleased with himself, Cutler thought. He saw Johnny Angell watching Frank with that almost naked look of hero worship with which he had once regarded Martin Turnbull. Frank's chest expanded as he drew a deep breath before he continued:

"The men who are used to the ways of *themis* in Madison have contrived to give the form of legality to a murder. The issue is not that Martin Turnbull was the beloved friend and associate of many of us here. The issue is simply murder. Martin Turnbull had purchased, in good faith, a herd of cattle. The herd was promptly, and I believe cynically, claimed by another. A writ of attachment was issued by Judge Arthur. When this was protested, a warrant for Martin Turnbull's arrest was issued, and a posse deputized. There are many witnesses to the claim of the possemen that Martin Turnbull opened fire on them and that they returned fire in self-defense. There are only three witnesses to belie them. There are no explanations for the fact that Martin Turnbull was shot in the back of the head, or that his own revolver was found and had not been fired.

"What, then, are law-abiding men to do in order to advance the cause of *dikē* in this matter?" Frank asked. He folded his arms on his chest, threw back his head, and glared down his nose from face to face. "Yes?" he said.

Cutler turned to see a rancher with graying hair and a gray-stubbled chin stand forward. "It is war, Frank. They have started it."

"I do not believe wars solve anything but the question of who is stronger at a given moment," Frank said.

"The war of revolution that you mentioned did," Lily said in her clear voice.

"Martin was shot down in Jefferson County, not Madison," Dr. Prim said, thumbs hung in his vest pockets.

"Yes," Frank said, nodding. "One course is to see if Sheriff Timmons of Jefferson County will deputize a posse to arrest at least four members of that murderous Madison County posse. The four actual murderers are known."

"Clay Mortenson, Ed Duffy, Cory Helbush, and Bert Fears," Johnny Angell said from where he leaned against the wall with his boots crossed.

"What about Pogie Smith?" another man called out.

"The sheriff wasn't with them. He'd went around the back way with some others."

"I'd say somebody ought to go after Pogie Smith, Neill MacLennon, and Barry Arthur. And Ran Boland."

"I would say that also!" Lily said. "Are women to be listened to here, Frank?"

"Yes, of course, my dear!" Frank said, coloring.

"Then I say that to destroy a rattlesnake you do not merely draw the fang that holds the venom!"

Cutler's arms was pressed again. "She is very forward!" María whispered.

Stretching his wry neck, Joe Peake moved to confront Frank Maginnis at the top of the step. "I believe if we don't just stick to the four that did the shooting we're in a mess, Frank," he said.

"Hard to go against others than them without some true facts," Johnny Angell said.

Frank looked from face to face with the pomposity Cutler found irritating, as though making Olympian judgments. Men muttered and formed small groups, leaning together. There was a clatter of silver and china. Cutler watched Johnny Angell in conversation with Peake and Lily. Lily looked very beautiful in her emotion, with that soft, nakedness to her face that had always obsessed his eyes. Now she held a possessive hand poised over Peake's arm.

"I know that violence will only lead to more violence," Frank said, but he had lost much of his audience, men glancing toward him and back to their own discussions. He spoke more loudly. "I have loved the law all my life. How can I support it by supporting its contravention?"

"We will be doing everything legal, Frank!" Peake said.

"I'm afraid it is the same kind of spurious legality our enemies employed," Frank concluded sadly. A few moments later, with Lily back at his side, he came to speak to Cutler.

"Well, Pat, I am sure you are relieved that none of this is your put-in, as an army officer. Martin and I had simply underestimated their determination and their ruthlessness— their desperation, it may be. He was such a fine young fellow, wise beyond his years and yet an innocent as well."

"Innocence does not last long in this country, it seems," Lily said. Cutler watched her husband's eyes slide toward her. He wondered again how much Frank knew of the visitors to Lily's library.

In halting Spanish, Frank asked María if she was enjoying her life at Fort McLain.

"Very much, Señor Abogado," María said with the dip of a half-curtsy.

"Please tell your wife I think her very beautiful, Pat," Lily said. "And that you are a very lucky man!" She looked directly at him, in her dark eyes questions that were not of him and María, but of him who was her own. Her smile opened, the pink tip of her tongue touching her upper lip. She asked where they had met.

"In Guaymas, at a ball, where she broke an egg of confetti over my head." He translated Lily's compliments to María, who performed the small dip again, but warily. In feminine matters she seemed to him older than nineteen.

Angell came up, hat in hand, and said to María, *"Buenos días, señora."* To Cutler, "Guess we can't ask for any tunes on the piano, today; bad days. Maybe if I could talk to you a minute, Mr. Maginnis." The two of them moved off.

"That one is very noble, I believe," María said. He translated for Lily's sake, grinning to think that María might be very able to impart a little English, even if she couldn't speak it.

"He has taken it very hard," Lily said. "He holds himself responsible. He admired Martin so much."

For his part he admired Lily's stance, contrived for his admiration, the long S-curve of her body with the thickening of the skirt below her waist, the lift of her bosom. "Everyone did—" she had started, when he interrupted to quote Don Fernando: "It is a paltry life that has no tragedy in it."

Lily's face jerked toward him, eyes widening. He bent to translate for María, patting her fingers where they rested on his arm. It was time for them to take their leave.

In the buggy, headed back to the fort, darkness closed in, the mountains receding to invisibility. María said, "I believe the wife of the advocate is not virtuous, Patricio."

"No?"

"She is, what we say, very 'hot' with men. With the tall vaquero, and with you also, that I noticed."

He remained silent to that, until she said, "You have made love with her?"

"Yes."

Out of the corner of his eye he saw her chin tighten and her fingers pull her cloak tighter.

"That was before I met you," he added.

"Then she has made love also with Don Martín, who was murdered?"

"I think so."

"And the tall vaquero also?"

"I don't know."

"But what of her husband, who loves her very much, I think."

"I think he is not interested in women in that way."

"Ah! A *maricón!* The vaqueros—"

"I think he is just not interested."

She puzzled over that. Her hand sought his in the shy way that made him grimace with happiness. She whispered something he did not understand, in bad English.

"Pardon?"

"Dere ees bah-bee!" she whispered.

He embraced her wordlessly, while she sniffed in emotion against his neck. "Ysabel says it will be a boy," she said.

"That will please Don Fernando!"

"You also, Patricio?"

"I also! Very much!" He pressed his wife against him on the seat, grinning up at the cold stars as the buggy rolled back toward Fort McLain. Don Fernando would be informed immediately of the fruitfulness of María's womb, and now Ysabel could attack her knitting to more purpose.

Benny Dee brought Cutler the message that Bunch wanted to see him, so he rode Malcreado out to the reservation at Bosque Alto. Bunch was camped in a Sibley tent on a rise of ground overlooking the wickiups of his scout company, where smoke was rising. The camp of the scouts in training was just over the hill from the main Sierra Verde *rancherías.* The Nahuaque *campos* were several miles to the south, nearer the reservation headquarters. The Bosque Alto reservation had been treatied to the Nahuaques, who had been pacified fifteen years before. Because of their friendly reputation, there seemed to be no move toward relocating them at San Marcos or Fort Apache. The Nahuaques were cousins of the Red Stripe People, and the Sierra Verdes' presence at Bosque Alto had resulted in no friction so far; apparently Caballito and Young Eagle, the Nahuaque chief, ensured this by keeping the two bands well separated except on ration days.

Bunch had recruited fifty scouts from among the Sierra Verdes, and these were being trained within view of the rest of the band, according to General Yeager's plan for compromising Caballito's authority. Fully trained, they would not move to Fort McLain where Cutler's flying squad of Hoyas was quartered, but would remain at Bosque Alto as a kind of sea anchor for the rest of the Red Stripe People. A fat-faced young half-breed served as Bunch's interpreter. Bunch was well pleased with his scouts' progress.

"They are all right!" he said, as though he had not yet got over his surprise, he and Cutler seated on camp stools on the packed earth apron before the Sibley. Bunch had poured dollops of Scotch whiskey into not-very-clean glasses. He waved at a fly. "They'll make good soldiers, as good as my Crows!"

The sun hung over the western mountains, and the full moon was already risen, a pale wafer riding high.

"I'll tell you, though," Bunch continued, "I'd never thought of firing prone off the deck of a pony at a trot, until these birds showed me it could be done. McClellan saddle, too. You can't make them take proper care of a horse, though. I think they were calling me something like 'Nantan Ponyfucker' for a while."

"They had one for me like that. It had to do with a beard with a cigar sticking out of it; Nochte was embarrassed to translate. Then I graduated to Nantan Tata."

They sipped whiskey, watching the sun's descent. "Full moon," Bunch said. "There'll be dancing tonight."

"Who?"

"The Nahuaques. They'll dance all night, drums going to give you fits. You can hear them all the way over here. I've got a spy, my secret scout. She knows what's going on. Says they are raising the dead."

"What dead?"

"Mangas. Cochise. Victorio. The great *nantans*."

Cutler whistled.

"I thought you'd better come take a look before I get the colonel roused up." Bunch waved at another fly. "Agent Dipple doesn't think it's worth bothering ourselves aboot, but those drums going all night get on my nerves."

"Do they come out of the dances belligerent?" The peace-loving Nahuaques!

Bunch shook his head, sitting splay-legged on his stool, booted feet thrust out before him. "Thought you and me'd go up and take a look after it starts up."

"The general ought to know about it."

"Maybe. One of your Hoyas's been coming out—the one I sent with the note."

Benny Dee was married to a Nahuaque woman and had been requesting frequent permissions to visit her on the reservation.

"Listen!" Bunch said. The drums had begun, so quietly it might have been the droning of insects. Bunch poured another round of whiskey. The drumming pulsed more loudly once Cutler had identified it.

"Bird named Nakay-do-something," Bunch said. "Medicine man. Big power. My spy tells me he went to church school in Tucson and got excited about the idea of resurrection. He preaches that the Nahuaques can dance the great *nantans* back to life. Now he is saying it is so difficult because of the white-eye's presence. If the white-eye would all go away they could do it."

Cutler whistled again.

Bunch stood, hitching his belt. "Let's go. It'll be full dark by the time we get there."

They rode part way, tethered the horses, and proceeded on foot, pale moonlight falling on the path striped by the pines. The discordant squeal of Apache violins could be heard along with the drums. As the trail skirted narrow canyons, climbing up along the creek, the drums, the violins, and a kind of galvanizing *shush-shush* came more loudly. Cutler followed Bunch's back at a fast stride in the moonlight. Ahead was the red glow of firelight.

Bunch said in a low voice, "Up here. I don't think there's any danger, but no reason to make them nervous too." He led Cutler off the trail, climbing through the trees to a high, rocky flat. There he seated himself, with Cutler beside him.

Below, in a broad meadow, four fires blazed at what must have been the cardinal points. Between them were the dancers, maybe two hundred of them, Cutler estimated. They were arranged in eight spokes, broad at the perimeter, narrowing toward the center, the spokes wheeling slowly clockwise with the steady scuffing of moccasins, circling two men at the hub. One of these was a singer, chanting in a melodious bass voice, the other the medicine man, who stood with both arms raised. His breechclouted, naked body was painted in blue and vermillion stripes, his head covered by a white sack, also paint-striped and surmounted by a jagged pair of antelope horns. As the dancers shuffled forward, he turned slowly counterclockwise, raising and lowering his arms, sometimes with a different gesture, as though broadcasting seed—*hoddentin,* the sacred pollen. In an arc between two of the fires were the drummers and fiddlers, red gleam of light on brown flesh and glossy, unturbaned hair. The firelight appeared to quiver with the throbbing of the drums, which were rounds of bent branches with hide stretched over them, slapped with flat hands. The scene had a power and urgency to it that, innocent or not, made Cutler nervous also.

"They'll go on like that till moondown, at least," Bunch whispered. "Sometimes all night."

"I've noticed that Benny Dee is crusty the day after he comes back. I don't see any *tiswin* drinking, though."

"Something's got them cranked up. Looks like fun. I wouldn't mind going down and joining in."

They sat on the rough stone watching the dancers slowly wheeling around Nakay-do and the singer. Cutler shivered with the increasing chill in the air. The moving shapes cast long shadows in the firelight. There was no variation in the dance, the dancers shuffling one way, the medicine man turning the other.

Bunch said, "The new thing is that they can't really hope to dance back the great chiefs unless the white-eyes leave. That's what I don't like much."

"The white-eye doesn't plan on leaving, I'm afraid."

"Right. There's some of ours they can dance back, while they're at it. Seen enough?"

They started back down the trail to the horses, the scrape of strings, the shushing of moccasins, the drumming receding behind them.

"How's married life?" Bunch asked as they mounted.

"Better than it was."

"Nothing like a woman for cheering a fellow up."

"Nothing like it."

Bunch's tent was illuminated by a lantern burning inside, so it looked like a lighted Halloween pumpkin.

"Say, would you just give me a couple minutes?" Bunch said. "Looks like my secret scout's here." He dismounted to look in through the open flap, mutter something, then disappear inside. Cutler could see his shadow against the light, two shadows, a woman cheering a fellow up. He paced on the dirt apron. The throb of the drums crawled along his nerves. As usual, the man risked little, but if the woman was a wife she risked a nose-bob, or if an unmarried girl or a widow she risked never finding an Apache husband. A figure came out of the tent and disappeared into the shadows. Bunch called to him.

Inside the tent the captain poured whiskey into the two glasses and held one out to Cutler.

"She keeps me posted what's going on." His big face burned red.

"Verde?"

"Right. And I am damned fond of her, Pat." He combed fingers through his hair defiantly.

"Not of her nose."

"Her husband's in a white-eye prison. She's as good as widowed."

"She'll never get another then."

"You're damned sanctimonious now you're married! As a matter of fact, I intend to take care of her. I mean, she's damned useful to me here! Her name's Tze-go-juni, that's Pretty Mouth. I call her Junie." Bunch plumped himself down on a stool.

Cutler was trying to think what Sierra Verde was in a white-eye prison. "She's Joklinney's wife, then," he said. "Alcatraz?"

Bunch's smile vanished. "That's right."

"Yeager's planning on his coming back. You knew that."

"Shit." Bunch tossed off his whiskey and shrugged big shoulders. "So, what are we going to do about the Nahuaque dancing?"

"Dougal has to hear about it, and I'll send Yeager a report."

Bunch sat slumped, staring down at his empty glass. "Shit," he said again.

In the colonel's office the officers were crowded, standing. Dipple and Bunch had been summoned from Bosque Alto, and the interpreter, Dandy Bill, was also on hand. Colonel Dougal sat at his desk facing them, fingers drumming on the desk top.

"I will say that every time some religious fools try

educating these savages it turns out a mistake," he complained. "I'd better hold parley with this medicine man."

Cutler stood among his fellow officers with his cap in his hand, eying the framed photographs on the wall—the colonel's Civil War commands. On his desk was a photograph of his son, a cadet at the Academy, where he would learn to join in the Silencing of out-of-favor cadets.

Cutler shifted his attention to the interpreter, as Dandy Bill spoke disdainfully. "Nakay-do very bad." He wore the black, threadbare suit of his station, soiled white shirt buttoned tieless at the throat. His arms were folded, his mouth disapproving. Caballito refused to parley through him. Tells lies, he said. It was always a problem in interpreting—not even lies, just accuracy—when the systems of thought, and the importances, were so different.

"Well, it has seemed harmless enough to me," Dipple said, a thin man with receding hair and a walleye, Nantan Malojo. Disliking the army in its arrogance, disliking the Indians and his responsibilities, no doubt disliking himself who had once been a man of principles, he must have been sick to death of the lonely life on the reservation and an easy prey to cultivation by Ran Boland and his cronies. He was often seen drunk. At some times he was an honorable facto-tum and judge to his charges, at others transparently and cynically corrupt. He was not a particularly bad Indian agent.

"These are not *tiswin* drunks," Dipple continued, lean-ing a bony hip against the colonel's desk, in a reminder, Cutler thought, that it was the Bureau and not the army that ran the reservations—until there was real trouble, at least. "There are no regulations against dancing and drumming," Dipple said. "I have gone several times to watch the show. There is no hostility. The Nahuaques have been friendlies for many years, of course."

"Is Caballito involved?" Phil Tupper asked, risen to his toes to peer over Jud Farrier's shoulder.

"I believe I've seen a Striper or two watching," Dipple said. "I don't believe any are participating."

"I haven't seen any," Sam Bunch said.

"Oh, it's innocent enough," Dipple said easily.

"I doubt that!" Major Symonds barked. He stood with boots planted, facing the colonel across the desk. "If they are trying to dance the white-eye out of the country so the great chief can return, next thing they'll take steps to see the white-eye leaves the country!"

"Oh, to leave the country!" Farrier whispered, and there was a ripple of snickers, the Iron Major scowling. Cutler grinned, watching the two field-grade officers glaring at each other. The colonel's hatred of the Iron Major often led him to better decisions than he might have made without Symonds's advocacy to oppose.

"Well, I want to talk to this fellow," Dougal said. "What's his name again, Mr. Dipple?"

"Nakay-do. The Dreamer, they call him."

"Very bad!" Dandy Bill said, refolding his arms.

"I want him in here!"

"I'll volunteer to bring him in, sir!" Pete Olin said, red-headed, freckled, fiesty. His wife had come to call on María, along with Milly Tupper; at least Mrs. Cutler was not being Silenced along with her husband. Cutler explored gratitude, like a tongue after a missing tooth. The necessity only angered him.

"Please allow me to request that he come in for a parley," Dipple said stiffly, his bad eye wavering. "I am certain he will come. Why would he not?"

"Can't tell with these devils," the major said. The colonel set his jaw and leaned over his desk.

"What do you say, Mr. Cutler? You are better acquainted with these people than the rest of us."

"I agree with Mr. Dipple, sir."

"Very well, Mr. Dipple," the colonel said. "I turn this over to you. That will be all, gentlemen."

The scouts clustered in the shady corner of the parade ground, two sitting on the wooden bench there, the others squatting in front of it, Nochte leaning against the fence. Cutler could hear the hooting. They stood when he approached, not exactly at attention, but close enough. He returned their salutes, all grinning together. They were hardly regimental, in their cavalry shirts and high Apache moccasins beneath breechclouts, red cloths tied around their brows. Nochte wore the low-crowned gift hat with its ribbons.

Cutler called aside Nochte and Benny Dee, a skinny, five-foot boy with a thick head of black hair and a seamed, broad-nosed face. He nodded eagerly when asked if he had been at Bosque Alto last night.

"Ask him if he went to the dancing of Nakay-do."

Benny Dee glanced quickly at Nochte on hearing the name, his eyes avoiding Cutler's. Nochte translated the Spanish into Apache, and Benny Dee nodded and folded his arms. "*Sí*," he said.

"Ask him if the Dreamer is a good man."

"*Sí!*" Benny Dee said to the question.

"Ask him if the Dreamer preaches what is good for the white-eye and Indeh together."

Nochte asked, but Benny Dee did not answer, shifting his folded arms higher on his chest and scowling ferociously. "What do you think?" Cutler asked.

"I think it is not good, Nantan Tata."

"Have you heard the Dreamer preach? He has been educated at a Christian school."

Nochte shook his head with a disdainful expression.

"Who else has gone to hear the Dreamer?"

Nochte summoned Lucky, and Cutler dismissed Benny Dee. Lucky trotted toward them, a squat, proud-headed man with a broad chest and comically bowed legs. "Ask him what the Dreamer preaches."

Lucky giggled at the question, but sobered. He and Nochte conferred at length. Nochte said, "He says the Dreamer has very strong power in his dreams. He has learned of the white-eye spirits and how they are summoned after they are dead. He believes the great *nantans* can also return. The dancing at the full moon time brings more power and the dream comes very strongly. Sometimes it also comes to those who dance, which increases its power. It is believed that on one night of dancing the great *nantans* will return to life."

Lucky grinned and nodded as Nochte translated into Spanish.

"Ask him if it is true that the Dreamer says the great *nantans* cannot return so long as the white-eyes are here."

Nochte looked puzzled, questioned Lucky, and replied, "He has not heard the Dreamer say that, but he has heard that it is said."

"Is this a new thing that is said?"

Yes, new.

* * *

The happiness in Quarters 5 lasted through María's announcement of her pregnancy and then abruptly died. "I know that something has gone wrong," Rose Reilly said to him. "I hope I am not presumptuous in considering it my business, Pat. That poor girl—"

He sat with her in her parlor, flowers on the table, lace curtains ghostly in the sun through the window. Bernie was tending sick troopers at the infirmary.

"I can't think what's happened," Cutler said. "Everything seemed to be going well. It's almost like some kind of mental collapse. I know there have been letters from Mexico, but she won't admit there is anything wrong."

"Naturally her condition will affect her sensibilities," Rose said, frowning delicately. "I have not been permitted to experience what she is going through, but it is well known there are changes, in attitude as well as physique. One must perceive that one is not just a girl anymore. Life may look very different—" She halted.

María had, in fact, told him that her beautiful horse Güero had died. He supposed the information could have caused an overwhelming attack of nostalgia for Las Golondrinas and her youth. But he thought letters had come from Pedro Carvajal also. In her new misery María sought solace in prayer. A shrine to the Virgin, with a silver medallion, a red candle, and a spray of flowers, had been established on the mantel of the fireplace.

"She seems to me to be totally miserable," he said. "Much more so than when she first came here."

"Have you tried to get to the bottom of it with her, Pat?" Rose asked, her fadingly pretty face anxious for him and pink with embarrassment. "Have you thought that she might be worried that you do not love her?"

"I do love her," he said, irritated because his eyes would not meet hers. "Yes, I must," he said.

It seemed to him that Ysabel was on the verge, several times, of confiding something to him, but was held back by her loyalty to her mistress. Ysabel had mellowed considerably under the attentions of Corporal Brent. Maids were almost impossible to keep on the frontier posts, where lonely soldiers paid them desperate court. Married to enlisted men, they became camp laundresses and earned more pay than their spouses. Officers' wives recruiting servants from the

East always stipulated homely girls, but they were rarely homely enough to discourage courtship. Ysabel's witchlike profile had softened in the presence of the striker's blue eyes and broad shoulders, and her coquetry amused Cutler on occasions when there was little else to amuse him. But he must, as Rose Reilly had said, confront María herself, and not try to pry secrets from the *criada*.

He and María sat opposite each other at the dining table, María with her eyes lowered and hands clasped before her. Ysabel sat at her knitting just beyond the doorway into the parlor. Corporal Brent swept in with a cauldron of turkey ragout.

"Turnips and carrots compliments of Mrs. Reilly, Lieutenant! Out of her kitchen garden!"

"Thank you, Brent."

The clean white line of the part in María's hair touched him with its vulnerability. She raised her eyes to meet his, hers outlined with some dark substance out of a jar, but darkened also by her unhappiness. In her tragic mode she was beautiful, where the impish girl with the confetti egg had been merely pretty—the pouting, dancing girl spoiled by a doting grandfather. But something was wrong other than the vagaries of her condition.

"Can't you tell me why you are unhappy?" he asked.

She shook her head once. "It is nothing, Patricio."

"Would you like to go home? Would you rather have the baby at Las Golondrinas?"

She shook her head again, more vigorously. Once in his smugness he had been certain he could win her affection, if not her love; briefly he had thought that he had. Was she fearful of the displeasure of her grandfather, who had responded joyously to the telegram notifying him of her condition, if she returned to Las Golondrinas?

"Please tell me what makes you unhappy. For a while you were not. What has changed you?"

But she only made a gesture that might have indicated her belly and poked her fork at the stew Brent had ladled onto her plate.

"All right, I will be pleased if Bernie Reilly delivers the baby," he said. "Then, as soon as you can travel, you and the child will return to Las Golondrinas. I will come in a year, maybe less. Then we will begin again. At Las Golondrinas."

She did not raise her head again. He thought she was more depressed than pleased at this itinerary. She had told him that he had saved her from marrying Colonel Kandinsky, an old man. And that she was bored to extinction by her life at Las Golondrinas. Her grandfather would never let her go with Doña Hortensia to the capital and the grand *bailes* there. Fort McLain was a terrible place, and her husband was ostracized by his fellow officers, but she did have a few friends now, and Ysabel seemed to be flourishing. Somehow Pedrito, reliever of her virginity, must be involved, and the whole Spanish tradition and literature of dangerous loves and lovers.

He managed to laugh at his visions of himself as the grand *hacendado, patrón* of Las Golondrinas, in his silver-embroidered formal vaquero dress, greeting the peons, Juan and Pablo, Caterina and Adela, who revered him as they had Don Fernando, and would his son after him. And his wife who longed only for Mexico City or Paris or San Francisco— or Pedrito.

"One day we will be *patrón* and *patrona* of Las Golondrinas as your grandfather wishes," he said to her. "Will you continue to hate me then?"

She gazed at him mutely, patting her streaming eyes with her napkin. The black substance ran with her tears, giving her a clownish appearance that tugged at his heart the more. "I do not hate you, Patricio," she whispered.

She was shaking her head even as he started to speak. "There is only One who can bring me happiness, Patricio."

He thought from her expression that she was praying to her One now, God or the Virgin, or some other of her Catholic pantheon. He saw that her hand was tucked inside her shawl, telling her beads. Pity overwhelmed his anger. Perhaps it was her physical condition dictating her sensibilities, as Rose Reilly had said.

He poured ruby wine into their glasses and raised his. "To the child!" he said heartily.

"Yes, Patricio," María said, and drank with him.

The *rancherías* of the Sierra Verdes at Bosque Alto were about five miles from the stone buildings of the agency, in pine woods on both sides of a meadow with a creek twisting through it. Boys were calling and running in the woods in some game, and, in front of the wickiups, mothers sat with their daughters, picking in their hair for fleas. Breechclouted bucks watched Cutler as he reined Malcreado down through the trees. Further along the creek women were washing clothing and spreading it on boulders to dry. A cow had been butchered, and strips of red beef were laid over bushes on the sunny side of the wickiups. He saw Caballito waiting for him outside his jacal—blue cavalry shirt, dark, bare legs, and lean, lined face jutted like an ax blade. Other men emerged from the wickiups, and women's faces peered out. A baby on a cradleboard hung on a tree, brown eyes bright as beads in a square, brown face.

He dismounted to shake Caballito's horny hand. There would be a harangue in Spanish over the failure to bring Cump-ten-ae's women and children back from Mexico. He remembered a story of Caballito, whether true or apocryphal he didn't know. When he was a young buck, Caballito's mother and some other women had been captured by Mexicans and borne off to Sonora. Caballito had prayed to the thunder, which had instructed him where to find his mother. With three other braves he had ambushed the Mexican farmer who had purchased the women, and had slaughtered the family and peons. The Apache squaws had been freed and brought back to the Green Range. Now it seemed that Caballito had learned to depend upon the white-eye instead of the voice of the thunder. Cutler thought his friendship with the chief did not extend to making a joke of this.

"All is well?" he asked in Spanish.

The chief shrugged and pushed out his lower lip. Of course it was a *nantan's* duty to maneuver and pressure, to flee or fight, for the benefit of his band. Both of Caballito's breakouts could be understood as the direct result of mistreatment or the threat of it. Perhaps the attendant murders could also be understood, Cutler reflected. Was he beginning to understand these people too well?

Now Caballito shrugged and protruded a lip. "*Mejor que . . .*" he said, contemptuously waving a hand west. Better than San Marcos! But! Of course there was a *but*.

Nantan Malojo wanted the Red Stripe People to slaughter the cattle they had brought from Mexico, and had shouted and waved his arms when Caballito reminded him of the promises given by Cutler, whom they called Nantan Verdad.

"Good," Cutler said.

Still, Nantan Malojo's weights were bad. Not so bad as at San Marcos, Caballito said with his jaw thrust out. But the weights were bad.

"I will look into it."

Caballito continued excitedly in Spanish, mixed with sign language and posturings. The weights were not iron! They were not true weights!

Cutler said again that he would look into the matter, and Caballito's expression became almost amiable. Usually the sparring was continuous, and exhausting.

Caballito said that the Red Stripe People had been scraping the ground and planting corn, beans, and squashes. Nantan Malojo had come to look. The chief pointed to his eye: "Ver' good! Ver' good!" he said in English, and laughed explosively. Would the Red Stripe People remain at Bosque Alto long enough to eat those squashes? the chief demanded.

"Of course."

Caballito smiled gently with his head cocked to one side. He shook it once.

"Tell me about the Dreamer," Cutler said.

Caballito's smile changed to a frown. He hunched his shoulders, his hands illustrating antlers above his head. The Dreamer's power was very strong. He had seen it. The hands drew apart to indicate a full moon. On the night of the great moon the Nahuaque had danced. His shoulders suggested the dancing, and he shuffled his feet. Just before the moon was gone, there had been revealed, at the top of the hill—he paused for dramatic effect, straightening—the three great *nantans!* He mimed a body rising, swaying. Cutler felt the prickle of hairs at the back of his neck.

"Mangas Coloradas! Cochise! Victorio!" They had risen! Cutler slapped his chest, his belly, his legs. But they had sunk back. The moon had gone, and they had gone also. He stood motionless, gazing steadily into Cutler's face.

Did Nantan Tata not believe this had been seen?

"I did not see it, Nantan Caballito," he said in Spanish, indicating his own eye. "It is difficult."

Cutler said with a shrug that perhaps they had only been *pesh-chidin*. Cutler knew the Apache word for ghost. "The Red Stripe People do not dance?" he asked.

Caballito shook his head, grimacing. He held up a hand with two fingers bent into the palm. Only three.

"Young men?"

Old men who remembered the great *nantans*, evidently. Dawa would have danced but was not strong enough. Caballito seemed proud that so few of the Sierra Verdes had danced with the Dreamer.

Cutler managed to inquire if the thunder had spoken to Caballito in this matter, and for a moment he thought he had made a bad mistake, Caballito glaring at him with blazing eyes.

But the chief shrugged and said that the thunder had not spoken to him for many years, maybe it would never speak to him again. He raised his eyes to the sky, squinting, and remained in that posture for an uncomfortable time. Then he said that the Dreamer insisted that the great *nantans* could not return so long as the white-eye remained in the country of the Indeh. With a sly expression he added that perhaps the thunder would not speak for that reason also.

Cutler did not know how to respond. He saw Caballito's stern lips crinkle with amusement, and the chief said in Spanish, "I believe this of the Dreamer will pass, Nantan Tata. Now the Nahuaque are excited. They are restless, they move around, they talk together, they dance—long time! But there is no harm in it. I believe the night of the *pesh-chidin* will not come again."

"The *nantan* of the fort has sent for the Dreamer to come to him for parley, but the Dreamer has many excuses not to come."

Caballito shrugged elaborately.

"The *nantan segundo* of the fort believes that if the Nahuaque are told the great *nantans* cannot return because of the white-eye, there will be trouble."

Caballito pronounced the blue-soldier *nantan* a well-known fool. So were the Nahuaque also fools, and cowards as well. They were famous among the Indeh for being cowards.

"If there is trouble, what will the Red Stripe People do?" Cutler asked.

There was a dense silence before Caballito spoke again. The Red Stripe People were not cowards, but they were not fools either. Caballito had understood at Apache Pass, when he was a young man, that the Indeh were finished. He drew himself up, and his voice rose to its tone of harangue. They would have killed all the white-eyes there, if the wagons had not been thrown at them. By which he meant the mountain guns, Cutler supposed.

But then he had known the Indeh were finished. Dawa knew this also. Also Joklinney, who was in the white-eye prison. The white-eye would kill all the Indeh. And if the Red Stripe People must return to San Marcos, then they would die sooner. Sometimes it was better to go than to stay. Sometimes sooner was better than later. Sometimes it was better to die than to live—better to die like Indeh than live like coyotes. Caballito spread his hands wide, not in illustration of the full moon, but of Ussen's will.

"There has been too much killing, Nantan Caballito."

"Or not enough? *No bastante?*" Again the spread hands. Grinning, the chief said that he had been killing men before Nantan Tata was born.

Cochise and Mangas Coloradas had ambushed the California Column at Apache Pass. They would have killed them all if the mountain guns had not come up. It was not likely that any Sierra Verdes were on hand, but it had not been likely either that Mangas's Warm Springs and Cochise's Chiricahua bands would combine for a fight. Caballito, if he had been a young warrior then, must now be in his forties. It was impossible to guess the age of an Apache. Dawa, gray and senile, must be in his seventies at least.

"I killed a man when I was seventeen," Cutler said, and felt his face redden at what must seem a brag, but Caballito looked at him with interest.

Cutler pointed to his beard. "I have gray hairs and Nantan Caballito has none. These come from worrying about the Red Stripe People remaining at Bosque Alto, where they may live and not die."

Caballito cried out explosively, "I believe you, Nantan Tata! Look, here is a white-eye I believe!"

Cutler did not know what to do but grin at this outburst. Caballito folded his arms and gazed at him down his nose. Nantan Tata must explain to him why Nantan Lobo had forbidden the Indeh to make *tiswin.*

"For good reason."

But Caballito swept on. Nantan Malojo was much drunk, sometimes in the day, more often at night. And blue soldiers drank whiskey and beer, which was the *tiswin* of the white-eye. Hoya scouts came to Bosque Alto and bragged that they had drunk whiskey with the blue soldiers. If Nantan Tata knew he and all his people must die soon, would he not wish to drink *tiswin*?

"Nantan Lobo knows that before the Indeh drink *tiswin* they fast," Cutler said. "Thus the *tiswin* hits like the wagons thrown by the white-eye at Apache Pass. When the Indeh are drunk they fight and kill each other, and sometimes beat the women until they die. It is this that Nantan Lobo wishes to stop."

Did not blue soldiers get drunk and kill each other?

"Not often. Nor do they beat their women until they die, nor cut off the tips of their noses."

Caballito inquired if Nantan Verdad possessed a wife. "Yes."

"If this wife made two backs with another blue soldier, would he not beat her?" This required considerable illustration, Caballito grinning wolfishly.

Cutler said, "Yes! But not cut off the tip of her nose, because then she would no longer be beautiful. One trusts that she is chaste, as the women of the Indeh are known to be chaste among the Indian nations."

"They are chaste because if they are not their noses are cut!" Caballito said, and shouted with laughter. Then he sobered, squinted cunningly, and said that not all were chaste.

Cutler was certain Caballito referred to Bunch's "secret scout," the wife of Joklinney, but immediately the chief smiled to pass it off. From the nearest wickiups the Red Stripe People watched this conversation, some covertly, some obviously. Cump-ten-ae, carrying a rifle, waved a greeting to Cutler. Nantan Verdad, Chief Truth. It was a compliment, or more probably only a flattery by a man clever at the manipulation of his enemies.

When it came time for Cutler to leave, Caballito walked with him to the edge of the woods, Cutler leading Malcreado.

"This very fine horse," Caballito said in English. "You make gift to your amigo."

"No, for he was a gift to me from the grandfather of my wife."

Caballito scowled sullenly. In his tone of harangue he

demanded to know when Nantan Lobo would bring back Cump-ten-ae's people.

"As I've told you, I don't think it is possible. The Mexicans want money for them. Five or six hundred dollars for a pretty woman, half that for children."

"Catch mexicanas, make trade," Caballito said in English. For an instant his face was totally vicious, hard beads of eyes tucked into brown folds of flesh. They walked in silence. When Caballito halted, at the edge of the trees, Cutler drew himself to attention, saluting. He was gratified when the action startled the chief.

"I salute a great *nantan* and a good friend!"

"Yes, we are friends, Nantan Verdad!" Caballito bellowed in Spanish. "But do not forget the bad weights of Nantan Malojo!"

10

Cutler borrowed the true weights from the quartermaster depot and loaded them into a spring wagon for transport to Bosque Alto. It was an overcast day, yellow clouds moiling with ripples of warm and cool beneath, and once a mutter of thunder. Speaking to him in approval? It was ration day at the Agency and he felt some frets of compunction for the occasion he had chosen, but Dipple had been warned.

In the area before the Agency buildings the Indians swarmed, Nahuaques and Sierra Verdes, and in the pens the horns and brown and white heads of cattle pitched, in a smell of dust, blood, and cattle dung. Bucks sat along the fence railings or stood in idle circles chatting, while the squaws squatted and filed in a winding line, or trotted off with their blankets filled with bleeding chunks of beef and their other rations, also cloth-wrapped. Dipple looked down upon the scene from his high railing, while his clerk, the Nahuaque youth, and two more Nahuaques, stripped to the waist and splashed with blood, hefted the chunks of raw meat onto the scales. Elsewhere a crew was slaughtering, and others carried the quarters to the cutters at the scales.

A way was made for the wagon, Dipple straightening to watch Cutler's progress. He drew up at the scales, an old Fairbanks weighbridge with a graduated arm from which hung a poured concrete weight shaped like a gallon jug. Smaller weights were stacked nearby. Cutler jumped down and asked the pimply-faced, sweating clerk what weight was on the arm.

"That's the fifty, Lieutenant."

Blood was thickly puddled on the scale and the ground beside it. The working bucks stood staring, and a wall of brown faces watched, most of them Nahuaque, but many

159

with the striped Sierra Verde cheeks. One of the women had a sliced-flat nose tip, which she covered with her hand under his glance.

He hefted the iron fifty-pounder out of the wagon bed and dropped it onto the bloody platform. The arm tilted sharply.

"Looks like yours is a bit off," he said cheerfully. With adjustments from the round plates from the wagon, he weighed out the concrete jug at about thirty-two pounds, shaking his head and clucking, and watching for Dipple out of the corner of his eye.

Next he checked the twenty-pound weight, which also proved light. The clerk stood squeezing a chin pimple and watching him. The wall of faces watched silently. Further back, Young Eagle had appeared on his white pony to watch. Cutler recognized one of the Sierra Verde squaws, with her carrying cloths, ducking her head under his gaze.

"What the devil do you think you're doing, Cutler?" Dipple yelled at him from twenty feet away.

"Looks like your weights are off the way I said, Mr. Dipple!" he shouted back. "I'll just get the right weights marked on here if your fellow'd get me a brush and paint."

The clerk and Dipple glanced at each other over the black heads, and the clerk jerked his chin at the young Indian, who turned to bully his way through the crowd. He returned with a paint pot and brush. Sweating in the heat beneath the yellow clouds, Cutler tested, weighed, checked, and, almost as a penance, rechecked and reweighed, before he carefully painted the figures on each chunk of concrete. The clerk, the young Indian, and the working bucks, the blood drying on their arms and chests, stood watching him. Not one of the watching Apaches moved, including the young chief on his horse. Dipple had disappeared. Cutler swiped the sweat from his eyes as he continued his work, finally straightening and handing brush and paint pot to the tally clerk. When he had loaded his weights back into the wagon and departed, he was certain that Dipple had preceded him to Fort McLain.

At the quartermaster depot the sergeant said wanly, "I'll take care of these, Lieutenant. You are to report to the colonel as soon as you come in."

He did not hasten, crossing the parade ground, breathing deeply of the heated air. His heels thumped hollowly on the headquarters steps, above which the glossy, varnished sign hung: COL. ABRAHAM DOUGAL, COMMANDING.

The colonel, Adjutant Pizer, the Iron Major, and Dipple were seated in stiff poses in the interior dimness. He saluted. The major's red face illuminated the room. Colonel Dougal leaned forward with his goat beard almost brushing his desk top. Pizer hulked scowling at his desk. Dipple sat with his hat on his lap.

The colonel cleared his throat. "I am interested in hearing your side of the matter, Mr. Cutler."

Better not to ask what matter. "The weights, sir?"

"The weights, mister."

"I was informed by Caballito that the weights were incorrect at the Agency, and the Sierra Verdes were drawing short rations. The Nahuaques also. I took the quartermaster's true weights to the Agency for a test. The Agency scales were off quite a bit. Isn't that correct, Mr. Dipple?"

Dipple said nothing, folding his arms with his hands in his armpits, as though to keep them from doing violence. His good eye was locked on Cutler, his other wandered.

"You have embarrassed Mr. Dipple in front of his Injuns," the colonel continued. "You have made him a laughingstock. You have made his position impossible, he tells me."

"I would have thought Mr. Dipple would be pleased to have an error in the weights cleared up, sir."

"Did you have the quartermaster's permission to take those weights off the post, Cutler?" Major Symonds barked.

"No, sir."

The Iron Major looked significantly at the adjutant, who wrote.

"Mr. Cutler," the colonel said in a reasonable tone, but still crouched over his desk as though about to pounce, "does it occur to you that you may have gone about this incorrectly? It is understandable that in some cases you will make errors of procedure, since you did not have the advantage of a formal military education. But this is simply outrageous. Would it not have been better to notify Agent Dipple of Caballito's complaints? Rather than this bull-in-a-china-shop foofaraw?"

"I told Mr. Dipple he should see to correcting the scales, sir. He pointed out that it was none of my business."

"And so it is not!" the major said.

"It damned well is not!" Dipple shouted. "Damned snooping busybody!"

"Is he to be allowed to curse me, sir?"

"That will do, Mr. Dipple," the colonel said. "And how do you explain that it is your business, Mr. Cutler?"

"Sir, I serve as an aide-de-camp to General Yeager. The general charged me in the strongest terms to make certain that Caballito rests easy at Bosque Alto. I will remind you, sir, that the last time he busted out there were many dead as a result. At least twenty civilians, without counting Mexican nationals. Seven soldiers, including Lieutenant Helms. One of the chief reasons for the Sierra Verde breakout from San Marcos was their claim that they were being cheated on rations. Caballito's complaints are my business by General Yeager's orders, sir!"

"The military has no authority to interfere with the employees of the Bureau of Indian Affairs in their administration of the reservations," the colonel said mildly.

"And you know it, Cutler!" The Iron Major said. His face was glowing again.

"I do know it, sir. I took the only course of action I saw open to me."

"You have an answer for everything, don't you, mister? You are as slippery as Nakay-do with his excuses for not coming here!"

Dipple said sulkily, "Caballito broke out of San Marcos because civilian authorities had obtained warrants for his arrest for murder and stock theft."

"That was the immediate reason. But short rations was the continuing reason for both his breakouts."

"I see you would trust a Pache over a white man," Symonds said with a thrust of his chin.

He felt no need to respond to that.

Leaning forward over his desk again, the colonel said, "I believe you were pleased to embarrass Mr. Dipple, Cutler. As you have often been pleased to embarrass your superior officers. Your record of disobedience to orders, citing some vague superseding orders from the commanding general, is as shocking as the record of your impertinences. I must tell you that I have persuaded Major Symonds not to take action against you in a certain instance, although your own report on the Rock Creek affair is by no means satisfactory. Moreover, you have chosen to disobey a standing order of mine."

"May I ask what order that is, sir?"

"That the officers of this post do not frequent the Maginnis establishment in Madison."

"I would contend that a commanding officer has no right to dictate his officers' companions when they are not on duty."

Pizer hissed wordlessly. Cutler considered Bernie Reilly's warning, that he might force the colonel and the major into an alliance against him. His shoulders ached as though he had been carrying the quartermaster's true weights on them.

Dougal straightened to thrust a finger at him. "It is not a commanding officer's right but his *duty* to dictate on such matters as might be deleterious to his command! Lawyer Maginnis is a notorious troublemaker. He and his wife would like nothing better than to seduce junior officers to their cause, by plying them with fancy foods and liquors and evenings of carousal. You would have been called to account for this had it not been for the peculiar status you count upon so heavily, mister!"

After some heavy breathing the colonel continued. "Mr. Randolph Boland, whom the Maginnises slander and harry, is a force for stability and peace in this county. He had been a military man himself, as has the sheriff, and I am proud to call them old comrades-at-arms and friends! And you should be ashamed, Cutler, to have abandoned those who made you welcome in their midst. You have turned on the hand that nurtured you!"

"You'll be sorry if you meddle in Ran Boland's affairs, Lieutenant," Dipple said.

He did not inquire if the bad weights were Ran Boland's business, but he said to the colonel, "I don't think Mr. Boland's 'miracle herd' has been a force for peace and stability at Bosque Alto, sir."

"What do you mean, Cutler?"

"It's quite well known in the county, sir—the herd that never becomes any smaller despite Mr. Boland's sales of beef to Mr. Dipple. Perhaps it won't seem such a miracle now that Mr. Dipple's scales have been corrected."

"By God—" Dipple started, but stopped, his walleye

wavering. The scratch of Pizer's pencil was audible. The colonel crouched again, chin whiskers to the desk top.

"I see you have been well infected by the Maginnises' slanders. Mr. Maginnis had better guard his tongue. So had you, mister! Officers are forbidden to attend the Maginnis establishment just because of canards like that one that you have seen fit to repeat. Did you take down that statement of Mr. Cutler's, Mr. Pizer?"

"Yes, sir!"

"Mr. Cutler, one of these days General Yeager is not going to be available for you to fall back upon. One of these days, mister! Do you understand me?"

"Yes, sir. I believe you are threatening me. Will that be all, sir?"

The colonel rose to stand leaning his fists on his desk. "That is not all, mister! You will keep your nose out of Mr. Dipple's and Mr. Boland's business! That is an order, sir! You are witnesses, Mr. Dipple, Mr. Pizer, Major Symonds."

Cutler saluted and backed out of the office into the blaze of sunlight. Shading his eyes, he started for the lane of married officers' quarters. His stomach churned sourly, but he could hold it down by his tough will.

If Dipple had reported the foofaraw over the Agency scales to Colonel Dougal, he would also have reported it to Ran Boland. To forestall a summons, Cutler rode into Madison the next day.

He climbed the creaking stairs to the higher darkness of Usury, Malefaction, and Collusion, Inc., rapped on the door there, identified himself, and was invited in; inside there was a smell of cured leather and furniture polish. The curtains were drawn, a single lamp lit. Ran Boland sat at a high, rolltop desk, his tub of a body twisted to watch Cutler enter. His clown face was shaped into a luminous smile. Rimless glasses perched on the end of his nose.

"Come in, Pat; welcome!" He thrust himself up out of the chair with difficulty. In a platform rocker was a stranger to Cutler, a young man with a hard Irish face and a mat of rusty hair parted on one side and heaped up on the other so that his face appeared out of balance. He wore a black suit and black, high-topped shoes.

"Meet my new partner, Mr. Henry Enders, Pat. Just

come out here! Henry, this is my old friend Lieutenant Cutler we were just talking about." He winked at Cutler.

Enders rose to extend his left hand for Cutler's handshake. His right arm was crippled, a pale claw of a fist tucked against his chest.

Cutler shook Boland's fat paw also. Boland beamed at him with his red lips. His shirt was collarless and open at the throat.

"So you're a married man, now, Pat! Congratulations, my boy! A steadying influence, a little woman waiting at home. I imagine there will be a bit less chasing around on your part, eh?" Boland laughed. "Pat chases Injun when he's not chasing the ladies, Henry! Sit down, sit down, please, Pat!"

He perched on the uncomfortable chair to which Boland had assigned him, and Boland rambled on. "You'd never believe it but I chased Injun in my time, Henry. Apache Pass! They almost had us there. But pretty soon old Mangas was killed, and Cochise died. Looked like peace would come, but that's been twenty years now!"

Soldiers of the California Column had tortured Mangas Coloradas with red-hot bayonets until they killed him, and had cut off his outsize head and boiled out the skull to sell to a medicine show. For that murder many white-eyes had been murdered, and for that mutilation many, like Lieutenant Helms, mutilated.

"Twenty years, and now it looks like we've got still another war on our hands, eh, Henry? Band of wild cowboys calling themselves Regulators chasing around the county, not a speck of legality to them."

"Get to the point, Ran," Enders said; he was staring at Cutler with a hostile electricity in his eyes, under thick brows.

Boland laughed again. "Henry keeps me to the course. Henry's had experience bringing things back in line that've got out of hand. My new partner, Pat. I haven't had a partner since dear old Tim Perkins passed on. Now, Pat, what was this run-in you had with Chet Dipple? Henry and I can't make heads nor tails of it."

He found himself crossing his legs uncomfortably as he told the story. He did not know what he owed Ran Boland, except that they had once been friends, and he had enjoyed Ran's easy laughter and extravagant talk and the poker games in the big room next door, to which, at one time, he had been proud to be invited. It seemed to him that in the argument with the colonel and Dipple he had made himself sound committed to Frank Maginnis's cause. He was not committed to any cause in Madison, not to Frank or Lily or the memory of Martin Turnbull. Only to trying to ensure that the Sierra Verdes rested easy at Bosque Alto.

"Getting cheated regularly on their rations, so their wives and children go hungry—that's the main reason bands like Caballito's bust off the reservation." Ran Boland watched him with his eyebrows cranked up to full attention, the other partner slumped and silent. "When they bust out, the army had to go Apache-chasing. Soldiers get killed. I'll do whatever I can to keep Caballito and the Sierra Verdes on the reservation. I don't care who gets embarrassed in the process."

Boland leaned forward with a creak of his chair. "Do you know why a fine gentleman like Abe Dougal don't feel the way you claim to, Pat? Because it's in the fights that officers move up in rank. Just the way you wouldn't mind pinning some captain's bars on those shoulders of your, eh?"

Enders said, "The point is that we are warning you to stop interfering in matters that don't concern you."

"I've just been explaining how it does concern me."

Enders's face turned red in blotches, while Boland rocked, smiling, in his swivel chair. Enders said, "Do you think we're having a joke with you?"

Cutler turned to Boland. "I hope this is a joke. I hope your partner doesn't think he's threatening an officer."

"He's a hot-blooded young fellow, Pat! You will have to forgive him."

"No, I don't think I will."

"You are not aligning yourself with our enemies, are you, Pat?" Boland said with the forgiving smile.

"I came here to tell you I was not. Turnbull's death is not a concern of mine. But the Sierra Verdes' staying put is."

"That was a terrible tragedy, Pat. No one could have wanted such a thing to happen. I'd met Mr. Turnbull; why he would do such a foolish thing I can't imagine! But a touchy situation is not helped by a pack of crazy gunmen riding around the county swearing vengeance. They have used that fine young fellow's death as an excuse for pouring their venom on me!"

Enders cursed, the white fingers of the little hand twitching and rubbing together.

"Is it possible to ask this fellow to leave so you and I can talk, Ran?"

Enders jumped to his feet. His face was blotched again. The crippled hand clung to the lapel of his jacket. "Have your talk!" he said, and slammed out the door.

Smiling with his blood-red lips, Ran Boland said, "He is a hot-blooded young fellow, Pat, but he'll calm down. He's from Missouri, led a life of violence and contention there, but he was able to rise above it and make himself a considerable nest egg too. We ran across each other last year in St. Louis, took to each other right away. I needed help here, and he was looking for opportunity out west. He has a keen mind, brilliant! He takes it strongly that this is a time when we have to know who our allies are. People in town here are choosing whether they will stand by their old friends or go over to new acquaintances. You understand that, Pat."

"There is going to be more violence in this dispute, is there?"

Abruptly the smile was gone. Boland leaned forward with a squeak. "They have incited it, Pat. Now it's getting out of hand like a range fire. *That devil!* Frank Maginnis is a devil. It's his doing!"

"What about this crazy cripple you've taken on for a partner?"

"Pat, I am an old man. I'm sick. I just can't fight them by myself. Henry's just the man I need. He is young and hard the way I was once, before I turned into a barrel of suet. He'll fight for our rights!"

Cutler rose to take his leave. He could remember not even two years ago when Ran Boland had been hard-muscled, hearty, pink-cheeked, and full of genuine good cheer, not this slimy imitation of it. He had been a dedicated hunter, bringing home the carcasses of deer and elk, and the poker room was decorated with racks of horns like a thorn fence. Now he was old, dying, confused and bitter.

When Cutler came down the steps from the second floor, Henry Enders was not in sight. "How's Mr. Ran today?" the clerk asked.

"He doesn't look well."

"He's been poorly for some time and that's a fact," the clerk said. A gunman lounged against the far counter, watching.

As he rode through Madison, along the dusty curve of road with its dappling of sun and shadow, he felt watched, his presence and destination noted. A horseman passed on the opposite side of the street without looking his way. He dismounted before the low, tiled-roof Maginnis house and turned Malcreado into the corral with four other horses and the unhitched buggy.

Fat Berta answered the bell, and led him inside, disappearing as he trod the russet tiles and soft rugs. He circled the room, regarding the gleam of the piano on its dais, the tapestries on the walls, the fat vases with their sprays of artificial flowers. Curtains were drawn over the windows. As always at Lily's, his knees felt treacherous, his groin thick with blood. He tried to laugh at his excitement at the approaching tap of her slippers.

"Pat!" Her voice had exactly the expectant tone that he had imagined, exactly the note of surprise and pleasure. "You've come to see me!"

"I couldn't stay away any longer."

She flew into his arms, which encircled the roundness of her, the slimness, the softness. His hands ranged over her shoulders and back, silky slide of flesh over bone. Her gasp was as precise and expected as her cry of his name had been. She stretched her head back to expose the white round of her throat to his lips. He brought his hands up slowly beneath her breasts, as though raising great weight. Her hot mouth clamped to his and she caught his right hand to her, pressing and gasping against it.

In bed he stroked the milky wonder of her body, pink fingertips of nipples, black tongues of hair in her armpits, the broader swatch between her strong, blue-veined thighs. She lay with her eyes closed, gleam of teeth between her parted lips. From time to time she moved a hand to test the state of his desire for her. Presently he mounted her again. Her breath galloped in his ear.

"You are so strong, Pat," she whispered.

"All I have to do is think of you. At recall watching the flag come down, I'll think of your petticoat coming down. It can be almighty embarrassing."

Murmuring laughter, she caressed the small of his back with her boneless, burning hands.

"Doesn't your pretty wife suffice you?"

"No."

He spent in her like falling down a well. "Oh, my, Pat! Oh, my Pat!"

He rolled from her to think venomously of Martin Turnbull. Don't say anything about it. Don't just say something mean. He said, "I couldn't bear your fucking Martin Turnbull."

She was silent for a time. "He didn't use that ugly word. We made love." She raised herself to gaze down at him, swing of her breast against him. The pale wedge of her face drove downward from the dark swirl of her hair, her eyes searching his.

"It's something men cannot help, isn't it? After they've had their pleasure they must spoil it."

"I'm sorry."

"You mustn't spoil it for me."

"I want it to be the most important thing that ever happened to you. I couldn't stand it that making love with Martin Turnbull could be important too."

"It was very different. He was very tender, surprised, shy—do you want me to say this?"

"Yes!".

"I loved him very much. I will never forget him." Her voice began to shake. "Anything I can do—any way I can make those people—" She stopped.

"Are you making love with Joe Peake?"

She shook her head. A hardness showed around her mouth. "No. I might."

"Because he's tender and shy?"

"To maintain him on his course. He is furious and dedicated right now, but... Men ignite more quickly than women, but they burn more quickly also."

She gazed down at him, her features thickened by her posture. She resembled a wise lioness. He said, "Was that what you were doing with that suffrage minister in Albany?"

"So my past has followed me here," she said softly. "Yes, perhaps I was, although that was a very different cause. And I had thought I had a marriage tie that rose above the petrified customs of the past."

He didn't understand that. "I don't understand a single

thing about you," he said. As Yeager had said of Ruth Anna, she just *was*, like light and air. Was that it, then?

"Do you think I'm beautiful, Pat?"

"Yes. No. Yes, very."

"I am beautiful for this little while of my life. It's the gift I have been given. I must make the most of it, for it's my inheritance. It's what I have instead of the talents a man might have to make his fortune. But I don't choose to make my fortune by it."

"Just to—" he started, and was able to halt himself.

He could keep himself from mentioning Frank, who was never named in these sour conversations. But of course Lily knew what he was thinking. "I advocate equal opportunities and equal responsibilities for my gender, Pat. I am married in a free union. I am not simply a toy; I am myself! I know it is very difficult for men to accept that."

She lay down beside him again, curving her body to his. Jealousies washed over him, sometimes receding into clarities. The anguish that she would not be his alone never receded. He could not imagine her pact with Frank. The wonder that had been Ruth Anna began to fill his mind as he lay with Lily.

She asked about his wife.

"For a while I thought she was happy. When she was first pregnant. Now she's so miserable I don't know what to do but send her home. But she says she doesn't want to go."

"What could have happened?"

"I don't know."

He felt her lips against his shoulder. "Do you love her, Pat?"

It was what Rose Reilly had wanted to know also. He considered the possibility that María languished because he did not love her. He said carefully, "I would do almost anything to make her happy."

Lily was silent for a time, before she changed the subject. "Frank thinks he must go to see the governor. He thinks the war must stop or many will die of it."

"I've heard talk of Regulators."

"Joe and some others have been deputized over in Jefferson County. They've gone in pursuit of the murderers, the actual murderers—the murderers who don't matter." She was silent for a time, then: "There's no law for anyone but Ran Boland's people. So strong men like Joe and Johnny

Angell must call themselves Regulators. Frank thinks that it's wrong. But it's a war now."

Her back was turned toward him now, the sweet long S of her spine, the almost childish curve of her cheek as she gazed at the red curtains.

"Johnny hero-worshipped Martin," she said. "I think he may have more . . . perseverance than Joe. He's such a strange old-young man. He has a kind of glow about him, so that it's hard to keep your eyes from him. Have you noticed that?"

He did not say what it came to his lips to say.

She pressed back against him. "Oh! You still love me!"

"Yes."

In front of Quarters 5 he encountered Corporal Brent sweeping the brick walk. The striker worked straight-backed, elbows high, the broom flying. Cutler had a sense of having been waited for.

The corporal grounded his broom and saluted. "Permission to speak to the lieutenant, sir!"

"Certainly, Brent."

"Sir! Request permission to court Miss Gutiérrez, sir!"

"Who?"

"Miss Gutiérrez, sir!"

"Ah, well, of course, she is Mrs. Cutler's . . . attendant. I'll consult Mrs. Cutler, of course." He cleared his throat. "Are you sure it would be wise to marry a foreigner, Brent? She's a Mexican national, and a Catholic."

"I am very taken with the young lady, sir! And I have reason to believe my affections are returned. Of course I don't speak much Mex and she don't English, but it is surprising how we are able to converse."

"She was brought up very differently than you were, Brent. There are bound to be difficulties."

"Always be those, won't there, sir? We will just have to work harder being married than another couple. I will say, sir, that they are short of laundresses on the post just now. There is good money to be made. If you will not think that is my great concern."

"As I say, I will lay the matter before Mrs. Cutler. I'm sure she will want the best thing for Miss Gutiérrez."

A horn sounded officers' call. Cutler trotted off across the parade ground toward headquarters.

Dougal leaned over his desk, fists doubled up on the desk top. Gold spectacles were nipped onto his nose. Symonds stood spread-legged, arms folded. Jumbo Pizer sat at attention at his desk. Tupper trotted in, followed by Jud Farrier. Others were in the field or on leave.

"Gentlemen," the colonel announced, "I have just had a communication from Captain Bunch at Bosque Alto. He has had information that the Dreamer is now telling his Injuns that the white-eye will be cleared out of the country by the time of the ripening of the corn." He seated himself. "You will recall our last meeting on the subject of Nakay-do. That was almost a month ago! Mr. Dipple conveyed my order that the Dreamer present himself here for parley. But Nakay-do does not present himself."

"Has he refused, sir?" Farrier asked.

"He has had a dozen excuses. He is treating someone who is very ill. There is a ceremony he must attend. Gentlemen, I believe it is time to bring Nakay-do here. If force is required, force will be employed."

"Absolutely right, sir!" the major said.

"Sir!" Cutler said. "I request permission to go to Bosque Alto with my scouts and bring him here."

Glaring at him with a head-lowered, dogged expression, the colonel shook his head. "Denied. Major Symonds will be proceeding to the reservation in force, mister. Major, you will take F and H troops."

"Sir," Tupper said, "if there is reason to believe there may be a fight, what does Captain Bunch say of the Sierra Verdes?"

The colonel merely shrugged.

"Sir," Cutler said, "Caballito told me that the Sierra Verdes did not concern themselves with the Dreamer or the dancing. He also told me he saw no danger in them."

"Yes, yes," Dougal said, waving a hand.

"Request permission to accompany the major, sir," Pizer said.

"Granted, granted."

Bernie Reilly panted in, and the situation was explained. He glanced at Cutler and said, "I have heard that the ghosts of the three great Apache chiefs are counseling the Nahuaques to live at peace with the white-eye."

"The white-eye is not leaving the country in peace by the time the corn is ripe, Sawbones!" Symonds said.

"You will be prepared to set out in the morning at eight o'clock, Major!"

"Yes, sir!"

Cutler gazed at the colonel's white fists pressed to the desk top, and sympathized with his predicament. Dougal could not permit himself to be put off by the medicine man in his fashion, but if the wrong actions were taken, a scrape with the Nahuaques could lead to a breakout. If the Nahuaques broke out, or got into a fight with the blue soldiers, the Sierra Verdes would rest less easy. The star the colonel was probably never going to get was in the balance, and whether Cutler was or was not to telegraph General Yeager at Fort Blodgett was on his own conscience.

"Sir!" he said. "I request permission to accompany the detachment." He thought it better not to add, "as an aide of General Yeager's," for no doubt Dougal understood that anyway. He said instead, "Since there may be danger of Caballito becoming involved."

"Granted," the colonel said.

Early the next morning Major Symonds led two cavalry troops up the Encinal Valley toward the hills of Bosque Alto. The bugler, Dandy Bill, and the adjutant rode with him. Lieutenant Farrier led F Troop, Lieutenant Olin H, the troopers following their officers in columns of fours. Pale dust drifted southeast from their passage. Cutler, on Malcreado, rode to windward of the column. He had taken to confiding in the big horse, who pricked up his ears at his master' voice.

"Look at the Iron Major," he said. "*A la brida*. Headed out to teach the Injun devils a lesson." The major rode like an armature attached to his saddle, stiff-shouldered, belly sucked in, fist curled on his thigh. From time to time he rose in his stirrups, peering behind him to make sure there was no straggling. In a scabbard alongside his leg was his saber. These had not seen service for many years in the Indian Wars, being useful only in the close quarters Indians had more sense than to engage in. An officer drawing his sword in the sights of an Apache's breechloader was only going to wave it once.

The trail led along the bony ridge with jagged outcrops of rock and slashes of yellow sand. Below them grazing land was spotted with cattle that might be Boland's "miracle herd," and beyond was sloping terrain speckled with dwarf mesquite dark against the pale earth. On a higher cornice an Indian on a gray pony watched their approach. He was stripped to the waist and bushy-headed, and Cutler could not make out whether or not he sported cheek stripes. After minutes he swung away and disappeared over the ridge.

The column strung out into single file where the trail narrowed between the pines of higher elevations, sun and

174

shade dappling across the troopers. From the third ridge they could look down on the big Nahuaque *rancheria*, wickiups patched with cloth, tarps, and faded tent-sections. Cutler saw the women and children scurrying upward on the far side of the rocky bowl. Bucks, mounted and on foot, followed more slowly, halting when the main body of troops came into view. All the Apaches were armed with rifles.

Bunch, in a broad-brimmed and unregimental hat, urged his bay up the shale slope toward the major. His mustached face was red with sunburn and exertion.

Symonds stood in his stirrups to call out to him. "Have you received a message from the colonel that you are to hold your scouts out of this, Captain?"

"I have, sir. Sir, I think you ought to parley with Young Eagle and Nakay-do before you go in there."

"I have my orders, Captain! We are to bring out the medicine man."

"Those fellows are stripping for trouble," Jumbo Pizer said, pointing. His horse had taken on his nervousness, wheeling while he jerked on the reins.

Symonds signaled the column forward, and they started down into the bowl, horses sliding in the shale. Bunch rolled his eyes at Cutler. They proceeded toward the *rancheria*, and wound among the first wickiups. All these were empty. Cutler felt a shoulder-aching tension, aware of the half circle of bare-torsoed bucks among the rocks above them.

"What about the Sierra Verdes if it comes to a scrape here?" he asked, falling back beside Bunch.

"I think they'll hold steady. Your trick with the scales pulled some weight. What's the colonel holding the scouts out for? Yours too?"

"He doesn't trust them, as you know."

"My spy says one of your fellows is hanging out with the Nahuaque, as a matter of fact."

"Benny Dee. He's AWOL. I'll have his breechclout."

"Feels damned scaly," Bunch said, squinting up at the Nahuaque bucks. "Everybody spoiling for a fight."

In front of a larger wickiup, a man dressed in an eagle-feather helmet and painted buckskin shirt sat on a bench chewing on a turkey leg. It was the Dreamer, in the ceremonial shirt he had worn the night Cutler had observed the dancing with Bunch. Nakay-do rose as the major and Dandy

Bill approached him. Holding the turkey leg in his right
hand, the Dreamer bowed and smiled. He was pale-
complexioned, with a thin mustache sprigging at the corners
of his lips. The smile was amiable.

"Welcome, Nantan," he said in English. "Welcome, blue
soldiers."

"We come for you!" the Iron Major bellowed. On the
high side of the bowl the Nahuaque braves stood with their
rifles ported. There was continual movement of brown bodies
among the rocks, although the women and children had
vanished into the trees higher up. Cutler was aware of his
own hand on the butt of his Colt.

"Why do you not come when the *nantan* of the fort
sends for you?" Symonds said. Cutler shook his head. Since
the major had not heeded Bunch's advice, he should simply
have loaded the Dreamer aboard a horse and pulled out.

Nakay-do chattered with Dandy Bill in Apache, then
spoke again in his Catholic school English. "I have sent to
inform the *nantan* of the fort that I cure some peoples here,
but cannot succeed if I leave just now. Soon I will come."

"The *nantan* of the fort orders that you come right now!"

"We're in a rat trap, Pat!" Bunch whispered.

"I know it." He glimpsed Benny Dee among the bucks
above them, holding his rifle at a slant across his body. His
eyes, gazing back down at Cutler, looked bigger than the rest
of his face.

The Dreamer waved his turkey leg. "If the *nantan* will
wait, I will finish my food."

"Very well!" the major said. Wrong, Cutler thought.

"*Shit!*" Bunch whispered.

"Tompkins!" Jumbo Pizer called in a shrill voice, and the
trooper with the led horse for the Dreamer spurred forward.
Nakay-do reseated himself and continued gnawing on the
turkey bone in his fist. The troops waited. The major's cheeks
burned like a lantern. Cutler glanced around at the troopers'
tan, set faces, eye whites showing whenever one glanced up
at the Nahuaques. Several of these were drifting back down
the hill.

The descending bucks halted about thirty feet from the
Dreamer and called out to him. He responded.

"What's he say, damn it?" the major demanded.

"He tell them not worry about him," Dandy Bill said.

"He say soldiers will only take him away for little while, for he has done no wrong thing. He say to wait for him return."

Some of the younger braves had edged close to the troopers. "Tell them to get away!" Symonds said, cursing as his horse jerked against the bit.

"*Ugashe!*" Dandy Bill called out. The braves sidled but did not really retreat, hard faces turned toward the major. The Dreamer slowly chewed his meat. Cutler saw the violence congeal in that slow helplessness of catastrophe observed in a dream. The major drew his revolver, cursing as his horse still pitched and jerked against the bit. Several troopers near him cocked their carbines. Symonds fired into the air.

Immediately there was fire from the canyon wall and the two troopers who had cocked their pieces were slammed out of their saddles. Others fired back, horses wheeling. Another trooper fell, yelling for help. Bunch spurred, dismounted, and helped the wounded man up behind his saddle. Cutler saw Benny Dee, rifle raised, aiming. Malcreado was caught among the other milling horses as he drew his Colt. He saw Pizer spur up to where the Dreamer had risen and empty his revolver point-blank. Instantly the adjutant was flung to the ground, his chest a bloody mush. Firing back, the command followed the officers retreating up the hillside. There was a steady yelling, hoarser from the troopers, shriller from the Apaches. The firing ceased when the troops had passed out of effective range. Cutler saw four, five, six empty saddles.

Two-thirds of the way up the shale slope, the troops were dismounted to take up firing positions behind the horses, their carbines with longer range than the Nahuaque rifles. Two of the ammunition mules had been captured. Higher on the ridge, brown bodies could be seen filtering among the trees, cutting off further retreat.

After ten minutes a wounded trooper limped panting in, promptly sinking to his knees and loudly thanking his Maker. The officers circulated, determining that two troopers and the adjutant had been killed at the first volley. Another trooper was still missing, and four were wounded seriously. Below them the Nahuaques could be seen swarming around the wickiups. There were occasional shots from higher up, and the major stationed sharpshooters. It was very hot on the flat, exposed to the afternoon sun. Cutler was appalled at the stupidity of this tragedy.

Bunch sank to the ground beside where Cutler sat cross-legged, holding Malcreado's reins. "What an absolute balls-up!" Bunch said. "Why didn't the colonel just send you and your Hoyas to bring him in? They must've thought the blue soldiers'd come to wipe them out!"

"This way Dougal can prove the Iron Major's a fool, and not give the general's pet scouts any credits."

"Christ! And perishing hot on top of everything else. Did you see your AWOL Hoya?"

"I saw him."

"*That's* bad too," Bunch said.

Sweating troopers were digging in, rolling rocks and stacking shale to fort up. The officers assembled around the major. Farrier had a bloody scrape on his cheek. Nearby a corporal tended a soldier with a bandaged arm and leg.

"Sirs!" the wounded man called out. "You wouldn't leave a good soldier behind to be cut up by them devils, would you, sirs?" He stretched his good arm out pathetically.

"Here, stop that!" the corporal said.

"We won't leave you behind, Matthews!" Olin said, striding up. He wore his binoculars on a lanyard around his neck.

"These are the possibilities," the major said. He had lost his cap and tied his bandana around his head, as Cutler remembered him at Rock Creek. "We can fort up here and send for reinforcements. Or fight our way out. Or attack and punish these treacherous savages. And that is what I think we should do."

"H Troop is ready, sir!" Olin said. Farrier, who had been harder hit, did not second the motion.

"Why, it's Custer Junior!" Bunch said with a laugh, and ignored Petey Olin's glare. "Major, if we go back down there, it is a chance we are biting off too much to chew and maybe bringing the Sierra Verdes into it too. If we fight our way out, they can brag they scared the blue soldiers away. I say send for reinforcements."

The major paced in the restricted space, squinting up at the hilltop and down at the *rancheria*. There was sporadic firing from above, none from below. The horses were corralled in a grove above and behind their position. Troopers lay or sat behind their breastworks. Cutler was aware of their glances toward the officers' parley. They were outnumbered better than two to one by the Nahuaques, and the odds would rise dramatically if Caballito decided to come to the aid of Young Eagle. He did not think the Sierra Verdes would do that, but he considered it a real possibility that Caballito would pull out and head for Mexico again.

"I'll volunteer to ride for help, sir," he said to Symonds. "I have the fastest horse."

Symonds squinted as though it hurt to look at Cutler directly. Three dead soldiers, maybe more, due to his blundering, and his concern was still the invocation of the Silence.

"What'll you do, head out at sundown?" Bunch said, as though it was settled.

"Better just before sunup, I think."

Apaches would never attack at night but might do so at dawn, unless Young Eagle had had second thoughts and wise counsel by then. The Nahuaques must be in an absolute fury over the murder of the Dreamer, but forted up as it was, the major's detachment could hold them off until help arrived.

"Very good, Cutler," Symonds said, and set Olin and Phil Tupper to figuring the range of all the landscape features in case of a dawn attack. Jud Farrier suddenly got to his feet and stamped over to where Cutler sat with Bunch, their backs against the stacked-up shale. Farrier glared down his nose from under his cap brim.

"Just wanted you to know I didn't want anything to do with their shitting Silence, Cutler," he said. "It was the major and that fat-ass State-of-Mainer, Pizer, that called for it. They got us into this mess too!"

"Thanks," Cutler said, maybe more sullenly than he had intended. Farrier stamped off, ducking as lead whined overhead.

"Gracious Pat Cutlery," Bunch said. "Symonds came to me too, you know. I guess he had to do something after the colonel told him he'd make a damned fool and worse out of himself if he went after you in an inquiry or court-martial."

"I thought he'd probably come to you."

"You're welcome," Bunch said, laughing.

Cutler kept Malcreado close by him that night, saddled and bridled. It was well he did so, for the Nahuaques struck the corral just before dawn, driving off seventeen horses. In the ensuing fuss he started out, leading Malcreado up the slope and over the first ridge.

The valley stretched out before him, still smoky with darkness, when the sun came up, sudden warmth on his back. He descended the hillside, squinting back to see dust rising against the yellow glare and gritting his teeth in disgust at the whacking of his heart. He halted and dismounted to tighten Malcreado's girth, the beautiful horse turning his head to nuzzle Cutler's chest. He slipped the carbine from its scabbard, braced it on the saddle, and, shielding his eyes, followed one of the fast-moving shapes with the front sight blade. The stock jarred against his shoulder as he pulled the trigger. They drew up for one static moment, six of them, then disappeared. He remounted and started on at a faster clip.

He saw another trace of dust to the north, where other Nahuaques must be riding to cut his route to the fort. The horses they had captured were being put to good use. He urged Malcreado into a long lope, heading southwest, heat of the sun on his left cheek now. The big horse bore him through the strips of ochre sand, through the clumps of mesquite, veering from a long promontory of rock resting in the desert like a gray lizard. Experience and intuition warned Cutler away from it.

Maddened bumblebees snapped overhead, one, then two, then two more. Glancing back he saw the first six riders again. "*Vamos, Malcreado!*" he whispered. The flowing stride increased, and he laughed, looking back to see the Nahuaques as though standing still in his wake. Soon he was out of range, and he slowed Malcreado to a steady pace while he searched the northern hills for signs of the other bunch whose dust he had glimpsed. The six still continued their pursuit, although fallen far behind. Which meant—

"*Vamos!*" he whispered, swinging further south at a dead run.

There were four in the second bunch, streaming out of the depression of a lateral canyon, brown antic shapes on their mounts, black hair streaming, rifles flourished, faint yipping cries. Malcreado flowed on south to turn the corner on them. More bumblebees zipped past, shots from horse-back not worth worrying about. Around and past, he halted on a height of land, to rest Malcreado and drop some shots among his pursuers. The second bunch was a thousand yards back, scattering under his fire, disappearing. They were uncanny at discovering defilade in which to shelter.

He pushed on, gradually increasing Malcreado's pace. They were intent upon his track because he was heading for the fort for aid, and, just as likely, because they coveted Malcreado. Some kind of corollary there: that the very thing that made escape possible ensured pursuit.

They continued to follow him, although far behind. Now the first group had shortcut closer, and the next time he had a clear view of them, he halted to fire again, while Malcreado panted. He did not waste cartridges when they scattered. He poured water from his canteen into his hat for the horse to lap. The sun was high and murderous.

Still they had managed to keep between him and a direct route to Fort McLain. He mounted again and patted Malcreado's dripping shoulder. "Vamos, mi lindo!" Onward again, south and west, the sun burning down, wet hat cooling his head. Heat waves shimmered above rocky ridges. He led the two bands as though pulling them along by strings, the first group the closer now, the second only occasionally visible against the hills. Malcreado covered the ground at his swinging lope. Cutler knew his disadvantage was that he did not intend to kill his horse in this run, their advantage that they did not care whether they killed theirs or not. Twice more he halted to fire, some gunsmoke showing in response. He let the horse move on at a walk.

But soon he began to feel the unease again. He picked up the pace, then nudged the horse to a dead run when he saw a defile that by great exertion they might have reached. As Malcreado raced past it, three of them burst from it as though out of the ground, yelling and firing. He ducked close the laboring neck, whispering, "Más rápido, por favor, mi lindo!" This time a few bees whined closer, but now he had turned the corner at last, heading north along the river.

It was the Nahuaques' last gasp. As soon as he had crossed the river, hooves kicking up little white tents in the shallow water, he knew he was shed of them. He halted to let Malcreado drink, dismounting to splash water into his own mouth. Then he leaned on the saddle with his carbine braced, watching for them. But it had been the end.

At a trot he cut up Byow Hill to avoid one last place they might be waiting for him. From the hill he could see the fort, tan sweep of the parade ground, the cottonwoods along Officers' Row, the heart-lifting bit of color at the top of the flagpole.

"Let's go!" he whispered to the big horse that had saved his life.

When Colonel Dougal and Captain Smithers, with A, B, C, and E Troops, rode out of Fort McLain to the relief of the major at Bosque Alto, Cutler was in a stall in the officers' stables, rubbing down Malcreado. The big horse stood with four hooves planted, flexing his neck as Cutler scrubbed him with soft straw. Then he washed the horse with soapy water, and again rubbed him dry with straw. From time to time Malcreado made a deep rumbling of pleasure, like a cat purring.

The sun was low when he finally made for Quarters 5. Strangely, he was again feeling uneasy, and his steps quickened into Officers' Row. Lamplight showed in some of the quarters, but none in 5. The door clapped open emptily and his footsteps seemed to echo. In the parlor he lit a lamp. Probably María was with Rose Reilly or Milly Tupper, but where was Ysabel? He swung around at a knock. Corporal Brent was at the door.

"Where's Mrs. Cutler, Brent?"

Brent's face was puckered into a grimace. He gestured meaninglessly. "Gone, sir! Both Mrs. Cutler and Miss Gutiérrez. A gentleman came to fetch them back to Mexico, a relative, as I understood it, sir."

That was it, then; that was what it had been all along. "A young man, soft-looking, almost pretty?"

"That would be him, sir."

"I suppose if I had given you permission to pursue your courtship of Miss Gutiérrez you could have persuaded her not to accompany her mistress. I'm sorry."

The striker said nothing, turning his cap in his hands.

"How long ago did they leave?"

"This morning, sir."

It seemed that the departure might have been timed to coincide with the expedition to Bosque Alto. The closest route south was along the river. He must have passed close to them on his flight from the Nahuaques.

His heart swelled in his throat like a hand choking him.

Cutler again set out before dawn, this time with Corporal Brent and the scouts: Nochte, Tazzi, Kills-a-Bear, Lucky, Skinny, Jim-jim, and Chockaway; Benny Dee AWOL. By first light Chockaway and Skinny found tracks along the river.

When he rode up on Brownie, both trackers had dismounted to squat, rolling cigarettes and lighting them. Chockaway, who spoke some Spanish, raised his hard, dark face to him. He jabbed a finger at horse droppings.

"*Caballo Mexicano*, Nantan Tata." He raise his hand with the fingers stretched apart. "Five—two man horse, three woman horse." He pointed to hoof prints and the dried runnels of urine. Mares ejected behind the rear hoofs, horses before. Mounted on two horses and three mares were María, Ysabel, Pedro Carvajal and two others, probably peons.

The Hoyas watched Cutler out of the corners of their eyes, embarrassed for him, whose wife had been stolen. Corporal Brent sat very erect in his saddle, gazing toward Mexico with round blue eyes in his brown face. The striker was thinking of the same thing he was, which they did not discuss: not of Pedro Carvajal, but of renegade Apaches.

He clucked Brownie into motion again. Following the tracks of the Mexican horses was easy enough, and they continued south when the river swung east—flat country with distant peaks floating on the horizon, ahead only distance extending into Mexico. Skinny suddenly raised his rifle in both hands, muzzle pointing. Cutler stood in his stirrups to peer east. A string of riders had appeared out of space, strung out in single file in exactly their own formation, but more of them. Seventeen, eighteen, nineteen—not Apache but white-eye, from their big hats, glint of the sun on rifle steel. An armed band.

Cutler, Brent, and the scouts rode in parallel formation for some time before Cutler, with Nochte beside him, angled off to intersect these others. Two of them immediately rode out for a meeting. He recognized them from a hundred yards away and realized what this band was—the Regulators, the posse pursuing the murderers of Martin Turnbull. Joe Peake in his sugarloaf hat rode on a big black. With him Johnny Angell was a slighter figure on a paint horse.

Peake waved in greeting. "Howdy, Lieutenant! What's those with you? Scouts? Thought they might be broncos."

"We're looking for five people headed for Mexico."

The man Lily might decide to make love to shook his head. He swept off his hat and combed fingers through his thinning, matted hair. Johnny Angell came up, high-colored fair complexion beneath a layer of dust, twist of hair protruding from beneath his hat brim.

"There's been a bustout from Bosque Alto," Cutler said. "There may be hostiles around."

"We'll chew 'em up and spit out the seeds," Peake said. "Any luck of your own?"

"Two out of four." The tall cowboy indicated with satisfaction the chain of riders headed south. They were headed into Jeff City with their captives.

"Come along easy as picking berries from a vine," Angell said. "Sitting in the cantina in Three Rivers drinking sarsaparillas."

"Two to go," Peake said.

"Who busted out?" Angel asked. "Verdes?"

"Nahuaques." He told them about it.

"See you in Madison!" Angell called back to him, as the two of them took their leave. His revolvers were girded high around his waist.

Cutler guided Brownie at a slant back to his own column. They continued in parallel with the posse for a time, before the others diminished to the south, disappearing into heat waves. Ahead the cactus plain stretched out over the shoulder of the world, while mountains marched closer from the west.

He became aware of an increased tension among the trackers, Chockaway and Skinny leaning out of their saddles to examine the ground, Nochte and Kills-a-Bear joining them. Nochte drifted back toward Cutler, his fine-featured dark face knotted in a frown.

"Nahuaque, Nantan Tata."

He had already anticipated it, his heart swelling to choke him again. There seemed to be a pattern. On the beautiful horse, a gift from Don Fernando of Las Golondrinas, he had escaped the Nahuaques. They had pursued him the more relentlessly in hopes of taking Malcreado, while he was forced to lead them south and west. Now their tracks had joined those of Pedro Carvajal's little party, which included the granddaughter of Don Fernando, pregnant with the heir to Las Golondrinas.

"Cuánto?" he asked.

"Quatro." Four of them.

"Cuándo?"

Kills-a-Bear, who had come up, pointed straight overhead to the noon sun, then back toward the horizon. Corporal Brent also rode in close. "What do they say, sir?"

"Four Nahuaques. Maybe six hours ago."

He spurred Brownie into the lead with Nochte, the other scouts watching him out of slanted eyes, their faces pointed away. The trail now was easy to follow, for the Nahuaques were not fleeing but pursuing, a broad path of hoofprints puckering the sand. He urged the trackers to a faster pace, Chockaway and Skinny coming up with him and Nochte, Corporal Brent bringing up the rear with Jim-jim. There was a general stripping-off of shirts, that signal of anticipated action. He gestured to them to ride spread out, in case they were heading for an ambush. He laid a hand to his chest to feel the heavy beating of his heart. Skinny exclaimed in Apache, pointing.

Pedro Carvajal had made his stand on a rocky outcrop. The sun gleamed on the white bodies streaked with the black stains of dried blood. The first Cutler came upon was Ysabel. She was headless, but seemed enormous. Her arms and legs had been severed and reassembled, each limb a foot away from its stump, lined up with care. Her severed head had been set upright gazing outward from her crotch. He stared down at her from his saddle, panting shallowly. He found he had taken off his cap and held it in his hand. He was aware of the sound of Corporal Brent retching.

He said to Tazzi, "Why did they do this?"

"*Porque bruja*, Nantan Tata."

He didn't take the meaning right away. Because they had thought her a witch. He himself had thought she looked like a witch. One of the peons lay nearby, arms curled over his belly, terrible wound in his exposed temple, swatch of his scalp severed and laid on the ground beside his head. The Apaches had never been scalpers like the Plains Indians, although their own scalps were purchased by the Mexicans. Sometimes they made the gesture, as though not quite certain what they were supposed to be doing. Mutilation was enthusiastically engaged in, however. Another body was spread-eagled, on its back, toes, genitals, nose, and chin cut off and heaped in a blackened mess on the chest. Soon they must come upon María.

The third man had been savagely tortured, tongueless mouth opened in a graphic O, eyeball-less sockets staring upward at the sun. This was Pedrito Carvajal. Brownie shied from the cadaver and Cutler rode in an increasing circle, looking for the fifth corpse.

Corporal Brent's horse was riderless, the striker on his knees turned away from Ysabel's terrible cadaver. The scouts were bunched together, carbines in hand, looking from one to the other of the white-eyes. Cutler ordered them to make wider swings. The thought had come to him that the Nahuaque had taken María with them. Relief made him sweat so that salt liquid ran into his eyes. Brent had struggled to his feet to cling to his saddle.

"Corporal, you'd better head back to bring a detail to pick up these bodies."

"Sir!" Brent said, facing him with a gesture like an aborted salute. "Sir, if you are going after those..." He hung fire on the word.

"As far as the border, if they are headed that way."

"Sir, you will need all of us if you catch up with them! Even if it's only four of them." He halted again, panting; his face was dead white.

"All right, come along." He sent Nochte back to the fort with a note. The scouts had not found María.

They started on again, Chockaway and Kills-a-Bear in the lead now, brown backs bent along their mounts' necks as they followed sign. Once Skinny slid to the ground, plucking up something. Remounted, he waited for Cutler to come up, and passed him a bit of blue cloth. Cutler touched it to his nose. He knew the dress this had been torn from, he knew the scent also.

Mid-afternoon they came upon a dead Mexican shepherd, shot and mutilated, but without the fine attention that had been paid the bodies on the rock outcrop. Now the

Nahuaques would be moving more slowly, herding the flock of sheep, which, however, concealed their tracks. A flock like this was moved swiftly by lashing the rams' horns together to form a living wall enclosing the other animals. Sharp hooves had diced the ground, and the trackers cut back and forth searching for horse dung. Corporal Brent again brought up the rear, cocooned in his misery, his uniform blouse soaked dark with sweat. Foothills humped up before them, the Boot Range.

The scouts halted to confer. He was summoned. Squatting, turning his good eye up to Cutler and down again, Kills-a-Bear scratched the ground with the point of his knife. He had copied the profile of the Boots, where they loomed above the hills ahead. He pointed. "Nahuaque!" He scratched a roundabout line to one of the higher peaks, then indicated, with jerks of his finger, Cutler, Corporal Brent, the scouts, himself. He stood up and, miming a carbine, aimed down at Jim-jim's moccasin toes. "Bom-bom-bom-bom!"

Other giggled. Corporal Brent said in a shrill voice, "He means he knows where they're going?"

Cutler said in Spanish to Tazzi, "There is a place where they will make camp?"

Tazzi nodded vigorously. He pointed to Kills-a-Bear's map, nodding.

Cutler glanced up at the sun quartering down the sky. He said to Brent, "We'll get above them tonight."

Kills-a-Bear aimed down his carbine. "Bom-bom-bom-bom!"

All the Hoyas laughed, Lucky bouncing and slapping his thighs in excitement, Skinny also simulating a carbine shooting. They started on, no longer following the sheep track, but hurrying straight toward the peak Kills-a-Bear had indicated. Cutler was relieved that they kicked up no dust in the thick sand, nor could he see any dust from the herd ahead.

At dusk they drank from a rill of water in one of the finger canyons that ran up toward the peak. They wet hardtack and munched the tough starch. Often the scouts conferred, with glances toward him and Brent. He understood that they thought they should take over this operation, knowing better than he how to ambush Nahuaques, attack Nahuaques, free the prisoner of the Nahuaques. No doubt they would handle it better without him and the striker, and he felt a queer rush of emotion to think they were debating

whether or how to tell him just that. But evidently it was
decided not to embarrass him further by asking him to
remain behind with Corporal Brent.

In the darkness they ascended Kills-a-Bear's peak, solid
dark against the lighter dark of the sky, the horses left on a
picket line among the cottonwoods at the bottom of the
canyon. In the stars' faint illumination he could make out the
shapes of the Hoyas climbing ahead of him on all fours,
carbines strung across bare backs, a small scraping and scuf-
fling. Once Brent knocked a stone loose that rolled noisily,
everyone freezing against the slope, Brent whispering, "Sorry,
sir!"

They kept on, Cutler taking hold of a growth of stiff
brush, testing it, boosting himself up, panting. They ascended
for what seemed hours, once descending steeply before they
climbed again. A thin moon rose above the craggy shape of
the peak above them.

It had turned cold and he shivered continually. A hand
touched his; he was aware of a chain of hands coming back
from Tazzi, in the lead, crouched to peer over a ridgeline. He
reached back to halt the corporal. Moving carefully, they
came up alongside Tazzi. Cutler saw the white glint of his
grin, the mass of his extended arm.

A fire had burned down to red-glowing coals on a shelf
opposite and perhaps two hundred feet below them. The
queer, light-gray mass that caught glints from the fire must be
the flock of sheep. Another dark mass further along the
canyon would be the horse herd. He could smell, faintly, the
rich aroma of broiled meat, and was suddenly famished. He
could see no movement around the fire. He had no idea what
time of night it was, but below him were the four Nahuaques,
probably the same four who had chased him, the murderers
of his wife's lover, two peons, and her personal attendant.
María's captors. He reminded himself that Apaches were
never rapists. If she was their captive they probably would
not harm her.

On one side of him was the line of scouts' heads, to his
right the slant of Brent's forage cap. He backed off to the
reverse side of the slope to consult with Kills-a-Bear and
Tazzi. The Hoyas would work their way further down the
slope, closer. It would be best if he and Brent remained here.

No one was to fire until Cutler fired first, and care was to be taken for the *nantan's* wife.

"Bom-bom-bom-bom!" Tazzi whispered, giggling. Then they were gone, the other scouts slipping down the bank after them. Cutler worked back up to the ridge beside the striker, and whispered instructions; the two of them were to remain right there until first light.

He heard no sound as the Hoyas positioned themselves lower down. He marked the slow progress of the moon, sighting it against a stub of juniper. The embers of the fire cast less light, and the pale mass of the flock faded into shadow. Now in this waiting his mind poked at the terrible scene they had passed, María watching as her beloved cousin was destroyed, listening to his screams. The moon hovered close to the juniper snag, and slid from sight. He was not aware for a time that the world had lightened, but all at once, shapes were visible—Corporal Brent's stone profile beside him. A buck was seated on a rock above the broad shelf, head bowed, rifle held upright. Two others were bundled in their blankets by the fire, no sign of the fourth, or of María.

Brown backs were crouched among the rocks below him, Lucky's bushy head, Jim-jim's face turned briefly up toward him. Now he could make out the wickiup of woven branches further back in the shadow of the cliff. María would be in there. Waiting had become a kind of physical pain, arms, legs and back aching, grate of a pebble beneath his knee that he did not remove because of some need of that small gripe. The figures below came up slowly out of the shadows, the two beside the fire sitting up, the guard stretching. Now he saw the fourth man, in fetal position in his blanket before the wickiup. Kills-a-Bear's face turned questioningly up to him.

He had estimated the range to the sentinel at fifty yards. He fixed his sights on the man, dark arm protruding from his blanket to support himself, tangle of hair. His finger gently stroked the trigger. The sentinel disappeared, and a volley of shots echoed between the peaks, stink of powder in his nostrils as he strained to see through smoke the activity below, two of the Nahuaques leaping free of their blankets. A second volley knocked down one of them.

Brent was half leaping, half falling down the slope. Cutler slid down the talus after the corporal and the scouts.

He heard the thin wailing of the death song beginning, and snuffed out.

He ran to the wickiup and stooped to peer inside. María screamed as he reached in for her, and jerked away from him. Outside the Hoyas whooped and yipped. He pulled María, still screaming, out of the wickiup. The Hoyas capered around the shelf, brandishing their carbines. He held his arm around his wife. He tried to stop her mouth with his hand but she twisted her face away.

He couldn't make out what Brent was doing, dodging through the flock of sheep, the wooly mass shifting one way and another with his progress. It seemed to him that the corporal had gone mad, feinting with his carbine one way, then leaping in another, straddling a sheep's back. Chockaway pointed at him, shouting with laughter.

When he let María go, she flew back inside the wickiup again.

Brent must be pursuing a Nahuaque who was crawling among the sheep. As though he had forgotten the use of a carbine, he swung it wildly over his head. Finally he brought it down like a pickax, muzzle first, yelling as he plunged it down again and again. Then he waded back through the milling sheep. Kills-a-Bear, Chockaway, Lucky, and Skinny dragged the dead Nahuaques to fling them into a heap. Cutler could hear the corporal panting. He started to duck into the wickiup again, but, crouched inside, María began to scream shrilly. He backed out.

"*Cabezas*, Nantan Tata?" Tazzi said, standing spread-legged between the dead Nahuaques' legs.

He couldn't think why not, easier to bring the heads back to Fort McLain than dead bodies. General Yeager had offered a modest reward for the heads of the bloody Tonto raiders led by Delshay, and scouts had brought them in and arranged them in a neat line on the ground, facing his quarters. In fact, a number of heads resembling Delshay had produced themselves. If he ordered these heads taken, their Nahuaque owners would wander headless through eternity, like Mangas Coloradas.

"Take their heads," he said, and left María in the wickiup until the process was finished. The head of the Nahuaque Corporal Brent had killed was not worth taking.

The other head that had been destroyed was María's.

Her screaming began again when he extricated her from the wickiup the second time. She screamed at the sight of him. When she was not screaming her mouth gaped open in the terrible silent scream of the tortured O of Pedro Carvajal's mouth. His wife was insane.

What they found out was: There were thirty-two men in the posse Sheriff Pogie Smith had deputized and led out of town to arrest Mr. Turnbull and attach the herd with the disputed title. When they did not find Mr. Turnbull at the ranch they split up, the sheriff and nine others going after the herd, and the bigger bunch heading toward Joe Peake's spread thinking to find Mr. Turnbull there. Right off it was interesting that the bigger bunch had gone after the man, and the smaller after the herd.

The four out in front had been Clay Mortenson, Bert Fears, Cory Helbush, and Ed Duffy. So they were the four that had done the killing. There were some in the main body of the posse that thought Mr. Turnbull had come out shooting. There were others that had been shocked at straight-out murder.

What Johnny wanted to know was how far back up the lines the orders had come from. To Clay Mortenson from Pogie Smith. To Pogie from Judge Arthur, who would have issued the warrants, and Neill MacLennon, who would have requested them. In behalf of Ran Boland. There was another layer to it, which was Jake Weber, in Santa Fe, that you heard carried mortgages on the store and its properties, and Governor Dickey himself. It tired his mind to think it through further than Ran Boland, from the store to the Ring.

He had quarreled with Joe over the fact that their posse had right off started calling themselves Regulators, like Mr. McFall's old gun-toting outfit, which hadn't ever had two cents' worth of legal claim to it; and he didn't like it either that right off they were operating outside their jurisdiction of Jefferson County, where they'd been deputized. There were fifteen of them, half Turnbull hands and half south-county cowboys and small ranchers, some of them McFall people. Jack Grant had not volunteered, probably because Jay-O-Joe was heading up these Regulators.

They caught Cory Helbush and Bert Fears in a saloon in Three Rivers, just about as easy as falling off the back stoop.

That same day, heading back for Jeff City, they ran alongside Lieutenant Cutler and his scouts on the track of Nahuaque renegades. At suppertime they held up to cook some beef and beans and boil coffee where there was shade and water. Cory and Bert had been dumped out in full sun, however. He didn't think that was right, and helped them crawl over to a patch of shade, squatting while he asked Cory questions that concerned him.

"I didn't do anything!" Cory said. His unshaven face was slick with sweat and he kept twisting his shoulders to rest more easy with his hands tied behind him. "Goddamnit to hell, my goddamn arm is falling off, Johnny!"

"Who was paying you?"

"Told you and *told* you! We was deputized all proper, to bring in the Englishman and that herd! Clay told him we had papers on him, and he started yelling and throwing lead!"

"You're a liar!" Bo Becker said, coming up. He prodded Cory with his rifle muzzle, Cory groaning and twisting his shoulders some more. "We know what happened!"

"Then what're you pestering me for?"

Some of the others laughed at that, where they lounged around the fire, watching the coffeepot and the meat smoking on the grate. Bert lay on his side with his face turned away, sick. He'd been puking up blood from being slammed in the belly with a rifle butt.

Johnny wished Bo would leave and let be. He said to Cory, "Tell us who was paying you."

"Told you. County, deputy pay."

"Tell us all of it," he said, hunkered down, looking into Cory's face very close. Out of the corner of his eye he could see Joe pacing up and down on the other side of the fire, spurs chinking. The horses were tethered over by thick brush. Cory squalled when Bo screwed the rifle muzzle into his ribs again.

"You better answer Johnny!"

"Just hold off, will you, Bo?" He never would understand people. He was trying to get some sense out of Cory with Bo banging him in the ribs, and Cory spitting mad and scared.

"Well, I know you are some big punkins, Johnny-A," Cory said in a breathy voice. "You've killed five men or maybe it's nine. But I'm not escared of you, Johnny-A!"

"Never asked you to be. Just want to know who paid for Mr. Turnbull killed."

"You're going to kill us anyway!"

Joe came over to stand looking down at the two prisoners, arms folded on his chest and his lip curled as at a bad smell.

"Clay did it!" Bert said in a muffled voice. "Clay shot him."

"Shut your face!" Cory yelled at him, and squalled again when Bo kicked him in the thigh. He cussed awhile, then he said, "What the hell do you expect, the Englishman throwing lead—"

"Johnny found his Colt unfired," Joe said.

Lying on his side with his arms bound behind him and his cheek against the ground, Bert said, "Pulled iron like he was going to use it, so Clay shot him."

"How was it he was shot in the back?" someone called from over by the fire.

"I guess it was Clay had him covered from behind when he pulled iron," Bert said in the tired, muffled voice.

"They're going to kill us, Bert," Cory said.

"You boys wouldn't do that, I know," Bert said in the worn-out voice. He gazed up at Johnny with glazed eyes in his gray face.

"Tell us who paid for it," Johnny said. He wanted one of them to say it; he didn't want to put words in their mouths, scared as they were.

"Maybe we'll just cut off your balls and cook them up for your supper!" Pard Graves called over.

"I know you boys is just funning us," Bert said.

"I just can't believe anybody'd be so stupid," Joe said in his stifled voice. He had sounded that way ever since Mr. Turnbull had been killed. "All you had to do was take up his Colt and fire it off and leave it there. Instead you just left it. And the rock somebody beat his head in with, too."

Cory cussed in a low voice until Bo kicked him.

"Well, Clay did it," Bert said. "He had some bad spleen

in him against the Englishman. He told me once but I forget why. It was Clay, all right. You've got the wrong fellows here, boys."

"What I want to know," Johnny said patiently, "is who paid Clay to do it? How was it you four was out front like that?"

Bert just shook his head, cheek scraping against the ground, drool spilling out of his open mouth.

"Who?"

"I just don't know what you're saying, Johnny. We was deputized perfectly legal to bring in the Englishman and that herd. He started waving that Colt—"

"Liars!" someone yelled.

"Tell me who was paying you."

Bert only shook his head. He looked pretty far gone sick, but more afraid of the store than them still. Squatting there trying to keep a cool head, Johnny could smell the coffee on the boil.

"Any point feeding these bull pizzles, Joe?" Cookie called.

"Not much," Joe said, rocking on his heels.

"You'll hang, you sons of bitches!" Cory yelled.

Johnny hunkered closer to Cory who was panting and twisting his shoulders. "What I want to know is: Did Ran Boland or Henry Enders tell Pogie they wanted Mr. Turnbull dead? And Pogie told Clay Mortenson and you-all that?"

Cory stared at him with his mouth hanging open, chicken watching a snake. He whispered, "I'm not escared of you, Johnny-A!"

"What I want to know," he said patiently, "is what Pogie Smith said to you four ducks. Who it is pretty hard to believe was ever deputized possemen in the first place. Did he tell you all to kill Mr. Turnbull?"

No answer. He was aware that everyone was watching him, waiting quiet for him to continue. Bo stood by with his rifle pointed down at Cory, Joe with his arms folded on his chest like he was cold, the others by the fire.

"Where's Clay and Ed?" Pard called out.

"I expect they have headed for Texas, boys," Bert said.

"Now why would that be?" Joe said. "When everything was done proper and legal, including shooting Mr. Turnbull in the back of the head and then beating his brains out with a rock?"

Bert didn't answer that.

Johnny prodded Cory's shoulder until he opened his eyes, shivering like a poison pup. "I want to know if Pogie Smith told you-all to kill Mr. Turnbull."

"Maybe he told Clay," Cory whispered. "Johnny—you're not going to let them kill us, are you?"

"You boys better hunt up Clay," Bert said, heartier. "Clay could tell you that."

"Tell us what?" Joe said with a harsh laugh.

"You're pretty as a girl but you are pure bad, ain't you, Johnny-A?" Cory said, staring up at him.

When they got back from Jeff City, with all that done for, Johnny and three other Turnbull hands who had ridden with the Regulators headed into Arioso for the grand *baile* with masks everybody'd been talking about—Pard his best friend, with his wild ways and jokes, Carlito the Mex, who carried his guitar along with him in case he was asked to play a tune or two, and Paul Tuttle, a quiet young fellow turned quieter still after the stint of Regulatoring.

Arioso was the closest to Mr. Turnbull's spread of any of the south-county hamlets called *placitas*, and the biggest too. There were pretty girls there, with their honey-brown skin, flounced skirts, and neat little bosoms, smoking their *cigarrillos* and laughing and flirting—the five Soto girls, daughters of Don Teodoro, the town *presidente;* and the half-breed daughter of Pete Fulton, who'd lived among Mexicans all his life, ran a big riding stock and drayage business, and alternated with Don Teodoro as mayor of Arioso. There were other town girls also, and cousins and friends in from the south-county ranches for the festivities. If you craved the company of white-skin American girls, you were out of luck in the territories, for those in the big towns like Santa Fe and Tucson did not associate with cowboys. Johnny Angell could not imagine any girls more delightful than those of Arioso.

They rode west along the ridge trail north of the canyon country where the Old Ones' ruins were. The western sky was still alight with the sun just down behind the mountains, and all around them were juts of rusty rock, ocotillo whips, and saguaro like railroad semaphores. All of them knew not to mention Cory Helbush and Bert Fears and spoil the fun of riding into town to a dance.

"Girls, here we come!" Pard whooped, spurring and reining in at the same time so his pony jumped and sidled. He had been saying it at intervals as they approached Arioso.

"These pretty little girl surely do like dance with cowboy!" Carlito said.

"No fighting now, you ducks," Johnny said.

"No fighting, no, sir!" Pard said. "What an idee!"

The three of them would get drunk, and often enough Pard would end up proddy. Now they were laughing at their jokes, and he reflected on the pleasure of the anticipation of the *baile*, and of the pretty girls of Arioso. He loved the masked balls, although often they knew who he was, even masked, because he was small. He laughed out loud in his pleasure. Laughter was a kind of drunkenness in itself. It had to do with a release of responsibilities and vexations and all the weights of being a man; laughter and pretty girls and trusted friends to enjoy yourself with and look after when they got drunk.

But on the ridge trail in the gathering dust, laughing with his friends, he had a sudden, queer, and incomplete vision: Joe dead, and Pard terribly hurt, and—with a jump to his heart, as though he glimpsed it a long way off—another lying dead with hands folded on his chest and the glint of a silver medal in his fingers. And he knew it was from the war. The vision came to him so vividly that he sobbed out loud, and then laughed the harder to cover it.

The *baile* was already in progress in the plaza between the general store and the cantina, the building fronts decorated with paper flowers, and the space between crisscrossed with twisted colored-paper streamers. Paper lanterns glowed, and on the bandstand a *banda* of guitars, fiddles, and two trumpets played. The dancers in their masks revolved and swayed—hermits, conquistadors, clowns, Moors, grand court ladies, girls with domino masks, red masks, blue ones, all in their lacy dresses. Their partners were young Mex fellows and some cowboys, masked and not. Masked girls and older women sat on benches watching.

Pard whooped one more time. "Oh, you pretty little women, here I come!" They dismounted and tethered their horses, and started along the cobbled street into the plaza, boot heels cracking and chinking to the rhythm of the music. The papier-mâché masks were for sale at the general store.

Johnny dropped a pace behind the others to survey the Anglos on hand; as far as he could make out all of them were south-county fellows, friends and acquaintances; not much worry in south county about meeting the sheriff or Madison hardcases. Sometimes he would see Jack Grant at these fiestas, recognizable even with a mask by six-four and pole skinny.

The first girl who set herself in his way wore a black and white domino, with red lips and red flowers tucked into a coronet of black hair—Valentina Soto, no question about it. He swept her into a dance, marveling at the suppleness of her waist with his arm about it. She laughed up into his face, eyes moving like mice behind the eyeholes of her mask.

"'Allo, Juanito el Ángel! You have come to dance with me?"

"I have come to dance with all the señoritas!"

She laughed into his ear, and they swayed and stepped to the melancholy, slightly-sour strains of "Cielito Lindo." Pard and the others had disappeared into the store to buy their masks.

He danced with most of the other Soto girls, not sure which was which in their masks. He recognized Elizabeth Fulton in her dead-white mask with round spots of crimson on the cheeks and lips; she was as tall as he was, and the slimmest of the Arioso girls, bold with her mask on, who was usually as shy as she was slim. One of the cantina waiters, in a soiled white apron, threaded his way through the dancers to tell him Don Teodoro asked to speak to him.

A bunch of cowboys and Mex *muchachos* were drinking at the bar, everybody friendly because all were south-county in the town-against-county fuss. They called out to him, "Hey, Johnny-A!" and "Buenas, Juanito!" and "We are sure with you, Johnny!" and "Don't let her cool off, now!" He waved a hand and greeted them by name, those he could. As he passed on by he felt that prickling of attention on his back that he both liked and didn't, like after that Fourth of July target shoot in Jeff City.

In the back room of his cantina, Don Teodoro Soto rose up out of his chair like a mustached, black-suited whale, offering him a pillow of a hand to shake. The mayor of Arioso smiled at him with his thin dark lips, but his eyes, tucked in above fat cheeks, smiled less.

"It is good to see you, Juanito! You sit down, eh? A glass of good whiskey with me?"

"Just one finger, Mr. Soto," he said. As he seated himself, his piece knocked against the wooden arm of the chair with a startle of sound. "Sorry!"

The mayor waddled to the mantel and poured Old Crow into two glasses, handing him the half-filled one. *"Salud!"*

"Y pesetas!"

"Y vida larga!"

"Y muchas muchachas!"

They laughed together, and Don Teodoro maneuvered his massive behind back into his chair. On the walls were painted squares of metal depicting Biblical scenes. There was a framed oleo of Jesus with the crown of thorns and trickles of blood. Behind the desk was a squat safe.

"You are a great hero, Juanito!"

"No reason for it."

"Yes, yes, the *gente*, our people, have loved Don Martín very much, that good man. May his soul rest! Nor do they like the men of power in Madison, who have done this thing. For they have also been very hard with the *gente*."

"Sure, I know that." He sipped the whiskey; he did not like its taste, or its effect either. He liked his clear head. Outside, the band, which had been silent, struck up again with a wail of trumpets: Cucurrucucu, Paloma.

"We are good friends, Juanito," Don Teodoro said, leaning toward him. "You have been a good friend to the *gente*. El Angelito!"

Something wanted here, he thought.

"I must tell you some things that trouble my heart," Don Teodoro said.

"Surely," he said, and wished he were back outside dancing. He had still to get a mask. He rubbed an itchy spot on his back against the chair back.

"Once this country was ruled by England," Don Teodoro said, like a schoolmaster. "A great war was fought. For freedom and justice, you understand. Many sad wives and mothers. After, in ten, in twenty years, how much more freedom and justice did your country have than Canada, which had not fought for those beautiful ladies? Not much, I think."

He didn't know what Don Teodoro was getting at.

"Listen. Mexico was ruled by Spain. A terrible war was fought, for freedom and justice. How much more justice does poor Mexico have? I think, Juanito, that no war for freedom and justice can be worth the terrible things that are done in war. Nor do we ever capture those beautiful ladies that we pursue. Do you know of what I speak, my friend?"

"Well, I guess I don't rightly understand, Mr. Soto." It seemed he had come to a position in his life where he must listen to lectures on freedom and justice when he would rather dance with pretty girls.

"It is well known that Señor Boland is sick," the mayor continued. "Very sick! It can be said he deserves his fate for his many crimes. Soon he must die, Juanito."

"They say his new partner is a cripple-arm duck, about as friendly as a she-grizzly."

Soto gazed at him worriedly, breathing hard, nostrils swelling and narrowing. He tossed back his whiskey.

"Listen, Juanito. I have many friends in old Mexico. These friends hate the Estados Unidos. And why? There are many insults, many wrongs, much arrogance. Without permission, the cavalry chases *indios* into Mexico. Parties of revolution meet in Texas, or in Arizona territory, and they raid into Mexico hoping the government of Don Porfirio will fall. Every week, every day, the periodicals of Mexico are full of rumors of war with the Estados Unidos. Do you know what I tell my friends?"

"I think you tell them that wars make things no better."

"Yes, that is what I tell them," the mayor said sadly. He rose to stand by the mantel, fat fingers gripped around the neck of the whiskey bottle, with a melancholy expression.

"My friend," the mayor continued, "cannot the lives of these two men shot in *ley fuga* be traded for Don Martín's life?"

"Joe is going to have to have Clay Mortenson," Johnny said, harder than he had meant. He added, "It does look like Ed Duffy has left the country."

"Then I see this. There will be an exchange for Clay Mortenson. Maybe that will be Joe Peake, or you, Juanito. And the others in the end must take Señor Maginnis, for you see it is a game of chess, and he is the one they will have in the end. But the pawns and then the kings will go, until none remain."

The mayor poured himself another glass of whiskey. "There was a bad bunch in the county ten years ago, Juanito. Maybe you have heard of them, Davey Stovall was the leader. They hated the *gente*."

He had heard of the Stovall gang, of course.

"They would come to a *placita* and cause trouble. Some of our young men decided that these bad ones must be met with force, for they were no better than Apaches. So there was a shooting, and one of the gang was killed. For this they attacked a *baile* at Corral de Tierra, and three young men and a young woman were killed.

"I went to Señor Boland and asked him if he would put a stop to Davey Stovall and his gang. I do not know what he did, but those bad ones left for Texas and did not return again. If they had not gone, our young men would have killed more, and they more—until the game of which I have spoken was played out." He stopped, standing before the mantel with his big belly, his fat legs tapering to tiny feet in black, shiny town shoes.

"Well, that is it, you see," Johnny said, as easily as he could manage. "Ran Boland from olden times ran Madison County, so he could tell Davey Stovall to clear out and Stovall had to do it. But when Mr. Turnbull is a nuisance and will not clear out, then he is shot and his head beat in with a stone. Now that is maybe just Clay Mortenson thinking to do Ran Boland a favor. And the judge the same, putting out some bad writs and warrants on a herd Mr. Turnbull had bought with good money."

Don Teodoro was nodding like he was thinking of something else.

"Come to think of it, Clay Mortenson rode with Davey Stovall at one time," Johnny said.

The mayor crossed himself silently. Johnny rose. "Well, I had better go out to the *baile* before all the pretty girls get danced away with."

"We remain friends, Juanito," Don Teodoro said, with a little bow and a handshake.

Later, up the ladder in the hay barn, with his clown mask pushed up on top of his head, he stroked Valentina Soto's breasts until her nipples felt like hard little fingers under his palms. He pushed the cool coin of the Virgin of Guadalupe medallion aside so as to kiss between them.

"The terrible pistolero Juanito el Ángel kisses the breast of Valentina," she giggled. "Tell me, does Juanito also kiss there Adelita and Celestina and María Dolores and Carmen, and Elisabeta Fulton?"

He raised his head to kiss her mouth that smelled pleasantly of *cigarrillos*. "Only Valentina."

"Not Elisabeta, who is like a boy there?" She giggled.

"Not Elisabeta."

"Not Celestina?"

"Celestina is very Católica."

"Elisabeta sighs for el Angelito the famous pistolero of the beautiful sad eyes."

"Valentina has the prettiest bosom," he said, and brushed her nipples some more while she sighed and stretched. She caught his hand, though, when he tried to slip it inside her shift.

"Forbidden! My Lady guards what is below."

"From angels?"

"From *pistoleros!*" she said, laughing, and firmly pushed his hand away. They lay back side by side on the sweet-smelling hay while the band in the plaza played sad love songs. It was of Elizabeth Fulton, whose breasts had never been uncovered for him, that he was thinking.

Fanny Peake served them flapjacks, fried steaks, and black coffee, Joe sitting tall and scowling at the head of the table with slicked-back hair and an ironed blue shirt. Johnny and Pard sat on one side of the foreman, Carlito on the other, stuffing their bellies, nobody talking much till the coffee took hold. Clay Mortenson had been seen over toward Bosque Alto, and they were heading after him.

Chuckie played on an Indian blanket that had been spread out on the bare planks. He had a cowboy doll Joe had constructed of empty spools strung on twine, with a beanbag head. The spool cowboy rode a straw horse, the kind the Mexes were clever at making.

Fanny set down another platter of flapjacks and stood with her bent wrists braced on her hips, gazing down at Joe.

"I just wish I thought you knew what you were doing, Joseph Peake!"

"Never mind it, Fan," Joe said. He had a short fuse, but Johnny had never seen him blow up at his wife. When she nagged at him he would get a wrinkle across his forehead like trying to remember something that wouldn't come back. Now he stretched out his wry neck, rubbing his knuckles along it.

"You see he is careful now, Johnny!"

"Yes, ma'am," he said.

"I just don't like it," Fanny Peake kept on. "Last time Sheriff Timmons deputized you properly, but this time you are just too uppity to bother."

"Uppity! Huh!" Pard said, grinning.

"Governor went and relieved Timmons," Joe said. "Well, they say Dickey's going to get relieved himself pretty soon, too many guns starting to go off out here." He grinned also.

"You think it is all just boys' games, Joe Peake," Fanny said.

Johnny watched Pard and Carlito dig into the flapjacks, pretending not to hear Joe and his wife bickering back and forth. He would choose one of the Arioso girls any day of the week over a back East American woman. Fanny was all nag, whine, and complain for all he'd ever heard, but Joe prized her above gold bricks.

"I would like to know there are more than the three of you going," Fanny said. "He is a notorious, dangerous gunman!"

"We are going past Batesons'," Joe said with a mouthful. "There'll be a bunch there."

Fanny started back for the range, where flapjacks were smoking, but turned and came right back again. "Well, if you're going that way I need some supplies in Riveroaks. It seems like we go through two of those Arbuckle coffee packets a week. We could save money if you'd buy green and let me do the roasting."

"Last time you burnt the whole batch," Joe said. He rose, swiping at his mouth with his napkin. "Well, let's go, if you-all are ready." Johnny and Pard stood, chairs jarring back.

"Da!" Chuckie said from his seat on the blanket, holding up the spool doll and shaking it.

From Riveroaks they headed up into the foothills along the rim of the reservation. A Mex friend of Carlito's had seen Clay Mortenson up near Cooper's sawmill, just off Bosque Alto. Probably Clay was thinking about rustling some Apache stock. Every cowboy with larceny in his heart had ridden up to cast an eye over that fine herd of the Sierra Verdes, though it was known to be well guarded.

"Sooner or later Clay was bound to start making plans on that Caballito herd," Joe said.

"I'd be satisfied to see those Red Stripers take after Clay with a cutting knife," Jimmy Bateson said.

Everybody was feeling chipper today. With Ed Duffy gone the Regulatoring would be over if they caught up with Clay Mortenson. The sun bore down like a hot mattress, but there was a little breeze breathing down out of the hills to cool faces, six of them now, including Chad and Jimmy Bateson, and Paul Tuttle. At the sawmill Cooper's wife would feed travelers for a few bits a meal.

They would single file up through the weedy, second-growth pines. Johnny pointed out two Apaches on spotted ponies watching them from a ridge, that kind of still, hard examination of Indians. You could make out from here the red stripes on their cheeks. Those stripes had once been enough to give a settler, a prospector, or a cowboy heart failure, no need even for the Sierra Verdes to waste a cartridge or unsheathe a cutting knife. Caballito was famous for bloody bustouts, though it was the Nahuaques, from the other side of the reservation, that had broken out on a raid most recently.

Joe raised a peace-sign hand and one of the Paches returned the gesture. "Painted-face devils!" Chad Bateson muttered as they rode on toward the scarf of smoke from the sawmill.

They were seated at dinner in Mrs. Cooper's kitchen, when Carlito rose to crouch pointing out the window. Everybody scrambled up, bumping together, and Johnny had to stand tiptoe to see past the taller men. Through the dusty glass there was Clay Mortenson, aboard a mule, headed this way. His black hat was mashed down on his head, there was a rifle in a boot, and he was lurching with the mule's gait like he'd been all day scouting the Sierra Verde herd.

Clay and Jesse-Jay Clary were sidekicks and the same kind of bird, who had once been decent fellows up from Texas, working at whatever came to hand, but had grown hard and harder like a callus in a too-tight boot. They would hang out in cantinas or saloons spoiling everybody else's good time, looking on the prod and sour, and it was like the first time Clay Mortenson rode out to scare an arrears farmer into paying up on store usury or clearing out of the Territory, he had gone all the way over, first pretending to enjoy that line of work, and then not even having to pretend it.

Clay's bearded face glanced right and left and straight ahead, so some of the men jerked back away from the window. Luckily they had tethered the horses out back. Clay wore a bandana knotted at his throat, a flannel shirt and unbuttoned vest, the tags of makings dangling from the pocket. He halted by the rail to dismount and tie the mule. Carrying the rifle he sauntered on up the path at a splay-legged saunter, disappearing around the corner of the building.

Joe hitched up his cartridge belt, and, without a word, boot-cracked across to the door. Mrs. Cooper stood at the range with a plate of boiled potatoes steaming in one hand, the other braced against her neck as though she was holding her head on. The others followed Joe outside, with Pard and Johnny bringing up the rear.

He could smell fear stronger and sourer than the meat, potatoes, and turnips smell from Mrs. Cooper's kitchen. Sweat darkened the back of Carlito's shirt. The four backs blocked the doorway. He could just see past Chad's shoulder Clay Mortenson coming up on the veranda, foot raised but held suspended there and a poker set to his face on seeing them. Clay raised a hand very slow to scratch in his chin whiskers.

"Well, hello, Joe. Chad. Jimmy. Fellows."

Joe said in a too-loud voice, "Clay Mortenson, we are here to arrest you for murdering Martin Turnbull!"

Through the slot of space Johnny watched Clay's intense bearded face, scar on his cheekbone like a three-pointed star. Clay licked his lips, left to right on the lower, right to left on the upper.

"Why, Joe, you don't have no authority for arresting any man."

"Get 'em up, Clay!" Joe yelled, and Chad's elbow jammed back into Johnny's belly as he drew his Colt. Johnny flung himself aside, knocking Pard out of the way as the doorway exploded with everybody yelling at once, and, behind them, Mrs. Cooper screeching.

The Regulators jammed together, retreating into the kitchen, slamming the door behind them. Everything at times like this came to Johnny very slow and clear—Joe with his smoking Colt, face white and mouth open; Jimmy holding up his right hand, which streamed blood; Carlito with a shoulder jammed against the door; Paul stumbling back; and Chad with his piece up, aimed in two hands and smoking.

Pard shouted, "What happened? What the Christ happened?"

"Gut-shot him!" Chad said.

"Look at my hand!" Jimmy cried.

Johnny jerked out his bandana and caught Jimmy's hand, which was pumping blood, and bound the cloth over the stump of thumb. In a moment of silence he heard Clay groan on the other side of the door, then a dragging sound and a door slam. That was the door to the anteroom of the mill, he knew.

Jimmy kept whispering. "Shit! Shit! Shit!" through his teeth, wounded hand gripped against his chest with his left hand. The rest of them continued their retreat across the room. Mrs. Cooper had disappeared. They all took up their rifles.

Johnny saw that Joe didn't know what to do now. "He'll get himself forted up in the mill," he said.

Joe gave him a dazed look. "We'll get out the back and shoot for the windows."

"If he is gut-shot you could just leave him be."

"He's gut-shot, that's certain!" Chad said, checking the loading of his Springfield. Jimmy sat at the table, bending over his shot hand and whining like a hurt puppy.

Joe seemed to be getting in charge of himself and the situation. "Outside!" Joe said, setting his shoulders. He jammed his Colt back in its holster and took up his rifle. "Come on, Johnny, we've got to roust him out of there!"

He shrugged to Joe's crazy glare; he didn't want to challenge Joe's authority here. Outside the sunlight was painful, and the others slapped on hats like they were helmets. The mill hulked up with the feathers of smoke leaking from the tall chimney. Clay would still be in that anteroom, hurt and dying and dangerous as a wounded grizzly.

Joe hustled them around a corner and behind a stack of timbers. A shot rang out and lead chipped wood behind them. Joe sent the others to the sides of the mill, while he and Johnny remained behind the timbers. Johnny considered the situation for a minute, then he sprinted across open space to a pile of rusty sawmill junk, worn-out gears and circular blades and corrugated iron troughs. He hunkered down there where he could cover the anteroom window from one angle while Joe bore on another. The muzzle of Clay Mortenson's rifle poked out and slanted this way and that. Kneeling behind the junk pile with green runners of morning glory snaking through it, Johnny braced his rifle and waited.

In the slow clarity he saw Joe's hat rising like a muffin in the oven, behind the top timber, half of Joe's face showing between hat and timber, following that his rifle sliding out and tucked to his cheek. Before Johnny could yell a warning the hat flew off. For an instant there was Joe bare-headed, patch of blood glistening on his forehead; then his face disappeared. From the window Clay Mortenson shrilled, *"Gotcha!"* leaning forward into Johnny's sights.

Of the two dead men at Cooper's mill, both shot through the head, Clay Mortenson in the belly as well, one was buried on the spot, the other packed aboard his horse to be taken home.

13

So Cutler came again to the Hacienda de las Golondrinas,
the mud ramparts against the green corduroy of the agave
fields, and the cornfields moving in the wind like a tan sea.
He rode the beautiful horse Malcreado, which had saved his
life, beside the closed buggy and its driver hired in Hermosillo
for this sad journey inland. He had not sent ahead word of
their coming, for he had not known what word to send. They
passed in through the enormous gate and halted in the
shadow of the oaks. The thick-necked, frowning *mayordomo*
did not remember him.

"I am Lieutenant Patrick Cutler," he said. "You will
summon Don Fernando here."

The man stuttered apologies, and hurried inside. He
returned with the old man, who walked more stiffly than
Cutler remembered. Both sides of his face were frozen in
dismay, as though in his long life he had come to expect the
worst but still some new form of the worst could surprise
him. Cutler embraced him, frail as kindling.

"Patricio, you have come—you did not warn me—" He
wrung his hands in silence, staring at the closed window of
the buggy.

"She will not come out if she knows I am here. If she
sees me she will begin to scream."

"Ah, Mother of God, what have you done?" Don Fernando
stepped toward the buggy, but hesitated there; the straw-
hatted *arriero* sat above his team, gazing down at the scene.
Others materialized—fat Doña Hortensia, the aunt of Ysabel;
two servants in their striped vests; Padre Juan with hands
tucked inside the sleeves of his cassock like a Chinaman. All
of them looked shabbier than Cutler had remembered, the
reality not so grand as the remembered, and shattered,

dream. They congregated at the door of the buggy, Don Fernando's white head taller than any of the others as, before he opened the door, he called out to his granddaughter inside.

Cutler led Malcreado hoof-clopping along the cobbled way past the *casa grande* to the stables, to wait there until they had taken his wife inside.

In the high, cool, dim *sala*, the ornate gilt frames of the family portraits caught glints of light from the high windows. They sat around a table, Don Fernando facing Cutler across it. Doña Caterina snoozed in her chair, her polished stick propped beside her. The padre leaned over hands clasped ostentatiously in prayer, sheen of sun on his pale bald pate. Doña Hortensia had fled from the room at the news of her niece's death. María was in her bed, with sedatives.

"He suffered very much at the hands of these evil ones, then," Don Fernando said, and cleared his throat.

"The worst I've ever seen. She must have witnessed it."

"May God forgive her. And Pedro Carvajal. I pray that he was able to die with honor."

"I think the extremes to which they went indicated that he did." Cutler had had time to rehearse all this on the railroad journey into Mexico.

Padre Juan stirred and glanced at him with swimming dark eyes. Don Fernando inclined his white head over his own clasped hands. A small snore emanated from Doña Caterina's chair. This jerked her awake, and she peered around her with confused, bright eyes.

"She still—carries the child?" Don Fernando inquired.

"It is clear from her figure," Padre Juan said. "It is four months now, Don Patricio?"

He nodded. Don Fernando glared at him out of the paralyzed mask of his face. "It is your child, Patricio?"

His scalp prickled with anger that quickly passed. "I can only believe that it is." There was a press of waiting silence. "She was very unhappy," he said. "Each day she was as miserable as the last, or more. I thought it was life on a military post, and missing this place of her childhood. Once she said to me that there was only one who could bring her happiness. I thought she meant... her Maker. But she was in correspondence with her cousin. I've found that he waited in Jefferson City with two peons until she was able to send word that I was away. I had accompanied a column to the Apache reservation, where there was a fight that resulted in a break-out. That resulted in this horror."

"Sometimes God seems to me very far away," Don Fernando said, big-knuckled hands locked together on the table before him. "Sometimes not so far."

"Never far, Don Fernando," Padre Juan said reprovingly.

"I ask that you pray for the soul of Ysabel Gutiérrez, and that of Pedro Carvajal, Padre."

"I will hold a Mass this very evening."

"And for the salvation of my granddaughter and the child she carries."

"Of course, Don Fernando."

Cutler continued. "We pursued the renegades and killed them. However, most of the Nahuaques, including the chief, remained on the reservation, and everything has quieted down. My general gave me permission to bring María to her home. The doctor who is my friend says he thinks there is nothing to be done at this time. Possibly in the months to come she will be better. After the birth of the child, perhaps. But I do not know if she will ever change towards me—for reasons I can understand."

The little old woman stared at him with a birdlike cock of her head. María's tragedy seemed to interest her much more than María's grand wedding had. "What reasons, señor?" she asked in her blurred voice.

"She betrayed me. The result was the terrible death of her lover."

Doña Caterina nodded. Padre Juan stirred.

"Do you still honor your marriage vows, then, Don Patricio?"

"I do."

"I sympathize with your position, Patricio," Don Fernando said tiredly. "You and your wife made the profoundest of vows to one another, and she . . ." He paused to recover his emotions. "And yet she was only a spoiled child in love with dancing."

"We will trust in God," Padre Juan said, bending over his clasped hands.

"We will trust in God and the advice of the best physicians I can summon from the capital."

"There are herbs that are known to be effective," Doña

Caterina chirped. "I will consult with the *curandero* of San Gorgonio, who is very famous."

"When she is delivered of her child I believe she will begin to heal in her mind," Padre Juan said. "I will pray for this every day."

"We will pray also that the child is a boy," Don Fernando said.

Two days later Colonel Kandinsky arrived, in his gray, exotically embroidered uniform, a silk handkerchief in his sleeve with which he brushed the dust from his face before he offered Cutler a strong handshake. Cutler was glad to see the *rurales* commander, who seemed to bring a sense of strength and purpose with him. They took sherry with Don Fernando in a verdant patio with sunlight dripping through the leaves. Kandinsky had visited María in her apartments.

"Very bad," he said, shaking his head. "The religious fervor is intense. The beads are told, Hail Marys proliferate. I do not at this time criticize the padre, you understand. Still, I cannot believe María fails to recognize her Lalla."

The colonel strode across the burnished tiles in his high boots to halt before the parrot's cage, peering in at the gorgeous blue, red, and orange bird. His colorless hair was combed into a careful pompadour. He dipped a finger into his sherry glass and inserted it through the wire bars. The bird sidled toward it on its perch, opening its yellow beak.

"Careful, my friend," Don Fernando said, slumped in his tall chair.

"*Rurales* have no fear, of man or beast," Kandinsky said. The parrot inclined its beak toward the damp finger, touched it with a gray wad of tongue, and sidled away. Kandinsky chuckled, drying his finger on the silk handerchief.

"I would prefer Hail Marys to screams," Cutler said.

Pacing, frowning, Kandinsky halted, facing him. "We in Mexico have also had experiences with Apaches," he said. "And I, in my position, have had more than most men. I ask you to consider this, Patricio. Why did María not share the fate of Ysabel? It is well known that Apaches will take young women captives, as they will take children, believing it good to bring new blood into the band. It is also known that savages respect madmen, believing them possessed *of* magic as well as *by* magic. There are many tales of their victims, driven mad by the horrors they have witnessed, who have themselves not been harmed. Also of those who have escaped their fate by pretending madness.

"I postulate this. That María was preserved not by her screams, which she reserves for her husband, but by her Hail Marys and the telling of beads. By holding up the holy crucifix, by loud prayers, by her pretense of religious fervor, in fact! Having preserved herself in this way from savages, she seeks to protect herself from further unpleasantnesses by the same devices. By this continuing pretense, she has slipped in part into the condition of the pretense."

He bowed to Cutler. "I have known many women in my life, señor. In many lands, in my career as a condottiere. In Poland, in London, in Paris, in all Italy, in Mexico. I have come to understand that insanity lurks always in the sanest of women. And sanity in the most mad, of course."

"It seems that the sight of me drives her to the extreme of her condition," Cutler said.

"Time will heal," Don Fernando muttered. As Las Golondrinas seemed to Cutler shabbier on this visit, so Don Fernando seemed perceptibly older and frailer; as the aged sister seemed brighter in the face of tragedy, he seemed confused. Still the affection that had been engendered on that first visit remained.

"When will you return to the United States, Patricio?" Kandinsky asked.

"Tomorrow, *mi coronel*."

Kandinsky raised his glass. "We have our duties, we who serve our nations. There are duties of the heart as well. To our duties, señores!"

Cutler raised his glass. Don Fernando lifted the leather-covered bottle. "We will finish this, my friends."

"I have spoken with General Ordaz on the subject of hot pursuit, which troubles your General Yeager," Kandinsky said. "We see no reason to bother Porfirio Díaz with such a trifling matter. Our conclusions—unofficial, of course—have been communicated with some force to Governor Molino. Incursions of the kind of which you speak are indeed to be tolerated. Perhaps I should say ignored. Although such incursions will not approach any place of habitation, and will be broken off if effective contact with the savages is lost or contact made with Mexican soldiers. Will that suffice your general, do you think?"

"I believe it will, Colonel."

Don Fernando stood, tall and bent, to empty the bottle into the glasses they held. Again Kandinsky raised his in a toast.

"I salute the heir of Las Golondrinas!" he said.

In the morning Cutler went to bid his wife good-bye. She was seated in a chair by the window, her back to him, her lustrous, dark red hair fanned over the shoulders of her dressing gown. A servant girl was brushing her hair, María raising her face to the sunlight streaming in the window.

Suddenly she thrust the girl aside and swung toward him. Her beautiful face, that was no longer a girl's face, contorted into ugliness. He had no defense against the hoarse scream of horror she wrung from her throat, the sound as awful and echoing as that snatch of the death song of the trapped Nahuaques—not loud, just long, profound, total. Her eyes above her open mouth with its ululating tongue were wide, black, blank.

Back at Fort McLain he found that Benny Dee had been condemned to death by a court-martial. Sam Bunch assured him that there was nothing he could have done. Percy Robinson came down from Santa Fe to notify Cutler that the general would not interfere with Benny Dee's sentence. He stood in Cutler's room in the Bachelor Officers' Quarters, round-shouldered, red-nosed, shaking his head. "He feels there is nothing he can do."

"I gather it's considered my fault."

"Let's say it would have been better if it hadn't happened. This is the only occasion on which an Apache scout has proven disloyal to his oath. The general doesn't wish to appear to be trying to cover up the incident, but he feels his enemies have used the incident to discredit his policies. It's been a setback."

"A setback for Benny Dee, too."

"Military policy," Percy said, and sighed. He plucked up the copy of *Anabasis* from the marble-topped table that held the lamp. "Dear old Xenophon."

"A good deal of military policy to be encountered there," Cutler said. "A good deal of it wrong, too."

Percy laughed and nodded, thumbing through the heavy little volume.

"Let me tell you the Apache view of military policy," Cutler continued. "You can pass it along to the general."

"Pat, Pat."

"My Hoyas say the reason the white-eye can't read sign is that he won't bend down to look. There's a word for knees that won't bend, but I forget what it is. Maybe that's lower policy."

"I will certainly pass that along, Pat: that is interesting," Percy said. "Well, there were some interesting things to be learned from history also." He gestured with the book. "Did you know that the battle of Cunaxa illustrates the strengths and weaknesses of cavalry warfare?"

"No, I didn't know that."

"Artaxerxes deployed his cavalry well in advance of his army, disguising his own movements while keeping himself informed of those of Cyrus. As a result he gained an initial advantage that almost ensured victory. However, by receiving Cyrus's charge when stationary, the Persians were broken by a force numbering only a tenth of their own. Thus demonstrating the potency of cavalry on attack, and its weakness on defense. Right, Pat?"

"Oh, yes, right!"

"But after this triumph Cyrus failed to rally his cavalry. Of course that's a difficult feat, with men and horses excited by battle and the prospect of plunder. This failure cost Cyrus the battle. And the campaign that followed showed clearly the interdependence of cavalry and infantry. Without good infantry the Persians couldn't attack the Greek mercenaries, who were only a quarter of their own numbers. With no cavalry of their own, the *hoplites* couldn't contemplate attacking the Persians."

"A long walk home for Xenophon."

Percy smiled at him tiredly. "Alexander would soon demonstrate the irresistibility of an army in which that interdependence was exploited to the fullest."

Cutler waited for him to finish.

Percy sighed and said, "The general sends his sympathies in the matter of your wife, Pat."

He nodded. "As I wrote him, Colonel Kandinsky says there's an informal permission for hot pursuit."

"Of course he hopes there'll be no need. Caballito is

apparently content at Bosque Alto. Unless the Bureau decides they want the Red Stripes moved back to San Marcos."

"Wants them destroyed, that is," he said.

"Can we go and have a glass of whiskey at the post trader's, Pat?"

"All right. I'm being spoken to again. The Silence seems to be off. Something else you learn at the Academy," he added.

"I understand your bitterness, Pat," Percy said.

Over whiskey he confided in Cutler that certain politicians had been in touch with the general to see if he might be interested in nomination to a high political office. The general had been writing letters to find out what support he had.

Cutler burst into laughter that hurt in his chest.

"Is the prospect so ridiculous?" Percy asked, frowning.

"The fact that it isn't ridiculous is what's funny," he said.

The Silence had indeed been abandoned after his wife's tragedy, which was, of course, connected with his own desperate ride for reinforcements when the major's column was besieged at Bosque Alto. Sam Bunch had also staked the claim that the Sierra Verdes had not joined in the Dreamer fight precisely because of Cutler's disclosure of the faulty Agency scales. Cutler, however, considered that the chief reason for his forgiveness was the mutiny of Benny Dee, which had brought General Yeager down a notch. Officers who disapproved of Yeager's insistence on the employment of Apache scouts now had proof that mutiny lurked in every Apache heart. For his part, Petey Olin had forgiven him simply because he and his wife had now moved back into Quarters 5, abandoned by Lieutenant and Mrs. Cutler.

When he received the wire from Don Fernando that he was the father of a boy, even Captain Smithers congratulated him. A half-breed kid, he supposed they were saying, but nevertheless he ordered a case of Veuve Cliquot through the post trader, and one evening when Sam Bunch had come in from Bosque Alto, he held a celebration at the officers' saloon in honor of the heir of Las Golondrinas.

Bunch stood beside him at the bar, big-shouldered, red-faced, with his piratical mustache—protective, Cutler knew. They drank health and long life in pale, warm bubbly. He knew that Sam, and Bernie Reilly, were worried that he had been drinking too much these last months. They were right.

"And here's to the boy's mother!" the surgeon said. "How is the mother, Pat? Any help from those famous Mexico City doctors?"

"Better, better!" he said, pasting an amiable smile on his face. His fellow officers were grinning at him and holding up their glasses, though the major had claimed duties that kept him away, and Captain Smithers looked preoccupied.

He had taken to playing the drunk even when he was not, and sometimes he could not separate cause and effect.

"A big old castle down in Sonora, I hear it is, Pat," Olin said, his freckled face gleaming in the lamplight.

"How is it you speak Mex so well, Pat?" Jud Farrier called to him.

"Told you. Brought up in a Mexican whorehouse." He made a face at Bunch, who grimaced back. Others were laughing at his clowning—*at* him of course, not with him. Of course he was only a mustang officer who did not have their fine advantage, with Cavalry Tactics and the battle of Cunaxa studied at the Academy. He told himself that he did not mind their disdain, for it did not match the reciprocate. He considered announcing that his son had been named for his wife's dead lover: Pedro, first in a string of Catholic given names, Cutler.

"How's your secret spy?" he asked Sam Bunch instead.

"Just fine," Bunch said, and shook his head at him.

"Had one of your pets turn sour on you," Smithers said in his Alabaman accent from down the bar. "How do you feel about that, Cutler?"

"Bad, Smithers," he said. "Couldn't speak out. For the good of the service. Higher policy and all that. Orders to keep my mouth shut." Why was he embarking on this? It would be well if he kept his mouth shut right now, which was what Bunch was glaring at him to do.

"What do you mean, Pat?" Jud Farrier said.

"Fellow's wife was Nahuaque. He was there visiting when along comes a gang of blue soldiers firing at him. He fired back, like only a Pache would do."

There was silence. He was pleased to have alienated his fellow officers again; they were standing at the bar or seated at the tables looking embarrassed or angry or only puzzled, some still holding up their champagne glasses. Champagne to your friends and pain to your sham friends. Bunch took hold of his arm.

"Come on, Paddy." Carrying a green bottle, he urged Cutler toward a table. "Let's not get into any more cutlery here." Cutler sat down a little harder than he had intended. Leaning toward him, Bunch said, tight-lipped, "You know that little Hoya fart was AWOL!"

"Did I forget to mention that?"

"What the hell is it?" Bunch said, looking at him in a way that made Cutler glance away. "You just can't stand good times, can you? Everybody's here celebrating you on your kid. Why do you have to be the most disliked son of a bitch on the post?"

"Might hurt my feelings if they didn't have some good reason for hating my guts. I could read them the letters I've had from Emily Helms!"

"You ornery toad!"

"More at home with my dirty-face Hoyas than with you people. Here's to the Good Gray Battalion on the Hudson!"

"Christ!" Bunch said. Bernie Reilly came over to sit with them.

"Here's to your son, Pat!" Bernie ticked his glass. Cutler's friends both regarded him worriedly. He didn't need friends.

"Gain a son and lose one of my trackers," he said.

"Next week, isn't it?" Bernie asked.

The gallows had been set up before the flagpole in the center of the parade ground, the white shaft and limp red and white stripes of the national banner looming over the ugly structure beneath. Benny Dee, naked except for his loincloth, squatted beneath the rope with its loop and fat knot. Two troopers stood at attention three feet behind him. No one cast shadows in this noon sun. Cutler would give the signal.

Sweating brandy in the heat, he bellowed, *"Ten—SHUN!"* A and E troops snapped to attention, hard brown faces beneath forage caps all slanting in parallel lines of attention toward him. The scouts had been ordered to attend this affair, and his Hoyas and Bunch's Sierra Verdes were directly behind him. Bunch stood rigidly alongside them, his scouts all in clean cotton with red headbands, more regimental than

Cutler's. The Hoyas appeared grubby by comparison, except for dandy Nochte under his jaunty straw hat. To Cutler's right stood Captain Smithers and Lieutenant Hotchkiss, Adjutant Pizer's replacement.

Cutler had borrowed a saber from Jud Farrier. When he drew it from its scabbard, the two troopers stepped forward to pull Benny Dee to his feet and adjust the loop over his head. The rope and the knot seemed much too substantial for so little a man. Benny Dee stood calmly, hands tied behind him, loose hair tented around his face. Cutler could not make out his expression at the distance. One of the troopers pulled the black sack over the scout's head and fastened the ties. The two of them stepped back, waiting for Lieutenant Cutler, Nantan Tata. He raised the saber.

When he slashed it down the trap was sprung and Benny Dee disappeared. The rope twitched, then steadied and hung taut with strain. He sheathed the saber. Sweat dripped from his chin and trickled down his neck. He waited, although there was no reason to hold these men at attention any longer. Except that they were here to witness a man's execution. The colonel had been vociferous on the therapy of the scouts witnessing the death of one of them who had betrayed his oath. Cutler stood watching the rope for long moments before he about-faced and dismissed the troops.

He marched to the platform beneath the gallows, ducking through the low door there. They had cut the body down and placed it in the coffin, two troopers with bare torsos gleaming with sweat in this oven beneath the structure. Bernie Reilly had his stethoscope in hand. "Hello, Pat."

"Properly dead?"

"At twelve-oh-six. How did the scouts take it?"

"It probably didn't seem any more mysterious than any of the other things the white-eye does."

"They are as familiar with ritual murder as the Anglo-Saxon race," Bernie said, patting his face with his bandana. "Well, nail him up, nail him up. We'd better get him under ground before he spoils. And out of here before we do."

One of the troopers flipped the joined pine boards of the coffin cover over the little Indian corpse, and the other began driving in nails.

"May I treat you to a whiskey, Pat?" Bernie said, mopping his face.

*   *   *

After he had reported Benny Dee's death to the colonel,
Cutler joined the contract surgeon at the post trader's saloon.
Sam Bunch and Jud Farrier were also there.

"Abe pleased?" Bunch asked. "Maybe he'll want to make
a regular thing of it—one a week?"

He supposed that he should be amused that Sam, training his company of Sierra Verde scouts, had become as
partisan as he in his sympathy with the brown savages.
Colonel Dougal hated them, hated any one with skin that was
not white, hated the necessity of depending upon them for
anything. Benny Dee's mutiny had been a great satisfaction
to him. He had all but congratulated Cutler on the offense
itself.

"Little fellow died pretty brave, I'd say," Farrier said.
"Of course it's impossible to know what they're thinking."

"He was thinking about dying," Cutler said. He took the
glass of whiskey Bernie held out to him and went to sit down.
Bernie came with him. Bunch remained with Farrier at the
bar.

"Any news from Mexico?"

Don Fernando had written in old-fashioned Spanish
script, tall, jagged, difficult to read, and uncertain of translation. María spent her days in prayer. She prayed many times
each day in the chapel of the Wounds of Christ. She confessed
her sins to the padre. The child was beautiful. She seemed
almost a whole person when giving the child suck. Surely
within a year this madness will have subsided. Within the
year he must come to Las Golondrinas to see the beautiful
child, Pedrito, that was his and María's.

He said, "Her grandfather writes that the child is very
beautiful. I've written back to ask if he has all his arms and
legs and a prick."

"It is a tragedy," the doctor said, tossing back his whiskey. His lumpy, sweat-salted face was earnest. "But tragedies
can rectify themselves."

"Well, we got Corporal Brent transferred."

"That poor fellow." Bernie gazed at him steadily. "And
how are you in yourself, Pat?"

He managed a grin. "Better."

"I had thought you should be putting in for a transfer
also."

He shook his head. Yeager would never release him.

"Everything quiet on the reservation?" Bernie asked, as though he had known what Cutler was thinking.

Things were almost too quiet. Caballito had not summoned him with complaints since the affair of the scales, and, except for Percy Robinson's visit, all was quiet also at Fort Blodgett, the general more preoccupied with political considerations than Apache affairs. If he resigned to seek nomination to a "high office," Lieutenant Cutler would no longer be an aide-de-camp in charge of a detachment of Hoya trackers and of the welfare of the Sierra Verdes at Bosque Alto. Lieutenant Cutler, in fact, would probably be assigned to the 13th Cavalry and the command of Colonel Abraham Dougal.

Presently he returned to his cube of a room in the BOQ, which was not quite as hot as the room beneath the gallows where Benny Dee had perished. He was thinking about Lily Maginnis. Joe Peake had been killed in one of the savage, vengeful little scrapes of which the "war" now consisted. Johnny Angell was reputed to be the leader of the pro-Maginnis—or were they anti-Boland?—forces. He supposed the handsome little gunman was the latest to be admitted to Lily's library. Sometimes the need for her was a physical wanting like a dry mouth for water or an empty belly. Did he restrain himself from riding into Madison because of this new jealousy, or because of his mad wife or his beautiful child, Pedrito?

He was roused in darkness by someone knocking insistently. "Sir! Lieutenant Cutler, sir!" A tall sergeant of D Troop leaned anxiously over him. "Mr. Cutler, you had better come!"

At what time of night he didn't even know, he hurried across the starlit parade ground following the sergeant. No windows were alight but his own, behind him. Gradually the gallows revealed itself, a gross, squat collection of shadows at the base of the pale vertical of the flagpole. The sergeant's bull's-eye lantern cast its light right and left and straight ahead. They had almost reached the platform when Cutler saw the taut line of the rope, which was strained as though Benny Dee's corpse had never been removed. This weight, however, had not passed through the trap, but hung suspended above it—a bundle of old clothing, it looked at first glance. But it was a squaw. How had she contrived this suicide?

Climbing the scaffold and jumping, the rope around her neck. Her hands were not even tied.

"It is a damned squaw!" the sergeant said in a strangled voice. "How did she get here, I'd like to know. How'd she—" He shone the light on her—terrible stretched neck, hands caught in the noose. Benny Dee's Nahuaque wife.

"It's his wife," he said. "Cut her down and see she is buried with him."

"But she's not—but what the devil's she doing here, sir? A Pache squaw! What—"

"A human being!" he said savagely. "Do as I say!"

"Sir!" the sergeant said in a shocked voice.

14

When Johnny told Mrs. Maginnis Joe was dead, she covered her face with her hands. Mr. Maginnis put an arm around her, gazing at him with his bugged eyes and his jaw shot out.

"We have lost our good right arm, Johnny!"

The others gathered around them in the Maginnises' parlor as he told of Joe's death, and Clay Mortenson's. Dr. Prim had bound up Jimmy's hand, and he carried it slinged up against his chest, face beard-dark and put-upon. Tom Fletcher was there, and so was Penn McFall, come in town on some errand. Mr. McFall usually bulked up so big and old in a room, barging around the way he did, that it was hard to keep your eyes on anything else. But just now it seemed that everybody had eyes fixed on Johnny. It was that Fourth of July feeling again, and it came to him that he had been elected to Joe's place.

Mrs. Maginnis dropped her hands to gaze at him with her hot, wet eyes. "Poor Fanny Peake! And the little fatherless one!"

She was so much of a woman she made every other one he knew seem like a silly girl, but sometimes there was a falseness about her that irritated him like a spider bite he couldn't get at to scratch. But other times she would show she was her own person in a way that only he was also. Just now she looked at him as though she knew exactly what he was thinking.

"What will Fanny do now?" Tom Fletcher asked.

"I think she will return to her people in Pennsylvania," Mr. McFall said, in his rain-barrel voice. Mr. McFall always had an opinion on everything, right or wrong.

"That is what I will advise her to do when I go there on

my way back to the Citadel"—the Citadel being the PM Ranch home place. "We all must see that she realizes as much as possible from the sale of Joe's ranch and its assets."

Dr. Prim asked if the shoot-out at Cooper's sawmill was to be reported to Sheriff Smith.

"I will be going there directly," Johnny said. "There is going to be no more Regulatoring here."

"Is that wise, Johnny?" Mrs. Maginnis asked, with her eyes fixed on him.

"We had better do things right, ma'am."

Mr. Maginnis nodded in his ponderous way. "You are absolutely correct, Johnny. We must show by our every action our belief in the processes of the law."

He saw Dr. Prim roll his eyes at Tom Fletcher.

"Would you have Johnny risk his safety to show our belief in the law, Frank?" Mrs. Maginnis said.

"Yes, my dear, I would." Mr. Maginnis laid a heavy paw on Johnny's shoulder. "And I must believe that if we act as though we honor the law in Madison County, that that honor will have its force."

"I hear it that Governor Dickey is to be replaced by another man," Penn McFall said.

While they were talking about that in their way that never really came to any point, Johnny took his hat and left. He crossed the street to the courthouse and climbed to Pogie Smith's office on the second floor.

The sheriff was a slight, short-legged duck of about fifty, with eyes so far apart he appeared to be looking at two things at once, and short-cropped, gray whiskers yellowed at the corners of his mouth from chewing tobacco. A silver star with the brass showing through was pinned to his vest. Sometimes he was called Cap from the rank he had held in the war. It was well known that he and Ran Boland and Judge Arthur had been in the California bunch that was ambushed at Apache Pass by Cochise and Mangas Coloradas. It was like that fight gave them a ticket to do what they saw fit forever.

Pogie sat with one buttock braced on the corner of his desk, his deputy, George Kimball, in a straight chair tilted against the wall. The windows of the sheriff's office looked out on the street, the hotel across it, the Maginnis house down one way and the Boland & Perkins store the other. Pogie Smith had a good view of what went on in Madison.

"You just write up a deposition and sign her, Johnny," he said. "Can you write?"

He said he could write.

"Write her up and sign her. I expect Jimmy's deposition will be about the same, and Chad's; who else? Carlito Rivera? What about Mrs. Cooper at the mill?"

"I don't expect she had a handle on what was happening."

"So you and Joe and these others was sitting at dinner in the kitchen there when you saw Clay riding up, is that right?" Pogie squinted at him down his cocked-up nose. "Tell me this, Johnny: what were you and Joe and these other south-county fellows *doing* there at Cooper's mill?"

"Looking for Clay Mortenson."

Pogie laughed right out, and when George Kimball had seen it was not only all right to laugh but probably required, he let out a chuckle also. He was a slight, tight-wired man whose boots didn't touch the floor when he leaned back in his chair. As Johnny knew it, Pogie had been appointed sheriff by Governor Dickey pending an election that had never been held, and Pogie had appointed George Kimball deputy. No doubt Ran Boland was consulted in both appointments. So they were only Regulators in office, and there wasn't much real law in the county to honor. The complications of that made him feel shaky.

"You are a one, Johnny-A!" Pogie said. "A man gets so used to hearing lies in this office he can't believe his ears when the truth is told."

He waited for the two of them to finish laughing. Pogie shot a long squirt of brown juice into the spittoon.

"Well, Johnny, I guess a man's been known to attack four armed men looking for him, but I thought you was one that didn't believe it."

"I saw both," he said. "Both of them. This one happened that way, since we are talking truth."

Pogie's face braced into the squint again. "Now, Johnny, just why was you and Joe and them out looking for Clay Mortenson?"

"Arrest him for murdering Mr. Martin Turnbull."

"Well, what *authority* was you carrying? A warrant? I mean, Sheriff Timmons being relieved of his job . . ."

"Afraid you'd have to talk to Joe about that."

They both grinned. He didn't like either one of them

one bit, but he had been put off by the crowd at Maginnis's this time too. They had stunk of fear and confusion. These stank of smugness. Being all alone made him feel shaky, and at the same time he felt so much his own-owned person that it was like being wrapped in oiled silk.

Pogie rocked forward and back on the corner of his desk, his jaw moving in and out with his chaw like a camel's. "Looks to me like things have about canceled themself, Johnny. What would you say to a little chin with Mr. Boland, maybe everything could get itself straightened out. Might be worth your while."

"Might be at that," he said. If you talked to people like Pogie much, you would get used to never saying a thing straight. George Kimball leaned forward until all four chair legs touched the floor.

"You wouldn't mind walking over to the store, would you?" Pogie said. "Ran is a sick man and don't get out much." Both of them rose to stand looking at him. It was easy to give them relief saying he wouldn't mind walking across the street.

Going back downstairs took a bit of managing, for Johnny preferred to bring up the rear in this company. George Kimball threw nervous glances back at him as they kicked through the dust of the street. In the dim interior of the store was a long counter with bolts of cloth on it and stacks of shirts and trousers, the old clerk holding down the far end. Beyond him were three store hard cases, all with their heads turned toward him, one lanky duck with a shotgun and two others hunched over motionless like he had frozen them flat in their tracks, coming in off the street like that.

Pogie asked him to wait while he went upstairs, see if Mr. Boland was feeling well enough for a talk—ailing as he was.

He waited with George Kimball, keeping one eye on the three down at the end of the store while he moved to the counter where there was a little chest of drawers that held sewing supplies. He pulled out the little drawers to handle the spools of thread, taking pleasure in the colors—pinks and blues, reds and oranges. There were neat envelopes of needles also.

"Johnny," George said. He looked up to see Pogie beckoning from the stairs. He took his time replacing the spools and packets, then climbed the steps with the clerk, George, and the other three watching him.

Pogie showed him in a door to a room with windows that had the opposite sweep of those of the sheriff's office. Mr. Boland sat in a chair swung away from a pigeonhole desk as big as an organ, fat legs splayed apart so his belly could hang between his thighs above polished high-button shoes. A cane leaned against the arm of his chair. Spectacles were perched on his nose, with blinking old tortoise eyes behind them.

"So this is the chap they call Johnny-A!" Mr. Boland struggled to his feet to lean one hand on the head of his cane and extend the other. Johnny reached out to give the fat, cold hand a shake.

"How do, sir? Sheriff said you might want to talk to me."

Boland slumped back down in his chair again, twist of pain griping his face and, with it, disgust. Johnny thought the disgust must be at that gross, unmanageable body dying. He had a clear sense of what it must be like—the mind still capable and clear, but the body that supported it disintegrating. A person then became two people, the one hating and disgusted with the other, and the other resenting the one. Not only that, but just when he had everything in the county running his way, here comes Mr. Maginnis and Mr. Turnbull raising a dust, and now a wind was blowing that would not quit. All that hate, disgust, and resentment behind the courteous fraud of Mr. Boland's exterior.

Mr. Boland called out, "Henry, would you come in a moment, please!"

Appearing promptly in the far doorway was the Irish-looking fellow with the crippled arm, Mr. Boland's new partner. Johnny felt another flashing of hatred and resentment in this one also, but radiating outward instead of inward. Henry Enders shook hands with him left-handed and cordially enough. He was in his shirtsleeves, the sleeve gartered upon his good, left arm. The white little hand at the end of his right arm was laid up against his chest, and he wore a revolver tucked into a shoulder holster under his bad arm. Everybody sat. Pogie related the sawmill shoot-up, to which Enders made no comment.

"Mister Angell," Boland said. "How can we persuade you that you are working for the wrong people?"

"I believe you would have to show me that it was them sent out to kill Mr. Turnbull."

He was pleased with the quality of silence that met that, Mr. Boland sucking his lips into a rosebud shape and Henry Enders radiating that fury he could feel through his oiled silk wrappings.

"Well, sir," Mr. Boland said, "wouldn't you say that was marked paid to the whole business, Joe and Clay finishing each other off like that, not to speak of Cory Helbush and Bert Fears?"

"Maybe that is the kind of trade a store makes a profit on," he said, "but it is no kind of trade." Which brought on another silence.

"Let me tell you, Mr. Angell," Mr. Boland said, "a great mistake was made when young Martin Turnbull was shot. A great tragedy! They say he started the shooting, I don't know, but a posse of that size should have been able to take a single man into custody. It was a great error. I can only try to understand some overzealous fellows thinking they were doing Henry and me a favor. But that sort of thing does no one a favor. Am I right, sir?"

"I believe you are right about that," he said. "But I will tell you something I heard from Don Teodoro Soto in Arioso. That the Davey Stovall gang was giving the *gente* down there fits. There were shootings and scaly times. He asked if you would help, and the Stovall gang straight off left for Texas. So he is grateful to you."

Mr. Boland smiled grandly.

"You told them to go and they got."

Mr. Boland didn't want to understand what he was talking about. "Those were different times, Mr. Angell. Simpler times than these. In many ways better times. Allow me to return to my original point, which was that this strife has run itself out with the killings at Cooper's mill."

"No, sir," he said. "Mr. Turnbull is still murdered."

"Of course everybody liked that young limey," Pogie Smith said quickly. "I liked him myself. The fact remains that there was a writ to be served, and a warrant for his arrest."

"Well, those ducks served it shooting him in the back of the head and then pounding his brains out with a rock. What kind of serving is that, Sheriff?"

Mr. Boland sighed like a ferry coming into a slip. "I have

admitted to you that it was a great mistake, my boy. But let us now discuss who the real culprit was."

He was supposed to ask about that.

"Maginnis!" Enders spat out.

"Yes, I am speaking of Frank Maginnis."

"I am a friend to Mr. Maginnis," Johnny said.

"And Mrs. Maginnis too, I'll bet," Henry Enders said.

He turned to face the crippled-arm man. "That is correct. And I hope I take your meaning correctly, or I would ask you to account for yourself."

Enders started, "Acc—" and left off. His ears had turned red.

Mr. Boland said, "I will grant you that Lawyer Maginnis is a very pleasant-seeming and friendly gentleman, but I ask you to consider the fact that there has been nothing but contention in the county since he and Mrs. Maginnis have arrived here.

"When my partner died—Tim Perkins, who was one of nature's true noblemen—his share of the store was bequeathed to me. Frank made a great, a totally unnecessary, fuss contesting the will in favor of some distant cousins of Tim's living in Maine. He got himself made executor of the estate, and I can only say that money passed through his hands that was never properly accounted for. Not to speak of certain ranches and herds that Tim had acquired. One of these, the Peters place, and several herds, were sold to Mr. Turnbull through Mr. Maginnis's offices. It was one of these that the sheriff, by court order, had gone to attach that tragic Friday."

"Not to speak of a new store in town," Johnny said, and wished he hadn't. He thought Mr. Boland could take an argument and turn it sideways and inside out and look at it from different ways until there was not much of it left.

"We will speak of it, by all means," Mr. Boland said easily. "But first let me add that it was Frank Maginnis who poisoned young Martin Turnbull's mind against us. Thus a contention arose, when cooperation is always the better course."

He said, "Well, Mr. Boland, it looks to me that things are not marked paid at all, and won't be until you have rid yourself of Mr. Maginnis."

"And his gunslinger too!" Enders almost shouted. "We

know how to handle cowboy fancy-shots here!" His good hand snapped to the butt of his revolver.

Johnny drew his own Colt and held it in his lap, finger pointing along the barrel at Henry Enders's top vest button.

"See here, now!" Pogie Smith said, half rising. "Hold on here!"

"Tell him to take his hand off his piece," Johnny said.

Pogie Smith was gazing at Johnny's Colt with his lips puckered into a kind of whistle.

"Henny, Henny," Boland said. "We are trying to have an amiable discussion here. Your temper does not help matters. Take his weapon, Pogie!"

The sheriff finished getting to his feet, stepped over to where Enders sat on the horsehair sofa, and relieved him of his revolver.

Enders seemed bursting with fury, a crazy man; but Johnny had a sense that this scene had been contrived to frighten him of the violence in Enders and to assure him of Mr. Boland's good will in case that would bring him around. He thought they would also offer him money.

Mr. Boland sat with his jowls jiggling with disapproval, sighing and clicking. "You're a young fellow still, Mr. Angell. Eighteen? Nineteen? With a young man's loyalties, and a young man's needs. I am prepared to offer you five hundred dollars if you will depart from the Territory. I'm certain that the charges that have been instituted against you can be voided! I would strongly recommend California as a place where an ambitious young man may build his future. What do you say to that, my boy?"

"Sounds like a generous offer to me," Pogie Smith said.

"I guess I will stick it out here. Interested in seeing how things work out."

"Don't be a stubborn fool, Mr. Angell! Take my advice and clear out."

Johnny pushed to his feet. "There's things I want to know yet. Like your saying it was just some overeager fellows thinking to do you a favor. That is one way of looking at it. But there are others, you see."

There was another of the digestive silences, before Mr. Boland cleared his throat. "And what are the others, my boy?"

"Well, for instance, there is Davey Stovall and that crew

clearing out when you said to, which means a word from you carries a pretty good freight. And there is my being offered five hundred dollars to clear out. So it may be that the whole thing was rigged like that, only you could think of it as favors. Papers from Mr. MacLennon and the judge, and the sheriff picking up the kind of posse it was. Rigged all the way. There are some that hold that that is the way it was."

"And you are one!" Henry Enders said in a strained voice like his collar had got too tight.

"I am one who is trying to find out what the true fact is."

"Ah, what is truth?" Mr. Boland said.

"Yes, sir, that is what Pilate said. But he did not care much about anything, did he?" Johnny excused himself and walked out past Pogie and down the steps to where George Kimball was sitting in a chair, looking up at him, and the clerk was waiting on a farm woman in a bonnet. The other three were hunched up together like he'd caught them stealing candy—all of them watching him without a word spoken as he passed by them, heading outside into the brilliance of the street.

That was a thing to remember, coming half-blind out of a dim place into the sun glare.

He sat in the cool patio with Mr. Maginnis, listening to Mrs. Maginnis playing the piano, some tune with a melody so long and flowing it seemed to drift in the room like silk scarves. It was a different kind of melody from the ones they played in the bunkhouse—mouth harp, guitar, and sometimes banjo, with Pard beating time on a bucket bottom—or the kind of old-favorite songs Lieutenant Cutler had played that time. He listened to the soft pat of the serving woman's slippers as she passed over the tiles inside the glass-paned doors. Mr. Maginnis had his legs crossed, one gaitered shoe waggling out of rhythm to the piano, a cigar clasped in his knuckles like a billiards cue. He tapped ashes into a big pot of ferns. Johnny respected and trusted him except for those queer froggy eyeballs.

"Will you go on my payroll, Johnny? I must go up to Santa Fe for a week, legal business. I would like it if you'd look after the place here, keep Mrs. Maginnis company."

"Surely," he said, "my pleasure." Fanny Peake was staying

with the Batesons, who would look after her and the boy until they left for Pennsylvania.

Mr. Maginnis sucked on his cigar and exhaled smoke. "I have been in correspondence with Martin's brother," he went on, "in Manchester, England. He has connections with the Foreign Office. Questions of an international nature are being asked. I think the governor may be asked for some explanations. I would not be surprised, in fact, if he tenders his resignation. Such is the rumor.

"Mr. James Turnbull also intimates that funds may be forthcoming for the pursuit of justice. You are aware that the Santa Fe Ring is the parent of the Madison Ring, and Ran Boland enjoys the protection and financial support of Jake Weber. In addition to his post as U.S. attorney, Weber is a partner in one of the two powerful law firms of Santa Fe. I have reason to believe the other firm may be interested in taking a bite out of his hide, and I'm going to Santa Fe to confer with them."

The frog eyes rested on Johnny speculatively, a hard, flecked, golden glitter to them. It made him nervous to remember what Mr. Boland had said were the causes of his quarrel with Mr. Maginnis, for there was no doubt that Mr. and Mrs. Maginnis liked money and lived well.

"I cannot imagine that there is anything to fear here," Mr. Maginnis continued, crossing his legs the other way to show the other gaitered shoe. He wore a heavy tweed suit and vest, with a gold chain laid over the beginnings of a corporation. The suit looked so hot Johnny took out his handkerchief to wipe his own forehead.

"I think our enemies may be reconsidering the fruits of violence. In any case, Johnny, Manuel has a loaded shotgun in his quarters, and there are arms in the stables. Mrs. Maginnis is bound to be nervous with me gone, so I will ask you to keep her spirits up. She enjoys a game of double solitaire of an evening."

"I do admire listening to her at the piano. She will have to teach me solitaire."

Just then the piano fell silent, and Mrs. Maginnis appeared in the doorway. She raised one slim arm to lean on the jamb, and smiled down at the two of them a step lower. Her dark hair framed her face with its high, flushed cheekbones and the flat planes beneath them, her lips folding out with her smile, taut upper, full lower. Her deep bosom rose and fell in her violet-purple gown as though from the exertions of her playing.

"Frank is leaving me for a week, Johnny!"

"I will not believe that justice cannot be found in the Territory," Mr. Maginnis said, in his voice that sounded as though he were addressing a packed hall. He tapped his cigar into the fern pot. "It has not been proven to me yet," he said, "although many have warned me."

"Well, I will be staying here to look after you, Mrs. Maginnis."

"Oh, that's good, Johnny!" she said, smiling at him, both of them smiling at him.

Dr. Prim came for supper, a plump, florid, very polite man with sharp little eyes glinting behind thick spectacles. The four of them ate at one end of the big Mex-carved table. Johnny watched carefully how Mrs. Maginnis used her knife and fork, and how she set them down after use, she and Dr. Prim considerably more refined than Mr. Maginnis, who left his utensils propped off the side of his plate like the hands of a clock, and tucked his napkin in at the top of his vest.

After supper Mr. Maginnis disappeared into his office, and Johnny watched Mrs. Maginnis and the doctor play double solitaire at a low table just big enough for all the cards laid out, the doctor's big, clean, black-haired hands and Mrs. Maginnis's slim ivory ones darting out to slap down cards. They laughed at their game, and it seemed a precious thing to him, laughing like that with Mrs. Maginnis, with her sparkling eyes and a high flush on her cheeks. They talked about Lieutenant Cutler, whose wife had been captured by Nahuaques in their bustout and who had gone off her head.

"Was she—" Mrs. Maginnis said, watching her hands as they swiftly dealt the cards. "Did they—"

"That is one bestiality that is not their practice," Dr. Prim said. "Their religion forbids it. But she was forced to witness the torture of her lover."

"I understand Pat is drinking heavily," Mrs. Maginnis said.

"I have heard that is the case from Dr. Reilly," Dr. Prim said, laying out his cards in the neat row.

When Mr. Maginnis returned they talked about Dr. Prim's letter to the President in Washington about the mur-

der of Martin Turnbull. There had not yet been a reply. The
doctor and the President had gone to school together back
East and had kept up a correspondence since.

"I cannot believe he will continue to countenance the
state of affairs I have described to him," the doctor said
grimly. "I have never asked for a favor for myself, and I ask
none now. I only ask his examination into a poisonous situation." He took out his fat watch, frowned at it, and said he
must be going home.

Mr. Maginnis, planning to leave at first light, went to
tend to his packing, leaving Johnny listening to Mrs. Maginnis
playing the piano. She seemed unaware of him, swaying as
she placed her ivory hands right and left, sometimes hum-
ming a phrase. He nodded off in his chair, waking with a jerk
like coming out of a dimness into sudden light. He rose and
announced that he must go to bed or his eyes would drop
out.

She showed him his room, preceding him down a hallway with the lamplight throwing giant shadows on the
whitewashed walls. It was a little room—a door, window, bed,
and a washstand with a basin, pitcher and folded towel on it.
In the close space he breathed the violet scent of her. "Good
night, Johnny," she said, and was gone, leaving the lamp
behind her. He fell into bed and down a black chute. In his
dreams a piano tinkled distantly.

He wakened to first light and activity in the corral
outside his window, a breath of dust filtering through, and
Mr. Maginnis's voice in a long monologue. He had drifted
back to sleep when he heard the opening squeak of the door,
and he jerked up to snatch at his Colt hanging in its holster
from the bedpost.

"It is I," Mrs. Maginnis whispered. He sat up with the
sheet pulled up over his bare chest as she seated herself on
the foot of the bed, small pressure on the mattress beneath
him as she did so. "Frank has gone," she said in a normal
voice, a dark figure against the gray light from the window.

"I heard him getting off."

She sat looking at him; he couldn't see her features yet,
silhouetted there like a madonna.

"Think he can accomplish anything in Santa Fe?" he
hurried to say. He was shivering.

"I suppose it is worth his efforts. He is a dear, foolish man, but a fine one."

"Yes, ma'am, he is that!" He tried to get a grip on his belly to stop the shivering. "He is surely set on justice," he said.

She laughed a little. "Sometimes I'm afraid I play a very second fiddle to that blindfolded lady!"

"Beautiful ladies in Mr. Maginnis's life," he managed, and was pleased that she laughed again.

"That's very nice, Johnny!" Now he could make her out better, sitting with her head bowed. After a time she said, "They will kill him. They hate him so much." In the increasing light he could see the pale plane of her cheek beneath her pinned-up hair. She wore a blue robe. Her hands were clasped in her lap.

"But you, Johnny-A," she said, "you are no longer a boy, are you?"

"No, ma'am."

"It is very noticeable. Once, in Florence—Italy—I saw some sculptures by the great sculptor Michelangelo. Michael Angel!" she said and laughed. "They were incomplete, men emerging from great blocks of marble. Coming out of the stone to *be*come. It is like that."

He didn't know what to say. She was rubbing her arms as though she was cold, as though she was shivering also.

She said, "I thought it was Joe Peake coming out of the marble but I was wrong. It was Johnny Angell."

She rose suddenly against the pale rectangle of the window and moved to the black vertical of the doorway. Then she was gone and the door pulled closed behind her. He lay back on the bed panting once, his hands jammed down over his groin.

He was an old Mex with a white mustache and a bald head, his hat in his hands. "There is a thing I must tell you, Juanito."

Johnny moved with him across to the far side of the corral from where Manuel was pitchforking horse turds into a wooden-sided wheelbarrow. In the street a freighter was passing, the ox team raising dust, the top half of the high, white wagon cover sliding along the top of the adobe wall.

"They will shoot the *abogado* when he returns from Santa Fe," the old man said.

"How is this known, señor?"

"My cousin has heard this at the store, where he washes the floors each morning. He heard this spoken of this very morning."

"Who?" he asked, leaning against the wall with a boot propped up on two stacked 'dobes. He could listen to this with a quiet mind, where earlier he had been shivering like a pup with the pip.

"Señor Enders and the sheriff and Jesse Clary, Juanito. These, he is certain. Others also, but he is not certain."

Jesse'd been in Texas for a good while working for Boland's enterprises there, and if he'd been called back it probably tallied out with what this bird was saying. Jesse-Jay had always been what the Mexes called "hard to the *gente*," which might be one reason for this information coming his way, who had always been friend to them.

"Did your cousin hear where this was to be, señor?"

"In this very place! A man will watch for Señor Maginnis returning past Sheepshead Hill. Then they will become ready. They will shoot him here, just outside the wall. There. They laughed when they said it should be there."

"I will get you some money for this favor, señor."

"It is unnecessary, Juanito. We do this for you, and the *abogado*. You will send to warn him, then?"

"That, and maybe we will be waiting here."

"There are young men who will come, if it is necessary. These men are not friends of the *gente*."

"Your name, señor?"

"Jesús Cárdenas. They will know where to find me at the González store." He waved a hand in the direction of the Mex *tienda*, standing there with his broken-down boots set apart. He clapped his hat back on his head, a bleak grin opening beneath his white mustache. "So, perhaps you will surprise these evil ones, Juanito!"

"Something," he said. "Thank you, Señor Cárdenas. Señor Maginnis will know of this also."

"One knows that what you decide will be well done, Juanito," the old man said. He saluted and trotted off across the corral yard.

Johnny waited for Mr. Maginnis in San Elizario, halfway

to Santa Fe. He had brought along a spare Springfield and a
Colt, although probably the lawyer would refuse to arm
himself. He had not told Mrs. Maginnis of this danger. He
was seated on the old buggy seat resting on its springs in
front of the cantina when Maginnis rode down the dusty track
toward him, city-suited on his black gelding, laden mule in
train.

Maginnis looked at him with surprise from under the
brim of his hat, then with displeasure. "What brings you
here?"

"Waiting for you, sir," he said. He helped Mr. Maginnis
secure his animals to the rail. Inside the cantina, over bottles
of El Paso beer, he told the lawyer what he had learned, and
his plans.

Maginnis stared at him with his lips pushed out in a
pout. "What if I do not choose to believe this tale you bring
me?"

"Well, sir, believe it or don't. But I am asking to ride
into town with you, and for you to come in around the back
way."

"I will not do that!"

"Front way then."

"What if I choose to consider these preparations presumptuous?"

"You left me to take care of Mrs. Maginnis. I am trying
to take care she is not Widow Maginnis."

"It is my policy to believe in the legal processes of this
territory until I have clear evidence to the contrary!"

"Yes, sir, you have got that with Mr. Turnbull shot dead."

Mr. Maginnis took a long pull on his beer and wiped the
back of his hand across his lips. "Some rumor circulated by a
Mexican who probably didn't understand what he was hearing."

"Yes, sir. But maybe did."

Down toward the door the Mex barkeep was leaning on
the bar gazing into the slant of sunlight from the street.
Twists of flypaper clotted with flies curled down from the
rafters. Maginnis set his bottle down with a sharp rap.

"I propose to ride into Madison as though no doubts had
been brought to my mind!"

Johnny had found that it was possible to dislike a man
while admiring him, but he knew that Mr. Maginnis was

frightened. "Yes, sir," he said. "But I propose to ride right along with you."

"Very well, then."

It was mid-afternoon when they passed around the low rise of ground with its north-facing rocky outcrop like a sheep's face. The river cut in close to the Santa Fe road there, and they halted to water the animals. Johnny saw no sign of a spy departing for town with the news of Mr. Maginnis's arrival, but his forehead prickled with the sensation of being watched. Mr. Maginnis had been sullen and silent all afternoon. The sun slipped down the sky, the heat encasing Johnny like a wool blanket, and frequently he fanned his face with his hat. In his heavy suit the lawyer seemed impervious to the heat. Whenever the road wound close to the river, there was a hint of cool breathing up out of the willows.

They rode past the first houses of Madison, Mex 'dobes, brown children playing along the sides of the road, and plump brown women hanging out washing. Four men standing on the veranda of the González *tienda* watched them pass. He recognized Jesús Cárdenas by his white mustache and raised a finger to tip the brim of his hat. He unshipped one of the Springfields and held it on a slant before him, Mr. Maginnis riding ten yards ahead of him, trailing the pack animal. Two stubborn mules, he thought, the second with its neck stretched by the lead rope, the first gazing straight ahead with an expression he didn't have to see to know.

Two freight wagons were drawn up outside Boland & Perkins, and, further along, farm wagons were parked under the trees. Sun glinted pinkly on the second-story windows of the courthouse, brown haunches of horses tethered there. He found his lips puckered to a silent whistle as he followed Mr. Maginnis more closely toward his house, its red tile roof just showing now through the trees.

He kept an eye turning from one possible cover to another: the windows of the courthouse, the deep shadow of its entry, the far side of its steps, a buggy stationed before the hotel, the vacant space where a house had burned, dead trees surrounding the lonely brick chimney, thick brush there. He glanced again at those six steps up to the courthouse doorway.

"Keep an eye on that brushy place right over there," he said, just loud enough for Mr. Maginnis to hear. The other paid him no heed; he had not turned his head right or left yet that Johnny had seen. The wall along the street side of the corral came into view, the whitewashed adobe gray in shadow. In this very place, Jesús Cárdenas had said; they had laughed that it would be there. He rode up almost alongside Mr. Maginnis, maybe a hundred feet to go before the wall—

He spotted one in the brush close by the burnt-out chimney, dark hat in a tangle of foliage that reminded him of a grackle glimpsed in a pear tree. There would be a second one at least. Mr. Maginnis was slanting his mule past the wall toward the gate. He saw the thin gleam of a rifle barrel ease up over the top courthouse step.

He snapped his rifle to his cheek and fired twice, a hair before smoke showed above the step. He cranked one off at the man in the brush, set spurs to surge up beside Mr. Maginnis and slam over against him, knocking him from the saddle and bearing him down in a bellowing tangle. He scrambled up to brace his rifle on the gelding's saddle, but now there was silence, no movement except his own horse trotting riderless on down the street.

He hustled the lawyer in through the crack in the corral gate, Pard's pale face there, inside three others with rifles propped over the top of the wall. Pard jammed the gate closed behind him.

"You sure got that one by the chimney!" Carlito called to him. "I never even saw him, Juanito!"

"Where was the other one?" Pard yelled.

"By the courthouse steps."

Maginnis slumped against the wall just inside the gate, hat gone, dust all over the front of his suit, one hand inside his coat as though making certain his heart was still beating. He was puffing his cheeks and blowing his breath out as though he had almost drowned. Manuel Torres came out of the house with a shotgun, behind them Mrs. Maginnis's face a pale heart shape peering out.

"Nobody hurt?" Johnny said loudly.

Nobody hurt on this side of the street, except Mr. Maginnis's dignity; the lawyer also looked as though he had had a scare that would last awhile. "You were right, Johnny," he said as though it came hard to say it.

*   *   *

A hard case pal of Jesse Clary's was dead in the bushes by the old chimney. Dead behind the courthouse steps, hunched over his Winchester, was Sheriff Pogie Smith.

Mr. Maginnis sat slumped in his chair, legs stretched out before him. He still had hardly brushed the dust from his suit. His head hung like a bulldog's and he continually puffed his cheeks and blew his breath out noisily like he was having difficulty getting enough air. Johnny stood beside his chair, looking out at twelve or fifteen men who had gathered in the parlor. Mrs. Maginnis was at the piano, playing; he wished she wasn't.

"It is a complete breakdown of the judicial and police systems," Mr. Maginnis said, in his short-of-breath voice. "It is disorder at its worst, it is malevolent disorder! I intend to fight."

"Go it, Lawyer!" someone called out—Pard, Johnny saw. He felt a bit foolish standing beside Mr. Maginnis like a lamppost.

"I am endangered," Mr. Maginnis went on. "So is Johnny, here—as much as I! Johnny has killed the sheriff. The sheriff of this county was not only party to a conspiracy to murder, he was a hired murderer himself! We are all in danger. When Martin Turnbull was murdered I did not understand the extent of the evil that has infected this county. The scales have been removed from my eyes. I owe my life to this young man!" He laid a heavy hand on Johnny's arm and left it gripping there.

"Yes, sir, but what are we going to do?" someone called out from back.

"There are many *gente* who will come, Señor Maginnis," one of the Mexes said.

"Good—Good—I believe our only course is one of action, gentlemen!"

"What kind of action is that, Mr. Maginnis?" Paul Tuttle asked.

Johnny was glad when Mr. Maginnis released his arm. The lawyer straightened in his chair and stopped the silly business of blowing out his cheeks like that. He wished Mrs. Maginnis would stop playing the kind of music she was playing.

Mr. Maginnis said, "It is clear that there is no coherent system of law in the county. I propose that we then take the law into our own just hands. I propose that a force be

gathered from the honest citizens of this county to arrest Mr.
Boland, Mr. Enders, Mr. MacLennon, Judge Arthur—"

"Jesse Clary too!"

"George Kimball!"

"Yes, yes, all those we know to have been involved in
this latest outrage," Mr. Maginnis said, holding up his hands
for order. "We will take them to Sante Fe to the governor—"

"Better take him along too!" There was broken-off laughter.

"I do not mean Governor Dickey. A new governor has
been appointed by the President of the United States!"

Just when Johnny was wondering what Mr. Maginnis
thought he was using for authority, the lawyer continued.
"We will present our malefactors to this new governor. He
will have to face the problems of this county, then, for he will
have them on his hands! He will have to judge!" He paused
dramatically, before he said, "And I must believe that he will
see where justice lies!"

There was a silence. A moment later everybody began
talking at once. Johnny grimaced at Mrs. Maginnis, swaying
at the piano with her loud pedal on. Mr. Maginnis rose to his
feet with his arms held up again. He was talking about
collecting an army against the malefactors, south-county men,
Anglo and *gente*. County versus town. Johnny was uneasy
with the sound of it, but a lot of folks would be ready to load
up and ride out against the store. And some for the store,
that was a fact too.

"They will be collecting fellows too," he managed to get
in. Mr. Maginnis didn't pay any attention.

"We will not seek violence," Mr. Maginnis was saying in
his speaking-hall voice, while Mrs. Maginnis played loud
music on the piano. "But if violence comes, we will be ready
for it!"

It had a bad sound of Regulatoring to it, but Johnny did
not see what else they could do here. Put up with or fight.

15

Colonel Dougal, whiskers bristling, strode up and down in his office before his junior officers, the contract surgeon, the major, and Cutler. He made a gesture as of fitting a too-small jacket to his back, fists clenched.

"Served with me in the Wilderness!" Dougal said. "Brevetted captain there. Minié ball through his shoulder there! Doctoring then wasn't what it is now, I can tell you—eh, Dr. Reilly? But he came through. To be murdered by one of Maginnis's gunmen, by God! Wife—sweet, plump little woman—three children! By God, this bill will be paid! By God, I will not sit here twiddling my thumbs in this instance! His deputy has taken over, man named Kimball. By God, we will offer Sheriff Kimball every cooperation! Major, you will take A troop and ride down these murderers. Bring them in to Sheriff Kimball!"

Cutler had known that Dougal and the sheriff had served in the same regiment late in the war, but he had not expected the colonel to be galvanized into such a fury by the shooting. Usually it was the major who proposed violent action, and the colonel who prudently pulled back from it. He said, "May I remind the colonel of General Order 28?"

Dougal halted and swung to face him, chin whiskers erect with rage. Cutler was aware of other eyes sliding toward him, the major seated, Jud Farrier with a boot resting on a chair rung, Petey Olin standing at a stern parade rest, Bernie Reilly frowning warningly. Bunch, not present.

"I will interpret the General Orders on this post, Mister Barracks-Room Lawyer!" the colonel said. He paced and turned, paced and turned. Cutler thought he could deflect the colonel if he played it right. He was, after all, an aide-de-camp of the general's. General Order 28 forbade the involvement of troops in civilian quarrels.

"I suppose you will tattle to General Yeager, Mr. Cutler?" the colonel said, hunched facing him with his fists balled.

"No, sir."

"No, sir; no, sir; what do you mean, no, sir?"

"I will not 'tattle,' sir." He supposed in future time he might find this amusing to remember; now it made him feel as though he had been punched in the belly.

The colonel flung himself down in his chair, glaring. "I can tell you that you are not quite the general's pet you have been, mister. Since your Injuns showed their true colors."

"What colors were those, sir?"

Dougal swung around and leaned forward until his chin whiskers brushed the desk top. "Mutiny, mister! Perhaps you have already forgotten the execution at which you presided!"

"One man was hanged, yes, sir."

"Convicted of mutiny, am I right, Mr. Cutler?"

He hesitated for what would seem a pause of consideration before he said, "Yes, sir."

The admission appeared to dissipate the colonel's wrath, which was his purpose here, was it not? The colonel called for his orderly who stepped into the room, saluting. "A bottle of whiskey and glasses, Corporal!"

Bernie Reilly glanced at Cutler and shook his head once. The colonel was staring at him in his crouched-to-spring stance, bright-eyed. Some tactic here. The officers waited. The other version of the shoot-out in Madison had the sheriff and a couple of gunmen setting up an ambush for Frank Maginnis, only to run into an ambush themselves.

Whiskey was produced, and Roberts poured portions into the glasses. Dougal rose, holding up his glass. "To our friends in Madison!"

The others raised and drank, who had as readily toasted General Yeager's denunciation of the Indian Rings at Ojo Azul. Was it military hypocrisy, or merely military failure to make connections? Cutler folded his arms. Dougal's nostrils flared white. Disloyalty to old friends!

"I notice you do not participate in this toast, Mr. Cutler. Have you at last forsworn the fruits of the grain?" He looked pleased at his sally.

"I believe you are offering a toast to the Madison Ring, sir."

"I resent your designation of our friends as a Ring, mister! Our friends who were your friends also, until you discovered a more attractive Ring. Moreover, you are maligning men who have served their nation in the war!"

"Maligning, sir?"

"Yes, maligning! These men who have served their country well deserve something for their services! They are in business to make money. The Bureau of Indian Affairs and the Department of the Army *want* them to make money, Mr. Cutler, so they will continue to serve the Indian reservations and these godforsaken military posts. I tell you, without the store we would get mighty hungry out here."

The colonel straightened at his desk and peered around at his officers. "And I will tell you gentlemen something else. Something that I believe Mr. Cutler knows very well, but chooses to dissemble for reasons of his own. We are not here this close to the Mexican border because some so-called Ring chooses that we be here for its profit. Gentlemen, another war with Mexico is a certainty. I believe that we are here to lead the attack that will acquire for this great nation the Mexican states of Chihuahua and Sonora. And what do you say to this, gentlemen?"

"Praise be!" Major Symonds said.

"May we ask how you know this, Colonel?" Captain Smithers asked. He was turning his fat gold Academy ring on his finger.

The colonel's hard little eyes fastened upon Cutler again. "I believe Mr. Cutler knows, since he spends his time in the company of a certain general, on protracted scouts in northern Mexico. Eh, Cutler?"

He thought the expedition to Madison had been defused. "The Mexicans certainly do anticipate an invasion, sir." Out the window three blue-clad troopers were herding horses down the company street, manes blowing, heads bobbing, gleam of sun on brown haunches. The three men's bodies floated above the moving mass of horseflesh. It was a sight, like the first glimpse of the colors of the flag from the pass, that stirred him, as for a time María had loved the different bugle calls of the day—the few little splendors of military life that drowned in the dinginess and stupidity.

"One can understand certain loyalties you might have in the case of our southern neighbor," Dougal said spitefully. "Even in the case of your brown pets. But what can be said of your allegiance to a criminal troublemaker of lawyer?"

He was shocked at this new attack but maintained his silence.

"And his wife who is a public scandal," Dougal said.

"Sir! You will not malign Mrs. Maginnis in my presence!'

Dougal's face turned dark with blood. Symonds stared at Cutler almost cross-eyed: the colonel might detest him, but the major hated him implacably and abidingly. Bernie was moving his lips in a mime of caution. Petey Olin gazed sideways at him in horror.

"And just what do you mean by that, mister?" the colonel said.

"Things might be set in train we would both come to regret," he said. He tensed his muscles against the shake in his belly.

"And what might those things be, Lieutenant?"

"One would be for me to demand a court-martial so that my side of this matter might be examined by my fellow officers."

"And the other?"

"Would be for me to resign from the service and demand satisfaction." As always, he had gone too far; fat in the fire now, in what had begun as a decent cause. He was a poisoner of the wells he had, in the end, to drink from. He felt his heels come together to attention.

"You threaten me!" Dougal bellowed, jarring his chair back as he lurched to his feet. "I have been threatened, and you gentlemen are witness to it! You are under arrest, Mr. Cutler, general's pet or not, sir! You are confined to your quarters. Major Symonds, you will set a guard."

The major rose, swelling out his chest, scowling smugly. Cutler saluted and preceded him out the door. At least he had drawn the teeth of the expedition into Madison.

He sat in his chair in the darkness, trying to concentrate on Xenophon by lamplight. According to his modicum of Greek, that *Xeno-* must have to do with being a stranger, an enemy, up-country in Persia with every hand against you. At least the Greek mercenaries had known who they were and what they came from. Emily Helms thought she knew who he, Patrick Cutler, was—her seducer, the only man she would ever love and who consequently must love her also. Her latest scented, importunate letter lay in its stiff envelope on the little table beside his chair, beneath his service revolver in the cone of light from the lamp. He could hear the steps of the guard pacing the corridor outside his room, but he was listening for the rat. The rat was probably listening to the rustle of turning pages. They did not rustle regularly, since his concentration on the adventures of other troubled soldiers was affected by his listening for his rodent.

He heard it, in the corner past the doorway. He thought he could make out the pink reflective glare of its eyes. He let his hand holding the *Anabasis* droop to the table, released the book and slid his hand to the revolver's butt, cocking the piece as he lifted it. Humans were supposed to kill rats as their avowed enemies, but he would regret this fellow, the rustling progress, the pink glare, the nibbled edges of his boots, the neat rat turds deposited like payments here and there. Still he raised the revolver and sighted down the barrel.

Footsteps sounded in the corridor, a muttered conversation, three raps on his door. Bernie and Jud Farrier entered, gleaming buttons, stiff faces, Bernie's screwed up anxiously, Jud's long, sideburned, and dutiful. It gave him pleasure that they had come as Dougal's ambassadors, now that the colonel had had time to rethink his position. Farrier sat on the bed while Bernie remained standing. The lamplight made his eyes look like a bandit's mask.

Cutler placed the *Anabasis* on top of Emily Helms's letter. "Abe send you?" he asked.

"Well, Pat," Bernie said, "he realizes you've had a tragedy, you are under a strain, and so forth and so forth."

"He's going to let the whole thing pass, Pat," Jud said.

"I'm not."

"Oh, for Christ's sake!" Bernie said.

"What's he done about Madison?"

"The major's gone in with a detail to guard the store against looters. That's all."

"No military posse?"

"No more mention of that," Jud said.

"So your outrageous performance accomplished something, Pat," Bernie said. "But you'd accomplished that before

you challenged your commanding officer to a duel. Why mus
you always carry a thing beyond any bound of human
sympathy?"

He saw Bernie glance at the revolver on the table
Should he reassure them that it was only cocked to shoot a
rat, an action well within the bounds of human sympathy?
No.

"Pat," Bernie said, "sometime you're going to push him
so far he won't be able to back off. If for some reason you lose
General Yeager's . . . *support*, he would stack a court-martial
like a cold deck. Or if the colonel ever relinquished his
command to the Iron Major. Symonds wouldn't hesitate
generals or not. You push Abe too far, and then you won't let
him off the hook when *he* goes too far."

"I saved him from a violation of General Order 28. I
don't suppose he'll thank me."

"He's a lunatic on the subject of a Mexican war," Jud
said. "At least he got sidetracked onto that."

"You did threaten him," Bernie said, looking at Cutler
steadily. "I mean the Mrs. Maginnis business."

"He made her a proposal in the coarsest terms, Bernie
The old goat. He'd never bring that before a court."

Bernie and Jud glanced at each other. Bernie sighed and
said, "Pat, there are certainly rumors. Now it's that she's
carrying on with this boy gun-toter. You've heard them."

He managed a laugh. "I can't threaten all the rumor
bearers."

Farrier said quickly, "I think if you'd apologize he'd
forget the whole thing."

He shook his head.

"Don't be so damned self-righteous!" Bernie said.

"Let him stew. I've got a good book. Did you know that
the Battle of Cunaxa illustrates all the strengths and weaknesses
of cavalry warfare?"

When they had gone he went back to Xenophon with
even less attention, listening for the rustling, watching for the
pink eyes watching him out of the darkness, listening to the
pacing of his guard.

The next day he was relieved of his arrest, whether
because the colonel was afraid of offending General Yeager or
because Dougal realized he had been saved from a foolish
action, he had no way of knowing. The stated reason was that

word hád come from Sam Bunch that Caballito wanted to see Nantan Verdad at Bosque Alto.

Because of his trip to Mexico, he had not been to Bosque Alto for almost three weeks, since the tragically stupid killing of the Dreamer. He rode to the reservation by way of the sawmill where Joe Peake had been shot by one of Boland's gunmen, who had in turn been ventilated by Johnny Angell. Since then Johnny-A had also shot the sheriff, and Madison had become a powder keg, south-county ranchers swarming in to support Frank Maginnis, and the store also calling in its IOUs, with Henry Enders and a badman named Jesse Clary in command. Ran Boland was known to have departed for Tucson for medical treatment.

Urging Malcreado into the piney hills that sloped up from Cooper's Creek, where Caballito had established his *rancherías* more than ten miles from the agency, Cutler was aware of observation by the Sierra Verdes, brown bodies on brown horses glimpsed between tree trunks. One stood revealed on a bare hill, an arm raised and pointing.

Cutler altered his course to parallel that of his guide, and they passed between hills into a long valley. The grass flattened in long ripples in a little breeze blowing down-creek, and the floor of the valley was dotted with clumps of grazing cattle—the Sierra Verde herd. A wisp of smoke rose beyond a thickly wooded peninsula that ended in a tongue of boulders extending into the meadow.

His guide stopped at the meadow's edge, watching him as he headed on toward the smoke, Malcreado breaking into a swinging trot as he surged through the grass. Cattle turned blank faces, clumsily ran a few steps, then forgot their fright to muzzle down to the grass again. Rounding the point of rocks he came upon two wickiups covered with faded brown canvas. A fire unwound a curl of smoke between them. Naked brown children played there, and a squaw in her voluminous layers squatted on a flat rock by the creek, doing her washing. The Apache lounging in a camp chair by the fire was Caballito.

The chief rose in greeting, bare-torsoed, with the long Apache breechclout and high moccasins. His face was decorated with the horizontal stripes, and his hair hung to his shoulders, glossy and loose. He was unsmiling, eyes studying

Cutler not quite with hostility, mouth flat and bitter as a snapping turtle's as he inquired in Spanish of Nantan Tata's health and complained of not having seen him for many suns.

"My health is good, Nantan Caballito," Cutler said, dismounting and dropping his reins to the ground. "And the *nantan's* health?"

Caballito laid a hand on his chest over his heart. He was well except in that part.

Camp chairs were arranged facing each other. Cutler produced cigars, and the chief grunted with pleasure. He fished a coal from the fire with two sticks, and lit the cigars.

Leaning back contentedly, he commented that the white-eye did some things very well. The tobacco! He had heard that Nantan Verdad had gone to Mexico.

"I have taken my wife to her home in Sonora."

Did Nantan Verdad have no more liking for his Mexicana wife? Perhaps she could be traded for Cump-ten-ae's wife who was a captive of the Mexicans.

"She is mad, Nantan Caballito." He made the appropriate finger-to-temple gesture. "Driven mad by the terrible things done to her companions by evil Nahuaques. You have heard of this?"

Caballito had heard. He turned in profile to gaze off across the meadow, commenting that there were many women.

"The white-eye is permitted only one wife."

Caballito wondered about the wives of the blue soldiers who had been killed. Surely they must become the wives of others who already possessed wives. Moreover, he had heard that certain white-eyes to the north had many wives. What did Nantan Verdad have to say of that?

It came to Cutler that the chief, who was famous for his ambushes, also enjoyed the ambushes of conversation. If he could not understand Cutler's attempts to explain Mormonism, still he would enjoy Cutler's discomfiture well enough.

Changing the subject, Cutler asked what troubled Caballito's heart.

The chief squinted at the coal of his cigar, holding it upright so the smoke threaded upward past his nostrils. Many days he had gone to the mountain to pray that Ussen would speak. But today he had known that Nantan Verdad would come! And he had come!

Cutler waited for the *but.*

Caballito rose to stand half-crouched, his hand holding the cigar waving its smoke right and left. Nantan Lobo had promised that the Red Stripe People would remain at Bosque Alto. That they would receive their proper rations. That their cattle would remain their cattle. He straightened to fling a lordly hand in the direction of the herd. Was all this not true?

"I have promised these things for Nantan Lobo, yes."

Was it true that blue soldiers had killed the scout Be-jah-di? Why had this been done?

"He made promises he did not keep, and he shot at the blue soldiers in the fight of the Dreamer."

Caballito squinted at him through smoke. So the white-eye killed those who did not keep their promises.

Ambush. Cutler said, "It is like the number of wives of the white-eye. It is not always the same."

Not the same for the Indeh as for the white-eye, Caballito said.

Cutler sighed and said, "Tell me."

It seemed that Dipple had told Caballito that in White Father City they would soon decide that the Red Stripe People must be sent back to San Marcos. Also that their cattle would be taken away. Dipple had also said that Nantan Lobo had lost his power. Caballito sank back into his chair with the cigar clamped in his jaw and his fists clenched on his knees.

"Tell me how this conversation came about, please."

Caballito glowered at him.

"I think Nantan Caballito said something to Nantan Malojo that caused these things to be said."

The other aimed his cigar at Cutler like a pistol, spitting words: Everyone knew of these things! The wagons came to Bosque Alto full, moving slowly. The mules worked very hard! They brought the rations of the Nahuaques and the Red Stripe People, flour, coffee, salt, sugar—all except for the cattle, which came on their own feet to be slaughtered. But when the wagons returned to Madison they moved more swiftly. The mules did not work so hard.

"Because they are empty."

His face splitting with a white grin, Caballito waggled a negative finger at him. No, because the road led down instead of up!

"What does the *nantan* mean?"

The wagons brought supplies, but they also took supplies

away. Caballito had told Nantan Malojo that this was known. It was believed that Nantan Malojo counted so many Nahuaques and so many Sierra Verdes, but there were not so many as he counted. So some of the supplies returned in the wagons.

"Nantan Malojo was not pleased that this had been observed?"

Nantan Malojo had shouted and waved his arms, and said much. Was it true that Nantan Lobo had lost his power?

"It is not true."

Caballito nodded vigorously, his lips crinkling. So the blue soldiers would break Nantan Malojo's neck because of this lie.

Cutler saw that although Caballito had contrived an elaborate joke, his essential ferocity lurked at the corners of his grin. "I will speak with him," he said.

Caballito shrugged.

"I will tell him if he troubles your heart again I will break his neck."

"Only talk," Caballito said, folding his arms and glowering off across the meadow. The squaw was squatting by the fire now, and there was a smell of burning meat.

Caballito announced that he had had a dream. He had seen Joklinney in his dream, who had been thought dead, but was not dead. Joklinney would return soon from the white-eye prison.

It was a message, Cutler thought, for Sam Bunch. Caballito studied his face, still with a trace of the wolfish smile. Then he waved a hand to dissipate the cigar smoke and the subject as well.

"Here is food, amigo. You will eat."

The plump little squaw scurried over with the meat, with its delicious smell, on a platter of bark. It was a water rat, broiled whole, the skin half burned away exposing blackened flesh. The head had not been removed, nor the intestines. Apaches were not called gut-eaters for nothing. Cutler rose quickly.

"I must go to speak to Nantan Malojo!"

Caballito laughed and waved him off.

The Agency bordered on Bosque Alto Creek, stone structures in a broad L, the agent's house at the east end, set up on pilings adjoining the office, the store and warehouse ranged along the side of the corral, out of which the beeves were distributed each week. At the far corner of the yard was a flagpole with a droop of flag. A row of bucks was seated on the corral rail across the dusty area. A squaw carried a plump sack by a tumpline from her forehead, the men ignoring her as she passed them.

Dipple came onto the porch of the house in his vest and shirtsleeves as Cutler dismounted, draped his reins over the tie rail, and climbed the steps to confront him. "Caballito says you are threatening to send him back to San Marcos."

"It's possible," Dipple said, folded his arms, and stood at a slight backward slant. His walleye roved. Cutler was pleased to realize that the agent was afraid of him.

"General Yeager promised he would not have to live at San Marcos."

"The army does not determine the Bureau's policies, Lieutenant. The Bureau does. The policy of the Bureau is to concentrate the Apaches. It may be more convenient for the Sierra Verdes to be sent back to San Marcos than for them to remain here. There are strains with the Nahuaques. It may be that those strains contributed to the Dreamer troubles."

"Is that what you're telling the Bureau?"

Dipple did not answer, tilting his head and gazing down his nose. "Would you mind stepping back inside here?" Cutler said. "I have something private to tell you." Dipple retreated, Cutler following him closely. Just inside the door he removed his gauntlets from under his belt and slugged the agent full in the face. Dipple stumbled back, squalling, to trip and fall.

"What was that for?" he spluttered, rising to his hands and knees. He halted there as Cutler stood over him.

"So you wouldn't be embarrassed in front of your Injuns. That was for Lieutenant Helms, killed trying to get Caballito back on a reservation. Not to speak of dead enlisted."

"I'll report you to Colonel Dougal!"

"Do." He backed up a step so Dipple could rise, hand covering his cheek and nose, eye rolling. "You can tell him I'm threatening you too. If you cause Caballito to bust out of here, I'll kill you. That's a promise. The general's orders are for me to make sure Caballito stays on the reservation. I'll do what I have to do to see to that."

Dipple assumed the backward lean again. His face was blotched with red.

"You're still using the corrected weights?"

The agent nodded sulkily.

"What's this about loaded wagons heading back to Madison?"

"It's happened once or twice," Dipple said, with an elaborate shrug. "No room in the warehouse, so I'll send some things back for storage."

"Boland and Perkins storage?"

"That's right."

"Does this happen often?"

"Well, several times just lately."

"Let's have a look in the warehouse."

"As a matter of fact it's almost empty just now."

"Higher head count, is that it?"

"Two thousand five hundred and sixteen last week," Dipple said. He backed up a step when Cutler moved toward him again.

"Why more last week?"

"They come and go."

"You are supposed to report any large movements."

"In my judgment the movements have not been large enough to cause any concern."

"Let's take a look in the warehouse." He beckoned Dipple past him, and followed the agent outside and down the steps under the gaze of the Nahuaques perched on their rail like so many black-topknotted birds. The agent walked at a long-legged scissoring pace. At one side of the warehouse door was the window where the clerk passed out the rations to the squaws lined up to receive their flour, coffee, salt, sugar, and bleeding hunks of beef.

The warehouse was vast and dim, dirt-floored. The roof was held up by unpeeled log posts set upright on flat stones. Sawn boards had been nailed into ten-foot-square closets, a few of these partially filled with fat gunnysacks. The place smelled of flour and coffee.

Cutler gazed around him, waiting for his eyes to grow accustomed to the semidark. "I'm trying to imagine this so full you have to send wagonloads back to the store's warehouse."

"Well, of course it's not really *full*," Dipple said. "It's when those hundred-pound sacks have to be hoisted eight feet up that I send them back."

"What about not purchasing so many in the first place?" Dipple was silent.

"The fact is that the store is cheating the Agency and the Indians with your connivance."

"Sometimes I lend Mr. Boland back some of our supplies. You may depend on it that they are always returned. Not that it is any of your business."

"I believe you told me that once before," he said. Dipple stepped quickly back away from him as Cutler made a show of slapping his gauntlets against his leg. "I'm paying close attention to your business," he said. "I'm concerned with what kind of vise you are putting the Sierra Verdes into. Promises were made to Caballito to induce him to return to this country. One was that he wouldn't have to go to San Marcos again. Another was that they could keep their herd—"

"Their herd!" Dipple said. "There's no reason for the government to provide them with beef when they possess the finest herd in the county!"

"It was a promise! I made that promise to them for General Yeager. I made one to you just now!" He flourished the gauntlets, turned and stalked outside, blinking in the painful glare. The Indians on the rail watched him, and gazing back at them, he felt drained by futility. Caballito would bust off the reservation again for one good reason or another. Even if he succeeded in bullying Dipple, there was still the Bureau of Indian Affairs with its policy of concentration. There was still the Madison Ring and the Santa Fe Ring, greedy merchants, officers anxious for the advancement that only came with combat, civilians who detested army authority—so many forces.

En route back to the fort late that afternoon he met a buggy, a farmer in overalls, his sunbonneted wife, two towheaded children staring at him with round eyes. The farmer called to him, "Say, soljer, all hell is busted loose in town. You fellows had better git in there!"

The popping ahead reminded him of Chinese New Year in the San Francisco of his youth. He urged Malcreado on, feeling the same kind of reluctance in the Las Golondrinas horse that he felt in himself; yet still he tipped in his spurs and pressured with his thighs. In a lull in the firing the silence was oppressive. Now he could see the flagpole atop the courthouse cupola, the swing of tan road into Madison's main street. The tempo of rifle fire picked up again.

A train of three wagons, ox-drawn, plodded toward him, farmers, farmers' wives, farmers' children staring at him in strained-face fright as he trotted past them into the dust of their passage. Congealing in the dust was a blue-clad trooper on a gray horse, slant of his visor over his eyes, cartridge belt slanting across his chest, slant of carbine held out before him, inverse V of corporal's chevrons on his sleeve. Cutler reined Malcreado up short. The corporal saluted.

"What's going on, Corporal?"

"It's the war they've been talking about, sir! Colonel sent in a detail this morning to watch out for women and children. They got shot at, so B and E Troops come in. Colonel's down by that burnt-down house with the chimney, but you don't want to ride along the street there. That's where we got shot at. Maginnis's people it was, from his place there. Boland's people's in the store and in the courthouse and all around. Then further down there's another big bunch of Maginnis's, at the González store. He has brought in a pack of gunslingers to try to arrest the sheriff and the store people, take them up and deliver them to the new governor, but he has plain run into a buzz saw!'

Ducking, Cutler rode on past the courthouse, glimpse of faces mashed against the glass of the second-floor windows, rifle barrels poking out. He swung off the street where he could see the adobe walls and red tile roofs of the Maginnis house. Ahead of him mounted soldiers were milling. A Sibley had been pitched inside the rectangle of the burnt house, beside the solitary chimney. Colonel Abraham Dougal stood straddle-legged before the tent, jabbing a finger at the chest of Lieutenant Tupper.

The colonel glanced Cutler's way with an irritated twitch of his cheek and jabbed at Tupper's chest again. "You tell that rabble down at the González store that if they are not out of town in half an hour I propose to unlimber the mountain gun and start dropping rounds on them! I will not have a pack of south-county toughs coming in here adding to trouble-enough!"

"Yes, sir!" Tupper said, saluted, mounted, and started off at a trot. Cutler saw the canvas-booted gun on its trail, beside

he ammunition caisson. Horses were tethered further back,
a fire had been built, and there was a smell of boiling coffee.
Troopers stood waiting, no one lounging, hard, attentive
faces. The colonel swung toward him, Uncle Sam jut to his
chin whiskers. Cutler saluted.

"Well, mister!" Dougal said shrilly. "There is full-scale
insurrection in this place. We have been fired upon!"

"Yes, sir. I heard your ultimatum to Lieutenant Tupper. I
assume you've issued a similar one to the store gunmen."

"I have not, mister! They have been properly deputized
to keep the peace here."

"Then you have sealed the fate of the occupants of the
Maginnis house."

The colonel's face turned purple. "I have orders for *you*,
Mister Cutler! You will take a detail and approach the Maginnis
house. Presumably they will not shoot *you*. You will demand
their surrender to properly constituted authority!"

The firing picked up again and the colonel scowled
toward the street. Cutler said, "Sir, I'm certain the Maginnis
faction does not consider Deputy Kimball properly constituted authority."

"*Sheriff* Kimball, Mr. Cutler!"

"I would refuse to execute an order that would put
innocent people into absolute jeopardy!"

The Iron Major and Lieutenant Hotchkiss had come up.
The new adjutant was a lanky young man with a sweating
face. "By God—by God—" the colonel spluttered. "Direct
disobedience of an order, mister! Major, did you hear that?"

"Yes, sir," Symonds said, squinting one eye at Cutler as
though this was only to be expected. Soldiers were staring,
some of them drawing away from this disturbance among
their officers.

"I would ask that they surrender to *you*, Colonel,"
Cutler said.

There was another fusillade, the splintering crack of lead
against planking, squeal of a ricochet. The colonel folded his
arms on his chest and glared at Cutler more calmly.

"Very well, mister. Yes, that will do."

"And I'd rather go alone."

"Suit yourself," Dougal said, and turned away from him
to speak to Symonds. Cutler saw Hotchkiss gazing at him
with a queer mixed expression of amazement and respect.

He made his way through the brush to the edge of the road, and started obliquely across the street toward the Maginnis house. The sun was low over the western ridges, striking brilliantly off the snow cross on the face of Mount Wade.

The firing had died away again, the quiet even more oppressive. He could feel the cool of beaded sweat on his face, the clamp of his hatband on his forehead. Bullets had pitted the walls of the house. A window was smashed, its splintered frame hanging half open. There was a long split in the planking of the corral gate. Rifle muzzles pointed over the corral wall, some at him. The peak of a hat moved there. A white smear of face peered out of the broken window. He heard a faint tinkling, music—the piano! The sound was so unexpected, so brave and ridiculous, that tears clawed at his eyes. He raised his hands to shoulder height.

He had a glimpse of the four or five defenders of the corral before he was let into the house, unfamiliar rifle-armed men in both places, Johnny Angell coming up to join him, hatless, with a dust- and powder-stained young face. He carried a rifle and wore revolvers on both hips. Inside the dining room was a mess of smashed terra-cotta pottery, earth, flowers, ferns, and potted plants. The piano was louder—Liszt. Maginnis appeared among the gunmen in his dark tweed suit, vest with its arc of gold watchchain, unarmed.

"What is this, Pat?" The others gave way as he came to face Cutler.

"I've been instructed by Colonel Dougal to tell you that you may surrender to him, Frank."

There were nervous, scoffing laughs. Maginnis gaped at him with his queer, bugged eyes. Lily continued her playing, invisible from here. Smiling confidently, Frank said, "Oh, I don't believe we need do that, Pat. Tell me, what is the cavalry's role here? Are you arrayed against us also?"

"It seems that someone here fired on troopers."

"That's a lie!"

"Maybe not," Johnny Angell said, standing with a boot braced up on a cracked pot. "There is some itchy-finger ducks out there in the corral."

"Just what do you all think you are doing here?" Cutler demanded.

"Well, we got this kind of posse together for Mr. Maginnis

to arrest us some malefactors," Johnny said. "But they were good and ready for us!"

"It has given the colonel a reason for coming in on the side of what he calls 'legally constituted authority.'"

"Oh, my!" Angell said. "That is a jawbreaker!" In this situation, and with his growing reputation as a gunman, Angell possessed an authority Cutler had not noticed before. He was self-assured and cheerful but no longer a cheerful boy. The others looked to be small ranchers, no doubt from the southern part of the county. Lines were not yet well defined there, and probably some of these were as much rustlers as ranchers. It was said of the south-county stalwarts that some ranched, and rustled on the side, while others rustled, and ranched on the side. And they rustled for themselves until they possessed large enough herds to be rustled from. It was a short route for an ambitious young cowboy to become county gentry like Penn McFall. Gangs of rustlers formed and dissolved, though some, like that of Jesse Clary, rustled as a trade, selling stolen beef to merchants like Boland or to the Texas army posts. For the most part, though, these men were of the old restless stock that moved westward, generation by generation, and they might be thieves, but they were not murderers. Now they were the stern-faced and frightened supporters of the Turnbull and Maginnis cause.

"As you see, we are well supported, Pat," Maginnis said. "We believe we possess as strong a legal position as George Kimball. Many men have ridden into Madison to our support."

"You have probably lost those who were gathered at the González store," he said, and explained. There was silence, broken by one shot from the defenders still in the corral. Lily appeared. She looked feverish, her face vivid with color. She wore jet beads, at which one hand told and tugged, and a long, full-skirted, dark blue gown. Her hair was tied back with a blue ribbon.

"Pat, can this be true?" she said in her clear voice. "That you have turned against us too?" She leaned so tragically against the corner of the wall that he wanted to shake her.

He ignored her question to say to Maginnis, "I told the colonel I thought you might surrender to the protection of the army."

"Tell me something, Pat," Maginnis said loudly. He

stood in an oratorical pose, chest thrust out, fingers inserted in his vest pockets. Cutler felt like shaking him also. "Would *you* trust Colonel Dougal in this matter?"

"I think you must trust him."

"I don't know how we are going to make out, Mr. Maginnis," Johnny Angell said. "Fighting Henry Enders and Jesse Clary and George Kimball, and the army too."

"Yes, I think Colonel Dougal is also our enemy," Frank said.

"Who's afeared of soljers?" another young man said, heavy-shouldered, with a round earnest face. "What's so fine about cav'ry? Just a bunch of farmers and Bowery boys, ain't they?"

The question was addressed to Cutler. "That is all they are," he said. "But they have had training you have not had. They are led by experienced officers, and have the discipline not to run home when things get tight."

"Tight right now, and nobody's runnin'!"

"Mister, you are saying we're going to run out on Mr. Maginnis?" another said pugnaciously.

"I think those who were at the González store have probably run out already," he said. He said to Lily, "I advise you to surrender, Mrs. Maginnis. You are in an untenable position here."

She tightened her lips and glared back at him. Maginnis said flatly, "We trust our friends, you see, Pat."

He felt a gripe of rage at the orator's stance and bullfrog expression that proclaimed Frank's faith in the law, justice, the right, and the inevitable victory of *dikē*. He was a fool, and yet that very irritating, smug faith that made you want to shake him made it essential that he be served by men of common sense.

"I can't permit you to drag Lily into a massacre, Frank."

"I will remain with my husband, Pat!"

He wondered if Johnny Angell was already trapped by the frontier's speedy mythologizing in his role as the boy avenger, the newest six-gun nonpareil. If so, Lily would have helped to ensnare him in it. For a moment the pulse of his anger beat so powerfully he could not look at her.

"What about you, Johnny?"

Angell said, "I heard it said once that an old soldier is one that run when he was a young one. I'd say we'd better plan on clearing out soon as it's full dark. If it is so about those fellows down at the *tienda*," he added.

"Well, I'm stickin' it out!" another said. "You count on us, Mr. Maginnis!" Others joined in. From his expression, Frank was enjoying these expressions of loyalty.

"Take care of Mrs. Maginnis," Cutler said to Johnny Angell.

"Surely. Do my best to get everybody out of here intact, if it comes to it."

Cutler thought it would come to it.

"You may return to your colonel and tell him we do very well here," Maginnis said, teetering on the balls of his feet. "And that he should be ashamed of the company he keeps." He turned away.

Angell gave Cutler a tight grin with a shrug of his shoulders. He rested his hands on the butts of his pair of revolvers.

Cutler stamped outside past hostile faces. Across the silent street, half in shadow now, he could see the troopers in the brush.

He started toward them, the flesh of his back crawling. As soon as he was out of the street the firing began to pick up. He went to report his failure to the colonel in the Sibley tent.

The men of the Maginnis faction, Anglo and Mexican, and Mexican bravos from the south-county hamlets like Arioso, Corral de Tierra, and Puerto del Sol, had indeed departed on the threat of a cannonade, and Cutler estimated that some fifteen rifles in the Maginnis house and corral faced the new sheriff's fifty or more. Henry Enders's men succeeded in firing the north wing of the house with kerosene, although the fire produced more smoke than flame. Kimball, a short, slight, self-important man, came to confer with the colonel, with him Jesse Clary, lean and ugly in a battered leather jacket, who spat tobacco juice just missing a guard's boots as he followed Kimball into the Sibley. Henry Enders was conspicuous by his absence. Cutler was not invited to the conference.

He found a coign of vantage in a corner against the chimney of the burnt house, with a view of Maginnis walls through the brush. Sometimes greasy flames licked out the broken window in the north wing.

His nerves ached with overextended anxiety, and he had the same sense of stupid tragedy slowly impending that he had felt in the final moments before the firing began at Bosque Alto. He had to depend upon Johnny Angell's good sense overriding Maginnis's obduracy. There was nothing to be done about Colonel Dougal's.

He could see the hunched backs of Enders's gunmen as they moved closer to the smoking house in the dusk. The firing from the corral was sporadic, ammunition saved for the final outbreak. As the dusk thickened there came a lock of tension, for the breakout must be soon. Smoke swirled in the street, and the firing had almost ceased. From time to time he thought, or imagined, he could hear the brittle notes of Lily's piano. None of his fellow officers came near him. He lit a cigar and tried to savor the perfumed smoke.

"Here they come!" someone shouted. He leaped up to rush toward the street as there were shrill yells from the besiegers and the firing increased to a roar. He could dimly make out two parties fleeing, the larger group sprinting out of the corral to disappear toward the creek, the other appearing from the house itself. Someone from the house went down and rose again only to be sent sprawling. Cutler crossed the street at a trot. Maginnis had been hit, lying face down with arms pinned beneath his body. Three gunmen stood over him, one firing a coup de grace as Cutler came up. All of them were laughing, and all around store men were yipping with excitement.

He ran inside the house into choking smoke. More store men were silhouetted against the flames of the north wing, with Lily among them. Her hands were raised not in surrender but as though to ward off a blow. One man grasped her arm. There was clotted laughter. Cutler rammed into the man who held her, caught her away, drew his revolver, and presented it.

"Come on, Lily!"

Arm around her, he hurried her outside. Faces glared at him, one man shouting a curse, another yelling, "You just leave that hoor to them that—" Cutler jammed his revolver muzzle into the bearded face and the man spun away. Lily was coughing from the smoke, straining against his arm.

"My *piano!*"

"Your *life!*" he panted in her ear, trying to keep between

her and the madmen standing around Maginnis's body. There must have been twenty of them. They had heaped boards on the corpse, and a man poured on kerosene, to cheers. Flames leaped up.

"How do you like the fire, Diablo!" They milled, retreating before the heat of the flames. Henry Enders was among them, revolver in his good hand. He was spinning, stooping, hopping up, gesticulating—almost, Cutler thought, dancing. His withered arm was caught up against his chest as though he danced with it. Red light flickered over his face, his mouth open as though he was chanting. Jesse Clary pushed past him, rifle in hand.

"Jus' a minnit there, soljer!" Clary shouted, leveling the rifle at Cutler's chest. His mouth looked stuffed with teeth.

"We are here to protect women and children!" Cutler shouted, showing Clary the muzzle of his revolver. "Get out of my way!" He brushed past, Lily gripped on his side away from them. He breathed the stink of kerosene and scorching flesh.

Lily cried hoarsely, "They are burning Frank! They are burning my husband! They have killed Frank!"

"Jus' hold on there, soljer!" Jesse Clary bellowed behind him, but he did not stop. Beyond the burning planks Henry Enders capered.

There was a yell. "Burn Madam Jezebel with Diablo!" Cutler shoved Lily on away. Then they were out in the street in the gathering dark. Troopers sat their horses watching Henry Enders and his men celebrating the death of Frank Maginnis.

"Johnny got away!" Lily panted. "They were in two groups, those from the house and those from the corral. Johnny's were supposed to draw the fire—then Frank—but he would not hurry! Oh my God, Pat, they are *burning* him!"

"Where can you go?" Now he kept between her and Frank's murderers so she would not see Enders's insane dance.

"Billy Prim's—Berta's there." She was shaking convulsively. Mounted men rode past with a creaking of saddle leather. Cutler breathed dust along with the broiling stench. He hurried Lily along the far side of the street toward the doctor's house, where a lamp burned in the surgery. Flames reddened the sky behind them. Singing started up, hoarse, harsh, triumphant: "We'll hang Frank Maginnis to a sour apple tree..."

When he released Lily she ran awkwardly up the walk to Dr. Prim's front door, holding her skirts with both hands, not looking back. She disappeared into darkness. He heard voices. A door slammed, cutting them off. He turned back toward the flames, the shouting and the song. Johnny Angell had got away, but Frank had waited too long in his obduracy, in his disbelief that *dikē* could lose even a battle in the Madison County War.

BOOK TWO

The Secretary of the Interior came around his vast, cluttered desk to pump Underwood's hand. He was thick-bodied in his claw hammer coat, pink-cheeked, fair-whiskered, with the perspiration of his responsibilities beading his forehead.

"The President is grateful that you have accepted this very difficult commission, General Underwood. Or, as I should say now, Governor Underwood." The Secretary flashed his winning smile.

Underwood reclaimed his hand and smiled reservedly in return. He was not grateful for this commission as governor of a miserable frontier territory populated by outlaws and Apaches and celebrated only for its lawlessness. It had seemed to him that his services to the Republic during the war, and to the party as Chairman of the Indiana State Republican Committee, warranted an ambassadorship, and such had been his request. But as every military man knew, timing was the essence of success. Unfortunately he had demanded his reward just when the President was faced with appointing a new governor of New Mexico Territory.

"What questions have you, Governor?" the Secretary said, motioning him to the leather chair that faced the desk and retreating to seat himself with a flourish of coattails.

"Might as well ask an Eskimo if he has any questions about camel herding."

The Secretary laughed more than was necessary at Underwood's sally. "Your official residence in Santa Fe was built when Shakespeare and Cervantes were alive, Governor. That should interest you as an historian."

"Indeed it does. I do have some facts from the only reference book I could locate. The Territory came to us after the war with Mexico and was supplemented by the Gadsden

Purchase. The population is largely Mexican, with the addition of American miners and stock-grazers. And savage Indians."

"Navajos and their cousins, the Apaches. The Navajos have taken peaceably to confinement. The Apaches continue to be restless. Are you acquainted with General Yeager?"

"We have met," Underwood said. Yeager was not popular with his fellow officers, twenty-five of whom he had jumped in rank to reach his present eminence. There was no question that his Indian campaigns had been successful, and no question either that he was insufferably arrogant.

"Once the Territory has quieted down you will find time for your literary endeavors," the Secretary said. "And what are you working on at the moment, Governor?"

"I have been doing some reading on the conquistadors other than Hernán Cortés. Pedro de Alvarado in particular. I will use the coincidence of my location to learn Spanish, so as to continue my researches in that language. Coronado, of course, passed through New Mexico, and probably so did Cabeza de Vaca, who was the first European to traverse the continent."

"The President mentioned how much he enjoyed reading *Washington Under Siege*," the Secretary said. "And of course everyone is familiar with *The Mississippi War*."

Underwood nodded with reserve. The Secretary did not mention *Victory in Virginia*, which completed his trilogy of the history of the war and had been a failure. The reading public had grown weary of these memoirs of old soldiers passed off as histories—so his publisher had told him. He had moreover been attacked in print by a number of military men whose wartime conduct and tactics he had criticized. In early morning wakefulness he would alternately blame a cabal of old soldiers and publishing ineptitude for the failure of *Victory in Virginia*. Which failure had led directly to his writing to the President to ask for an ambassadorship.

Out the window the roofs of Washington glistened in the sunshine after the morning's rain, the Washington monument raising its clean white spike against the green shore. How exciting the capital had been during the war—the soldiers, the pretty women, the rumors of victories and defeats. His own greatest hour had occurred not twenty miles away, at Pike's Junction, where he had saved the capital from Jubal Early! What wondrous years those had been for a young lawyer from Richmond, Indiana, commissioned a captain, within a year brevetted colonel, and inside two a general. In disgrace after Shiloh, then the hero of Pike's Junction, but he had never regained Grant's favor.

The Secretary was speaking of matters in New Mexico. Madison County was located in the southern part of the Territory, adjoining both Texas and Mexico.

"The Madison County War, whose bloodshed and violence fill the daily press, will of course require your immediate attention. I am embarrassed by it. The administration is embarrassed, and the party, and most importantly the President. He looks forward to a day when the front pages turn their attention to other items than the latest outrage in Madison. There are, in addition, very strong protests from Her Majesty's Government over the murder of the British subject, Turnbull. The man's brother is demanding an investigation.

"The county is almost a fifth of the Territory in area," the Secretary continued. "Fifteen thousand square miles, with some four thousand inhabitants, a majority of them, as you say, of Mexican extraction, and with perhaps more loyalty to Mexico than to the United States. The tracts along the border are mainly deserts, some rangeland, few settlements. Consequently there is not the political action there is along the Texas-Mexico border, where revolutions are continually plotted against the Mexican government.

"Originally the cattle herders of the county regulated themselves by common understanding. In the usual pattern, two or three of the biggest ones succeeded in appropriating most of the watered land and driving the smaller operators into bankruptcy. These then began stealing from the larger, who retaliated by importing gunmen—some of these criminals of the vilest stamp. Lynch law reigned. These range wars were predecessors of the present violence. That, and frontier independence and contempt of law. And allegiance to warlords."

Underwood listened to the Secretary's account of the Madison County War, down to the most recent violence—the murder of the lawyer, Maginnis, by a mob. "The press has severely criticized the army's actions," he commented.

"Indeed it has! There is another embarrassing aspect. Not only is Maginnis's widow raising a row, but a partisan of hers is a certain Dr. Prim, who was a schoolmate of the

President's. The President turns Prim's indignant letters over to me, and I will include copies in your portfolio. They are violently prejudiced upon the side of the murdered Englishman and lawyer."

"A young warrior named Angell has been celebrated in the papers."

"One of Maginnis's men. There have already been fictions about him in *The Police Gazette* and elsewhere, I understand. In the Territorial papers he is held to be a murderous delinquent—slayer of his stepfather, a kindly old employer, and perhaps four men in the 'War,' including the sheriff."

Underwood inquired what the situation was at the moment.

"Quiet except for the outpouring of letters I have mentioned. Things may in fact settle down now that the leaders of the anti-Boland movement are dead. But surely one of your first official acts must be to appoint a new sheriff in the county. And this man will have to be a titan of probity and courage."

"Is martial law a possibility?"

The Secretary squinted at him. "Affairs would have to grow much further out of hand to justify such an unpopular course. Any such use of the army would have to be arranged with General Yeager, whose headquarters is at Fort Blodgett, near Santa Fe."

Underwood blew his breath out lengthily, remembering his dream of an ambassadorship to Austria or perhaps Peru. Instead this unsavory mess within the continental boundaries of the United States.

The Secretary plucked a newspaper clipping from an open file on his desk. "Here is some local opinion, from the weekly paper in a town called Las Vegas. 'Although the adherents of these parties have been guilty of "killing their enemies," there is no murder in the matter, but a contest for "the best of the fight." Here in the East we would consider this an unusual theory of jurisprudence.'"

"It would seem that the 'best of the fight' would tend to go to the party with the bigger artillery. Will I meet Governor Dickey?"

"He is bound to take your replacement of him as a rebuke to his administration, and I'll wager he'll be gone by the time you reach Santa Fe. He has been rather a creature of Jacob Weber, the United States Attorney, and an associate of Randolph Boland's. Thus the Madison Ring interconnects with the Santa Fe Ring, of which Weber is the chief. Weber has important friends in the Senate. I name no names, but I will say that the old soldier network is very strong."

"Certainly there are loyalties," he said.

"There are also party loyalties," the Secretary said, frowning. "The Santa Fe Ring is the Republican stronghold in the Territory. Such matters must be considered, but of course will not affect the Jovian judgment a governor is expected to possess."

"I assume, in my Jovian judgment, that peace and quiet is the desired end."

"Peace, yes. With as little fuss, time, and expense as possible. But *quiet* at any price! May I ask how you propose to proceed, Governor?"

"First I will seize the reins of office firmly. I'll search for this titan of a sheriff for Madison County while interviewing and trying to placate the remaining principals in the conflict. I'll see to the training of some kind of militia, threatening, but not employing, martial law."

"Very good, Governor!" the Secretary of the Interior said.

In Richmond Underwood turned over his law practice to his partners, who arranged a picnic in his honor in Masonic Park. There successive speakers lavished encomiums upon him as the "hero of Pike's Junction," and "our renowned historiographer," referring to him as both General Underwood and Governor Underwood. He spoke briefly, mentioning new challenges and new services to the Republic. Clara would remain in Richmond, tending Mother Curren in her lengthy illness. When the old woman had finally gone to her reward, Clara would join him in Santa Fe.

Three days in a sleeping car brought him across the great plains to mountains that rose like teeth against a vivid sky. The railroad had not yet pushed through to Santa Fe, and, in Pueblo, he transferred to the narrow-gauge line to Trinidad. From Trinidad he made his way through the Sangre de Cristo range by buckboard.

He wrote to Clara: "A deadlier instrument of torture was never invented by the Inquisition. Without a stop except to change horses, it was jolt, crash, jar, bump, bang; no rest, no sleep in the deep cold of the mountains even with two blankets..."

In the plaza at Santa Fe at last, he crawled out of the torture machine and booked into the Fred Harvey Hotel. No one seemed to have been notified that a new governor was arriving.

Cater-cornered across the square was the oldest building in the United States, over the centuries a barracks, fortress, administrative headquarters and Palace of the Governors—a low sprawl of mud-brick walls and tile roofs. He strolled along a covered plank sidewalk, rotted and broken through in many places, beneath sagging rafters. Inside, the place stank of rodents, mildew, and urine, with a kind of historical chill that made him shiver.

A functionary caught up with him, wearing a black clerk's jacket, plump and pasty-faced, a secretary named Logan. "We had not expected you so soon, Governor Underwood!"

"You will find me punctual, Logan."

Logan showed him through the palace, disappearing now and then to bellow Mexican names. Two sandaled, dark-skinned servants eventually appeared and were ordered to begin cleaning the governor's quarters. These proved to be barren rooms of peeling plaster with windows giving onto the square, a threadbare rug on the floor, and a corner fireplace in what must be the parlor. In the office was a scarred rolltop desk, surmounted by a lamp with a missing chimney, and a single straight-backed chair.

"Governor Dickey took almost everything away with him, Governor," Logan said, frowning nervously around the room.

"I see that," he said. He was feeling a profound depression at his surroundings and his prospects for getting back to work on Pedro de Alvarado. He had done a little reading on the death of Alvarado on the train. Rolled on by his charger in his last battle, borne dying to Guadalajara, when asked if he was in pain, his last words had been, "Only in my soul." The words did not fit Underwood's own picture of the salty old adventurer.

One of the Mexicans appeared with a bucket and mop

and began sloshing water onto the tile floor in a slovenly manner.

"Instruct that man to do that correctly," Underwood said to Logan. "The mop is to be thoroughly wetted, with the excess of liquid squeezed back into the bucket. That procedure is to be frequently repeated during the mopping process."

"Well, sir, you see they have their own ways of doing things. They have been mopping that way for a long time."

"They will now change their ways in accordance with my instructions," he said, amused by his own severity.

"Yes, sir!" the secretary said, drawing himself to a semblance of attention. Presumably he had once been a military man.

"Where may I find General Yeager?"

"Out at the fort, sir."

"There is a conveyance to take me to him?"

"There is a nice buggy, sir."

"Please have it sent around. Who else should I be seeing besides the general?"

"Oh, Mr. Weber, Governor. I'd say you ought to be seeing Mr. Weber first of all. And the archbishop."

"Mr. Weber is the United States Attorney? No, I will call upon the general first. Have the buggy sent around."

"Well, sir, I don't know if I can get hold of anybody—" Logan stopped, looking relieved when the cathedral bells began chiming. "It is Sunday, you see, sir, and we wasn't expecting you so—"

"Then bring the buggy around yourself, man!"

Logan started another excuse, thought better of it, and trotted away, leaving the servant still mopping in his inefficient fashion. Underwood strolled outside, enjoying the warmth of the day, the sun and shade of the plaza, the bracing air of the altitude out of the chill and gloom of the governor's palace, until the buggy spun around the corner, drawn by a fine, high-stepping sorrel.

Fort Blodgett possessed the same splendid vistas of snow-capped mountains as the plaza at Santa Fe, and Underwood, the general, and a captain sat at ease in a sunny patio with chilled fruit juices a young corporal brought them. Yeager wore his famed personal uniform, a many-pocketed khaki jacket and high, laced boots with his trousers tucked inside. The captain was more conventionally garbed and had his notebook in hand to catch the pith and wisdom of the great Indian campaigner.

Underwood calculated that Yeager was some five years older than he was. He knew that Yeager had been one of Old Brains Halleck's pets in Washington, and, if he had seen action, it had only been toward the war's end. It was galling that his own swift advancement should have been terminated by the humiliation of Shiloh and only partially redeemed, while there had been no such desperate chances in Yeager's career, which had blossomed in the Indian wars. Now Yeager was being mentioned as a strength to the Republican ticket as a vice-presidential nominee.

"So you have replaced that old fraud Dickey and will bring the bounties of decent government to this benighted place," Yeager said. His features looked curiously squeezed between bushy, rusty sideburns.

"There seems to have been an accumulation of difficulties."

"Oh, things are very quiet just now," Yeager said, with a lazy flick of a hand indicating the mountainous landscape. "They have been quiet so long, a less experienced man might be reassured that they were quiet for good. More probably they are quiet for bad, eh, Perce?"

The captain smiled, nodded, and wrote.

"We are prepared, however," Yeager went on. "The Apache scouts have proven themselves blessedly useful. Once it was thought that the scouts must belong to a different band than those they pursue. Now I believe we can employ, say, Sierra Verdes to pursue Sierra Verdes. Those who break out of the reservation cause a great deal of difficulty for those who remain behind. The principle of 'good Injuns' and bad ones is well understood."

"I'm afraid the immediate concern of the Secretary of the Interior is the Madison County War."

"Ah, yes!" Yeager said, taking up his pale pink decoction. No doubt, Underwood thought, he was uninterested in civilian matters. With his radically cut sideburns and his pink drink, he resembled an Oriental potentate taking his ease.

"This Colonel Dougal at Fort McLain seems to have become unfortunately involved in the situation."

"He is a great fool," Yeager said.

"The Apaches call him Nantan Tonto, which means just

that," Captain Robinson put in. Yeager, Underwood knew, was proud of his own Apache appellation, Nantan Lobo, Chief Gray Wolf.

"Unfortunately he cannot be removed," Yeager said. "You understand the army, General Underwood. Colonel Dougal's sister married into the very highest army circles." He laughed and ticked off the stars pinned to his shoulder, adding one more. "Still, our concerns are the same, Governor," he continued. "For I presume your charge is to bring decent government to the Territory. Your enemies will be, then—as mine are—the Indian Rings."

"I presume you are referring to Mr. Jacob Weber. I have not yet encountered that gentleman."

"He will do his best to cultivate you. His Republican caucus is in fact the Santa Fe Ring. Like the even more influential Tucson Ring, it favors Apache war over Apache peace. They will not admit it, of course, but their profits depend upon the size of the military forces that are maintained here. Consequently they will find a hundred different ways to keep the Indians stirred up. And hell alone knows the fury of a capitalist whose profits are threatened. They derogate me in every way they can, and, if you displease them—and I hope to heaven you will!—so will they you."

Having delivered himself of his peroration, the general set his lips sulkily and reached for his drink.

"I mentioned to the Secretary the possibility of martial law in Madison County."

Yeager looked at him sharply, and he had a glimpse of a keen intelligence behind the foppish sideburns and eccentric uniform. "I would advise against it in the very strongest terms."

Underwood watched the captain writing, bent over his notebook with his red, swollen nose pointed at his work.

"If I were you, Governor," Yeager went on, "I would hie myself down to Madison to look over matters there in person. You will find little to choose from between the factions. A strong hand is needed. A sheriff should be appointed who is not aligned to either side."

"The Secretary mentioned that also. I have been wondering how to locate the proper fellow."

"Surely the right man will turn up," Yeager said. "And

how are you enjoying your habitation in the Palace of the Governors?"

"My predecessor seems to have made off with the furnishings."

"Ah, a thief to the end! We can help you with your furnishings. Captain Robinson will introduce you to the quartermaster with carte blanche."

"Thank you, General," Underwood said with political respect, rising. Although he was governor of the Territory and Yeager the general commanding the department, Yeager was a favorite in high Republican circles and could be a help or a hindrance depending upon their relationship. Underwood saluted smartly in deference before departing.

He walked in the plaza with Jake Weber, a short, mild, balding man in a frock coat, who regularly removed his broad-brimmed hat to mop a pale scalp with his handkerchief. The cathedral bells were tolling, and a mule team drooped before an enormous freight wagon with a soiled white cover.

"I have heard it said that the so-called Madison County War is a fight between rival storekeepers," Underwood said.

Weber managed a laugh. "It's not so simple as that, Governor! Do you know the term 'brown gold'?"

"Cattle?"

"Cattle. Cattle raising. Cattle rustling. The rustlers are Texas men for the most part, southerners, lawless men. Fighting each other over brown gold, but closing ranks against the law in Madison County. Brown gold, Governor!"

"Ah! And the young Englishman was involved in this?"

"He found the life these fellows led attractive, you see. The Robin Hood ideal! The British! It's difficult for them to understand that we must deal with real life out here, not old romances." Weber looked momentarily worried, as though that might have offended, but continued: "Our own Robin Hoods! The James gang, the Daltons, the Youngers. Our own Johnny-A! To anyone else but a frontier people these would be common murderers. I don't believe the British on their island would honor an ignorant young lout who murdered a sheriff."

"I seem to remember that Robin Hood's foe was the Sheriff of Nottingham."

"Ah, it's impossible to inform an historian!" Weber said. "But of course Robin Hood was no murderer." He removed his hat to mop his pale skull. "I wish you could meet Ran Boland. But he's ill—too ill to travel, I'm afraid."

"I hope to meet everyone involved in this tragic business," Underwood said.

"A devious and worried man," he later wrote in his notes, "but a pleasant companion. He is in the difficult position of trying to impress me that my predecessor was unjustly dismissed by a distant government which gave ear to libels and lies, while pretending to greet my appointment with delight. He has taken pains to acquaint himself with my history. Party loyalty is invoked. He does not rant against 'certain elements' in Madison, he speaks more in sorrow than anger, but I am informed that the 'certain elements' are lawless, unreconstructed confederates, Democrats all.

"I have also informed myself of his history and circumstances. He is widely liked and admired in Santa Fe, and moves in the highest social circles—indeed the term *rings* has a very graphic application here, in its suggestions of interlockings and wheels and gears. He is accepted by the old Mexican and Catholic hierarchy, and he and the crotchety old archbishop are bosom friends. He is also the friend of the newer American element, especially, of course, the Republicans, whose leader he is. There is a general dislike in Santa Fe of Texans, no doubt stemming from the Texan invasion early in the war. Texans are equated with Democrats. Weber himself arrived here with the California Column, which chased the Texans out. There is a solid bond of loyalty among these Californians.

"Needless to say, he is held up as a paragon in the pages of *The Territorial Call*. He has a charming and handsome wife, who chooses to garb herself in the old Spanish style, and two charming daughters."

"Surely the right man will turn up," General Yeager had said of the titan sheriff who must be found. The most promising interview with the protagonists of the Madison County War in this regard was with the cattleman Penn McFall, a white-thatched old swaggerer who walked as though his knee joints were sprung.

McFall was cynical of all motives but his own. The "store," which seemed to be the term for all the Boland enterprises, was totally corrupt, but the Englishman, Turnbull, had been a "crazy lad" who had had more money than was good for him; the murdered Maginnis had been a "lawyerer." References to Mrs. Maginnis were accompanied by man-to-man winks and nods, as though men of the world knew what to make of women of that stripe. It was apparent that McFall considered himself the principal and most disinterested cog in the Madison County gears. Underwood had the sense that half of McFall wished to brag of his successes, while the other half was secretive and fearful of envy.

Underwood said, "I'm looking for a good man of independent sympathies and some stature in the county whom I might appoint sheriff until an election can be organized. Can you recommend anyone to me?"

McFall nodded ponderously, as they paced together in the thin sunlight of the plaza. "Happens I know just the man, Governor."

"And he is?"

"My range foreman, Jack Grant. I believe him to be a natural lawman."

"But of independent sympathies?"

"You mean because he is *my* foreman?" McFall laughed his hard, flat bark, swinging along at his aching-knees gait. "No, he will give full change to whoever he works for."

"You mean he has no sympathies in this fight?"

"Ah, well, you can't find a person in the Territory that doesn't have some of those. I would guess Jack would rather call Johnny-A friend than Jesse Clary, but he is a law-and-order man first of all."

"How does one get in touch with this paragon?"

"I'll take care of that, Governor," Penn McFall said.

Cutler had been invited to the colonel's quarters, where Colonel Dougal poured two glasses of whiskey, smiling and briskly friendly. What did it mean? He sat in the comfortable chair to which he had been directed, holding his glass in one hand, a panatela in the other.

"I remember General Underwood well," Dougal said, pacing, head forward, chin whiskers jutting. "We campaigned in southern Ohio together. The old Eighth! We ran those rebs out of there pell-mell! He'll remember me—I was his quartermaster. 'Mr. Dougal, you will see that the men have good meat today and not sowbelly. They deserve a real meal!' And I did it, never mind how! He will remember me all right. Little Dick Underwood. The brigadier was Richard also. Big Dick and Little Dick.

"The Hoosier Zouaves!" Dougal continued. "He was a great advocate of Zouave training, Little Dick Underwood. Of course General Grant was sour on him after Shiloh."

Cutler sipped the colonel's excellent whiskey and savored his cigar. Dougal halted to stand spread-booted before his chair.

"The fact is that Mrs. Maginnis has requested an escort into Santa Fe to present her case to General Underwood. Now, mister, I will not say a word about that lady's morals or motives. The fact is that she has requested a military escort. She is fearful of what she calls 'the Jesse Clary gang.'"

"Yes, sir," he said.

Dougal stepped over to the sideboard, pad of one boot on the dusty Belgian carpet, crack of the other on bare pine floor. The colonel emptied his glass, smoothing a hand down his wattled neck as though following the liquor's downward progress. He poured himself another.

"Did Mrs. Maginnis request that I escort her to Santa Fe, sir?" Cutler asked, having added two and two.

"She did, mister, and I have decided to comply with her request."

They smiled at each other. The colonel was worried about the lawsuit Lily was threatening, not to speak of the board of inquiry into his actions during the Battle of Madison.

Dougal resumed his pacing. Something else was also on his mind. "It is interesting to me, Cutler, that a military man has been selected to replace Governor Dickey."

Cutler did not find it interesting. Military men had been selected to fill most administrative positions since the war.

"I understand that General Underwood and General Yeager have conferred," Dougal continued, flinging himself down in a chair. "I am sure that one of the subjects of their conference was the matter of violence in this county. I happen to think there was another subject."

"What could that be, sir?"

"I am not a brilliant man, Cutler."

No, sir.

"But I learned at my mother's knee to do my sums. I have done my sums, Cutler. Two general officers conferring, one of them the newly named governor of this territory bordering on Mexico, and the other very familiar with northern Mexico from several expeditions in pursuit of renegade Apaches there." Colonel Dougal winked at him solemnly.

"Add one of the junior officers from my post, who speaks Spanish well, and is married to the daughter of one of the principal landowners of Sonora." The colonel touched a forefinger to his temple. "I have done my sums, Cutler. The invasion of northern Mexico was also a subject of this conference. And I think you are aware of these plans, mister!"

"No, sir. I'm sorry, but I am not."

"Then I think you may be apprised of them soon. Tell me, on a visit to Santa Fe, an aide-de-camp would no doubt pay a call on his general, would he not?"

"I would, sir." He watched Dougal push himself to his feet and pace again. The seat of his trousers hung slack, his legs were skinny and bowed, his pale hands were clasped behind his back.

"I will ask you a favor, mister. I ask you to keep your ears peeled. I am very interested in this invasion. I am certain that it must come. Cutler, the only means by which field-grade officers can expect a promotion is combat. I believe that war is very near. I understand that the Mexican newspapers are filled with expectations of it. Also that there are many well-connected men in Chihuahua and Sonora who would welcome us with open arms. Then, of course, General Yeager could solve the Apache problem once and for all! And a nation which becomes embroiled in a new revolution every few years would possess a stable government at last. I believe it is this invasion that occupies the highest level of military planning these days, Cutler, and I ask that you keep your ears peeled in Santa Fe and at Fort Blodgett for any news you can bring back."

He was being permitted to accompany Lily to Santa Fe in return for feeding Colonel Dougal's obsession with an invasion of Mexico. The colonel, who had accused him of tattling to General Yeager, now wished to be the recipient of some reciprocal tattle. Cutler said, "I will report to you anything that is divulged to me, unless I am sworn to secrecy, Colonel."

Dougal smiled down at him paternally, combing his fingers through his chin whiskers. "Our relations have not always been good, Cutler. I have been suspicious of your loyalty to me. But I want to like my junior officers. It is the only way in which the army can function. Loyalty and respect, Cutler. Officer to officer, officer to enlisted. Mutual trust!"

"Yes, sir," he said, blowing smoke from the colonel's cigar.

"Mexico, Cutler! Very well, you will accompany Mrs. Maginnis to Santa Fe, even though she is trying to cause trouble for me."

In the buggy Lily was swaddled in a linen duster with scarves tied over her hat and two carpetbags stacked beside her on the seat. Cutler rode Malcreado alongside, with a corporal and two troopers following.

The buggy rolled over the packed red sand, slowing through the washes etched into the desert. Below was the river and the dense green of treetops. Cloud shadows crept over the ground ahead, the clouds sailing west like the white canopies of westering wagons.

Lily's whip dipped over the back of the trotting mule with its brave red tassel nodding. She held a bright-breeched rifle across her knees, her own defense against the Jesse Clary gang, who had threatened her in an illiterate note left at the hotel desk. Cutler was armed with a carbine in his saddle scabbard and a service revolver on his hip. The flap of his kepi kept the sun from the back of his neck, but sweat dripped from his chin. Just when the heat became unbearable another cloud drifted over.

"I have reason to believe that Governor Underwood is a just man," Lily called to him, so that he was obliged to incline Malcreado closer to the buggy. "A sensitive and rational man. He is the author of histories. He is not merely a military man."

If he rode near the buggy she would talk to him in this voluble way that embarrassed him. If he did not ride close enough for conversation she gazed at him reproachfully. Although he was sympathetic to her cause, he was apparently not sympathetic enough.

"I do not demand retribution—and protection!—as a woman!" she continued. "I demand them as a citizen! I know now that when men like Jesse Clary and Henry Enders make threats, they intend to carry them out."

The trailing edge of the cloud glided by, and he felt the heat of the sun again. He brushed at his chin with his soaked bandana, glancing back at the three troopers, who looked as wilted as he felt. He had wanted to bring the Hoyas, but the colonel had insisted upon a more respectable escort in his efforts to placate Lily. Cutler did not believe there was any danger of an attack by Jesse Clary.

"My husband has been murdered," Lily said, gazing up at him from under her scarves. "His body burnt by *dancing, singing* men! No one has been arrested for *that* crime. Instead his friends and companions, who stood by him in his final hour, are hunted men. With warrants for *their* arrest!"

He resented her demand that he share her fury over Frank's murder, muttering that no doubt the courts would sort out these matters in time.

"There is an attorney in Santa Fe of whom Frank thought highly. I believe Mr. Redmond is exactly the man who will have the courage to come to Madison and institute proceedings."

"Where's the on-the-shoot boy wonder?" he asked.

She pulled an unhappy face and turned her attention to her reins. Sorry; he didn't say it aloud.

"I imagine he is dodging George Kimball's posse," she said in a stilted voice, "although I hope we will encounter him along our route."

"Gunslingers fighting for you, soldiers escorting you, lawyers instituting proceedings for you."

"I would prefer that they were doing it out of duty and principle," Lily said, but she seemed to decide his statement had been intended as a compliment.

The road swung up toward sandstone bluffs and threaded through a defile there. It was where one once would have been watchful for an Apache ambush, and he whistled to the corporal and made an encircling motion. The escort lit out at a good trot to flank the right hand scarp. Cutler unshipped his carbine and spurred forward to lead the buggy through the slot in the cliff.

Johnny Angell and three others waited there, with the corporal and the troopers reined up above and beyond them, carbines in hand. Cutler was pleased that the soldiers held higher ground as he signaled for a relaxing of armaments.

Johnny-A reined his pinto to his rear legs, waving a hat at Lily in the buggy. A lock of fair hair fell over his forehead, and Cutler noticed again that hint of luminescence, as though he loomed against the sun. With him were two of his own "gang," although it must be supposed that this gang was morally superior to Jesse Clary's because warrants had been issued against its members by a corrupt county judge. One was older, mustached, with a twist of red bandana at his neck; the younger, who was not much older than Johnny-A, was grinning and squinting. Both were heavily armed. The corporal was scowling at them disapprovingly.

"Morning, Mrs. Maginnis!" Johnny-A called. "Morning, Lieutenant! I guess this is your regiment on the hill here." Johnny also wore a red bandana at his throat. Cutler wondered if it was a kind of uniform to distinguish them from other gangs, as the Apache scouts wore red turbans, and the Sierra Verdes red stripes on their cheeks.

Cutler watched Lily extend her hand as Johnny rode close to the buggy. The hands embraced briefly. Johnny's beard-stubbled cheeks were creased by his smile.

"Those ducks have showed up down by Three Rivers, ma'am. They won't be bothering up this way."

"Thank you, Johnny."

"We'll ride along aways, if that is all right by you, Lieutenant. I surely do enjoy riding downwind of a lady's perfume."

They started on, Cutler and Johnny on one side of the buggy, the other two on the other, and the troopers bringing up the rear again. Lily sat up very straight, attentive to her reins and whip, the mule trotting briskly. Cloud shadows drifted over the sandstone outcrops.

Johnny-A said to Cutler, "I do appreciate your getting her out of that mess at the house like you did, and over to Doc Prim's. She's fearful of Jesse Clary from that night. And Henry Enders too."

"It was a terrible show."

"The worst yet," Johnny said grimly.

They toiled up a long incline and at the top came out into the full sweep of desert, red ramparts far ahead, the sandy floor checkerboarded with cloud shadows. Cutler was aware of Lily watching the two of them in conversation.

"Mighty fine-looking landscape, if you are inclined to it," Johnny said in a different voice.

"I'm inclined to it," Cutler said.

The boy nodded solemnly. "Place I know, where what they call the 'Old Ones' lived—caves dug into the cliff, and there's ladders up to second and third stories—I go out there when I get fussed. Kind of peace out there that lays right into you. Well, the desert has got some of that in it too, those mountains off at the edge of things, and clouds floating over. But right now it seems to me there is a bad pollution on it."

He considered Johnny's meaning and nodded. "Yes, I understand what you mean."

"This county has got poisoned, and everybody's sick on it."

Cutler asked if Johnny knew an antidote to the poison, and the other looked at him for a moment with hard blue eyes and then smiled.

"A fellow has to make certain the antidote don't get everybody sicker than the poison." Johnny took off his hat to fan his face. "I went all wrong in the house at the end there," he said. "I was to get us all out of there, and I thought I had everything fixed. It was dark enough so nobody was going to see to shoot worth a nickel, and us in the corral was to draw fire while Mr. Maginnis and those others got away down to the creek, and Mrs. Maginnis out the back to Doc Prim's. But Mr. Maginnis was one to take his time, and everything jammed up. I should have seen to it he *went*."

"Maybe he never believed he was in danger." Maybe Lily had not either.

"I don't think anybody's going to hire me for safekeeper again. I haven't been much good at it."

"Johnny-A!" one of the others called from the other side of the buggy. "When's eats?"

"Another half hour to Stony Creek!" Johnny called back. He swung his pinto along beside the buggy again, and Cutler watched Lily's brightened face turned up to him with emotions he remembered from watching her with Martin Turnbull.

"We'll ride along as far as Stony Creek, ma'am," Johnny said. "When will you be coming back this way, do you suppose?"

"I hope I will be bringing Mr. Redmond back with me on Thursday."

At Stony Creek only a trickle ran between a shallow chain of pools in red rock, glints of gold flashing through the purling water. In mesquite shade they consumed the picnic Berta had packed, chicken laid out in bronzed splendor on a blue-and-white-checked tablecloth, enough for everyone. Johnny-A's young sidekick was Pard Graves, the older one was called Pauly. Both of them had worked for Martin Turnbull.

Lily presided in the lacy shade, straight-backed, ringed fingers rearranging her hat scarves, which, Cutler thought, prettily displayed her bosom to male admirers. She proffered chicken, potato salad, and cold pinto beans, and made conversation with men who were usually more interested in feeding than in dialogue.

Aware of his eyes she cocked her head and stretched her neck slightly to rid her chin of the little pad of slack flesh beneath it and smiled at him with perfect teeth. He felt jealousy, irritation, and lust.

"A penny for your thoughts, Pat!"

He supposed it was to punish her that he said, "Oh, I was wondering why Frank was hated so much."

Johnny-A grimaced in embarrassment. Pard glanced aside

while Lily carefully put down her chicken breast and regarded Cutler with tragic eyes. "Frank was righteous, Pat. It is a quality that infuriates the unrighteous and perhaps those tolerant of unrighteousness as well."

"He was that way," Johnny Angel said. Cutler saw that his two sidekicks looked at him with more than respect. "It is queer that even fellows you trust more than anyone can get under your skin. Mr. Maginnis was on the right side of everything, though. Everybody knew that. Him and Mr. Turnbull was the decentest men I ever knew." His companions nodded to his summation.

"There was a bunch of people in this county that wished they had come into town that day," Graves said in a rough voice.

Cutler turned his attention to Johnny-A. He was a killer by reputation but still hardly more than a boy, with his forelock of fair hair and his stubble of beard, his youthful slimness and that luminescence that was surely in the eye of the beholder. It seemed that he was kindling into a demigod, already celebrated in such magazines as *The Police Gazette* and *Frank Leslie's* as the plucky slayer of a corrupt sheriff. Johnny-A!

After the picnic they took leave of Angell and his confederates, who would not accompany them further. "We will look for you back this way on Thursday," Johnny said to Lily Maginnis, hat in hand. "I hope you will find this new governor a better one than the other." He stood dismounted beside her buggy, while Cutler and the military escort swung into their saddles.

"And I hope you will find this Mr. Redmond the lawyer you are looking for, ma'am," Johnny Angell said.

Governor Underwood received Mrs. Maginnis and two attendants, one a Lieutenant Cutler, a compact and muscular officer with a short-cropped beard and a rather hard, appraising, and supercilious eye, the other a local lawyer by the name of Redmond, a strutting, fractious fellow with an irritating manner of flinging a finger at any addressee as at a hostile witness. The two men clearly detested one another.

Underwood wrote of Mrs. Maginnis in his notes: "Instinct tells me not to trust her very far, although her listing of the outrages done her is convincing and is in some part corrobo-

rated by the lieutenant. She is a combination of feminine
guile and frontier ingenuousness. Her stance or pose is to be
completely candid with me, but a native wiliness intrudes.
No doubt frontier women learn, from the inordinate value
placed upon their gender, to pay equal deference to all the
males within range. Mrs. Maginnis manages this very well,
playing her escorts off one against the other, and even I found
myself attracted to her person and her cause. She gives the
impression of a lady who has spent a deal of time before a
looking glass, discovering her best angles. On close examination she is not beautiful, but she has an extraordinary power
of eye, a handsome left profile, and a fine bosom. She seems
also to have protected her complexion, which is fresh and
pale and not the shoe leather of many a female cheek in these
parts.

"I am anxious to meet the young gunman, Johnny Angell,
who rumor has it is her lover as well as her protector."

"Redmond is an ambitious young man, son of the foun-
der of the local law firm of Redmond and Settle. He practiced
law in Chicago before returning to his father's firm last year
when his father became incapacitated by illness. He makes it
clear that he intends to establish himself at the expense of the
Santa Fe Ring in general, and Jake Weber in particular. We
will see."

The governor's barber, a Mexican redolent of lotions and
face powder, brought along with his towels and razor a
cheap-paper book, *Marlow's Nickel Library*. Beneath this
inscription was the depiction of a five-cent piece, the number
123, and below that a crude woodcut of a cowboy-hatted boy
leveling a six-gun at a huge, snarling Indian, while a girl
cowered behind, as though warding off the Indian's advances
with an elbow: "JOHNNY ANGEL MEETS THREE-FINGER JACK!"

Inside, in prose as careless and exaggerated as the cover
drawing, was the tale of a hero, "scarcely more than a boy,"
and his trusty revolver, on the trail of the giant Comanche
renegade who had kidnapped pretty, young Elsie Fetters.
Another drawing showed Johnny Angel promising a grieving
father in a storekeeper's apron and a corseted, bustling,
fashionably dressed mother that he would bring their Elsie
back "instanter!" Underwood did not read much of the text,
which was prolix as well as ungrammatical, for it was clear
that the hero's exploits were to be farfetched in the extreme.

Moreover, he found this fiction troubling. This invention of the adventures of the author's Johnny Angel, based upon a real person, gave him an historically uneasy suspicion that invention intruded into the adventures of Pedro de Alvarado and the other conquistadors, even in the memory of honest old Bernal Díaz del Castillo! So his own pursuit of facts became meaningless in that blur of memories, of self-serving distortion, of enmities and friendships and convenient forgetfulness, which made of history only the "fiction agreed upon," of Napoleon's cynical sneer. And now in the latter part of the nineteenth century invention became instantly solemnized by print into facts for future historians to be guided by. Violent boys were given heroic stature by cynical writers who fulfilled the craving for excitement in a public that had been taught to read without having been taught to question.

The nickel novel, printed on coarse gray paper with ink that left smudges on his fingers, left smudges also on his disposition—an irritation, a depression, not so much for Johnny Angell, who had been so cheaply glorified here, as for himself. It was as though cracks had appeared in a smooth and intact surface whose integrity he had never questioned before.

Redmond, acting for Mrs. Maginnis, sent him a copy of the agenda for the board of inquiry which was to deliberate upon Colonel Abraham Dougal's actions during the Madison County War:

I. Did Colonel Dougal conspire with the Boland-Enders party and assist in measures of violence against the Maginnis party?

II. Did he allow the Maginnis house to be fired, thus endangering the lives of women and children therein and in the adjacent buildings and structures?

III. Did he fail to protect the women and children after they had fled the burning house and adjacent threatened structures?

IV. Did he fail to prevent the killing of Maginnis when it was in his power to do so?

V. Did he cast aspersions on the character of Mrs. Maginnis?

At the bottom of the page Redmond had written, in a sprawling, confident hand, "Mark my words, the good colonel will not be found culpable on any of the above."

On the veranda of General Yeager's quarters at Fort Blodgett, with its sweep of views toward the Sangre de Cristo, Cutler came upon an Apache sitting on a wooden bench. His hair was close-cropped, and he was neatly dressed in a white shirt, store trousers, and scuffed city shoes. A servant, Cutler thought first, but the Indian exuded a certain force. The white-eye haircut made his features look outsized, strong jut of a nose, slash of a mouth, close-set eyes. He rose from his bench to face Cutler just as Captain Robinson came out from inside.

"Here is Joklinney, Pat," Percy Robinson said. "Just back from San Francisco. He is Dawa's youngest son, you know."

He extended a hand and Joklinney gripped it, shook it once, and released it, continuing to stand stolidly before him. The husband of Pretty Mouth. He had been tried by a native court at San Marcos for murder and stock theft, and sentenced to the white-eye prison. He was another of Yeager's weapons against Caballito.

Joklinney's lips slanted in a trace of smile and he regarded Cutler in the Apache manner, with his face turned aside from the object of his gaze. "Nantan Tata," he said.

Cutler was surprised that the Apache knew of him.

"Carries his scouts around on his back," Robinson said, grinning and scratching his red nose. "Checks the agent's scales. Come on in, Pat."

Joklinney remained on the veranda as Robinson led Cutler inside. Yeager sat behind a desk in a sunny room with a red and black Navajo blanket on the wall, a potted fern on a wrought-iron stand, a wall of books. Yeager indicated a chair, and Robinson also seated himself.

"Well, Pat, what of Caballito? 'Quiet to quick bosoms is a hell,' of course. Is anything threatening that quick bosom?"

"Yes, sir. Dipple tells him the Bureau of Indian Affairs may decide to move him back to San Marcos, and Dipple may be advising them to do just that. There's also that herd of the Sierra Verdes' that a good many people have their eye on. Maybe including some friends of Dipple's."

"I am well aware the Bureau wants the Sierra Verdes

back at San Marcos," Yeager said. "I have told them it will mean destruction. We are prepared for a pursuit if he goes out again, are we not?"

"Yes, sir. My trackers are ready, and Captain Bunch has done a fine job training his Red Stripe scouts. Of course he's been reporting to you directly."

"He is well pleased, very well pleased," Yeager said, nodding. He squinted censoriously. "But that fellow of yours who was hanged—that was a setback, my boy."

When he tried to speak in defense of Benny Dee, the general waved a hand in front of his face as though at the pestering of a fly. "We accept our losses, we do not excuse them. We see that they do not occur again."

"Caballito seemed to know that Joklinney would be returning, sir."

"Pat encountered Joklinney outside," Percy Robinson said.

"They do have powers of perception, these medicine men," Yeager said. "Such matters can be unnerving, to a white man raised in the belief of the evidence of his five senses. I think something can be made of Joklinney, Pat. He's the hereditary chief and an intelligent young man besides."

"He was a bloody-handed murderer before he was an intelligent young man," Robinson growled.

"You know he's Caballito's nephew, Pat," Yeager said. "Besides being Dawa's son."

Cutler searched the general's face and demeanor for some clue, as though at the mention of paternity his own became the issue. He fumed at himself, and Yeager glanced casually at Robinson as the aide said, "San Francisco's accomplished quite a regeneration, from the look of him, sir. Speaks fair enough English now."

"I'll expect him to be a restraining influence on his uncle. He's seen how many white-eyes there are. 'Multitudinous as the leaves that fall on Vallambrosa . . .' The presence of Joklinney, in addition to Captain Bunch's company of scouts, should provide enough weight on that unquiet bosom to make my charge to you an easy one, Pat. My charge that you are to see that nothing jars Caballito off that reservation." He squinted an eye threateningly.

"I will deal with the Bureau as to San Marcos," he

continued, and laughed. "I'll even go to Mexico on another goose chase, if necessary!"

Cutler found himself shaking his head. He felt sour and stubborn. "He'll go out sooner or later. There are just too many things to jar him loose."

Yeager gazed at him stonily for a long moment. Then he shrugged. "Since you are here, you will accompany Joklinney back to Bosque Alto. Make friends with him if you can, get to know him. If the Red Stripe People are not destroyed by the willfulness of Caballito, Joklinney will become their chief. He can be very useful."

"Yes, sir," Cutler said.

The general relaxed in his chair, hands clasped behind his head, an amiable expression on his homely face. "How is your wife faring, my boy?"

"Better, I'm told."

"And your son?"

"His great-grandfather's pride."

"I will become a grandfather in the fall," Yeager said. "A son is important to a man, Pat. My own has always been a disappointment. He has not a jot of humor to him. He is a persnickety, finicking dry stick and I can't bear to be around him."

"I'm sorry to hear that, sir." Cutler thought about his own son, and listened for his own pulse. He said, "Don Fernando is very old. I think within the year I will have to retire from the army and go to Las Golondrinas permanently."

Yeager sat up again with his hands flattened on the desk before him. His eyes were suddenly hard. "I believe my charge to you takes precedence, Pat. You owe me a thing or two. I know you are aware of that."

"Yes, sir. And I owe my wife and son and Don Fernando a thing or two also. I have been warned that if you were to retire I had better leave Fort McLain and the service in a hurry. Or even if it happens that Major Symonds takes over command of the 13th from Colonel Dougal."

"Yes," Yeager said. "With your talent for antagonizing your superiors, if for any reason my protection—my often invoked protection, Pat—if it fails, I do advise you to set out for Sonora on the first express train. Meanwhile, I reiterate my claim to your services, although perhaps within a year a number of things will have concluded themselves."

Yeager sat watching him with a hard, unfriendly gaze, as Cutler said, "I've promised Colonel Dougal that I would inquire of the general if an invasion of Mexico is being planned. The colonel is interested in such an eventuality."

Yeager tugged at his side whiskers with both hands, so that his grin turned into an ape's grimace. "Why, of course it is being planned, my boy! In the army every eventuality is constantly being planned. How little of that planning is ever set in motion!" He made a quick little gesture toward Robinson, which Cutler took as a signal that this was to be recorded.

When he left the general's presence he found that his shirt was soaked with sweat.

Cutler lounged on the rocky bank of the river beneath red-brown cliffs, watching Joklinney at the river's edge, busily bending, straightening, arms in motion as though weaving something from the reeds and sticks he had collected. A quarter of a mile further along, Lily and her Santa Fe lawyer strolled along the riverbank, Redmond looming over her. The corporal and one of the troopers sat on a rock nearby, and the other trooper tended to the horses. Remaining in the vicinity of Lawyer Redmond abraded Cutler's nerves, so he kept company with the future chief of the Red Stripe People—if Caballito didn't destroy them all first.

Joklinney stepped back toward him among the pale rocks, bare dark legs beneath his coattails. He squatted to breathe upon the little fire he had built. His eyes slanted toward Cutler lounging on the warm stones.

"What are you making there?" Cutler called.

"You eat rat, Nantan Tata?"

"White-eyes don't like rats the way Indeh don't like fish."

Joklinney grinned in his mechanical way, as though clockwork gears and levers in his cheeks had to muster themselves. "Joklinney eat fish every Friday in San Francisco."

"Friday fish for good Catholics."

"White-eye don't like guts," Joklinney said.

Cutler raised himself to his elbows to rest an aching back. Little gusts of cool drifted up from the river. On the far bank a deer showed itself, to bounce off into the brush flaunting the white flag of its tail. Downstream Redmond was now seated on a down timber, lecturing Lily on one of the many subjects he knew more about than anyone else in the world.

"Soldiers at Fort Point call Joklinney Joe King," Joklinney continued. "Hey, you, Joe King!" He mimicked an irritated, shrill voice of command. As Percy Robinson had said, Joklinney spoke English well enough, but often it was as though the Apache chose to use the pidgin his white auditors expected.

"Hey, you, Joe King!" Cutler echoed, and they both laughed, he and the bloody-handed butcher of Joklinney's Raid.

"Nantan Tata has wife?"

"I have a wife in Mexico."

"Joklinney two wife, one San Marcos, one Bosque Alto."

He knew well enough of the wife at Bosque Alto, and the thought of Sam Bunch's secret scout with her nose bobbed made the backs of his legs crawl. There was a commotion where Joklinney had built his trap, a stick springing erect with a water rat suspended, struggling. Joklinney moved swiftly to squat beside the rodent on its gallows. His knifeblade flashed. He brought the rat back to the fire, holding it by the tail. When he laid it on the coals, hair fizzled in the flames.

"Plenty rat San Francisco," Joklinney said, squatting by the fire. "Plenty guts," he said, grinning sideways at Cutler.

"Were the soldiers at Fort Point good to Joe King?"

"Some good, some no-good, some plenty bad. Lieutenants take Joe King San Francisco." He made motions indicating hills. "Take Joe King ferryboat," he pidgined. "Chinee eat. Take Joe King hoorhouse."

"Whorehouse in San Francisco?"

Joklinney made the hills motion again, but differently, illustrating breasts. "Big house! Many white-eye squaws. They fuck with Joe King, lieutenants pay."

He asked if the house had been on Nob Hill, but Joe King didn't know that, and of course San Francisco was famous for the number and variety of her whorehouses, famous also for her madams. It seemed a curious bond with this Apache. Face pointed toward the fire, eyes slanting toward Cutler, Joklinney said, "Joe King fuck two squaws that place."

"Good-smelling women!" Cutler said. One night in his sixteen-year-old vigor he had fucked four of the girls in the house on Delight Street, and two on many occasions. Then he had fallen in love with one and shot dead her pimp, who had discovered she was giving away free tricks to Pat Cutler and had beaten her terribly. If Pat Cutler had remained in San Francisco after that, the Hounds would have had their revenge. Thus he could make a case that Ruth Anna had sent him east to save his life, not to be rid of him. "Apache needs two women," he said. "White-eye only needs one."

Joklinney nodded seriously to this, tending his rat. Cutler knew of his raid, an offshoot of Caballito's breakout from San Marcos, as a two weeks' horror, Joklinney and six other bucks killing, torturing, crippling sheep, maiming cattle, riding stolen horses to death—killing and maiming for the sheer hell of it, for sheer hatred. Along with Johnny Angell, Joklinney was another murderer Cutler found himself rather liking.

The smell of roasting meat circulated with the hot air from the fire. Joklinney prodded the carcass with a stick. "San Francisco many white-eye," he said.

"Many more white-eye in New York, Chicago, Baltimore, Cincinnati, New Orleans—"

"Too many white-eye."

"Too many white-eye for Indeh to fight," Cutler said. "Indeh must settle down. No more raiding."

"Not San Marcos," Joklinney said grimly. Downriver Redmond was up and pacing, gesturing, watched by an audience of Lily and the soldiers.

Joklinney pried the rat off the coals with the tip of his knife, dropped it on a flat rock and cut off a hind leg. He passed this, steaming, to Cutler, who burnt his fingers and dropped the gobbet back on the stone, to Joklinney's laughter. Joklinney watched him with his close-set eyes as Cutler picked up the leg again, and nibbled at it. His stomach lurched.

"Joe King thinks he die at Alcatraz of white-eye sick," Joklinney said. "But Nantan Lobo send him to Fort Point to the soldiers, so he don't die." He cut and munched, nodding to himself, occasionally pushing steaming tidbits toward Cutler. Cutler tried another. This time his stomach didn't rebel.

"No guts, Joe King."

"At Alcatraz many bad white-eye," Joklinney said with his mouth full and juice dripping down his lip. "Bad white-eye try cross water." He made motions of ocean waves, or of swimming. "Four bad white-eye die. They think die is better than Alcatraz. Indeh think die is better than San Marcos."

"Red Stripe People live Bosque Alto now," Cutler said, in the same pidgin that Joklinney employed.

Joklinney shrugged and said, "Nantan Lobo want Joe King think like white-eye, come back to Red Stripe People like white-eye Indeh. Joe King don't think like white-eye..." He paused to grapple with the expression of his thought. "Joe King don't think like Indeh anymore." He sat hunched and scowling into the fire.

"Joklinney's father is Nantan Dawa. His uncle is Caballito. Joklinney will be *nantan* one day."

"Joe King don't think like Indeh anymore," Joklinney said again.

"Joe King knows what he comes from, though," Cutler said. The Apache's eyes slanted toward him, puzzled. Cutler pried off his boots, shucked out of his trousers and shirt, and made his painful way barefoot over the stones to the river's edge. He tried a foot in the murky, slow-moving water, then plunged in. He swam a few strokes, splashed up out of the water, and yelled, "Hey, you, Joe King! You have to swim to bust out of Alcatraz!"

Joklinney sat scowling at him from beside the fire. Further along the riverbank Redmond and Lily were standing, staring at him, the lawyer with his arm around her waist. The troopers had risen also, and the corporal started in his direction but halted when Cutler waved.

"Live Bosque Alto or die!" he shouted at Joklinney. It felt good to yell like that, but he did not yell "Paternity is the father of invention!" which was too complicated a sentence. He paddled back to the rocks along the bank and pulled himself out of the water. Shivering, he limped back over the rocks to join Joklinney beside the fire.

There was a fair-sized party of them headed back from Santa Fe—Mrs. Maginnis and her lawyer Mr. Redmond, the lieutenant, the corporal, two soldiers, and a short-hair, store-clothes Apache the lieutenant was taking back to the reservation. Johnny, Pard and Paul Tuttle met them in San Elizario, and Chat Bateson joined up with them pretty quick, who had been keeping an eye out on Jesse Clary. So then Pauly went home, where he had work to do.

The lawyer was such a big man his shoulder stuck out of the buggy, and Mrs. Maginnis was scrunched over onto the far side, with scarves tied over her hat and under her chin so she looked like an Arab woman.

The lieutenant didn't like Mr. Redmond one bit, and kept company with the Pache more than anybody else. The corporal muttered to Johnny once that Cutler was famous for preferring Paches to his own kind. The other officers didn't like him much, especially since Cutler had shown some of them up at an ambush the major had got them into.

The lieutenant kept to himself with his town Apache, and Mr. Redmond didn't care for Johnny riding alongside the buggy for conversation, either, and whenever they stopped to stretch their legs he acted as though he had taken a lease on Mrs. Maginnis, helping her down out of the buggy and ushering her this way and that, and contriving to keep his arm around her or his broad, black claw hammer coat back between her and anybody else. It did appear that he didn't want anybody interfering with his client. Pard and Chad made jokes about it until Johnny squint-eyed at them to quit it. The troopers watched, grinning sideways, and the lieutenant pretended he wasn't interested. The simple fact of it was that Mrs. Maginnis affected men so they seemed like dogs around a bitch in heat.

Redmond had a fair leather satchel with a high polish on it, straps, brass buckles, and a fancy handle, and the initials on it, JHR. He tended to his little case even more carefully than to Mrs. Maginnis, so Pard whispered, "Wonder what he's got in there. Greenbacks, probably."

"Lectures he's going to give once he gets really warmed up to it," Johnny said, and Pard laughed, for the lawyer was a great one for lecturing. He had a way of shaking a finger out in front of him when he spoke, like a teacher instructing plowboy scholars.

Seated on a down timber where they stopped once, Mrs. Maginnis on one side of him and the shiny satchel on the other, Redmond patted the case, shook his finger out, and said in his bugling voice, "I have spent two nights writing writs and torts and charges that I have got right here. We will see how this justice of the peace deals with these! I believe we will see the law hopping in Madison!"

"Are you sure you should proceed so quickly to battle, Mr. Redmond?" Mrs. Maginnis murmured from under her scarves. She glanced at Johnny and he thought she was blushing. It seemed to him too that Pard and Chad were expecting him to do something about this fool of a lawyer.

"My dear little lady, did you not come to my office praying for someone to pursue your case?"

Lieutenant Cutler, lounging in the shade with the corporal and the Apache, made a face like eating pickles.

"And what have you to say, Mr. Angell?" the lawyer inquired.

"Well, sir, I don't know that much'll get done until the governor appoints a sheriff, like he said he would do."

"The sheriff is only the spout of the pipe," Redmond said. "We are talking about the veritable springs on the mountainside! You young fellows"—he waved a big hand at the three of them—"think the law has become a joke. The law does not suffer contempt, my friends! We will summon it back from the grave, we will pump it full of life, we will give it direction and purpose! The law of the gun will become as extinct as antediluvian beasts!"

"Oh my!" Pard said, pretending admiration.

Johnny watched the lawyer lay his thick arm around

Mrs. Maginnis's waist, squeeze her once and release her.
"We will flay this little lady's enemies! And I include Colonel
Dougal." He turned to peer at the lieutenant, as though
Cutler might make some objection. "Madison has not seen a
real lawyer yet!" he declared.

That seemed a bit hard on Mr. Maginnis. It seemed to
Johnny that Mr. Redmond had a whole different set of faults
from Mr. Maginnis and was not going to serve anyone well
but his own self. But both of them had that same trust the law
would work everything out, or said so anyway. Mrs. Maginnis
looked wilted inside her cocoon of scarves, and he thought
she might be wishing for a different lawyer than this one.
Still, the fair leather satchel did looked stuffed with legal
papers.

While Redmond was loading Mrs. Maginnis back in the
buggy like she was a piece of luggage, Pard said, "What's a
man do, learning law? Just read books so he can jabber like
that?"

"Too many laws anyway," Chad said.

"He has got a good portion of them in that satchel of
his," Johnny said. One night in the cantina in Corral de
Tierra he and Jack Grant had sat late talking about law. Jack's
point was that laws were there to be enforced. Frock-coat
gentry sat in the legislature thinking up fine new statutes, but
out at the lawing end somebody had to load defensive iron,
saddle up, and ride *out*. Just the few laws, like the shalt-nots
of the Commandments, enforced hard, that was the proper
system, Jack had said.

It did gall him a bit that Pard and Chad were looking to
him to deal with Redmond somehow. They had taken to
accepting whatever he said like orders in the army, but at the
same time expecting of him what he wasn't always certain he
could perform. Just to let them know he had the problem in
mind, he set them to looking for a rattler the next time they
stopped. Chad found a granddaddy, long as he was.

They had a bit of luck when Mr. Redmond left the fair
leather satchel behind going off into the brush to relieve
himself, and Mrs. Maginnis went in a different direction.
They unloaded the rattler from the tarp onto the satchel,
poking sticks at it to keep it there, until it coiled and headed
up very mad, head wheeling and jerking at one end, and the
yellow buzzer going it on the other. The way you caught a

rattler was walking around and around it fast, until it couldn't keep up watching and you could catch it behind the head. He started walking fast around the snake buzzing away on top of the satchel, Pard and Chad joining him, so the three of them were hurrying in a kind of loco lockstep, yelling back and forth. The corporal came running up, and the troopers, and the lieutenant and his pet Pache. The corporal unshipped his revolver, but Johnny signaled to the lieutenant and Cutler told him to put it away, the rest of them standing well back from the three hustling around the snake with its turning head. And finally Redmond rushed out of the brush demanding to know what was happening.

When he saw the rattler buzzing off its fat, diamondback coils, head turning and tongue flickering, he stopped in his tracks. "What's that snake doing on my case?"

"He is pure in love with it," Johnny said, almost panting from his trot. "It is a fact that some of these big diamondbacks will fall in love with a shiny thing like that."

"By Golly, he is a big fellow!" Chad said, and Pard said, "That is a ten-year rattle if I ever saw one!"

"Shoot him!" the lawyer bugled out. "But be careful of my case there." Mrs. Maginnis had come up too, to stand well back with the lieutenant.

Johnny acted like he was too busy stamping in a circle around the case to answer right away.

"Tell one of your men to shoot that snake!" Redmond yelled at the lieutenant.

"Johnny Angell usually knows what he's about, Mr. Redmond," Cutler said.

"Shoot that big fellow and his mate'd be here in a minute," Chad panted.

"Not only that," Johnny said. "See those kind of reddish marks underneath those diamonds? That is a *king* rattler!"

"Oh my, it is one at that!" Pard cried out.

"Shoot that king rattler and every other rattler in the district'd be swarming up here!"

They stamped around their circle. He hoped the rattler wouldn't get dizzy and fall off the satchel.

"It is *king* rattlers that love shiny stuff," he said. "Love to look at their reflections, is what it is. How're we going to get this fellow off here, Pard?"

Pard made a grating sound trying to hold back laughing,

and Johnny saw Mrs. Maginnis staring at him with her hands
folded under her chin.

"Get a stick! Knock him off!" the lawyer yelled. He was
bouncing around them, going counterclockwise.

"Oh my God, you can't do that, that is the worst thing!"
Chad panted.

"Well, do something!"

"Not so close there!" the lieutenant called out. Johnny
could see the corporal grinning. The Pache was standing with
his arms folded and his nostrils flared out. They charged on
around the coiled snake.

"I—b'lieve—I—can—hit—that—duck!" he panted. "He'll
just give us one chance, though. Everybody's got to be ready
to hightail it! Everybody mounted up and ready to go, hurry
up now!"

They all hustled off to their horses, Mr. Redmond gathering up Mrs. Maginnis and rushing her to the buggy. Pard
doubled over once with his hand to his mouth like he had a
stomach seizure. Johnny signaled to the two of them to
mount up too, while he continued to fix the snake by trotting
around it.

"Be careful of my case there!" Mr. Redmond yelled at
him.

Finally everybody was mounted up and watching, Chad
holding his horse ready. Johnny drew his Colt and blew the
snake's head off, messing up Mr. Redmond's case quite a bit.

"Get out of here!" he screeched. "Every snake in the
territory will be here in one minute!" He snatched up the
satchel from under the writhing rattler, skinned into his
saddle, and led the way out of there at a dead run. They
raced on away from the mesquite grove, raising dust on the
Madison road, Chad and Pard whooping to cover their laughter, and the army galloping very soldierly but grinning when
he looked back at them. The buggy slowed pace first, and the
rest of them dropped back to a walk. He reined over to hand
the satchel back to Mr. Redmond.

"Afraid it got some mess on it."

"I see it did," Mr. Redmond said, giving him a long,
gauging kind of look. Mrs. Maginnis's upper lip looked like it
had got stuck to her teeth. Johnny rode on ahead with Pard
and Chad, feeling some better about things.

A couple of miles from town the lieutenant and the

Apache cut off for the fort and the reservation, leaving the troopers to accompany Mrs. Maginnis on into town. Johnny and his friends rode on along with them, Mr. Redmond having promised them that because of the governor's assurances they had nothing to fear from Kimball or any outstanding warrants.

"Watch out for snakes, Johnny!" the lieutenant called after them, when they had parted company.

They took supper at Dr. Prim's house, Pard and Chad in the kitchen with Berta, but Johnny dragooned into the dining room with the gentry. The doctor sat with Mrs. Maginnis at his right, Mr. Redmond at his left, and Johnny across from him. The candlelight made soft shadows of Mrs. Maginnis's eyes and her mouth when she laughed, and shimmered on the ivory flesh of her shoulders. He could watch her without looking at her directly, for she was fuzzily reflected in the black glass of the windowpane. The other three were drinking red wine. Mr. Redmond was not so noisy as usual, though he claimed it had been a satisfactory afternoon.

"No, I cannot say it was a successful interview with Governor Underwood, William," Mrs. Maginnis said. "He is suspicious, naturally. Who am I, after all, but a very special pleader?"

Berta, the Mex cook of the Maginnises' who now kept house for Dr. Prim, waddled in with the beef roast. Dr. Prim stood up to hone his carving knife. Good smells!

"An historian for a governor," Dr. Prim said, red-faced from the heat and exertion as he sawed meat. "Perhaps we will all become a part of history. It is to be remembered that the victors write the histories, as in Shakespeare's Tudor bias against Richard the Third and his English one against Joan of Arc."

Johnny watched in the mirror of the windowpane the long, smooth line of Mrs. Maginnis's throat, her hand to her cheek, shadow smudges of her eyes. "Yes, how will we be spoken of, William?" she said.

"The impression of Governor Underwood in Santa Fe is favorable," Mr. Redmond said. "He certainly is not indebted to Jake Weber as Dickey was. He's been to call on General Yeager. He's supped with the archbishop. It seemed to me he lent a very sympathetic ear to Mrs. Maginnis. An historian must be used to trying to get at the facts of a case."

"Johnny has already entered history," Dr. Prim said, "although on a cheap grade of paper so far."

"I'd be embarrassed if anybody I knew read that cock-and-bull," Johnny said. His cheeks burned. He didn't know whether he should laugh or get mad at those stories in *The Police Gazette*, and a nickel novel too, with drawings like the artist was in a hurry and had a sore hand. The ones he knew of took him for the hero, but they could just as well do you the other way, so they told lies about you to make you into Three-Finger Jack instead of Johnny Angel.

"Ah, there is some reading going on tonight!" Mr. Redmond said, laughing. "I've presented Judge Arthur with papers he'll be poring over far into the early hours. And I notified Mr. Henry Enders that the day of reckoning is at hand. The man was positively livid! Suggested I would do well to leave town while I was still able. I have yet to ride out to the fort to encounter Colonel Dougal, but I intend to do so tomorrow!"

In the window glass Johnny watched Mrs. Maginnis watching the lawyer as he spoke. A dim figure congealed beside her, that at first he thought was Berta again. Redmond was still talking when the glass burst. Johnny had his Colt out a hair too late, yelled too late. The room exploded, Mr. Redmond flung over backward, Mrs. Maginnis rising, screaming, acrid smoke billowing. Through the smashed window he had a glimpse of two faces bent over rifle barrels. His finger was pointed along his piece fixed on Henry Enders when a red-hot poker slammed into his shoulder. Then he was under the table, scrambling in broken glass.

When he slid over to peer out they were gone. Keeping his head down, he straddled the sill and dropped outside. In the pitchy dark with the lighted room behind him he was all but blind again—the other way round this time. He trotted out to the street. No one. One of the second-floor windows of the courthouse was lighted. Behind him voices shouted his name.

"Who was it, Johnny?" Pard's voice.

"Henry Enders and Jesse Clary," he said loudly, in case they were still in earshot. "Maybe one other, but them for certain."

Back in the turmoil of the house he sent Chad for

George Kimball. A blanket had been thrown over Mr. Redmond's dead body, flat on his back with one foot still hooked in a chair rung. Blood was soaking through the blanket. Mrs. Maginnis was seated in the parlor with a shawl over her head like a Mex woman, and Pard was standing by her with a rifle.

Dr. Prim took him into the surgery, stripped off his shirt with its blood-soaked sleeve, and mopped blood away from a two-inch furrow in his shoulder. He stanched the bleeding, dressed the wound, and clucked over Johnny's glass-cut hands. Bound up with his left arm trussed to his chest, Johnny refused the dose of laudanum the doctor offered him.

"The trouble is," Johnny said, "you just don't believe people's going to be as bad as they can turn out to be."

"No," Dr. Prim said, fussing with his instruments. "I know. Yes." He seemed pretty badly shaken up.

"Next time around I don't intend to come in second."

"Yes, I am afraid of that," Dr. Prim said.

George Kimball arrived, wearing the sheriff's star on his shirt pocket. He bustled around outside with a lantern, inspected the window as though making sure the glass had blown inside instead of out, and peeled back the bloody blanket to look at another dead lawyer. Finally George Kimball got around to him, and Johnny found it interesting that it was not that the deputy didn't believe he had seen Henry Enders and Jesse Clary through the glass just before the shot, it was that he had to make a considerable business of *pretending* to doubt it—not an easy expression for George Kimball to figure out how to jam his features into. No mention of warrants or old fights either.

It was decided to leave the body covered up where it lay, until morning.

In bed Johnny stared up into the darkness, considering the likelihood of his own death by some violent means, like this tonight, or otherwise. He groaned when he remembered the rattler trick he had played on Lawyer Redmond, whom the snakes in town had brought down. When he got to playing tricks instead of tending to his business, people died that he ought to have been responsible for.

Late that night Lily Maginnis crept into his bed for the first time, to comfort or be comforted.

*　　*　　*

Five days later Johnny was at Penn McFall's line camp east of Puerto del Sol, where he found Jack Grant. They sat in the mud-daub hut with its one window and smoke from the center fire sucking out through the eaves, though still thick inside—he and Jack and a lean old PM cowboy, with white whiskering and no front teeth. They squatted by the fire drinking black coffee. Johnny's eyes were running from the smoke.

"What'd you do with Maginnis's missus?" Jack asked.

"She's got a sister she's gone to stay with in Santa Fe."

Jack wrapped his long, scarred-up hands around his coffee cup. His own was almost too hot for his right hand, his left still bound in a sling that was filthy as everything got out here.

"Thought I'd talk to you before I talked to Mr. McFall, Big Jay," Johnny said. "About a bunch of us riding into Madison. Maybe it is up to us to clean out that nest of rattlers."

Jack's long, earnest, stubborn face turned sour. "Maginnis tried that. That is no good, Johnny. I remember once you spoke out strong against Regulatoring. Just a posse against folks you don't like."

He was tired, and his shoulder hurt with a steady throb that didn't give him much sleep. A good many people had volunteered for that posse or Regulators or whatever it was of Mr. Maginnis's, Anglo and Mex alike, that the cavalry had run out of town. But he understood well enough what Jack was saying.

"Maginnis ought to known better, being a lawyer," Jack said. "No proper authority, what's a posse but a mob of men?"

"I just don't see any other way—" Johnny started, but quit.

"Times when a mob o 'men's the onny way," the old cowboy said, spitting into the fire.

"Not to my mind," Jack said.

"That was no proper posse that gunned down Mr. Turnbull, Big Jay."

"Proper posse acting improper, the way I look at it," Jack said. "The way I heard it, anyway. I'd rate Joe's posse a step down too. Both of them, just a way of murdering with some kind of OK stamp on it."

"I was with Joe's posse," Johnny said. He thought to speak of what Mr. Redmond had said of the spout and the mountain springs, but he just felt played out.

"I expect there'll be a proper sheriff soon," Jack said, with his lower jaw stuck out like a mackerel's.

Johnny took a deep breath and said, "It was all Mr. Maginnis knew to do. He had just been shot at by the *sheriff* and two others set to dry-gulch him. It was all he knew to do, get his friends together and face down the people that'd killed his partner and tried to kill him. The law was out to kill him too. It is no better with George Kimball, and you know it, Jack. I've come to ask you to ride into Madison with us. Some others is out rounding up other fellows."

"I won't do it. I wouldn't before, and I won't now. I won't go with a mob of men. I don't think many others will either, after that last time."

The cowboy muttered and scrubbed the back of his hand over his mouth.

"They gunned down Mrs. Maginnis's lawyer and almost got me, Jack. It is run, stand and wait for next time, or go after them."

Jack reached for the tall, blue enamel coffeepot and poured more coffee. He waved a hand before his face to thin the smoke. His pants had ridden up over his boot tops to expose narrow, white shanks.

"Little Jay, you and me've been friends," he said. "We have gone hunting together, and chasing poontang together in town, and got drunk as seven hundred dollars and howled at the moon, and rid home next day with a head like a punkin. But times is changing, and they're changing us different ways. You got a bellyful of Regulatoring before I did, but maybe I got sicker on it in the end than you did—since now you are talking it again. I say stand and wait. Ran Boland and Henry Enders is like a chicken with its head chopped off that don't know it is dead yet. Let it die."

"I have had some experience lately to show it is pretty lively," Johnny said.

Jack said, "Little Jay, I had better tell you—Penn McFall has told the new governor I would make a good sheriff for Madison County. He has asked me, and I'm thinking I'll do it."

It was like a mule kick in the belly, but he managed to say he thought Jack would make a good sheriff.

"I'll have to serve any warrants against you if I do her, Johnny."

"There's other warrants than mine to be served. That Santa Fe lawyer had a satchel full. Writs and charges anyway. There is the colonel probably. Maybe Caballito too."

"What's there'll get served without fear or favor," Jack said. The old man sat beside him cross-legged, glaring into the embers.

"Well, I'd better clear out before all this serving starts," Johnny said, setting down his cup and rising. His knees had gone shaky on him.

"You don't have to go, Johnny!" Jack said, squinting up at him through the smoke. "Where you going, anyway?"

"Thought I'd head into Arioso. Good luck to you, Big Jay!"

Jack uncoiled himself to stand up, so tall he had to straddle and still bend his head under the roof. Jack reached for his hand and gave it a hard shake. "Good luck to you, Little Jay. You take care of that shoulder, now!"

"Surely," he said. His eyes kept running from the smoke.

"You are in the right, Johnny-A," the old cowboy said, rising also and holding out a hand. "Whatever this prickly bird says."

"Thanks! Thanks for chow, Jack." He went on outside and stood for a long moment looking up at the stars, so high, so cold and far off. Then he mounted and rode on toward Arioso to call on Elizabeth Fulton. He rocked a little in the saddle with the ache in his shoulder, trying not to feel bad about Jack Grant, trying not to feel sorry for himself.

Elizabeth was sitting in the window when Johnny rode down the cobbled street, as though she had been waiting for him, dim shape of her with the lamplight behind her, so there was a nimbus around her hair—light brown hair the *gente* called *güera*. Pete Fulton was a principal citizen of Arioso. He and his plump Mex wife lived in a fine house with a leafy central patio and barred windows giving on the street.

Elizabeth sat in the iron cage of window bars with one hand raised to him in a high-necked dress, with a glint of silver on the chain around her neck. Her tan face, in profile to him, caught some light—her face too long, her eyes set too close together. It was a nagging irritation to him whenever he saw her that she was not beautiful, that her honey-colored skin, her pale hair, her features did not combine into beauty.

He reined up at the window, where he was on a level with her. Her hand was curled around one of the bars, her face showing in the interstice, dark blossoms fastened in her hair.

"Are you in trouble, Juanito?" she whispered.

"Things are not going as well as they might," he said, grinning at her.

"But you are hurt!"

"It is only a graze." He slipped his hand from the sling and raised it to show, gritting his teeth not to wince.

"You must come in and I will dress it," Elizabeth said, rising swiftly. "Mamacita has a salve that is very potent. I will make you chocolate."

He watched her narrow form sway, diminishing, blocking the light until she disappeared through a far door. He dismounted and led the pinto around the corner just as a *mozo* unbarred the big door in the wall. He turned the reins over to the servant and passed on into the lamplit *sala*.

Pete Fulton advanced toward him, jamming a hand out to wring his, unshaven and whiskey-smelling. "Johnny, you are always welcome!" His Mex wife stood by, smiling: "Welcome, welcome, Juanito!" Elizabeth's brother, Tommy, sullenly shook his hand and excused himself.

Elizabeth spoke rapid-fire to her mother, who said, "*Sí! Sí, Elisabeta!*", and hurried away. Pete Fulton held up a bottle.

"Whiskey, Johnny?"

"No thanks, Mr. Fulton."

"Heard they tried to gulch you up in Madison."

"Not much more'n a scratch."

Ranging between them as though to separate him from her father, Elizabeth drew up a chair, pushed Johnny into it, and helped him strip off his shirt. She hissed to see his shoulder. Her mother came back with a basin of water and a sponge and disappeared again. Elizabeth bent so close he could feel her breath as she patted warm water onto the wound. He grinned up into her worried brown eyes.

Her mother reappeared with the famous salve, that

stunk like gone-bad turnips and burned like chilies. This time he could hear his own hiss of breath. Elizabeth gave him her slim hand to hold, and he wrung it until he saw her face twist with pain. While she was binding up the wound, Pete Fulton stood with his back to them, his bald spot showing when he threw back his head to drink.

When Elizabeth left the room with the basin, Pete swung around toward him. "What're you going to do, Johnny? Getting out?"

"Oh, I think I'll stick around just to see what's going to happen."

"Jesse Clary's looking for you, I hear."

Johnny grinned and indicated his bound-up shoulder. "I'm looking for him."

When Elizabeth appeared with cups and a pitcher of chocolate on a tray, her father excused himself and strode unsteadily from the room in his polished boots. Elizabeth poured a cup of steaming chocolate and brought it to him. He inhaled the heavy sweetness.

"Juanito, everyone thinks you must leave the country; for your safety, you understand—" She left off there, as though it had been a prepared speech that did not quite apply. She looked as though she had a headache, passing a hand over her forehead. He thought she was probably a virgin.

The chocolate tasted very good, sweet as it was, and hot down his throat to his belly. It was as though the heat and sweetness had loosened a knot there that had been clenched tight too long. He leaned back in his chair and smiled up at Elizabeth Fulton, and wished that she was beautiful.

"Why, then they would think that they had us beat," he said.

"I know that is important to men." She sat down opposite him, her face bent over her cup so that the neat part of her hair showed between the red blossoms. "I will try to understand... But the *gente* know you are a good man, Juanito."

She continued in a rush. "We admire you very much, young and old, men and women. All. You know this. But I must tell you that there are some who carry jealousy for el Angelito."

"I understand. I don't like just everybody either."

Her face had turned a dusty pink. Sipping his hot chocolate, he reflected that he had thought he and the fellows could collect another gang of south-county men, and ride into Madison . . . But Jack Grant had not thought he could do it, after the army had threatened them with that cannon. And now Elizabeth was trying to tell him that not all the *gente* in these south-county *placitas* were the friends he had considered them. But he was not running out of country yet.

He saw Elizabeth's hand reach out a bit, and just when he thought to cover it with his hand, he heard excited voices and footsteps. Don Teodoro Soto hurried across the patio with Pete Fulton a step behind. Johnny got to his feet.

"Juanito," Don Teodoro said, coming halfway into the *sala* on his tiny feet like goat hooves. "Jesse Clary and three others are here. Clary and another in the cantina, and two in the barbershop. I think they know you are near."

He had been thinking his luck had run out. He drew his Colt and checked the loading.

"What will you do, Johnny?" Pete Fulton asked.

"Is there anyone that will back my play?" he asked Don Teodoro. "Just to see the two in the barbershop don't get into it."

"Rafael and Roberto Gómez are here. Others will produce themselves."

"It's enough. Just to keep those two out of it."

Elizabeth stood facing him, tall as he was, her hand touching the silver medal at her throat. Pete Fulton said, "By God, if I was younger!"

Don Teodoro said, "I ask one thing. The mirror behind the bar is new. It has come from Santa Fe, before that from St. Louis. It was very expensive."

Johnny nodded. His lips felt like a grin. He grinned. "I go to save the expensive mirror," he said, with a little bow to Elizabeth. "Thanks for fixing me up, and for the chocolate."

"I will pray for you, Juanito," she said, standing straight, and very near to beautiful.

He came into the cantina through Don Teodoro's office, the back way, so he would not be facing the mirrors. The two of them stood against the bar, Jesse Clary mostly out of sight behind the other fellow, who was beefy in a checked shirt, with his hat off and lamplight gleaming on his pale forehead. The side of Jesse Clary's face was visible in the expensive mirror, slant of his hat across his face, and that mouth going, talking, that didn't look big enough to hold all the teeth in it. Nobody else was in the cantina except for the little barkeep, who glanced once sideways at him as he stepped out into the room.

"Looking for me, Jesse-Jay?"

He shot the beefy one in the gun arm, and the fellow fell halfway across the floor, yelling. Jesse Clary had his piece half out, angled like a lazy Z in his aiming crouch, when Johnny centershot him.

Near the *rancheria* of Bunch's Sierra Verde scouts, Cutler encountered a detachment. They streamed out of pinewoods to half surround him, almost fifty of them mounted on good cavalry California horses, legs bare between blue shirttails and high moccasins, the red flannel turbans—the mark of their identity—on their heads, no stripes on these tamed cheeks. Sam Bunch rode out between the files, broad-brimmed hat, unbuttoned shirt, not so regimental since he had been with the scouts. He hailed Cutler with an arm raised, big, sweating face, Viking mustache. They shook hands, Brownie and Bunch's gelding shifting counterclockwise under the gaze of the Sierra Verde scouts.

"I have got these birds in fighting trim, Pat. Ready for action. Time for Caballito to make a run for it!"

"Don't even think about that."

"How's your crew?"

"Perishing of inaction. I'm afraid if you brag too much about yours, the general'll send mine back to civilian life, no more blue-soldier dollar."

"My Sierra Verdes are natural cavalry, I'll tell you. I just wish I could scare up some cartridges for target practice. Dougal's got none to spare, he says, and I've got more sense than you about going over his head."

"Your Verdes've probably already fired more shots in anger than any troopers do in practice."

"They are used to stealing their ammo," Bunch said. He indicated a tall Apache with a face like a snarling mummy and a sergeant's chevrons on his sleeve. "My sergeant says why not bust into the magazine at the fort? Or clean out an ammunition train coming in. Might not have to kill many blue soldiers. These birds have a sense of humor, I'll tell you!

One of them's horse stepped in a squirrel hole, and the fellow took a fall, broke his neck. They just about died themselves, laughing at him."

He knew. The horses shifted sideways again, and he faced the semicircle of impassive faces under the red headbands. He missed his own Hoyas and that sense of humor where life was a joke and death a part of it. When he returned he'd take some cans of pears out to their *ranchería* behind the stables at the fort, and they would have a feast.

Bunch said in a low voice, "Junie's over at Caballito's *ranchería* with Joklinney. It's bad. I guess I should have listened to you. She wanted me to take her away with me. I can't take her away, I'm stationed right here! It's a fucking life sentence. So she's gone back to him." He rubbed the back of his hand, hard, across his mouth. "Shitfire! She said he was dead. He was supposed to be dead! Do me a favor, Pat."

No response was expected, and Bunch continued in a roughened voice. "You tell that son of a mule if he cuts her nose, I'll kill him. I mean, I'll kill him. You tell him that for me!"

"I think I'll put it to him differently."

Bunch squinted at the ranks of scouts, in their watching immobility. His face flamed. "I mean, Paches always die pretty quick in a white-eye prison, what does the fucking gut-eater mean, coming back?" He slapped his gauntlets against his thigh.

"The general brought him back to help us keep Caballito on the reservation. Which is what we're here for, if you'll remember."

"I may be what you're here for. But me and the scouts're here to go after them when they do go out. Let the sons of bitches go! We'll be on top of them in a day. Then don't think I won't put that fucking nose-cutter under!"

The Red Stripe People had built a dam in a gully where two eight-foot banks leaned toward each other, and, in the Mexican fashion, were now digging a mother ditch to bring water to the dam. Barring the way was a rock outcrop, craggy and gray-lichened. Cutler stood with Caballito watching the squaws heaping faggots and pine knots on the fire that blazed against the side of the rock. Flames leaped with each tumplined load, the squaws giggling in horseplay as they hurried up laden with wood. Two of them staggered along with a black-and-white, tight-woven Apache basket filled with water. This was handed up to bucks atop the rock, where water was flung in a gleaming sheet onto the heated rock. With a satisfying crack, a washtub-sized section of stone flaked off. The squaws shrieked in triumph and scurried off for more wood and water as the flames struggled upward again.

Cutler estimated that it would take a month to wear through the outcrop. "Slow," he said in Spanish.

"*Rápido, no*," Caballito said, nodding. He stood with his arms folded inside a red blanket. But when the ditch brought water Nantan Malojo would give them seed.

"Nantan Malojo should give you dynamite."

Caballito shook his head, mouth slashed down in a scowl.

"I will bring dynamite," Cutler said. They strolled back among the wickiups together. On a blanket outside one a naked child lay beneath a sunshade of woven reed, one leg propped up. The leg was terribly swollen, dark red shading into black on the calf. The child lay motionless, an arm crooked over his eyes. From the wickiup opening a squaw's round face watched over him expressionlessly.

"Rattlesnake?" Cutler asked.

Caballito's jaw shot out grimly as he nodded.

"He must have a doctor."

Caballito shook his head. When Cutler lingered, he marched on ahead. Unfeeling bastard, Cutler thought. The mother's black eyes fixed upon him, but there was nothing to do but follow the chief. They sat together on a log near the creek.

"He will die," Cutler said.

Caballito nodded savagely, gestured savagely toward the sun. The child would die before the sun dropped.

"*Ha-tip-e-ca?*" Cutler said stubbornly. Why?

"*Dah-koo-gah!*" Caballito snapped, the Apache "just because" to unanswerable questions. "I have seen it!" he added in Spanish.

On the other side of the creek squaws were working. Cutler could smell mescal baking. Caballito gazed off across the meadow with a jaw like a snapping turtle's. Cutler asked where Joklinney was.

Joklinney was with Dawa, with the cattle herd. Caballito

was in a foul mood, and there was no use prolonging the conversation. When Cutler took his leave the chief would not look at him directly.

"Nantan Verdad brings dynamite," Caballito called after him.

He bribed the quartermaster sergeant with a bottle of whiskey and the next day returned to Bosque Alto with a case of explosive, a drill, and a sledge. He commandeered one of the giggling squaws to hold the drill while he hammered it with the sledge. A growing group of Sierra Verdes, the men with red-striped cheeks, collected as he banged the drill, instructed the squaw to turn it, banged again. He removed his shirt, sweating immediately in the high sun, single-jacking the drill into the rock. Caballito appeared with Dawa, whose face was so seamed with wrinkles his eyes looked like glittering beads all but lost in folds of flesh. Joklinney stood, arms folded, watching. He wore an eagle feather fastened into his short hair.

Cutler beckoned Joklinney to help him hammer the second hole, another squaw substituting for the first. This one was pretty, glossy hair falling in a black wing over her forehead. Was this Bunch's Junie, Pretty Mouth, the secret scout? If so, the tip had not yet been sliced from her nose.

He took over again for the third hole, exchanging with Joe King again on the fourth. Other bucks clamored for a turn, but he was afraid one of them would miss a stroke and break the arm of the squaw holding the drill upright. Joklinney, he figured, had had some experience with rock breaking at Alcatraz or Fort Point.

He dropped sticks of dynamite into the holes, lit the fuses and shooed the Red Stripe People from the rock out-crop. The explosive blew with a hollow thump. When the dust cleared, the rock was broken in a V, with water from the mother ditch already surging through it. There were yells of surprise and triumph, the squaws shrilling. He felt vastly pleased, and amused at his pride. He walked with Caballito, Big Ear, Cump-ten-ae, Joklinney, and the toddling Dawa, back toward the rancheria.

There was no sign today of the snakebitten child. Squaws had laid strips of red beef on a flat rock beside a fire, and the six men squatted by them. Cutler had brought a brown pint of whiskey, which he produced. He passed this first to Dawa, who tossed off a swallow, murmured approvingly, and passed it to Joklinney. The pint circled from lip to lip.

"White-eye make Injun drunk!" Joklinney said, grinning at him. "Indian go crazy!" There was conversation in Apache, nods, glances of approval in his direction. He had their approbation again—Nantan Tata.

When the pint was finished, he strolled with Caballito and Joklinney across the meadow and into the shade where the trees began. A rattlesnake was plastered, yellow belly out, against the trunk of a pine, rattle buzzing. It had been nailed to the tree with one spike through its tail and one through the throat, jaws open to show a white mouth and curved fangs. The snake was curiously immobile except for the vibrating rattle, until Cutler realized that the black specks on the belly were the heads of smaller nails that had been driven in along either side. Apache torture. He had heard of the terrible torment of arrows driven into the body of a victim, each with excruciating care to find a nonlethal spot, as many as a hundred shafts, while the subject writhed and screamed in his agony. He saw the handful of shingle nails on a leather pad at the foot of the tree. Caballito, who had yesterday seemed insensitive to the child's death, plucked up one of these, jammed it into the snake's belly, and hammered it home with a fist-sized stone.

Joklinney looked into Cutler's eyes with his hard, black, close-set ones. He picked up a nail and rock, held the rock poised as though expecting Cutler's interference, then, with a grin, hammered it in.

"Why do you do this?" Cutler heard himself demand.

"*Dah-koo-gah!*" Caballito said, turning away.

Joklinney said, "This evil one has killed Key-del-koni's son. For this, many rattlesnakes will die. This is the first." Cutler thought that Joe King, caught—as he had said he was—between white-eye thinking and that of the Indeh, was trying to explain complex matters to him. It seemed, as well, that here he was confronted by the immutable, and that the clash of a modern race with a Stone Age one must result in the destruction of the Indeh. Caballito would not remain much longer at Bosque Alto, planting the seeds the agent grudgingly gave him. The Red Stripe People could not, in this tiny slice of their history, be turned from raiders into farmers and herdsmen. They would never become brown-skinned white-eyes, nor would their hatred for those who had doomed them subside. They were savages. They might become, at best, half-savages like Joklinney. They were truly doomed.

Later when he and Joklinney wandered together among the pines on a low ridge from which they could survey the activities of the *ranchería*, Joklinney said, "Nantan Tata does not like this of the snake."

"It made me think of the Indeh and their enemies. I am one of those."

Joklinney halted, shrugging. He gazed at Cutler half seriously, half mockingly. "The Indeh are few, enemies many," he said. "Always it is that way. For each Indeh who dies, many enemies must die."

They stood on a point of land watching the smoke from the fire where the strips of beef were broiling. Feathers of smoke drifted also from the mescal oven. Squaws toiled around the rock the dynamite had split. Three mounted braves were riding in from the cattle herd in the next meadow. It was a peaceable scene, except for the rattlesnake nailed to the tree, which he couldn't even see from here. He felt like Joklinney, who could not think like a white-eye or any longer as Indeh; he felt burdened with the responsibility for this people who must eventually be destroyed, and the dream of a future in Sonora was like a door that had opened to invite him into a beautiful garden only to slam shut before he could enter.

He was gratified that Joklinney no longer maintained the pretense of speaking only a crude pidgin and had admitted that one of the lieutenants at Fort Point had labored daily with him to improve his English. But Cutler was wary of intruding into Joklinney's affairs by inquiring if Caballito had welcomed him back, or if Yeager's purpose was suspected. He did ask if Joklinney's Bosque Alto wife had been pleased by his return.

Joklinney glanced from him to the women laboring around the split rock and shrugged. "She had gone to live with another, thinking Joklinney dead in the white-eye prison."

Cutler ventured further. "Does Joe King think she must be punished?"

"Joe King white-eye Indeh," Joklinney pidgined. "White-eye punish wife fucking other man?"

"Sometimes there is no fault."

"Indeh think fault," Joklinney said. "The snake is fault. You understand, Nantan Tata?" His intense, curiously inhuman eyes peered into Cutler's, and the tiny gears and levers accomplished their work, producing a hard grin. "Tell Nantan Bigotes Joe King don't cut," he said.

"That's good."

Joklinney shrugged again, disinterestedly.

"How is Caballito in his head?" Cutler asked.

The other gazed at him impassively for a moment, before he said, "Caballito nervous at Bosque Alto."

"*Ha-tip-e-ca?*"

"*Dah-koo-gah!*" Grinning again, Joklinney said, "No fault! Caballito long time Bosque Alto."

"Is Caballito nervous because Joklinney has returned?"

Joklinney laughed a single bark. "Indeh not like white-eye," he said.

Sheriff Grant's narrative:

The governor was a tall, good-built man with hair black as an Indian's that came loose in two hooks to frame his forehead, and which he would push back with one hand or the other, and a deep voice with some Hoosier in it. He told me his instructions from the Secretary of the Interior were to bring order to the Territory, and peace and quiet to Madison County in particular. And quiet came first, he said. Did I think I was the man for the job? I told him I did not know of a better one.

So we settled on my salary, a salary for a deputy it was up to me to pick, and the turnover of the horses, arms, and supplies now in the possession of George Kimball. I would need a fair salary living in Madison where Callie Tomkins was, and I will say Callie was some of the reason I was anxious for the job.

We sat in the governor's office, with its window out on the Santa Fe plaza, the governor in his rocker with his black boots set together and his hands tented.

He asked me, "Just how long do you propose to take to settle matters in Madison County, Sheriff?"

I said, "Well, sir, when I came through Madison I looked in on George Kimball. He has got warrants stacked it would take six months and fifty armed men to serve. Not to speak of court running in continuous session."

He pulled a long face at that information. On the desk beside him was a lamp with a green glass shade and a sheaf of papers an inch thick, corners neatly squared, in the exact center of the green blotter. He wrote histories, but I had not read any. My daddy told me war stories enough, who left a foot at Gettysburg and never quit hating rebels because of it. The governor was a general who had fought rebels also, and it was rebels in this county he was up against and hiring me to deal with, for there are rebels other than Confederate ones trying to fight their way out of the Union. It seems that rebels are the natural best for settling new country, but there is a time when they must be lawed into quietening down so the new country can settle in with the old.

The governor said, "The President and the Secretary of the Interior are embarrassed by the continuing violence."

I said, "The news of it anyway, as I took your meaning."

"Yes. What would it take to conclude matters in sixty days?"

I said, "Martial law."

"That is the most drastic course, and I do not yet consider it a possibility. I wonder if we could induce Colonel Dougal to participate in a bit of undeclared martial law."

I said, "I believe he will be treading pretty light these days, with Mrs. Maginnis snapping at his heels. Where has she got to, anyway?"

"She is here in Santa Fe," he said, hooking a horn of hair back from his forehead. "Staying with a sister who lives here, I believe." And he said, "I will ask Colonel Dougal if he will not mount some maneuvers in the county for show, but martial law will be a last resort. There is another course I am considering. A declaration of amnesty. A general pardon."

"You mean everybody concerned?"

"The slate wiped clean as of a certain date."

I didn't like that. It seemed to me bound to weaken the law, which did not have much more give to it in Madison County. Men ought to be responsible for their doings. I said so.

"Nevertheless, I would make such a proclamation if I thought it would spell finis to the war. Just now there seems to be a seesaw of aggression and retaliation that will find no end but sheer exhaustion. It is claimed that Henry Enders and Jesse Clary shot Lawyer Redmond and wounded Johnny Angell. In retaliation Angell has killed Clary and wounded a man named Murphy. Do you think Enders can be persuaded to forgo a retaliatory action?"

I said I guessed there was only one way to find out.

"Very well, we will put the question to him. He has come to Santa Fe to give me his side of the matter. He is advised by a prominent attorney here."

I knew who that would be.

"I hope you will remain here to attend the meeting with Enders and Mr. Weber, Sheriff."

"I'd better be here in case Johnny-A decides to lay out Henry Enders and Jake Weber the same way Redmond was laid out."

The governor looked a bit nervous at that.

It is not a sheriff's business to like or dislike the people he has to deal with, but Henry Enders would be a hard one to take a shine to. Callie said the girls at Mrs. Watson's did not like him at all, for the things he would call on them to do for him. He was a mat-haired, feisty fellow with his crippled arm tucked up tight against his chest. He had a chipmunk grin that was a pure fraud when he pulled it, and he was so full of beans he would jump out of his chair to strut around the room, and then fling himself back into his chair like he was trying to smash it. I know his kind. Something was left out when the Almighty put him together, and he does not consider that the laws and rules and Commandments that other people must pay heed to apply to him, since he is what everything else in the world is *for*, the solid diamond jewel at the center of everything. I had heard he had a reputation as an enforcer and bushwhacker back where he came from, lame arm and all, and that things had got too warm for him there. So he had come west to join up with the store, where Ran Boland was looking for new blood because of his illness.

A warrant had been sworn to by Johnny-A, Mrs. Maginnis, and Dr. Prim, that Enders and Jesse Clary had fired through Dr. Prim's window to kill Redmond at the supper table, although according to George Kimball Johnny was the only one in position to see the murderers. Enders might be feeling nervy because Johnny had already put Jesse Clary under in that seesaw the governor had mentioned.

"It has all been too much for poor Ran," Weber said. He sat very easy in the governor's office, one leg crossed over the other, high black shoes with a Mexican polish. "Not a well man," he went on. "Very ill, in fact. Army service," he said, with a severe set to his face. Old army comrades meshed through the Territory, strong as hog fencing, but I didn't think the governor would be having any. He wanted things settled, and that quiet first and peace second he had laid to me.

"Yes, things in Madison got too much for an ailing man," Weber went on. "Somebody shot out the window of his office. The sheriff murdered. Constant violence. He has gone to Tucson where he is under a physician's care."

George Kimball had not spoken of that Ran Boland window shoot. I asked who had done it.

Enders pulled his chipmunk grin at me. "Well, now, who would you think, Sheriff? Johnny-A, Pard Graves—you know those fellows pretty well, don't you?"

"Oh, yes," I said. "No witnesses to this particular window shoot, though?"

"Middle of the night!" Enders spat out. The little white fingers of his withered arm looked like the hand of some midget he had strapped under his coat. He plumped himself down in his chair again. "Mr. Weber will speak for me here," he said. "I am an outspoken man. Get myself in trouble with my mouth often."

"You are newly come to the Territory, Mr. Enders?" the governor asked.

"From Missouri," Enders said with a tight little jerking of his head. "Up near Baconsville."

Missourians were known for being scratchy, it came from the state being fought over and burnt and robbed and shot up by Federals and Confederates, turn by turn, in the war.

The governor said, "I understand Mr. Weber holds mortgages on the store and other Boland and Perkins properties." There was a graveyard silence to that. The governor's eyes flicked past mine with just a hint of his hard-winter smile.

Weber said smoothly, "The firm has been financially distressed by all this violence. I was pleased to be able to help out my old friend."

"Oh, I see, these mortgages are recent ones," the governor said, though everybody knew they were not. He went on then, leaving that hanging so Weber would have to interrupt him to set things straight, which he did not do. I was beginning to see the governor was a slick article.

"I am interested to know—and so is Sheriff Grant—if Mr. Enders is planning any renewed violence."

I saw Enders's ears turn red, and he started to pop to his feet again, but Weber made a kind of pencil stroke of his finger to stop him.

"Would you explain your meaning, Governor Underwood?"

"Certainly, Mr. Weber. Sheriff Grant and I have been discussing means short of martial law for halting the pattern of retributory violence that seems to be the curse of the county. My question is whether or not Mr. Enders feels able to cooperate in breaking this pattern."

"Mr. Enders has only acted in self-defense, Governor. His life is in danger. Threats have been made, shots fired. In a frontier situation, such as we have here, those men remain alive who are quick to defend themselves. If Mr. Enders had not possessed that quickness, he would be as dead as Sheriff Grant's predecessor."

I said, "And Jesse Clary too."

Enders snarled silently at me, the chalky little fingers scratching at his chin.

The governor said, "I am proposing an amnesty, a general pardon."

Enders snorted. "Madam Jezebel will never consent to that. Or her mad-dog killer, Johnny-A!"

"What if they would?"

"Oh, he will do what she tells him! Pup-dog sniffing a bitch in heat."

Weber made the pencil scratch again, and I saw the governor's face turn red. He did not like that kind of rough talk.

"Mr. Enders, I will not have that lady maligned in this office!"

Enders managed to snarl and chipmunk-grin both at once. "Sorry, Governor! That lady and her husband have put us through so much molestation I just can't stop myself sometimes. Told you my mouth gets me in trouble!"

The governor let that sit awhile. Weber crossed his legs the other way with a strong glance at Enders. I uncrossed my own, which were longer and took more doing. Finally the governor said, "And my proposal?"

Enders bounced up again, to strut up and down before the governor. He said, "I will mark all my accounts paid and settled if the other side will. The general pardon, I mean. My word on it!"

"Very well, Mr. Enders. We will speak with the other side in this matter." I noticed when the governor got up he made no move to shake hands with either Weber or Enders, ignoring Enders's pushed out good hand. When the two of them had gone he went to stand at the window looking out on the plaza.

I said, "My old grandmomma back in Pennsylvania said she never met a man she couldn't like. She never met Henry Enders."

"Would you put any faith in his word?"

"Not a bit. I would Johnny-A's."

He squinted like that worried him, forking back one of the locks of hair. He said, "Angell is a friend of yours?"

I· said, "Yes, he is. Johnny has got his faults, but you could bundle them and they'd fit right into that bitsy hand of Henry Enders's."

He wanted to know what those faults were. He had a very lawyer way of boring in at you.

I said Johnny just would not put up with the way things had got to be sometimes. "He doesn't understand how you can go wronger trying to fix a thing than it was wrong in the first place. He is a fellow who will take a pure outrage, like the store murdering Martin Turnbull, and let it ride him so hard he will never get over it. And now there's other things to add to that. I believe Turnbull's murder has ruined Johnny Angell, that was as good-hearted a boy as I have ever known."

The governor looked at me hard, as though thinking that over. He said, "I see you are not so impartial in your opinions as I had hoped you would be."

I said, "Maybe my opinions and the sheriff's are two different things."

He nodded to that and said he must prevail upon Mrs. Maginnis to bring Angell here for a meeting, and I agreed with him.

The next meeting was five nights later. I was anxious to get down to Madison to take up my duties, relieving George Kimball, and show Callie the star on my vest, but I was anxious to see Mrs. Maginnis also, now that she had become "Madam Jezebel," as Henry Enders had called her; and to see how the governor put himself forward with Johnny. There had been a piece on Johnny's shooting Pogie Smith in *The*

Police Gazette, taking the view that it was the plucky lad's duty to ventilate that conniving brute of a sheriff, though I found myself a bit tender now of that kind of talk of sheriffs. There'd been other pieces about Johnny published also. One fellow would tell you what he'd read, half mad at it, while another would tell you laughing. It gave me some pleasure to think of those stories about that slip of a boy, solid grit, holding out against the forces of evil that couldn't be anything else but the store, driving Henry Enders wild. On the other hand, the Territorial newspapers were for the most part hooked up with the Santa Fe Ring, and there Johnny was the "mad-dog killer" Enders had called him. It came on me about this time to wonder if I was going to get caught up in this magazine and newspaper cross fire over Johnny-A.

Mrs. Maginnis seated herself where Weber had sat, in her black gown as fashionable as a lady in a magazine. She wore a cameo brooch at her throat, and her face was as pale as the stone, her dark hair caught up in a knot in back, glossy in the lamplight.

We were waiting for Johnny, who had promised to show up—Mrs. Maginnis, the governor, and I. I confess I kept an eye peeled on the window, all of us pretending to patience nobody felt. The governor treated Mrs. Maginnis a good deal more politely than he had Weber and Enders.

She said, "He will come!" smiling at the governor, who returned her a better one than his hard-winter model. When she turned her smile on me it was as though the motion spread her flowery scent. I had never seen her so close up before, and she was a fine figure of a woman, and a face you could hardly bend your eye away from. Whether there was anything to the gossip about her or not, I didn't know and made no judgments, but Callie would speak up for her. There were not many proper ladies in the Territory who would greet females like Mrs. Watson's doves on the street, or even pass them by without pulling their skirts aside like out of the mud. But Mrs. Maginnis was always friendly and would even stop to pass the time of day.

I got up when there was a single rap on the door, and the governor said, "Please come in."

The door swung open and Johnny stood there, wearing his vest and blue-check shirt, striped trousers stuffed into his

boots, revolver on his right hip, rifle in his left hand. He
glanced around at the three of us.

"It's all right, Johnny," Mrs. Maginnis said in a gentle
voice. It seemed to me her voice had changed, like she was
talking to a child, or a sick person, or a pet that she loved.

He came on in, saying, "Hello, Big Jay." He shook hands
with the governor. "Pleased to meet you, sir!"

"I am glad you have been able to be with us, Mr.
Angell," the governor said. "Please sit down." I was interested to see Johnny glance once at the window before he sat,
and I thought that never again in his life would he look at a
night window the same as he once had.

The governor explained the idea of the amnesty, Johnny
sitting straight-backed, frowning, his rifle balanced against
the wall beside him. I wondered who was going to be in
charge between him and Mrs. Maginnis. When the governor
finished there was a silence, as though the two didn't know
themselves. It was Johnny who spoke first.

"Well, sir, I can see it's a good idea from your point of
view, for it might stop some things that have got going like
that seesaw you spoke of. But you'll pardon me if I say it just
won't do."

The governor said over his tented hands, "Why is that,
Mr. Angell?"

This time Johnny glanced toward Mrs. Maginnis. I studied his features to try to make out what was different. He had
always been pretty as a girl, but he had lost some baby fat,
and there was a hard line to his jaw and a kind of hard,
flashing squint when he glanced up at the window again. But
I understood that what was most different was the way I was
looking at him, which was a sheriff looking at a fellow he
might have to deal with some day. And I thought that it was
true what I had said of him to the governor, that Martin
Turnbull's murder had been the ruin of as fine a young fellow
as you would ever know, a man you would rather ride range
with than anybody else, or head into a *placita* to a *baile* with.
That Little Jay was as dead as Martin Turnbull.

Johnny said, "Well, sir, there's two kinds of wrongs—
what you called just now outrages. There is the general kind
that happens to other people, or somewheres else, and you
feel bad about it in a certain way, but you forget about it and
it blows away. But there is the other kind, the particular kind

that is done to you or people that are important or dear to you. That kind won't blow away."

"Bravo, Johnny!" Mrs. Maginnis whispered.

"There are things that have got to be punished for," Johnny went on. "By law is best." With a nod to me, he said, "Jack and I have talked how it beats Regulatoring. But this country—I mean the whole country, too!" he said with a wide motion of his arm, "—will never amount to anything if those things are just let be. I mean, there will be a kind of poison on everything."

"Yes, yes, I understand your strong feelings," the governor said. "Everyone has seen such instances in his own life, of course. Everyone has had to swallow some."

"A thing my mother used to say to me," Johnny said, "a man has to go to his Father's House justified. It is part of that, you see."

There was a silence like there just wasn't any answer to that position of Johnny's. Mrs. Maginnis said, "We in Madison County have had more than our share of outrages, Governor."

"No doubt you have, ma'am, but you must understand that your enemies also have their grievances and justifications. Mr. Enders is willing to accept a general amnesty, and, as he put it, mark everything paid and settled."

"He has nothing to lose, Governor!" Mrs. Maginnis said.

"And may I ask what the Maginnis party has to lose?"

I saw Mrs. Maginnis touch Johnny's arm as though that was for him to answer. He said, "What I just said, sir."

"Vengeance," the governor said, raising his head to peer at the two of them along his nose.

"It does sound bad when you say it that way," Johnny said, "but maybe it is the only thing that will blow away the poison. Like I said, it would be better if there was a proper court of law doing it."

"I try to speak fairly, Governor," Mrs. Maginnis said. "There is terrible faction in Madison. People are forced to choose one side or another. Each has its violent adherents. Of course we believe—and with a great deal of evidence, with *many* outrages suffered—that we are in the right. We also know there can be no justice for us while Judge Arthur is on the bench. There is false swearing, bribery, intimidation, and shameless manipulation."

"Barry Arthur is a store man, all right," I said. I thought Mrs. Maginnis had spoken well for her side of the fight.

The governor looked down his nose at me for butting in. Mrs. Maginnis said, "My husband would have wanted us to pursue every legal means of retribution, Governor Underwood, and it is still my resolve to do so."

"Of course, ma'am."

"There has got to be punishment," Johnny said. "It is not going to all just blow away."

I said, "Johnny, if you go outside the law for your punishment, then you will come up against the law."

He looked at me with those eyes that sometimes seemed to see right inside. "Why, I understand that, Jack. What is wrong is the law thinking that if it does nothing it is all right to do nothing. It is not all right."

"I will tell you what my husband came to believe, Governor," Mrs. Maginnis said. "He loved the law, you see. But he came to see that the processes of the law could fall into the hands of criminals. In that case, the citizens—who had handed the power of the law over to certain sheriffs, judges, and prosecuting attorneys—could take that power of the law back into their own hands."

The governor said, "I believe that is called lynch law. I would feel compelled to fight harder against that corruption of the law than the other you claim to perceive."

"My husband was seeking to arrest the malfeasants of Madison, Governor—Mr. Arthur, Mr. MacLennon, and Sheriff Smith—when the cavalry was quite illegally ordered into action to protect those people."

I said, "So what will you do now, Johnny?"

He looked at me tight-lipped. "I just don't know yet. You know, that posse that killed Mr. Turnbull. There was four of them that did the killing. Three of them are dead, Ed Duffy got away to Texas—"

"You would know as good as anybody that three of them's dead, Little Jay," I said.

He shrugged as though cold murder and hot were all the same, which was the way he had changed or else the way I had, thinking it. He said, "If I just knew those four had been *told* to do that. How far up that *told* came from. That's what I just don't know for certain yet."

The governor said, "I have heard you both say that legal punishment should take precedence over lynch law."

"Yes!" Johnny said, and Mrs. Maginnis nodded.

"And you are certain you recognized the men who shot Mr. Redmond, Mr. Angell?"

"Yes, sir."

I said, "One is dead."

"That is not what we are talking about, Jack," Johnny said. "He was out looking for me."

The governor said, "Would you give evidence if Henry Enders is brought to trial?"

"Yes, sir."

"Will you surrender to Sheriff Grant and protective custody until the trial takes place?" I saw him fix his eye on Johnny like he had set all his will power behind it.

"Governor, there are warrants against him for murder!" Mrs. Maginnis said.

The governor leaned back a bit and folded his arms. "I will guarantee that he will not be prosecuted, or that if he is prosecuted and found guilty, that he will be pardoned."

I said, "That is a kind of one-way amnesty, Johnny."

"I don't know. . ." Johnny said. "I don't know if I can stand being cooped up. I don't know if—" He was rubbing his hands on his knees and I saw him glance at the window again. He looked sideways at Mrs. Maginnis.

"You did say—" the governor started.

"You have to give me some time to think it over," Johnny said.

I saw that did not please the governor, who had got himself set thinking he had worked it out and everybody else ought to see it the way he did.

"I advise you not to take too long about it, Mr. Angell," he said.

Cutler's son was a year old when the signal sergeant handed him the flimsy of a telegraph message from Hermosillo: "Don Fernando ill suggest Patrick Cutler come Las Golondrinas earliest instance. Kandinsky."

His footsteps left rotten spots in the half inch of snow that had fallen during the night, evenly frosting everything visible except for the broad circles of bare ground beneath the trees. His hands ached with cold, holding the paper. He

had walked a hundred yards before he retraced his steps to
send a telegram to General Yeager at Fort Blodgett, requesting
leave to visit his wife in Sonora. Colonel Dougal would think
he had been sent on another expedition of espionage, further
evidence of a coming invasion of Mexico.

Permission for a two weeks' leave came before noon,
over Captain Robinson's name.

It was very cold at the Hacienda de Las Golondrinas,
within deep walls, on tile floors. A fire burned in the huge
fireplace in the great *sala*. Dr. Bellaguer was a pudgy little
man in a frock coat. His plump white hands patted and
rubbed together as he spoke.

"I believe his health will improve when the weather
becomes warmer. In the spring, when flowers begin to bloom
again, and life is renewed, you understand. He is old, he has
seventy-nine years, there is not much warmth in such old
flesh. But the spirit remains strong! Be assured that when the
sun warms the land again, he will be restored. I tell him he is
like a lizard, who must sun himself upon warm stones so that
the blood will continue to flow in its courses!" Dr. Bellaguer
chuckled as he smoothed imaginary cold cream into his soft
little hands.

Cutler asked of his wife.

The doctor assumed a solemn expression. "Ah! She improves, she improves, but slowly, slowly. But please, Teniente
Cutler, Don Fernando begs to see you upon the point of your
arrival!"

The old man lay on a chaise longue in a sunny, south-
facing room, with a fire blazing and split wood neatly stacked
beside it. He was propped up by pillows and wrapped in a
gaily striped coverlet. His beard and mustache were white
with yellow veining, hair thin and fine as cotton with the pink
scalp showing through. His face looked as though the skin
had been stretched over bone. There was warmth in the hand
Cutler held for a moment, and a small smile tilted one side of
Don Fernando's lips.

"You are better, I see, Don Fernando."

"So I am told, Patricio. When I asked Lalla to wire you it
was thought the sands were running out. I am grateful that
you have come." His frozen cheek glistened with a tear.
"Please, here is a chair. Please, sit." The frail hand made
motions. Cutler sat. Out the window the leaves were ruffled

by the wind, turning silver, turning dark. He noticed some new, pale green growth. Beyond yellow fields were low hills spotted with grazing cattle, beyond the hills distant mountains.

He said, "The doctor says María is better."

Don Fernando frowned delicately. His waxen nose looked like a jib. "She takes great interest in her religion, it is true. And an interest is better than no interest, or so I tell myself. She prays, she observes Holy Days one had not known existed. She confesses her sins. It is excessive, and sometimes the irritation at these excesses rises in me like bile. There is no doubt that she has been damaged, Patricio. And yet I must try to believe the good doctor, who claims that she recovers."

"Does she know that I am here?"

Don Fernando closed his eyes and shook his head. "I do not know what she will do when she knows, Patricio. But I thought—you must see your son. He has one year now."

"He pleases you?"

"Ah, he is purely a marvel! You will see! How he lights up the dark days of one's winter." Don Fernando's face seemed to have lighted as he spoke of the child. "The strong little body, the beautiful little face. He looks at one—so candidly! I tell you, Patricio, that when she is with the child, the mother is not mad! For Peto is only sweet sanity of mind. Those candid eyes ask, why are you ill, Abuelito? Why are you mad, Mamacita? And pouf, it is gone!"

"He speaks already?"

"Many words! You will see how he tries them out, first very softly to himself, then aloud."

Cutler cleared his throat and said, "Peto?"

"It is true she insisted upon naming him Pedro," Don Fernando said. "But he is called Peto, not Pedrito." The old eyes, one bleared, one clear, fastened upon his. "You will remember that once I inquired if the child was yours. There is no question. You will see."

Cutler leaned back stiffly in his chair. "I must see María."

"In a moment," the old man said. "We will wait." He closed his eyes. Cutler sat watching him, not understanding. After a time a bell outside began to toll. The corner of Don Fernando's lips tilted into the smile again. "Now if you will stand by the window just here, Patricio. There is the chapel. Do you see it?"

He looked down from the window on the chapel, with its stone figure of Christ foreshortened from here, a hand raised in blessing, stone lamb held in the crook of His arm. The figure of Padre Juan was foreshortened also, standing at the top of the steps in his black cassock, gleam of winter sun on his tonsured head.

"At the hour of eleven she comes to confess her sins," Don Fernando said in a thick voice. "What sins can she have committed that she must do these penances—the candles, the rosaries! A girl of twenty-one years!"

Cutler did not answer, as he thought of María's sin. His heart accelerated as the padre bowed, then stood erect smiling at someone just outside Cutler's range of vision, lips moving in greeting. Then she came in sight, a slim figure in black, black shawl covering her head and shoulders like a peasant woman. Twenty-one years old! Was she truly mad, driven so by the furies of Apache hatred? She would not have been the first, nor perhaps yet the last. Yet he could understand and even forgive her need to feign madness. He watched her mount the steps to the chapel, pale hands tucking up her skirts as she climbed.

"She is there?" the old man asked.

"Yes."

He continued to watch even after María and the padre had disappeared through the dark entrance. Far off an animal brayed.

"You will see the child, in any case!" Don Fernando said. A bell sounded with a startling clang, and Cutler turned with a hand extended as though to halt this. But a *mozo* in a striped vest had already appeared.

"See that Peto is brought to his father!"

He had no doubts that the boy was his son, but profounder intimations of illegitimacy moved in him. Even if María's father had been shot for treason, on her side the child had a history that could be traced back at least three hundred years. On his own there was only terra incognita—his mother a whore, his father a pimp or a client, or his mother a madam, or his father a young lieutenant at the Presidio. He could assure himself that it did not matter. Don Fernando had picked his stock over any other available. This very lack of heritage was what had made his own country powerful, while this older one was mired in dictatorship and corruption, in poverty and religious obsession. But those old unresolved lacks remained clenched in his mind like a fist.

The *mozo* returned with a plump-bosomed Indian girl in an embroidered blouse who carried the child upon her hip, his legs drawn up like a jockey's. He had expected a child in arms. The boy clung to the wet nurse's shoulder, thick, dark, neatly combed hair, an oval, olive-complexioned face—a Mexican child. Then the child's eyes met his—candid, deep-set, and blue. The eyes he saw in the mirror whenever he trimmed his beard gazed back at him. You will see, Don Fernando had said.

The *criada* put the boy down, and he toddled over to his great-grandfather. Cutler felt weak with blunted emotion as he watched the old fingers patting the little back, the limber side of the *hacendado's* face suffused with pleasure. The boy wore a tiny, white, ruffled shirt, short trousers, red shoes. His face, when he turned to gaze at Cutler, had an extraordinary quality of calmness, a pursed, waiting-to-see mouth, those examining eyes.

"This is your father, Peto," the old man said, in a ragged voice. "You will go to him."

The boy approached at his tripping gait, halting ten feet from Cutler. Don Fernando watched with a sheen of tears on his cheeks. The wet nurse watched big-eyed, her hands caught together in her apron. The *mozo* watched from the doorway.

Cutler seated himself a little harder than he intended in the stone alcove of the window. The boy approached another step.

"I've come to see you, my son," Cutler heard himself say.

Now the boy stood at his knee. Cutler smoothed a hand over the dark hair. He had an intense sensation of the importance of every move. His son looked up into his face with the searching eyes. Cutler restrained his restraining hand when Peto started away, tripping back to his great-grandfather. The boy leaned his face into the old man's side again, one eye watching Cutler. Then he spoke, unintelligibly, in a tone of complaint, and turned toward the Indian girl. He rubbed his eye with a curled fist.

"Peto is tired," the girl said, and seated herself to receive him when he ran to her. She took him onto her lap, shrugged a shoulder and pulled up her blouse to free a plump breast. Cutler saw drops of milk spurt from the nipple, and his son pressed his face to the breast. The wet nurse smiled at the child, pink-faced. "This little one is very hungry."

The old man had closed his eyes and seemed to be napping, the sun in his face, once his lips moving as though whispering to himself. Cutler sat watching his son nursing, the Indian girl smiling and stroking his head. The little head with the V of dark hair that pointed down the thin neck looked very vulnerable. His mind ached trying to think what the life of the heir of Las Golondrinas would be.

Two days later, still without having visited María, he rode into the hills on a quail-shooting expedition with Colonel Kandinsky and a young officer of the *rurales*, his aide, in their embroidered, dove-gray uniforms and high-crowned hats. Kandinsky rode beside Cutler on his twelve-hands gray gelding—lean, gray-mustached, ageless face, shotgun in a boot alongside his pommel.

"He was certain he was dying," Kandinsky said. "He was frightened, the dear fellow. In the hour of extremity there are terrible anxieties of incompletion. He felt there were promises he must exact from you."

"I will keep the promises I have made."

"Ah, but you have not yet met with your wife."

"No."

"That is, of course, his terror. That you will increase her madness, and so his carefully made plans will have become worthless. Except, of course, for Peto."

"The doctor says Don Fernando is recovering."

"It is, of course, what doctors always say," Kandinsky said in his lazy, heavily accented Spanish. "And I believe he is correct in this instance. Still, this death must come to pass, my friend."

"Yes."

"I remind you, merely," Kandinsky said. Cutler found that he both resented the condottiere's reminder and was grateful for it, for here was a colonel who possessed almost too much good sense, while remaining loyal to his friends. Mexico had been good to him, he had told Cutler. Don Porfirio Díaz had been good to him, as had Don Fernando also. He repaid these beneficences with loyalty.

"My friend is fearful that his granddaughter will never accept her husband again," Kandinsky continued. "And that the husband, in his pride, will not try to effect a reconciliation. He is also exercised at her theological obsessions. The sins that obsess her obsess him."

Ahead of them the peons were laughing at some joke. The aide had stationed himself just out of earshot.

"She was sinned against as well as sinning," Cutler said.

"Ah!"

"Her grandfather treated her as no better than livestock when he wed her to a gringo lieutenant who carried her off to places strange and unfriendly to her. Who thought her merely spoiled and selfish, and gave her little sympathy in her misery. She was only nineteen."

"I see you blame yourself, Patricio."

"I do not blame only María."

"She blames herself too much. I tell you I have no faith in priests, with whom this unhappy country is too numerously endowed."

The horses scrambled up through a cleft in the rock rim onto a mesa, where the peons spread out right and left, trotting ahead to a tract of brushy swales. They would beat back toward the guns of Cutler and the *rurales* officers. Black mountains reclined across the horizon.

"I do not blame her if she refuses to see me," Cutler said.

"Nevertheless, this problem must be faced if promises are to be kept," Kandinsky said lightly.

With a flapping fury a quail shot up before them. In one fluid motion, Kandinsky snatched the shotgun to his shoulder and fired. The bundle of feathers tumbled to the ground. The aide spurred forward to dismount, pluck up the bird, and flourish it above his head.

They rode slowly on, the horses weaving through the brush. "I tell you something in the greatest confidence, Patricio," Kandinsky said. "Already you no doubt realize that if Don Fernando had not met you in Guaymas, he would have asked me to marry his granddaughter." He laughed harshly. "What dispensations in my heart would have been necessary for such a union! For I had been the lover of her mother—she who Don Fernando thinks died of shame for her husband. She died of the typhoid, but indeed her husband, my friend's son, was an unparalleled failure as a husband, a soldier, and a man."

"Are you María's father, then?" Cutler asked.

"Ah, no!" Kandinsky said, laughing. "Understand that Don Fernando saw in young Pedro Carvajal all the weaknesses of his own son, perhaps unfairly. Nevertheless, Patricio, I think one must not look at tragedy and say, had this or that been done differently, there would have been no tragedy. Tragedy is rooted in the very hearts of the actors of the drama, and may be surmounted only by character! Your shot, Patricio!" he sang out.

Cutler fired, the butt slamming his shoulder, the bird tumbling. One of the peons plucked it up and flourished it at him. "A fine shot for a gringo!" Kandinsky said, laughing.

It was the aide's turn to shoot the next rocketing bird. Then two more flailed up. Cutler and Kandinsky both shot the same quail, the other escaping low through the brush. Kandinsky clucked reprovingly.

"The important thing," he said, "is that tragedy not compound itself."

"I don't know what you mean."

"I mean that character must rise above tragedy, my friend. I believe that it will do so!" Kandinsky spurred off to ride with his aide. Peons picked their way through the brush, stuffing the birds into game bags.

In the high sun of noon they rested on the pebbly shore of an island between branches of a creek, enjoying the warmth of the sunlight and the fire, over which the peons broiled quail on spits. Cutler found himself seduced again by the pleasant pastimes of an *hacendado* in Mexico.

The lieutenant of *rurales*, sugarloaf hat beside him on the ground, lounged next to Cutler. "The señor serves in the cavalry in New Mexico?"

"At Fort McLain, yes."

The other had a round, brown face with a toothbrush mustache. "That is near a city called Madison? Does the señor know of a *pistolero* of the name of Juanito el Ángel?" The lieutenant had read of Johnny-A in a periodical. He leaned past Cutler to tell Kandinsky, "This *pistolero* explains his method of firing the pistol. He lays his finger along the side of the barrel and simply points his finger. It is simple, no?"

"This angel of death has killed many men?" Kandinsky asked.

"Not so many as he is credited with in the periodicals," Cutler said. "But he is a dangerous man. I think he is a good man in bad circumstances."

"The *rurales* of Sonora would not permit such a one to live so long," the colonel said. "Or else we would recruit him, eh, Tomás?"

Tomás laughed dutifully. He said to Cutler, "You have no *rurales* in the Estados Unidos, señor?"

"Nor much of anything else in Madison County." He explained the issues and forces of the Madison County War.

"The army of the United States does not concern itself in these disputes?"

"It is not supposed to concern itself with civilian matters."

With an eyebrow raised, the lieutenant asked, "Is it true that the army of the United States prepares itself to invade Sonora?"

"I know nothing of that. There are no preparations that I have seen."

"Mothers frighten their children with such stories," Kandinsky said, yawning. "The Apaches will come if you are bad. The gringos will come if you do not eat your dinner."

The lieutenant said, "Is it true that el Angelito shoots for the arm of the pistol, and not for the heart?"

Cutler had counted thirteen patios in the *casa grande* of Las Golondrinas, but he thought there might well be more. He reclined on a leather chaise on one of these, which had in its center a murky pool surrounded by a low rim, watching his son chasing ducks. A different nursemaid this time watched from a stool across the patio.

A waddling duck trailed a line of fluffy ducklings. Peto with his tripping gait followed along behind these in circuits of the patio. He would almost catch up with the last duckling when it would accelerate and flee, the line of them thrown into disarray, rushing this way and that. The mother would take to the water to regroup her brood, while Peto lingered along the pool rim as though the ducks were of no concern to him.

From time to time he stopped by Cutler, who sipped from a glass of fruit-flavored water and shared it with the child. "When you are older I will take you quail shooting and dove shooting and turkey shooting, and when you are older than that, deer hunting," he said to his son. "You will have your own pony until you have your own horse."

The child gave him a long look before he started on another duck stalk. This time he ran at the flock, which scattered squawking. Peto captured one of the babies and brought it to Cutler, cupped between his hands, the yellow feet treading water on either side, long neck and yellow beak poking right and left.

The child's lips were testing words—*pato*, Cutler thought, duck. The boy said, a little more loudly, "*Mi papá*."

His heart convulsed. It was as though a solid wall as tough as brick and mortar within the hollow of his skull had cracked across. It was what he was!

He paused in the broad hallway with plants springing from Ali Baba pots on either side and a brilliant four-pane window at the end. He did not knock but swung open the right half of the iron-braced door and stepped inside. Light fell into connected rooms in long slants, and there seemed to be dark mirrors everywhere, reflecting him in tight-fitting vaquero garb as he strode past them. His son was seated in a pool of sunlight stacking blocks into three towers. Beyond the boy were the wet nurse and the other *criada*, frightened faces jerking toward him. Turning the corner he saw María, standing facing him as stiffly erect as a knife that had been hurled into a plank, vibrating there. Each of her hands gripped the opposite wrist before her breast, and her face was so luminously pale it seemed to float toward him across the space between. She wore a long dark blue gown with lighter facings, and her dark red hair hung loose to her shoulders. The power of her eyes halted him. He had thought she might burst into loud prayers, into the hymns and incantations with which Kandinsky thought she had confronted the Apache butchers, but he could only hear the sibilance of her breathing.

She took three quick steps to her right, to a marble-topped table which held a lamp and an empty goblet. She smashed the goblet on the marble, plucked up a sliver, and gashed her wrist with it. Blood spurted like the milk from the wet nurse's nipple, but red.

In the chaos that followed, of screaming maids, of Dr. Bellaguer summoned, of blood and bandages and helplessness, he thought that his wife looked at him with triumph in her eyes.

"What will you do, Patricio?" the old man asked. He seemed frailer after the alarms and stresses of the day, his cheeks sunken and pale, with startlingly dark smudges beneath the eyes, which had a queer, oily gleam of apology or resignation in them.

"I must go, but I will come back. Perhaps it will be different when I do."

"One must pray for that. But even if it is not . . ."

Cutler understood. Life could be lived separately in a *casa grande* of thirteen patios and numberless rooms, and no doubt compliant women were available to an *hacendado*. Don Fernando's damp eyes communicated all that with urgency.

"I must go back now," Cutler said. "You see . . ." How to say it? That between the Sierra Verdes and extermination stood their one friend, Nantan Lobo, whose aide he was. Against his will the fate of the Red Stripe People had come to matter to him. "I have promised my general," he said. "But in a year it will be over." Only after he had said it did it seem to him true.

Don Fernando nodded, just perceptibly, the frozen side of his face grim. "I will live another year, then, Patricio."

In that same rush of emotion he had felt in the patio with his son and the ducks, Cutler went to gaze out the window at the little chapel with its stone statue of the shepherd Christ. He said, "If I could take a horse and a pack animal, I would ride north from here instead of returning to the railroad."

"The Sierra Madre is very difficult from here, but there is a route. The vaquero Ramón knows it well and shall accompany you."

"I must be alone, to think things through. You understand."

"I understand, Patricio," the old man said.

20

The rock ledges slanted steeply in dense shadow, the footing so treacherous—dry pine needles on slick granite—that he was panting steadily as he led the saddle horse, Negrito, keeping close to the steep bank. The pack mule trailed behind.

The mule screamed like a human when she slipped. Pressed back against the rock, Cutler forced himself to watch the fall. The mule crashed on a ledge with the load exploding like a burst trunk, then stiff-legged, slowly revolving, the long free fall, until the toy animal lay motionless among the black rocks of the stream at the bottom of the gorge. Panting, Cutler stroked Negrito's jerking, warm muzzle.

At last the ledge widened, slanting downhill. Ahead, ridge on ridge of the Sierra Madre shimmered in the heat. When the sun passed behind western peaks, he made camp. He still had dry tortillas and some sour beans from lunch, but everything else had gone with the pack animal. He shivered all night, dozing and jerking awake, huddled close to his little fire.

He supposed this was the kind of hardship, danger, and pure misery he had sought when he had fled Las Golondrinas in despair—some kind of melodramatic notion of tracking northeast from the hacienda through this rumpled country even Colonel Dougal could not suspect of being militarily valuable, although somewhere in these mountains beyond the Sonora-Chihuahua line must be the Sierra Verde redoubt for which Caballito headed when he broke off the reservation. Beyond here also was Pascual Molino's filthy SP army, and a promise of a firing squad. Maybe that also had entered the equation of his melodramatics. It was as though his observa-

336

tion of the long fall of the pack animal had brought him back
to his senses.

The next day he passed through canebrakes where saw-
tooth leaves scarred his boots and drew blood from his hands.
Clouds of tiny flies enveloped his head and danced before his
eyes. Something had bitten him on the calf, and the place
itched fiercely. Scratching was the kind of pleasurable agony
he supposed he had thought this fool's expedition would be.

He came into a broad valley—greener, rolling country
with outcroppings of black, tangled lava, overburdens of
grassy earth thick with young pines. Negrito picked his way
among the abrasive stones. Once a man traveling in this
country had been as good as dead from Apaches or bandits,
but the Apaches were on reservations and the bandits had
been wiped out by the *rurales* and the Chihuahua *seguridades
públicos*. Young Pascual Molino's death's-head face hung in
his mind's eye.

A scattering of white buildings shimmered ahead. The
town grew larger, a miserable collection of adobes, several
with new coats of whitewash. Along a hundred yards of
roadway were three smelters, one smoking. A drunk who
looked American lounged on the wooden stoop of the cantina.
When hailed, Cutler pretended not to understand English.
In the cool dimness of the *tienda* he purchased a blanket,
canned peaches, chunks of chocolate, and a dozen cans of
oysters. He arranged forage for Negrito and took supper with
the storekeeper—*carne seca*, tea with boiled milk, and a
glutinous concoction of dried apples. Everything came to this
town on burro- or muleback, the storekeeper explained.
There were no wagon roads. At Sahuaripa there was a wagon,
property of the priest there, that had been brought on
muleback and assembled, but never used.

The storekeeper wondered if Cutler was looking for
mineral. There was much mineral in these mountains, and
prospecting was now safe, with the Apaches confined in the
Estados Unidos—although who could know when they would
return to raiding? In the next, larger town was a mill with
sixty stamps in fine working condition. The border was fifty
leagues to the north, more or less. He had never heard of
Madison or Fort McLain, and Cutler was not certain he
understood "New" Mexico. This was Chihuahua.

The next day Cutler followed in a northeasterly direction

the stream that watered the valley. He was uncertain, now, of how many days he had been en route and was concerned about overstaying his leave. His calf was swollen and throbbed steadily.

Late in the afternoon he came upon a fortified ranch, a high wall of volcanic rock built against a gray escarpment. A flag that was surely the Confederate Stars and Bars flew from a flagpole behind the wall. Women walked up from the stream, swaying gracefully as they carried red ollas of water cushioned on their heads, to pass through a slot in the wall only wide enough for a single horseman. He followed them into an interior courtyard slashed across with the shade of the cliff. Under porticoes women were spinning and weaving, and four fat hogs dozed in a pen. There was a corral, with the dark faces of mules thrown over the top rail. A bearded man watched him, seated on a veranda, with a boot propped up. Three dusty children sat on the veranda step.

"Gringo?" the man asked. He held a shotgun across his lap.

He identified himself as Patrick Cutler.

"Captain Ferriss Wilkison, C.S.," the man said in Southern-accented English. "Come up, Mr. Cutler." When Cutler had limped up on the veranda past the dirty-faced urchins, Wilkison rose to offer his hand, his other still gripping the shotgun. His eyes were set close together and wary, his beard was stippled with silver.

"Military man?" Wilkison asked.

His uniform had vanished with the pack animal. He was aware of the flickerings of shadow from the flag on its pole. "Cavalry. Indian wars. Fighting Apaches."

"Sit down, sit down, Mr. Cutler. Apaches! I can tell you some Pache stories. You see how this place is built? Built that way against Paches. Rosa!"

A plump face appeared from interior dark. "Bring some of the cool tea!" he ordered in Spanish. He said to Cutler, "It is a rule with me not to drink mescal until that shadow touches the veranda. You don't have any whiskey with you?"

"A little brandy."

"Ah!" Wilkison said, and put down the shotgun. He rubbed his palms together. Cutler went to get the half bottle of brandy from his saddlebag. Wilkison seemed to be transported into drunkenness with the first glass of brandy mixed

into his tea. He had not set foot on American soil since
leaving Texas after Appomattox. He had served in the Turkish
army in the Turko-Russian War, then he had come to Mexico.
There were others like him. They were called "irreconcilables,"
Cutler knew. Wilkison appeared to maintain a considerable
harem in his little fortress, with many children. No other
men were in evidence. There were herds of sheep and goats,
and the hacienda made its own corn meal, mescal, clothes,
and shoes. An Apache attack two years ago had easily been
driven off.

As the shadow of the cliff crept toward the veranda,
pigeons fluttered along the cliff face. Wilkison took up his
shotgun and fired. Two birds plummeted down. The children
ran out like bird dogs to bring back the dead pigeons.
Wilkison reloaded.

"Paches've been quiet since." He grinned, showing a
mouthful of decayed teeth. "Too quiet."

"They are on reservations, most of them."

"Ah, there is some around, my friend. They will take a
sheep sometimes. Just don't happen to be killing *gente* just
now." He leaned forward, to stare into Cutler's face with
unfocused eyes. "But I'll tell you, I will take Pache over some
of the mongrel bastards taking up room in this country.
Remind me of some people at home, you know—niggers!"
He poured more brandy into his tea, showing his teeth again,
a man who appeared to have produced a good many mongrel
bastards of his own.

"You keep an eye out for Pache when you leave here," he
said, "but you keep a better eye out for SP. Those evil
bastards will rip off your hair and dye it black and collect
bounty for Pache. Rip it off and call you albino Pache! *Gente*
in this country keep their hair cut short, I can tell you!"

Cutler said he had had occasion to meet Colonel Pascual
Molino.

"That evil, scalping, son of a bitch!" Wilkison drank, and
fixed his bloodshot eyes on Cutler's again. "I will take Pache
over filthy mixed-blood, but I will take anything over a
Yankee!"

This seemed to call for a silence. Wilkison picked up his
shotgun again, to bring down another pigeon. Cutler poured
more brandy than he wanted in his own glass in order to
empty the bottle. He gingerly scratched at his swollen calf.

"Where are you from, friend?" Wilkison asked, squinting at him.

"California."

"Cal–eee–forn–eee–yuh! My uncle went out there in forty-nine, never heard from again. You didn't run across a Beezy Wilkison out there, did you?"

"Not that I know of."

"You'd have knew it you'd run into Beezy!"

Cutler leaned toward the irreconcilable to say, "You left your country, never to return—served in Turkey, live down here—all because you hate Yankees?"

Wilkison thrust his face close, with its swamp-gas breath. "They had no right, I tell you! Runnin' us around, tellin' us how to conduct ourself, freein' niggers to rape our women! But I will tell you why I hate Yankees, Mr. California Cutler; it is because they want to cut every man out with a cookie cutter shaped like a Yankee!"

"Long time to carry a hate," he said. "Eighteen years."

"A good Southerner is a damned good hater," Wilkison said, reloading. He fired again. Yelling in competition, two boys ran after the fallen bird.

Long hates! Was María an irreconcilable? Maybe he himself had been. The thought startled him. He said, "I recall the Bible saying we should forgive those who trespass against us."

"Says a lot of things," Wilkison said with a shrug. "What is wrong with your leg there? Looks like it is swole up."

He said something had bitten him several nights ago, he didn't know what.

"Could been anything—scorpion, tarantula; centipedes in this country you could tan and buckle for a belt. Pull up your pant leg there and let me take a look."

He did so, and Wilkison stroked the inflamed, swollen muscle with soft fingers. "That don't look so good, friend," he said. "I better lance it." He grinned at Cutler. "Oh, I was a sawbones once. Took off so many limbs at Gettysburg we'd fill a wagon in half a day. This one sure needs lancin'. Get some quinine into you and one of my wives to make a poultice. Efram, my knife!" he called in Spanish, and one of the boys scampered inside.

When a thin-bladed, evil-looking knife was brought to him. Wilkison honed it with a bit of whetstone that had been stored in a crack in the railing. He whistled softly as he did this. When he cut, Cutler hardly felt the knife, only the release of hot pressure. He gritted his teeth as Wilkison squeezed out the pus. A fat woman, a different wife from the one who had brought the tea, appeared with a basin filled with a stinking concoction that Wilkison buttered onto the wound. Then he packed on leaves and bound the calf with clean white cotton. He split open the pant leg so it would fit over the bandage.

"Can't nobody say travelers get turned away untended from Hacienda Manassas Segundo," he said. "Even Cal—eee—forn—eee—yuh Yankees!"

The next day, however, the wound was just as swollen and painful. Cutler lanced it himself, with a shaking hand. When he encountered a stream of water running between rock pools, he let himself down into one, fully clothed except for his boots, and soaked for an hour in the cooling water. His leg felt like it belonged to someone else.

Later, halted in the shade of an oak tree on a ridge, he watched a detachment of Mexican soldiers quartering across a dry valley below him, infantry, about forty of them, with two mounted officers. The white-clad line snaked through the brush. He couldn't make out whether they were regulars or SPs. Probably they didn't have a surgeon along anyway. Take this gringo out and shoot him. His leg throbbed all the way up into his groin.

When the soldiers had passed from sight, he circled around to the north. That night he made a little fire and sat shivering by it, eating the dried meat and tortillas Wilkison had given him. Wrapped in his blanket he lay staring up at the stars, which, not much farther to the north now, must be American stars, and wondered if he was dying.

In his fever his head seemed clearer than it had ever been. If he died, his son would be fatherless, as he had been, raised by women as he had been—no matter if these were an insane, God-obsessed mother and her servants instead of a madam and her girls. Even if, in the end, the boy was not cast out of a soft berth into a ruthless world, something might happen to his heart which must not be allowed to happen. That encumbering and emotion-quelling armor in which he had encased himself—against what he could not even think now!—must not be passed along to Peto Cutler.

The boy must be reared as Don Fernando would wish, to take his place as the future *patrón* of Las Golondrinas. The difference in the two blood strains that had made the boy was important to the old man; the old, proud, but inbred and decadent strain and the new, brash, vital if illegitimate one. In this dangerous fever of his body he must ensure that the fevers of his brain were healed! If María was to be insane, he must be sane, for the sake of that child who had called him *papá* in the testing, small voice. He must live through this travail just as Don Fernando, with that sigh, had steeled himself to live another year.

The next day the sun burned on his face uncomfortably hot before he managed to sit up and pull on his one boot. His leg felt as though it weighed seventy pounds, and he had to hop one-legged when he saddled Negrito. In the saddle he sat panting with his eyes closed for minutes before he clucked to the horse and felt the forward motion beneath his aching thighs.

Once he fell, catching himself at the last instant with a hand on the pommel and slamming so hard against the side of the horse with the swollen leg that he screamed. Faintness swelled and shrank in his head, and he hopped to a flat rock to seat himself, taking out his knife again. He pricked the black gourd of flesh. Pus and blood spurted. He wept. Later he heard himself laughing. He managed to clamber into Negrito's saddle again, and clucked the horse into motion. North to the Estados Unidos to resign his commission so he could return to Las Golondrinas and his family.

That night or maybe it was the next, he lay wrapped in his blanket in a queer stone patio. Peering down at him were the empty eyes of door openings cut into sandstone, a second layer and a third, connecting ladders. All was empty and silent, a dream; maybe it was a dying dream. With a great effort he turned his head to see the black horse, unsaddled, cropping grass nearby. Hawks wheeled high above him. Like the Hacienda Manassas Segundo, this town—or city!—was built against a cliff, into the cliff, in fact. Swallows darted along the facades, and swooped low over the stone walls that jutted and angled out of the cliff face.

When he touched his thigh it almost burned his fingers.

He was afraid to extend his fingers lower down. His head was pillowed on a wad of clothing. Dimly he remembered someone helping him out of the saddle. He was disgusted to find that he was weeping again.

Turning his head with care, he saw a small fire licking up in a protected angle of wall. He admired the transparent orangeness of the flames. He heard a scrape of boot leather. A man was coming up a path toward him, bareheaded, a lick of fair hair curled over his forehead. He was carrying a canvas pail slopping water. He wore a revolver holstered on his hip, and he looked like Johnny Angell.

Cutler closed his eyes. Help.

Johnny squatted beside him, frowning at his leg. The pant leg had been cut to above the knee, but Cutler did not want to look at what was revealed.

"Gave it a cut and it squirted ten feet," Johnny said. "Get the thing aimed right you could kill rattlers with it." His lips tightened with worry. His cheeks were roughened with a week's growth of fair beard.

Cutler closed his eyes in a lassitude of exhaustion. "Where are we?"

"South of Corral de Tierra about thirty miles. It's a place I come to sometimes when I've got something on my mind. It's a old Injun ruin."

"Lucky for me you had something on your mind just now."

Johnny chuckled. "I better give this another poke, Pat." Cutler felt only the release of pressure this time. Johnny hissed and clucked. When Cutler opened his eyes the sun was behind the boy, framing his head and shoulders in gold.

"We'll wait for tonight, and I'll rig some kind of litter between the horses. Get you to that doc at the fort."

"Good."

"Raving like a crazy man a while back," Johnny said, shifting sideways so Cutler no longer had to squint into the sun. "Afraid I know more about you than'd please you. I did know you had a wife in Mexico—baby too. So you come back north through the Sierra Madre. Rough country, I expect."

"Blowflies so bad you can't hang venison. Centipedes you could tan and buckle for a belt. Scalp-hunters."

"I have thought of heading down that way myself,"

Johnny said, squatting beside him, face creased thoughtfully.
He turned away. "There's the coffee boiling."

Cutler closed his eyes again. Black edges pressed in
upon him, languor filled him. He could no longer feel his leg.
Then he was shivering. Johnny helped him prop up his head
to sip hot black coffee.

"Are you on the run?" Cutler asked.

"Just thinking over whether I want to turn myself in or
not," Johnny said. "Well, I heard your sad story, so you can
sit still for mine. I got called up to meet the governor, and he
promised me a pardon if I'd turn myself in to the sheriff and
give evidence against Henry Enders. I come down here to
think it over. I just don't know what to do. I know Mr.
Maginnis would've said it is my duty, and I believe I would
trust Jack Grant—but there's a batch of others I surely don't.
I just don't know. Like I said, I've been thinking of heading
for Mexico. Or up to Colorado, though I do have a poor
feeling about running out. If I turn myself in, I'll be in a real
tangle from here on, pardon or not.

"But I just don't think a person can look at the things out
of whack in Madison County and not have a try at straightening
them out, if it is in him. There is still Mr. Turnbull shot
down, and Ed Duffy, one of them that did it, just back from
Texas and walking around town bold as brass. And Mr.
Maginnis and Mr. Redmond shot dead—and Henry Enders
still in business."

"What would you do to straighten things out—shoot Ed
Duffy and Henry Enders?"

"I could do that, I expect, and head out," Johnny said.
Cutler listened with his eyes closed, shivering again. "Sure, I
have thought of just that. I expect Mrs. Maginnis would want
me to turn myself in like the governor said. She would like to
see the thing done legal. But I just don't think the law is
going to punish those fellows."

"Is it the punishment that will set things straight?"
Cutler heard himself ask.

"Why, surely!" Johnny said in a shocked voice.

He asked about Lily. Now in his mind's eye Lily was
luminous on her bed, with Johnny looking in from the little
library, hat in hand.

"She is waiting for Mr. Turnbull's brother to show up,"
Johnny said in a faraway voice. "He is settling up some

business over in England before he comes over. Mrs. Maginnis believes he will make the fur fly. She has it in her mind that some man will come along and set things right for her. Like Mr. Redmond was to do. Now it's Mr. Turnbull's brother."

"Like you."

Johnny laughed softly. "And you," he said.

Cutler wakened to the smell of broiling meat. The late sun made black holes of the Old Ones' doorways. Johnny squatted before the fire. Cutler lay breathing the aromas, staring up at the stone facades above him. High clouds sailing over made the cliff appear to be toppling.

Johnny came to squat beside him and press a hot bit of meat to his mouth. Cutler lipped it in, chewed, swallowed. "Look how the cliff keeps falling over," he said.

"Look at that!" Johnny said, peering up. "Kind of the way a man lives his life, isn't it? Notice how you can almost hear the quiet here? How long ago do you reckon the Old Ones was here?"

"Two, three thousand years ago?"

"Don't that make you think?" Johnny pressed another gobbet of venison to Cutler's lips. "Two, three thousand years, what'll it matter if Mr. Turnbull and Mr. Maginnis and Mr. Redmond was murdered like that? What will *I* matter? It kind of gets the *I* out of things, don't it?"

Cutler dozed. He saw María's triumphant smile, blood spurting from her wrist like milk from the wet nurse's nipple, like pus from his leg. Eighteen years of hatred. Was there a term to hatred, to old lacks and loss? Could you determine that as of *now* all that was over, or did it take two thousand years to get the *I* out? In eighteen years Peto would be the same age his mother was when she had married Patrick Cutler, who had not loved his bride as much as the Hacienda de las Golondrinas, which she represented. Johnny Angell must decide whether to give himself up to the new sheriff or run to Mexico, whether to murder Ed Duffy and Henry Enders or not. What must he, Pat Cutler, decide? He might not have to decide anything, dying instead, his leg flung onto a wagon with all the other amputated legs, including Ysabel's. In the end the *Apache*, which meant "enemy," which was death itself, killed you.

Dozing, he heard Johnny speaking: "The thing that happens is that you are just not yourself any more. You are what you have done in your life, and when you are still wet behind the ears you are not careful enough. And when you are older you are too careful. So when I think about it cold, I think that Jack Grant will kill me. Better that than some crazy duck shooting through the window. Crazy kind of Texas blood-for-blood people. That is not what I am! What I want is justice done for murder in cold blood, but it is not that kind of Texas windowshoot eye-for-an-eye that is the answer!"

When Cutler realized he had pissed himself he began to weep.

He looked up to see Johnny standing over him.

"Time to head for the fort, Pat. How're you feeling?"

He could only manage to shake his head. He saw that Johnny had the two horses lined up, head to tail, Negrito behind. Trimmed poles were lashed saddle to saddle, with a tarpaulin stretched over them for a litter.

He groaned as Johnny hauled him to his feet and half dragged, half carried him to the litter. The process of hoisting him onto the tarpaulin was painful and comical. They panted together, Johnny standing beside the litter mopping his face with his bandana.

"Thanks," Cutler said. His head was clearer with the pain in his leg.

"*De nada.*"

"I thought I heard you say something earlier—that the new sheriff intends to serve all the warrants that have collected in his office?"

"Told me he'd serve those old warrants without fear or favor. I was saying one would be against your colonel out at the fort. Mr. Redmond drew up papers against him and about everybody in town."

"And Caballito?"

"Sure, there might be at that."

"It was warrants against him that caused Caballito to bust out of San Marcos."

"I heard that," Johnny said. "Well, here goes the Ark of the Covenant heading for high ground." He mounted, glanced back down at Cutler, and the Ark of the Covenant lurched into motion. Immediately Cutler slept.

*   *   *

His senses buzzed on and off like a telegraph key. There was brightness. Cloth brushed his face: a sunshade of a jacket hung over a curved branch. Stretching his neck he could see Johnny's back, on the lead horse. There seemed a stiffness of tension in it, and he saw the butt of the rifle tucked under the boy's arm. Johnny swayed in the same motion that swayed him.

Turning his head, he saw the cloud of dust, the hurrying fringe of riders preceding it. There must have been twelve of them, fanning out as they approached. He didn't connect for a moment. Sheriff Jack Grant serving warrants without fear or favor!

He yelled, "It's a posse! Cut me loose and get away!"

"Never mind it, Pat," Johnny said, without turning. "I had decided to come in anyway."

"Johnny!"

"Don't exercise yourself. It is what Mr. Maginnis would've wanted. I have just got to trust the governor, I guess."

Then they were surrounded by milling, rifle-wielding, hard-faced riders, with the dust cloud drifting over them. Sheriff Jack Grant was a gaunt man, wearing a leather vest with a tarnished star pinned to it. He wore a hat like a steeple.

"Throw down your iron, Johnny."

"Just coming in to take up the governor's amnesty, Jack," Johnny said in a cheerful voice. "I have got one pretty sick lieutenant here, that needs to get to a doc in a hurry."

Men's faces peered under the sunshade at him. His consciousness began sputtering again. The Ark of the Covenant rocked into motion. Once he roused himself to stretch his neck, peering forward from under his sunshade. Johnny Angell's wrists were caught behind his back with bright hoops of steel.

In the infirmary of Fort McLain, Bernie Reilly told him that the leg might be saved, but another half a day and nothing could have been saved.

The jail was the south side of the second floor of the courthouse. Bars had been installed on the windows since the last time Johnny had been in Madison. There was one door out, with a jog one way to the stairs and the other to Jack Grant's office. Harry Williams was the jailer, a friendly little fellow with a squinty eye and a limp from one leg shorter than the other. They didn't keep him ironed but in handcuffs, and Johnny had already calculated that he could slip those cuffs if he was prepared to lose some skin doing it. In the sheriff's office was a closet where the shotguns, rifles, and sidearms were locked up.

His trial was set for a month off. They had appointed a lawyer for him that he had seen once, a red-nosed, bald-headed old fellow they had scraped up somewhere, who smelled like his kidneys had rotted out with cheap whiskey. Jack Grant had said the governor's offer might not stand, since (1) he had taken too long making up his mind to come in, and (2) they had apprehended him instead of his giving himself up. He had got his drunken lawyer to help him write a letter to the governor on that score, but no reply yet. He was just as pleased not hearing from the governor, since he was not optimistic about the governor's response. He was not much worried about hanging for shooting Pogie Smith. He knew he was not going to die that way. It was his part to die of gunshot. Who soweth the wind would reap the whirlwind, and who sheddeth the blood of men, by men would his blood be shed.

He could see the street from one of his windows, and what galled him was the sight of Henry Enders strolling along the boardwalk, sometimes glancing his way. He would be in his black frock coat with the little crippled arm braced up against his chest, either headed for the Bird Cage Hotel for supper, or back the other way, picking his teeth. Henry Enders had been indicted for the murder of Lawyer Redmond but was outside, and he was in. Sometimes he would see Ed Duffy also, who had put on weight and walked with a confident waddle. More than once he saw the two of them together. He did not see how there could not be among those warrants that Jack Grant was serving without fear or favor one for Ed Duffy, who had been one of the four that had shot Mr. Turnbull and then beat his head in with a rock, but Jack swore there was not. Still, seeing Ed Duffy back from Texas did not gall him the same way the sight of Henry Enders did. He was pleased that Ed Duffy was available, for sometime soon they would sit down to a talk.

He had a letter from Santa Fe from Lily Maginnis, who was trying to see the governor to plead in his behalf. So far the governor had been too busy to see her. Lieutenant Cutler was recovering his health and had not had to lose his leg. That was a blessing.

Jack Grant was out of town a good deal, on the track of what was left of the Jesse Clary gang, which was still raising dust in south county. There were also rustlers coming west to steal stock and run it back to Texas. These fellows were proving a good deal harder to catch up with than he had been, when everybody had considered Jack Grant the royal nonesuch for bringing in Johnny-A so easy. Now he could joke Jack for Regulatoring for McFall, only with a nickel-plate star on, though Jack said it was the star that made the difference. He had also teased Jack a bit that he was the only prisoner in the jail, for all Jack serving those fear-or-favor warrants. Later he began to worry that he was kept the only one on purpose.

Three times a day the waiter from the hotel brought meals to him. He was eating well and regular at least, though once or twice just before dawn, when he would lie awake with a poor brand of thoughts, he would think of Henry Enders heading for the hotel every day. He thought of asking Harry to take a bite of food that might have poison in it, but then he thought there was no more use worrying that than worrying bullets in a fight. So he only complained to Jack that the coffee was always cold by the time it got to him, and if he decided to bust out of the jail it was probably going to be because of that luke coffee.

For calls of nature Harry accompanied him to the outhouse out back. The only time he really had his privacy was sitting in the two-holer with its comforting stink, and the only time he had his hands free of the handcuffs. He would sit there until Harry began banging on the door and yelling was he going to take all day at it?

Often he and Harry played cards, sitting across the battered table from each other, taking turns playing red dog, which was his choice, or a simpleminded business called pet, which was Harry's. The jailer loved to slap the greasy old cards down, shouting, "Pet! Pet!" Slapping cards down was difficult with cuffed hands, so Johnny played more sedately, and he usually lost. His mind was often on saving butter to grease his wrists and the possibilities for snatching Harry's Colt. This could best be done by calling Harry to the window to point out Henry Enders or Ed Duffy. The sill was seat-high, and, when Harry braced his hands on the sill to peer out, that was the moment.

Sometimes he thought about the Sonora hacienda Pat Cutler had raved about in his fever. It had sounded a fine place to end up, but he kept remembering a green little box valley in the foothills up in Colorado where he had spent a night once.

"Another newspaper fellow looking to talk to you," Jack said.

"I'm not looking to talk to him."

"What I told him," Jack said. He stood just inside the door, arms folded over the nickel-plated star, and hardware dangling from his cartridge belt, so tall he had to duck under the lintel coming through the door. His store pants were always too short, riding up on his boots. Today he wore town shoes, with four inches of white stocking showing.

"Why, Big Jay, I understand you're throwing a party," Johnny said.

"What's that? What do you mean?" Jack said.

"Ask your shoes up to meet your pants," he said, and burst out laughing. Jack looked like he would like to bust him one.

"You are damned cheerful for someone that doesn't have a damned thing to be cheerful about," Jack said. He long-legged over to the table and sat down. "Henry Enders is free on his own recognizance. Besides that, he is marrying that Boswell girl from over toward Socorro. Next thing he'll ask change of venue to Socorro, and all that Boswell kin for the jury. Mark my words."

"All right," Johnny said. "You look a bit broody about it."

"Law and justice in the Territory," Jack said.

"Just the same," he said, "they have got to call me for a witness, Socorro or not, don't they? I saw Henry Enders and Jesse Clary shoot that lawyer through the window clear as I see you now."

Jack shrugged. "They don't have to call you for a witness if they have hung you first. There'll be change of venue and delays, you mark my words. Still, Henry Enders is not one to put all his eggs in one basket."

"I don't know what you mean by that."

"There is talk of some people wanting to help you bust

out of here. You just take a good look that someone trying to help you bust out isn't Henry Enders."

"Oh, my! That has got some corners to it. So I am not to bust out of here because of the cold coffee, just because Henry Enders might be waiting for me?"

Jack scowled at him. "Just telling you to look before you leap."

"Well, I do sympathize with you, Big Jay. It must be a hard pill Regulatoring for the likes of Henry Enders, Mr. MacLennon, and Judge Arthur. For me, I just have to sit it out and wait for the governor's pardon."

Jack wound his long arms around his chest again. "Johnny, you know he doesn't have to do it. He told you not to take long making up your mind, and you took ten days. And then we caught you fair and square."

"Coming to turn myself in."

Jack just shook his head once.

"I would hate for news to get around that General Underwood's a four-flusher," Johnny said.

Jack shook his head again. "Something's come up. Board of inquiry out at the fort. You'll be asked to give evidence. Army's part in the killing of Maginnis."

"Pleased to have the outing."

"I just wish you'd be serious one time," Jack said.

"If I get serious I might just remember your telling me I don't have a damned thing to be cheerful about."

Lily Maginnis came down from Santa Fe for the board of inquiry and visited him in the jail. Jack was out of town, and Harry nervous of letting in a caller Jack might disapprove of. But after dithering awhile he decided it would be all right if he remained in the jail room with them.

Lily still wore black for Mr. Maginnis—complicated black skirt with black aprons made of some frothy stuff looping in from each side, tight black jacket with shiny buttons like jet marbles, black bonnet with black ribbons. The black made her face look very pale, her eyes startlingly dark in it. She sat opposite him at the little table, and laid her spread white hands over his cuffed ones. Harry sat across the room in a tilted-back chair, with a sour persimmon expression.

The front legs of the chair slammed down and the jailer rose when Lily fished in her reticule. She brought out a

cheap-paper magazine called *Western Adventure*, folded back
some pages, and presented it to Johnny. It was not the first
one like this he had seen: "Johnny-A and the Mexican
Princess, by Louis P. Rutherford."

There was a drawing of a youth in chaps and a queer
pyramid kind of hat, like the ones Mr. Turnbull had worn.
Ribbons hung off the back. The youth was pointing a Colt half
as long as his arm at a snarling, mustachioed Mexican giant,
while a pretty, dark-skinned girl peered over his shoulder.
"Johnny-A rides to Mexico to save the daughter of an old
friend from a terrible fate!" it said, in smaller print.

"Oh, my!" Johnny said.

"This man has written four of these untrue stories about
someone named Johnny-A," Lily said. "Of course Johnny-A is
the hero."

"I guess that is better than the other way round."

"Don't you want to read it?"

"I guess not." His face was burning. "Might go to my
head," he said.

Lily laid her hands over his again. "A minister friend of
mine once said that the sin against the Holy Ghost was
turning human beings into *things*. Mr. Rutherford has made
you a hero, but in some of the newspapers I have seen you
are a villain of the deepest dye. *The Territorial Call*, you
know, is owned by business associates of Mr. Weber's. So
there is this ridiculous fiction on the one hand, and lies
passing as facts on the other."

"I guess I don't want to see any of it."

"I am afraid it is where the Madison County War is now
being fought," Lily said.

Harry limped over to pick up the magazine and squint at
it. "That is some sombrero, Johnny," he said.

"Ain't it."

Lily continued to gaze into his eyes. "Maybe it is that
the newspapers tell lies with facts, but fiction like this is
trying to make some truth out of lies."

He didn't understand what she meant. The trouble was
that when she looked at him like that, or touched him like
that, or just when he caught the flowery smell of her, his head
was apt to get mixed up.

"When they tell lies about you they can change what you
are," she said. "So you are helpless not to be changed. It is

something that women know very well. Before her marriage a pretty girl is treated like a princess. Then she becomes her mate's pretty bauble, his toy—but of course his chattel. She can never be simply herself, because of the petrified, cruel fashions that are passed from generation to generation. She becomes a wife. She becomes a mother. President Lincoln granted emancipation to black slaves. No one will grant it to white women."

He had heard her go on like this before. She would get herself so worked up she would look as though she had taken a fever.

"Durango!" Harry said. He had retreated to his chair with the magazine. "You have went down to Durango because this greaser that saved your life once has sent for you to come help. I didn't know you had spent time down in Mexico, Johnny."

"It's not so, Harry," he said. "They have made it up on me."

Lily took a lacy handkerchief from her sleeve and patted her forehead with it. "I am afraid I don't have any good news to bring from the governor," she said.

"He won't do it, huh?"

"He says he will make his decision after your trial, and Henry Enders's trial, and this board of inquiry into Colonel Dougal's actions. I do know that Pat Cutler has written him to say that you saved his life and that was how you were captured."

"Jack Grant says Henry Enders will try for a change of venue to Socorro. He is marrying someone from over there out of a big family of veniremen."

"I have talked to Mr. Tarkenton—the lawyer from Globe I wrote of—who has a similar idea for you. But he thinks it will be better on appeal."

So there was not much question in anybody's mind he was going to be found guilty of murdering Pogie Smith. And the thing Lily and her Mr. Tarkenton would turn him into was something no better than Henry Enders.

"Mr. Shields—that is the lawyer that got appointed for me—is not of much account."

"He is a joke," Lily said in a tragic voice.

"This Johnny-A, he just shoots for the gun arm," Harry

said. "Never been known to miss. But this big Mex comes off either side—ambi-something."

"Ambidextrous," Lily said, but too quietly for Harry to hear. She smiled tremulously at Johnny with her pale, full lips, her eyes reminding him of secrets between them.

She said, "We must trust that the board of inquiry will find that Colonel Dougal far exceeded his authority at the so-called Battle of Madison."

"Sure, we must trust to that," Johnny said. It struck him that he had been a good deal happier before this visit of Lily's.

"Dr. Prim has written the President again, in your behalf," she said.

"You shot him in both arms!" Harry said. "And he is howlin' like a timber wolf!"

That evening there was a folded bit of paper under the beefsteak brought over by the waiter. When Harry was out of the room, he managed to read it through the grease that had soaked it:

"Jonie A we will com fer yu wen yu say. lok outwindo firs lite tomorrer. thum up yes. thum don no. finner up fer day, 1 sunday, like that. Pard."

At first light the next day he peered out the window at the empty stretch of street with long westward shadows striped across it. There was the wing of the hotel, the boarded-up Turnbull and Maginnis store, and further along the burnt-out ruin of the Maginnis house. Its sentinel chimney faced the similar one across the street. He jerked his down-pointed thumb up and down, then flipped the palm of his hand back and forth for wait. Then, yawning and scratching, he went to bang on the door to rouse Harry from his cot in the hallway to take him to the outhouse.

The Palace of the Governors
Santa Fe, New Mexico Territory
March 2, 188–

My Dearest Clara:
    I have not, of late, been permitted much time with Pedro de Alvarado, although I have learned one thing of interest, oddly enough from a novel I purchased in a local bookstall, an ill-written affair with a water-damaged cover. In this book, *Great Captain*, is a version of the case-hardened old conqueror's final utterance that rings absolutely true, and it will be my duty and pleasure to track down the novelist's sources—unless he has merely exercised his novelist's prerogative of presenting what should have happened instead of what actually took place. According to him, in the fatal expedition against the rebellious Indians who had invested the hilltop of Nochistlan, near Guadalajara, the horse of a notary named Quevedo slipped on the steep slope and rolled down to crush the great captain. Alvarado's last words, then, were not the pious platitude that he hurt only in his soul, but: "Anyone who takes with him such a fool as Quevedo, deserves his fate."
    I have, in fact, decided to set the conquistadors aside for another project which has kindled my imagination. I have realized that, as an historian, I am living in a history, and indeed am a participant of considerable account. The history is that of the American frontier encapsuled in that of New Mexico Territory late in the nineteenth century: the Madison County "War," the Sante Fe "Ring," the Madison "Store"; the soldiers of Fort Blodgett, Fort McLain, and the other posts of this department; the Apaches of the reservations. I have

recently held conversations with General Yeager, the arch-bishop, the United States Attorney who is the chief of the Santa Fe Ring; with Johnny Angell and Mrs. Maginnis of the Maginnis faction, and Henry Enders of the store faction; with my appointee, Sheriff Grant; with an old Indian fighter, Don Rudolfo Perosa, who was fighting Apaches and Navajos in these mountains and deserts before the Mexican War; with Chester Baskerville, who was one of Kit Carson's lieutenants when that legendary gentleman pacified the Navajos; and with Tom Beak, a renowned scout. These last men, still very much alive and resident in Santa Fe, connect an almost mythological past with a turbulent present. My envisioned new work is nothing less than a history of New Mexico, and the project has seized me in its grip as I sit in my office in this building that was built before the United States of America was even thought of.

In the present, with which I am concerned at the moment, I believe I can see here, in small, the last frontier of a vast continent and a nation of boundless possibilities. I see that end plainly in the embers of the Madison County War, which may, in fact, glow for a while longer, and in the flurry of lawsuits that have been filed against the principals of that war. I see it in the railroad pushing west, close to the border, with its Irish laborers unaware of and uninterested in the events that swirl around them, while consuming the beef the rustler bands sell their commissaries. I see it in Johnny-A's having been captured by Sheriff Grant, for I see Grant as the symbolic figure in these death throes of the frontier.

The outlaw languishes in jail in Madison, awaiting his trial next week. He is not much more than a boy and can hardly be expected to understand that he has become a legend in his own time owing to the modern swiftness of the printed word and the national demand for quantity, rather than quality, in print. He is denounced by the territorial press, which is for the most part Ring-controlled, and cele-brated in the national pulp-paper sensationals and illustrated weeklies churned out by the great new steam rotary presses.

In order to document my history, I have begun collecting newspaper clippings, letters, official papers, and the like. I will attend Angell's trial and possess myself of a copy of its transcript. It may be that my attendance will cause the officers of that event to conduct themselves with more propriety than has been their wont, but it is a foregone conclusion that Angell will be speedily found guilty of the shooting of Sheriff Smith.

Meanwhile I have begun organizing a troop of volunteers into the "Santa Fe Guards," which I propose to train in Zouave drill and tactics. Colorful uniforms have been ordered. I remind myself that without the battalion of Zouaves I trained as military governor in Baltimore—deserters, suspected traitors, convalescents, who had been given some pride by "fancy duds" as well as by my faith in them—there would have been no core to the defense I was able to assemble at Pike's Junction. Jubal Early could very well have swept on into the capital. He could not have held it, of course, but he could have demanded ransom by threatening to burn the city, and the Federal cause would have suffered an irreparable blow.

Bird Cage Hotel
Madison, New Mexico Territory
March 8, 188–

(JOURNAL ENTRY)

This has been my second visit to Madison. On both occasions, those with whom I was able to hold conversations were of the store persuasion, except, of course, for the President's correspondent, the redoubtable Dr. Prim. It seems to me that the town has given its approval to the store, as the Madison Ring is known, and its minions of the local judicial system, because they represent order at least. Outside of town there is utter disorder. In other words, they view Sheriff Grant, and even such a biased and knavish court as the one I have seen today, as preferable to the mayhem, larceny, and brigandage that has seized the county since the Battle of Madison. Sheriff Grant I believe to be a great force for order, and I am assured that he is cutting wider and wider swaths in the outlawry south of here.

I had been advised that the trial would be a farce. It was held in the courthouse, with a full gallery of store partisans, although often even they murmured against the arbitrary decisions of Judge Arthur and in approval of the aplomb and gentlemanliness of Angell, whose conduct was exemplary. I had sent an official missive from Santa Fe, requesting that the trial be delayed until after that of Henry Enders, at which proceedings Angell would be the principal witness for the prosecution, but this was rejected at the outset, as I had been certain it would have to be.

The judge is a frightened and obdurate old reprobate with a pouter pigeon figure, a mat of gray hair, and heavy jowls, which tremble with his pronouncements. He resembles a bloodhound leaning over his bench. The prosecutor, Mr. MacLennon, is even more corpulent, and these two rotund gentlemen, in their frock coats, vests, and cravats, might have been comic if they had not been so efficient. Angell readily admitted to shooting Sheriff Smith, but his attorney, a timid incompetent named Shields, was not allowed to summon any witnesses to the effect that the sheriff and another rifleman were also shooting at Angell and his deceased employer, Maginnis. Witnesses friendly to Angell were routinely challenged, and the challenges routinely sustained.

I say the judge and the prosecutor were frightened men. I at first thought they must be frightened of a raid by Angell's supporters. Later I thought they must be frightened of me, and of the change in administration I represented. But I finally came to believe that it is change-to-come itself that has frightened them. They have run their course, as probably Angell in a different way has run his. They are a part of the frontier that I see ending here, of its old freedoms and laxities, friends and enemies, codes and feuds. They must know that they are soon to be swept into the dustbin with the store whose creatures they have been, with the south-county rustlers and their six-shooters, with the Apaches who are already incarcerated on the reservations. A pallid civilization will then come to this country, like cool evening after the blaze of afternoon.

Johnny Angell was found guilty in a little over an hour and sentenced to be hanged on April 1.

After the trial I received a message from Judge Arthur that he and Mr. MacLennon would like to meet with me at my convenience. I replied that it was inconvenient and that I would expect a copy of the transcript of the trial at the earliest instance, etc.

In his office Sheriff Grant said to me, "It is a trial like

that that takes the starch out of anybody that has to do with the law."

I told him that I had seen at least six instances of grounds for a mistrial, and when I had perused the transcript I had no doubt that I would find more.

He then inquired if it was my intention to pardon Johnny-A, and I replied that I saw no need of it at the moment, for it was clear that an appeal and a change of venue would see Angell a free man. I promised Angell that if he would give himself up I would grant him a pardon. He was captured by Sheriff Grant before he could surrender. I do not maintain that my promise is voided, only that it need not be exercised immediately. Time passed before his decision and thus can reasonably be expected to pass before mine. Nor will I ever again embark my regiment too precipitously upon an unscouted road!

Underwood perused the clippings he had collected with unusual care, for he had to take into account the attitudes expressed toward his administration, and the forces behind those attitudes. But not the attitudes expressed toward him personally! The facts were still what was most important here, and he saw the facts were as difficult to establish after two weeks as they had been for crusty old Bernal Díaz writing of the Conquest after fifty years. Of the two Santa Fe periodicals, *The Territorial Call*, the Ring newspaper, was critical, and chiding. The *Santa Fe Bulletin* was friendly. His own involvement in history made his researches more interesting, but he had to beware of personal bias. He recalled with amusement his eighteen months as military governor of wartime Maryland, where, because of the censorship, newspapers did not dare criticize his administration.

From the *Call*:

"March 9. Yesterday was an auspicious moment in the annals of Madison County, for Johnny-A was judged guilty-as-charged for the murder of Sheriff Smith by a jury of good men and true. Everybody in the Territory has by now heard of the famous outlaw who for so long infested the country and filled the newspapers with accounts of his crimes, and every law-abiding man will be delighted to hear that he has been sentenced to be hanged on April 1, in Madison. For the great

boon of his capture honest citizens owe their gratitude to
Sheriff Jack Grant and his posse of brave men, and for the
boon of his judgment and sentence, Judge Barron Arthur and
his jurymen."

From the *Bulletin*, an interview with John Angell, dated
March 8:

"Well, I had intended at one time not to say a word in
my own behalf, because persons would say, 'Oh, he is a liar
and afraid for his neck!' Mr. Newman [editor of *The Territorial Call*] did give me a rough go of it. He has created
prejudice against me. He sent me a paper which shows it,
and I am advised that he has tried to incite a mob to lynch
me. I have complete faith that Sheriff Grant would protect
me against such a business. I think it is a mean advantage
to take of me, considering my situation and knowing I
cannot defend myself. But I suppose he thought he would
give me a kick downhill, as his friends are my enemies.
But I believe the *Bulletin* will give both sides of the
matter.

"EDITOR: Do you feel you have been well defended in this
trial?

"ANGELL: Well, it has come out with me slated for hanging, so I must say I was not so well defended as I had hoped
for. I expect Mr. Shields did the best it was in him to do. It
did seem like whenever things got interesting for our side,
Mr. MacLennon would pop up and call out, 'Objection!' and
the judge would call out, 'Sustained!' I took it poorly that Mr.
MacLennon objected to some witnesses for our side that
were not allowed to testify.

"EDITOR: Do you expect a pardon from Governor Underwood?

"ANGELL: Considering the friendly relations that existed
between him and me, and the promise he made, I think he
ought to pardon me. I believe he is an honorable man, and I
believe he will. I would take it very hard that out of the war I
would be the only one to suffer the extreme penalty of the
law."

From the *Bulletin*, March 15:

"The following item appeared in the *Call* at somewhat
greater length: '. . . it is significant that the Governor Underwood requested a delay in Johnny-A's summons to justice,

which request Prosecuting Attorney MacLennon rejected with quite proper indignation.' The *Call*, by this little story, endeavors to show the governor's partisanship and to reflect ridicule upon him.

"The facts are these. Johnny-A was a very conspicuous actor in the Madison County drama but has committed no overt acts since Governor Underwood has occupied the Palace of the Governors, except for an affray in the hamlet of Arioso, where in self-defense he shot the notorious Jesse Clary and wounded a henchman in a four-against-one situation. Not even his most implacable detractors have sought to blame him in this instance. Therefore, he can properly plead the governor's pardon. He was, however, an eyewitness to the dastardly murder of poor Redmond, for which Henry Enders has been indicted. And the fact of his being an important witness against one of the favorites of the *Call* accounts for the milk in the coconut."

From the *Call*:

"There has been a considerable outcry over Governor Underwood's practice of giving instructions and directions to the military in his attempts to clean out the noisome sewer that is southern Madison County, as though he had command of the United States soldiers at Fort McLain and of incarcerating prisoners on that post. His reason in the first instance is that he is merely 'showing the flag' to the outlaws and their sympathizers, and in the second that the jail in Madison is small and inadequate. It has, however, been entirely adequate in holding the notorious Johnny-A.

"We are not disposed to join the hue and cry against the governor but believe he has done some good in arresting murderers and thieves, with one conviction and sentence of death for the most notorious offender. It does seem to us that while the governor's zeal has been vigorously applied, his partisanship is widely deplored. He should be advised of the old frontier adage that 'A good outlaw is a dead outlaw' and conduct himself accordingly in the face of misguided efforts to obtain a pardon for Johnny-A."

The grammar, spelling, and punctuation of Johnny Angell's letter were polished enough to suggest that he had had an emendator, probably either Mrs. Maginnis or Dr. Prim, or perhaps the lawyer, Shields:

March 17, 188–

Gov. Richard Underwood
Governor's Palace
Santa Fe, New Mexico Territory

Dear Sir:

This is to request confirmation of your promise to pardon me for the crimes for which there are warrants out against me and for my conviction of murder in the first degree in the death of Sheriff Smith. In return I stand ready to testify in the trial of Mr. Henry Enders, which has been scheduled for April 10 in Socorro. My own execution has been scheduled for April 1.

I am told you requested a delay in my trial, which was not allowed, and I saw you were present there. I am told my trial was a miscarriage of justice. The lawyer appointed to defend me was not much use, and the judge and Mr. MacLennon did act like they had practiced shutting him off when he did speak up. Mr. Graves and Mr. Rivera were not allowed to give evidence in my behalf, and Lieutenant Cutler was not allowed to be called either. Mrs. Maginnis had been threatened with harm if she came down from Santa Fe. It does seem that justice is in a bad way in Madison. I have been advised to file for an appeal, but I trust that your Excellency will not go back on your promise.

Sheriff Grant says there is some question because I did not take up your offer quick enough. I was bringing Lieutenant Cutler to the fort for medical attention when I was apprehended. I told the lieutenant at the time that I was heading in to give myself up, and I believe he will swear to this for me. I remain as ever,

Yours
Respectfully,
John Angell

Underwood stood behind the rail fence with Charley Harkins, editor of the *Santa Fe Bulletin*, watching the Santa Fe Guards at drill. The sight thrilled his heart with memories of younger and better times, the blue jackets, the red breeches, the yellow-gaitered boots swinging with fair precision. A skinny young bookkeeper had shown himself adept at learning the drill and had been appointed sergeant, and the twenty-seven young men, almost all members of Santa Fe's four baseball teams, were agile and athletic enough. They were drilling without arms still. The bayonet manual would come after the marching and countermarching, the perfect turns, halts, quick marches, downs and ups had been perfected. Now the guards strode along in fairly good line, red trousers fluttering handsomely in the chilly wind that blew down off the Sangre de Cristos.

Harkins was a tubercular young man with a slouched posture in his sack coat and cloth cap. He said, "I would be concerned that these fellows in their fancy duds might be called palace guards, eh, Governor? You say they are just for having parades and exercises, where they'll make a fine show?"

"They could be useful in future disorders in the Territory, Charley." It irritated him inordinately when people made fun of the Zouave uniforms.

"Mark my words, Newman will call them a private army."

"No doubt he will. But I thought this interview was to be on the subject of the Zouave drill."

Charley grinned at him, impertinent but likable. He brought his notebook from his jacket pocket. "Yes, sir! The Zouaves were a tribe of Algerians, tough fighters! The French Army established some Zouave regiments, and the Americans took it up in the War. I believe you once founded such a company before."

"I organized a company in Richmond, Indiana, in 'fifty-nine. We addressed ourselves to Hardee's *Military Tactics* and reached a high degree of proficiency. A magazine containing a description of the French Zouaves fell into my hands at the time, and I reduced what I read of their training processes into a system comprehensible to American soldiers, especially the extensive bayonet exercises. The Richmond Guards were so pleased with the drill they purchased their own Zouave uniforms."

"And you took these fellows in their red trousers off to fight rebs?"

Underwood laughed. "That was neither permitted nor desirable, Charley. The uniform is not the important thing, though it does give its wearers a deal of honest pride. No other form of drill enables the individual soldier to give such

a good account of himself in battle conditions. No veteran will
sneer at a soldier fighting from his belly as well as his feet.
The use of bugles instead of shouted commands makes for
clearer communications, and double-quick time is twice as
rapid as quick time. I believe all armies will eventually come
to Zouave tactics."

He kept one eye on Harkins scribbling, and the other on
his little troop, now striding off in the direction of the
mountains. He knew he had spent too much time organizing
the guards, but they had been his one pleasure in his lonely,
disagreeable, and frustrating duties.

Two men on horseback were approaching, Don Rudolfo
Perosa on his noble white horse Caro Blanco, mane and tail
lifting in the breeze. With him was Chester Baskerville, a
gauntleted hand raised in greeting. Don Rudolfo must have
been in his late seventies, a shriveled, shrewd-eyed, stiffly
erect monkey of a man. Baskerville had been with Kit Carson
when the Navajos had been defeated at Canyon de Chelly;
now he was a drunken town character who ranted in saloons
of old adventures and triumphs. His head, covered by a tall
sugarloaf hat, looked undersized above his barrel of a body.

Underwood shook hands with them when they had
dismounted, one huge paw, one tiny one. "They are going to
get those red trousers dirty crawling on their belly like that,"
Baskerville observed.

"Good trainin', crawlin' like Paches," Don Rudolfo said,
nodding in approval. "Seen Paches crawlin' through two-inch
grass not even showin' any rump. Those trouser'd put your
eye out, though."

"The governor says they wear soberer outfits for fighting
in," Charley Hawkins said.

"Modern time!" Don Rudolfo said. "Old time you'd train
with a rifle before goin' to fancy uniforms."

"I've applied to General Yeager for rifles and bayonets,"
Underwood said. "As you know, nothing involving the general
is simple."

They all laughed with him, Baskerville spitting a wad of
brown juice. "But what're they *for*, Governor?" he said. "Not
for fighting Injun, surely! Bunch of ribbon clerks and haberdashers?" He rubbed his swollen nose.

"I hope they will only be used to furnish color on state
occasions."

"Modern time!" Don Rudolfo said. "What's your intention with el Angelito, Governor?" he asked, with a sideways glance out of his shrewd old eyes. A crease of a scar ran down from his left cheekbone into his white mustachio.

"Nothing needs to be done until he has appealed the verdict. There were many irregularities in the trial. Now I am told that even the transcript has been lost."

"He is loved by the *gente* very much," Don Rudolfo said. "They think because he is their friend he will be betrayed. There is a saying, 'He who is the friend of the *gente* will become as poor as they are.'"

"And the army clearing the colonel of charges," Baskerville said, and spat tobacco juice again.

That was, of course, not his concern, but the three of them stood watching him, not the quick-stepping ribbon clerks, bank tellers, and haberdashers. Always it would come to him that his auditors were thinking of Shiloh and the regiment that had bogged down on the river road, and not of the proud stand at Pike's Junction. In the field the Santa Fe Guards wheeled gaudily.

The Secretary of the Interior had sent him a copy of the latest letter the President had received from his old schoolmate, Dr. William Prim. Underwood found himself accused of being a partisan of the Boland-Enders party because he had not fulfilled his promise to pardon John Angell. The Secretary wrote:

"I believe the President finds these epistles from his old friend more of a bother than a source of information. I have not troubled to have copies made of the several letters I have received from Mr. James Turnbull, the brother of the murdered Englishman. I find the letters pompous, arrogant, and insulting. I am afraid you may be inflicted of a visitation from his personage, which he threatens.

"What counsel can I give you in this maelstrom of accusations and counteraccusations, demands and counterdemands? It may be that the time for action has passed, to be replaced by one of inaction. But of course I leave that to your Jovian judgment.

"You will not be pleased, I know, by the progress of Colonel Dougal's case. The verdict of the board of inquiry, exonerating him of all charges, was disapproved by the commanding general, who directed that courtmartial proceedings be instituted. The Judge Advocate General's office, however, has reported to the Secretary of War that the evidence did not substantiate the principal charges against the good colonel, although it was granted that the presence of the soldiers had given a degree of moral support to the sheriff's posse and stimulated them to more violent measures than they might otherwise have undertaken. No action seems to be the policy of the War Department, from which I draw the substance of my own advice to you. Colonel Dougal, however, is by no means out of the brambles, with civil charges filed against him by Mrs. Maginnis."

(JOURNAL ENTRY)

I am interested in a controversy that I have been following in the pages of the *North American Review,* between the so-called scientific historians and the literary ones. The "scientists" seek to deliver history from the indiscriminate enthusiasms of the man of letters by the "German method" of minute analysis and sweeping generalization. Henry Adams suggests that an accumulation of evidence, scrupulously authenticated, will of itself reveal such generalizations. He criticizes Parkman because of "his natural inclination to follow action rather than to analyze," and for focusing his histories upon some hero (La Salle in this case), describing his adventures rather than analyzing the slow and complicated movements of society.

The scientific historian's contention is that history has meaning and validity only if it provides generalizations so comprehensive as to apply to more than a particular sequence of events, for in discovering the laws by which history operates, lessons may be learned that will contribute to social betterment. His emphasis, then, is upon source materials rather than narrative; it appeals to the intellect rather than the emotions, is analytic rather than synthetic, seeks to bring the past to the reader rather than transporting the reader into the past, and presents the evolution of society by means of concepts that prove larger than their exemplifications, rather than focusing upon specific events or the career of a hero.

In contemplating my blessed and fearful *History of New Mexico* (which must, after a manner of speaking, be written backwards as well as from inside out), I will stand with mentors such as Macauley, Michelet, Prescott and Parkman, although Henry Adams suggests that their histories are little more instructive than the historical romances of Walter Scott or Alexandre Dumas. Certainly I seek, by examinations in this local history, to uncover generalizations having to do with the progress of this nation and, further, of that stage in civilizations at large when a society's creative and expansive energies must be tamed to more mundane uses. According to the German method, I will accumulate all the source documents that I can in my unique position, but my "natural inclination," with Parkman, is to seek a hero upon whom to focus the events of my narrative, for a narrative it will be. That hero must become a generalization for the forces that are changing history in the way I have described. I believe that my hero is Sheriff Grant, for in his energies, his will, and at the same time his subservience to the law and higher authority (and this becomes me!) I believe he exemplifies the evolution of a frontier society in its "taming" and incorporation into the geographical society of which it has been the cutting edge.

And yet I find myself constrained in my double role as historian and actor-in-history. How can I analyze myself, with my charge from the President by way of the Secretary of the Interior, and my ambition as an historian? When present facts conflict with the truths I strive to reveal, will I suppress those facts or change those truths? Already I must admit that I have not answered Johnny Angell's letter for fear that such a document will be used to my discredit by other historians in other times. Does my consciousness of my inner role make me overcautious in my outer one?

Greater pressure has been brought to bear upon me from the two sides of the matter, Angell's friends urging me to pardon him immediately, his enemies urging his immediate demise. If I choose either course I have ensured myself of a store of enmity from the side chosen against. And I must not make the wrong choice *historically*! I am reluctant to take my place in history as the governor who pardoned a murderer as ruthless as the Apaches who not so long ago made this land untenable to whites. I am also certain that it would be a great error to allow Angell, who is viewed as a shining young hero by many, to be hanged.

I pray that some eventuality will make action on my part

unnecessary. May this cup pass from me! I see that it is Angell's tactic to delay filing an appeal in order to force me to honor my promise, while my own is to withhold action as long as possible. In such a battle of patience, I believe I am the more experienced.

In any case, at present the leader of one faction of the Madison County War is under sentence of death and securely incarcerated. Freed upon appeal, or pardoned with the proviso that he leave the Territory, he will ensure the conviction of the leader of the other faction. Moreover, Boland & Perkins is reputed to be on the verge of bankruptcy. Events in the Madison County War have withered away to Mrs. Maginnis's lawsuit against Colonel Dougal!

Clara had mailed him an undated clipping from the *Indianapolis Star* headed, "A Murderous Career":

"Although he has been burnished of late into an outlaw-hero by the more sensational examples of cheap journalism concerned with melodramatic fiction instead of hard facts, the hard facts in the case of Johnny-A have been revealed, and they show his career to have been one of cold-blooded murders instead of heroic fights for noble causes—if not one for every year of his short life, at least an impressive number of documented cases.

"He is a native of this state and at an early age murdered his stepfather, a blacksmith by the name of Gleason in the town of Broadfield. He seems then to have directed his murderous temper to Denver, where he is said to have shot his employer in an argument over wages. From Denver he moved to New Mexico Territory, where he volunteered for a vigilante crew that dealt frontier justice to cattle rustlers. It is not known how many lynchings he participated in. From these beginnings he turned to avenging the shooting of his employer, a young Englishman of decent reputation named Turnbull. His score stands at three in this affair: Clay Mortenson, Cory Helbush, and Bert Fears. This was followed by a gun battle in which the sheriff of Madison County and a deputy fell before his unerring rifle. One more murder followed, that of a gentleman named Jesse Clary.

"Thus eight notches in young John Angell's gun are accounted for, and there may be more. At this writing he has been tried, convicted, and sentenced to hang for the murder of Sheriff Smith, and so it will be unless his receives the governor's pardon, toward which his friends are bending their efforts."

Clara had written in the margin of the clipping, "Can you truly be considering pardoning this monster, Richard?"

At the table after lunch, dealing the cards for pet, Harry was less noisy than usual. Squinting at Johnny with his mouth switched to one side, he said, "Jack has put in a requisition for lumber."

"That so?"

"Gallows lumber," Harry said, making a face as though smelling something bad. "Takes one heap of lumber. Jack has put in for it. Takes some carpenters too."

"Got to build it strong for a heavy fellow like me."

Harry tended to dealing the cards out. Without looking up, he said, "You ain't going to let them hang you, are you, Johnny?"

"Nope."

"That trial was no good. Everybody knows that trial was plain no good. Ain't you appealing?"

"Have to speak to some people first." He did not have any hopes for the governor anymore, and he was fretting other possibilities.

Harry leaned across the table to halfway whisper, as though Jack Grant might be listening, "Your partners've been hanging around, did you know that? Pard and them, and they say the greasers've been meeting at the cantina. You know I can't do anything, Johnny—but something has got to be done!"

"Don't exercise yourself, Harry." Johnny meshed his fingers on top of his head and stretched to show he was feeling no worry himself.

"I tell you Jack has went and requisitioned the *lumber*!"

It tickled him he should have to reassure his jailer that he was not going to hang. "I promise you they are not going to hang me, lumber or not," he said.

370

It was the same with Jack. He told Jack he'd had to cheer up Harry telling him they weren't going to hang him.

"I wouldn't bet much money on you," Jack said, leaning in the doorway with his arms folded over his sheriff's badge. "Unless you get busy and appeal that judgment."

"Oh, well, you and me both heard the governor promise he'd pardon me."

"Listen—" Jack said intensely, but didn't go on, shaking his head instead. Finally he said, "Nothing to me, Little Jay, what he does or doesn't do. I do my job."

"That is what Harry tells me too. You are an uncommon jobly bunch here. The governor is a lucky man having such responsible ducks working for him." Johnny held out his hands before him and made to be admiring the handcuffs. "I reckon you are going to ask me if I'm going to bust out of here before you go to the trouble of building a gallows."

"No, I am not going to ask you that. I am telling you you are a dead man unless you find legal means to get things changed around. And I don't mean the governor, either."

"Plenty of time."

"There is just two weeks of time!" Jack unwound his arms and then wound them up the other way. "It is a miscarriage of justice," he said, like it hurt to say it.

"Proper trial done improper."

"You think I like requisitioning lumber to hang an old friend? I tell you, it is hard. Start out lawing, and this is the first thing you've got to tend to."

That tickled his funnybone again. Now he must comfort Jack Grant for his hard lot as sheriff.

"I just wish you would be serious about this, Johnny," Jack went on. "It is damned *serious*, I tell you!"

When Jack had gone Johnny went to watch out the window, wagons and horsemen passing, a cluster of four girls from Mrs. Watson's establishment, and Ed Duffy pushing a wheelbarrow with some bundles in it. After a minute or two Henry Enders strolling following him, that little arm tucked up with the hand under his chin and a derby hat on his mat of hair. After a while Ed Duffy slouched back the other way, picking at his teeth with a toothpick, fat waddle to his walk and an eye squinted up at the jail. Working for Henry Enders; they'd just had lunch at the Bird Cage together. Johnny practiced slipping his handcuffs, greasing his wrists with a wad of rancid, stinking butter he'd stowed back in the little drawer of the table, waiting for the waiter to bring his lunch across the street from the hotel.

Pat Cutler came to call. He looked fitter than the last time Johnny had seen him, at the fort at the board of inquiry, but his collar still looked about two sizes too big. He was decked out a good bit more soldierly than he usually appeared, blue jacket and shoulder bars, and boots shined up. Cutler was not so much taller than he was, but there was heft through his shoulders, and a white speckling to his short beard. He had a crooked nose from some bash, and hard, bright blue eyes looked out from under a shelf of eyebrows. He carried his cap under his arm. Evidently Harry thought it was safe to leave him untended with a cavalry officer.

Cutler took a little revolver from his cap and laid it on the table.

"What's that for?"

"In case you need it."

A pack of warnings rang in Johnny's head. He remembered that Cutler used to play poker at the store with Boland and the others, before he had taken up with Lily Maginnis. Look before you leap. He didn't need the revolver, all he had to do was call Harry to the window to look out at something.

"What would you want to do this for?" he asked. "Get you in trouble, won't it?"

"Why would you think I'd do it?"

"Lily?"

Cutler stamped over to the window to stand there with his blue back turned. "Why, man, you saved my life," he said. "And got yourself into this fix in the process. The governor has never responded to the letter I wrote him about it."

Johnny had to keep telling people not to exercise themselves over him, who was not going to die on any gallows Jack Grant hadn't even had built yet.

"Well, I *had* made up my mind to turn myself in. It's just I might've made a miscalculation depending on the governor. Looks like it just now, anyhow."

Cutler turned toward him with his jaw stuck out. "Any news from Lily?"

"Just she is not having much luck with the governor."

"I heard about the trial. It made the board of inquiry sound like serious business."

"Lily is bringing a fellow over from Globe, lawyer that's never lost a case. She has got a considerable faith in lawyers."

"Having been married to a lawyer too many people put their faith in," Pat Cutler said.

"That is right, isn't it?" Johnny said. "It is funny looking back on a thing you felt so strong about and seeing some fuzzy edges to it."

Cutler stepped back to the table and frowned down at the shiny little revolver. "I would feel better if you had this tucked away somewhere in case this lawyer doesn't work out."

To oblige, he asked Cutler if he had any string on him, and with a good deal of disarrangement of his uniform the lieutenant managed to pull the drawstring out of one side of his underdrawers. Johnny ducked under the table to tie the trigger guard by a slipknot to the drawer support. This relieved the lieutenant.

"What do you hear from your wife down there at that hacienda?" Johnny asked.

Cutler just shrugged.

"Sounded like a fine place, that day you was raving."

"If you need a fine place when you get out of here, you'd be welcome there," Pat Cutler said.

"Well, that is good to know; thanks. But there is country up on the east slope of the Rockies I have been thinking about; place I saw once."

Cutler stamped around as though he wished there was more to be said and then took his leave.

"Those durn officers from the fort strut around like they've got a poker up their ass," Harry said. "What'd he want?"

"Wanted me to promise I wouldn't let them hang me," Johnny said.

Lily's latest lawyer was a narrow-shouldered fellow with strands of black, greasy hair combed straight across his bald scalp, and a voice out of the cellar. Harry brought in two more chairs and stood by the door, watching them, as the lawyer sat at the table with a lined tablet, making notes with a pencil. Johnny sat answering Mr. Tarkenton's questions while Lily went to stand watching out the window, slim and tall in her black.

Mr. Tarkenton's opinion was that an appeal could be made on the basis of the transcript of the trial not having been filed, and, apparently, having been lost. There were at least twelve other procedural errors, in case that was not enough. Judge Arthur should have disqualified himself, for one thing. The venue should have been changed from Madison, for another. Mr. Tarkenton would see that the appeal would be made in Globe. There was no question that there would be an acquittal. Still, the gist of it was that Mr. Tarkenton would work it as manufactured one way as Mr. MacLennon and Judge Arthur had done the other.

"Just a minute, here," Johnny said. "It looks to me like we are riding off in the wrong direction. Mr. Turnbull was murdered, and Mr. Maginnis murdered, and Mrs. Maginnis and I want to see the men punished that did those things. Getting me to Globe is not what we are after here, Mr. Tarkenton."

Mr. Tarkenton rocked back in his chair, which creaked, and his knee knocked against the table. The little tap of Pat Cutler's revolver swinging was audible. Harry was leaning in the doorway with his fists stuffed into his pockets.

"The first thing is your safety, Johnny," Lily said, sweeping back from the window. She smelled like a flower garden.

"Well, I believe the first thing is me giving evidence against Henry Enders."

She shook her head at him as though he was talking foolishness, and the lawyer scowled and stuck out his lips.

"I was hired to keep Mr. Turnbull from harm," Johnny went on. It galled him when his voice went shaky. "Well, I didn't, nor Mr. Maginnis either. But being safe was not what I was paid wages for. Now I have made a promise to the governor, and if he does not keep his side of it that is not the point. And it is not the point getting me to Glove for a retrial. Henry Enders is the point."

He was in some discomfort watching Lily Maginnis's tricks, which he had never thought of in that way before—the way she would blink her eyelashes when Mr. Tarkenton addressed her, or move her hands up to her bosom to show her helplessness. Even though he knew she was trying to help *him*, Johnny wished he did not see all this so clearly.

"Have you ever seen a hanging, son?" the lawyer rumbled.

"No, and I am not going to, either."

"Let me put this to you, my boy. I can absolutely promise you that you will not hang for the murder of Sheriff Smith if certain procedures are followed."

"Johnny, I will blame myself if anything should happen to you," Lily said. She raised her hands to her bosom, but he could feel the force of her. He would have to do what she wanted of him, which was to be got out of Madison jail by hook or crook. It was the hook or crook that galled him. He watched the lawyer shuffle papers from his battered satchel.

"You will proceed, then, Jarvis?" Lily asked.

Mr. Tarkenton swung his head ponderously to look Johnny square in the face. "I must tell you that my fees are high, and I expect to be paid for my labors."

"You will be paid, Jarvis," Lily said. "I will personally guarantee it."

"How high, mister?"

"I would estimate two thousand, twenty-five hundred dollars."

The air whistled out of Johnny's lips. It was more money than he had ever had to deal with. He was worth that much! "I will pay your bill myself, Mr. Tarkenton," he said.

"There are means by which you can earn considerable sums of money, you know," Lawyer Tarkenton said. "I am acquainted with Colonel Russell of Colonel Russell's Wild West Show, and I am sure you would be well paid for appearing as a trick shot artiste. Or for appearances merely. And there are gentlemen of the magazines and newspapers who could be called upon to contribute to your legal defense for certain favors on your part."

He shook his head wordlessly. The idea of being in a Wild West show, like an animal in a cage for people to gawk at, made him dizzy. Nor did he want anything to do with the birds who wrote about him without knowing anything about him, plain liars.

When he said good-bye to Mr. Tarkenton, he almost said, "Stay away from windows!" It was advice he should have taken himself.

That evening he stood watching who was passing in the street before the courthouse, thinking of Elizabeth Fulton, her slim, long figure and long, almost beautiful, honey-

colored face; the way the golden hairs grew in a little swirl at
the nape of her neck; and the tiniest of brown moles beneath
her lip. If Mr. Tarkenton got him out of here without his
having to bust out and go on the dodge, he could ask Pete
Fulton if he could marry her. He could almost see them then,
himself with Elizabeth on two ponies, heading up the eastern
slope of the Rockies into Colorado, starting over where
everything was green, and water running everywhere in the
spring from the snow melt. They would settle into their own
little cove in the foothills there, start out with a couple of
hundred head of stock. He could just see the little house he
would build, adobe walls but pole-raftered, and he would
split the shakes for the roof himself, while Elizabeth—

The windowpane exploded over him. He reeled back
and stood shaky-kneed, brushing glass splinters from his
clothes and carefully out of his hair. Harry cursed, glass
crunching under his boot heels as he approached the smashed
window. He thought better of it, backed off, and limped out
of the jail, forgetting to lock the door behind him.

So Henry Enders was worried about Lawyer Tarkenton
of Globe. After a while Johnny eased back to the window to
watch the street that had emptied of people. No more
daydreaming, then, where anybody could get him in his
sights.

When he picked up the cup to sip the lukewarm coffee,
Johnny saw the square of paper beneath it. He set the cup
back down. There was trampling up and down the stairs and
calling back and forth, as Jack Grant and a posse got ready to
ride out of town. When Harry stood in the doorway, back to
him, watching the men trooping out of Jack's office and down
the stairs, Johnny unfolded the bit of paper. On it was drawn
a crescent moon crossed by a handgun. It seemed to him a
clock had started running with Mr. Tarkenton's visit, the shot
through the window, and Jack Grant and his deputies headed
out today. Look before you leap.

He finished his coffee reflectively, before he announced
that he needed to visit the outhouse again. Harry limped
down the stairs and outside into fierce sunlight with him,
unlocked his handcuffs and assumed his stance of impatient
patience outside the door with its crescent hole. Inside,
Johnny turned the bit of wood to lock the door and squatted

to push a hand through the stack of newspapers on the platform seat. The Colt was an old one, lead slugs showing in the cylinder slots. He flipped the cylinder out to inspect the loading, and levered the cartridges out into his hand, heavy bits of brass, copper, and lead. He checked the firing caps, the alignment of cylinder and barrel, the firing pin. He pulled the trigger and thumbed the hammer as it came forward. The firing pin had been filed down useless.

He squatted looking at the five bullets and the damaged gun. Then he tossed the gun through the hole, where it splatted into the mess below. The cartridges he dropped in one by one. The clock was running faster.

Handcuffed again, he preceded Harry back to the courthouse and up the stairs. In the jail room he walked to the window and bent to gaze out with interest. "Well, look at that!" he said, beckoning to the jailer.

Harry didn't come. When Johnny turned the jailer has his Colt out and leveled,

"What's this, Harry?"

"I know you got a gun out there!" Harry stuttered.

"Not me!"

"Sure you did!" Harry's knuckle on the trigger showed as white as his face.

Johnny staggered as he said, "You are going to kill me!" He slumped into the chair at the table as though his legs wouldn't hold him, and bent over the table like his backbone had gone. "Why would you do it, Harry?" he whispered. His fingers touched Pat Cutler's revolver.

"I need the money, Johnny! My wife—"

Johnny fired on *wife*, squeezing the trigger five times with the best aim he could contrive in one deafening continuous roar and cloud of smoke. Harry slammed across the room, falling against the wall with his head propped up.

Still leaning over the table, Johnny jerked open the drawer and fingered up the last of the butter there, greasing his wrists and slipping the cuffs off. He left the lieutenant's revolver where it was and jumped to scoop up Harry's Colt. Harry was pretty dead.

The clock was clicking away as he trotted into the sheriff's office. It took two shots to blow the lock off the gun closet, the door banging open as though someone had pushed it from inside. He slung a cartridge belt with a holstered Colt around his waist, stuck the barrel of Harry's piece into his belt, and took up a Winchester and checked the loading. Boot heels banged on the stairs and he flattened himself behind the sheriff's door as a man panted upstairs, shotgun in hand—a bristle-chinned hard case named Mike Piggot. Mike tramped on into the jail room.

He waited, for more footsteps were ascending, Henry Enders this time, in his black jacket and derby, revolver in hand. Following came Ed Duffy with a rifle. Henry Enders stalked inside.

"Drop it!" Johnny said to Ed Duffy, showing himself.

Ed stood facing him with his mouth gaping. Both hands jerked loose from the rifle, which dropped onto his boots with a clatter.

"Colt too."

Ed cautiously drew his piece and let it fall also, raising his hands shoulder high. His mouth still hung open, eyes like peeled grapes.

"Get inside!" Johnny moved quickly into lockstep behind Ed Duffy. Inside the jail Mike leaned over Harry's body. Henry Enders stood by the table with his Colt in his good hand. When he saw Johnny, Mike straightened, bringing the shotgun to bear.

Johnny shot him in the right arm, and Mike squalled and flopped over Harry's body with the shotgun under him.

He fired past Ed Duffy and Henry Enders fell back, knocking the table over. When Enders tried to untangle himself and get his Colt up, Johnny shot him in the good arm, knocking the piece free. Enders lay staring up at him, mouth opening and closing like a trout pulled up on the bank. His little white fist was clutched up beneath his chin, his right arm a mess of blood, and blood all over his belly.

"Dirty little pissant—"

He shot Henry Enders dead. Then he turned back to Mike, who had managed to roll off Harry with a hand raised like a schoolboy with the answer. *"No, Johnny!"*

He prodded Ed Duffy with the rifle muzzle. "Let's get out of here."

"Johnny. Johnny! I didn't—"

"Out!"

Ed started out and down the steps ahead of him, hands

shoulder high. Toward the bottom his legs gave and he fell and tumbled on down, screaming, "*Johnny, don't!*"

Ed struggled to his feet, trying to hold his hands higher than his head, white and blue-chinned blob of his face turned over his shoulder.

"You and Mike have horses out there?"

"Yes!"

"Go it."

Prodding Ed's back Johnny walked him out onto the front stairs of the courthouse, blinking in that full sun, and down the steps beside which Pogie Smith had concealed himself, even though four witnesses had testified he was only standing watching, not even armed.

The street was empty. He saw a face in one of the hotel windows, and the brown haunches of horses were lined up at the tie rail there. He could feel the forehead prickle of eyes on him. He caught himself thinking of New York writers scribbling: Daring Escape! Johnny-A Flees Madison Jail! Not a Hand Raised to Stop Him!

Not a hand was raised. "Get on your horse," he said, and Ed hustled to mount a white-faced gelding. Johnny swung up on the one next to it, keeping the rifle pointed. "Head out south."

Ed started out at a walk, triangle of face perched on his shoulder looking back. "What're you going to do, Johnny?"

"Just keep going."

He followed the fourth of the killers of Mr. Turnbull past an incoming farmer in a spring wagon with a team of mules plodding. His wife and two dark-haired children stared from the seat. Tell their children they had seen Johnny-A escape from Madison jail. The farmer clucked a gee-hup to his team.

Johnny directed Ed south out of town. He doubted that any kind of pursuit could be organized, with Jack Grant away, but after four or five miles he turned Ed off the wagon road and they wound through the hills.

"What're you going to do, Johnny?" Ed called back to him again.

"Going to find out exactly who paid you and Cory and Bert and Clay to kill Mr. Turnbull."

"Oh, I'll tell you that, Johnny! Not a bit of secret about that. It was Mr. Enders. And Pogie Smith in on it."

"Neither of them can give you the lie on that, can they? I

want to know it all, Ed. We'll stop and chat after a bit. You think about it till then."

He sat cross-legged in the shade, the rifle across his knees, squinting up at Ed Duffy saddled on the white-faced gelding. Sun sparkled in bright patches through the leaves. Ed sat up very straight with his hands tied behind him and the rope around his neck and looped over the branch.

Johnny had made a little slingshot out of a branch crotch and rawhide, and he flicked a pebble with it high toward Ed's shoulders. "You're sure, now?" The gelding pawed once or twice.

"I surely am, Johnny," Ed said in a high, rapid voice. "I have got no cause to lie for Ran Boland, you know that."

"Tell me again."

"Well, it was in that room upstairs at the store, like I said before. Mr. Boland and Mr. Enders, and Clay and Cory and me. Bert wasn't there just then. Pogie was there. He said we would ride point, and who would ride drag. He and some others would go around the other way. There would be people with the limey, he said, but we was to go just for him."

"Kill him."

"Well, Mr. Enders said, 'Kill the limey devil'—well, he said 'Diablo,' that's the way they talked about Mr. Turnbull and Mr. Maginnis. And Mr. Boland said, 'Just make certain you make everything look right, boys. Appearances is everything in this business.'"

Johnny thought he could hear Ran Boland saying that.

"'Getting rid of Diablo number two and Diablo number one is what's important'—something like that—Mr. Enders said. And Mr. Boland said, 'Appearances is appearances, and business is business. But just get us rid of the fellow.' Something like that, Johnny."

"A hundred dollars apiece," Johnny said. He fitted another pebble into the leather mitt of the slingshot.

"That was for Cory and Bert and Clay and me. I don't know about Pogie."

"Tell it again," he said, squinting up into the gleaming patches of light coming through the leaves. Ed and the horse were in silhouette, line of the rope from his neck to the branch. He aimed the slingshot and slung the pebble over the horse's haunch. Ed gasped. "From the beginning," Johnny said.

But as Ed started over it again, he knew he was never going to know the whole truth of it. What is Truth? as Pilate had said.

During Cutler's convalescence Colonel Dougal had obtained permission from General Yeager to release the Hoya scouts from active duty and resettle them at Bosque Alto. Cutler's telegrams of protest to Captain Robinson elicited no response. On the day after the news of Johnny Angell's escape from Madison jail, a telegram arrived ordering Cutler to prepare a report on the state of the Sierra Verdes at Bosque Alto. Spring was the traditional time for breakouts, when there was the prospect of summer-long natural sustenance and less need of white-eye rations.

Cutler wheedled three cans of pears from the mess sergeant with some kind of farewell to the Hoyas in mind, and set out for Bosque Alto aboard Malcreado. It was only the second time he had been on horseback since his recovery, and his seat was tender.

At the Agency the flag on its whitewashed pole floated lazily, like a sleeping animal in a striped sack. Indians milled in the area between the corrals and the Agency buildings. As he dismounted, one of them trotted toward him, bony dark legs churning beneath a filthy blue shirttail. Skinny skidded to a stop before him, with a broad white grin and a parody of a salute. "Nantan Tata!"

Cutler returned the salute. Nochte limped toward them, bare chest, soiled white trousers, his jaunty hat with its blue ribbons cocked on his head.

Cutler was so glad to see them his mouth hurt. Apache men did not embrace. "I have brought pears!" He took the squat cans from his saddlebag and presented them to Skinny, who cradled them against his chest, stroking them like small animals. He rattled in Apache to Nochte.

"What does he say?"

"He says we have heard you are dead. Are you a ghost? He says we have heard the Mexicans have made you sick. We will go to Mexico and kill Mexicans!"

"Tell him it is not necessary. I am well now."

Nochte smiled his prim little smile and relayed the message. Skinny rattled on excitedly.

"He says Nantan Tata's scouts perish of boredom at Bosque Alto. Also they are very poor without the blue-soldier dollars. He says it is very bad that Nantan Bigotes's scouts have blue-soldier dollars, and Nantan Tata's do not."

"I have sent telegrams to Nantan Lobo asking that the scouts go back on the payroll." It came to him that Yeager was aware that he intended to resign, and held this hole card over him.

"It is difficult when one has become accustomed to the white-eye dollars," Nochte said with dignity. His handsome, aquiline face was dirty also. He raised an eyebrow and said, "Perhaps the Red Stripe People will go out soon."

Cutler asked if Caballito rested easy.

Nochte looked thoughtful. Skinny wore an expression of listening to something a long way off. The two of them conferred staccato, too fast for Cutler to catch much except that Caballito and the Sierra Verdes did not rest easy. Nochte confirmed this. "Red Stripe People are like that, more than others."

"What of Joklinney?" When he explained to Nochte what he meant, Nochte said only that Caballito was *nantan* and Joklinney his nephew.

"Is it thought the Red Stripe People will go out?"

Nochte shrugged elaborately, regarding Cutler down his nose. "If the Red Stripe People left Bosque Alto it would be good for the Hoyas. We would have the blue-soldier dollar again and would no longer perish of boredom."

They moved away from the Nahuaques lounging in the area before the Agency buildings, Cutler leading Malcreado, Skinny with the fruit cans cradled to his chest, Nochte limping. Even the scouts were impatient for a Sierra Verde breakout. He was caught again, in the service of Yeager and Caballito.

He was informed that Tazzi had been sick in the stomach but was better, Jim-jim had been stung by a scorpion, Kills-a-Bear had heard that his wife at Fort Apache was dead. If Nantan Tata would come to their *ranchería* on Broken Tree Creek they would all feast on canned pears together, and perhaps some *tiswin* could be found.

"Nantan Malojo is fair with the Hoyas?" Cutler asked.

Skinny scowled when Nochte translated. They both shrugged, Nochte standing balanced on his good leg, the flat medallion toe of his other moccasin just touching the ground. "Nantan Malojo likes best the Nahuaque. He does not like Red Stripe People." Nochte made an in-between gesture rocking his hand. "The squaws complain that he does not like Hoyas, but it is better than with Red Stripe People. Nantan Bigotes has come to shout at him."

"I must go to speak with Caballito and Nantan Bigotes."

Skinny spoke at length, Nochte glancing sideways at Cutler and reddening. "He says Nantan Bigotes fucks Red Stripe People squaw."

"Is it known which one?"

"Yes, it is known," Nochte said, and he made a motion indicating a swelling belly.

In Caballito's meadow women squatted on flat rocks along the creek, washing clothing. To Cutler their laughter seemed shrill. Beyond them cattle grazed, brown moving backs in the high grass. Cutler sat cross-legged with Caballito, Joklinney, Dawa, Big Ear and Cump-ten-ae. Caballito would not speak to him directly, only through Joklinney, nor would he meet his eyes. The chief's face was savage, wrinkled like pie crimping around the mouth. He spoke harshly to Big Ear, who jumped up and stalked off toward the wickiups.

"He goes for whiskey," Joklinney said. His hair had grown longer. He wore a wrinkled but clean blue shirt, jeans pants, and moccasins.

Caballito glared around him. He looked as though he had already been at the whiskey, eyes with a red glint to them. There were mud stains on his bare brown legs, the mud lighter than the flesh. All of them but Joklinney had painted stripes on their cheeks.

"Who sells you whiskey?" Cutler asked.

"There are always white-eyes selling whiskey. Selling guns, selling cartridges."

"Who sells guns and bullets?"

Caballito barked in Apache at Joklinney. It seemed a bad sign that he would not communicate directly.

Joklinney said, "Caballito wishes to know if it is true Angelito has escaped from the white-eye jail."

"It is true."

"Killing men?"

"Three men were killed."

Caballito pulled his blanket more tightly around his shoulders, his mouth pushed out sulkily. Big Ear returned, carrying a brown bottle. "Drink, Nantan Verdad," Caballito said in English, still without looking at him.

He tipped the bottle to his lips, swallowed the rank liquor, and passed the bottle to Caballito. Cump-ten-ae squinted at him and spoke at length. Cutler gathered from the laughter and side glances that this was a joke at his expense.

Joklinney said, "He says Nantan Tata look very bad, very white. This whiskey makes him brown like Indeh."

Caballito muttered in Spanish, "Indeh cannot make *tiswin* so he must buy bad whiskey!" At last he scowled directly at Cutler, his face graven with downward-slanting wrinkles. "It is very bad at Bosque Alto, Nantan Verdad!"

"What is bad now, Nantan Caballito?"

The bottle passed around again. Dawa belched appreciatively and patted his fat belly. Big-Ear also belched. Cutler swallowed a little that seemed to bounce in his stomach, as though to come right back up again. There was discussion, Caballito not participating.

"They say that the Red Stripe People must return to San Marcos or men will come with papers," Joklinney said.

"Nantan Malojo says this?"

"Nantan Malojo has said it. The Nahuaques say it also. Nantan Malojo has said it is foolish to plant crops. It is thought he means the Red Stripe People will not be here much longer." Joklinney grinned bonily at him.

After more discussion, Joklinney said, "It is believed that Nantan Malojo and some other white-eyes wish to take Caballito's herd from him."

Cutler took a deep breath. "Nantan Lobo has promised that Caballito will keep his herd. It is true that the Bureau of Indian Affairs wishes to concentrate all the Indeh at San Marcos, but Nantan Lobo will not allow this to happen to the Red Stripe People."

Joklinney spoke at length in Apache. The others stared at Cutler. Big Ear spoke contemptuously.

"What does he say, Joe King?"

Joklinney looked at him with amusement at the name. The bones of his face could be traced exactly through the

skin, like the frame of a kite visible through the fabric. His
hair hung below his ears.

"It is said that Nantan Lobo has lost his power."

Cutler replied that he knew nothing of that. The others
stared at him.

Caballito spoke and Joklinney translated: "He asks what
white-eye believes happen when he dies." Caballito's hard
black eyes with their reddish glints were fixed on Cutler.

"White-eyes believe good people go to a good place and
bad people to a place where they are punished."

Joklinney said, "Indeh believe all will go to a good place.
All Indeh." His cheeks creased with his mechanical smile.
"No white-eye there."

Caballito demanded to be told what Nantan Verdad
believed.

Cutler said he didn't know. Big Ear gently straightened
old Dawa, who was snoring. Cutler said, "Tell Nantan Caballito
we will see each other again, one place or the other."

Joklinney looked pleased, nodding to him, as he relayed
this. Caballito grinned and flourished the whiskey bottle, as
though to unheard music. The grin vanished and he spoke at
length.

Joklinney gestured toward those present, and, more
widely, toward the wickiups. "He says all here, all the Red
Stripe People, all Indeh, will go to the good place. They will
go there very soon. He has the power to see this. They will
wait for Nantan Verdad there, who is a good man though a
white-eye."

Emotion combined with bad whiskey to wrench at his
belly. He bowed his head. "I will look forward to meeting the
Red Stripe People in that place, but I do not think this will
be soon."

Joklinney said quietly, "He thinks all are to die soon.
All."

"Why?"

"*Dah-koo-gah!*" Joklinney said with a shrug. Then he
added, "He has heard an owl call."

"Jesus."

"It is difficult for Joe King, who believes these things but
has been taught by the white-eye not to believe them."

Caballito rattled at Joklinney, who responded carefully.
The chief embarked upon a long speech, with gestures,

expressions of hatred, of despair, of conciliation, and of hatred again. His fist traced violent patterns. He halted, head held up proudly, waiting for Joklinney to translate.

"He tells of the great *nantan* Juan José. This was a chief of power, and friend to the white-eye. When his father was murdered by Mexicans he became very savage toward them, but to the white-eye he remained friendly. The white-eye was safe in Juan José's country. Juan José was friend with a white-eye named Johnson. This man kept a store, and sold whiskey and bullets, and Juan José trusted him. The Mexicans offered Johnson money for the scalp of Juan José, also for the scalps of his people. So Johnson invited Juan José and his people to the store, where they were given whiskey to make them drunk. He had a big gun—a cannon—and when the Mimbreños were all drunk he fired this at them. Many were killed. Others were killed by Johnson's men. Johnson killed Juan José, who had been his friend. And took his scalp and sold it to the Mexicans."

Cutler said nothing, watching Caballito gazing off across the meadow toward the laughing women. Boys were playing tag among the trees. Dawa sat bolt upright now, arms folded, with a severe expression. Cump-ten-ae and Big Ear kept their faces averted as Caballito spoke again.

"He speaks of the great *nantan* Cochise," Joklinney said. "He was a chief of great power, and a good friend to the white-eye. A blue-soldier *nantan* came with fifty-four men—"

"Lieutenant Bascomb," Cutler interrupted. "He is famous for the war he started that day."

"He accused Cochise of stealing a white-eye boy. This boy was not stolen by Chiricahuas but by Pinals. When Cochise came to the soldier *nantan* to parley, they took him with three others and put them in a tent. He must stay there until the boy was returned to his parents. With his knife Cochise cut the tent and ran away. The soldiers shot at him. The others, his brothers, did not run away.

"Cochise captured many white-eyes. The soldiers would not exchange his three brothers for the white-eyes Cochise had captured. So Cochise killed these white-eyes. The soldiers hanged his brothers. More white-eyes died. And more Indeh. More and more Indeh. And Caballito says that in the end it will be all the Indeh."

Cutler said, "The white-eyes have been very sorry for the wrongs done by the great fool Lieutenant Bascomb."

This was translated. No one looked at him directly. After a long silence Caballito spoke savagely again.

"He speaks now of the great *nantan* Mangas Coloradas of the Warm Springs band. He was a chief of power, and a friend to the white-eyes. He knew the white-eyes craved the yellow metal, and he offered to lead them to where they could find all they might desire. But they did not trust him because he was Indeh. So they tied him to a post and whipped him with whips until they thought he was dead. But he was not dead. It is said that ten white-eye miners died for every scar upon the back of Mangas Coloradas.

"But again Mangas Coloradas became a friend to the white-eyes, this time to the soldiers of California. It was thought the soldiers of California were friends to the Indeh because they had chased away the soldiers of Texas. But the soldiers of California made Mangas Coloradas prisoner. They heated their rifle-swords in the fire and pressed them against his legs and feet. Yes, it is known! And when he cried out, 'Am I a child that you treat me so?' they shot him. Many would die of it, many white-eyes and many Indeh. The Indeh have killed many for each one dead, but there are too many white-eyes."

Cutler sat gazing down at his hands in his lap. He knew that despite announced government policy, despite General Yeager's good will, despite his own feeble preventative actions, Caballito was right. In the end the Indeh would die. Caballito continued his denunciation, of treaties broken, always by the white-eye. The Red Stripe People had been promised the heart of the Sierra Verde range, but settlers had pressed in, copper and silver had been found. The treaty had been broken, and the Sierra Verdes sent on the "trail of tears" to San Marcos. They would not allow themselves to be sent there again.

Glancing from the chief's savage face to Joklinney's calm one, Cutler said quietly, "Is he telling me they are going out?"

"I think it is not decided."

"But he wants to go."

"I believe he will go," Joklinney said.

"And he knows they will die."

Joklinney nodded once. "The one called Angelito who has escaped from jail, does he know that he will die?"

"I think so."

"The Red Stripe People will die," Joklinney said, with the bony grin. "But white-eyes and Mexicans will also die."

Caballito was watching intently. He proffered the whiskey bottle to Cutler, who sucked a small swallow, wiped his lips, and said, "Why does Nantan Caballito tell me these things I already know?"

"*Dah-koo-gah!*" Caballito said explosively. The horizontal red stripes on his cheeks gleamed.

Cutler felt shaken and exhausted when he left the circle of Sierra Verde elders, Joklinney walking with him to where Malcreado grazed.

"There are too many things, you understand?" Joklinney said.

Cutler managed a laugh and said, "Hey you, Joe King! Will you go with them?"

The other shrugged. "Joe King does not wish to go. He has learned from the white-eye that it is better to live than to die. Perhaps he will go. Perhaps he will not."

"Will many wish not to go out?"

"The women. It is very hard for the women, running, running. They remember how it was the last time. Many were hungry. Many died. Children were hungry." He laughed shortly, and said, "The white-eye's rations make them remember being hungry."

"What of the scouts of Nantan Bigotes?"

"Nantan Lobo is very clever! Dollars are stronger than blood, as the white-eye knows." Joklinney smiled bleakly, exposing brown gums. He moved closer as Cutler mounted, gazing up at him with his head cocked. "Nantan Bigotes knows many secrets of the Red Stripe People from one whose belly swells with her secrets."

"Joklinney—" he stated.

"Hey you, Joe King!" Joklinney said, still grinning. "Be at ease, Nantan Tata. Nantan Bigotes is your friend, and so is Joe King. But others know of this also."

It was a warning. Riding up the ridge, across a wooded flat and over a shoulder of hill toward the Sierra Verde scouts' *ranchería,* Cutler tried to understand Joklinney's emotions—a man who could not think like a white-eye but no longer

thought like the Indeh either. So he was aware that his
wife—one of his two wives—was pregnant by her white-eye
lover and brought him also Sierra Verde secrets. But Joe King
could no longer think like a vengeful savage, so he became a
complacent husband like Frank Maginnis.

For his part, what must Caballito feel about the disarray
of the Red Stripe People? Almost half his fighting men had
been corrupted by the blue-soldier six dollars a month. Old
Dawa's heir had been weaned from the Indeh's faith by his
sojourn in San Francisco. The women were reluctant to face
the hardships of a flight to Mexico, where running, hunger,
and death were their lot. Once a chief had decreed a movement of his people and there had been no disaffection. Now
Cutler felt sadness, like a weight on his shoulders, for what
Nantan Lobo's friendship had done to the Red Stripe People.

Bunch lounged in front of his tent in a camp chair. With
him was his interpreter, a moon-faced half-breed in greasy
buckskins, long-haired. Two squatting scouts leaned on their
carbines. They rose to attention as Cutler dismounted, Bunch
rising also, in his undershirt with suspenders drooping in arcs
alongside his hips.

"*Ugashe!*" Bunch said, and the scouts departed, the
interpreter following more slowly. Bunch shook Cutler's hand.
"You look positively puny, Pat!"

"I'm healthier than I look, and grateful to still have two
legs."

"Makes for a better understanding," Bunch said, laughing. He produced another camp chair and they sat together,
squinting at the great red ball of the sun poised over the low
western peaks.

"It looks like Caballito will be busting out, Sam."

"So I've been hearing."

"Dipple's been hinting again they're going to have to go
back to San Marcos. Other things too. Somebody's been
selling them whiskey."

"An old bastard's been around. I went out to give him a
rush, but he said he was selling Bibles. Gives away a quart of
rotgut with every Bible. Would I interfere with his enticing
the heathen to Bible study?" Bunch chuckled. Then he said,
"Of course, first thing they'll go to thieving to get money to
buy those Bibles to get that whiskey. I've seen *that* before.

Speaking of which," Bunch said, and went inside the Sibley
to bring back a whiskey bottle.

Cutler sipped the liquor that tasted like milk and honey
after Caballito's potation. "There's also a rumor that Sheriff
Grant may try to arrest Caballito and some of the others on
warrants for civil crimes."

"I'll tell you what Agent Dipple says. It is the Bureau's
policy that Indians off the reservations can no longer be
protected from civilian authorities. Their *own* reservation.
Understand?"

"San Marcos."

"I can't believe the sheriff would be such a damn fool.
Anyway, a man who couldn't keep Johnny-A in jail long
enough to hang him is not going to make much show out
here."

"I'd better tell you that your secret scout isn't much of a
secret."

Bunch flushed crimson.

"My Hoyas mentioned it. So did Joklinney. They know
she's pregnant."

"What's that son of a bitch going to do about it?"

"He said nothing. That he's taken up white-eye ways to
that extent."

"Shit," Bunch said, combing his thick fingers through his
hair. "Pat, I love that girlie. The thing is—I've never told
you, I guess—I've got a wife in Maryland. I can't abide her,
nor her me. But she's—you know—Catholic. She is an absolute
bitch, she has never approved of one thing but maybe her
father in her whole life. Well, you'll see Junie tonight. She'll
show up after dark. She comes and fixes supper. We can't—
you know—*talk* much, but all the white squaws I know talk
too much. Shit, I don't want anything to happen to her
because of me!

"You'll stay the night, won't you? You ride out of here
after dark people'll think you're *pesh-chidin*—you're that
white. Junie'll fix us supper. No, guts, I tell her!" Bunch
managed to laugh, but his face had fallen into heavy lines.
"Shit, what's to become of her? She's such a pretty little
thing. So slender. You know the older women get pretty stout
from carrying burdens, but when they are young they are so
wonderfully slender." He held his hands spread-fingered with
the tips almost touching in illustration.

They drank Bunch's good whiskey and watched the sun go down, and Cutler tried to resign himself to Caballito's breakout. The general had charged him with preventing it and had promised to back any play he had to make. Like Johnny-A and the governor's promise, he thought. There are too many things, Joklinney had said. If the Red Stripe People go out it will be good for us, Nochte had said, for the blue-soldier dollar would be restored. Fires blazed here and there in the scouts' *ranchería* below. Bunch had utter faith in them. He was willing to bet good money he would not lose a man to Caballito in a breakout.

If a breakout was imminent, it was just as well that the Hoyas remain at Bosque Alto, Cutler thought, with someone to ride for him while Nochte took others in pursuit.

In the chill air the captain rose to put on his tunic. He paced the edge of the platform before the Sibley tent, peering into the darkness. The woman appeared suddenly, laden with cloth-wrapped bundles, halting when she saw Cutler, then silently putting down her bundles on the platform edge. Bunch jumped down beside her, the two of them murmuring together. Cutler heard her say, "Junie bring *choddi*."

"Antelope steaks," Bunch said, stepping back up onto the platform. Pretty Mouth squatted beside the firepit. Flames climbed in kindling, the secret scout a shrouded figure against the light. Presently she mounted the platform past them, her shawl drawn over her face, slim in her voluminous skirts, which effectively concealed her pregnancy. She came out of the Sibley carrying pans.

"*Pezá-a*," the girl said.

"That's frying-pan," Bunch said. "She's teaching me Pache. Very difficult language, as you know. You've got to get a word exactly right or it means something else. Put plenty *inchi!*" he called to Pretty Mouth.

"That's salt," Cutler said.

Soon there was the aroma of broiling meat. Bunch poured another round of whiskey and sat with glass in hand and his face tipped up toward the stars. "She's damned clean!" he told Cutler. "She bathes a sight oftener than I do."

They ate inside the tent by lantern light. Pretty Mouth brought them broiled steaks, a stew of green vegetables with red veins, a hard, dry bread, black coffee. She would not sit with them but knelt beside the table watching the men eat.

Her hair was long and glossy, her face a delicate brown. A little dart of white scar ran up into her lower lip, swelling it attractively. Her face pointed at the food on the table, her eyes examined Cutler. She ducked her head when Bunch complimented her cooking.

She pointed to the bread. *"Zigosti!"*

"Zigosti!" Bunch said, nodding vigorously. "Made from *ikon,*" he told Cutler. *"Tu-dishishn,"* he said, taking up his coffee cup.

"Tu-dishishn," Pretty Mouth said, nodding. Her eyes slid toward Cutler. *"Nantan Tata."*

"Tze-go-juni," he said. He pointed to his plate. *"Gun-ju-le."* It is good.

Pretty Mouth ducked her head again. She knelt with her small tan hands clasped at her breast, watching them eat the food she had prepared and drink the coffee. From time to time Bunch patted her fondly. Cutler heard the owl cry in the woods behind the tent. When he glanced at Pretty Mouth again she looked so stricken he jerked his chair back as though something had threatened her. "What is it, Junie?" Bunch cried. "What's the matter?"

"Hû!" she whispered.

"Owl," Cutler said.

"They are damned scared of owls!" Bunch said.

"Hû!" Pretty Mouth whispered. Now she held her two hands to her cheeks as though holding her head up, staring at nothing. *"Cha-ut-lip-un!"* she whispered.

Cutler knew that word: very bad!

Sheriff Grant's narrative:

I've been going out with Ben Gibson and but four others lately. A big posse is a good deal slower. It will raise a dust you can see five miles off. It carries news of itself right with it, so to speak. If a man doesn't learn lessons as he goes along, he's a fool. Now I take but five men with me on a sweep, but they are men I trust.

I knew I had to catch Johnny where he wasn't watching for me. He's an amigo to the Mexicans in those south-county *placitas*. He killed three men in his bustout, and whatever the right and wrong of it, he is pure outlaw now, but a man in trouble in Madison is *muy simpático* in Corral de Tierra or Arioso. We're going to have to catch up with Johnny in a place like that, at some fiesta or *baile*, where he will not be on his guard. I'll have to take my chances of him getting some backup from the local caballeros, like he did in his Jesse Clary fight.

I rode into Arioso with my five fellows. None of them had any bad record with the Mexicans. I went right to Mr. Soto, the mayor, and told him I was there to arrest Juanito Ángel when he came to town, and I didn't want any trouble.

Mr. Soto said there would be no trouble since somebody would have already ridden to warn Juanito not to come into town for the dance.

I said, that being the case, we were wasting our time and would return to Madison. We left town, but we did not go far and came back in a hurry. I can't claim it was not good luck more than anything, but a man makes his good luck with careful planning. So it was we met Johnny-A, Pard Graves, and Chad Bateson riding into Arioso from the south, carefree as mockingbirds.

I called to them to surrender, but they commenced firing. On our first volley Bateson went down, his jaw shot away. He died jerking and screaming in the dust. Johnny and Pard lit out with us on their heels and better-mounted. I had seen to that too.

We chased them five miles across the cactus plains, hard to make shots among those clumps of paddle cactus high as a mounted man's hat, and the two of them switching back and forth between the cactus stands and some saguaro. We hit Graves's horse to lame him, so Johnny had to take Graves up behind. That slowed them some, but kept us back with Graves firing off the poop deck. Finally they forted up in some tumbledown adobe walls, and kept up a slow firing that made things uncomfortable for us out in the sun. The temperature was up around a hundred. I had no way of knowing how much ammunition they had, or water, but we had plenty of both and could send for more. I sent our best shot to see if he couldn't kill the horse so they were stuck afoot. He came back to say he had done so. So the two of them were trapped in those adobe walls, and only a matter of time until they had to surrender or try to make a break for it, which they could only do after nightfall.

I raised up a white cloth for a flag of truce and called out that I wanted to come in to parley.

Johnny called back, "Come on, but leave your iron behind!"

I walked in with my hands raised and no sidearm. They sat in the shade with their backs to a wall, Johnny balanced on the three legs of a busted chair, Pard on the ground. Pard's shirtsleeve was soaked in blood where he'd been hit, and a tourniquet was cinched up tight against the shoulder with a stick through the knot. I recalled the way we had taken Johnny before, when he was bringing Lieutenant Cutler to a doctor.

I said, "You'd better get that to a doc, Pard."

"Pleased to," he said. He was a likable young fellow maybe a couple of years older than Johnny, but a soft center to him Johnny didn't have. "You take me along, will you, Jack?"

I said, "Not without your partner."

Johnny grinned like he'd known exactly what I'd be up to. He said, "Why, I don't need any doctoring, Big Jay."

"Pard does, though."

"Ready to go along, too."

I said I couldn't take Pard along to town to the doctor without him, for it was my duty to capture Johnny Angell.

Johnny said, "You always was one for duty, Jack. What will you do if Pard plain surrenders?"

"Why, I'll accept his surrender, but I can't take him to town till you've surrendered too."

Johnny said he was not going to do that.

I shrugged and waited to see how far it would roll on its own.

Johnny said, "Sorry, Pard."

"Luck of the draw," Pard said, but his face was drawn up anxious.

Johnny said to me, "I call that hard choices. Sheriffing has changed you. That is not a choice you would've put to a fellow once."

"Outlawing has changed you," I said. "I remember not long ago, nor far from here either, when you came in because a fellow you were tending was in a bad way from snakebite or whatever it was."

"That was before I was slated for a sore neck. So it's times that's changed. But I take it poorly that you won't send Pard into town."

I said it was a come-along I had to use, and he did nod to that.

"Maybe you'd better go along with Jack anyhow, Pard. Maybe they can do more for that arm than I can."

"Oh, I think I'll stick it here, Johnny," Pard said, trying to grin like none of it counted for much.

Johnny said to me, "Keep your head down, out there."

I asked how they were set for water. It was melting hot, even in the shade of the wall. Flies were swarming on the dead horse, and Pard had to keep waving them off his shoulder.

"We're all right, thanks."

I said, "I'll just leave this here," meaning the white cloth, which I spread over the top of the wall.

"Take it along with you, Sheriff," Johnny said, pretty tight, and tossed it to me. He was changed, all right. He was a desperate man now. Though it was told of Johnny that he had shot his stepfather in a fuss, and some claimed to know that he was the one that had put Bert Fears and Cory Helbush under *ley fuga*, I thought that before he was Johnny-A and the sheriff-killer out of the nickel novels, he would not have centershot Henry Enders after he'd broken his gun arm, or hanged Ed Duffy like he had done. That had shocked a good many people, say what you want to about Duffy. But I still don't believe things would have run the way they had if the governor had made good his promise.

I went on back. The rest of the afternoon was spent sniping. Once he almost got me. The slug chipped fire off a rock outcrop about two inches above my head, where I was crawling to give instructions to Ben Gibson.

I sat there brushing rock dust off my hat, thinking that that one had had my name on it. It seemed to me that my trying to take him in was one thing, part of my duty that we had spoken of, but his trying to kill me was another and part of his being outlaw and on the dodge for his life. So there was no more Little Jay and Big Jay between us.

I still thought he might give up to save Pard Graves, but as dark came on it was clear they would try to sneak past us after nightfall. I figured they had to try for the horses then, and I'd been laying the trap with Ben when Johnny's shot almost got me.

At full dark we were ready, but time passed and maybe we were not as ready as we should have been. Ben yelled that someone was out. It was Johnny alone, for he had left Graves behind in the adobe walls.

I couldn't think where Johnny might have hid himself. We scoured that place in the dark, and patrolled all night, and scoured it again by daylight. By then I figured he had sneaked clean away, but later I figured he had crawled right inside a stand of cactus, and waited us out. He is no slight of frame he could've slithered in among the thorns like a snake, and lucky he didn't meet a rattler in there. So he was clean away one way or the other.

We took Pard to the old sawbones at Riveroaks, and then on into Madison. Doc Prim had to take the arm off, saying it hadn't had to be. But I was doing my duty, which was first and foremost to bring in Johnny-A, and though I hadn't done that, I had taken off two of *his* right arms, which were Chad Bateson and Pard Graves.

I quarreled with Callie about Johnny, too, her sitting on the bed in her shift, hands in her lap turning the ring I had given her on her finger. On the table beside the bed were the white crockery pitcher and bowl. I told her Johnny had tried to kill me.

She said, "You were trying to kill him, Jack." Out in the parlor some cowboy began chording a guitar, soft music like a stroking.

I said, "I was trying to bring him in. It's my duty. I am sheriff here."

"If you bring him in they'll hang him," she said. She raised a hand to fix the loose hair over her forehead, and it was like she was brushing it over her eyes so as not to look at me directly. "That's killing him," she said. "He's your friend. I've heard you say so right here!"

I said that didn't cut any ice with me, but I felt foolish standing there before her in my long johns. I didn't like it that she looked afraid of me, although there was a mulish set to her jaw. The chording had stopped.

She said, "Can't you just talk to him, Jack? Tell him he has to leave here?"

"It's late for that," I said, feeling mulish myself. It's queer how a woman can do that to you.

"You can do something for a man who's your friend, even if you're sheriff. You're not just a—a locomotive!"

She had never said anything like that to me before. When I thought about it I could see that I had got fired up about bringing Johnny in, as though his bustout had been bad marks on me, with the governor badgering me and people remarking behind my back. Callie knew how to calm me down well enough, but now it was as though I was supposed to calm her down instead. I had to get her out of that place before she got to be like the other girls.

"Well, just you remember that we're not going to tie the knot until I've brought Johnny in," I said, "or else I hear for sure he's cleared out of the Territory."

Lily's sister's husband owned a pharmacy in Santa Fe, and Lily was putting up with them in their house on a street that wound above the plaza, the Harvey Hotel, the governor's palace, and the cathedral with its spire reaching up into the night sky. Lily let him in, a full-figured black cutout against a lighted room. "Johnny!" Her hand caught his tightly. He followed her, feeling like some kind of war wagon clanking along, Colt on his hip and Winchester in hand, weight of his cartridge belt and defensive iron, rap of his boot heels on bare planks and then muffled by a rug.

Her sister and brother-in-law sat on either side of a table with a lace doily covering it under a pulley lamp, their eyes slanting sideways at him like a couple of raccoons at the garbage as he passed. Johnny-A! He could smell Lily's flower scent, with a taint of something else with it, maybe fear. He was not used yet to people being afraid of him.

In the pitchy parlor there was a click as Lily closed the door behind him. The smell was stronger, and he could hear her breathing. Then she was up against him, bosom and belly heat, her fingers pricking the small hairs at the back of his neck. Right away he was shivering like a puppy with the pip. The pressure against him relaxed, and a little light drew the pale curve of her cheek bent close to the lamp with its glass shade like a tortured blossom. A wick flared up, and her face drew away from it.

"You killed Henry Enders," she whispered.

"And Harry Williams too." Of course she would know all about his bustout from the newspaper. He didn't want to know what they had said of him.

She led him to the settee and half pushed him onto it, seating herself before him on a low chair. "What will you do?"

He shook that off; that wasn't the point. "Ran Boland ordered it done and paid cash money for it," he said, more loudly than he had intended. "Ed Duffy swore to that."

"Was there any doubt?"

"I had to know for sure. So I am leaving for Tucson. He is there."

"Then you must keep on going."

"I guess so."

There was a silence before she said, "I must continue here. Martin's brother is on a ship bound for New York."

He felt snappish. He couldn't make out her face, her back to the light the way she was sitting. "I am finished after Tucson."

He heard the small intake of her breath. "I am not!

There is still Colonel Dougal. Who condemned Frank to death, and has called me a debauched woman!"

He wiped the back of his hand over his mouth, feeling his teeth.

She seemed to remove herself further from him. He knew it was the end. "I didn't mean I was asking for your help," she said. "You've done . . . enough. Mr. James Turnbull has resources."

Another lawyer for her to depend upon, this one called a barrister and rich. He breathed her scent. He had never known anyone like her, but she was only a woman, with breasts like Valentina or Carmelita, only larger, and a cunt that might be hotter. Yet she wore some kind of intensity like her fancy clothes, something she exuded like the flower perfume she must have bought in a bottle.

He said, "I meant I was finished because that is all that has to do with Mr. Martin Turnbull."

He thought she laughed, although it might have been a different kind of sound. "You have found that Ran Boland ordered it, so that is all," she said. "Do you know who owns the store now? It is bankrupt, and all its assets have reverted to Jake Weber, who lives not half a mile from here! The United States District Attorney! And I believe the track will lead on from him to former Governor Dickey, who I believe now resides in Denver. There is also Judge Arthur, and Mr. MacLennon—"

"I am through!" he half groaned.

"I am not asking you anything, Johnny! Only telling you that it is so much more complex than—" She halted herself. Then she said in a strong voice, "With the necessary resources we can get to the bottom of it."

"I have just about run my course, Lily."

"I have asked too much!"

"You have not asked anything I did not ask myself."

"Mr. Turnbull has promised to help with Mr. Tarkenton's bill."

"I don't want Mr. James Turnbull paying my bills and I am not running any lawyer bills anyhow. It is too late for that. Procedural error, or whatever Mr. Tarkenton'd call it—my busting out."

Her face was cast down, her fingers woven together in her lap. Was she weeping for him? He would not have it that she had used him to her ends! Their ends had been the same, after all! Only he could not see it as far as she could, as complexly as she could. No doubt she was yards smarter, and educated besides. But it did seem to him that, aside from Ran Boland, all of justice had got so blurred and mixed together he could not make sense of it anymore; and there were other matters he did not see how he could attend to, such as the governor holding off too long with his pardon, if he had even meant to give it at all, and Jack Grant holding off so long Pard had lost that arm.

He began to shiver when Lily leaned closer. Her mouth pressed to his, wet and warm. When she knelt before him he closed his eyes, despising his lack of will. It was not right, it was not even enough.

Aboard Trey-spot, rifle in its boot, bedroll and plunder strapped on behind the saddle, hat pulled down to his eyes, in the darkness he jolted down the steep street past the floating, insubstantial rectangles of windows. Passing these magic lanterns in his tight store pants, shirt and buttoned-up vest, boots and gauntlets, press of his hatband on his head, he felt intact, contained, pulled together—himself, John Angell, not the Johnny-A, the Juanito Ángel, the Angelito of others, who must make him into something he was not. Himself! He had taken his last leave of Lily Maginnis.

Trey-spot jolted from one hoof to another in this descent. Behind the windows were people of regular lives—storekeepers, lawyers, schoolteachers, businessmen, Mr. Jake Weber somewhere not far off. He felt a lightsome freedom that he need no longer concern himself with Maginnis concerns.

He came down past the high loom of the cathedral against the starred sky. Low trees threw the plaza into a tangle of shadows, dark bulks of wagons parked along the far side. He turned along the long, low, porticoed mass of the governor's palace, where one window was alight.

From the saddle he could see into the room where he had met Governor Underwood. The governor sat at his desk there, back to him, triangle of bearded cheek showing. He was writing, bent with the intensity of the task, elbow moving, hand brushing across the paper before him. He halted once to straighten, fidget his shoulders, then dip his pen into the inkwell and lean forward again.

Johnny pulled his bandana up over his nose and mouth and urged Trey-spot up onto the boardwalk under the porticoes, ducking his head under the rafters. The governor continued his writing. What document? A pardon too late? Treaties he did not intend to carry out? False warrants? False history? He drew his rifle from its scabbard and held it across his body.

Finally the governor turned, turned further, stared, brushing a hand over his eyes as though at a cobweb, jumped up and pushed his chair back. He stepped closer to the window, his face startled, red lips in his black beard, black hooks of hair framing his face. Johnny urged Trey-spot closer.

The governor fled out the far door of the office, and Johnny could hear his muffled shouting. He guided Trey-spot off the boardwalk and into the plaza, and away at a good trot. He began to whistle.

Tucson was an old Mex town with Yankee fringes, adobe buildings haloed in heat, dusty streets, dogs, horses, mules, burros, buggies and wagons, stink of dogshit, piss, chilies, beer, dust. He followed in the wake of a water wagon drawn by a span of mules. Shimmering water sprayed from its tail end to disappear into the dry dust. Two men were fighting on the high boardwalk before a saloon, heavy, slow blows; one of them had blood leaking from his nose. Trey-spot danced with pleasure in the rainbow wake of the water wagon.

Johnny stopped at the next saloon to inquire for Randolph Boland, a fat old man sick in bed. A Mex boy was found to guide him to a respectable, white-painted clapboard house with fancy turned-wood trim and lace curtains in the windows.

A purse-mouthed woman opened the door for him, gray hair drawn back so tight it pulled her eyes up at the corners like a Chinaman's. She wore a white uniform and pince-nez glasses on a chain around her neck.

"He takes a nap two to five. Come back after."

"Oh, I'd expect he'd want to see me. Old friend from home."

"You can't stay long. He's very weak. He don't hold up."

"I won't be hard on him, ma'am."

She led him to a back bedroom, away from the passing racket of the street outside. A great mound of Ran Boland snored on the bed, sheet-covered. The table beside the bed was covered by a towel, some bottles and a glass of water standing on it. The room stank of piss and medicine, smell of mortality.

"I usually clean him up when he's waked up from his nap," the woman said.

"I'll just sit here by him awhile." He swung the chair around and sat watching Ran Boland over the back of it. Boland snored open-mouthed, spittle running out of the pink corner of his mouth. The last one.

Vengeance is mine, saith the Lord.

After a time Johnny caught his head nodding, he must have snoozed off. One of Ran Boland's eyes was wide open, gazing at him.

"Come visiting, son?" Ran said.

"Not exactly," he said.

The pale, round, rubbery face shook, then settled and steadied like a pond after a stone had been dropped into it. "Come for what then, son?"

"Can't guess?"

"Just a minute—just a minute—" A fat hand, white as tallow, swept back and forth before the single eye. Like the governor brushing away the sight of him, Johnny thought. "Is this another. . . visitation."

"I don't know what you mean, Mr. Boland."

"Are you Johnny-A, truly?" Boland began to laugh, shaking all over again. "Or the angel of death?"

"Maybe both, Mr. Boland."

"Come to kill poor old Ran Boland? May I ask why?"

"You sent the posse out to kill Mr. Turnbull. I got it finally on Ed Duffy's say: you telling those people to go out and get rid of Mr. Turnbull."

Ran Boland continued to shake with laughter, or maybe it was something else. "Did he say it under compulsion, Johnny? I imagine that he did. My goodness, Ed Duffy wasn't at any meeting where such a thing was discussed! Who would say such a thing before the Ed Duffys of the world? And who would believe such a thing from the lips of an Ed Duffy anyway? Of course you are young and unacquainted with the intricacies of the world's turnings."

"I have got acquainted lately," he said.

"I will put this to you as pure gospel," Ran Boland said. "Such a thing was never said in the presence of Ed Duffy."

He was depressed at the thought of calling a dying man a liar and by the probability that he was not lying.

As though the other had read his thoughts, the single eye winked roguishly. "Mind, I do not deny having said it, son. I do not deny its having been said. Nor that it was a terrible error. A misjudgment that unleashed the hounds of hell. The angel of death, in fact," he said, and chuckled.

He hated Ran Boland jiggling and shaking like that, whether it was from laughter or from fear.

"My boy, do you know how cancer has its name?"

"No, sir."

"Cancer the crab. The crab gnaws at the innards, finding the tender places to chew on. Without laudanum I begin to moan. Sometimes with it. Without my potion of opium I begin to scream. The crab gnaws at some times more cruelly than at others."

He heard himself saying he was sorry.

Ran Boland took up the laughing-crying again. "Sorry! Oh! Oh! Oh! My dear boy! Let me say that I am not sorry that the angel of death has come! Let me tell you how I welcome your mission here. Life is sweet, even in its bitterest moments—of course the angel strikes terror—but what a blessed relief!" He wept, the eye closing, the mound of him shaking, bedsprings creaking.

Johnny closed his own eyes with embarrassment, smelling the stench of death. As much to himself as to the dying man, he said, "It is something that had to be done. I couldn't just leave be and think anything of myself. I don't see how I could've done any different!"

"My boy! My boy, you have done it! You have killed us all! We are punished! You must be satisfied!"

He said there was not much satisfaction in it. It was just that someone had had to do it.

"All for Martin Turnbull! What a misjudgment I made!" Boland began the shaking chuckling again. His cheek gleamed with tears.

"Mr. Maginnis too."

"Diablo!" Boland said, shaking his head. "Just wait, my boy. If the doctor is late—he is often late!—you will hear me start to groan. When he comes you will hear me begging. That should please you! If he does not come, you will hear me scream! Then you can . . ."

The eye closed, the rubbery smile faded to slackness. Ran Boland was silent for so long Johnny thought he might have died. Then a small snore purred.

He tiptoed out and told the woman Mr. Boland was still sleeping, he'd come back after five. At the crossroads outside town he gave Trey-spot his head, and of course the horse headed back for New Mexico Territory.

He sat at the pigskin-topped table with Elizabeth Fulton, so tired he could hardly keep his eyes open. He could not afford to get so tired. He could not afford to doze, just as he could no longer stand close to windows. He had pushed Trey-spot hard returning from Tucson. He had had the thought that he was headed for the Old Ones' cliff dwellings, but it had been Elizabeth he was headed for. She poured more chocolate in his cup and watched him anxiously.

"Think about you when I am not here," he explained.

She averted her face. "I think of you also, Juanito."

He took a breath and said, "I thought I would come and ask you to marry me. Talk to Pete about that."

She still kept her face averted. He watched her slim hand gather itself into a fist and then relax.

"But I am on the run," he went on. "I can't ask you to go on the dodge with me. Even if I did, you mustn't think of doing such a thing."

She nodded once.

"Even if Pete would allow it."

She looked up at him with glistening beads on her eyelashes.

"I can't stay here very long, I know. Someone will tell Jack Grant I am here. But I had to come and tell you—"

There were round spots of color in her cheeks. He decided that although she was not pretty, she was very close to beautiful. He wrenched his eyes open to feed them on her face.

"I've got to get some money together," he said. "I'll talk to some fellows I know and we'll get some stock together and take it over to Texas and sell it to the army there. Then I'll get another herd together and head up toward Colorado. There are some little valleys I remember on the east slope of the Rockies where I'll claim a little spread. When I have done all that, I will come back and ask you to marry me. Of course it'll be taking you away from your people here. I am sorry for that. But this country isn't safe for me anymore."

"I understand, Juanito," Elizabeth said with the tears shining in her eyes.

He knew that the tears were for him. She probably believed none of this. He did not believe it himself, except a little sometimes. Yet picturing it would make his eyes ache, the little rancho in one of those green coves, with a great bushy tree like a green, benevolent elephant's head bowed over the shake roof of their cottage. A safe harbor with Elizabeth there, and everything to start over. He was ashamed to pray to his Father for it.

"If you would wait for me till then," he said.

"I will wait as long as I have to wait, Juanito." The bright tears slid down her cheeks. He moved his hand to cover hers, and hers swiftly clasped his. Little muscles caught along the edge of her jaw.

He staggered to his feet. "I must get some sleep... I just can't keep my eyes open..."

She rose swiftly also. "You will sleep in my bed. No one will bother you there." And she whispered, "I will wait for you always!"

The next day he visited Don Teodoro Soto in the office at the back of the cantina. The mayor poured them each a glass of Old Crow.

"If you will not mind my giving you advice, I think you must clear out of this country, Juanito."

"That is my intention, Don Teodoro. I would just not want certain ducks thinking I was clearing out because of them."

He grinned, but Don Teodoro did not smile in return. Short, straight-backed, big-bellied, he paraded back to his chair on his hooves of feet. He reseated himself still with the solemn expression.

"I speak of matters that may not be pleasing to you, my friend."

"Forewarned is forearmed, as somebody said. A man does need four arms sometimes!"

Don Teodoro did not smile at that either. "Juanito, there were many young men prepared to endanger themselves to help you against the Jesse Clary gang. But things have changed."

"*Dígame.*"

"The sheriff, you know, is responsible for the collection of taxes. Sheriff Smith did not bother with the *placitas* in this matter, but now comes Sheriff Grant."

"To collect taxes."

"He has spoken to me of the matter. Not only taxes for this year, but for past years. He does not say this is because Arioso has been the friend of Juanito Ángel, but he does not need to say it. Money is important to the *gente*, who have so little. Money alters one's thoughts in certain matters, you understand, Juanito."

"Surely not yours, Don Teodoro!"

Finally the mayor smiled tiredly. He drained his glass and leaned forward to place it carefully on the blotter of his desk. "Perhaps even mine, a little, my friend! It is sad, is it not? One is ashamed! Still, there the matter lies."

"So I do not have so many friends in Arioso as I used to."

"You have many friends here, Juanito. You are a hero to the young men, even to some whose *novias*' hearts you have stolen! And you are the friend of Teodoro Soto! Never will this fact change!"

"Still, there is some interference from the taxes."

"It does not affect the essence!" Don Teodoro said, and clapped his pudgy hand to his heart.

Johnny was beginning to feel seriously hemmed in by Sheriff Jack Grant.

Back at Pete Fulton's, he asked Elizabeth's brother Tommy to ride to the Walkers' ranch with a note from him. He wanted to talk to Red. The Walkers lived with their widowed mother on their ranch outside Riveroaks. They were halfway friends of his who had done some rustling, off and on, and were a rough and ready bunch. Red was the roughest and readiest of the three brothers, a wild rusty-thatched bird with green eyes you could see a half-mile off.

Johnny was wondering how to get at that famous Sierra Verde herd at Bosque Alto, laughing at himself to think of riding with a bunch like the Walker brothers and going up against Red Stripers and maybe cavalry too, just for a stake. Jack Grant had Pauly Tuttle in jail in Madison now, had scared Carlito into running south to kin he had in Sonora, and had pushed him, Johnny Angell, into pure foolishness at last.

Worse luck, he and Red Walker were out on a Bosque Alto scout when they ran into Pat Cutler and one of his trackers, heading up the trail above the sawmill where Jay-O-Joe Peake had been killed. Pat was in uniform with a slouch hat, sitting his big gold-colored Mex horse, the Pache bare-legged under a blue shirt, wearing a fancy low-crowned straw with blue ribbons dangling off it.

"Well, hello there, Pat!" Johnny called.

Pat tapped his fingers to his hat brim. He looked a good deal better than he had when he'd brought the little revolver to the jail, filled out some and color in his cheeks. He looked too as though he knew exactly why they were riding up to the reservation this back way.

"What is this expedition, Johnny?"

"We're just out taking the air. Meet Red Walker here. Lieutenant Cutler, Red."

They nodded to each other. He could see from Red's stance he wasn't going to take any truck off soldiers, and especially not an Injun.

"Don't even think of it, Johnny," Pat said, looking at him hard out of his blue eyes set under a shelf of brows.

"Don't even think about what, mister?" Red said in a proddy tone.

"Never mind it, Red," Johnny said. He had come to see in these last days that Red required a good bit of handling, and he did not have much patience for it. He said to Pat, "Well, we have been thinking about it, and that's a fact."

"Everyone who has to make a quick stake gets to thinking about it," Pat said, leaning on his pommel. "The sheriff knows that too."

"What if he does?" Red said. He took makings from his pocket and started a cigarette.

"That doesn't scare me much, Pat," Johnny said.

"It scares me," Pat said. "You two going after that herd doesn't, because the Red Stripes know how to watch out for their herd, and now I've seen you Captain Bunch's scouts will be on the lookout too. What scares me is the sheriff and a posse barging around the reservation, since it was a sheriff serving papers that ran Caballito off San Marcos. And a dozen or so people killed."

"Huh!" Red said, and lit up. The tracker was leaning on

his pommel like he was copying Pat Cutler exactly. He had a dark, almost pretty face.

"Do you follow me, Johnny?" Pat said, not looking at Red. "My orders are to see nothing jiggers Caballito out of here."

Of course every cowboy with larceny in him got to thinking of the fine Sierra Verde herd one time or another. Johnny had told the Walkers and the three others they had brought along that he thought they had about a twenty percent chance at it. Still, he had got himself into a box, for if he did not make some move pretty quick his gang would start coming unraveled. It was either the Bosque Alto herd or Mr. McFall's stock, and he had strictures against thieving from a man he had worked for. "So it's not us that's scaring you, it's Jack Grant," he said.

Pat took off his hat and scrubbed the back of his hand over his forehead. He said, "I'm scared of anything that might spook the Sierra Verdes."

Johnny pulled a big shrug and swung Trey-spot's head back downhill. "Let's go, Red. I don't believe this is the place for us."

Red came along, green eyes glaring and a face like a thunderclap. He hunched over his pommel with his hand-rolled burning in the corner of his jaw. Pat Cutler and his straw-hat scout sat their horses watching them heading back toward the sawmill.

"He surely talked you out of that Red Striper herd," Red groused.

"Did, didn't he? Well, I'll tell you, him and me have a kind of bargain going. I saved his leg once, and he saved my neck; now it's my turn again."

"Huh!" Red said.

"Besides, I told you we had about a twenty percent chance. Now he's seen us it's come down to about ten, and that's too long odds."

He felt bile spoiling in his belly, and a bad, hemmed-in feeling of fences and bars and old bargains heading him off the true. He was sick of himself that he would be ashamed before Pat Cutler of riding with one of the Walker brothers, and ashamed before Red Walker that he had seemed to give way before Pat Cutler. Had he come to it that he had to worry things like that, and fret about the Walker brothers taking his orders without a fuss? He was sick that he had to worry any of that trash. He said, "You didn't help anything back there sounding your toot. From now on keep it shut, you might learn something."

He gave Red a hard look, and Red started to speak but didn't, a flush coming up into his cheeks.

"Understand me?" Johnny said, with an edge on his voice.

"Sure, Johnny," Red said, nodding jerkily and hunching his head down a bit as they rode on down toward the sawmill.

24

Caballito and most of the Sierra Verde band slipped away from the Bosque Alto reservation after a thunderstorm during the night of April 20, 188-. His numbers were estimated at 140 of the Red Stripe People, plus 40 Nahuaques and a few Comanches who had drifted onto the reservation—perhaps 90 bucks, believed to be well armed with repeating rifles. The rest were women, children, and a few old people, and Caballito had taken the precaution of bearing away a number of the squaws of the Sierra Verde scouts. He had also driven along with him a large part of the cattle herd, and a *caballada* of remounts. It was a major breakout.

Captain Bunch immediately set out in pursuit with his company of Sierra Verde scouts, none of whom had defected to Caballito. Two of Lieutenant Cutler's Hoya trackers accompanied them, and five troops of cavalry from Fort McLain followed their lead. General Yeager's orders to the border posts were that detachments proceed to the waterholes and main passes of the routes into Mexico.

Cutler was delayed until he received orders from Captain Robinson reenlisting his Hoyas. He knew that the last act had begun, and hopes for the salvation of the Sierra Verdes were reduced to a candle glimmer. As with the Hoyas and the cavalry, as with so many others in the Territory, it had come to be to his benefit that the Sierra Verdes commit this final act of their destruction, for when it was finished he was free to pursue his life in Sonora, at the Hacienda de las Golondrinas, with his son, with his wife.

The *ranchería* of the Red Stripe People at Bosque Alto was by no means deserted, although most of the wickiups had been stripped of their coverings. The frameworks of dead branches were already almost indistinguishable from the brush

410

and meadow grasses. Cutler left the Hoyas and the pack animals on the ridge and rode down toward the wickiups. He was feeling a profound awareness of time passing, a ticking of impatience and reluctance, of anticipation and dread—and an irritating inattention, his mind skittering off to the future when there was still this equation of the present to be solved.

A few squaws were visible by the split rock, but there were no sounds of merriment today. They were old women, and old men squatted in a circle, brown backs, turbaned heads, wrinkled faces slanted toward him. Joklinney rose from among them. His cheeks were red-striped, and his hair hung loose to his shoulders. He approached Malcreado.

"You remain here, Joe King!"

"As you see," Joklinney said. "Among these old ones. All young men and women have gone."

Cutler swung down to shake his hand. "I am surprised you were allowed to remain behind."

Joklinney moved away out of earshot of the others, squinting sideways as though deciding whether or not to reveal a secret. "Joe King said that one that was not blue-soldier scout or old one must remain behind so the Red Stripe People would not be forgotten."

Joklinney called himself Joe King when he was thinking like a white-eye. So he would become the renewal of the Red Stripe People if they were destroyed. Cutler realized that his own renewal was already provided for, Pedrito at Las Golondrinas.

"Did the thunder speak to Caballito?"

Joklinney shrugged, leaving his shoulders high. "It was the *hû*."

"The *owl*?"

"Yes, Nantan Tata. The owl cried in the night. Then the thunder spoke."

Cutler's laughter hurt in his chest. So Caballito had also heard the cry of the owl, which was *cha-ut-lip-un*. Joklinney gazed at him mockingly.

"Joe King did not wish to die for fear of the *hû*. This is the gift of Nantan Lobo."

The gift of Fort Point, of San Francisco, of a whorehouse on Nob Hill. Was it worse to die of fear of the *hû* or of the white-eye papers? Cutler said, "The women of the scouts were taken?"

"Yes, five," Joklinney said. "The woman of Nantan Bigotes was also taken."

"Tze-go-juni!"

"Yes, that one."

"Will he kill the women if the scouts press him?"

Joklinney merely shrugged, as Cutler mounted Malcreado. "So it ends, Nantan Tata," he said, grinning.

Cutler swung away. On the ridge Nochte, Lucky, Jimjim, and Kills-a-Bear waited. Out of sight were Chockaway and the pack animals. Skinny and Tazzi had accompanied Bunch's scouts. He spurred to a trot, signaling to them to start after the others in the pursuit of Caballito.

From the messengers and cavalry units they encountered he learned of the mounting toll: three soldiers who had been guarding a horse herd, two miners, two teamsters slaughtered, but four, who had been able to fort up, safe, and a wagonload of ammunition saved from the marauders. No doubt there were unrecorded casualties.

They overtook and passed F Troop in a desert in bloom, tall creamy explosions of yucca blossoms, red flares of ocotillo, a varicolored carpeting of blooming ground cover. Lieutenant Farrier thought Bunch and the scouts were half a day ahead, approaching the flanks of the Baldy Range.

The trail left by the Sierra Verde herd, the scouts, and the cavalry troops still ahead was broad as a highway. They came upon two dead herders, stripped naked, black with blood and already swollen in the heat—the familiar stench of Apache depredations. There were also the carcasses of wantonly slaughtered sheep, and a dead cow. A wind-broken horse waited forlornly. Beside Cutler rode Nochte and Kills-a-Bear, the others stringing out behind, all in their red headbands, wearing blue troop shirts, bare-legged above high moccasins. The scouts were in high spirits, their long boredom and poverty ended.

In broken country the trail bordered the river, which was broad and shallow here, gleaming in the sun. Here many animals had watered. Kills-a-Bear splashed across to the far side, where he dismounted to lead his horse, peering at the ground, often squatting to study; he was the master tracker of them all. He stood and beckoned. They crossed to join him,

Kills-a-Bear grinning as he pointed to scuffed earth and a twig broken loose to reveal a pale pith.

Kills-a-Bear pointed to his eye, pointed south, pointed to Lucky and Jim-jim. Immediately the two set off, riding in arcs, hunched, cutting for sign. "Ho, Tazzi!" Kills-a-Bear grunted, grinning. Tazzi and the Sierra Verde scouts had apparently been fooled.

Nochte said, "He thinks Nantan Bigotes has followed the cattle herd. Caballito has gone that way."

Cutler thought there were no question. Chockaway led the pack mules across the river, calling ahead in Apache. Two hundred yards away Jim-jim was holding his rifle by the barrel and the stock and pumping it up and down; many. Caballito was headed for the Boot Range, not the Baldies. Lucky was instructed to ride after Bunch to tell him of Caballito's ruse, if he had not discovered it already. Caballito had been willing to sacrifice his precious herd, which was a drag on his speed. Another could be stolen in Mexico.

They rode on following sign, the Hoyas merry as Cutler had not seen them since before Benny Dee's death, pleased with themselves because they had not been outwitted, as Tazzi and Skinny had been. Nochte had decorated his hatband with a chain of yellow blossoms. They trotted on southeast through the spangled foulards of flowers on the desert floor.

Cutler decided to make camp early, in the foothills of the Boots on the banks of a creek that poured through a chain of granite tanks. He did not want to blunder into an ambush before Bunch came up, and he sent Jim-jim back over the trail to lead in the Sierra Verde scouts.

They came in just before dark—Bunch, the interpreter, and the ugly sergeant with the yellow chevrons on his shirtsleeve in the lead, all in a foul mood from their expressions. The rest of the scouts rode in good order, regimental enough in their white cotton, and red headbands, none with cheek stripes. Tazzi, Skinny, Lucky, and Jim-jim rode apart.

The Hoyas lounged on the rocks munching on baked mescal and jerked beef. When they were not joshing Tazzi and Skinny, they watched the Sierra Verde scouts expressionlessly, their eyes slanting at Cutler when he went to greet Bunch. The sergeant squalled in Apache, and Cutler admired the company's maneuver across the creek, where it dismounted and the horses were led off to picket lines in groups of four. He wondered if any of the Sierra Verdes had been aware of Caballito's trick but had chosen to ignore it.

"They've been straight salt!" Bunch said loudly, as he and Cutler wandered in the gathering dusk. "Bishi-do'd figured out what'd gone wrong about the time one of your fellows did. We were on our way back."

"Pretty Mouth is with Caballito."

Bunch halted to stand motionless. "Shit," he said. "Of course we knew he'd taken some of the squaws along, but I didn't think of that. Shit. How do you know?"

"Joklinney told me."

"Well, it doesn't change anything, does it? Duty's duty. Herd him back to the reservation or kill him. Shit." He sat down on a rock, massaging his face with his big hands. "That bloody bastard Joklinney. That raid of his Yeager had him sent to Alcatraz for was pure butchery, I've heard. They ought to've hanged him." He rubbed a hand over his mouth. "I've thought what I'd do to him if he cut her nose. I'd cut his cock off by inches and feed it to him. I'd cut a piece of his gut and nail it to a fence post and whip him to running till he degutted himself. I catch myself thinking like a fucking Pache! Shit, now Caballito's got her. Saw some of *his* work along the way."

"My Hoyas think we're not far behind him. That he won't think he has to move so fast now."

"We'll leapfrog," Bunch said. "You go full out first thing. My flying squad'll come up and relieve you. There ought to be cavalry units spread all over the place up ahead. We can chancery him against one of them, or maybe one of us can get ahead of him."

"We'll go out at first light."

"Shit," Bunch said, holding his head in his hands.

That night the Hoyas and the Sierra Verde scouts danced together. The drum was a camp kettle partially filled with water, a soaked canvas stretched over it. Its rhythms were accompanied by an Apache fiddle, carved from soft, pale wood. A scout drew a stick over its string, producing the sound of a cat in sexual agony. The scouts danced naked except for breechclouts and moccasins, flourishing their carbines, copper glint of firelight on brown skin. They pirouetted, charged, filed and counterfiled through each other's ranks, bounded into the air with belligerent shouts, chanted a monotonous refrain. From time to time one would step before the others to deliver some aggressive message. The Hoyas danced less wildly, more hunched, and kept together.

Nochte squatted with Cutler, Bunch, and the scout sergeant, Bishi-do. "They say what they will do when they catch Caballito tomorrow," Nochte said in Spanish. "They will kill these bad ones who have betrayed the Red Stripe People. Who make trouble for all the Indeh. They will take their rifles and horses and women. They will take back their wives, who have been stolen."

"What is *sikisn?*"

"*Sikisn* is brother. All are brothers here. Tomorrow they will kill Caballito's people as brothers. All are brothers here, as Nantan Bigotes and Nantan Tata are brothers."

The drum beat monotonously, the fiddle squealed to the eerie harmonics of the chanting. The scouts and trackers pranced, now some of them dancing together.

Cutler explained to Bunch what Nochte had told him. "All are brothers here, as the *nantans* are brothers. May I have this dance, brother?"

Bunch propped his chin with a forefinger and affected a shrug like a curtsy. He pushed himself to his feet. They danced together, Cutler's left arm around Bunch's waist, Bunch's right arm around his, booted feet extended and planted, dipping, retreating, a turn maneuvered. Dark faces watched obliquely as they danced their brotherhood, danced the destruction or the capture of the Red Stripe renegades, the acquisition of their rifles and horses, and the recovery of the women.

That night after his watch Cutler dreamed of Las Golondrinas, the swallows twittering along the eaves of the *casa grande,* the swirl of horseflesh and the prickle of dust as the vaqueros drove a horse herd into the corrals. Malcreado bore him through the great gate, out of the sun into that sudden Mexican shade that was so much denser than North American shade, and there was his son, standing with his mother and one of the nursemaids, calling to him in that silence of a dream, his mouth shaping the word.

Caballito's trail was easier to follow now, the Sierra Verdes taking less care to cover their tracks: a horse with its throat cut, which Nochte said might indicate a shortage of ammunition; the remains of a butchered steer; once a litter of abandoned plunder, dresses, a half-burned saddle, a scatter of letters, which meant raiders had hit a wagon train or an isolated ranch house.

The Hoyas rode hard, preceding Bunch's scouts. Ahead in the blue ridges of the Boots smoke was rising. "Hsst!" Tazzi said, riding beside Cutler. He tapped his ear with a dirty forefinger. "Plenty gun!"

Cutler realized he had already been hearing it, like the ticking of his pulse in his ear, the *slump! slump!* of rifle fire. He sent Lucky back with a message for Bunch to hurry.

As the firing grew louder the Hoyas stripped for a fight, shirts bundled behind saddles, carbines in hand, black hair streaming, flashing grins. No one was perishing of boredom now.

Nochte and Tazzi in the lead, they proceeded at a pounding trot toward the sound of the guns. The canyon narrowed into thick growths of flowering trees, creamy blossoms floating down in the flurry of their passage, blue of jacaranda, red berries among white blooms. From a thicket two scared-looking black-faced troopers peered out at Cutler over half-raised carbines. They were guarding a string of cavalry mounts, shifting heads along a picket line. They gaped at the half-naked scouts.

"What outfit is this?" Cutler called.

"A Troop, 6th Cavalry, sir! We are catching hell up ahead, sir!"

Cutler sent Nochte and Tazzi toward the opposite canyon walls to scout, while he and the others followed Skinny on up the trail. Skinny's dark back crouched and wove, once he glanced back with white teeth. "Caballito, Nantan Tata!"

They halted in dense undergrowth on the edge of a grassy clearing, sporadic firing from the canyon walls ahead—a classic Apache ambush site. He couldn't see the troopers, concealed in the high grass of the meadow. The 6th was a Negro regiment stationed at Fort Snelling, east of the mountains, and was no doubt trying to intercept Caballito on General Yeager's orders. Caballito had intercepted them instead. The Red Stripe warriors were equally invisible, except for the puffs of smoke of their firing, forted in behind rocks on the canyonsides. Lucky tapped Cutler's arm and pointed. By the loop of the creek, under a rock face, two troopers were sprawled motionless.

Nochte and Tazzi reappeared almost simultaneously with the arrival of Bishi-do and Bunch's flying squad. Cutler sent Tazzi with Bunch's scouts to flank the north wall, Tazzi rolling his eyes once at the sergeant's parrot-beak scowl, then beckoning them on with a superior expression.

Cutler lay prone behind a down timber, carbine propped and aimed at the south wall, Kills-a-Bear and Nochte close beside him. Time wore past, and the firing had diminished to an occasional shot, when Tazzi's force struck with a crashing volley. Immediately brown bodies were moving and dodging behind the rocks on the north wall. Cutler caught one in his sights, following movement with the front sight blade, squeezing the trigger. The butt smacked his shoulder just as the man sprawled and disappeared. He had one more hurried shot before there were no more movements to be seen. Then on the south side two bucks stood up to dance, one brandishing his rifle and the other flipping his breech-clout defiantly. Before he could shift his barrel around they were gone. There was a heavy silence.

A soldier rose cautiously out of the grass, peering around him, dark as an Apache. Other black soldiers appeared. They all flung themselves down at another spate of firing, although it came from a distance. Cutler sent Nochte to scout.

Bunch, coming up, had run into hostiles circling to get behind Cutler. One of his scouts was dead, one slightly wounded, but he was very pleased at their conduct in the fight with their fellow Sierra Verdes, and, Cutler thought, relieved. *Sikisn!* It was impossible to determine if any of the hostiles had been killed, for Apaches carried their dead away with them whenever possible. It was at least the standard cavalry victory, which was possession of the field after hostiles had slipped away. But more than that, Cutler thought.

The A Troop lieutenant, hardly more than a boy, was in despair, blaming himself for the ambush. Three of his Negro troopers had been killed. They had come up from the eastern slopes, headed for high ground to try to catch a glimpse of the renegades, and had discovered a horse herd guarded by two Indians. They had chased the herd only to find themselves trapped in this meadow. Caballito had got away with one of their pack mules carrying ammunition—about two thousand rounds, the lieutenant thought. However, his black soldiers had handled themselves well enough in their first fight.

They left A Troop to bury its dead, and hurried on in their pursuit, camping that night without having reestablished contact. The scouts sat around four small fires, feasting on mule meat from an animal the hostiles had abandoned and shot—no longer so sparing with their cartridges, as Nochte pointed out. The Hoyas lounged around their own fire. The relations with the Sierra Verde scouts seemed still friendly, but there was no dancing tonight. The moon rose, vast and yellow, above rock crags and mountain juniper. Cutler, seated cross-legged between the Hoyas' fire and a Sierra Verde one, noticed that the Apache chatter had abruptly ceased, to a silence of singing insects celebrating the moonlight. But it was not insects.

"That is somebody *singing!*" Bunch said.

Nochte slid over to seat himself beside Cutler. "It is the song of Caballito!"

Kills-a-Bear and Lucky slipped closer also, with a white flash of eyeballs.

"It is Caballito's medicine song!" Bunch's interpreter said.

"He sings to the Red Stripe People," Nochte said.

The sound seemed to Cutler sometimes close, sometimes far off, sometimes floating away entirely, only to swell again—impossible to determine where it came from. It made his flesh creep. Sometimes it resembled the distant chatting of coyotes. Sometimes a rhythmic chanting rose to a long shrilling. There was utter silence from the Sierra Verde scouts gathered around their fires.

"He asks the Red Stripe People to leave the white-eye and come with him to Mexico," Nochte whispered. "He says his medicine is very strong. His power is great. He says they go to live among the eagles. He says they cannot trust the white-eye *nantans*. The white-eye lies to them. He sings of his medicine."

Cutler sat watching the Sierra Verdes, hunched brown backs around their fires. He could feel Sam Bunch's tension. The song rose and fell in its long periods. Sometimes a slow, dirgelike drum could be heard in accompaniment. "Well, shit!" Bunch said, flexing his shoulders.

Cutler thought of the blue-soldier six dollars a month balanced against living among the eagles in Mexico with their chief of strong medicine. Joklinney had learned that the white-eye medicine was stronger, as the white-eye numbers were greater. "I think I'll send a couple of men to scare him off," he said to Bunch.

"Do that," Bunch said.

He sent Kills-a-Bear and Skinny, but they had hardly left the circle of light of their fire when the song faded, became distant, became silence and the hum of insects. He and Bunch stood watches during the night, and, at first light, all the scouts were present and accounted for.

By the second day they had left behind all the cavalry units that had been trying to intercept Caballito. Increasingly Caballito seemed harried by their pursuit. This the trackers inferred from the spacing of hoofprints. That horses were tiring could be determined by a jerky fall of hooves, by long strides gradually shortening, becoming long again when the animals were pressed on by jabs of a knife. It could be seen that they had moved by night rather than by day if a mesquite bush had been run over rather than gone around. The temperature of horse droppings told how long ago the animals had passed.

Twice there were brief encounters with a rear guard, braves sniping to slow the pursuit. More animals were abandoned, either left alive or again with throats cut or speared through the heart. Springs were shat in or fouled with a disemboweled coyote. Once there was an attempt at an ambush, a herd of a dozen horses grazing for the taking in a cove in the foothills. Cutler sent the Hoyas in a flanking movement, but they were caught in an intense fire and forced back until Bunch's scouts came in to drive the hostiles to flight again.

That night Cutler and Bunch planned an ambush of their own. If Caballito suffered a defeat and lost some of his bucks, others might also desert him, and he might then be induced to parley. By moonlight Cutler and Bishi-do took the Hoyas and the flying squad on a long arc to try to head Caballito. This was mountain terrain Kills-a-Bear professed to know well, and by first light they were bearing on a saddle peak above long blue ridges. Kills-a-Bear, riding ahead, pointed

toward the saddle and raised his rifle above his head. There
was a spring the Sierra Verdes would head for.

Cutler saw everyone forted in behind the rocks beyond
the spring when the first of the Red Stripe People straggled
in, an untidy parade of them on horses and mules, most of
the women afoot with their bundles and cradleboards, wornout
cattle hustled along with them. Cutler watched with his
throat dry as ashes. He had ridden north from Ojo Azul with
these people, he had drunk bad whiskey with Caballito and
the elders and discussed the hereafter. They had called him
Nantan Truth. What was the truth here? That the Sierra
Verdes must be destroyed because of their intransigence and
their savagery? That they must be preserved to furnish the
blue-soldier dollar to his Hoyas and Bunch's scouts, advancement to the military, and profits to the Indian Rings? What of
his own freedom and his own servitude? He could not
distinguish Caballito among the hurrying figures.

The scouts had been ordered to hold their fire until his
signal. The hostile braves continued to ride in, giving over
their ponies to half-grown boys and spreading out to guard
the watering. And there was Caballito, wearing a broad-
brimmed hat and white-eye vest, on a skinny buckskin pony.

Cutler took slow aim, the head beneath the hat jiggling
atop the sight blade; he cinched tight the whole connection of
shoulder, arm, forearm, wrist, hand, trigger finger. The tip of
the sight rode just above the hat as he pulled the trigger. The
hat flew. From all around came the almost simultaneous
volley. Smoke roiled. Caballito disappeared. Hostiles ran
shouting, falling, disappearing. Fire was returned. Bodies
were stretched out in the grass, one still writhing.

He had hoped to hold them in combat until Bunch came
up, but they were gone as though the earth had swallowed
them. He crouched still with his carbine propped on a rock,
cheek against the stock. Duty is duty, Sam Bunch had said.
He had held the end of the Sierra Verde breakout in his
sights, the end of his own service also. It seemed that his
hand, which had lifted that sight a sixteenth of an inch, had
considered that his duty was still to try to induce Caballito
back to the reservation.

This time the Sierra Verdes had been unable to carry
their dead away, a squaw and five bucks—warriors Caballito
could not afford to lose.

When Bunch came up they pushed the pursuit in a running fight eastward, trying to get between Caballito and the border, until the Red Stripe People gained some heights too dangerous to attack frontally and too formidable to try to flank. But it had been a terrible day for the renegades, at least six dead and probably more, and twenty-two head of the blown horses captured, so more of the Red Stripe People were afoot.

That night they camped below the cliffs above which the Sierra Verdes must be licking their wounds. One of the scouts walked up and down, yelling—calling to his wife to run away, Nochte said, calling to all the squaws to desert the chief and join the scouts. Cutler gathered from Nochte's embarrassment, and some laughter, that the invitation was bawdy. The scout stalked up and down, alternately visible and invisible in the stripes of moonlight and dense shadow. Where was Caballito's medicine now? Where was his power? What of the home among the eagles now? The squaws should come to the friends of the white-eye, who were rich, who would treat them well, for they would soon all be widows. There were other reasons they should come down from the cliffs that Nochte did not translate.

Shrill voices replied, in chorus and singly. The white-eyes would never take Caballito! His medicine was powerful! He would never return to San Marcos! They would live in peace with full bellies in Mexico where the white-eyes could not follow! One voice continued to shrill.

"What does she say?" he asked.

Nochte said carefully, "She says, if Caballito dies—the squaws will eat him. No white-eye will ever see him again." Cutler thought then that Caballito had been wounded.

During the night Caballito's band managed to fade away, the trail leading south again, contact broken. But the trackers reported that twelve horsemen had left the main band, and these they believed to be Nahuaques sneaking back toward the reservation. By noon they were out of the mountains into desert, with the vertical flats of mountains lining all horizons but the south. The heat was tempered by a little breeze. He and Bunch sat their horses face to face, Bunch with a bandana tucked under the back of his cap to protect his neck from the sun, big-mustached face scarlet with sunburn and stubbled with beard. The scouts surrounded the two *nantans*, watching them make their decision. They were close to the border, if they had not already crossed it.

"Hot pursuit," Bunch said, wiping his face with another bandana.

"Do we go on?"

"This is surely 'unpopulated country,' and the scouts qualify as 'uniformed soldiery' so long as they keep their red headbands on."

"We don't want to get the scouts in any ruckus with the SPs. They'd as soon cut scout hair as hostile."

"We've got a fortune in hair here!" Bunch said, with a sweep of his arm. "Shall we go in?"

"Let's go."

"Let's go," Bunch said, nodding, and signaled forward. They started into Mexico on the trail of the Red Stripe People, who now made no effort to disguise their tracks. They would be thinking they were safe from the white-eyes now.

Two days later they were deep in Chihuahua. They were living off the land, as the Red Stripe People must be also: acorns from the stunted oaks of the foothills, mashed into a paste and baked; cactus fruit and the fruit of the Spanish bayonet, which, roasted, tasted like bananas; mescal roasted between heated stones, very sweet; and the nests of ground bees raided for honey. This country, the bottomlands of the San Bernardino Valley, was a different kind of desert. Fields that must have once grown corn, wheat, and barley now showed only an odd brown stalk protruding from a thick mass of semitropical vegetation—fields gone fallow and returning to wilderness, the riverbanks choked with canebrakes. They came upon a deserted hamlet, ruined adobe walls melting back into the earth. A walled town raised its ramparts higher on a mountain flank, and Bunch and the interpreter went in to purchase supplies, while Cutler rested with the scouts in the shade of willows on the riverbank.

Bunch returned to say no supplies were available in the village. "Poor!" he said, squatting in the shade beside Cutler. "Rags! Hungry kids! Though none of the hombres is so poor he doesn't have a sombrero big as a washtub, with a silver band on it. And a blanket over his shoulder. This country's a ruin!"

"Apaches have been raiding down here for hundreds of

years. They could fight them off till the Apaches got repeating rifles."

"Just when they start thinking they are safe, Caballito's on the loose again."

Late that day they came upon the bodies of six Mexicans in a streambed. Cutler kicked through the grass on the edge of the creek and found brass shells. One of the bodies was powder-singed; it was evident that they had been shot from a few yards away and had not been dead long.

They rode silently on through lava formations, rising ground, ahead the loom of the Sierra Madre. Just before dark Skinny and Tazzi exchanged shots with Caballito's rear guard. They were in contact again.

That night the mountains flamed before them, fires set by the Red Stripe People to cover their trail and hinder pursuit. The scouts worked through the night setting backfires. The animals were badly frightened, and the air filled with clouds of insects flying from the flames. Higher on the slopes pines blazed like torches, and fringes of flame moved downward to meet the faster moving backfires.

The next day they circled the blackened mountainside. Jim-jim found the trail again, and they moved deeper into the range. Snowy peaks rose ahead. In conference with Bunch, Cutler, the interpreter, and Bishi-do, two of the Sierra Verde scouts claimed to know where Caballito was heading, and to know a shortcut where they would not have to guard against ambushes.

"But he'll know we've been told of this other route," Bunch said. The interpreter translated; he spoke with his fingers moving near his mouth like a second pair of lips. The two scouts looked at each other, one almost cross-eyed with self-consciousness, the other lowering. Both muttered.

"They say he will not know," Worthing said.

"Get up there ahead of them for another ambush?" Bunch said.

"I don't think so," Cutler said.

Bunch leaned back with his hands clasped at the back of his neck. "What's your idea?"

"We've given him a lot of punishment, and we're hard on his track—in Mexico where he thought he'd be safe. Maybe I can persuade him to come back to Bosque Alto."

Bunch spat. "He's not going to Bosque Alto, Pat. He's going to San Marcos or hell."

"Maybe by now San Marcos will look better than hell."

"You never give up, do you?" Bunch said.

They were all day beating up narrow canyons and along knife-edge ridges, terrain similar to and not far from that of his journey north from Las Golondrinas. A pack mule fell at one of the crossings, the canyonside so steep the *aparejo* knocked against a rock protrusion, throwing the animal off balance. It fell with one desperate bawl; the scouts laughed to watch it fall, slapping their thighs, holding their sides, pointing; the laughter of the Indeh!

Toward evening they could see the smoke of the cook fires of Caballito, on a mesa ahead. Cutler, Bunch, Kills-a-Bear, Nochte, the interpreter, Bishi-do, and one of the scouts who had claimed to know this route, held a council to plan an encirclement that would cause Caballito to surrender. First thing in the morning the scout would make his way to Caballito and try to arrange a parley.

By first light the scouts began moving to the positions that had been located the afternoon before, the mountain vast and black against the greenish paling of the sky. The scout was back before the sun had broken free of the eastern peaks.

"He says Nantan Verdad and one other will come," Nochte translated.

The scout led them part way and pointed up. From a crag a hostile with red-striped cheeks watched them, rifle slanted across his body. Cutler, unarmed, in uniform except for the broad-brimmed hat, toiled up the slope with Nochte limping behind, crowned with his own fancy hat. The sun appeared, feathers of smoke visible against it, above a rock reef, just below the tipped-up summit of the mesa. Below, ridge on ridge disappeared into morning fog. On higher peaks to the south were slashes of snow banks and snowy hoods, and the vast range swept away over the edge of the world with peaks and ridges protruding from the mists. Even as they climbed, the sun burnt the fog away so that more and more of the tangled terrain became visible. From above, the sentinel watched them tensely.

There was a crump of distant rifle fire, single shots nearer, a volley. The guard disappeared as Cutler and Nochte scrambled up over the rocks. From here the camp of the Red

Stripe People was visible, brown bodies milling and running. They were abandoning their cook fires and making for the higher ground at the far end of the mesa, the rifle fire continuing. Cutler couldn't understand what had gone wrong until he saw the white uniforms appearing over the rim from the west, where Bunch had been headed. New yelling mingled with the screeching of the Sierra Verdes.

"It is SPs that come, Nantan Tata!" Nochte panted, coming up beside him.

He squatted where he stood. "Tell Nantan Bigotes he must see that the scouts get out of the country—" But the SPs had come up the side where Bunch should have been! "Nochte, all of you back across the border. I'm going to try to reach Caballito—" He stopped, trying to think. The firing had risen in tempo. White uniforms were running forward. He took a page of notepaper and a pencil from his breast pocket and scribbled:

"Sam. SPs here. If I'm caught get Col. Kandinsky, Rurales Hermosillo. Pat Cutler in trouble in Chih. I'll give it one shot to try to get Caball out. Pat."

He said to Nochte. "To Nantan Bigotes. Or to Nantan Lobo!"

Nochte folded the note, tucked it into his breechclout, and went flying down the track up which they had just come. Once he pitched and almost fell, his fine hat rolling free, picking up speed like a cartwheel. Cutler had started on toward the wickiups the Red Stripe People had assembled and the still-smoking firepits there, when a bullet screamed past his head. He pitched himself prone onto lichened stones. Caballito would consider this fluke of coincidence another white-eye betrayal. He slid forward to break a long twig from a dead shrub and tie his handkerchief to it by two corners. Holding his flag of truce, he rose to his knees. Not twenty feet away a white-uniformed Indian with a dark, ugly face was aiming a rifle at him.

He jerked up his hands crying, *"Norteamericano!"*

The Tarahumara hesitated. There must have been a hundred of them, swarming through the wickiups. Three others came up to level their rifles at Cutler.

Holding his hands up, his handkerchief higher, he stood at attention before his captors, shivering in the morning chill. "I am an officer of the army of the United States."

It was as a prisoner, seated on the ground guarded by two Indian SPs, that he watched the destruction of the Red Stripe People by the soldiers of Colonel Pascual Molino.

Caballito had made his last stand in the brushy canyon between two low peaks that rose at the south end of the mesa. The SPs fired from positions behind rocks and brush, moving forward steadily. The return fire was more and more sporadic. Cutler heard the first wavering notes of the death song. As ammunition was exhausted and the rifles in the canyon were stilled, the song rose in duets and trios, in a chorus, shrill and trembling, defiant. He forced himself to watch as though it were a penance, for one who had not understood enough, sympathized enough, made sufficient effort, who in the end, like too many others, had simply wished to see the problem of the Red Stripe People disposed of. The SPs in their filthy white uniforms crept on up into the canyon, firing. By noon it was over.

The SPs moved through the brush and rocks, bending, straightening, sometimes firing a coup de grace. Cutler watched the practiced motion, as of farmers harvesting some tough, low-growing crop, as they cut and wrenched scalps from bloody skulls. The captured women and children were herded on down the mesa. He watched a white-capped officer shoot a half-grown boy, then shoot another even younger. Soldiers knelt or stooped to harvest the scalps. These black, bloody, valuable trophies were collected on a tarpaulin. Colonel Pascual Molino strutted before the growing pile.

The SPs had been lying in wait for Caballito's band. Mingled with Cutler's fear that Pascual Molino would have him shot and his grief for the Red Stripe People was a terrible anxiety for Bunch and the Sierra Verde scouts, who must have blundered into the SPs as they tried to encircle the mountaintop, and for his Hoyas.

The women and children, guarded by soldiers, disappeared over the rim of the mesa. He supposed Pretty Mouth was among them, and the squaws of the scouts. Probably they were safe enough, the young women in particular more valuable alive than dead. He watched a Tarahumara cut the throat of a boy, the boy's bushy head pressed to the man's side almost affectionately, the knife slashing once. Then the cutting and wrenching.

One of the guards prodded him with a rifle muzzle. An

officer in a white cap like a street-sweeper's stood over him, a spoiled, dour, dark face, a lieutenant's pips on the shoulder boards of his white shirt. Blood had splashed upon one sleeve. Cutler rose.

"*Norteamericano?*" the lieutenant demanded.

"I am Lieutenant Patrick Cutler of the Army of the United States. We are here in pursuit of Caballito."

The lieutenant jerked a thumb. The rifle prodded Cutler into motion. Trailed closely by his guards, he started down the mountainside after the women and children. The trail led steeply down, along a ridge, down again. In front of a brush jacal with a mud roof, Sam Bunch sat on a rock, hatless, hands raised to either side of his head as though holding it on. He looked up at Cutler with blank eyes. Bloody matter was smeared on his neck.

"Sam!"

Bunch slowly lowered one of his hands to regard it. Blood and brains were smeared over the side of his head. He had been shot behind the ear.

"*Shit, Sam!*"

Bunch did not seem to hear. More soldiers came by, to form a half circle around the gringos, silently watching Bunch. Four came past carrying the heavy tarpaulin, dripping blood. Bunch pressed both hands to his head again, sitting patiently on the stone before the jacal. "You shot him, you fucking greasers!" Cutler said in English.

The SP standing beside him stank of blood. Saliva leaked out of Bunch's mouth and glistened on his mustache ends. With careful movements he let himself down to a seat on the ground. Then he lay on his side, his knees pulled up. He died that way. The lieutenant who had ordered Cutler down the mountain came by and ordered him on again.

The SP camp appeared to have been in existence for some time, adobe buildings that had been roofed with mud-covered brush, a collection of jacals and tents, a log cantina. Before the largest tent a red, white, and green Mexican flag hung slack from a staff. The Red Stripe women and children had been penned in an enclosure, only the black heads and braids of the women visible as Cutler was directed into one of the huts. He sat in a creaking chair made of woven branches, facing his guard. A pale scorpion fell from the roof to crawl across the floor, and the guard stamped on it and ground his boot, grinning at Cutler triumphantly.

Presently Colonel Molino appeared in the doorway, two of the white-capped officers with him. They were accompanied by a stench of mescal. The guard stood to attention, the rifle held before him.

"I have promised to shoot you if you come to Chihuahua again," Molino said pleasantly. "And here you have come!"

"We came to Mexico to persuade the Apaches to return to the reservation or to destroy them!"

"But we have destroyed them, señor! And you lie. You have come with these savages to make war against Mexico, and so you will die."

"We are in Mexico by agreement with General Ordaz in hot pursuit of hostile Indians. I am in uniform and so was Captain Bunch."

"So now gringo spies come to Mexico in uniform in their arrogance! You will see that I keep my promises, señor!" Molino snapped his fingers like a pistol crack and spouted commands. Cutler's hands were lashed behind his back, and he was pushed outside into blinding sunlight. A bandage was bound over his eyes, but not before he had seen the three soldiers with their rifles grounded before him.

He stood at attention, sweating, as an officer called out: "*Listos!*" There was a clash of bolts.

"*Apunten!*"

He managed to say calmly, "General Yeager has been sent the message that I am held prisoner here. He will notify General Ordaz in Guaymas and Colonel Kandinsky of the *rurales* in Hermosillo. Who will inform the President of the republic, his friend."

There was a silence of intensity while he waited, his calves trembling as though they would give way. Silently he cursed them. The bandage was snatched from his eyes.

"I will give you life for this one night in celebration of our victory!" Colonel Molino said in a jovial voice. "Enrique, you will shoot him if he tries to escape!" The commander of the SPs shimmered before Cutler's eyes, receding. He was led back inside the hut and his aching hands unbound.

"You are a lucky man, señor!" the guard said. Cutler sat dazed in the chair, listening to drunken voices outside. "They rape the women," the guard said. The racket continued for hours. He wondered if there was any hope of Nochte getting his message to General Yeager, and thought of scorpions falling from the roof, and listened to the SPs celebrating the destruction of the Red Stripe People.

As a prisoner, he rode with Colonel Molino's SP army into Chihuahua City. Parading the last few miles, the soldiers carried poles cut from pine branches, each one decorated with a black-haired scalp, seventy-eight of them. One was quite gray, old Dawa's; others would be those of Cump-ten-ae, of Big Ear, and of Caballito himself, who, it was said, had stabbed himself rather than be shot by the SPs. Pressed together among the ranks of soldiers were the women and children, who would be sold or bartered—Tze-go-juni, carrying Bunch's child, among them. One of the white-capped officers displayed a memento, the whittled ball in a cage that Sam Bunch had presented to the chief of the Sierra Verdes so long ago.

Cutler did not witness the nailing of the scalps to the beam ends of the porticoes in the *plaza mayor,* for he was confined in a stone dungeon beneath the municipal palace. The place stank of piss and rotting wood. Fat gray rats crept along the rafters. When two encountered each other, one swarmed over the other in a process that made Cutler grimace with disgust. It seemed that the rat coming from his right always prostrated himself to the one from the left. There was a high window through which he could hear the festivities, a band tootling and thumping, drunken singing of sentimental songs, speechmaking. The Chihuahuans had been harried, robbed, tortured, and murdered by Apaches for many generations. How could he blame them for their celebration?

Sometimes booted legs were visible through dusty glass. Horses' hooves clopped past, carriage wheels keened and rattled. Two rats approached each other on the rafter. The one on the right flattened himself, the other slid over him.

In the morning, pale light falling through the window, the harelipped jailer brought him dry tortillas, dry bean paste, and weak coffee. Carriages rolled by outside. He grieved for Sam Bunch, for his Pretty Mouth and unborn child. He grieved for Caballito and the Red Stripe People, who had been his charge. He fretted over the safety of the Hoyas. He wondered, here in Mexico, if he was ever to see his son again, his wife, Las Golondrinas—that Mexican life of the pleasant hours that once he had been certain would be his.

Five days later he was warming his face by the brief afternoon sun ray falling through the high window, when he heard the crack of boot heels and a Polish-accented voice calling, "Don Patricio! You are here?"

The key rattled in the lock, the heavy door swung open, and Kandinsky strode inside, gleaming boots and beautiful dove-gray embroidered uniform. His graying, colorless hair was neatly combed, his cap carried under his arm. It was so good to see him that Cutler's eyes ached.

"What a stink there is here!" Kandinsky said, stamping across the floor to embrace him. "And how you stink, also, my friend!"

"And how lovely you smell, Colonel!" He was laughing a little hysterically. "I had despaired that my message would reach you!"

"I have come as swiftly as possible! You are free, my friend. Kandinsky has resorted to threats. He has mentioned his friendship, and that of Don Fernando, with Don Porfirio Díaz. But there is one concession that must be made, which is that the unfortunate North American captain shot first at the soldiers of Don Pascual."

"I cannot say that because I did not see the shooting."

"You will admit the possibility," Kandinsky said grimly.

"If necessary."

"It is necessary. Come, then! We reside at the palace of the governor, where you will bathe before sensitive noses are required to smell you. A barber will come. You must be made presentable for our council with the governor."

"How is Don Fernando? Does he continue to recover? And my son, does he remember me?"

"We will speak of all that when this business before us is completed," Kandinsky said. He smiled at Cutler through his silky mustache. "And all will be well if you do not forget our little concession."

"I believe I would have rotted here if you had not come. I am grateful to you!"

"Good!" Colonel Kandinsky said, clapping his hands briskly together. "For later there are decisions to make."

Scrubbed, shaved, barbered, talcumed, and scented, in

a washed, mended, and pressed uniform that was still warm and a little damp, Cutler marched beside Kandinsky down the red-tiled central hallway of the governor's palace, alongside a colonnaded patio filled with sunlight and greenery, birds in wicker cages hanging from pegs on the columns, a fountain spraying with a micturating sound. Kandinsky carried a woven leather swagger stick, which he slapped against his thigh in rhythm with his steps.

The governor, Don Victoriano Molino, rose from his throne of a Spanish Colonial chair. He wore his sash of office over a double-breasted blue uniform. His nephew, commander of the *seguridades públicos*, also uniformed, stood gazing at Cutler with disinterest. Kandinsky beamed, standing with his gleaming boots set ten inches apart, nodding and bowing and murmuring greetings.

Cutler reminded the governor that they had met during the visit here of General Yeager of the Army of the United States.

"Ah, yes! The North American general, yes! What an unfortunate occurrence here, Lieutenant! Your captain killed, a tragedy! We are informed that our soldiers merely returned his fire. They are *indios*. No doubt he thought them the Apache enemy, eh?"

He felt a slight pressure of Kandinsky's elbow. "I cannot dispute their word, Señor Governor."

"So many unfortunate occurrences in war!" the governor said. "Now we will drink to the end of these evil savages who have been the curse of this country for so long."

A servant entered with a tray of bottles and glasses. Champagne was served, glasses ticked together, a toast drunk. Pascual Molino glared at his libation. The governor remained standing; no chairs had been proffered. The meeting was to be brief as well as uncomplicated.

"Señor Lieutenant, you and the unfortunate captain had come to Chihuahua to urge these savages to return to their reservation in the United States?"

"Yes, señor, in accord with the responsibilities the United States has accepted to prevent the Apaches from raiding in Mexico. General Yeager and General Ordaz had made arrangements for hot pursuit in certain cases, of which this was one."

The governor stared at him with a raised eyebrow of

incomprehension, Don Pascual Molino with the skull-like expression of total contempt. "I believe the two gringos commanded Apache troops," Colonel Molino said. "We have killed some of these."

"We commanded Apache scouts, it is true," Cutler said. "They were ordered to return to the United States as soon as contact was made with Mexican soldiers, in accordance with the agreement I have mentioned."

Kandinsky's elbow nudged him again, this time he thought approvingly. Colonel Molino's eyes bored at him. Cutler was thinking of SPs taking scalps of the Sierra Verde scouts they had killed along with Bunch, of Hoya scalps.

"Gringos employ Apaches to fight Apaches," Colonel Molino commented. "For this purpose we employ Tarahumaras, who hate Apaches."

"Yes, I have seen them," Cutler said with a bow.

"And they have been magnificently successful!" Kandinsky said swiftly. "Congratulations, *señor coronel!*"

"I would advise gringos to distrust Apaches," Colonel Molino went on. "Those who have trusted the Apache have always come to regret it."

Cutler said, "And yet those very Apache scouts were the other jaw of the nutcracker that brought Caballito's band to the mercy of the *seguridades públicos.*"

"Yes, yes!" the governor said. "Of course this is obvious! I will make another toast, señors!" He raised his replenished glass. "To the continuing friendship and cooperation between two great nations, which has led to the destruction of these devils and the freedom of our lands from their terrors!"

Cutler drained his glass with the others. To mention the captive Sierra Verdes would be an idle exercise. In this conclusion of an amicable meeting, hands were proffered, and all but Colonel Pascual Molino bowed in farewell. Cutler and Kandinsky retraced their steps down the broad hallway, past the sun-filled patio and the birds chittering in their cages.

"It is finished!" Kandinsky muttered.

In Kandinsky's apartments the windows looked toward the cathedral and the *plaza mayor.* Heavy, high-backed chairs were stationed between them. Cutler stood gazing out, lighting the cigar Kandinsky had offered him. The array of scalps was not visible from here.

"And what now, my friend?" Kandinsky said, pacing behind him.

He held out his cigar and watched the smoke rise. "Tomorrow I will take the Ferrocarriles de México to El Paso."

"And what of Las Golondrinas?"

"I will come there soon."

"Don Fernando told me that you believe much time must pass before you come again. I believe a woman who slashes her wrist unsuccessfully will continue to be unsuccessful in such dramatic attempts. Moreover, you must understand that you are now of more importance to the presence of Las Golondrinas than María, and your son more important to its future."

"I understand that."

The heels continued to pad behind him. "I believe that if you come now, no wrist will be slashed," Kandinsky said. "In the end there will be an accommodation. Perhaps, best of all, a reconciliation."

"I want what will be best for the boy," Cutler said. He sat down in one of the stiff chairs. Kandinsky stood over him, his own cigar in hand. His hair gleamed like polished metal in the sunlight from the window.

"But would not that *be* the best, Patricio? The boy is a beautiful, intelligent child who will be spoiled by too many women worshipping him and infected with a sickly religion by a fat priest. Without his father the boy will not become a man worthy of the respect of men, a man who will hold, defend, and keep prosperous the Hacienda de las Golondrinas of the centuries. Already the hacienda shows the lack of a strong arm directing its fortunes, Patricio.

"You have asked about my friend. He is better, but then he is ill again. I think he will not see the end of this year. Sometimes he despairs of your coming."

Cutler sucked the smoke of Kandinsky's expensive panatela. "I can come immediately to the Hacienda de las Golondrinas, and write a letter to General Yeager tendering my resignation from the Army of the United States."

He saw Kandinsky's eyes light, but Cutler shook his head and continued. "Or, more properly, I can return to the

United States on the Ferrocarriles de México tomorrow—to the general, to whom I owe much, and submit my resignation in person. Or, most honorably, I can remain in the United States to give evidence in the inquiry into the things that have happened here in Mexico—the slaughter and enslavement of the Sierra Verde band, and the death of Captain Bunch. I think that is my proper course, Colonel."

Kandinsky bowed his head and sighed. "I also am a military man, my friend. Of course you must do what is honorable and proper. Only, may it be done with all possible speed."

How could he explain to Kandinsky that when he resigned from the army he also severed himself from General Yeager, and certain connections would be lost forever. He had assured himself a hundred times that there could be no revelation because there was no secret, there was nothing but manipulation and mischief. Was he not the father of his own son? And yet— He said, "I am as anxious to be there as Don Fernando is to have me."

Cutler rose, flexing his shoulders, to face the window again. The sun gleamed upon the red tile roofs of Chihuahua City, and on the saints in their niches on the facade of the cathedral. When he thought of his confrontation with General Yeager he felt a core of leaden dread that the general still held some trump card that he did not know how to anticipate.

25

The afternoon of the day after he had crossed the border, on an airy veranda at Fort Cummings, he related to a military audience the pursuit of Caballito, the incursion into Mexico, Bunch's death, and the slaughter of the Red Stripe People. This informal tribunal was presided over by General Yeager, with whom Cutler had had no chance to speak before it convened. There were five colonels, six majors, four captains, and a lieutenant recorder. Captain Robinson also took notes. All were seated on camp chairs or benches, except for the general, who rocked gently in a platform rocker, smoking his pipe. Cutler would have felt easier standing facing his questioners, for he was continually having to lean forward or back, switch his head one way or another. Most of the expressions of the officers were unfriendly, suspicious anyhow; one of the issues here was the employment of Apache scouts.

One colonel, Brewster, with an irritating drawl and eyes that would not meet Cutler's directly, was the most persistent questioner. Yeager himself rarely spoke, although occasionally he pushed his lower lip out in a pout or fingered his side-whiskers.

"How far behind were the regular cavalry units when you crossed the border?" Brewster demanded. He was clean shaven with short-cropped hair, and not much older than Cutler: it was a matter of resentment to the line officers that staff officers received more frequent promotions.

"I don't know that, sir."

"Would you not say the normal function of scouts is to inform the regular units of the movements of the enemy?"

Cutler looked to the general for assistance, but Yeager

435

was intent upon refilling and relighting his pipe. "Yes, sir," he said. "But we were not in a normal situation."

"Just what did you consider your mission to be?" a major inquired.

Percy Robinson glanced up with an eyebrow raised. Cutler said carefully, "Once the Sierra Verdes had left the reservation they were subject to punitive action, and our mission was their destruction. However, there was the possibility that Caballito could be out-maneuvered in such a way as to effect his surrender. We were strong enough to engage him. At the end we had as many fighting men as he had, and we were better armed and supplied."

Yeager produced a considerable smoke cloud as he pushed his tobacco pouch into one of the many pockets of his tunic. He gave Cutler a dim smile out of the unused corner of his mouth.

Brewster said, "So you made no effort to keep in contact with the regular units in this situation that you say was not normal."

"No, sir, not in any regular way."

"Why not, mister?" another colonel snapped.

Dah-koo-gah! He said carefully, "We had left them far behind. We traveled much faster than they could. They are quite a bit limited to flat country because their supplies are carried by rolling stock. We carry our own supplies."

A major with a thick Southern accent said, "Your own tracker outfit is Western Apache, I believe, Lieutenant—no friends to the Sierra Verdes. But Captain Bunch's company was all Sierra Verde?"

"Yes, sir." He realized he was going to have no help from General Yeager or Captain Robinson.

"Did you and Captain Bunch not have any suspicions that these scouts might be less than dedicated to running down their own kith and kin?"

Another officer said, "You yourself have told us that the trail was lost the first day, and your own scouts discovered the trick."

"We were convinced that they were dedicated to running down the renegades of their own band, because renegades and raiding causes trouble for all the other Apaches. Caballito was considered a 'bad' Apache. They were 'good'

Apaches, and on the payroll besides. He had also kidnapped some of their squaws."

"That does not answer my question, Lieutenant."

"Very well, sir. Of course the possibility occurred to me. I cannot speak for Captain Bunch. We did not discuss the possibility." This answer seemed to please the Southern major, so Cutler added, "The fact is that it was on the advice of Captain Bunch's scouts who were familiar with the Sierra Madre terrain that we were able to run Caballito to earth."

"You ran him to earth, but it was Mexican irregulars who finished him off," another colonel growled. Cutler had already felt the current of frustration that Mexican irregulars should have accomplished what American regulars had failed to do.

The Southern major persisted. "Yet treason has not been unknown among the scouts. One of yours, I believe, was hanged?"

We accept our losses, we do not excuse them, Yeager had said. "Yes, sir," he said.

"Consequently I am surprised by the degree of trust you and Captain Bunch seem to have manifested, Lieutenant."

"Yes, sir," he said.

"So you would persuade us that Captain Bunch was murdered by these Mexican irregulars rather than by his own scouts," Colonel Brewster said.

"There is no question in my mind, sir."

"Which, as you have told us, is a very trusting one insofar as Apaches are concerned." Brewster looked as though he had scored a fine point there, glancing around smiling at the others.

Cutler waited for his pulse to slow before he said, "The Mexicans insisted that I concede the possibility that Captain Bunch fired upon them first. I have no doubt that they killed him and that they fired first. They also would have been pleased to blame his murder on the Sierra Verdes."

He saw Yeager frown at that *also*. Be careful.

"A certain laxity of uniform is permitted scouts' officers," a bespectacled major said. "Could the Mexicans have mistaken Captain Bunch for an Apache?"

"Captain Bunch looked a good deal more like a Viking than an Apache, sir."

"It is interesting that the Viking was fired upon but you were not," another said.

He thought he could ignore that, but Brewster did not. "I understand you are married to a Mexican national, Lieutenant."

This caused a stir, as though grounds for suspicions had been uncovered that might lead to the reason why Mexicans and not Americans had disposed of Caballito.

"Yes, sir," he said.

General Yeager took his pipe from his mouth and said, "The grandfather of Lieutenant Cutler's wife is a very influential citizen in Sonora. It was through his intercessions that we have an informal hot pursuit agreement with General Ordaz. It is also through his influence that Lieutenant Cutler escaped imprisonment in Mexico and very possibly a firing squad. When I was informed that Cutler had been captured, I immediately contacted Colonel Kandinsky of the Sonoran *rurales,* who effected his released. Pat, tell the assembled something about the Chihuahuan irregulars."

"They are called *seguridades públicas*—public security forces. They are scalp-hunters; Mexico pays a bounty on Apache scalps. They are the private army of the governor of Chihuahua, who is the largest landowner in the state and has suffered a great deal of loss from Indian depredations. The soldiers are for the most part Tarahumaras, old enemies of the Apaches. The officers are white or mestizo. The men receive a share of the loot, scalp bounties, and proceeds from the sale of the Apache women and children."

"Oh, come now, Lieutenant!" a major called out. "Are you implying that there is enslavement?"

"The Mexicans have been taking Apache and Navajo captives for hundreds of years, sir. When New Mexico was still a part of Mexico it was fashionable for young women of the upper class to receive an Indian cub as a wedding gift. I was informed by Colonel Molino of the SPs that a pretty young woman can be worth as much as six hundred dollars."

Although others were interested in this information, Colonel Brewster was not. "Mr. Cutler, I must believe that if there had been a couple of troops of cavalry along when Caballito was cornered and these irregulars encountered, the whole affair might have been settled without bloodshed. I refer, of course, to Captain Bunch's tragic death."

"I believe there would have been more bloodshed, sir. And international repercussions. The arrangement with General Ordaz would have been violated if Americans did not immediately retreat upon contact with a Mexican force."

He was relieved when General Yeager at last spoke up in his support. Holding his pipe a foot from his lips, and squinting once to make certain Robinson was taking down his words, he said, "I believe that Captain Bunch and Lieutenant Cutler acted with great vigor and good sense throughout the campaign. If it had not been for the unfortunate coincidence of the encounter with the Mexican irregulars, they might very well have forced Caballito's surrender or wiped him out themselves."

It seemed to Cutler that the general's summing up by no means swept the other officers' suspicions away, and he remembered Caballito's vision of Nantan Lobo losing his power. The dissatisfaction remained that it had been Mexicans who had disposed of Caballito; if the scouts had waited for regular units to come up, perhaps this shame would not have existed. The record of the cavalry in its encounters with Caballito had been, almost without exception, one of defeat and failure. Caballito had gone to his death undefeated by Americans except in the field of making and breaking treaties.

Cutler could have pointed out that Mexicans had been fighting Apaches for more years than the United States of America had been in existence. He thought also that the officers here were disappointed that the Apache wars, the last of the Indian wars, were finally over. If they wanted to focus their displeasure on him, that was fine. He was on his way out.

Later, in General Yeager's quarters, he sipped whiskey with the general and Percy Robinson, the general standing spread-legged before him. Through the window Cutler could see the gleaming whitewashed cubes of the Mexican town just across the Rio Grande.

"You handled yourself pretty well, Pat," the general said. "As you are no doubt aware, there are officers who would not hesitate to strike at me through you."

"Colonel Nathaniel Brewster for one," Robinson said. "General Schofield's white-haired boy." He was seated in a painted wicker chair. He tossed back his whiskey with one jerk of his head.

Cutler watched the general; back to him, Yeager seemed smaller, older. As though conscious of Cutler's stare, he straightened his shoulders.

"All the surviving Sierra Verdes are aboard a train headed for Florida, Pat."

Cutler choked on his whiskey. *"What?"*

"The bad ones did the good ones in, as you pointed out. Caballito's last breakout was one too many. It has embarrassed me very seriously with the administration." He turned, grinning like a scar.

"All of them!" Cutler heard himself say.

"Yes, my boy, all. *All!"*

"You ordered this?"

"It was ordered by the President upon my recommendation. My recommendation was made just before the order, which I knew to be forthcoming. I believe I got in under the wire."

"Nantan Lobo, the friend of the Indians," Cutler said.

The general smiled frostily. "I advise you not to exercise yourself, Pat. The deed is done. Caballito's breakout was the last straw. The government is fed up with Apache depredations. *I* am fed up with them also. I am also fed up with being ripped up, down, and sideways by the Territorial press—as the friend of the Indians, as you so courteously put it. Sour are the uses of adversity, which like a toad, ugly and venomous, sticks in my craw! I am fed up with blame and vilification." Yeager tossed down the rest of his own whiskey, and nodded to Robinson to refill the glasses. Cutler blocked his with the palm of his hand. He was shaking.

"They are bound for Fort Parsons," the general continued. "It is an abandoned military prison on the Atlantic coast. They will be interred there as prisoners of war. This will at least keep them out of the hands of vengeful civilian authorities. And lynch mobs. Public opinion, Pat, is very strong against them. I would say explosively strong."

Nantan Lobo. "Even Sam Bunch's scouts?" he said.

"All, Pat."

"Even Joklinney?"

Yeager raised a helpless hand. "Pat seems to be having difficulty understanding the situation, Perce." Red-faced, he said to Cutler, "I realize you have had a tiring afternoon, my boy, but try to pay attention. *All* of the Red Stripe People who are still alive. If any more seep back from the Sierra Madre massacre, they will also be sent off to Fort Parsons. *All* of them."

"To die of tuberculosis in a damp climate."

Yeager made an irritated gesture. "No doubt some will die, but they are a hardy people—"

"'Hardy people'!" he almost shouted. "When they are shot, they bleed, those hardy people. When a man is hanged, his wife hangs herself out of human grief! When they are *betrayed*—"

"I will not be addressed in this hectoring manner!" the general shouted back at him. More calmly, he said, "You will simply have to understand that they are only an historical process, Pat. They have historically been raiders, hated and feared by their neighbors. A superior people has appeared and has tried to make an accommodation with them. These efforts have failed, perhaps often in bad faith. The raiders will now be swept under the rug of history."

Cutler felt as though his head were encased in a buzzing cocoon of heat. "Too many lies," he said.

"What are you muttering about?" the general said. He gesticulated with the hand holding the glass, and whiskey slopped onto his khaki tunic. Robinson leaped up to wipe at the stain with his handkerchief.

"Listen to me, Pat," Yeager said. "This action became inevitable as soon as this last breakout occurred. Those left behind were immediately shipped to Florida because Caballito, if he returned, was to be sent there also. I had promised that he would not be sent again to San Marcos, and he would not be allowed to return to Bosque Alto, where his restlessness had affected the young Nahuaque bucks. There was simply nothing else that could be done. This country was fed up with Caballito! Therefore Joklinney, the older men and women, and five squaws who had hidden themselves rather than leave the reservation were to be used as a lever to induce Caballito to follow them peaceably to Fort Parsons. Well, that was not to be. The Sierra Verde scouts on their return, however, were also sent east. There is simply no point, now, in fulminating against these decisions, even if I cannot persuade you that they were wise ones."

"Nantan Lobo had taken such trouble to turn Joklinney into Joe King."

"I do not consider those efforts to have been wasted, Pat. Joklinney is the Sierra Verde chief now. Unfortunately—" His face reddened again.

"Joklinney escaped from the train," Robinson put in.

"Good for him!"

"That is a stupid thing to say, Pat. He will have to be killed."

"*Why?*"

"Soon there will be reports of horse theft, cattle butchery, murders, probably tortures and mutilations. Such bronco Apaches are hunted like wild animals, as you know. People will kill their enemies and blame it on Joklinney."

Yeager turned toward the window, his back to Cutler again. "Joklinney will revert to Apache methods of justice and revenge. It is unfortunate, because he might have led the remnant of the Sierra Verdes out of Egypt. You and your Hoyas will have to track him down and kill him."

"No, sir, we will not!"

He watched the shoulders stiffen. After a hesitation Yeager jerked around to face him again. "What is this, Pat?" he said quietly.

"I'm resigning my commission!"

The general blew his cheeks out, staring at him. Then he managed the chill smile. "I will not accept your resignation until you have accomplished this last chore for me."

Cutler shook his head. He didn't trust himself to speak.

"This country, this Territory, and *I* are sick to death of Apache depredating, and I predict that Joklinney will cut a bloody swath. He did so before we sent him to Alcatraz, you'll remember. The sooner he is stamped out, the less bloody the swath will be, and you and your Hoyas are the men for the job."

"I'm resigning from the army and leaving for Sonora to take up my responsibilities there."

"I think you must consider the welfare of your trackers."

Cutler thought about what that implied as Yeager produced his pipe and tobacco pouch, loaded and lit the pipe, and gazed at Cutler through the smoke.

It seemed that the Hoyas had returned safely, at least, but he felt as though the hot balloon had congealed around his head again. Captain Robinson sipped his whiskey nervously.

Yeager said, "You will return to Fort McLain and await

communications from Perce. I believe that Joklinney will eventually show up bound for the Green Range. I do not think, in view of Caballito's end, that he will head for Mexico. You will place yourself and your trackers in readiness. You will be kept informed by telegraph."

"And when we've performed this chore for you, you'll ship the Hoyas off to Fort Parsons to join the Sierra Verdes."

"No, Pat, I will not do that. My boy, if officers of the Army of the United States cannot trust one another's word, our military system will simply cease to function."

"It's already ceased to function as far as I'm concerned."

Yeager's face glowed pinkly through the smoke that wreathed it. "I've tried to be your friend, Pat," he said quietly.

"And the Apaches' friend. Nantan Lobo. Nantan Mentira!"

Yeager looked as though he had been struck, and Robinson half rose from his chair. Yeager stammered, "There is a bond between us, Pat."

"There is not!"

"We both loved the same woman."

Cutler waited, a knot of constriction swelling in his throat. Was there more? But Yeager said no more, and Cutler pushed himself to his feet. Robinson's eyes seemed to reach out to touch him.

"Lieutenant Cutler," Yeager barked. "You will acknowledge that order!"

"I comply but do not obey," he said in Spanish, one of those grand Mexican phrases. But Yeager had played his trump.

Cutler stopped at the signal office twice a day to see if there had been a telegram from Percy Robinson, although the signal sergeant would have sent a messenger for him if there had been. In the month since Joklinney and another Sierra Verde had escaped from the train bound for Fort Parsons, no bloody swath had established itself. A sheepherder had been killed here, a lonely ranch house attacked there, but with no evidence that it had been Joklinney. The depredations had been in Texas, nothing in the Territory so far. Meanwhile the Hoyas were established in tents in their own *ranchería* out behind the corrals, collecting their six dollars a month and awaiting orders—all but Lucky, whose scalp decorated the *plaza mayor* in Chihuahua City, along with those of two Sierra Verde scouts also killed by the SPs.

This afternoon the signal sergeant told him Colonel Dougal wanted to see him. His life seemed bounded by colonels.

"Mind my words, the wars of the future will be fought with communications," the colonel said genially, seated at his desk with Cutler opposite him. "Next year a breakout such as Caballito's will be impossible. We would know his whereabouts at every moment! The telegraph, the heliograph, the telephone. General Yeager saw fit to ignore my suggestion that a system of surveillance by aerial balloon be established—never mind!" He leaned with his chin whiskers closer to the desk top. "The signal sergeant tells me you sometimes receive reports from Fort Sill and Fort Cummings on the whereabouts of your bronco Apache. Matter of time before he is apprehended. Then I suppose they will hang him."

"I doubt he'll be taken alive, sir."

"Ah, you knew the fellow, did you not? Protégé of the general, I believe."

Cutler did not feel he needed to defend General Yeager to Colonel Dougal.

"Tell me, Cutler," the colonel continued, "what was your observation of the state of the military in Mexico?"

"Fearful of an invasion from the north," he said promptly.

"Preparing then, are they?"

"Not particularly."

The colonel nodded as though that had been meaningful. "I have come to the conclusion," he said, straightening, "that General Yeager will not command the invasion. Too many of his pet policies have been discredited. A colonel becomes adept at reading the signs! In fact, there are rumors of his imminent retirement. What do you think of that, mister?"

He said that he had not heard such a rumor.

"At one time it was thought that the general would be retiring in order to seek the Republican vice-presidential nomination, but of course the Caballito debacle has writ finis to any such aspirations. I believe he will be retiring upon request, if you understand me, and the invasion of Chihuahua and Sonora put into the hands of another."

"Yes, sir," he said tiredly.

"Now, Cutler, you may know all this, modern communications being what they are," the colonel said. "The fact is that Mrs. Maginnis has recently returned to Madison bent upon causing trouble. She is accompanied by the brother of the unfortunate Englishman, who seems to have money to burn on lawyers' fees. A number of suits have been filed with me as their object. It is simply a persecution, in matters upon which I was exonerated by a military board of inquiry." Colonel Dougal cleared his throat and added, "Among these lawsuits is one for libel."

So this was why he had been summoned.

"I am aware that my language is sometimes intemperate," the colonel continued. "An old army man will forget his niceties sometimes. Mrs. Maginnis claims I referred to her as a less than respectable woman—as a common tart, in fact. She claims there are witnesses to my saying such things of her. I have been wondering if these lawyers of hers have asked for your testimony."

"No, sir."

"We have not been close friends, Cutler," the colonel said. "I have not been the old uncle a commander often is to his junior officers. Not my style, mister! Moreover, we have had our differences. But I am a straightforward man and I will put this to you in a straightforward manner. Would you be inclined to give such testimony?" The muscles at the corners of his mouth contracted in an attempt at a smile.

It did not seem unreasonable that he enjoy the colonel's anxiety. "I doubt that they'd ask such a thing of me," Cutler said, "knowing that it would be a very serious matter for a junior officer to give evidence against his commander in a civilian court."

"Yes, of course," the colonel said with relief. "Whatever their differences, officers should stick together when under civilian attack."

"Yes, sir."

"You reassure me, then, that I have nothing to fear from your testimony?"

"Certainly not so long as I'm an officer, Colonel."

"I appreciate this," Dougal said, tenting his fingers together. "This is a very wise decision of yours. I can tell you that you have many enemies within this command, I will stand between you and their enmity, even when General Yeager has retired, which, as I say, I believe to be imminent.

"Now, Cutler, surely it is common knowledge that you and Mrs. Maginnis have been more than merely friends. And that since that time there have been others who have been more than friends. As one has been aware of your friendship with the unfortunate Mrs. Helms. Well, as I say, mister, I am a straightforward man. Would you be disposed to give evidence in my behalf?"

Cutler was almost breathless. The misjudgment, the slur on *him*, the *insult* was so vast he could not even take it seriously. "Oh, you mean evidence to the fact that Mrs. Maginnis is, in fact, a common tart?"

Colonel Dougal grimaced at the word, his face as dark as broiled meat.

"I'm trying to understand your thinking, Colonel," Cutler went on. "I can only take it that because I did not attend the Military Academy and so did not become acquainted with the kind of honor disseminated there, I might be inclined to further my career by impugning a woman who has been a good friend."

The colonel's lips popped open to let out a bubble of air and closed again.

"The answer is no," Cutler said, and rose, saluted, and took his leave.

He stopped in again at the telegraph office on his way back to the officers' quarters. This time a telegram from Captain Robinson awaited him. A Mormon rancher had been shot dead, and his wife seriously wounded but not otherwise molested, by two Apache renegades near the hamlet of Bosworth. If it was Joklinney, he had crossed at last into New Mexico Territory. Another depredation or two and the trackers would have enough of a line on his movements to go into action.

The second shoe, however, did not fall. It was as though Joklinney and the other, Nah-kut-le, had disappeared or had dropped down into Mexico after all. It seemed to Cutler that there might be no more appearances, that everything was finished, and he could demand that the Hoyas be sent west to the reservation at Fort Apache, where their people were, submit his resignation, and head for Las Golondrinas and whatever accommodation or reconciliation awaited him there.

In this waiting time in which he now felt the ultimate die

had been cast, even his life at Fort McLain seemed less disagreeable. He checked with the signal sergeant twice a day, he finished Tacitus and began Plutarch. A piano had been installed in the officers' saloon, and some nights he played sentimental Jimmy Blazer melodies. Bernie Reilly, Jud Farrier, and the adjutant, Dick Hotchkiss, would collect around the piano to sing, while the other officers watched. Major Symonds's enmity was solid, palpable, almost comforting, but the admiration of Second Lieutenant Hotchkiss was disturbing.

The summer passed, as hot an August as he had ever experienced in the Territory. His scouts perished of boredom, but lived well on the blue-soldier dollar.

Often he supped at the Reillys'. Rose had forgiven him Lily Maginnis because of the tragedy of María, and he felt none of the pressure in this company that he felt at the officers' mess or the saloon, where his offensive behavior would now be tolerated by Jud Farrier and viewed with hero-worshipping eyes by Dick Hotchkiss. He realized that he had become a colorful character to some of the young lieutenants, a scouts' officer who disdained uniform regulations and read Plutarch in his room, who was known to have disobeyed direct orders from the colonel and had shown the Iron Major up as a fool and a coward, whose Mexican wife had run off with a lover only to be captured by Apaches who tortured her lover to death. The wife was now incarcerated in her madness in a feudal hacienda deep in Mexico.

Bernie Reilly asked his wife's permission to smoke, and produced cigars from a leather humidor. They lit up, the surgeon's pug-nosed face illuminated by the match in the shadowed room. They sat at the table with its white napery and glasses containing ruby wine, sweating in their uniforms. The plump Mexican *muchacha* cleared the supper plates away.

"Are things really better out here?" Bernie asked philosophically. "I wonder. The railroad, the telegraph, the *telephones*—have you seen the office of the Bird Cage Hotel, Pat? Vats of acid—batteries—powering the thing. Installed by Mrs. Maginnis's lawyers. The end of the Apache wars and the Madison County War. Caballito dead and Johnny-A reduced to a south-county rustler."

Cutler patted his sweating face with his handkerchief. "I wouldn't count Johnny-A out yet."

"I wonder if he is even aware of his legend," Bernie said.

"What about the Apache who escaped from the Florida train, Pat?" Rose Reilly asked. Crooked tracks of perspiration marred the powder on her face, and damp patches showed beneath her arms when she passed the coffee cups.

"I don't think we've heard the last of Joklinney either."

"Pat and his squad of cutthroats are waiting to pounce on him if he raises any dust," Bernie said, cigar in one hand, wineglass in the other. "Poor Yeager! His star has gone down faster than Johnny-A's. His enemies rejoiced when Caballito went out, and again when Joklinney escaped from the train."

"Well, I thank General Yeager for pacifying the Indians!" Rose Reilly said. "It was terrible when we were first assigned out here! The anxieties, the bad dreams! Why, *your* poor wife's tragedy was only two years ago, Pat! Any time the command rode out of the fort I worried myself sick. Many times not all came back, either! And the poor women on those lonely ranches, with children to protect! To live day after day after day, never knowing when those savages might kill you. Steal your children. Worse than that!"

"One of my scouts told me he was full grown before he understood that men died any other way than killed," Cutler said.

"They were the ones who chose their way of living! And of dying!"

"No sympathy for them, my dear? Now that they are finally conquered and confined, or dead?"

"None! Never in this world!"

"Now that we are down to two Pache outlaws and one white-eye one," Bernie said, "I repeat my question: are we better off? An age of large terrors, large tragedies—even large comedies—has been replaced by one of merchandise and salaries. I for one am sorry to see Johnny-A merely a rustler hiding out among the *placitas*. Even Pat Cutler, the famous mustang lieutenant, the burr under the regimental saddle, now plays the piano for his friends and admirers in the saloon." He laughed, and Cutler managed a grin.

"Once, no doubt, certain men cast longer shadows than were warranted, but perhaps the shadows were more important than the realities. To reexamine Plato's figure." The surgeon blew smoke at his profundity. Cutler watched Rose frowning at the girl pouring the coffee. She looked relieved when the operation was successful.

Bernie said, "I am about to betray a confidence, Pat. Tell me, do you enjoy a surprise party—where guests leap out from behind the sofa crying, 'Happy birthday'?"

He said that he did not, carefully knocking the ash from his cigar into the tray. He was still mulling Bernie's "friends and admirers."

"I prepare you for just such a surprise. I have it from Dick Hotchkiss. You will be receiving the Congressional Medal of Honor."

"*What?*"

Rose cried, "Oh, Bernard, you never told me! Oh, that's wonderful, Pat!"

Cutler cleared his dry throat to ask, "What for?"

"Heroics in Mexico."

"Yeager," he said. It must be a trap, an ambush like those Caballito had once been adept at setting. Visions of the dismay when he refused it danced before his eyes. But the Medal of Honor! It was a trap. "I'll refuse it," he said.

"You'll do no such thing," Bernie said. "There is a captaincy also."

"Oh, Pat, it is wonderful!"

He began to laugh. When he managed to control himself, his shirt continued to shake over his chest. He was thinking of Colonel Dougal confronted with this information, of Major Symonds, of Captain Smithers. Of his friends and admirers.

"I'll refuse both."

"Then I'm glad I've betrayed the confidence, for there is time to persuade you otherwise," Bernie said earnestly. "It may mean nothing to you that this honors the regiment also. But I think you'll not want to dishonor Sam Bunch's memory."

"What do you mean?"

"Sam is being awarded the medal posthumously."

Now he could laugh. He met the surgeon's anxious eyes and nodded in capitulation. Bernie and Rose raised their glasses in a toast.

"But why would you even think of not accepting it, Pat?" Rose inquired.

"Because it's Yeager's doing. Sam wouldn't accept his

either, if he had any say. Yeager sent all his scouts off to rot in prison in Florida. Joklinney is Yeager's doing. I believe Yeager is responsible for every murder Joklinney commits." He halted himself.

"But there must be others who also think you deserve it?" Rose insisted.

He only shook his head, irony undermining irony.

Still holding his glass aloft, Bernie said, "I began this conversation by saying one era had ended and another begun. I think the winner of a Congressional Medal of Honor can afford to slip out of some old clothes."

"What do you mean?"

Bernie's face turned red. "Pat, Rose and I know you for a sensitive, lonely, overproud gentleman—who can be very charming. To most of the other officers and their wives on this post you have showed yourself rude, crude, and contemptuous. On the colonel's side of it, you can make a 'yes, sir!' sound like a slap in the face. You make your fellows feel stupid and incompetent, and you are *not* a good example to the younger officers, who perceive you as something of a hero. I wish that that clothing—armor, perhaps—could be changed."

Cutler looked down at his own glass. "A mustang acting as a mustang is expected to act," he heard himself say.

"You're not the only mustang officer in the army, Pat."

"I haven't told anybody but the general," he said. "I'll be resigning my commission as soon as Joklinney has been disposed of. I'll be going to Mexico."

"Do you think you'll be happy in Mexico?"

"Why yes," he said. He summoned up a grin. "I can change my clothes down there."

On the lot next to the courthouse the gallows had been erected, awaiting Johnny Angell's recapture—an eight-foot-high structure surmounted by a six-by-six upright, the L of the arm supported by a diagonal brace. The wood was faded from weather, and rust streaked the timbers below the nailheads. There was no rope. Cutler reined up Malcreado to gaze on the squat, ugly structure. He could not feel any of the ironic detachment General Yeager had claimed to be a necessity when considering the wrongs done the Apaches. It was a machine for killing what had come to be an embarrassment to a self-confident society turning its interests to merchandise and salaries, away from the old frontier values. It was an implement that men employed to rid themselves of the criminals who were the product of society's crimes. Benny Dee and Johnny-A; Joklinney, if he was captured alive. So General Yeager did not interfere in the execution of Benny Dee for fear of being thought soft on Apaches, and the governor, for political reasons, delayed pardoning Johnny Angell until other forces had sprung Johnny from jail, with more murders chalked against his name.

The people passing paid it no attention, men in overalls, straw-hatted against the sun, unarmed, slim beside plump, poke-bonneted wives in Mother Hubbards, many with children, a couple of Mrs. Watson's girls in their finery. Two Mexican horsemen rode by on the opposite side of the street, wearing ornate sombreros. Customers passed in and out of the Boland & Perkins store, which was under new management. The other store was boarded up, and the Turnbull & Maginnis sign had been removed; it had been open only briefly, before Turnbull's murder had closed it. He tied Malcreado to the rail before the Bird Cage Hotel and mounted the steps to the veranda. When he turned for another look at the gallows across the street, he saw Lily.

She was crossing from the courthouse between two men, one of whom held her arm—a tall, broad, frock-coated fellow wearing a derby hat. The other man was smaller, older, and walked as though his feet hurt. Lily's hands lifted her skirts free of the dust. She wore a dark blue gown with geometric black facings. Her pale, naked face was raised to one, then the other of her companions; then her eyes fixed on Cutler on the veranda, her lips opened, and a hand was raised in a greeting that carried its galvanic charge across the fifty feet of Madison's main street.

He was introduced to James Turnbull, whom he disliked immediately, a red-faced, big-bellied version of his brother, who regarded him with dislike in turn and managed always to interpose himself between Cutler and Lily. The other was a lawyer, Mr. Pettit, with a pinched gray face framed by side-whiskers, and a hand like a turkey claw.

"How do, Lieutenant," Pettit said. "We have been hoping to see you soon."

Lily's face gleamed with perspiration, which she blotted

with a handkerchief from her sleeve as the four of them maneuvered through the door of the hotel. Cutler had a glimpse of the telephonic equipment, thick glass cases filled with clear liquid like aquariums, wires and gleaming copper and brass. A man sat at a desk wearing a wire headdress. Turnbull ushered them toward the end of the lobby, where he almost physically seated Lily. The waiter hurried to assist in the arrangement of chairs, skinny and nervous in a white apron. As he snatched one of the chairs from the waiter, Turnbull's coat gaped open to show Cutler a revolver in an armpit holster.

When everyone had been seated to his satisfaction, Turnbull sat with one fat hand covering Lily's on the arm of her chair. His eyes, gazing at Cutler, were set close together above a thick nose, so that he resembled a shrewd collie dog. The little lawyer had removed his hat to reveal a lumpy bald head. He demanded a glass of water, and counted pills out of a silver pillbox. Lily smiled at him, smiled at Turnbull, smiled at Cutler. Her smile for him communicated that the two of them realized that all this fuss of seating was ridiculous but well-meaning.

Pettit washed each pill down with a swallow of water and a jerk of his Adam's apple. He wiped his lips with a napkin. "Now, sir, Lieutenant Cutler," he said, squinting an eye. "We are trying to establish Colonel Dougal's culpability in the tragic death of Mrs. Maginnis's husband and the burning of her home. Murder and arson, sir! The colonel has made certain statements about her as well. Are you prepared to assist us?"

"Not in court, Mr. Pettit, although I'll be glad to tell you what I saw that afternoon."

"You will not testify?" The little lawyer set his lips in a hard line.

Turnbull scowled beefily. He looked like a bad-tempered John Bull. "Why, man, Mrs. Maginnis has counted upon you as a good friend and a reliable witness. What is this?"

"I can't give evidence against my commanding officer in a civilian court."

Lily's smile had vanished. "If honest citizens will not do whatever they must do to serve the cause of justice, justice will not be served. I'm sure you remember Frank saying that, Pat."

"Yes."

"Frank always said that one must do right—not just what is not wrong—whatever the consequences."

"Lily, I'm afraid I think the consequences have been too hard. I'm afraid I think that Frank served the right too rigorously."

"I cannot believe that such an excess is possible," Lily said. She looked worn as he had not seen her before, traceries of lines at the corners of her eyes and mouth, a papery quality to her cheeks. She made a motion with her hand. "This little group is dedicated to serving the right, whatever the cost. I am dedicated to serving it within the law, as Johnny has tried to serve it outside."

"I've just been looking at the machinery across the street," Cutler said. "I'm afraid that Johnny is going to die there because of Frank's principles." He paused before he added, "I've promised Colonel Dougal that I would not testify against him in a civilian court."

"I see," Lily said, smiling.

"This man is not the friend you thought him, my dear," Turnbull said.

"Oh, yes he is, James! And always will be."

Outside in the street there was a plodding of hooves, the creak of a dry axle. Peppery dust drifted inside. The lawyer sneezed into his handkerchief, replaced it in his pocket, and brought out a small lined tablet.

"I think the Madison County War ought to be over, Lily," Cutler said.

"It cannot be over until justice has been served. That is what Mr. Turnbull, Mr. Pettit, and I are dedicated to, Pat."

"Now, Lieutenant," Pettit said. "If you would just go over the events of that tragic day . . ."

He recalled the events of the Battle of Madison as best he could, careful not to impute motives or faulty judgments to Colonel Dougal, who had been officially exonerated by the board of inquiry. He was very tired now of the whole complex of loyalties and moralities of the Madison County War. He wished that it would fade into what Bernie Reilly saw as an earlier, and perhaps more heroic, era of history. All the while Turnbull watched him with a scornful expression, Lily with her brave smile.

When he had finished, she rose abruptly. "I must speak

to you in private, Pat. If you will pardon us, James, Mr. Pettit..."

Rising also, Turnbull said, "I think, my dear Lily—"

"Never mind that now, James. Please, Pat!" He followed her blue-gowned wake through the chairs and gleaming brass spittoons and men pretending not to watch their progress. Her room was the second down the hall. A pigskin suitcase rested on a rack, ranks of gowns marched in lockstep in the closet. Lily leaned back against the door to close it, rich curve of her bosom, of her arms arched back, of her white throat with her face tilted up to him.

"Pat, it is all right—what you say you cannot do. People are moved differently, I know. But Frank was my beloved husband!"

He nodded, watching the color sweep up from her throat to her cheeks. "I am to marry James Turnbull," she said.

"Don't—!" he started, before he could stop himself.

"I am not a young woman anymore. The years have been hard, Pat."

"You're still a beautiful woman," he said.

She smiled pinkly. "There are traps that in the end must close on any spirit seeking to be free," she said. "They are not even the traps of men, for nature has set them. They are the traps of time and age, and of the need of financial supports in order to live the way one is accustomed to living."

Her speech sounded as though she had practiced it. "I see that Mr. Turnbull is very much in love with you," he said.

She shrugged. "Yes, I hope so. We will live in England. But I must speak of Johnny, Pat. That terrible structure across the street— You see, I am afraid that they would sacrifice him if it would aid our cause. And I cannot have that weight upon my soul, whether justice is served or not! You spoke of it just now as though you knew what aches in my heart."

He drew a long breath of her flower scent that could still make him ache well below the heart. "What can I do, Lily?"

"He must leave the Territory. Surely, one of these times Sheriff Grant— And he must be told he is not to trust anyone, anyone claiming to be helping *me*— Pat, if you could find him and tell him he must leave the Territory *on my account*! There's a Mr. Soto, I think he is mayor of Arioso, who will know where to find him. There is a place Johnny hides out—"

Cutler knew the place.

"Tell him I will be destroyed if they destroy him. Tell him Frank would not want that—for the sake of any principles."

"I'll tell him."

She swayed toward him. "Oh, Pat, we used to love each other so! Then—all this!"

His arms had raised to her despite himself when there was a sharp rap on the door.

"Lily, are you all right in there?"

She sighed and retreated. "Yes, James," she called. "I will be right out. Pat and I have finished our conversation."

He remembered Johnny saying the Old Ones' ruins were about thirty miles south of Corral de Tierra. He found the place where he and Johnny had encountered the sheriff's posse, and then backtracked from there into a mesh of canyons opening out of a riverbed with a summer's trickle of water running through. From here his tracking experience came to use, and he cut back and forth until he made out hoofprints in the red sand where cattle had come through. He followed the track along cliffs rising on his left, caves appearing where one stratum had separated from another, reds, browns, and whites in long waves like the flow of the centuries. The trail of hoofprints continued, the caves came more regularly spaced, more frequent, more rectangular. The horizontal lines of the cliffs straightened, with levels set back one above another, ladders connecting the levels. He smelled wood smoke.

He saw the cattle first, brown backs penned by a low adobe wall topped by a barrier of branches—fifty head or more. Horses grazed further over, on a greasy bank this side of willow thickets. He came into a broad, level area of stone terraces bordered by the eroded walls of the Old Ones. Five men were congregated around a fire, two lounging with their backs against a wall, two squatting, one standing watching him with his rifle in his hands. The others scrambled to their feet. Cutler held up his hand in a peace sign.

One of them trotted toward him—Johnny Angell, bareheaded. Cutler dismounted and dropped the reins to the stones. They shook hands.

"Look some improved from the last time you dropped in," Johnny said, grinning, brown moss on his cheeks and chin. His face was thinner, like a face burned in high wind, careful blue eyes above the boyish grin. He wore his familiar vest over a blue shirt, pants stuffed into battered boots, a holstered revolver. They sat together on one of the low walls, the ranked vacant eyes of the doorways of the Old Ones gazing down. The cliff top rode against the September sky, the fringe of brush, cactus, and stunted trees leaning east from the prevailing winds.

He told Johnny Lily Maginnis's message.

The outlaw rolled makings from a sack drawn from his vest pocket. "Get out while the getting can still be got," he said, nodding.

"I'm to tell you it's for her sake, and that of Martin Turnbull and Frank Maginnis."

"That is powerful saking," Johnny said, applying a match to his cigarette. "Well, Mrs. Maginnis is a natural wonder for getting what she wants. I hear she is pretty well lawyered in town there."

"She's pressing charges against Colonel Dougal."

"Wouldn't want to be in his boots."

Better his than yours, Cutler thought. He said, "It's quiet in Madison except for the rustle of legal documents."

"Quiet down here except for the rustle of stock," Johnny said, and laughed. "Well, I knew Jack Grant would make a nonpareil lawman. One way or another, everything has got itself sorted out except me. And I hear there's short odds on that."

"That's why Lily wanted me to come."

"Took a little trip to Tucson," Johnny said seriously. "Bad business on my mind. Mr. Boland is terrible sick, blown up like a colicky calf, and he smells rank too. I had thought I would go to the springs instead of the spout! Well, the mill grinds slow but it does grind fine. A young fellow gets nervy from that slow grinding, but I believe next time I will just let her grind.

"Older and wiser is what I have got to be," Johnny went on. "It is easier to think let-be now it is all gone past, but a young fellow does go a bit loco thinking something oughtn't to be allowed to happen in fine country." He held his head in his two hands and rocked. "It is like coming out of a fever.

Well, you would know about that, Pat! I surely thought you would be losing that leg!"

"I'm going to the hacienda in Sonora pretty soon. You would be welcome there. It is like a great fortress, with trees, flowers, birds, good hunting. There are thirteen patios, and servants in livery."

"Oh, my! And pretty girls?"

"Dozens."

"*Bailes?*"

"Every week."

"I do enjoy riding in to the *bailes,*" Johnny said, his cigarette raising a pencil of smoke from the corner of his mouth. "Well, it is all one grand masquerade ball, isn't it?" Sobering, he said, "That is fine of you, Pat, but I will not be heading for Mexico. Might look like I was on the run. No, sir, I am not running from Jack Grant, or the militia I hear the governor is training up in Santa Fe. Or even cavalry, if you will pardon me. I will be heading out on my own time, and before it is too late, too—if you would tell Lily that."

"I urge you also."

Johnny nodded. Over by the fire one of the cowboys was standing, relating something with extravagant gestures to an appreciative audience. "They are good fellows," Johnny said. "We will sell this bunch to the railroad camp up on the new line. And I'll head north to take up land on the east slope of the Rockies. There is a pretty señorita who has promised to come along with me."

Cutler was thinking of Joklinney depredating again and Johnny-A thinking he could quit rustling.

"That is PM stock," Johnny went on. "You know, Jack Grant and me worked for Mr. McFall once. This is how he got his herds together in the first place. Mavericking, rounding up strays, and plain thieving. Rustling land, too. He would scare off settlers coming in to those creek bottoms he figured he had more right to than they did. Maybe everything got rustled by people that came first and then ran off people coming later. Hired sheriffs to keep people from stealing what they had stole in the first place, putting a high moral tone to it.

"Maybe I know what those bronco Paches are feeling. Every man's hand against them, and pushed tighter and tighter into a corner. They are dead men, but they have got folks froze-up scared worrying about them now—what they did to the Floreses. It is hard to understand what makes people do like that to live human beings."

"What happened?" Cutler's dry mouth said. "*When?*"

"Wiped out a family name of Flores yesterday, north out of Arioso. Luz and Carlos and a four-year-old kit Mr. McFall was godfather to. Bad," Johnny said, with a grim shake of his head.

Joklinney had reappeared. Tortures and mutilations, Yeager had prophesied. Joklinney's other raid, four years ago, had been a month's horror. But this one had had to begin in order to be finished.

"How many were killed?"

"Five of them," Johnny said. "I went over there. Bad," he said again. He sounded as though he had a cold in his head.

Cutler stood. It was time to return to Fort McLain. At least there was something now to be done. "They have more outrages against them than even you have," he heard himself saying. "Backed into corners. Betrayed. They don't know who to get back at except any white-eye or Mexican they come across."

"There are things a man don't do and still call himself a human being," Johnny said in the stuffed-up voice.

"We will have to kill them," Cutler said. "I expect they'll kill more before we do."

"If I could put those broncos under, I would do it," Johnny said. "That is something a man could go out on!"

Bernie Reilly had wondered if Johnny-A was aware of his legend. When Johnny spoke of the little spread on the eastern slope of the Rockies, he must have known it was never to be. When he said he could go out on an act of public service, *out* did not mean heading north. So he was aware of his meaning to others, at least.

"I just want to enter my Father's House justified, Pat," Johnny said, turned half away from him.

Cutler thought then that he would never see Johnny alive again and that there was no point in urging him to seek the safety of Colorado or Mexico. "Maybe you will, Johnny," he said.

Cutler and the Hoyas encountered the sheriff with four or five of his men in the meadow where the burned-out adobe was, roof burned black against the leafy green of the willows pluming out of the creekbed beyond. The posse men were grouped around a campfire and there was a smell of boiling coffee against the pervasive stink of char and rotten meat. Everything had been cleaned up and buried except for dead cattle and a dead horse further along the meadow. As the trackers spread out hunting sign, the sheriff, gaunt, unshaven, tall and tall-hatted, like a caricature of himself, slouched toward Cutler on Malcreado.

"Hello there, Lieutenant. Glad to see some cavalry, even if it's only scouts."

"Looks like you've cleaned up already, Sheriff."

"We did and puked a good deal. There was some neighbors here earlier. They are scared gray in the face."

"There's no doubt it's Joklinney."

"Nope."

"At least there's something to go on now. Which way'd they go?"

"Left out over there where those two fellows of yours is at," Grant said. "One of my boys followed along a way, and took a fright and come back." He rubbed a hand over his dirty face. "Hounds of hell," he said.

Squatting on the ground, Kills-a-Bear slanted his good eye up toward Cutler and rattled at Nochte in Apache.

"He says there is no more sign, Nantan Tata. Joklinney is very clever."

"Can't they keep cutting?"

Nochte questioned Kills-a-Bear, Jim-jim and Chockaway leaning out of their saddles to listen. Kills-a-Bear shrugged, the corners of his mouth pulled down harshly.

"He says we can do that, Nantan Tata. There is too much sign—the sheriff, other Mexicans—but there is no Joklinney sign."

Cutler hugged his arms to his chest, impatience like a rowel in his side. "We have to do something."

More conversation, Skinny coming to squat beside Kills-a-Bear and join in. Kills-a-Bear scowled from face to face, shook his head, addressed Nochte.

"He believes Joklinney must come to one of two places, Nantan Tata. He says you must send Chockaway to one place,

Jim-jim to the other place, to watch. He says you must wait to hear that Joklinney has come to one of these places."

"All right," he said.

Nochte glanced at him worriedly. "Joklinney is very clever, Nantan Tata."

"I believe the Hoyas are more clever."

When this was relayed to Kills-a-Bear, the ravaged face relaxed. He grinned, and nodded once.

So there was nothing to do but send out Chockaway and Jim-jim as Kills-a-Bear demanded, and to wait.

Sheriff Grant's narrative:

There was criticism that I went ahead and had the gallows built, with Johnny on the loose, but the gallows put a serious set to a lot of fellows' minds that might have been considering kicking up some dust, and I hoped just hearing about it would cause Johnny to clear out of the Territory. Meanwhile the governor sent me telegrams and letters demanding an accounting of what was being done in the campaign to recapture Johnny-A, for he had taken a bad scare one night to find Johnny looking in his window at him. For he had not played Johnny fair, and he must know it too.

I could write the governor back that I had got rid of Graves and Bateson, at least, and Tuttle in custody, and it was only a matter of time, etc., etc. Probably Johnny would make tracks when he had got himself a stake together, rustling. He was riding with the Walker brothers and some others that were not doing his reputation any good, and I had heard he was often to be seen in Arioso, being interested in a young lady there. I didn't see any way to talk turkey to him as Callie had said I must do, for there was a lock on the door now, we weren't anymore Big Jay and Little Jay, we were sheriff and outlaw, and I knew he had taken hard against me because of Pard Graves's arm. I was going to have to go into Arioso again after him sooner or later, unless he listened to somebody's reason and cleared out.

Meanwhile Mrs. Maginnis was back in town with Martin Turnbull's brother and a high-price lawyer. I went looking for her at the Bird Cage, where they were all putting up, and managed to cut her out from her menfolk for a talk. She was dressed in her fine clothes, with a purple feather on her little hat that nodded over her forehead like a warrior plume when she talked. But she looked tired, like somebody that had stayed scared too long and hadn't slept well, tight little lines around her eyes I had not noticed that last time I'd seen her, which had been in the governor's office. We sat facing each other in the *sala* of the hotel, with the Englishman watching us from across the room.

I said to her, "You have got to tell him to get out before it's too late."

She said with her little chin stuck out, "Are you pretending to still be his friend, Sheriff Grant?"

I said I wasn't pretending anything, only telling her this, for I knew she knew how to get in touch with him.

She said, "I assure you that I do not!"

I said, "Mrs. Maginnis, I don't want Johnny caught and hanged. You can believe that or don't. But I am going to have to catch him and hang him."

"You will never take him alive!"

"Or that. So I am asking your help."

Her eyes misted over. It is too bad that I had the idea she could do something like that on call. But she laid a hand on my hand and, her purple feather nodding, said, "I believe you. Yes, he must get out. I will try. I have already sent someone—"

It may be I looked at her too sharp, for she broke off. But she laughed a little and said, "To think that I find sympathy in a sheriff of Madison County! There are those who would not believe it."

I said, "Yes, ma'am." Martin Turnbull's brother had been watching us across the *sala* all the time, scowling like a fat eagle, and I said, "I will let you go now, ma'am, for I see I am making Mr. Turnbull nervous."

"He has heard so much of the terrible enmities of this place, you see, Sheriff," she said.

It was soon clear that that lawyer of Mrs. Maginnis's was giving the judge and the prosecuting attorney fits. MacLennon would shy at him like a mare at a rattler; he had his number. Pettit would ram things at him before Judge Arthur, and each time it was like chopping one of the posts that held up the veranda. With each chop the whole thing sagged more, and pretty soon it would all come down. If MacLennon didn't put this or that to the judge, Pettit would draw up complaints to the federal court in Santa Fe, which Jake Weber no longer ran like a private railway car. And Pettit had his telephone to talk to his people in Santa Fe right this minute! Seeing all of this gave me and a pack of others in town some amusement.

As my daddy used to say, as soon as you get the door closed, here they come through the window. With Johnny-A fenced in, here came Apaches! Two of the Red Stripers that had been shipped off to prison in Florida had busted off the train. For a while nothing much was heard of them, though everybody assumed they would be heading west for their home stamping ground in the Green Range. They killed some people, sheepherders mostly, and shot two troopers guarding a horse herd and ran off twenty head.

I had announced that I would take up the warrants in my office as they came, but bronco Apaches on a raid will take precedence over everything else. Everybody knew they would pick up meanness as they went and every strike was apt to be worse than the last one. So I started receiving telegrams from the governor on the subject of Joklinney instead of Johnny-A, for some of the newspapers were calling him "Governor Do-Nothing."

And then a Mexican rode in from south county on a lathered horse to say Joklinney had hit a Mex ranch down there, killing everybody and bad. It was a good chance for me to show the Mexicans I was their friend even if I was on Johnny's trail, so I pounded out of town headed south with a big posse. This was serious business now that they were hitting so close. Nana's raid had covered a thousand miles and killed more than fifty whites and Mexicans, Chato's at least half that many, and Josanie's maybe thirty-eight in twelve hundred miles. Joklinney's other raid, that they had sent him to Alcatraz for, had killed a couple of dozen, not including what Caballito killed in the San Marcos bustout; and now this one was becoming a butcher-shop business too. When Apaches were on the vengeance trail they killed hard, no tooth for a tooth for them, but ten for one.

The adobe ranch house at Willow Meadows was close by a bend of creek, with the sun shimmering on the dry grass, and ugly patches of black burn. A little breeze was rippling the grass, and it brought with it a sickly stink of spoiling meat.

You see one of these things they call depredations and you would like to skin alive some of those Congressmen and East Coast newspapermen that claim Apaches are only good, simple folk driven to savagery by white men stealing their land and wiping out the buffalo. I say let them come out and look at a thing like this, *smell* it too. Any decent person couldn't even think of what they had done to that poor Mexican ranch family, things I will not even set down in this record. Two women among them, or what had been women, and a four-years' boy: torture them to death and mutilate the remains. I don't believe white men can hate that hard.

All of us puked in the course of digging a hole and laying the bodies and pieces of bodies in, and covering them over, stink of vomit on top of the other.

Chuck held his bandana over his nose and said, "I say kill all the devils, squaws and papooses too. Florida prisons're too good for them!"

Frank said, "What I heard they used to do in the old days up north—they'd get blankets from somebody'd had smallpox, give them to the Injun. Wipe out a whole village that way."

A dozen Mexican fellows had come to watch, neighboring ranchers with brown faces turned gray at the edges. I had a queer feeling at the back of my neck Johnny-A might be about, for I knew these people had been friends of his.

I sent Ben to see if he could cut any track on Joklinney heading out of here. He found the trail easy enough and followed it a way, but got to thinking of Apache waiting for him and came back to where the rest of us were having a good wash in the creek.

Back in Willow Meadows Lieutenant Cutler and his Pache trackers came in in single file at a good trot, some of the scouts in blue cavalry shirts, others in filthy cotton manta, bare brown legs, high moccasins, red headbands. Most remained mounted, gathering around Cutler, but three piled off to squat peering at the ground. Cutler was a tough-looking cavalry officer, hard blue eyes and a chewed-up stogie stuck in the corner of his jaw. He agreed with me it had to've been Joklinney, while the trackers circulated around the meadow and the house. Then they all set off, in single file again but one of the trackers leading, on the track Ben had come back from.

* * *

We hadn't been back in Madison half an hour, and I was sitting in my office by lamplight, too tired to go see Callie or even home to bed—and too low as well—when Ben Gibson came in to say there was a *muchacha* wanted to talk to me but wouldn't come inside.

She was standing in the shadows by the stoop, where just a little light out of the office window showed a slim figure and a rebozo draped over her head. I could make out she was young by the curve of her cheek. She said she had come about el Angelito.

"You come Arioso *el Día de los Muertos*," she told me. That was the Day of the Dead, when Mexicans celebrate their dead ancestors, take picnics to the graveyard, eat candy skeletons, and have a grand *baile* that night, with masks—a Halloween sort of business.

"Juanito come Arioso *el Día de los Muertos*," the girl said. Sometimes she swayed a little so her face almost came into the light, and then pulled back. "Jack Grant come Arioso *el Día de los Muertos también. Máscaras!*" she said, and laid her hands over her face inside the rebozo.

"*Baile de máscaras!*" she said. Masks! Johnny would come into the masked *baile* the night of the Day of the Dead, and I was to come in and take him with the help of this little Judasita.

"Juanito your sweetheart?"

She shook her head like she was angry. It was well known that el Angelito cut some swath among those south-county muchachas, and I figured he had passed over this one for the one he was supposed to be keeping company with now. No fury in hell like one of these cigarillo-smoking chili peppers spurned.

"Jack Grant come *baile de máscaras*," she said. She covered her face again. "Juanito come. *Yo también*, I come. *Flores!*" She tapped her bosom and pointed to each side of her head. "*Tres flores. Aqui, aqui, aqui.*"

I said, "Three flowers. Here, here, and here."

That is the way it works. You stop worrying Johnny-A to worry Joklinney, and a señorita comes to turn him in. Now there was a date by when he had to clear out of the country, and that was by the night of the Day of the Dead, in early November.

Three days later the governor came down to Madison with his Apache-hunting militia.

What I knew of General Underwood was that when Jubal Early was raiding up the Shenandoah Valley toward Washington and things got tight, Underwood threw together a makeshift army of state militia and raw recruits, and delayed Early long enough for reinforcements to come up from City Point and run Early back down the valley. The governor got a medal for it.

Which might go a way to explain why he showed up in Madison on a Thursday, with such a queer gang out of Santa Fe that right away my temperature began going up. In the lead with the governor was Don Rudolfo Perosa, an old-time soldier from the Mexican days, wearing a flat, broad-brimmed hat and dirty buckskin shirt, and between them his wolf's face so wrinkled you could hardly make out the features in it. With them was Chester Baskerville that Underwood must have scraped up off some saloon floor, having a fine time waving his hat at a couple of Mrs. Watson's girls; and the old scout Tom Beak, grown fat and rich as a Santa Fe trader. Next came a couple of dozen Navajo scouts on spotted ponies, wearing straw hats and striped blankets on their shoulders like Mexican caballeros. Last of all were the governor's Zouave guards in their clownsuits, about thirty of them, all of them mounted and bouncing along like plowboy riders.

The governor rode straight as a stick and proud on a seventeen-hands bay. He was not wearing his Union uniform but a gray suit that looked Confederate, if anything. With his slouch hat on he looked, except for his black beard, like photographs of General Bobby Lee aboard Traveller.

They came on along the street toward the hotel and I didn't know whether to kick dust or spit. Everybody was coming out of stores and buildings to watch the show. Some fool took to clapping and others joined in, though no one could have known what all the show was in aid of. But I knew that the governor had another Pike's Junction on his mind, and this pack of bank clerks, misfits, drunkards, and Navajos had come down to save Madison County from Apache depredators.

I trotted along the boardwalk to where the general was dismounting, handing his reins to a city-suited young fellow and slapping dust from his own fine clothes with his hat. I heard old Baskerville croaking, "Where is the nearest saloon, boys?" and somebody else called out, "By George, it is a long ways between drinks down this way!" Everybody laughed at that, like it was a joke they were familiar with.

"What is this, Governor?" I said, more exercised than I wanted to be, for all this did seem an insult on me. "What kind of unlawful assembly is this you have brought down here?"

He gave me a cold look and said, "Some of these men were fighting Apaches while you were in kneepants, Sheriff."

I said I could see that easy enough. The Zouaves were dismounting, fitting bayonets to their rifles, and forming up in lines, an officer pushing and growling at them like a sheepdog. The governor settled his Bobby Lee hat on his head, and took a cigar case from his coat pocket. He made a business of selecting a cigar, twirling it under his nose, and lighting up. He didn't bother to offer me a cigar to turn down.

In the street the Navajo scouts were riding past in groups of two and three. One of them had a regular bouquet of eagle feathers stuck in his hair.

And now with some bellows from the Zouave officer, the Santa Fe Guards began to march down the street all in a pack. They strutted with their red bloomers billowing and yellow gaiters flashing, rifles propped on their shoulders and high glitter of bayonets above their heads. They broke into double time, then reversed, and all at once fell down on their bellies like one man, and squirmed in the dust that way. In an instant they were up and strutting again, the fronts of their uniforms caked with Madison dust. I don't know why they made me so mad, except they were so fancy all-for-show. If they were for fighting Apaches, it would be trying to swat a mosquito with your elbow.

"Joklinney has struck again," the governor told me, very cool. "Whites this time, near Crescent Station. The Territorial newspapers are demanding action, Sheriff. And so am I!"

"Something must be done!" Underwood said to Yeager in the general's office at Fort Blodgett, the general half reclining behind the desk in his many-pocketed jacket, fingering a sideburn as the governor leaned toward him. The general

seemed listless and uninterested, which Underwood found
irritating in the extreme.

"A family of Mormons has been slaughtered," he went
on. "Unspeakable atrocities! I am sick to death, General, of
being called Governor Do-Nothing!"

"They have run out of epithets for me," Yeager said with
a pursed smile. "They have roasted me in sulfur, washed me
in steep-down gulfs of fire. The Paches' Pal, General Nuisance! I can only advise you to grow a tough shell and be
patient, Governor. Joklinney's raid will come to its end in
good time."

It was like hearing himself talk lately. Even Charley
Harkins had turned on him, and he had been shaken when
the rancher McFall had appeared in his office, fierce as some
jungle beast, to curse him hysterically because his godchild, a
Mexican boy, had been tortured and burned by the raiders.

"Tell me," Yeager said, tenting his fingers together
superciliously. "Are we more distressed because of the personal attacks or because of these terrible slaughters?"

Underwood took it as just such a personal attack. "The
cavalry is blind without its scouts," he retorted. "And the
scouts have all been sent to Florida."

"Lieutenant Cutler's Apache trackers are on continual
reconnaissance," Yeager said coldly. "I expect results any day.
Each of these depredations makes Joklinney's apprehension
more certain."

"I am considering employing Navajo scouts."

Yeager shrugged. "They have proven themselves less
than effective in dealing with Apaches."

General Yeager's position had been that scouts should be
recruited from the same tribe or even band as those they
might have to pursue. But of course he had received a
setback both military and political because of the Sierra Verde
breakout, and because of Joklinney's escape from the Florida
train and his consequent bloody raiding. For his own part,
Underwood had come to realize the danger that history
would indeed show him as Governor Do-Nothing. His principle of considered delay had worked in the case of Johnny-A,
but in the hysteria that attended these Apache horrors, action
was absolutely essential. No doubt Lieutenant Cutler's trackers
would eventually run Joklinney to earth, but meanwhile the
governor must produce some determined show.

The general instructed him to take his list of necessities to Captain Robinson and assured him of the quartermaster's cooperation. "I have suffered the attacks of the Territorial press for much longer than you have, Governor," he said, standing to shake Underwood's hand, "and I am thankful that I will not have to suffer them much longer."

So it was with determination and the unease of embarking upon a new River Road that the governor called the Santa Fe Guards to active service, sent Perosa to the Navajo reservation to engage a company of scouts, and mustered a corps of citizens who had had Indian fighting or Indian tracking experience. He was pleased that all this mustering and equipping was done with the same facility with which he had assembled his little army for the march on Pike's Junction to confront Jubal Early. Within two days' time he was on the way to Madison, the nearest town of any size to the quarter of the Territory that had been the scene of Joklinney's latest depredations.

Looking back from a ridge at his motley militia, he felt a surge of pride such as he had not experienced in years. His sergeant bore the Stars and Stripes on its staff, leading the guards in their Zouave uniforms—although there had been no time for cavalry drill, and they did not appear at their best on horseback. Next came the well-mounted Navajos, with their bright blankets and straw hats over dark faces; the civilian riders straggled behind, with the six wagons last of all, a brown dust cloud blowing east from the column's progress.

The civilians constituted a growing disciplinary problem, for they had brought whiskey along and its effects in the hot sun were first audible and presently visible. Underwood had to resort to strong language to extricate Beak and Baskerville from the cantina in San Elizondo, where they seemed to have settled down for the afternoon.

"Why don't we just put up here, Gov? This is a fine place," Baskerville said, and Beak added, "Joklinney'll probably show up right here, and we'll snap the trap on him!"

The guards were becoming saddlesore, and it was difficult for them to keep up with Don Rudolfo and the scouts, who had taken the lead. The civilians continued to straggle. Underwood was able to reassemble the column into fair order for the entrance into Madison, but there he found Sheriff

Grant in a petulant mood, as though the militia were intended as a rebuke for his failure to bring in Johnny-A.

Underwood supervised the erection of the tent camp on the edge of town, the digging of latrines, and the setting up of the mess kitchen with the chuck wagon and the two complaining cooks he had brought down from Santa Fe. The civilians were ensconced in the Bird Cage Hotel and were already at sundown deep into drunken revelry, as though this whole expedition were just some kind of old school reunion. To escape the racket they were making in the saloon and to placate the sheriff for the disturbances of the peace that certainly lay ahead, he took his leather map case and crossed the street to the courthouse in the starry darkness.

Grant seemed to have gotten over his pet and looked with interest at the map Underwood spread out on his desk. Underwood had gone over it with Don Rudolfo and Tom Beak, marking with red circles the places where Joklinney had struck and with crosses the passes to the Green Range, also circled in red in the center of the Territory.

"We have devised some patterns for trying to catch these murderers," Underwood said. "And I will be counting heavily on you and any good local men you can recommend."

"You're not going out with those ribbon clerks dressed up in Mexican admirals' uniforms, are you?" Grant asked.

"No, I am not," he said with irritation. "They are for show, Sheriff. It is imperative not only that I take some of them, but that I seem to be taking action. Do you understand me? I am being crucified by the press for inactivity, along with General Yeager."

Grant grunted, perhaps approvingly, still leaning over the map. His arms were so long, six inches of bony wrists protruded from his shirtsleeves.

"Your former employer came to Santa Fe and all but attacked me physically in my office," Underwood said. "It seems the boy who was killed with the Mexican family was his godchild."

Grant grimaced at him, nodding, before turning to pore over the map again. "Old Mac loved that kid. He'd visit over there at Willow Meadows a good deal. Did he come along with that bunch of yours?"

Underwood shook his head. "I've brought a number of expert trackers with me," he continued, raising his voice as there was a swelling of the drunken noise from across the street. "If we come across Joklinney's trail I have no fear that we will lose it, but I also hope to station detachments at various points where they might intercept him—at some pass or water hole. For we can only assume that he will eventually head for the Sierra Verde hunting grounds. I hope you will have some ideas of your own from your hunts for Johnny-A."

"I believe you could use those Hoyas of Lieutenant Cutler's."

"I think we must do without them," he said.

Grant grunted again, swinging around as the door was jerked open. Underwood gasped. A frightening figure filled the doorway, a pure white skull face under a tall hat, the muzzle of a Colt swinging back and forth between him and Grant. A muffled voice commanded, "Just keep those hands up away from your iron, Sheriff."

The skull face was a mask. Queer gray stripes lined out the bones, the eyes and mouth were black cutouts, a cigarette burned in one corner of the skull mouth. The eye pits focused on Underwood, and the iron ring of the revolver muzzle pointed at him. His heart began to convulse.

"What do you think you are about, Johnny?" Grant said calmly.

So it was Johnny-A behind the mask. "Show you," the muffled voice said.

The outlaw had held one hand behind his back. Now he brought it around, holding a red stick of dynamite with a gray twist of fuse. He tucked the dynamite stick under his arm in order to touch the burning tip of his cigarette to the fuse.

"Hold steady now!" he said, and tossed the stick under Grant's desk. Underwood stooped to snatch for it, but the voice sharpened. "Hold still, I said."

Underwood could hear the fizzing of the fuse. Sweat stung in his eyes. Grant looked frozen, hands half-raised, his face gray, and his mouth gaping open. The gleam of the outlaw's eyes were visible within the mask's eyeholes.

"That ought to do it," Angell said. He jumped back with one last wave of his revolver and slammed the door. There was a dragging sound outside, of something shoved against the door.

Grant was scrambling beneath the desk. He lurched back out from under it, uncoiling erect with fingers snuffing out the burning fuse and the dynamite stick jerked back to be flung through the window glass. Then he halted the motion, grimacing.

"Get rid of it!" Underwood yelled, but Grant only grinned bonily. He stripped the red paper from the dynamite, which proved to be a stick of kindling. Outside, louder than a peal of drunken laughter from the saloon, came a shrilling of rebel yells and taunting yahoos.

When the sounds had quieted, Underwood mopped at the sweat on his face. The panic he had felt had turned to an icy rage. "I want you to rid me of that fellow, Sheriff," he said through his teeth.

Grant grinned again, long knife slashes showing in his cheeks. "Why, Governor, it was just a joke. Don't you think we owe Johnny a joke or two?"

27

Cutler sat with another cavalry officer's widow in her weeds, the wife Sam Bunch had said he hated and who hated him, in Officers' Quarters 1, which the colonel had vacated for her stay at Fort McLain, Sam's widow sitting stiffly erect on the settee, Cutler in the platform rocker, a broad swath of morning sun flooding in across the table with its crocheted cloth and bowl of geraniums. Mrs. Bunch watched him steadily, hands folded in her lap, as he told of her husband's last campaign.

She was about thirty, with colorless hair pulled back into a severe bun and a sallow face drawn tight as though facing into a strong wind. There was a monochrome effect to her face, hair, eyes, pale lips—and an intensity also, as though the wind she faced came from fire. One of her hands was adorned with a gold wedding band.

"So he died a hero," she said. "My father was also decorated posthumously." Her chin tilted aggressively. "Did he ever speak of me?"

"Why yes," Cutler said uncomfortably. "Of course he did, Mrs. Bunch."

"Did he say he hated me?"

He blew his breath out between his lips before he said, "Yes, he did."

"And that I hated him? I told him I hated him the last time we saw each other. I told him he would give me some vile disease if he continued his . . . filthy habits."

She halted to gaze at him challengingly. He did not want to know any of this.

"I told him he would infect the child," she said. "Children can be born blind, you know."

473

Bunch had never mentioned a child. And in Mexico, by now, there must be a darker half brother or sister.

"I didn't know Sam had a child."

"A son," she said with that thrust of her chin. "Daniel. For my father. Sam never saw him." She looked down at her hands in her lap. The morning sun ray brightened her black skirt and the tips of the black sensible shoes protruding from beneath it. "I wrote Sam he would never see him."

"I see," he said.

"At Fort Belvoir, where we were stationed, he was famous for seeking out low, vile women. Women of color, in fact, Lieutenant Cutler. He did this from malice, of course. I was carrying Daniel then. I told him he would blind Daniel with his vileness. I sent him away. Then he was transferred to Dakota Territory."

Cutler's shoulders ached as though he had held them raised defensively for too long. "He was my friend," he said.

"So I may expect that you will judge me harshly." Her eyelashes were the same color as her skin, which gave her eyes a strange, naked look. "I am very sorry that Daniel will never have known his father," she said.

That other child of Bunch's would never know his father either. If Bunch had hated this woman, he had loved that other of color, Pretty Mouth, Junie, whose release must be arranged, and that of her child. But maybe they were better off in Mexico than in a Florida prison with the other Sierra Verdes. There was Las Golondrinas. It was a debt he owed Sam.

"He will have a medal to remember his father by," he said. "He will have a name that he will know as his own. He is not fatherless in that way, and he will have a mother to tell him her best memories of her husband. There will be a document to show him his father died a hero."

"Yes, that is just what I had of my father," Olive Bunch said, and her lips tightened in what must have been an attempt at a smile.

He thought it might have been her father whom Bunch had first learned to hate. Was her accent more Southern than Bunch's had been, with his Marylander's *oots* and *aboots*? He asked if her father had been a Confederate.

"Yes, he was!" she said. "I was twelve when he was killed."

"Where did you and Sam meet?"

Her expression softened, and for the moment she was almost pretty. "At an Academy dance. My cousin was his classmate. Sam loved to dance. He was a fine dancer for such a big man! We simply *flew* around the floor. But after it was too late, I discovered the brute that was in him."

"You have had two tragedies in your life," Cutler said. That seemed to satisfy her, her expression firm-lipped but almost smiling—almost in fact, smug, although tears glittered in her colorless lashes. He was very sorry for the child Daniel Bunch and determined that that other child and its mother be saved. Everything seemed to him interconnected, woven together inextricably, part of some whole, a continuum that taunted him for recognition. For of course his own son was part of it, the boy whose paternity had become so much more important than the empty shroud of his own.

When he rose to take his leave, Mrs. Bunch thanked him for telling her of her husband's death and for the comfort he had brought her.

In full-dress parade, the troops not out searching for Apache raiders stood at attention before the flagpole, facing Colonel Dougal; Major Symonds; the adjutant, Lieutenant Hotchkiss; and Captain Robinson, come down from Fort Blodgett as General Yeager's emissary. Cutler and Mrs. Bunch, a slim erect figure in black, black-hatted and -veiled, stood twenty feet apart, backs to the troops, facing the colonel. Cutler stepped forward when his name was called.

The adjutant had stepped forward also. He cleared his throat explosively, and announced:

"Awarded: by the President of the United States, to Captain Patrick Cutler, for bravery in action in the campaign against hostile Apaches in New Mexico Territory and the State of Chihuahua, Mexico."

Hotchkiss read the citation haltingly, pausing before the big words like a high jumper rearing back. The recommendations had been made by General Yeager, Commander of the Department, and by Colonel Burke, Commander of the 6th Cavalry. There was a supplementary commendation from Governor Molino of the State of Chihuahua.

The citation was for bravery in action in the pursuit of the band of the Sierra Verde chieftain, Caballito. In a series of pitched battles, in one of which they had rescued elements of the 6th Cavalry Regiment from almost certain destruction, and operating far in advance of other elements that might have come to their own rescue, Lieutenant Cutler and Captain Bunch had harassed, pressed, and weakened the hostile force. Crossing the border in hot pursuit, they had implemented an encirclement of the band in close cooperation with Mexican troops commanded by Colonel Pascual Molino. The hostiles had been annihilated. The action was exemplary in its cooperation between the two nations and carried out in the finest traditions of the U.S. Cavalry.

Giggles rose to Cutler's throat like bubbles in champagne, rising through layers of indignation and fury. Captain Robinson, breathing hard with concentration, his liquor-thickened nose like a red snail attached above his gray mustache, looped the ribbon bearing its heavy bit of metal over Cutler's neck. He pinned another bit of ribbon, a red, white, and blue bow, to Cutler's chest and captain's bars to his shoulder straps.

In the fitful shadow of the flag blowing and slumping in the little breeze, Colonel Dougal beamed at Cutler loonily. The Iron Major stood beside the colonel, glowering. Beyond the two field officers the parade ground shimmered in the heat, bounded by barracks and the corral fence. Four of the Hoyas were perched on the fence, watching the white-eye ceremony. The scouts had not been mentioned in the citation, other than as "their commands."

Cutler marched between Hotchkiss and Percy Robinson to be congratulated with what seemed an excess of effusion by Colonel Dougal. Major Symonds congratulated him with restraint, a set to his jaw as though he were munching nails.

"I thank you on the part of the regiment, many of whom unfortunately cannot be present to honor you and Captain Bunch," the colonel babbled. "Your honor is ours! 'Bravery beyond the call of duty!' 'Matching hostile ruse with honest tactic!' We are proud of you, Captain Cutler!"

"Thank you, Colonel."

He stood with the colonel and the major as the same citation was read posthumously for Captain Bunch. The shadow of the flag rippled over them, and the band began to play as Captain Robinson presented the medal to Bunch's widow.

Mrs. Bunch wept as the officers congratulated her, and Lieutenant Hotchkiss supported her from the field.

Cutler allowed himself one squint down at the medal that had been hung around his neck and sideways at the double bars pinned to his shoulder. When the troops had been dismissed, he waved a hand in the direction of the scouts perched on the corral rail. Percy Robinson took a grip on his arm. "We must have a few words alone, Pat."

They walked together in the shade of the cottonwoods beyond the parade ground, where Robinson halted to lean against a trunk, one foot braced back. "The general has submitted his resignation, Pat. General Schofield will be assuming command of the department."

The world whirled and dropped beneath his feet, and steadied. He thought that this news must explain the colonel's lunatic grin and greasy congratulations. Still, it seemed that Yeager had provided him with a line of defense.

"This was just about his last official act," Robinson said.

"I'll bet he thought it was funny."

Robinson shook his head. Flickers of light played over his rumpled uniform. "He thought the decoration might protect you when he was no longer on hand to do so, in case you changed your mind about resigning your commission."

"I won't change my mind," he said. He thought the Iron Major would like to see him shot out of hand, the more so because of the decoration. He had written Don Fernando that he would be coming to Las Golondrinas soon, but these days waiting for Joklinney to show himself were very long. Now he was wary of some new claim on him by General Yeager, for he found it impossible to believe the general capable of a gift that was not in some way self-serving.

"The general simply didn't realize what the consequences of another Sierra Verde breakout would be," Robinson went on. "Apparently the President was furious. Any prospects of a Republican nomination have vanished completely."

"I'm glad the Red Stripe People got something back."

Robinson frowned at him reprovingly for his lack of loyalty. His big face was flaming like a steamed pudding from exposure to the sun, and his nose resembled a piece of fruit that had gone bad.

"I don't owe him anything, Perce," Cutler said. "He's made a jackass out of me. He's strung me along with mysteri-

ous references, pretended— He made me think he was my
Nantan Lobo. I'm lucky he hasn't shipped me off to Florida
with the Sierra Verdes."

"I understand, of course, since I've been a witness to
much of this," Robinson said. "But if you will try to understand. He collects hole cards and trumps in case they should
ever become useful. He treasures debts that can be called. As
you know, I've been his amanuensis for his memoirs, which
he's been in the process of recalling, collecting, dictating—
even writing himself—for some years. I've recently seen
some of his own journals and run across a bit of information
that may be of interest to you."

Cutler smiled at the old sudden beating of his heart
rising like a trout to the bait.

"It was when he was stationed in San Francisco in
'fifty-two. He became the recipient of a foundling child,
which he thought to be that of an Irish laundress at the
Presidio. As he put it, it was one of the many duties for which
an officer had not received training at the academy."

"What did he do with it?" But of course he knew.

"He wrote that he was able to persuade a woman to take
the baby, a woman of the very highest social position in San
Francisco—this phrase afforded him a good deal of amusement, Pat. And a woman who had fallen in love with the
young lieutenant he was then. He is a braggart, as you know."

"Yes," said Patrick Cutler, son of an Irish laundress.

"I think in fact the young lieutenant was desperately
infatuated with the woman of high position," Robinson went
on, "and never recovered from it, as of course you have
realized. Because of your connection with her I think he half
blamed you for her treatment of him and at the same time
felt a kinship with you. You were a connection with her. That
was what he was trying to tell you in El Paso."

Robinson locked his hands behind his back and, frowning
severely, paced three steps past Cutler before turning back.
"His own son is rather a nasty prig. You have been like a son
to him, you know."

It seemed that these revelations at last should cause him
to vanish in some vast, comic explosion. He couldn't even
laugh. He had not wanted to discover that he was the son of a
laundress at an army post by some nameless enlisted man,
Cutler no doubt having been his mother's name. Nor had he

wished to be like a son to General Yeager. He had yearned for more than that! A man must define his own self, he thought, but did not enunciate it.

"Well, it's a relief not to have to worry that old business anymore," he said. "Thanks, Percy."

"I am pleading for some sympathy for the general," Robinson said, his face flaming.

"I'll never forgive him for what he's done to the Sierra Verdes."

"A desperate move to save a crumbling front, Pat."

"He finally ran out of hole cards," Cutler said. He felt curiously light. Dear Mother, dear Bridget Cutler or whatever your name was. Who needed a father at the age of thirty-two? Peto Cutler needed a father. So did Daniel Bunch, and the child of Tze-go-juni.

"He must keep men in his thrall," Robinson said in a thick voice. "And so he has kept me, of course."

"I know you could've been more than a secretary to a crazy general. *Have* been."

Robinson was grinning as though his teeth hurt. "But a *Presidential* secretary, Pat! That would have been something pretty fine, wouldn't it now?"

In the officers' saloon Cutler headed for the corner where Bernie Reilly, Jud Farrier, and Dick Hotchkiss waited for him at a table spiky with champagne bottles. The queer elation he was feeling after the session with Percy Robinson held up against the hostile faces at the bar that managed to watch and ignore him at the same time. Someone said for his hearing, "—general's pets."

Jud stood up to hold out a hand and offer congratulations. Cutler shook hands all around. He could feel the giggles coming on again, some bile churning with them. He did not think the crew at the bar considered his honor to be their own. Bernie filled his glass with champagne, and Cutler remained standing to offer a toast in a carrying voice: "Here's to Sam Bunch, the general's pet!"

They drank, those at the bar closing ranks. "Here's to you, Pat!" Dick Hotchkiss said. Friends regarded him with affection, but worriedly. He didn't have any friends in the army, with Sam Bunch dead with his brains leaking down his neck. Nor a general for a father or a madam for a mother. He felt hotheaded and loose-tongued with his first glass of Cordon Rouge. Bubbles!

"I thought I was going to break down out there," he said as they seated themselves.

"Emotional affair," Bernie said, nodding. "Sam's citation along with yours, and Mrs. Bunch collapsing like that."

"I mean break down laughing," he said, still loudly, and Jud grimaced and glanced over his shoulder at the officers at the bar.

"'Relentless pursuit'!" Cutler went on. "'Annihilation of the hostiles'! 'Cooperation between the two nations'! We were trying to head Caballito back for Bosque Alto. Instead we got him wiped out down to the last Red Striper buck, seventy-eight scalps for the *plaza mayor* in Chihuahua City. Women and children sold down the river, including Sam's Junie." He flipped the heavy medal on its ribbon. It rapped against his chest sternly. "Well, it helps to be a general's pet," he said. "Only nine years a first lieutenant!"

"Why don't you leave off this, Pat?" Bernie said, leaning toward him.

"Old Cutlery," Jud said patronizingly, grinning.

Dick poured more champagne. The adjutant had a mole on one eyelid that gave the impression of a permanent wink. "Hard to be a hero, Pat?"

"Do heroes go to their Father's House justified?" he asked.

That silenced his friends or whatever they were, confusion and irritation in Bernie's pug-nosed face, the anxious affection in Jud's, the hero-worship in Dick's made bearable by that winking eyelid. The honest hostility of those at the bar seemed to him preferable.

"Too quiet in here," he muttered, and got up to make his way to the piano, where he played in extravagant style, tipping his head back like Jimmy Blazer and flourishing his hands as though broadcasting seeds. Here's to your musicales, Lily! No one joined him or seemed to be paying attention, his friends embarrassed for him and trying not to show it. So he went back to join them.

"The only Medal of Honor winner who learned to play piano in a whorehouse," he said, not loudly. He tossed down champagne. He had been saddened remembering those evening at the Maginnises, and now he was grieving for Sam

Bunch, for Caballito, for Johnny-A, even for Joklinney—even, he was astonished to discover, for General Yeager. It took the heart out of his efforts to be insufferable.

"Four in one night was the best I could manage," he said. "I was sixteen then." Of course no one knew what he was talking about.

"The governor's come to Madison with his bank clerk militia and a company of Navajo scouts," Dick told him. "They're bound to track Joklinney down. The colonel is having fits."

"No militia is going to catch up with him if two cavalry regiments can't!" Jud said.

"They are all wasting their time," Cutler said. He eased a champagne cork and aimed it at the ceiling, where it made a satisfying rap.

"How about your trackers, Cutler?" someone called from the bar. "We don't see you even going out to look for sign."

"These Paches don't leave sign," he said. "But two cavalry regiments and the governor's militia won't catch up with Joklinney. Six Hoya scouts and a mustang lieutenant will. Captain," he amended.

Dick Hotchkiss looked pleased. Cutler supposed he should be flattered. "Anybody like to make a bet?" he demanded.

Those at the bar muttered among themselves. Symonds glared at him. No bets?

"How about it, Major? A hundred dollars?"

"All right then, Cutler!" Symonds barked.

"How do you plan to do it, Pat?" Jud asked.

"There are two places. They'll show up sooner or later at one of them. It's only a matter of time." Too much time, he thought.

That settled everyone down for a while. It did not seem that anybody here had heard yet of General Yeager's resignation and replacement, even Dick, who was able to keep his ears well peeled at headquarters.

Then he heard Smithers's Southern voice, "—Congressional Medal of Honor! My old daddy would turn in his grave!"

"Pat!" Bernie said, as Cutler jarred his chair back, rising and holding up his half-full glass.

"To the cavalry!" It was the obligatory toast, and even those at the bar turned with their whiskey glasses raised. "To Renny Smithers's daddy, the Johnny Reb general!"

In the silence Smithers moved swiftly to face him across the table, hard handsome face and jutted jaw, blue eyes electric with anger. Jud stumbled back out of the way.

"I will thank you to leave my father out of this, Cutler!"

"Well, all right, we won't mention the oath of allegiance he took—"

"Son of a whore!" Smithers said.

"Laundress," he said. Why had he hit that other captain in a Deadwood saloon? He was trying to remember as he tossed the contents of his glass into Smithers's face.

"Hit him!" the Iron Major bellowed. "Hit him, Renny!" Was it an order? Cutler had promised the general that he would strike no more superior officers. But he was a captain now! Nor did he any longer owe the general any promises, hole cards or trumps. But he had hesitated too long, for Smithers's arm was already swinging. The fist seemed to be coming for a long time, thrown overhand, good shoulder behind it, heavy gold Academy ring gleaming. The table and a considerable amount of glassware went down with him.

Bernie Reilly helped him back to his quarters, still drunk, with an aching jaw and his handkerchief pressed to his bleeding nose.

"That was damned foolish, Pat. Why do you have to insult everyone? We were drinking your health. They would have, too."

His voice sounded muffled. "Poison to them."

"You're the one who poisons yourself. Why did you have to incite Renny Smithers? What's the point?"

"He got what he wanted, I got what I wanted, everybody got what he wanted. Small price to pay."

"You have got more friends than you think, Pat. But you make it damned hard."

"This is a hard time for me, Bernie. Waiting."

"Waiting for what?"

"Waiting for Joklinney."

The next day everyone knew that Yeager had been replaced by General Schofield, and Cutler had a sore jaw and a nose as red as Percy Robinson's. After lunch he went automatically to the signal office, but now there was no one at Fort Blodgett to send him intelligence or orders. There was no one from whom he was required to take orders anymore! All promises were off now, and Yeager no longer held over him the threat of sending the Hoyas to Florida after the Sierra Verdes. He was no longer required to see Joklinney destroyed before he departed for Las Golondrinas. The realization of his freedom made Cutler shaky.

He saw Nochte trotting toward him on a brown pony, wearing a new hat, black, flat-brimmed with a low crown, very stylish. A Mexican coin necklace gleamed on his brown chest. His forefinger was raised in a signal. Joklinney had been located at last.

They had come this way before, on the trail of the Nahuaques who had tortured Pedro Carvajal and driven María Cutler insane. It was a place Kills-a-Bear knew, an Apache haven in the Boot Range. Skinny had been delegated to watch for Joklinney here, Chockaway in another place, closer to the Greens. Joklinney and two others had arrived in the Boots two nights ago, with a small herd of cattle and a string of spare mounts. The raiders had at last come to roost.

So in the late afternoon, hurrying away from the early sunset of autumn, sighting in on the tallest peak, came Captain Patrick Cutler with the five Hoya scouts, Nochte, Kills-a-Bear, Tazzi, Skinny, and Jim-jim. Chockaway still watched the site nearer the Greens, Benny Dee was dead by hanging, and Lucky dead in Mexico. Still the odds were good enough, six to three, even if one of the raiders had been educated to white-eye ways at Alcatraz and Fort Point and a whorehouse in San Francisco.

These five with whom Cutler rode, whom he would never understand, were precious possessions. His scouts, his: Nochte with his stylish hat, his jewelry, his crippled leg; Tazzi with his raffish grin and jeering speech; wise, careful Kills-a-Bear with his wrecked face; Skinny, small as a fourteen-year-old boy, spinkle-shanked, the tail of his red headband nodding with the motion of his horse dark, dour, shy Jim-jim. Five savages armed with the breechloaders that had made their people strong and dangerous enough to challenge the U.S. army and lay waste to tracts of northern Mexico. His Hoyas.

As the sun hung over the western ranges, their shadows trotted before them, tall silhouettes of horses and riders like arrows loosed across the red earth. Sometimes the scouts yipped with excitement, bent to their mounts *al jinete*, all but Nochte wearing the red turbans that were their uniform, cheerfully aiding the white-eye *nantan* in the pursuit of their own kind.

It was full dark and moonless when, on foot, they began their ascent of the peak. Cutler kept up with difficulty, panting, tired in some kind of accumulated way. His nose hurt. The scouts had stripped for a fight, and sometimes in the dim starlight he could see brown flesh in motion ahead of him. They paused to wait for him from time to time. It seemed to him that everything was suddenly moving faster than he could keep up with, his career in the army all but over, a new life in Sonora about to begin with even more puzzling problems of existence and relationship. Do you think you will be happy in Mexico? Bernie Reilly had asked him.

Once Tazzi whispered to him, "*No miedo*, Nantan Tata! Plenty scout, few bad fella!" He felt a queer flooding of emotion at the comfort of that "Never fear!" The male companionship of war, which he had never shared with any of his fellow officers except Sam Bunch, he had intensely shared with this ragged, dirty crew of aborigines. Somewhere on the other side of this peak, with Nah-kut-le and apparently a second associate butcher, was Joklinney, who had claimed he could no longer think like an Apache but had in the end reverted to Apache vengeance. His heart did not ache for Joklinney, it ached for the five Indeh climbing the mountainside ahead of him, with their carbines and cartridge belts slung over their bare backs. They paused to wait for him again.

This time they shared with him meat from their *piches*, cooked into long shreds like bootlaces, strong-tasting. He did not worry what part of what beasts it had come from, who had feasted on broiled water rat with their quarry. He washed the dried meat down with water from his canteen, which he then passed around.

They climbed on, a pale half-moon rising behind them. He grasped at stiff brush to hoist himself up this steeper slope, avoiding the paddle cactus and niggerheads as best he could. Frequently he called for halts to rest, the scouts squatting impatiently above him. He had identified a part of his fatigue as a draining reluctance for the culmination of this climb.

"It is not far now, Nantan Tata," Nochte murmured in Spanish. The others whispered sibilantly among themselves. One of them giggled. They were only a part of a historical process, but they were as human as he was and, he sometimes thought, more. They already knew, through some signal office of their own, that Nantan Lobo had lost his power and now there was a new great blue-soldier *nantan*.

"No more scouts, Nantan Tata?" Nochte inquired with elaborate unconcern.

"I think the new great *nantan* will not believe he needs scouts."

"Nantan Tata will go away also?"

"To Mexico. To my wife there."

Nochte conveyed this, and the rest chattered and clicked. Kills-a-Bear spoke at length.

"He says what will the blue soldiers do without Nantan Tata and the Hoyas? Other *nantans* are foolish, they ride around and around and they see nothing. The blue soldiers are like children. Bad Indeh will kill them like turkeys."

"These we seek are the last of the bad Indeh," Cutler said.

They discussed this notion, negatively, Cutler gathered. He asked where they would go when he had left for Mexico, if there were to be no more scouts.

Nochte said, "It is equal to us, Nantan Tata. Our people are at Fort Apache."

"I cannot tell you to trust the white-eyes," he said. "For you know better. Neither the blue-soldier *nantans*, nor the agents of the Indian Bureau."

Tazzi jeered in his fearful English, "Indeh no trust no white-eye never! Trust Nantan Tata plenty little!" He convulsed into silent laughter.

"Nantan Tata trusts Tazzi, Kills-a-Bear, Skinny, Nochte, and Jim-jim," he said. Nochte translated this, to a reverberating silence. Cutler rose, and the others scrambled up. They started on, outlined now on long, silver slants of light from the risen moon, casting their shadows ahead of them. Suddenly the ridge showed against a paler darkness.

From the ridgeline it was exactly as before, although this time there was no captive woman to be saved. Below, on the rock shelf, was the pale glow of coals in a firepit. He could make out the moving patch of the penned cattle farther down the canyon, hear their stamping and rustling and the trickle of running water in a stream. He delegated the placement of the scouts to Kills-a-Bear and lay on the ground with his cheek pressed to the oiled stock of his carbine. Sleepiness crushed him, and he fought his eyelids open time after time.

By first light he saw two men moving by the firepit, and heard the crackle of kindling broken. The two squatted by the fire as flames licked up. Presently Cutler could distinguish Joklinney on the right, in a slouch hat, a jacket, and trousers. The other was hatless but also wore white-eye clothing. The third was not in sight, but must be ensconced in the old wickiup from which Cutler had pulled María. The scouts were crouched behind rocks and brush lower on the slope. The light was still too dim for careful aim. He shivered in the predawn chill.

Gazing toward their cliff-face, Joklinney rose, wiped his hands on his pant legs and strolled to the rim of the shelf, clearing seen now out of the shadows of the canyon. The other still squatted by the fire.

Cutler rose to face Joklinney. It seemed to him that the outlaw was smiling, although he could not be certain in the gray light. The one by the fire rose also. The third still had not appeared.

"Hey you, Joe King! Don't move!"

"So, it is Nantan Tata," Joklinney said. His words had a sharp-edged clarity in the chilly air, across a hundred feet between them. Joklinney took off his hat and shook out his hair, which was Apache-long now.

"Where's the third one?"

Joklinney gestured toward the wickiup.

Holding his carbine half-aimed, Cutler called, "I want the three of you by the fire while we come down there. No weapons."

"We die here like Indeh, not coyotes," Joklinney said in a deep voice.

"Like savages," he said.

"Yes, Nantan Tata." Clearly now he could see that Joklinney grinned up at him with that Apache humor, knowing he was a dead man.

"*Ha-tip-e-ca?*" Cutler said.

Joklinney replaced his hat and took a cautious step in retreat. He bellowed, "*Dah-koo-gah!*" and turned to run.

Cutler stroked the trigger. Joklinney fell, sprawling, the hat flying off. Five carbines roared in a volley, then single shots. Joklinney lay prone, spread-eagled. The other lay on his back.

"They are dead, Nantan Tata!" Nochte called up to him.

When he caught up with them, on the rock shelf with the dead raiders, they had found the third one, a woman, in the wickiup. The same bullet that had killed the mother had killed the child. She was a young woman, pretty, with the little dart of a white scar beneath her lower lip, Tze-go-juni rescued from her captivity in Mexico, and her half-breed child.

He instructed Nochte to see to the burial of mother and child and to burn the wickiup.

"Cabezas, Nantan Tata?" Tazzi called to him.

He nodded, for the bodies would rot very quickly in the heat of the day. He went to sit on the higher ledge while these things were accomplished, gripping his own hands to his cheeks as though to hold his own head on and shivering as the shadows drew inward and the sun appeared. Nochte came to tell him they had found a bag of greenbacks and silver. Joklinney had learned the value of cash money from the white-eye.

By nine o'clock they were out of the mountains, with the heads of the bronco Apaches in gunnysacks lashed to one of the pack animals, over five hundred dollars in cash, twelve horses, and twenty head of cattle. Thus is was that they arrived in Arioso to learn that the sheriff had been badly wounded the night before in a shoot-out with Juanito el Angelito.

Sheriff Grant's narrative:

While the governor's old Indian fighters, Navajo scouts, and some Madison citizens were circulating and staked out east of the Green Range hunting Joklinney, I rode out with Ben Gibson for the *gran baile de máscaras* of the Day of the Dead, and the señorita of the three flowers who would point out Johnny-A to me. This was a fiesta with posters up in all the south-county *placitas* and Madison too, and there would be Anglo cowboys in from the county ranches. I had heard no news of Johnny leaving the Territory, so this time we were bound to take him.

I know that Ben and I cause people to grin just to look at us sometimes, since I am six-four in height, and he may be five-six with his high-heel boots on, and on the tubby side besides, but he is a good man and trustworthy in a scrape. We obtained masks at the González store in Madison for the occasion, his a Moor, brown-faced with a painted-on gold crown, and mine a *hermitano*, pale-faced with a nose like a potato and hanks of frazzled rope for hair.

We rode into Arioso a half hour after sundown as planned, for I did not wish to be recognized by my size in daylight. I had been in bad spirits all day, for I was sick that it looked like the Almighty had arranged it so that Johnny and I must come to it at last, and I remembered saying to him once that I would never work for a man who would send me against him.

No one took particular notice of Ben and me in Arioso, masked as we were, for the streets were jam-packed and almost everybody had masks on, young Mexican bucks and

their señoritas in long gowns and Sunday best, older *gente*
too, and cowboys moving among them, some masked and
some not, and more than a few into liquor already. I remembered going into these *placitas* in the old days with Johnny,
with that high excitement of not knowing what would happen
in a romance or a fight, and I would rather have been going
in there tonight with Little Jay than with my deputy.

Three different bands were playing, one in the plaza and
the others on street corners near enough so their music
thumped together with the notes mixing up. There must
have been a dozen people in skull masks like the one Johnny
had worn when he had the laugh on the governor and me
with his stick of kindling, and there were devil masks, goat
masks, shrouded faces, pale-lady masks, and half-masks with
fringes dancing on dusky cheeks. Some of the señoritas were
smoking cigarettes, the white tubes very pretty against brown
faces.

Ben and I made our way through the press in the plaza
and the street running into it. My shoulders ached from
stooping. Señoritas passed us in twos and threes, sometimes
breaking a painted eggshell filled with confetti on the head of
some favored young fellow. A cowboy on the stagger from too
much whiskey and excitement made grabs at passing girls,
but they giggled and slipped away. A Mexican fellow lay face
down in a puddle of puke. But for the most part it looked a
fine fiesta, flowers everywhere, little shrines to the Virgin all
candle lit, set into the walls, and papier-mâché skeletons,
skulls, and devils hanging about.

Ben had got his nerves jingling worrying that if we got
into a scrape with Johnny-A there would be cowboys as well
as *muchachos* to take his part, so we stopped in at the cantina
for whiskey to restore his grit. The place was packed with
men, many of them known to me from my years at the PM,
masks pushed up so they could get at their liquor with more
dispatch. If they took any special notice of me I didn't see it.
A table of older men was playing at monte, hoarse voices and
cards slapped down. There was a stockyard pitch of noise in
the cantina, and the music thumping outside.

There was dancing in the main plaza, cowboys stomp-
dancing, señoritas dancing together, many couples swinging
about, and older women sitting on benches watching the
show. It was a warm night, with Mexican town stinks mingled

with flowers, perfume, and sweat. Dogs scampered among the dancers. The music blared up toward those desert-country big stars, south-of-the-border songs with thin, melancholy brasses and strings to tug at your heart: "La Golondrina," "La Paloma," and the rest. Ben lashed up with a not-so-young lady with a tamale figure, and the two of them circled laughing, their arms pumping. I kept weaving through the dancers looking for the three-flowers señorita.

She found me first, touching my arm and pointing to her blossoms. She wore a pale-lady mask, and a red gown layered up like a Chinese pagoda, with her little black slippered toes peeking out from under the hem. I followed her across the plaza, not too close and stooping as best I could. She stopped shy of the far corner. She didn't have to point.

Johnny was dancing sedately with a girl as tall as he was, white flowers in her hair and a black domino mask. His back was toward me, but I knew his vest and checked shirt, and the Colt on his hip. The cord of his mask dented the fair hair at the back of his head. When they circled around I saw he was wearing the skull mask, and I ducked back out of his line of sight.

When the three-flowers señorita was certain I had spotted him, she slipped away.

I had set off to find Ben, the music jangling here from two bands too close together, when I saw that Johnny had left his señorita and was headed for the corner. Nothing I could do then but fuss at Ben under my breath and set out after the skull mask. He turned the corner out of sight, and I trotted along the narrow sidewalk after him, passing under one of the Virgin shrines with its tiny light. I saw him again, turning inside a gate where there was a lantern burning.

I hurried on along the narrow way, turning in at the gate also, coming into a patio with tile roofs sloping into it. There were chunks of black shadow between some hanging lanterns and plants in pots hung from the rafter ends. Keeping to the shadows, I made my way around the edge of the patio. I stretched my hands out before me so as not to trip over some bench or wheelbarrow. I slipped my Colt in the holster to make sure it was free.

One lighted room gave onto the patio. Inside there was an old man in a rocking chair, facing two little girls in pigtails and ribbons who were seated with their hands in their laps and ankles crossed. The grandfather lectured them in a low, monotonous voice. No sign of Johnny there.

I turned in an open door into a pitch-black room, waiting a long minute for things to take shape out of the dark—a bed, a bureau, a mirror like a black hole in the wall. I shuffled along through a door into the next room, with a hand held out before me.

"Quién es?" Johnny said, no question but it was him. *"Quién es?"*

I jammed my Colt toward him and said, "Johnny, you are under arrest!"

He gave me a shove that sent me back stumbling. We fired at the same instant, furry flame springing between us. I was slammed stumbling back again with a lightning bolt in my arm. Before I could get border-shifted I heard the crack of boot heels and saw the silhouette of him against the lighter dark, the white patch of the skull face pointed back at me. He was bent sideways in a queer way, so that I knew he was hit too, before he was gone.

I managed to get out of there, but I was bleeding bad and fainting. All of a sudden there were a bunch of people in my way and trying to help and yelling; then someone got a tourniquet on my arm. I heard a shout that Juanito had got away, and the girl with him. But he was hit! I swear he was hit!

They were heading up along the Purgatory River, Colorado country, under the cliffs there, he and Elizabeth pushing their horses along hard, *out of it all,* heading for that cove in the hills he remembered so well, with the great green tree bending over the cabin site like a guardian bear. There was not much water in the river here, but of course things dried up in the fall. Leaves were falling, coming down on them like bright-colored snow, but, oh, what a freedom it was, up north here out of the Territory at last, even if it was turning cold. Leaves flicked in his eyes and brushed his shoulders, and Elizabeth called to him sometimes through their autumn colors. Sometimes he couldn't even see her through them, shivering then in a queer aloneness. But of course it was colder this far north, probably there was real snow on the higher peaks ahead. Night was falling too, dimmer and darker, and it was urgent that they *get there* before full dark,

see to make camp, lay out their bedrolls, gather up fire-
wood. So they spurred the tired horses along, calling back
and forth through the falling leaves, the dusk, and the chill;
on and on upstream, not much more than a trickle running
here as they climbed into the hills, with the first faint stars
showing. There was the great tree.

They were *there* at last, *home*, dismounting and running
and hiding in the heaps of leaves in the chilly night, his side
hurting from the laughter, and Elizabeth's voice calling his
name like some child's game in the dark.

Leaving the scouts moving slowly west with Joklinney's
herd and the laden pack animals, Cutler rode hard for
Johnny-A's secret canyon with its cliff tenements of the Old
Ones. Señor Soto in Arioso, whom Lily had recommended as
a friend of Johnny's, had said he thought the outlaw had been
hit in his escape. Jack Grant had suffered a broken arm and
had been taken back to Madison by his deputy.

Malcreado trotted over the sandy canyon floor, echoing
clop of hooves, and rustling as they trotted through the heaps
of dead leaves under the willows where the canyon narrowed.
Then it widened out, the walls straightening into cliffs, the
cliffs pocked with the doorways of the Old Ones. Two horses
grazed on the grassy bank beside the bare willows, and a
woman stood on one of the ground-level terraces as though
she had been waiting for him.

She was dressed for a ball, a long gown, wilted flowers in
her hair. She was tall, slim, brown-haired, very young, a
half-breed. She spoke in charmingly accented English. "You
are the señor lieutenant?"

He said he was, dismounting beside her. "Where is he?"

She motioned. "He is dead," she said calmly. Cutler
broke into a trot. Johnny-A lay half in shadow along the side
of one of the eroded walls, his head propped on his saddle,
hands crossed on his chest. His shirt was soaked dark with
blood. The boy's face was clean-shaven and peaceful; gone to
his Father's House. His lashes were long as a girl's against his
pale cheeks.

Behind Cutler the girl said, "The blood would not stop.
We could not staunch it."

"He didn't get out in time."

She came up beside him. "He could not get out, señor

lieutenant. He could not run from Jack Grant, as he could not run from those of the store. He died as he would have wished—he told me that."

Sunlight gleamed in her light hair, with its coronet of browning blossoms. Her face was long, honey-colored, serene, and beautiful. "He spoke of the lieutenant as his friend," she said.

"We were friends."

She nodded as though at a contract confirmed. "No one but you and I will know. It must never be known that Jack Grant has killed him."

He almost laughed aloud, his breath leaping in his throat.

"So El Angelito is not dead," she added, as though he might not have understood.

"And you?"

"He has promised he will return for me. I will wait for him."

At his last meeting with Johnny-A in this same place, Johnny had wished that he could go to his Father's House justified. If I could put him under, Johnny had said of Joklinney. I could go out on that. Cutler almost laughed again, in his elation.

On the stones beside Johnny's body, face down, was a papier-mâché mask. He plucked it up and turned it over. A white skull face with grinning bared teeth glared back at him from empty eyeholes. "What is this?"

"It is his mask from the *baile*."

He asked her name.

"Elizabeth Fulton." She stood before him in her luminous beauty with her fingers whitely clenched. "He said we would go to Colorado. He knew a fine place for a rancho that he had seen there. We knew we would never go. Still we played this game. I promised myself to him."

Hat in his hands, he nodded as she spoke of her love for her Juanito, of the love of the *gente* for him, of what he meant to the Mexican-Americans of the *placitas* and ranchos of the Territory. El Angelito had been their knight errant, even though an Anglo. Cutler noticed that she did not look at her dead lover as she spoke. In Johnny's folded fingers was a silver religious medal.

The dead outlaw and hero was surprisingly light when

Cutler knelt to pick him up. He could feel the cool damp of blood that had not yet dried seeping through his own shirt as he carried Johnny to the foot of one of the ladders, calling back to Elizabeth Fulton to bring a rope.

The ladder was made of crossbars fastened into the uprights with doweling and thongs that had crumbled into dust. He climbed, testing each rung before he trusted it with his weight, to come out on the first terrace. Another ladder climbed to a higher terrace. This one was rickety, with a split upright, but it held. Elizabeth Fulton watched him from the rocky slope beneath as he descended again. She had brought a coiled lariat.

With the rope he hauled the body to the first terrace, then to the second. The girl ascended the ladders behind it.

He laid Johnny-A out on the packed earth floor of an empty cubicle scooped out of the cliff, in a long slant of sunlight that reached in from the doorway. Elizabeth protested when he removed Johnny's cartridge belt with its heavy appendage of holstered revolver, but she accepted his promise to explain later. He removed also the vest and boots and trousers, leaving the blood-soaked shirt.

Together, he bending, she kneeling, they arranged Johnny Angell in the exact center of the floor, head to the west, the body thin-legged in long underwear beneath his shirttail, barefoot, fingers clasping the silver medal with its worn-smooth depiction of the Virgin of Guadalupe. The girl carefully smoothed the fair hair into a forelock on the brow. Kneeling still, she bent her head over her folded hands and murmured a prayer.

She carried the clothing, Cutler the boots and cartridge belt, down to the lower terrace. There he wrestled the cracked ladder to the terrace edge and pitched it off. It crashed onto one of the adobe walls, bouncing into a dozen pieces of kindling. When they had descended to ground level it was impossible, squinting up at the cliff face that seemed to topple over on them, to make out the particular black rectangle that was the door of the final resting place of Juanito el Angel.

Cutler smashed the rungs of the lower ladder with a rock. He was panting with exertion when he seated himself on the wall next to Johnny Angell's clothing and gun. Elizabeth

Fulton stood before him, watching him with her amber eyes in her luminous face, as he told her what they must do.

Bird Cage Hotel
Madison, New Mexico Territory
November 4, 188–

My dearest Clara,
I am writing this late at night in my hotel room. I have had a warm bath and consumed a tot of whiskey, but sleep will not come.

The most difficult lesson a young officer had to learn in the rapid promotions of wartime was to delegate authority. Next came the ordeal when, having delegated it, he languished in some field headquarters awaiting reports from his subordinates that were delayed or never sent and that, when they came, might just as well announce fiasco as triumph. So I waited at Shiloh, only to learn that the greater part of my command would not extricate itself from a flooded road in time to join the fight.

Yesterday authority was delegated, and today I have been waiting all day. Don Rudolfo and Tom Beak have led the Navajo scouts south and west to take up stations at three passes and an important waterhole, where, in consultation, it has been decided that Joklinney is most likely to appear. Western Apache scouts have been sent for from Fort Apache, but it may be several days before they arrive. The Navajos were accompanied by a number of local men and some of those I brought with me from Santa Fe. My guards have remained here, and at least one old Indian fighter has disintegrated into a drunken derelict crying out against the pink snakes of delirium tremens. I have been unable, so far, to sympathize with his sufferings.

We will see if my efforts here do not blunt the savage edge of the criticism that has been directed my way these last several weeks. Meanwhile a new wonder has deflected the attention of the wolves of the press, for Sheriff Grant has traded revolver shots with his quarry, Johnny-A. He has suffered a broken arm and lost a dangerous amount of blood but claims to have seriously, if not mortally, wounded the outlaw. The fact of that matter is that he has failed in this his principal charge, but Angell has fallen to a position of minor irritant, a petty gunman of fading reputation drifting among the Mexican hamlets, "on the dodge," as it is called. Eventually, if Grant did not mortally wound him as he claims, Angell will be apprehended or shot down by a law officer, glory seeker, or even some Judas among his admirers. His legendary stature has eroded, and I believe the end to be unimportant.

In fact, except for the surely temporary clamor attendant upon Joklinney's raid, I believe that the Secretary of the Interior's charge to me has been fulfilled, for peace and quiet reign in Madison County. I am told that erstwhile enemies from the Madison County War have ridden out in search of Joklinney together.

How I long for this waiting to be over, so I can return to the peace and quiet and profound emanations of the Palace of the Governors, and the work on my blessed history. Writing history from the inside! Watching it take place around me, marshaling the facts toward perceived truths, the minute analysis and sweeping generalization of the "German method," but also the narrative plan with its protagonist of the "literary method"—the process is blissful pleasure to me. Once this last eruption of the frontier's old wildness is finished, I will take up my history with a vengeance. . . .

Underwood did not know what time it was when he wandered from his room to see if there were any signs of activity at the telephone operator's post, and then out into the night to gaze up at the stars in their courses. A light burned in the sheriff's office, and he strolled across the dusty street to the courthouse, where Sheriff Grant was probably sleepless with pain instead of anticipation.

Grant's right arm was supported by a sling, and lines of pain and anger were graven in his face. With him was Deputy Gibson, a short, red-faced fellow of a cheerful disposition. Grant slouched in the chair at his desk and sipped from a brown bottle of laudanum which he kept stuffed into his sling. The deputy watched him uneasily.

The doctor had taken two inches of shattered bone from Grant's upper arm, and the arm was permanently crippled. The pain and his failure with Johnny Angell had made Grant a bitter man. "Tell you what they do in hell," he said to Underwood. "They wait for news that don't ever come."

"Ha!" Gibson said.

"I am waiting also, Sheriff," Underwood said, "although I think we wait for different news."

"I just want to hear that kit-rattler's shot in the liver and died screaming for his mother," Grant said. "But I don't think I am going to hear it because we're sitting here in hell and don't know it yet. I've just told a pretty woman that was going to marry me that it's off. She don't want to be married to a cripple-arm fellow."

"You shouldn't have done that, Jack," the deputy said.

"I know you are in pain, Sheriff," Underwood said, "and I am sorry for it. But try to pull yourself together."

Grant glared at him, rearranging the slinged arm on the desk top. "Tell you what I've been thinking, Governor," he said. "If you had gone ahead and pardoned Johnny the way you told him you would, none of a lot of things would've happened."

"That line of thought will take you nowhere, Sheriff," he said firmly.

"I'm not trying to go anywhere," Grant said. He fished the brown bottle from his sling again. "I tell you he was hit!" he said.

In gray light Underwood wakened to taunting hoots and yells outside in the street, and instantly he felt a surge of hope that this was a messenger come to report Joklinney killed. He had risen and begun hurriedly to dress when a mechanical clamor began, metal beating metal. The sound was continuous and irritating.

Men were collecting outside in the dawn light, hurrying toward the gallows, and he trotted to join them. Suspended from a nail on the sturdy upright of the gallows was a filthy gunnysack, the bottom stained with some dark, greasy substance. It contained what appeared to be two large melons. On the platform stood the hotel cook in his stained apron, holding a metal pan and a long serving spoon. He began to beat them together again. Deputy Gibson also appeared on the platform, to stand with his hands clasped together and an anxious expression as he gazed at the stained sack.

"Shut that noise!" Sheriff Grant shouted, forging his way through the men standing below the platform, a head taller than any of them.

"What is it?" someone called, and others, "What's in the sack? What's all the fuss?"

"It was Johnny-A!" the cook shouted, over the other voices. "Him and another fellow with masks on. Climbed up here and hung up that sack. Then they yelled and spurred around a bit before they lit out of town!"

"It wasn't Johnny!" Grant panted, as a fat man in shirtsleeves helped boost him up onto the platform, where he stood, like Gibson, facing the gunnysack. "Tell you I shot him!"

"It was too, Jack!" the cook insisted. "I have seen Johnny-A a hundred times, and he don't fool me with any skull mask on."

"I saw him too," the deputy added. "It was Johnny, all right. He had been hit, like you said; dried blood all over his vest there. Wasn't there, Bobby?"

"Surely looked like blood," the cook said. "Other one had a pale-lady mask on." He looked as though he would like to go on beating his pan to increase the size of this assembly.

Everyone was staring at the greasy bag with its twin bulges, and Underwood had a premonition of what it contained.

"Bring it down, Ben," Grant said, grimacing as he gestured with his slinged arm.

The deputy freed the sack from its nail, and, grunting with the weight, let it down to the platform. He and Grant glanced toward each other. Gibson straightened for a moment, before bending to grasp the sack by its bottom, and invert it. Two black, hairy objects rolled out, one continuing to roll, eccentrically, almost to the sheriff's boots.

"Holy Jesus God!" someone whispered.

"Oh my God, they're *heads*!"

Underwood knew what heads they were, those of Joklinney and the other raider. Johnny Angell had beaten the cavalry, the militia, and the Navajo scouts, as well as Sheriff Grant. Grant stooped in sections from his lean height to jerk up one of the heads by the hair. He looked into the face, then swung it around, black features, crudely severed neck with a stump of bone protruding.

"Joklinney!" a stifled voice called out.

"*Johnny got him!*"

The sheriff stood there with his slinged right arm, and his left hand holding up the head, tilted against its weight.

His face was as terrible as the one he displayed, and, in the clamor all around him, Underwood had a queer congealing vision of a group of men gazing down from some Valhalla in the sky. Who were they, these huge, dim, troubling figures? Daniel Boone, surely, with that hat; Davy Crockett; Paul Bunyan with his ax, Mike Fink the riverboatman. Their eyes were fixed upon Johnny-A's apotheosis, and not upon the true historian with his facts, his considered conclusions, his history from the inside, for Johnny-A was one of their own.

When Cutler rode Malcreado into the officers' stables at the fort, the clean fume of horse manure was comforting after breathing too long the stench of rotting flesh. Cutler had swung out of the saddle when Sergeant Kinsey appeared as though tiptoeing as he hurried toward him, one big hand held up in caution.

"Captain, sir! Lieutenant Hotchkiss said for me to tell you to hold up right here until I run for him!"

"Hurry!"

The sergeant trotted out. Cutler paced. It seemed there was always to be one more thing before his departure, but surely all that remained now was to wash off the stink of dead Apaches, pack a few books and personal effects, sign his resignation at headquarters, and head for Tucson and the train south. Malcreado whickered and swung his head as though sharing his impatience.

"Going home, Malcreado!"

The adjutant rushed in, panting. "Pat, the colonel's had a stroke. He can't even talk, all he can do is roll his eyes. The major's in command."

Cutler almost laughed out loud.

'He's going to arrest you for theft of government property!" Hotchkiss said. "You took some scale weights, something like that—before my time."

He did laugh.

"Listen!" Hotchkiss said. "Everybody knows you're resigning. I wrote it out for you." He unfolded and proffered a paper and lead pencil. "You had better sign it and git, Pat!"

Cutler pressed the letter of resignation against the plank wall, licked the pencil lead, and signed with a flourish. "Do something for me," he said.

"Surely."

"There is a packet of letters in the drawer of the table in my room. They are from a crazy woman, but no one need know of it."

"I'll burn them," Dick Hotchkiss said with a knowing grimace. He drew himself up to attention when he had folded the resignation back into his pocket. "It has been an honor serving with you, Captain!"

"There's some greenbacks leafed into a book in that drawer too. A hundred dollars is for the major on the Joklinney bet." Grinning, he said, "I'll miss saying good-byes to all the chums. Tell Dr. and Mrs. Reilly I'll write from Sonora. Thanks for all this, Dick!"

"Better git!"

"When he swung back aboard Malcreado he felt light enough to fly. "Tell Nochte they are to meet me south of Madison, he'll know the place I mean."

He trotted out into the full sunlight, embarked for Las Golondrinas at last, for his son, his wife, Don Fernando, his duties, responsibilities, and pleasures as a *hacendado*. Surely nothing could stop him now. He headed across the broad shimmer of the parade ground toward the central pole, where he halted to salute the national banner, squinting up at it flexing its soft folds against the sun. So many times, returning to the fort with his spirits dragging the earth, the first glimpse of that flash of red and blue had raised them.

He saw the Iron Major, very *a la brida* on a cavalry gray, leading a squad of mounted troopers in their slanted caps.

"Halt!" Symonds bellowed. "You are under arrest, Cutler!"

Cutler leaned on the pommel, shaking with something more than laughter as they approached at a trot. The major's face glowed like a red lantern. With the troopers was Jud Farrier. It did not seem advisable to argue with the Iron Major that he had already resigned.

He waved once, casually, and kneed Malcreado away from them. "Vámanos, Malcreado!"

"Halt!" the major squalled.

Malcreado's long muscles began to work beneath his thighs. He leaned forward, breathless with pleasure. How else would he have wanted to leave the army? "Fire!" the major shouted.

There was a ragged volley. He bent lower to the horse's back, at a dead run now past the end of the parade ground and the officers' quarters. Once he glanced back over his shoulder to see the troopers spread out in his wake. Jud Farrier, riding behind the Iron Major, held up a gauntleted hand in a farewell.

"Fire!" the major bellowed again.

"Las Golondrinas!" Cutler called to the gelding's ears, as Malcreado's long strides left the pursuers behind.

He said good-bye to his scouts on a red sandstone outcropping from which he could see the great sweep of the desert into Mexico and the nearer parallel gleam of the tracks of the new railroad, pointing due west. A mile ahead a locomotive raised gusts of steam that marked the farthest extent of the road. He would ride to Tucson, and from there take the cars south to Hermosillo. Aboard Malcreado again, he would head east for the Hacienda de Las Golondrinas. He wore civilian clothing acquired in Corral de Tierra for his journey and civilian status—blue shirt, canvas trousers, new red bandana in his pocket, new Justin boots. A blanket-lined jacket and some supplies were bundled behind his saddle. Cold weather might be encountered this time of year.

He took the three cans of pears from his saddlebag and gave them to Jim-jim to open. The seven of them squatted in a circle within the larger circle of the ground-tied horses. Dirty fingers fished the pale pear halves from the thick juice. Heads waggled with approval, juice glistened on dark chins. Good! Good!

Cutler felt like Washington bidding farewell to his army. He said in Spanish, "Tell them I will never forget them. All of you."

Nochte spoke solemnly. Kills-a-Bear grimaced and hung his head. Skinny crossed his eyes. Chockaway also made a face, Jim-jim a more severe and juice-stained one. Tazzi grinned hugely in his embarrassment. Kills-a-Bear addressed Nochte, avoiding Cutler's eyes.

"He says Nantan Tata will also be missed. They will perish of boredom. They will also miss the blue-soldier dollar."

"Tell them they must not gamble with the money they found with Joklinney. Nantan Tata forbids it."

The translation elicited grins. "Nantan Cabezas!" Tazzi said in his jeering voice.

Cutler parceled out the remaining pear halves and passed the cans so the sweet juice could be drunk. He stood.

A handcar was progressing west on the rails, workmen at either end bending and straightening rhythmically. They halted their labors to gaze curiously at the band of Indians on the high outcrop. One waved. After a rest they started on again. Cutler swung into Malcreado's saddle.

"*Adiós*, Nochte!"

"*Adiós*, Nantan Tata!"

"*Adiós*, Skinny, Jim-jim, Chockaway. Tazzi. Kills-a-Bear."

Tazzi began to laugh and slap his thighs. He spouted Apache.

With a dignified grin, Nochte explained. "He says the Indeh chase the bad white-eye into Mexico!"

They were all laughing at this fine joke, and Cutler managed a grin also, raising a hand in farewell as he swung Malcreado away. When he looked back some were still laughing and pointing after him, others waving, Nochte swinging his stylish hat by its cord. When he looked back once more they were motionless, very small now, clumped together still watching his departure. And finally they were gone, with only a tan mist of dust above the rocky outcrop to mark their passing.

ABOUT THE AUTHOR

OAKLEY HALL was born in 1920 in San Diego, California. He attended the University of Hawaii and ultimately received his B.A. from the University of California at Berkeley in 1943. By then World War II was well underway and Hall interrupted his studies to serve with the Marines in the Pacific. In 1945 he returned to the States and married Barbara Edinger. His first novel, a mystery, was published in 1949; he continued to write mysteries under the pseudonym Jason Manor well into the 1950's. His first mainstream novel, *So Many Doors*, appeared in 1950, and he earned his M.F.A. from the University of Iowa in that same year.

Inspired by the mythical pulp magazines and dime novels that had been so popular since the turn of the century, Hall decided in 1955 to write a trilogy about the Old West. The first book, *Warlock*, was published in 1958 and was nominated for a Pulitzer Prize. It was also made into a major motion picture starring Henry Fonda. The second of the trilogy did not appear until twenty years later, but Hall wrote many other works in the interim, including *Downhill Racers* (1962, also a film, starring Robert Redford) and *A Game for Eagles* (1970). *The Bad Lands*, his second Western epic, appeared in 1978 to much acclaim. It won the Golden Spur Award from the Western Writers of America, and the *Los Angeles Times* called Hall one of "our most absorbing novelists." His third Western saga, *Apaches*, was published in 1986, and inspired *Kirkus* to say that Hall "may be the living master of the genre." Since he was first published, Oakley Hall's books have appeared all over the world in many languages.

The novel is not the only form of prose with which Hall has succeeded. He has written numerous short stories of which one, "Horseman," won the Spur Award in 1982. He also wrote the libretto for a modern opera, *Angle of Repose*, which debuted in 1976 as San Francisco's offering for the Bicentennial. Since 1969, Oakley Hall has served as Director of Programs in Writing and Professor of English at the University of California at Irvine.

Oakley Hall does not, however, spend all of his time in front of a typewriter. He is an avid sportsman and hiker, and, several years ago, climbed to the Base Camp at Mount Everest. Hall and his wife divide their time between San Francisco, Squaw Valley, and Irvine. They have four children and five grandchildren.

THE LEGENDS WEST TRILOGY

BY OAKLEY HALL

All the beauty and danger of the Old West come alive in these highly acclaimed novels by one of America's most respected authors, Oakley Hall.

☐ **WARLOCK**   27114-8/$4.50

Clay Blaisedell is a gunman first, a lawman second, who comes to Warlock to end the violence that has scarred the town. With a host of colorful characters drawn from history, the novel erupts with treachery, vengeance, and murder before justice is established.

☐ **THE BAD LANDS**   27265-9/$4.50

A young Easterner comes to the Dakota Bad Lands to escape a family tragedy, and is immediately drawn into the hard life of a cattle rancher—and learns a tough lesson in the politics of the prairie as vigilantes roam the land exacting a blood price from their enemies.

☐ **APACHES**   27541-0/$4.95

Based on the infamous Lincoln County War in New Mexico, this bold, brassy, bloody novel of human conflict is played out on a spectacular landscape of desert and mountain. This powerful narrative takes you into the heart and minds of the men and women of the frontier.

Look for these great novels wherever Bantam books are sold, or use this handy page to order.

- -

Bantam Books, Dept. OA, 414 East Golf Road, Des Plaines, IL 60016

Please send me _____ copies of the books I have checked above. I am enclosing $_____ (please add $2.00 to cover postage and handling; send check or money order—no cash or C.O.D.s please).

Mr/Ms _____

Address _____

City/State _____ Zip _____

OA—9/88

Please allow four to six weeks for delivery. This offer expires 3/89. Prices and availability subject to change without notice.

A Proud People In a Harsh Land

THE SPANISH BIT SAGA

Set on the Great Plains of America in the early 16th century, Don Coldsmith's acclaimed series recreates a time, a place and a people that have been nearly lost to history. With the advent of the Spaniards, the horse culture came to the people of the Plains. In THE SPANISH BIT SAGA we see history in the making through the eyes of the proud Native Americans who lived it.

THE SPANISH BIT SAGA
Don Coldsmith